THE
MAN WITH
THE GOLDEN
ARM

THE
MAN WITH
THE GOLDEN
ARM

50th anniversary critical edition

NELSON
ALGREN

WILLIAM J. SAVAGE JR. AND DANIEL SIMON, EDS.

SEVEN STORIES PRESS
New York • Toronto • London

Library of Congress Cataloging-in-Publication Data

Algren, Nelson, 1909–1981
The man with the golden arm / Nelson Algren. —50th anniversary critical ed., Seven Stories Press 1st ed.
    p. cm.
Text accompanied by critical essays.
ISBN 978-1-58322-007-8. — ISBN 978-1-58322-008-5 (pbk.)
1. City and town life—Illinois—Chicago Fiction. 2. Morphine habit—Illinois—Chicago Fiction. 3. Criminals—Illinois—Chicago Fiction. 4. Gambling—Illinois—Chicago Fiction. 5. Chicago (Ill.) Fiction. 6. Algren, Nelson, 1909–1981 Man with the golden arm. I. Title.
PS3501.L4625M3 1999   813'.52—dc21
           99-41331
           CIP

SEVEN STORIES PRESS
140 Watts Street
New York, NY 10013
www.sevenstories.com

Distributed in Canada by Publishers Group Canada.
Distributed in the UK by Turnaround, London.

9 8 7 6 5 4

PRINTED IN THE USA

CONTENTS

EARLY RECEPTION

NEW VIEWS

We had two goals in mind for this critical edition of Nelson Algren's *Man with the Golden Arm*. First, we wanted to advance the level of comprehension, and thus the expectation of pleasure, readers bring to this great novel. Algren has deserved more than he has received in the way of illuminating criticism; we wanted to create a context for correcting this historical neglect. Second, and just as important, we sought to get those of us who think and write about Algren to be more aware of one another. The quality of the interaction among Algren's supporters will tell you everything about whether Algren will be read and remembered a hundred years from now.

Luckily, the Algren community has usually been characterized by great generosity. Studs Terkel and Kurt Vonnegut will make time in their busy schedules when it is a question of an Algren publication or event. This is true also of Russell Banks, Stuart McCarrell, Art Shay, and Stephen Deutch, Algren's good friend who died several years ago, and who, until it became physically impossible, would always be there when it was a question of Nelson. And of Algren's friend and agent Candida Donadio, formerly blacklisted writer Clancy Segal, Jan Herman, and many others. These and many other stalwarts have always enfolded any new Algren aficionado who came their way in a warm and patient embrace.

And the younger generation of Algren supporters—people like filmmakers Marc Blottner and Louise Wardle, National Book Foundation director and author Neil Baldwin, the younger agents Neil Olson and Ira Silverberg and, in this volume, biographer Bettina Drew and scholar Carlo Rotella—have expressed this same generous spirit in their dealings with us and each other. We also thank Geoff Smith of the Ohio State University Rare Books and Manuscripts Department.

The community of Algren supporters also includes several marvelous and important voices, including Carla Cappetti, Lou Reed, Tom Carson, H.E.F. Donohue, and others, who because of time considerations or other factors were not included here; we look forward to having them join the conversation in any future revised editions.

We are also pleased to include on and in this volume a few photos of Algren. Several of Nelson's best friends were first-rate still photographers, especially Deutch, Shay, and Layle Silbert. It may have been that, just as some writers take their inspiration from music, Algren drew his from sharp-edged, usually black-and-white documentary photography that was sincere and clear—not photojournalism so much as portraiture. And so it turns out, ironically, that although Algren has been thus far one of the least understood of writers, he will always be one of the best photographed, since Art and Stephen and Layle were forever clicking away at him. And their shots of his beautiful and expressive face continue to challenge us to know him better.

Daniel Simon and William J. Savage Jr., eds.
Brooklyn and Chicago, September 1999

THE MAN WITH THE GOLDEN ARM

I
RUMORS OF EVENING

KUPRIN *Do you understand, gentlemen, that all the horror is in just this—that there is no horror!*

The captain never drank. Yet, toward nightfall in that smoke-colored season between Indian summer and December's first true snow, he would sometimes feel half drunken. He would hang his coat neatly over the back of his chair in the leaden station-house twilight, say he was beat from lack of sleep and lay his head across his arms upon the query-room desk.

Yet it wasn't work that wearied him so and his sleep was harassed by more than a smoke-colored rain. The city had filled him with the guilt of others; he was numbed by his charge sheet's accusations. For twenty years, upon the same scarred desk, he had been recording larceny and arson, sodomy and simony, boosting, hijacking and shootings in sudden affray: blackmail and terrorism, incest and pauperism, embezzlement and horse theft, tampering and procuring, abduction and quackery, adultery and mackery. Till the finger of guilt, pointing so sternly for so long across the query-room blotter, had grown bored with it all at last and turned, capriciously, to touch the fibers of the dark gray muscle behind the captain's light gray eyes. So that though by daylight he remained the pursuer there had come nights, this windless first week of December, when he had dreamed he was being pursued.

Long ago some station-house stray had nicknamed him Record Head, to honor the retentiveness of his memory for forgotten misdemeanors. Now drawing close to the pension years, he was referred to as Captain Bednar only officially.

The pair of strays standing before him had already been filed, beside their prints, in both his records and his head.

"Ain't nothin' on *my* record but drunk 'n fightin'," the smashnosed vet with the buffalo-colored eyes was reminding the captain. "All I do is deal, drink 'n fight."

The captain studied the faded suntans above the army brogans. "What kind of discharge you get, Dealer?"

"The *right* kind. *And* the Purple Heart."

"Who do you fight with?"

"My wife, that's all."

"Hell, that's no crime."

He turned from the wayward veteran to the wayward 4-F, the tortoise-shell glasses separating the outthrust ears: "I ain't seen you since the night you played cowboy at old man Gold's, misfit. How come you can't get along with Sergeant Kvorka? Don't you *like* him?" As if every small-time hustler in the district, other than this strange exception before him, were half in love with good old Cousin Kvorka.

"I got nuttin' against Kvork. It's just him don't like me," the chinless wonder protested. "Fact is I respect Cousin for doin' his legal duty—every time he picks me up I get more respect. After all, everybody got to get arrested now 'n then, I'm no better'n anybody else. Only that one overdoes it, Captain. He can't get it t'rough his big muttonhead I'm unincapable, that's all."

The veteran edged restlessly half a foot toward the open door.

"You're unincapable all right," the captain agreed. "Your brains are screwed on sidewise—Hey, *you!* Where you think *you're* goin'?"

The vet edged back.

"Ever been in an institution?" the captain wanted to know, returning to the 4-F.

"Sure t'ing. The time my girl friend Violet hit Antek the Owner wit' the potato-chip bowl I was in a institution: the Racine Street Station House Institution, it looks a little like this one. Only they wouldn't let me stay. I ain't smart enough to be runnin' around loose but I ain't goofy enough to lock up neither." The punk's enthusiasm was growing by the moment. "Any time you want me, Captain, just phone by Antek, he'll come 'n tell me I got to come down 'n get arrested. I *like* gettin' locked up now 'n then, it's how a guy stays out of trouble. I'll grab a cab if you're in a real big hurry to pinch me sometime—I don't like bein' late when I got a chance of doin' thirty days for somethin' I never done."

The captain eyed him steadily. "You ain't had enough dough your whole life to take you from here to Lake Street in a cab."

"Oh, I ride cabs all the time," the punk corrected him respectfully. "Every time I get drunk I hail a Checkerd, it seems."

"Good thing you don't get drunk every half hour, you'd have traffic blocked. What's your right name?"

"Saltskin."

"Who's 'Sparrow'?"

"That's me too, Sparrow Saltskin, it's my daytime name."

"What's your nighttime name?"

"Solly. Account I'm half Hebe."

"Half Hebe 'n half crazy," the wiser stray put in unexpectedly; but no one reacted to his comment and he shifted impatiently in the shifting light.

"What were you here for the last time?" the captain wanted to know of the Sparrow.

"For nuttin'."

"For nuttin'?"

"Yeh. For nuttin'. I jumped into the squadrol when that Kvorka stopped for the lights, so he had to bring me. I like ridin' Checkerds best though. How many times I been pinched now, Captain?" The punk bent curiously across the charge sheet. "You keepin' tract for me? When I hit a hunnert I'm gonna volunteer fer Leavenswort'."

"I'll keep tract for you all right, Solly," Record Head offered affably. "No trouble at all. When it's a hundred we'll hang you. You got ninety-nine now. Go on home—if you got one. Your roof is leakin'."

"Oney on one side," Sparrow protested with some dignity, putting on a dirty red baseball cap with the peak turned backward as if preparing to make a run for it.

"I think you're a moron," the captain decided at last.

"He ain't no moron," the veteran confided to Record Head, "he's a moroff. You know; more off than on."

The veteran's flat, placid, deadpan phiz fixed absently upon an oversized roach twirling its feelers invitingly at him with a half-drugged motion from beneath the radiator: Come on down here where everything is warm love and cool dreams forever. Then, feeling the law's eyes unwaveringly upon him, he recalled himself and advised the captain confidently: "We were pinched together, if the punk makes the street I do too. Otherwise it's double jeopardy 'r somethin'."

The punk turned upon the dealer leisurely. "Never saw this motherless lush in my life before, Captain. Ain't them bloodstains on his jacket? You catch the guy sliced up the little girl yet?"

"You're both a couple loose bums livin' off the weaker bums till Hawthorne opens," the captain concluded and called over their heads to someone unseen. "Throw these two in. It'll give the suckers a chance to break even for a couple days."

From out of the station-house shadows a hand snagged Sparrow by the neck and immediately he sounded as if he weren't so hot about sitting in the cooler overnight after all.

"Why does everybody grab me by the neck?" he demanded to know. "It ain't no damned pipe. You tryin' to get it offscrewed on me? Hey!" He wailed over his shoulder to the captain as they took the first familiar steps down to the basement tier. "Bednar! Bednarski! Captain Bednarski! You got to book me fer *somethin'!*"

"We'll book you for killin' that officer in Humboldt Park if you want," the turnkey offered, and a moment later the bars clanged shut. Behind his easy boasting the punk concealed a genuine terror of being caged—and every officer in the Saloon Street Station knew it.

"Bring up a couple fuses while you're down there," Record Head Bednar's voice called from the top of the stairs, "we're gonna fry the goofy one at 1:01."

"That's you, Frankie," the punk assured the dealer swiftly.

"No, that's you," the dealer corrected him slowly.

It looked like a long night for Solly Saltskin. Not even Frankie Machine would guarantee him that the officers had only been joking.

"There's some things to kid about 'n some you ain't s'pposed to, Frankie," the punk scolded him. "It's a libel suit when you do. I could sue right now. I could sue you. You got me in here. Record Head was gettin' me ready to make the street 'n you jammed the deal—false pertenses, that's all you are." He threw a long looping left that Frankie caught in one hand, then scrubbed the punk's wispy poll with it like a man fondling a mangy pup. If Sparrow had had a tail he would have wagged it then; if they'd been in the death house together he wouldn't be too frightened so long as Frankie Machine was by.

To manhandle him fondly and get him into jams and then get him out again, just like that, the very next day.

"If Schwiefka wasn't always tryin' to chisel on the aces we wouldn't get tossed in the bucket so much," he confided in Frankie in the tone of one giving strictly inside information. "Bednar had Kvork pick us up just to show Schwiefka he's a week behind wit' the payoff." Then turned from the dealer, as the lockup went past rattling his keys, and in the same hoarse inside-info whisper: "Sssss—Pokey! You got this door locked *good?* We don't want none of you crooked cops breakin' in here tonight!"

The tranquil, square-faced, shagheaded little buffalo-eyed blond called Frankie Machine and the ruffled, jittery punk called Sparrow felt they were about as sharp as the next pair of hustlers. These walls, that had held them both before, had never held either long.

"It's all in the wrist 'n I got the touch," Frankie was fond of boasting of his nerveless hands and steady eye. "I never get nowheres but I pay my own fare all the way." Frankie was regular.

"I'm a little offbalanced," Sparrow would tip the wink in that rasping whisper you could hear for half a city block, "but oney on one side. So don't try offsteerin' me, you might be tryin' my good-balanced side. In which case I'd have to have the ward super deport you wit' your top teet' kicked out."

For being regular got you in about as often as being offbalanced on one side. That was the way things were because that was how things had always been. Which was why they could never be any different. Neither God, war, nor the ward super work any deep change on West Division Street.

For here God and the ward super work hand in hand and neither moves without the other's assent. God loans the super cunning and the super forwards a percentage of the grift on Sunday mornings. The super puts in the fix for all right-thinking hustlers and the Lord, in turn, puts in the fix for the super. For the super's God is a hustler's God; and as wise, in his way, as the God of the priests and the businessmen.

The hustlers' Lord, too, protects His own: the super has been in office fourteen years without having a single bookie door nailed shut in his territory without his personal consent. No man can manage that without the help of heaven and the city's finest precinct captains.

> *What're you gonna do for Dunovatka*
> *After what Dunovatka done for you?*

the captains still sing together at ward meetings—

Are you goin' to carry the preesint?
Are you goin' to be true blue?

Offhand it might appear to be a policeman's God who protects the super's boys. Yet a hundred patrolmen, wagon men, and soft-clothes aces have come and gone their appointed ways while the super's hustlers linger on, year after year, hustling the same scarred doors. They are in the Chief Hustler's hand; they have been chosen.

The hustlers' God watched over Frankie Machine too; He marked Sparrow's occasional fall. He saw that both boys worked for Zero Schwiefka by night while the super himself gave them hot tips each day.

The only thing neither the super's God nor the super was wise to was the hypo Frankie kept, among other souvenirs, at the bottom of a faded duffel bag in another veteran's room. The barrel of a German Mauser and a rusting Kraut sword leaned out of the bag against the wall of Louie Fomorowski's place above the Club Safari.

We all leave something of ourselves in other veterans' rooms. We all keep certain souvenirs.

Sparrow himself had only the faintest sort of inkling that Frankie had brought home a duffel bag full of trouble. The little petit-larceny punk from Damen and Division and the dealer still got along like a couple playful pups. "He's like me," Frankie explained, "never drinks. Unless he's alone or with somebody."

"I don't mind Frankie pertendin' my neck is a pipe now 'n then," the child from nowhere admitted, "but I don't like no copper john to pertend that way." For no matter how Frankie shoved him around the punk never forgot who protected him nightly at Zero Schwiefka's.

Their friendship had kindled on a winter night two years before Pearl Harbor when Sparrow had first drifted, with that lost year's first snow, out of a lightless, snow-banked alley onto a littered and lighted street. Frankie had found him huddled under a heap of *Racing Forms* in the woodshed behind Schwiefka's after that night's last deck had been boxed.

"What you up to under there?" Frankie wanted to know of the battered shoes protruding from the scattered forms. For this was the place where Schwiefka, urged by some inner insecurity, piled dated racing sheets. He never had it in him to throw a sheet away, pretending to himself that he was filing them here against a day when age would lend them value; as age had in no wise

increased his own. Frankie used them, on the sly, for starting Schwiefka's furnace; but advised the shoes severely: "Don't you know this is Schwiefka's filin'
cab'net?"

Sparrow sat up, groping blindly for his glasses gone astray somewhere
among the frayed papers below his head. "I'm a lost-dog finder," he explained
quickly, experience having taught him to assure all strangers, the moment one
started questioning, that he was regularly employed.

"I know that racket," Frankie warned him, trying to sound like a private eye,
"but there ain't no strays to steal in here. You tryin' to steal wood?" Frankie had
been stealing an armload of Schwiefka's kindling every weekday morning for
almost two months and didn't need help from any punk.

"I got no place to sleep, Dealer," Sparrow had confessed, "my landlady got
me locked out since the week before Christmas. I been steerin' for Schwiefka
all day 'n he told me I could sleep in here—but he ain't paid me a cryin' dime
so it's like I paid my way in, Dealer. It's too cold to steal hounds, they're all
inside the houses. Some nights it gets so cold I wisht I was inside one too."

Frankie studied the shivering punk. "Don't shake," he commanded. "When
you get the shakes in my business you're through. Steady hand 'n steady eye is
what does it." He handed him a half dollar.

"Here. You'll get a double case of pneumonia sleepin' in here. Get a room by
Kosciusko *Hotel*. 'N the next time Zero don't pay you off come tell Frankie
Machine. That's me—the kid with the golden arm." He paused to brush back
the shaggy mop of dark blond hair under his cap, squinting a bit with the weak
right eye. "It's all in the wrist 'n I got the touch—dice, stud or with a cue. I
even beat the tubs a little 'cause that's in the wrist too. Here—pick a card."
Cold as he was, the punk had had to pick a card.

During the lonely months with Frankie overseas and Schwiefka trying to
deal his own game, Sparrow alone, of that whole semicircle of 4-Fs, from Blind
Pig to Drunkie John, had remembered that golden arm.

"I'd be over there with the dealer right now," Sparrow had mourned quietly
to himself those months, "if I just hadn't got turned down for admittin' I steal
for a livin'."

Frankie hadn't troubled to write anyone until he began coming out of the
fog into which an M.G. shell had put him: on his back in an evacuation hospital with a daylong aching from shrapnel buried in his liver for keeps. He'd gotten off a shaky V-mail telling Sophie he was coming home.

Sophie had put the letter on Antek the Owner's bar mirror, among other wives' V-mails. The night that Sparrow read it there all the cockiness which association with Frankie had lent him, and Frankie's absence had taken away, returned. Dealer was coming home.

"Guys who think they can rough me up, they wake up wit' the cats lookin' at 'em," he had immediately begun warning everyone. And spat to emphasize just how tough a Division Street punk could get.

He had looked forward to watching Frankie's bag of corny card tricks once more. All the tricks of which he had never tired; as Frankie's Sophie had so long ago tired of them all. As Frankie had so long ago tired of showing them to her; yet had never wearied of revealing them, the same ones over and over, for Sparrow's ever-fresh amazement.

"That's one Hebe knows how bad it can get," Frankie sometimes explained their friendship obscurely, "knows how bad it can get 'n knows how good it can be. Knows the way it used to be 'n how it's gettin' now. I'd trust him with my sister all night. Provided, of course, she wasn't carryin' more than thirty-five cents."

Frankie could never acknowledge that he squinted a bit. "If anythin' was wrong with my peepers the army wouldn't of took me," he argued, "the hand is quicker than the eye—'n I got a *very* naked eye." Yet he sometimes failed to see a thing directly beneath that same very naked eye. "Where's the bag?" he would ask. "Under your nose, Dealer," someone would point out. "Well, there's suppose to be six bucks in it," he'd explain as if that, somehow, were why he hadn't seen it right away.

He squinted a bit now, in the cell's dim light, with the ever-present deck in his hand. "I can control twenty-one cards," he boasted to Sparrow. "If you don't believe me put your money where your mouth is. I'll deal six hands 'n call every one in the dark. Name your hand. You want three kings? Okay, here we go, you get what you ask for. But watch out, punk—that hand beside you is flushin' 'n that bird with nothin' but an ace showin' is gonna cop with three concealed bullets." And that's how it would be whether he was showing off in a cell or in the back booth of Antek Witwicki's Tug & Maul Bar.

"I give a man a square shake till he tries a fast one or talks back to me," he warned the punk. To hear him tell it Frankie Machine was pretty mean. "When I go after a wise guy I don't care *who* he is, how much he's holdin'—when you

see me start *pitchin'* 'em in, then you know the wise guy is gettin' boxed."
Sparrow nodded. He was the only hustler on Division Street who still believed
there was anything tough about Frankie Machine. The times he had seen
Frankie back down just didn't count for Sparrow.

"What you got to realize in dealin' stud is that it's just like drill in the army—
'n the dealer's the drill sergeant. Everybody got to be in step 'n stay on their
toes 'n there can't be no back talk or you got no harmony left—I'm good with
a cue because that's in the wrist too. Used to get fifteen fish for an exhibition of
six-no-count. No, they never put my picture on the wall but I lived off the stick
three months all the same when the heat was on 'n that's more'n a lot of hustlers can say."

It was more than Frankie could say too. He would have starved in those
three months if it hadn't been for Sophie's pay checks. And although Sparrow
was seldom allowed to forget, for long, what a mean job that of an army drill
sergeant was, Frankie's report was still hearsay: he'd put in thirty-six months
without so much as earning a pfc's stripe. Somehow the army had never quite
realized what a machine he was with a deck.

(There were those who still thought he was called Machine because his
name was Majcinek. But the real sports, the all-night boys, had called him
Automatic Majcinek for years; till Louie Fomorowski had shortened that handle for him. Now, whether in the dealer's slot, at the polls or on a police blotter, he was simply Frankie Machine.)

The bottom card squeaked as he dealt to Sparrow on the gray cell floor, and
it irritated him that he couldn't get a second off the bottom without hitting the
card above. Though he never had sufficient nerve to deal from the bottom while
in the dealer's slot he liked to feel he had the knack as a symbol of his skill.

For he had the touch, and a golden arm. "Hold me up, Arm," he would
plead, trying for a fifth pass with the first four still riding, kiss his rosary once
for help with the faders sweating it out and *zing*—there it was, Little Joe or
Phoebe, Big Dick or Eighter from Decatur, double trey the hard way and dice
be nice—when you get a hunch bet a bunch—bet a dollar and then holler—
make me five to keep me alive—it don't mean a thing if it don't cross that
string—tell 'em where you got it and how easy it was.

When it grew too dark to read the spots on the cards Frankie pulled a tattered and wadded scratch sheet off his hip. "Took me ten years to learn this little honey—watch the lunch hooks now." Sparrow watched the long, sure fingers

begin to weave swiftly and delicately. "Fifty operations in less than a minute," Frankie boasted—and there it was, a regular Sinatra jazzbow with collar attached out of nothing but yesterday's scratch sheet. "If it was just silk you could put it on now," Sparrow saw with awe. "Why couldn't you just turn 'em out all day, Dealer? Everybody in the patch'd buy one—there's a fortune in it."

"I ain't no businessman," Frankie explained, "I'm a hustler—now give me five odd numbers between one 'n ten that add up to thirty-two."

Sparrow pretended to figure very hard, tracing meaningless numerals with his forefinger in the cell's grayish dust until it was time for Frankie to show him how. Somehow Sparrow never seemed certain which were the odd and which the even numbers. "Mat'matics is on my offbalanced side," he allowed, "I make them dirty offslips."

Yet he was as accurate as an adding machine in anticipating combinations in any alley crap game; he distinguished clearly between odd and even then—sometimes before they turned up. "Playin' the field is one thing, solvin' riddles is another," it seemed to Sparrow, and saw nothing unusual in the distinction. "It's what they couldn't figure in the draft, neither," he recalled. "I was either too smart or too goofy but they couldn't tell which. It was why I had to get rejected for moral warpitude."

Frankie was making a vertical row of three ones and a parallel row of two ones. Adding the first row, he got a total of three and, adding the second, a total of two: by the proximity of the two totals he had a total of thirty-two.

"There's somethin' wrong *somewheres,* Frankie," Sparrow complained, sounding distressed. "You got my big eyes rollin' 'n the lights goin' on in my head—but if I just knew some good old long division I could put the finger on what's wrong."

"Nothin' wrong at all, Sparrow. Strictly on the legit—just the new way of doin' things we have these days. Like the new way of makin' ten extra bucks for you out of every hundred you got in the bank. This I wouldn't show to nobody only you. Only me 'n the bankers know this one 'n they're sweatin' it out that the people'll find out 'n have 'em all broke in a week. Swear you won't tell?"

"Saint take me away if I tell."

"No good. Swear a Hebe one."

"I don't *know* no Hebe one, Dealer."

No oath was necessary. He would have died before betraying the smallest of Frankie's professional secrets. "Of course," Frankie warned him now, "in

order to get away with this one you got to give up your interest—you willin'
to give up your interest?"

The question worried Sparrow. "Is it a Hebe bank 'r a Polak one, Frankie?"

"What's the diff?"

"If it's a Hebe one maybe I got a uncle workin' there, he'll just sneak me a
fistful when the president ain't peekin'."

"You got no uncle in this one," Frankie decided firmly. "In fact you got no
uncle nowheres. You ain't even got a mother."

"Maybe I got somebody in the old country, Frankie." Hopefully.

"There ain't none left in the old country so quit stallin'—you gonna take a
chance or not? You can't make this tenner 'n keep your interest too."

"Okay, Frankie. I'll chance it."

"It's just this simple, buddy-o." He began tearing tiny squares off the hand-
fabricated jazzbow, each square representing ten dollars, until he was ready to
make a hypothetical deposit of ten squares—thus with an account of one hundred dollars he pretended to withdraw that amount, then replaced it beginning
with the last square he had withdrawn, in the old burlesque routine, so that by
the time he had replaced the hundred he still retained one square in his hand.
"And there's your daily-double money 'n you still got your hundred in the bank,"
he announced triumphantly. "You can do it all day, they can't stop you as long as
the sign outside says the bank is open for business. It's on the legit so they got to
let you—that's the new way of doin' things we got these days."

Sparrow removed his glasses, blew on them, put them back on and goggled
dizzily, first at Frankie and then down at the make-believe money. It was hard
to tell, when the punk goggled like that, whether he really didn't understand
or was just putting on the goof act to please Frankie. "Somethin' wrong again,"
he complained, seemingly unable to put a finger on the trouble at all. Before he
had time to gather his shocked wits Frankie had another sure-fire miracle
working for him.

"Here's how you always pick up a couple bucks in a bowlin' alley, Solly.
You're bowlin' 'n you get a perfect split railroad—the seven 'n the ten pins. A
guy offers you twenty to one you can't pick it up. 'I never seen it done my
whole life,' he'll tell you, 'Wilman couldn't pick it up.' He'll even show you a
record book where it says it ain't been done in years. You tell him, 'Put up 'r
shut up.' So he puts up a double saw 'n you just stroll down the alley 'n pick
'em up with the lunch hooks. That's all. Strictly on the legit."

"Is that in a Hebe bowlin' alley 'r a Polak one?"

"I done it on a guy on Milwaukee so I guess it's a Polak one."

Sparrow could see through that one right there. "That's out. I'd get my little head cracked for sure. Then I'd be offbalanced on *bot'* sides."

"That'd even you up then. You'd be just right."

For no seeming reason Sparrow suddenly pointed an accusing finger at Frankie. "Who's the ugliest man in this jail?" he demanded to know and answered himself just as suddenly. "Me."

Then sat down to brood upon that reply as though it had been offered by another. "What do I care how I look anyhow?" he assuaged the insult he had so abruptly dealt himself. "What counts is I know how to get along with people."

"If you could get along with *anybody* you wouldn't be in trouble up to your ears all the time," Frankie reminded him gently. "You wouldn't be one conviction away from Mr. Schnackenberg's habitual act."

"I'm *t'ree* convictions away from Mr. Schnackenberg," the punk assured Frankie, "so long as I don't catch no two alike." Then confessed his offbalanced state with a certain plaintive moodiness: "I can get in more trouble in two days of not tryin' than most people can get into in a lifetime of tryin' real hard—why is that, Frankie?"

"I don't know," Frankie sympathized, "it's just that some cats swing like that, I guess."

Whatever Frankie meant by that, Sparrow skipped it to supply his own explanation. "It's 'cause I really *like* trouble, Frankie, that's my trouble. If it wasn't for trouble I'd be dead of the dirty monotony around this crummy neighborhood. When you're as ugly as I am you got to keep things movin' so's people don't get the time to make fun of you. That's how you keep from feelin' bad."

Yet he poked more fun at his own peaked and eager image, the double-lensed glasses and the pipestem neck, the anxious, chinless face, than did all others together. He was too quick to take the sting out of others' jibes by putting them on his own tongue first—his anticipation of insult was usually unfounded, the others had not been thinking of Sparrow's ugliness at all. Others were long used to him, he alone could not get used to himself. All he could do was to smile his shrewd, demented little grin and just be glad he was Solly Saltskin instead of Blind Pig or Drunkie John.

Sitting tailor-fashion on the cement floor, he blinked up at the whitewashed walls as they were lit by the first half glow of the nightlights along the tier; blew the jailhouse dust off his glasses and brought his cap around till the peak was low over his eyes to express his feeling that he wouldn't be going anywhere before morning.

"I'll bet you don't have a cap on." Frankie was off again on his endless challenging of the punk; Sparrow fumbled a moment to be certain that he had, yet declined the challenge. "I'll bet you don't have shoes on, I'll bet you aren't smoking a cigarette. I'll bet I can get on a streetcar without a transfer, say nothin' to the conductor, pay him nothin' 'n walk right on in. I can't tell you the answer to all those, I don't want to expose myself."

"I won't expose you 'n don't you expose me," Sparrow offered, standing up to shake hands on that equivocal pact. And having shaken, began diverting himself by swinging, hand over hand, from the great beam directly overhead. "Look at me!" he demanded. "The Tarzan of the City!"

Frankie hauled him down by his spindling shanks.

"It's just the new way of walkin'," Sparrow explained, "we got all kinds of new ways to do things since you come back, Frankie."

"They'll get you in trouble the same as the old ways," Frankie assured the punk glumly.

That night, while the little twenty-watt bulbs burned on in a single unwinking fury down the whitewashed tier, Frankie Machine was touched by an old wound fever and dreamed, for the second time in his life, of the man with the thirty-five-pound monkey on his back. His name was Private McGantic, no one knew why; yet he stood, stoop-shouldered by his terrible burden, in a far and sunlit entrance to a ward tent where Frankie lay once more on his old army cot.

No other soldier lay along that double row of neatly made-up cots, but Frankie could tell that the private squinting into the tent had been sent by the dispensary. The winter's sun on his face revealed a hospital pallor; and the eyes looked so bleak below the dim and huddled mass on the shoulders.

"I can't get him off," he complained to no one in particular, with a certain innocence where one expected shame: a voice like that of a child confessing an unclean disease without sensing any uncleanliness. "Something has happened to him," Frankie felt. The private was pointing to where, on the ward sterilizer, a GI syrette, out of some medic's first-aid kit, lay with the GI quarter-grain ration of morphine beside it, melting whitely even as he watched.

"A shrewd one all the same, coming between shifts. He knows I'm the guy who knows how to get the monkey off, he waited till the corporal went to chow," Frankie decided, "I'm not getting into trouble on some private's account."

But the fellow kept looking at him in such dumb misery, afraid to come inside and too sick to leave while he had any hope of relief, that Frankie finally heard himself say, "You can use my tie." He looked up and the private was gone, so he got off the cot, the long dull pain in his liver began kneading the gut, the needle was full and ready and the tie was hanging neatly over the suntans and there was time, just time. He had the tie about his arm, trying to bind it with one hand an inch above the elbow but his fingers fumbled with a nervous weakness, he felt fevered and had to hurry and right outside the corporal's voice said, "I'm going to catch him at it today"—the needle curved softly into some soft sort of useless rubbery fever thermometer, someone put a flashlight right in his eyes and he wakened on his back in the cell to its accusing stare. With the old pain beating behind his navel.

The pain left off slowly. Some patriot down the tier was using a reflecting mirror to waken anyone it happened to hit. The cell was full of a drifting flesh-colored light and the murmuring rumdums were being let out of the cells to wash, break wind, hawk, stretch, spit and scratch their hairy bottoms.

Frankie got up and went to the bars, without waking Sparrow, to watch the Republic's crummiest lushes lining up to dip their hands gingerly and touch their foreheads, each with a single drop, as if it were holy water and each were on his way to confession instead of to twenty dollars or twenty days on the Bridewell floor.

Frankie Machine had seen some bad ones in his twenty-nine years. But any one of these looked as though all the others had beaten him all night with barrel staves. Faces bloody as raw pork ground slowly in the great city's grinder; faces like burst white bags, one with eyes like some dying hen's and one as bold as a cornered bulldog's; eyes with the small bright gleam of hysteria and eyes curtained by the dull half glaze of grief. These glanced, and spoke, and vaguely heard and vaguely made reply; yet looked all day within upon some ceaseless horror there: the twisted ruins of their own tortured, useless, lightless and loveless lives.

Though he had seen not one man of them in his life before, Frankie knew each man. For each was seared by that same torch whose flame had already touched himself. A torch which burned with a dark and smoldering flame from within till it dried a man of everything save a dark-charred guilt.

The great, secret and special American guilt of owning nothing, nothing at all, in the one land where ownership and virtue are one. Guilt that lay crouched behind every billboard which gave each man his commandments; for each man here had failed the billboards all down the line. No Ford in this one's future nor ever any place all his own. Had failed before the radio commercials, by the streetcar plugs and by the standards of every self-respecting magazine. With his own eyes he had seen the truer Americans mount the broad stone stairways to success surely and swiftly and unaided by others; he was always the one left alone, it seemed at last, without enough sense of honor to climb off a West Madison Street Keep-Our-City-Clean box and not enough ambition to raise his eyes back to the billboards.

He had not even been a success in the taverns. Even there he could not afford the liquor that lends distinction nor the beer that gives that special glow of health, leading, often quite suddenly, to startling social success. He had snatched snipes, on the fly, of the cigarette that clears the mind for the making of swift decisions in sudden crises with the fire still alive in the tobacco. Yet always, somehow, by the time the paper had touched his lips the tobacco had long gone stale. There must be something wrong with his lips.

All had gone stale for these disinherited. Their very lives gave off a certain jail-house odor: it trailed down the streets of Skid Row behind them till the city itself seemed some sort of open-roofed jail with walls for all men and laughter for very few. On Skid Row even the native-born no longer felt they had been born in America. They felt they had merely emerged from the wrong side of its billboards.

And yet they spoke and yet they laughed; and even the most maimed wreck of them all held, like a pennant in that drifting light, some frayed remnant of laughter from unfrayed years. Like a soiled rag waved by a drunken peddler in a cheap bazaar who knows none will buy, yet waves his single soiled ware in self-mockery—these too laughed. And knew not one would buy.

These were the luckless living soon to become the luckless dead. The ones who were fished out of river or lake, found crumpled under crumpled papers in the parks, picked up in the horse-and-wagon alleys or slugged, for half a bottle of homemade wine, in the rutted tunnels that run between the advertising agencies and the banks.

Then, only one day too late, they became VIPs at last. Front and profile photographs and a brass tag looped about the neck to await none other than the deputy coroner himself, a police hold order and a genuine pauper's writ.

Some the Demonstrators' Association would invite to attend an autopsy party. For these the cold white dissector's table would be the grave; there wouldn't be enough left to honor with American earth or the simplest sort of cross.

Yet some who had been unlucky so long might turn out to be the very luckiest after all: they were to be embalmed through the courtesy of the Balmy-Hour School of Beautification & Sanitary Bloodletting. Not many, of course, could be so lucky; for so few deserved such luck.

When thirty had gathered together, resigned to their fortunes at last, the merry county carpenters would come with bright new pencils behind their ears, black lunch buckets in their hands, nails in their teeth and Social Security cards in their pockets to make thirty clean pine boxes. Thirty stiffs in a white-washed basement room, heavy with disinfectant in place of flowers, listening, with an inscrutable disdain, to the cheerful ringing of happy hammers and the pleasant talk of living men.

Occasionally one of the stiffs, still stubbornly intent on making trouble for everybody, would require one longer or broader than he had any real right to at all. Gas and river cases gave the most trouble this way. There were not many giants any more.

When the boxes were ready and paid for the We Haul Anything Cartage Company would send around a moving van which fancied itself a hearse. The driver wheeled the dishonored dead out to Elm Forest, where a county sewer-digging machine excavated a trench long enough to hold thirty boxes, no more and no less. Over that single trench, in a cemetery like a forgotten battlefield, the inevitable and inimitable mimic, with the Holy Book in hand and hat held to the side out of respect to his modest fee, would say a few words—all holy—over these unholy dead.

This was all a part of their secret knowledge as they touched the jailhouse water to their foreheads, this was why they laughed so lightly from time to time. For they had had the ultimate joke played upon them prematurely: more ambitious men would have to wait a bit to find out. It was why they grinned so knowingly at the most casual of jailhouse companions; they'd all be taking the same road, down the same littered street, to the same single trench together. It was why they nudged each other familiarly and leered a little: "Take my advice, buddy. Don't die broke."

An old wino dragging a pair of mottled suspenders to the floor wandered in from somewhere and asked wonderingly: "You fellows remember me?" When none remembered he repeated the question to himself, with moving lips, as though he himself had nearly forgotten. Yet with each pulse beat his blood demanded to know, once and for all before it went cold for keeps, who remembered him and his mottled suspenders.

"Remember me? I used to be night watchman on the old Wabash." Not one remembered any night watchman off the Wabash, old or new.

"That's a good job all the same," Frankie explained earnestly to Sparrow. "You watch over people while they sleep. It's when everybody depends on you, nothin' bad should happen. When you're asleep, that's when you can't protect yourself; even Joe Louis is like a little kid then. It's why you shouldn't laugh at some old guy if he's been a good night watcher."

"I seen Fitzsimmons at the old Academy," the dodderer reported. "Remember the old Academy?"

"No," Frankie told him respectfully, "but I want to introduce you to a real live millionaire." He shoved Sparrow around so that the old man could take in all of the punk at once. "Look at that cap he's wearin'—Pop Anson give it to him, it's worth a fortune today." The old man sensed some mockery and, turning his behind upon them both deliberately and leaning so far forward he creaked, began a compulsive sort of scratching through the yellowed underwear, the fingers working with a life of their own, starting below the low sagging hill of the fallen thighs and laboring methodically upward as if pursuing the blood like a dog following its fleas; up over the hill and there paused, digging with blunted fingernails but yet without haste and even with something of pleasure. A full five minutes they watched him, he seemed to be pacing himself, knowing just how long this job would require; then up with the pants and, suspenders still dragging the soiled concrete behind, moved forward once more toward the one thing the blood asked as insistently as it itched in the buttocks: "You fellows remember me?"

The dying blood sought to renew itself by finding someone—anyone—to share a recollection of the old Wabash where so many nights had been shared. If but once somebody would say, "I remember," the blood would be touched; to make him for one moment as he once had been.

But those who remembered were gone with his strength, all down the drain with last year's rain; friends and family and foes together and the blood soon to follow the rains.

"Remember me?" Paused in his ceaseless scratching in that ancestral light, for it seemed that the men about him had all just wandered in off the old Wabash; they too had wandered away their lives in a flesh-colored light and now moved toward him for that final reunion beside a fog-colored trench. "They don't remember people around here any more," he complained aloud at last. So returned to his ceaseless scratching, rump pointed insultingly and suspenders trailing the mottled dust.

"A good turnkey can do better than a patrolman on a beat," Sparrow informed Frankie, "if he gets a houseful that's thirty-four bucks right there."

"It all depends on the neighborhood," Frankie told him out of his wider knowledge of the world. "You take a patrolman up there in Evanston, he's just walkin' around smilin' 'n tippin' his cap, sayin' how nice the lawn looks this morning, Mrs. Rugchild—he's like a watchman is all, up there. He's got to be polite 'cause that means good tips, it ain't like down here in hustlers' territory where they got to line up guys like Schwiefka by pinchin' guys like us before they can pick up anythin' on the side. It's why they got you dead to rights if they catch you duckin' through a Division Street alley after twelve—you're guilty the second that spotlight hits you 'cause you're a wrong guy in a wrong neighborhood out at the wrong hour. If it wasn't for guys like you 'n me guys like Cousin Kvork could be walkin' a North Side beat, they figure. It's why they're down on us, we interrupt their careers."

"Kvork ain't the worst," Sparrow put in, "he just does what he has to do. The time I was up for robbin' he didn't testify, he knew what one more conviction'd do to me."

"Kvork is the best," Frankie agreed, "he don't forget when you do somethin' for him. But it'd serve that pokey right if somebody slapped him silly. He's been shakin' down the greenhorns in here fourteen years. Someday he'll shake down the wrong dino."

"He's done that five-six times awready," Sparrow remembered, "but he always gets reinstated. How can a man get that hungry?"

"It's not hard to mistreat the homeless," Frankie explained.

A roach had leaped, or fallen, from the ceiling into the water bucket, where a soggy slice of pumpernickel and a sodden hunk of sausage now circled slowly, about and about, although there was no current. Belly upward, the roach's legs plied the alien air, trying dreamily to regain a foothold; while Frankie, leaning dreamily on one elbow, knew just how that felt.

It was, he decided, the same wanderer that had waved so invitingly to him from under a radiator while he was being questioned and felt half inclined to help the poor devil now just for old time's sake. He started to poke it over upon its belly so it could try for the bucket's walls, then decided against such charity.

"You ain't gettin' out till I get out," he scolded it aloud, recalling that he too had leaped, or fallen, between walls he couldn't scale; that he too plied the air at times. "We're in the bucket together for not watchin' them lights," he nagged the insect as Sophie so often nagged him; while Sparrow listened without laughter. "Maybe next time you'll look where you're drivin' "—he imitated Sophie's rattling whine—" 'yer fault, yer fault, takin' everythin' in yer own hands when you're stewed to the gills, all *yer* dirty fault.' Next time maybe you'll know better," Frankie consoled himself by consoling the roach. "This'll be a good lesson to you, bug."

The growing light began making a stairway to nowhere out of the shadows of the bars: a stairwell lit feebly by the reflecting mirror's glow as it competed with the lightening day.

"I'm no good but my wife's a hundred per cent," somebody down the tier confided aloud to everyone in hearing distance.

"Mine stinks," Frankie Machine thought softly; immediately his conscience kicked him in the shin. "I got a good one too," he answered loudly to make up for everything.

And his conscience kicked him in the other shin for lying.

The night's first shadows, nudging each other down the corridors, slipped quietly aside to let a paunch draped in a candy-striped shirt and a greasy black mortician's suit pass by: Zero Schwiefka threw out his big flat feet so that the soles squeaked painfully, like little live things being crunched beneath the full burden of his weight.

He stood before Frankie's cell rubbing his hands together breathlessly, clear to the elbows, like a great bluebottle fly preening its front legs, then tilting its head and body forward to preen the back ones; the hand-rubbing became an arm-rubbing, his head tilted darkly forward from the dark and twisted lapels till one almost expected him to tilt forward on his palms and start pressing his legs together with the same mechanical insectlike intent.

"Where *you* been, cabbagenose?" Frankie greeted him, sitting up. "Gettin' married?"

"Who'd marry *that?*" Sparrow asked from the cell's safety—"A woomin?"

"Got here as soon as I could, Dealer," Heavy-belly apologized, holding the belly up with the hamlike hands. Between his jowls, loosened by idleness and drink, the bulbous nose overhung a mouth like a half-healed knife wound. "You'll be out in half an hour, Dealer—leave Non Compis here till the dog-catchers go home." And spat to show his contempt for Division Street punks.

Sparrow spat in turn. Right into the water bucket where the roach now floated passively. "We ain't eat since last night," he accused Schwiefka. "How many suppers *you* eat tonight, Mr. Barrymore?"

"Do they have a charge?" Frankie interrupted politely.

"I made 'em put it down a misdemeanor. It'll be dismissed in the morning. They been holding it open."

"I'll still be open after they let me out," Sparrow pointed out, "open for any-thin'. You got somebody's legs you want bust, spigothead? T'ree-fifty fer one 'n two fer five—you save a deuce gettin' 'em both done at once 'n it's easier on the mark, too. He oney got to go to the hospital once, my way."

"When I want to hear from you I'll holler," Schwiefka advised the punk sternly, "and when I holler you come in on a shovel."

Nobody took Solly Saltskin seriously any more.

"You think I'm gonna sleep in this crum dump tonight again?" Frankie wanted to know. "Get us out tonight if you have to get Zygmunt to do it."

"Where you sleep is your own business," Schwiefka reproached him mildly. "What I said was you're gettin' out in half a hour 'n the super hisself couldn't put the fix in faster. The case'll be dismissed by noon whether you're in court or not. Depend on Big Zero."

"The oney place you're big is in the belly, bakebrain," Sparrow told him from behind Frankie, "you're the guy put his mother on a meathook for a quarter one time, I heard all about it from your old man, he was sore you wouldn't split wit' him."

"If your old man hadn't been out of work you'd never been born," Schwiefka told him, and lit a cigarette for Frankie, through the bars, with a silver lighter.

"Don't worry, Sparrow," Frankie spoke assuringly, "we can depend on Zero—he'll get us out if it takes ten years."

"I don't even ask how come you're in," Schwiefka complained, "I just come to spring you—what's the big squawk?"

"You know all right why we're in, that's the big squawk," Frankie let Schwiefka know. "Every time you duck Kvorka for his double sawzie he cruises down Division till he spots me or the punk 'n pulls us in on general principles.

This time he caught us together. The next time it happens you're payin' me off 'n the punk too."

"Next time they'll hang me," Sparrow put in moodily.

"We're layin' low a couple days," Schwiefka evaded the accusation, "till I get the tables moved back to the alley joint. We ought to get a loose crowd up there Saturday night. What time you be around?"

"Not early enough to move no tables, that's a lead-pipe cinch," and turned away.

Schwiefka was long used to the turned back. He had brought news of salvation to men before. Frankie listened to the retreating shuffle of those big flat feet in the oncoming gloom, testing each iron step of the stairwell as if each might be the last iron step of all.

"We won't have to see the old toad for a couple days, anyhow," Frankie sighed.

"You told him off just right, Dealer," Sparrow assured him. "He took off like a scalded dog. I guess you scared him, Frankie."

"Ain't nobody scared of me my whole life," Frankie conceded regretfully.

"Them Krauts was scared of you, Frankie," Sparrow reminded him in his rasping whisper, "you were a big man in the army."

"I was a big man awright—I was the guy had to pick the fly crap out of the pepper with boxin' gloves," Frankie mocked himself.

"'N that Nifty Louie been scared of you, too, ever since you caught him that time, tryin' to sell Soph them funny kind of cigarettes."

"Funny cigarettes ain't all that one pushes, it ain't no big secret," Frankie observed and thought bitterly: "If I didn't need a fix now 'n then I wouldn't even let that creeper take a hand at the table I'm dealin'."

"How'd you catch him that time, Frankie?" Like a child asking for some familiar bedtime tale.

"It wasn't him. It was Piggy-O. He wasn't sellin' 'n I didn't catch him." There was an old defeat in Frankie's voice now. "I just smelled 'em 'n asked her 'n she told me, 'Piggy *give* me four sticks,' that's all. So I told him to lay off her." Adding to himself: "One customer in the family is all we can afford."

"Tell you what's funny, Frankie," Sparrow promised, "Louie bein' scared of you, Zero bein' so scared of Louie, 'n you bein' scared of me—how come a little guy like me runs all you cheap hoods around, Frankie? How come a little guy like me bein' such a little terrer?"

"Just because you're so strong, I guess," Frankie conceded absently, his mind still occupied with Louie and Louie's many moods.

He'd been in short pants in the days when Louie Fomorowski was beating two murder raps. They'd gotten a one-to-life jacket on him for the second one, of which he'd served nine months in privileged circumstances.

Yet now Nifty Louie was pushing a heavily cut grade of morphine and having his own troubles pushing it. Where he got it only the blind bummy called Pig, who peddled it for him, might have guessed. Pig never cared to guess. "How could I tell where the stuff comes from when I can't even see where it goes?" he'd put it to Frankie. "It's why I'm the peddler, 'cause I can't see what the people 'r doin'."

"I never asked you where the stuff comes from," Frankie reminded him, "but I'll tell you one place where it *ain't* goin', 'n that's upstairs where I live. I'm kickin' the stuff altogether this week end, I don't want you hustlin' Soph onto no kick like that. I can't afford."

Blind Pig always agreed. "I never come around with the stuff till you send to Louie for me to come, Dealer," he pointed out. "If you're kickin' it I wish you luck. I hope you go from monkey to zero 'n never get hooked again."

Both Blind Pig and Louie knew there was no harm in wishing any man luck. They called those using the stuff only occasionally "joy-poppers" and wished them all great joy. For the joy-poppers had no intention of becoming addicts in the true sense. They had the will power, they felt, to use God's medicine once or twice a month and forget it the rest of the time.

Nor did Louie acknowledge that a student had ceased to be a joy-popper because he had reached a once-a-week compromise with his need. Once a week wasn't being hooked in Fomorowski's book. On a quarter grain a week a man was still just a student. It wasn't till a man needed a quarter of a grain a day that Louie felt the fellow was safely in the vise. "You're not a student any more," he would offer his felicitations. "You just graduated. Junkie—you're *hooked*."

"C'mon"—Frankie roused Sparrow—"hearts for noses," and they squatted together over the battered deck. Sparrow always played with some trepidation. For the winner was privileged to slap the loser across the nose with five of the cards ten times and Sparrow always lost. He would take his punishment then almost—but never quite—without flinching, trying very hard not to let the tears come into his eyes at the swift sting of the cards. For it always seemed a punishment, the way Frankie would slap him then, for something unspoken which Frankie held against him secretly.

So he stalled, knowing the turnkey was due with the keys, yet owed Frankie two games—twenty slaps—before the pokey appeared at last.

"Up in there!"

"I'll collect sometime when you got it comin' 'n I got more time," Frankie assured the punk as they reached for their caps. And Sparrow knew that, for no real reason he could name, Frankie had the right to collect, game or no game: that the game was really only an excuse to exact some ancestral tribute he owed the dealer.

At the open door Frankie remembered something. He grinned wryly with his flat pug's mug under the tawny tousle of his hair and went to the water bucket. "I promised to give him a hand when I got out of the bucket myself," he explained softly, eying the roach while the turnkey eyed him with deadpan suspicion. "Only look—it's too late awready."

It was too late all right. Too late for roaches or old Skid Row rumdums; it was even getting a little late for cripples and junkies and punks too long on the same old hustle. The water-soaked corpse was only half afloat, the head submerged and the rear end pointing to the ceiling like a sinking sub when the perpetual waters pull it downward and down forever. "I could have saved him," Frankie realized with a faint remorse. "It's all my fault again."

"Guys like you," the turnkey warned him, "I handle them every day," and watched the pair mounting the narrow steps toward a narrower freedom. On the street they waited for a northbound car.

A car that came on slowly, but not too slowly for Frankie Machine. If it would just sort of keep on coming forever, like streetcars sometimes did for him in dreams, without ever really arriving, he wouldn't have to go anywhere any more. The dealer didn't want to go home. Sophie did all the dealing there.

"Mama, deal yourself another hand," he hummed idly, deciding to himself, "If she starts that screaming about What was it for this time Why don't I get a broom in my tail 'n go to work on the legit Why don't we move out of the neighborhood the spades are moving in it's gettin' smokier every day 'n if it wasn't for me she wouldn't be strapped to no wheel chair when she could be out dancin'—Come on upstairs with me," he asked Sparrow, out of need of a barrier between himself and Sophie's crossfire.

Sparrow shook his head. He'd been trapped in that barrage before. She gave it to him first and hottest because she got so few chances at him. "I got to look for a job," he explained. Frankie understood.

Just as the street lamps came on the streetcar paused and went dark half a
block down. It had slipped its trolley and against the last light of evening the
pole groped blindly for the wire overhead, found it at last and came on again,
slowly, but with all self-confidence gone; yet bearing its precious load of light
caught from that magic wire with a sort of tenderness. And screeched to a stop
like Sophie's opening volley.

Frankie boarded it feeling done up and Sparrow followed whispering
hoarsely: "You want to bet on the transfer numbers?" Trolley transfers had a
serial number on the lower right-hand corner that could be bet on like a stud-
poker hand, the loser paying both fares. It was the one game which the punk
won more often than he lost against Frankie.

But Frankie held his transfer listlessly, unaware that he held it at all. Sparrow
slipped it out of his hand.

"Beat you again, Frankie, I got two pair. You owe me eight centses."

"You owe me twenty slapses."

"Call it square, Frankie?" He held onto Frankie's transfer.

"All square."

Both had won.

Yet, all the way home, Sparrow had the restless feeling that someone must
have lost.

"I'll buy you a drink by Antek," Sparrow offered suddenly when they
reached Milwaukee Avenue and Division Street.

They entered Antek Witwicki's Tug & Maul Bar together. At the corner table
the little terrier called Drunkie John was scolding Molly Novotny, a girl
scarcely out of her teens who supported both herself and John hustling drinks
at the Club Safari in the early morning hours. A small girl with a heart-shaped
face and eyes dark with exhaustion, she sat listening to John, a man close to
forty, with a sort of dull hopelessness. Each evening she had to listen here,
while paying for the drinks, to all the things she had done wrong since morning. She herself sat without drinking and without once moving her eyes off his
bitter mouth as if fearing to miss a single word.

Frankie noticed that John's hair, thin as it was, had been parted so precisely
in the middle it must have taken him ten minutes before the mirror to achieve
the part. His comb hand trembled, even as Frankie watched, when reaching
for his glass. The girl kept her own glass out of his reach. John's own had certainly been emptied too often and Frankie heard her pleading, under the rise

and fall of the uproar about them, to pick up his hat and come home with her, he had had enough.

Drunkie John never had enough. "The nuthouse is the best place for you," he began shouting at her for some reason, "babies your age 'r hoppin' up 'n down out there!" He reached for her glass just as she drew it back, his hand struck hers and sent the whisky trickling down the front of her flowered cotton dress.

"Have your own way then, have your own way," she placated him, not even knowing what way he wished to have next: her days were made up trying to guess what he might want next, a thing John could never tell himself. For he was a man with certain fancies on his mind. Once he'd gotten Molly drunk in here and had decided that what he really wanted to do next was "to make the people laugh" by pinning her dress up to the small of her back. She had staggered blindly about trying to unpin it while the barflies had snickered and she herself had laughed in a loose self-derision.

The next day John would have nothing to do with her, she had made such an exhibition of herself, how could a man like himself ever face his friends again?

John was as unpredictable as the weather in the streets. Sometimes he told her to put on her coat and leave him forever. And the minute she had it on would demand that she strip and get into bed right away, he was going to show her what a bull she had for a man. But once in bed the years of boozing would betray him and he would succeed only in showing her what a freak she had.

A good kicking around was what she had coming then, making a freak of a decent sort like himself. For he never used his hands on her. It was always a businesslike kick with the toe of his outworn dancing pumps, delivered not so much in rage as with a certain matter-of-factness, even a kind of contentment.

"Don't say you *won't,*" he warned her about something or other now. "Don't *never* say you won't *nothin'*."

"Just drink up," Molly pleaded, "the people 'r watchin'." She was trying to fit the nipple of a little blue balloon into the brown beer bottle beside her glass.

"What *you* doin' here anyhow?" he wanted to know as if only now realizing who she was. Then grinned slyly, bringing his face so close to her own that she drew back a bit. "You gettin' drunkie too, honey?" he asked insinuatingly, as if meaning that there was a great deal more between them than just getting drunk together again; and began shaking her by both shoulders in an access of drunken humor. "Now you're a big-time entertainer!"

She protested with strained laughter. "Johnny! *Stop* it!"

"Start singin' 'n dancin' 'n somethin'! Makin' the people laugh! That's right! Make the people laugh!" He added reprovingly: "I can't do it *all* myself, honey."

"Give that kid somethin'," Frankie told Sparrow, "I took her to a dance when she was fourteen 'n Soph slapped her face for goin' around wit' older men. I was twenty-one, I guess." He pushed Sparrow's change toward Sparrow. "Put a dime in the juke 'n give her a dime to sing along with it, she used to be singin' all the time."

Sparrow cocked his head to one side, studying Frankie dubiously. "Give it to the kid yourself, I don't interfere in fam'ly situations."

Frankie rose, handed a dime to Molly, and Drunkie John slapped it out of her hand.

"*I* pervide fer her," he told Frankie. "Who sent for *you?*" He really wanted to know. He wanted to know so badly that his head waggled weakly as he asked; and one shove, anyone could see, would send him sprawling. Frankie returned, red in the face from more than whisky, to his own table.

Down in the sawdust Molly saw the dime and studied it while Johnny studied her, waiting for her to make a move for it.

"Go ahead," he encouraged her, "you got no more damned pride left than to go pickin' up dimes off tavern floors—go ahead, the people know about you awready anyhow, what you are. They ain't forgot the time you danced around here with your fatal ass stickin' out—go on, let the people see how low a woman can get. It makes a man feel mighty fine, I can tell you, to watch his girl crawlin' on her hands 'n knees in a whisky tavern for a dime some cheap cardsharp tosses her. Go ahead, don't mind *me,* you're so low now you're two floors under the basement." He was trying to work up his anger like a man pumping a dry well; she touched him with real gentleness.

"Don't excite yourself, Johnny."

With the pointed toe of the dancing pump he kicked at her ankle, skinning the defenseless flesh. She turned and, with no further word, walked toward the door, bending once to rub the ankle as she went.

At the door bald Antek, with a plumber's plunger in his hand, blocked Drunkie John from following her onto the street. "All I ask is you give her a head start," he told Johnny. "I'd give a dog that much."

"You callin' my Molly a *dawg?*"

"No. I'm just calling you one."

"That's better, that's all right," Johnny assured him, actually gratified. "I don't care what you call *me.* I'm no good. But that girl is a queen, there's nothin' she don't deserve: I just hope I never catch her."

"I think what you need is a steady job hustlin' pins in the bowlin' alley,"Antek judged him. "All that's wrong with you is you don't know what to do with yourself so you take picks on that girl. Why she puts up with you you'll never make me understand." He let John pass to the street at last.

It was true. He was simply a man who didn't know what to do with himself, for he didn't yet know who he was. It's sometimes easier to find a job than to find oneself and John hadn't yet gotten around to doing the first. How could he know who he was? Some find themselves through joy, some through suffering and some through toil. Johnny had till now tried nothing but whisky. A process which left him feeling like somebody new every day.

There were days when he haunted the bookies without a dime in his pocket but with a pair of street-carnival binoculars, a child's toy strung by a cord about his throat: a big-time horse player but business had kept him in the city, he'd just dropped in to see how his stable was doing out there at Hawthorne.

Other days he sat at Antek's with a golf bag containing a single club between his scrawny knees. He had just come from the links, it had been too hot out there, he'd had to quit on the seventh hole.

In his room hung a yellowing photograph, thumbtacked to the wall, of a slack-jawed youth in loose black wrestler's trunks in the attitude of an advancing wrestler. He had been a wrestler in his youth, he would have the nerve to say while standing under this image, the proof lying in the signature below the picture. The photograph was without doubt of himself; no other could boast of a mouth as loose as the trunks themselves, those billiard-cue arms and that face of an underfed wanderoo.

He was many men and no man at all. He was a hysterical little bundle of possibilities that could never come true. He was a mouth at the end of a whisky glass, a knock-kneed shuffle in dancing pumps. Pumps—"for when I used to win them marathons all the time"—kept with the semblance of a shine by a girl with a heart-shaped face and the wonder gone out of her eyes.

"She got too big a heart, that girl,"Antek explained of Molly when John had left. "A guy can walk into her heart with army boots on."

Frankie and Sparrow sat silently a moment after Antek had passed. Until Frankie said at last, "There ain't many hearts like that no more, Sparrow."

"Sophie's gonna be real worried about you, Frankie," Sparrow chose the moment to remind the dealer. Frankie rose and pushed back his chair as though he thought it might somehow be Molly Novotny to whom he was going home tonight.

To the tenants of 1860 West Division Street Landlord Schwabatski was seldom referred to as the landlord. He was Schwabatski the Jailer. Though his
only uniform was a pair of faded army fatigues and his only weapon a hammer with which he pretended, from time to time, to repair a loose tread on
the stairs. To prove he really was the landlord he had hung a sign above his
desk on the second floor:

QUIET

Or out you go too

But both the desk and the sign seemed somehow lopsided. The whole vast
frame rooming house, and Schwabatski as well, seemed lopsided. If the desk
leaned a bit to one side it only went to show that the Jailer was no more skilled
in carpentry than at playing landlord.

He certainly appeared the kind of man more likely to be found behind cell
bars than the one turning the key in the lock. Yet he had to be a door-shutter
and key-turner for guests who insisted, summer or winter, on leaving doors
ajar. It was true that most of the rooms were small and close; but Schwabatski
felt it wasn't always for lack of air that tenants left doors a bit open.

"Maybe you mean to have only a little air all right," he would argue for
understanding, "but always somebody thinks it's an invitation and then comes
big fight, up and down, and who pays policemens for me then? If you want to
make carryings-on, please do in *family* way, door always *closed.*"

"I s'ppose I have to get dressed 'n go down 'n set on the curb like some bum
to get a breath of air," some stray would huff at him. But the strays were forever
huffing and the Jailer's argument never varied.

"You want to go out, go out. But you're in, don't be just *half* in—be *all* in.
You ain't in till door is *close.* A old man like me can't be run up, down stairs
every five minutes, see what goes on. Got work to do."

Schwabatski had work to do all right. He had a dim-witted, oversized, twenty-
one-year-old of a son whose sole and simple pleasure it was to plant paper daisies
in the cracks of the dark old stairs. Schwabatski never gave up hope of being able
to teach the boy carpentry; so brought him each day, with hammer and pencil
and nail, to watch the way in which a broken stair should be repaired.

The old man's patience was inexhaustible. How many times had that same
tread been pulled out and the work begun again because the boy's attention
wandered from the hammer's tapping to his precious daisies? Yet the boy's
patience surpassed even his father's. He waited as hopefully for the daisies to

take root as the old man hoped for some light to come into Peter's brain. Poor Peter—he touched each daisy to his heavy underlip before each planting: he prayed for rain to come to the dark stairwell.

There was nothing seriously wrong with the boy's understanding, the old man felt. It was just that, whenever the boy began to get the idea of the hammer and nails, one of those strays would start some uproar or other and hammer and nails and stair and son would have to be forgotten while he rushed to make peace at his own price before the Saloon Street aces made it at theirs.

Why would anyone want to eat peanuts in the dark with the door exactly two inches ajar? Yet there it was, the door open and swinging a little and a sound of peanuts being crushed and the shells tossed onto a newspaper in the darkened room. He couldn't tell whether it was a man or a woman, so he called in a voice good for either:

"That don't seem right to me in there! You like peanuts—eat them right. Turn on light. Close door."

A woman's voice answered, heavy with drink or sarcasm, "You got a house rule says I got to have the light on when I eat peanuts?"

"I'm an old man, I can't stay up all night to stop funny business."

"Nobody sent for you."

"Nobody sent for you, neither, lady. *Keep closed.*"

He would close it and closed it would remain, though he had to lock it himself from the outside and keep the key in his pocket all night.

Hardly a week passed but someone, on one of the floors commanding a view of the street, seeing a pair of aces from the Saloon Street Station making for the entrance, would give the old man joyous warning over the banister: "Visitors, Jailer! Company!"

And always it was the new ones who gave the most trouble. The old-timers, like the dealer and his wife, battled, like respectable people should, behind closed doors. Schwabatski's ears had long ago tuned out the sort of roarer that the dealer and his Sophie sometimes put on. To a stranger it would have sounded like one word short of murder; but the Jailer would shuffle past, explaining it to himself: "They want to love each other—but they don't know how." And shrug upon his way.

It was the rooms from which no sound came at all, while man and wife were together in there, that caught Schwabatski's ear. It was from such rooms that real trouble came, the sudden glass-splintering crash, the moment of panting stillness and then the unspeakable flat-level scream of straight terror as the woman stumbled out of the room with the blood down the side of her face and her particular prize behind her with the broken bottle in his hand.

Schwabatski never worried about the dealer's yellow door. There Sophie sat, her ash-blond hair in pin curls, one hand on the wheelchair's arm and her army blanket across her knees, toying aimlessly with a combination flashlight-pencil, pressing the tiny light off and on, on and off. A dog howling down Schwabatski's shadowed stairs recalled a casual promise made down her memory's spiraled stairwell.

"When you gonna get me the dawg you promised?" she asked as Frankie closed the door carefully behind him. "You promised me you was sure gonna bring me a sweet lit-tul dawg. Well, I'm still settin' 'n waitin' but I don't see *no* damned kind of dawg except a jailhouse dawg 'n that's you. *Why* you always promisin': 'I'm gonna bring you the cutest puppy-pup'—'n then a beat-out deck 'n a dirty shirt is what you really bring—I suppose you think I don't even know where you was again?"

"It wasn't no pet shop, Zosh."

"Who told me?"

"Who always travels the news around here? Piggy-O, the Information Bureau."

"*He* asks me how am I feelin', he don't just shove in here without even sayin' how's anyone feelin'."

"How you feelin', Zosh?"

"Don't call me 'Zosh,' I ain't no greenhorn, I wasn't born in Slutsk, I was born on eart' on Aw*goo*sty Boulevard 'n my name is Soph-*ee*-a—*say* it."

"How you feelin', Soph-*ee*-a?"

"No damned good at all. I got gas on the stomach. You got gas on the stomach?"

Something more subtle than gas weighed on her stomach. Behind the curtain of loneliness which had sheltered her childhood a sick dread had grown. Of being left, some final evening, alone in a room like this small room with no one of her own near at all.

A dread she sometimes evaded by reaching for an outsized album labeled, in her own childish and belabored hand, *My Scrapbook of Fatal Accidence*. When she had finished scissoring these letters out of red and green Christmas wrapping paper they had looked so large and cheerful she had gone on to embroider the title with comic-strip cutouts: Superman and Bugs Bunny, Tarzan and Little

Abner cavorted in a wanton carnival among lady spies in sheerest negligee and announcements of double-horror features and double-feature horrors from the tabloid movie directories.

She had begun the book with the *Times* photo of her own "fatal accident" and had gone on to add to it all manner of lurid cries from the depths: of unwed mothers who plunged newborn infants down dumbwaiters in an oatmeal box or tossed them into a furnace in a cornflake carton because "God told me to." To announce, when a visitor remarked that the house seemed rather warm: "I know. I just put the baby in the stove."

She loved to pull out the one captioned *Death Was Driving,* to which she'd added, in her own crude art, a skull and crossbones; because she had learned that that gave Frankie what he called "chicken flesh."

In fact she had been so altogether tickled with the crinkling effect it had had on his skin, reminding him as it did of the night when he'd supported her onto a cold white hospital bed with her eyes still dilated with shock, that she had gone on to wider fields: a whole family wiped out in a secondhand Chevvie one bright May morning at an Indiana Harbor crossing.

The movie directory captions she had clipped and hoarded like an aging coquette treasuring old dance programs.

EVERY KISS
EVERY EMBRACE
Brought a nameless terror . . .
A sinister jealousy!

ADULTS ONLY!
What do gorilla kidnapers do
with their women prey?

Do native women live with gorillas?
See: *A Beautiful Maiden in the hands
of the horrible Urubu Tribe.*

VOODOO SECRETS!

Best of all was the yellowing photo from the *Times* that proved to him, each day anew, that it had all been his fault. So much his fault that he could never leave her alone again.

"Wheel me a little, Frankie," she begged. There were moments when not even the scrapbook sustained her. She would feel she was falling and only being wheeled back and forth could arrest that endless plunge into nowhere.

Some nights she wheeled herself while he slept. When he wakened he would see her in the corner where the light and darkness met, half her face in the fading shadows of Saturday night and half in Sunday morning's rain-washed light. With her hair in papers, in crimpers or pins, she would be ready for the day and all day long would move, little by little, following the light, till the night's neon carnival began once more below.

All day long, alternately picking at the army blanket about her knees with her tinted fingernails and then at her chin. "Whiteheads, blackheads," she had a little song for the very loneliest hours, picking at the chin's flesh till it was raw: "I like to *tweeze* 'em 'n *squeeze* 'em, it's when I get in the mood."

Till the same old shadows took her anew.

Sometimes it seemed to Frankie there was no end to the wheeling at all. So now for reply he pulled a homemade drummer's practice board out from under the sink, seated himself before it, sticks in hand, on a little backless chair. He used the sticks lightly a moment, just enough to shut out the pleading punctuated by the flashlight's irregular clicking. Till he could get the feel of the drums again.

"That's right, just duck your puss over that dirty board 'n make off like I ain't even alive. I ask you to wheel me so you make like I'm dead—it's what you're hopin' all the time anyhow."

For one moment there was no sound in the room save that of the battered clock below the phosphorescent crucifix on the wall, its sturdy old pulse beating quietly, without a single flutter. He rapped out a long, sure, steady workmanlike beat.

Frankie liked the drums. That was in the wrist too. He beat through his own version of "Song of the Islands" twice.

"Cute," Sophie announced the moment he'd finished.

A single meaningless word like that: cute. But what and who and why everything had to be so damned cute there would be no telling.

"I knew that Gertie Michalek, the one wit' the birt'mark like a p'tato on her wrist," Sophie went on, "when she got preg'ant she could always tell if it was going to be a girl 'cause she'd get that cravin' for cold p'tatoes. 'N you know what, Frankie? To this day when Michalek's little girl eats a p'tato, the p'tato eyes come out on Michalek's birt'mark. What you think of *that?*"

No answer. He would be trying not to feel unnerved at her meaningless discontent. Around and around she would go now upon the breathless merry-go-round of her ceaseless mysteries; till his mind would be dulled by its whirling and he would try talking her back to reality.

"I'm lookin' for a job beatin' the tubs, Zosh," he told her, leaning forward to begin again just as she signaled to him with the flashlight—dot-dot-dash-dot-dot-dot—in a code she had just invented. "What am I signalin' now?" she wanted to know. She'd had enough drumming for one night. If he wouldn't wheel her he'd have to play games. He would have to guess something.

Brushing back his hair with his forearm, he felt the sticks growing cold between his fingers. "*My* guess is your roof is leakin'," he ventured at last. Knowing that if he didn't play the game she would rap-rap-rap with the metal against the wheelchair's arm, translating the secret code into an even more secret Morse while a faint and knowing smile would stray across her lips.

A smile that veiled her knowledge of his latest trickery: from the first night he'd lugged it up the stairs she had been on to him. Just one more excuse to keep from wheeling her, that's all the practice board was. All the talk about wanting to play in a real band, join the musicians' union and be on the legit were just so many more corny tricks to get out of doing his proper duty toward her.

Well, she still had a proper trick or two of her own up her sleeve. She watched him as he tried not to pay attention to the flashlight, wondering just what moment she'd begin signaling again.

For one moment she held the flashlight poised like a vicious little club above the wheelchair's arm while he held the sticks tensely above the board. Then shoved board and sticks back under the sink and lay his head on his arm across a soup plate. She put the flash down with a pervasive sense of triumph.

"That's right. Don't bother puttin' on no kettle fer dishes. Just lay wit' your head on the sink, that's the sure way to get 'em done."

Frankie raised up, took a battered deck off the shelf, shoved the dirty plate to one side and riffled the deck through his fingers.

"Sure. Just shove to one side fer the maid. Start dealin' to yerself now like a goof goin' soft in the head."

"There's only fifty cards in your deck tonight, honey," Frankie reproached her gently. "I think you got a little repercussion again today."

"You mean a *concussion*, dummy." For once she had him.

"No, I mean a *repercussion*. Like you been bounced on your head *twice*."

"My head is airtight. It's yours is leakin'—bot' ways. Your own stepmother said if you wasn't married you'd be settin' in the pen right now. Your own stepmother."

"She wasn't no 'stepmother,' " Frankie contradicted her flatly with genuine resentment.

"I s'ppose she was your real mother. Don't you think *I* know about you?"

"She wasn't no 'stepmother.' She was a foster mother 'n she done the best she could. She wasn't no 'stepmother,' the way you say it."

"She done so good you don't even know if she's dead 'r alive." Sophie knew when she had him in the vise and gave it the final turn. "She done so much she didn't even come to the school when you 'n them other punks got caught in the boiler room with the dice. If she'd of come you could have finished like them others."

"It wasn't she didn't *want* to come, Zosh," Frankie insisted. "She was ashamed, she couldn't talk good English, you know that. She done the best she could."

Sophie returned to the frontal attack.

"I got more brains in my butt than your whole scrumblebug fam'ly got in their heads—scrambled eggs is what your fam'ly got for brains. You gonna bring me a damned dawg 'r *ain't* you gonna bring me no damned dawg? *That's* what I want to know."

A plaintive howling came circling up the stairwell. Sitting with his slim back toward her, the dealer asked wearily, "You really want a dog, Zosh?"

No answer. She was studying the short hairs on the back of his neck. And waited, in the most cunning silence of all, to see whether he would pick up her thought. If he did, then she would know it was true, what old Doc Dominowski had told her about thought transference, how every mind was really a sort of radio set capable of both broadcasting and receiving thought waves.

"You couldn't keep no dog in here anyhow," Frankie pointed out.

"It don't have to be no damned wolf from a zoo, goofy t'ing. It could just be a soft lit-tul puppy-pup. Sort of smoody-like 'n cute, what I could pet. *You promised.*"

"He'd mess up the joint. What would you do when he had to go? Set him in the sink? So don't talk no more. I got scrambled eggs for brains 'n yours is poached, they ain't even settin' on toast—When do we eat?"

"As soon as you heave them greasy cards out the window 'n jump out after 'em," she informed him. "It's oney two stories."

"I'm afraid of losin' the joker that way," he told her with indifference, jamming a match, in lieu of a toothpick, between his teeth.

"You're the biggest joker around here." And studied him with a child's huge scorn: "*Some* toot'pick."

"Besides, the cards ain't even greasy," he decided, "I put your Saturday Night in a Whorehouse powder on 'em to make 'em slip good." He shifted the match between his teeth. That had been a pretty good one all right. "You don't let me practice on the tubs, I got to do somethin' to kill the pass-time."

"Where's *my* pass-time then? A dawg'd be my pass-time oney I don't count. I count fer nuts. It's just you 'n that secondhand drum box that counts." She wheeled up to him, her tone turning to a plea as she came: "'N it'd give *you* somethin' to do too, honey. You could take him out for air 'n bring back some beer."

She lay her fingers, so soft, so cold, upon his own hard hand.

"Beer ain't no good for you, Zosh," he reminded her, "the croaker said it wasn't no good for you account you can't exercise. It blows up your belly 'n the bubbles go to your head. Here"—he proffered the deck—"pick a card."

The fingers upon his own turned to bloodless claws—he drew his hand back fast. "*Ever*'thin's no good fer me," she wailed and slapped the cards out of his hand. "Little puppies 'n even havin' a little beer, to have somethin' to *do*. I'll be twenny-six years for Christmas 'n just *look* how I am—a old lady awready!"

Abruptly the loss of all her bright hours enraged her: "*Never* say 'croaker'— I don't *like* it when you say 'croaker.' "

"What do you like, Zosh?" He just thought he'd ask.

"What I like is when I mix that dark beer wit' the light stuff!" She had pinned him to the sink with the wheels of the chair touching his shoes. "It's *that* kind I like, what I really go for. Oh go*damn*it, don't you even know what I like *yet?*"

When her voice rose in that rattling whine he remembered the distant beat of artillery and the sudden applause of M.G. fire.

"Somebody was trying the latch last night," he told her, inching his toes back from the wheels.

"It's just the way the El shakes it," she explained. "It done that before you left 'n you wouldn't fix it then 'n it's gettin' to look like you never will now." Her hand tried to recover his own. "Everybody got to have a little bit," she told him pleadingly.

"A little bit of what, Zosh?"

"A little bit of beer, a little bit of fun," she told him in her thin sing-song. "A little bit of anythin', a little bit of love."

"What kind of beer you like best, Zosh?" Trying to get her back on the rails.

" 'What kind? What kind?' " she mocked him, her voice ringing as brainlessly as a ninety-eight-cent alarm clock in an unrented room running down to a whimper. "It's been so long since I had a beer I just don't know what kind I like no more."

With yesterday's empties crouching behind her chair.

"I don't *know*, Frankie," she complained with a distress like a tired child's. "How many kinds are there? I don't even know what kinds there *are* any more."

"There's Budweiser," he told her indulgently, as if enumerating distant relatives, "then there's Schlitz, and Blatz, and Pabst and Chevalier—

> *"Drink Chevalier*
> *The beer that's clear—"*

he hummed a radio commercial that sometimes softened her. Yet himself remained tense with the sense of being cornered by more than a secondhand wheelchair.

"Any kind wit' foam on, *that's* the kind I like"—her voice was happy at last, running over with imagined foam, drooling over her tongue in her haste to tell all about it. "*Any* godamned kind wit' lots of godamned foam—warm beer, cold beer, hot beer, winter beer—I *like* beer."

"I like beer too, Zosh," he assured her. She ignored his assent.

"I *like* beer. I just *like* it. Warm beer, cold beer, old beer, winter beer, big beers, bock beers 'n them little old teensy Goebbels' beers—I *like* beer, Frankie hon."

"I know, Zosh—"

"I like the Great Lakes too—you know why? 'Cause the navy's there. Godamnit, I *like* the navy, *any* navy, the Irish navy, the Mexican navy, I even like the Dago navy. I *like* beer, I *like* the navy, sunk navies 'n floatin' navies—I like them movie actors too. Give me them movie actors—go*damn*it, you don't know how I like *anythin'*." Her voice trailed off. "I like dancin' too, Frankie hon."

"Should I go down 'n get a half gallon?" Anything to get out of this corner.

"You can run down 'n get me a godamned dawg like you *promised,* you *promised,* you *promised*"—abruptly she realized that he'd deliberately side-tracked her desire for a dog.

"I spent thirty-four months havin' green-ass corporals chew me up," he told her with a bitter wisdom: " 'Dress up that salute, Private, no pass for you, Private, get the dust off that carbine, Private—pick up that butt you just stepped over, Private'—you think I come home to hear *you* quackin'? If I don't talk you get mad 'n if I say somethin' you tear my head off." He leaned his back against the sink, looking puffy-eyed, and heard his own voice pleading: "I don't know if I'm comin' 'r goin' no more, Zosh."

"You look to me more like you're goin'." She eyed him steadily, inching up till the wheels pushed the toes of his heavy army shoes back a fraction of an inch. "You know what the ruination of the world is?" And answered herself: "Stubbornness. You know what's wrong wit' you? You're a stubborn t'ing. It's why you're the ruination of *me*. It's why it's all your fault."

"You don't know anythin' about dogs," he defended himself.

"I know about dawgs, you don't know about dawgs."

"He'd run away," he told her, his eyes half closed against her.

"I'd keep him tied. The dawg'd be tied all the time."

"What you want a dog to be tight all the time for? Don't you think dogs like to sober up once in a while too?"

It didn't work. She thought it over one long moment and her mind ricocheted again: "Honey, you know about the girl wit' the strorberry on her behind? Whenever she ate strorberries it got real red."

No, he had heard about the girl with the blossoming butt.

"But that ain't *nuttin'*," she assured him. "On Saloon Street was a little kiddie-kid, her old lady got scared by a rat so bad she slipped her wig 'n you know how that kid come out? She had a birt'mark shapen like a rat right across her teeny face wit' the tail curlin' up onto the cheek, *hair 'n all*."

Then saw he was just sitting there listening to nothing but the ceaseless traffic's murmur and nudged the cup off the wheelchair's arm; he started as it shattered on the floor. She nudged the saucer after the cup.

"What you breakin' the dishes for?"

"'Cause I feel like it."

"Okay," he agreed amiably, "I feel like it too," and shoved a soup bowl off the sink.

She reversed the wheels swiftly, turned and raced to the cabinet in the corner as pale as the pillow behind her head. "You like to break t'ings?" she asked so softly he scarcely heard—and yanked the soiled newspaper out from under the stacked plates, bringing the whole shelf of them down with an explosive clatter and in a very frenzy of vengefulness wheeled the chair back, then swiftly forward over the remains of her best china, crushing fragments into further fragments.

Frankie grabbed his cap. He needed air. He needed sleep. He needed a good stiff drink. He needed anything, anything at all for just one short hour of peace.

"You 'n your *god*amned dog," he paused to tell her in the doorway. "You 'n your *god*amned dishes. You and your *god*amned chair—what you need is a good Polish beatin'." The door slammed behind him, then banged ajar with the impact and stood swinging a little in the gray, indifferent air.

"You're mad 'cause I like beer too!" she shouted after him.

"Up your dirty skirt!" he called back over his shoulder, almost tripping over the loose tread halfway down.

Again it had been all his fault, she realized: even the dog on the landing below began yapping up at him. And on top of everything else calling her dirty names—nothing could make up for a man calling his wife dirty names any more than broken china could be mended to look like new.

It struck her abruptly that her dishes were broken. There at her feet her own dear sweet dead mother's very best dishes broken just because that Frankie Majcinek had turned out so mean—*blaming* her now for being a cripple, breaking up the house to show how he felt just as if it hadn't been him who'd put her in the chair in the first place.

Yet her eyes took a sort of dry satisfaction at sight of the littered chards of crockery: she wouldn't pick up a single piece. Let it be like this when that henna-headed Violet Koskozka, always saying Frankie was too easygoing, came in. Let her see for herself what he *really* was like when you had to live with him. Let them all see what she had to put up with, chair or no chair. Let them all get a good look at what a temper that Polak had.

Not one of them must so much as pick up a single piece. Let it all lay and every time he came home he'd have to look at what he'd done until he'd finally understand that this was just what he'd done to one poor girl's heart: ten thousand fragments never to be repaired. Till at last, on some sad day he'd always remember, he'd have to pick up every last fragment on his knees and every one like a jagged edge in his heart. He'd come begging her forgiveness in that sweet hour. "It's too late, Frankie," she'd tell him. "You come to your senses too late.

"After all," she reasoned primly, "if he'd wheeled me a little like he should I wouldn't of shoved the cup in the first place. If it wasn't for him I'd be out dancin' by St. Wenceslaus tonight."

The dog accusing him on the landing below knew too how Frankie was forever breaking everything he touched: crockery, women's hearts or suckers' pocketbooks—then squealed in puppyish surprise and Sophie knew Frankie had kicked it in spite against all such dogs.

"He thinks he's gettin' even on me, kickin' somebody's little helpless pup—I ought to say I want a horse, maybe he'll break his dirty foot." A thin pang of pleasure went through her so deeply that she felt it between her withering thighs.

> *"I'm gonna lock my heart*
> *'N throw away the key,"*

she sang among the ruins.

> *"I'm wise to all those tricks*
> *You played on me . . ."*

and paused at the echo of a woman's voice or of some scolding girl's: that no-good little Molly N. giving her Frankie unmixed hell for kicking the dog. That one had something coming to her too. Ever since Frankie had taken her dancing that night. With a swift and babyish glee Sophie wheeled to the door, it wasn't every night there was this much excitement for her pale eyes to see or her ears to hear.

Yet the tingle of anticipation faded to an uneasy qualm as she listened and wondered dimly why her joy must always turn sick within her without her ever really knowing why.

"Next time you come downstairs feelin' mean go kick your own dog," Molly N. was telling him off down there. While doors all over the vast and drafty old house opened a crack to hear the battle on the first floor front.

To Sophie it sounded as though Frankie were buckling under down there. Not a peep out of him. Not a single dirty name of all the names he knew to call his wife. He mustn't say a one of them to a little tramp like that one. It sounded as if he were standing down there with his cap in his hand taking it big.

Frankie had his cap in his hand all right; but wasn't hearing a thing. Dark-eyed Molly stood before him holding her pup in her hands and so angry she'd

forgotten she wasn't wearing a slip and wasn't dressed to be standing in a doorway with the light behind her. Her anger subsided slowly before Frankie's
downcast eyes till she realized they weren't downcast from humility—and
slammed the door in his face.

Frankie didn't move a step. Just stood there grinning like a towheaded clown.
"Wow," he decided at last, "a shaft like *that* wasted on a clown like Drunkie John.
I got no dog of my own to kick, Molly-O," he called through the door.

Molly-O answered swiftly, urging him to go. "Sorry I hollered at you,
Frankie. Maybe the hound was makin' too big a racket, she deserved a little
kick." After all, what was the use of inviting trouble with the rent overdue?

He heard the scraping of the wheelchair's arm against the railing overhead.
Sophie had been listening up there the whole time. "Zosh is gettin' sneaky, she
never used to be like that," he realized uneasily.

The sign above the cash register of the Tug & Maul Bar indicated Antek the
Owner's general attitude toward West Division Street:

> I'VE BEEN PUNCHED, KICKED, SCREWED, DEFRAUDED, KNOCKED
> DOWN, HELD UP, HELD DOWN, LIED ABOUT, CHEATED, DECEIVED,
> CONNED, LAUGHED AT, INSULTED, HIT ON THE HEAD AND MARRIED.
> SO GO AHEAD AND ASK FOR CREDIT I DON'T MIND SAYING NO.

Antek's customers, from Meter Reader the Baseball Coach to Schwabatski
and Drunkie John, held the bar directly across the street in lively contempt. For
the joint across the way didn't even have the simple honesty to confess itself a
tavern: it was a club, mind you. *Club Safari,* Mixed Drinks Our Specialty.

Nobody mixed anything but whisky and beer at the Tug & Maul. To ask
Antek for a martini would have been the equivalent of asking him for a kiss. It
wasn't done. Antek kissed no one but his wife and served no man anything but
whisky and beer.

> Tug & Maul
> Shove & Haul
> Old Fitz, Old Crow or Old McCall—
> When you're broke go home—
> That's *all*.

That was not only Antek's own poetry: it was also his coat of arms. It was inscribed on the back of an oblong strip of tin originally intended to advertise Coca-Cola and leaned, against the pretzel bowl, to warn the barflies who buzzed all day long between the curb and the bar.

And all day long brought Antek news of the carryings-on in the Safari, who had just gone in and who had just come out. They could see right into the window of the Safari and thus could undo any man's reputation without so much as taking a foot off the rail. "I seen Nifty Louie steerin' some old swish in there again yesterday, what they was drinkin' was somethin' wit' leaves on top." That pretty well placed Louie on the Tug & Maul's social register.

For Antek held to the old days and the old ways, familiar whisky and well-tried friends. Neither bright neon nor a soft fluorescence lighted either his ceiling or his walls; but there was plenty of butchershop sawdust along the floor and an old-fashioned golden goboon for every four bar stools. He'd roll you for the drinks and give you a square shake, friend or passing stranger, every time; while penny-ante sessions went on, in one or another the booths, from noon till 4 A.M. If you came in already stewed you right-about-faced right back to the place you'd come from; but if you had had too much out of his own bottles he'd see you didn't get strongarmed on his side of the street.

He drew the line at television. "I give it a honest chance," he often told Frankie, "it don't work."

"Television don't work, Owner?"

"Well, it works in a way—but it don't work out at all. A customer orders a beer, looks at the screen 'n asks me, 'What's the score, Owner?' I dunno, I been too busy to follow. All I can do is ask some guy who been watchin': 'What's the score?' He dunno. He thinks it's 8–3 but he ain't sure. 'What innin' is it?' the new customer wants to know then. I dunno that neither, so I ask the guy who's been watchin': 'What innin'?' He dunno neither. He thinks it's the last of the sixth or the first of the sevent', he ain't too sure.

" 'Who's playin'?' the new guy wants to know. I still dunno. So I ask the old customer. He dunno neither. He thinks it's the Red Sox but he ain't too sure. 'N all afternoon it goes that way till I'm hittin' the bottle myself instead of pourin'.

"'N when I do get a chance to listen 'n look a little all I hear is: 'Here comes Luke Applin', he's breakin' the record for most games played at short, at third, I dunno. Last year he played so many games, this year he played so many awready, the record is two thousand—*will* he make it? I dunno.

" 'Luke would have broke the record sooner but he had to play third awhile, awready he got a better run-batted-in average than Everett Somebody. Yeh, but Everett Somebody was back in the days of the dead ball, you got to take all that into consideration'—why the hell do *I* have to take all that into consideration? Just because I work behind a bar? 'N the next time Luke comes up all I'm takin' into consideration is do I wait for somebody to holler for the Old Fitz 'r do I open it up just for myself."

Frankie would nod understandingly and call for the Old Fitz himself, television or no television.

"Why put up with a thing like that?" Antek with the bottle in his hand would want to know, making Frankie wish he hadn't said anything in the first place. "When I come up to serve a customer I don't hear nobody yellin': 'Here comes Antek the Owner! Last year he served 5444 beers, 11,220 shots of bar whisky and refilled the pretzel bowl twice a week fer fifty-two weeks! Up *to* 'n *in*cludin' last Sunday's double-header he got 3317 shots of Old Grand-dad to his credit, 2343 shots of Schenley's 'n God knows how many fifths of Old Fitz he has drunk by hisself!' What the hell, I got a record too—'n when they put *me* on that screen I'll buy it. Not before."

"They got wrestlin' at the Safari," Frankie informed his old friend. "The swishes come to drink the joolips 'n see the wrasslers."

No sawdust carpeted the Safari's floor and no penny-ante players were tolerated there. If you wanted to gamble you went to the 26-table or the bingo board. You received a receipt for every drink and a floor show was offered five nights a week. The tables had tablecloths, the lights were dim, music murmured from the walls and there were no drinks on the house.

Yet the strange cats of the Safari returned the contempt of the barflies across the way. They called Antek's boys "bummies" and considered Antek himself simply too *common*.

Now the old blind noseless bummy called Pig sat at the scarred bar of the Tug & Maul with the fresh sawdust beneath his soles and the old hope in his heart: he wanted a beer. But nobody would come to sit on the stool to his right nor on the stool to his left.

For he gave off an odor of faintly rancid mutton, moldering laundry, long dead perch and formaldehyde. He sat only one stool away from the lavatory, where Antek had long ago assigned him, claiming that the odor of disinfectant from that room somewhat modified the peddler's special odor. "I kill two birds

with one stinkin' stone," Antek had explained to Pig, "I use a extra half can of
Bowlene 'n people can't hardly smell you at all. Just don't try movin' up to the
front where the people who wash theirselves sit. When you move up that way
keep on movin' right through the door 'n take it all out onto the street."

"Some of them clean guys buy me drinks," Pig would point out in protest.

"When someone buys you somethin' they don't mean they want to drink
with you. You stay where you are 'n I'll bring it down to you. I can stand you,
I'm used to you, it's my job. But the customers come here to get numb off
Schlitz; not off you."

Pig was always secretly pleased at such insults, though he might pretend to
be a bit offended. "That Bowlene ain't as strong as you think, Owner," he would
challenge Antek. "Gimme six more months 'n you won't have to use it at all—
I'll just set here 'n the people'll think the can been disinfected even if it ain't.
Bowlene, that ain't *nothin'*. D.D.T.—that's the stuff."

A faded blue merchant mariner's cap was rolled far down over his brows
and his fingers drummed restlessly on the bar. Hearing others drinking all
about him, his thirst deepened and his fingers began working like an insect's
feelers sensing an obstacle in their path. Pig's obstacle was forever Antek.
Owner was getting harder to get around every day.

For Owner didn't like the way Blind Pig's fingers had of struggling upward
and wriggling excitedly against each other: they whispered obscene gossip
while pressing each other's flesh with an incestuous understanding.

"If I had fifteen cents I'd be all right!" he called gaily to the hubbub about his
ears. But the hubbubers heard only their own gaiety.

Nobody heard but Owner. And Owner, in his clean-shaven, bald and bespectacled indifference, cared not a bartender's button.

Yet the fingers crept slyly across the bar, slowly reversed and began a crawling
descent down the grimy vest into a tobacco pouch suspended from his neck; the
string left a line on the nape faintly whiter than the rest of this shapeless, ageless,
anonymous, discolored, mindless and eyeless sack of cold cunning and hot greed.

"I seen some crummy bums in my time on this street," Antek called out
defensively, "but you're what D.D.T. was invented for—you think 'cause you
can't see people they can't see you?"

Pig wore a creamy, dreamy smirk to veil a long-standing grudge against
everybody. He could smile like a chicken-fed tomcat while wishing everyone
bad luck without exception.

"They don't *have* to see me," he assured the black bar mirror of his mind with that smug and buttery smile, "they could just *thmell* me."

"They can 'thmell' you awright," Antek mocked him. "I'd borrow you the soap myself—only you ain't got the natural pride to use it."

Pig agreed, with the downcast eyelids of the man being warmly flattered. "I got *my* kind of pride 'n you got yours—I'm proud of bein' how *I* am too."

To Pig light and cleanliness were inseparable: if he could not have the one he would do without the other. From his eyeless malice he derived a sort of twisted glee in offending men with eyes.

The Eyes were a hostile race. They were those who washed themselves, out of a common pact, because they could see each other. Though he had been excluded from that pact, yet they wished him to be both helpless and clean all the same. They did not wish him to trouble their sight any more than they wished him to see. They asked too much.

Yet before the offense he so deliberately offered their noses and their sight they became a bit helpless too. *They* had to look at him, *they* had to feel their stomachs balk a bit at the smell of him as at the reek of spoiled liver.

"Look, Owner—I got twelve"—the blackened fingernails were prying at the pouch's strings and into the greasy little bag. One entered at last, then two, to return bearing a single penny, place it with caution upon the bar and return for a second like two black ants going for a heavy load, following tirelessly until a dozen pennies lay on the bar before him. "Look!" he told the darkness. "I got twelve." And pressed the fingers cunningly across the pennies, turning one over here and another there, for no reason apparent to Antek at all.

All the filth of West Division Street clung to those fingers and to the frayed ends of the army surplus underwear curling beneath the cuffs. He wore heavy underwear, an army overcoat and the mariner's rolled cap whether it were roistering August or mid-December. The accumulation of filth on his face and clothing made him appear nearer sixty than the forty-odd he really was. The pouch slipped out of his fingers and somebody stooped and picked it up for him.

"You dropped somethin', Piggy-O."

Nifty Louie, his amber eyes and two-tone shoes, his sea-green tie and soft green fedora with the bright red feather in its band above the pale, asthenic face touched faintly with a violet talc.

"Oh boy," Pig sighed with relief to feel the pouch between his fingers again. "What if I had a couple of G's in there 'n somebody else found it?" The thought caused the fingers to run so nervously over the pennies the coins themselves seemed to start sweating.

Louie seldom drank in the Tug & Maul and Pig got into the Safari only by the back door; so their little business was done between schooners for Pig.

"How you doin', Piggy-O?"

"I'm doin' wit' out—how's Fomorowski doin'? You gonna buy one or be one?"

"What you drinkin'?"

"Oh boy, what do I *want,* you mean? I want all I can get"—he waved the white cane, shouted into the beery air, shifted the cane swiftly under the armpit to get his drinking hand free and the cane stuck there as if caught by sheer grime.

"Service! A little service here!" Blind Pig demanded.

"Fomorowski, that's the name," Amber Eyes boasted of himself quietly, "Nifty Louie hisself from Downtown on Clark Street. Owner, give my fat friend here a beer." He rolled a new dime, with proper disdain, along the littered bar. Then nudged Pig and whispered obscenely: "What's your habit, Jack the Rabbit?"

For some reason this meaningless query amused the blind man. He tittered, leered and flushed to the temples. Antek came up with an eight-ouncer in a ten-cent glass and scooped up the dime.

"Here's a schooner, Piggy"—Antek winked at Nifty Louie—"here's that big sixteen-ouncer, fifteen cents to everybody else but only a dime to you."

Pig's lower lip loosened, he licked a string of reddish spittle off it, from where his gums bled constantly, licked at the beer with the weak half grin of a drugged lecher and said "aaaaaah" as if he were tickling himself with his tongue. Then felt the glass with those lewd feelers at last and cried out as painfully as though cut: "In yer mother-law's icebox it's a schooner! Yer mother-law's icebox! Yer mother-law's snatch!"

Yet quickly pointed that lascivious tongue so as to lose no more time, into the foam like a cat into cream, dipped swiftly and deliciously with its narrow pink point, lapped the foam loosely and aimlessly about for the sheer joy of knowing he could feel it in his throat any moment he wished now, then emptied the glass so swiftly it left his face smudged whitely about the lips like those of a dog trying to vomit. Felt the beer back up in his throat, half rose over the bar, clutching his throat to choke the precious stuff back; and sank back with utter relief.

This debauched, blunt-snouted, abject, obscene lush sloshed beer about his mouth in a way that made Antek want to hit him every single time. It made anyone want to hit him, there was that deliberately offensive manner about it. He sat there in all his veiled malice and secretly mocked them all. Knowing it made everyone want to hit him, knowing not one would dare.

And smiled, to reveal his gums. They were gray and lined by a livid margin of rawest red, where the teeth bled at the rotting roots; as he sloshed the beer around them it became infected with the pinkish spittle. Antek saw and backed off from that awesome breath, wishing he hadn't quit school so early.

Pig turned the glass to his lips till a stream of beer ran down both sides of his mouth and dripped in tiny rivulets down the grease of his clothes and formed a glistening boutonniere of rosy spittle on his lapel. Gasped, choked, sighed, grunted, put the glass down at last and every barfly in the place sighed with relief.

"Boy! Can I drink beer! 'N smoke too! All I can get!" he told the shrouded bar mirror he saw forever in his mind. "I'd like to get somebody's gir-rul in the back boot'—a guy's *wife* got drunkie once 'n mmmm—oh boy you in that back boot'—I can do that too, I take *all* I can get." His lips worked loosely at the memory. "Oh boy, oh *man,* if I just had more of that."

"You like girls, Piggy-O?"

"And how!"

"You like potatoes 'n gravy, Piggy-O?"

"Oh *boy*—them mashed potatoes 'n unyunz in the *gray*-vy!" Pig was drooling. "Gir-ruls too—you *thed* it. Your mother-law's big beer belly, you *thed* it!"

"Broke again, Piggy-O?"

"You *thed* it!"

He whistled slyly to himself, seeing, over Nifty Louie's shoulder, a slow and stiff burlesque moving down the curtained runway of his mind: an endless all-night carnival playing for blind Piggy-O alone. As it had played, off and on, since he had last had eyes.

His sight had first clouded watching the runway of a true burlesque, and for months after that final curtain had come his own inner stage had remained curtained; till the shock of blindness had worn off. Since then, clearly and more clearly with the months, he could see once more that last burlesque, peopled with clowns that had not been there before and with women more beautiful and more obscene than ever had danced before his lost sight. He never told men with sight of this private burlesque. And did not even wonder why the figures behind his shuttered eyes moved so stiffly, as if on strings. Though they looked as real as life.

Swaying on the stool like a pianist in the throes of a stormy concerto, the fingers pointed, retreated, advanced, curled, straightened tensely, wilted slowly and slid along the scarred bar leaving a damp little sticky track, like an insect's track, around and between the pennies.

"Do a small errint for me, Piggy?"

"I'll take all I can get."

"I'll fix you with a little honey—'n no back-boot' drunkie neither. Clark Street *hot*el stuff."

"Oh boy, that *hot*el stuff—lead me to it, Fomorowski." Then felt Nifty Louie's quiet nudge, knew someone had entered both knew too well and buttoned his trap in an old understanding.

Frankie Machine, looking beat to the ground, brushed past the pair of them without a word or a nod to either.

"Lookin' for someone, Dealer?" Louie asked, not so much to get a reply as to let Pig know that Dealer was out of the clink again.

But Frankie went on toward the back of the tavern, where a single drunk sat tilted perilously against a green 7-Up sign. There, crouched at the feet of the drunk while others watched in mild unconcern, Solly Saltskin was preparing a prairie bonfire.

Methodically he had piled papers, scratch sheets and emptied cigarette packs below the tilted chair and was filtering fresh sawdust around. "I'm givin' Shooie a hotfoots," he explained gravely to Frankie, like a man being paid by the hour.

"Looks to me more like arsony," Frankie commented, kicking paper and sawdust aside, "ain't we got enough troubles without you burnin' people down? C'mon, I'll buy you a beer just to keep you out of the cooler tomorrow."

The drunk raised his head and tilted forward as if he too had been invited: but the head returned heavily to the laboring chest and the mind returned to an argument with some bartender of his dreams. "Tell him Shooie's a regular guy! Tell him! What Shudefski promises Shudefski does! Keep me straight. Shake—here's the best pal you ever had. You know Shudefski? C'mere! I want you to meet the best pal a Polak ever had."

"I want you to get a dog," Frankie told Sparrow in the back booth, "'n I don't care where you steal him. Not one of your alley wolves though. Somethin' that's housebroke 'n won't be much trouble 'n don't have lices. Somethin' playful-like, to give Soph somethin' to do to get her off my neck. But no bitch that's gonna litter next week. You get it?"

Sparrow was happy to have a mission. He twirled his cap about till the peak pointed backward, started going somewhere and returned. "What's the matter with Rumdum?" he asked. "Rummy needs a home. Hey! Rummy!" And something moved in the shadows.

There, as his eyes became accustomed to the dark, Frankie discerned Antek's deaf-and-dumb cat nibbling affectionately at Rumdum's ear in an attempt to rouse him. But Rumdum only barked dreamily, pursuing some deaf dream cat. While above them the tilted drunk with the sawdust scattered across his shoes began humming softly to himself; then tilted forward again to ask loudly and clearly, "Who always lets the air out of these seats?" And tilted right back again.

The question wakened Rumdum. He rose, stretched his flanks, licked the cat tolerantly while it arched its back in feigned fright, and shuffled into the dim blue gleam cast by the juke box's dreaming glow.

Frankie felt a choking sensation as he surveyed this scandalous-looking freak. The dog was both bloated and ravenous-looking.

"He's a real pedigreed, Frankie," Sparrow asserted, reading Frankie's dismay, "a Polish airedale, sort of, 'n every crawlin' hair of him mine. I wouldn't trust him to nobody but you."

"I'll say he's a pedigreed—a pedigreed trampo. I couldn't keep a brewery horse like that unless I want to go to work days too."

"He'll bring back empties, Frankie. I got him trained how to do it." He whistled softly and the dog ambled toward him, one blear red eye showing like a warning signal in a fog—Frankie felt the cold and dripping nose shoved into his hand and heard the great hound break wind discreetly, then hiccough apologetically.

"Here, beauty," Sparrow ordered, and crouched with an empty in his hand for the hound to retrieve. Rumdum got the bottle securely between his jaws and lurched dutifully about in an erratic circle, like a circus pony with a fixed idea, for Frankie's admiration.

"He's one fourt' retriever is why he does that so good," the punk explained.

"Yeh. 'N three fourths stewbum," Frankie added. "He thinks he's earnin' a drink on the house."

"That ain't nothin' to be *ashamed* of, is it?" Sparrow reproached him.

"Maybe if he had a home he'd settle down," Frankie guessed hopefully.

"Maybe if I did I would too," Sparrow agreed wistfully, thinking of the Division Street kennel he called a room. Although he had abandoned his dog-stealing racket, save for an occasional foray "just to keep in shape," that room still smelled of the transients it had sheltered in the days before he had met Frankie. The room still held an assortment of secondhand dog collars, stolen dog tags, moldy muzzles and greasy leashes.

He remembered; while Rumdum went around and around, breaking wind politely with every step.

All it took, in the old days, to place an order with Sparrow for anything from a Pekingese to a sled dog was a fifty-cent deposit. "It ain't that your credit ain't red-hot wit' me," he apologized to a client, "it's all account of the hamburger shortage. You say you want to buy me a drink?"

He had never wheedled more than two shots out of a customer before he'd be on his casual way to the nearest hamburger stand. It had never occurred to the punk to go to a butchershop. "What's the hamburg stands for then? Besides, I like the fresh-ground kind myself. Leave the onions off one." He was fond of onions himself but had learned that some dogs, particularly chows, disdained them. Toward dark he would start tiptoeing down alleys, his eyes just over the back-yard fences and the single onionless hamburger in his hand.

"I knew the alleys pretty good when I had my dog-stealin' route," he told Frankie now, "I knew all the best windows, them days, 'n the quick short cuts to get there, account I run a peepin'-tom route before I caught on to how to snatch hounds. That's how I got to know the yards that had dogs in 'em 'n the ones that just had signs sayin' they did but they really didn't."

He would unlatch a gate quietly in the violet twilight and silently permit the hound to start snooping anxiously for the hamburger's scent. One glance would tell him whether the hound was bribable: he had yet to meet man or dog that wasn't. The animal's snout would trail the meat around the corner and up to the very door of the drafty old five-story frame tenement he called home.

Coaxed five flights up, an amiable puppy could be scooped up like a tired baby and softly encouraged to forget his past. But Sparrow had never forgiven the cynical, double-crossing spitz that had consumed three whole hamburgers, pickle and all, before he'd gotten it forty feet off its home grounds—then had sunk its teeth in his hand and set up a hysterical barking as if Sparrow had bitten it, bringing its mistress onto the punk's heels. He'd spent that night in the Saloon Street Station booked for dog theft until Record Head had advised the woman to drop charges and Sparrow to "stay in the light where we can see what you're up to after this."

Sparrow had planned to poison the dog's mistress after that one; but had ultimately contented himself with poisoning the spitz.

Once inside the room, any hound, regardless of pedigree, had become half drugged by the odors of the hundred breeds that had preceded him there. That close little room had never lost the special smell of shanghaied dogflesh: the captives had snuggled down on the shedded hair of some wayward collie to snooze like lotus-eaters. Sparrow would remove the collar and tag, substitute a less incriminating one and go for the shears. By dint of ingenuous hair clipping, a daub of black paint there and daub of white there, French poodles had come to impersonate "Cocky Spaniards" and Irish pointers had become "daubered-up pinchers."

A two-month-old poodle would waken looking like a debauched terrier: adhesive over a telltale marking on the left foot, dark circles under the eyes and the tip of one ear in the sink. Such a betrayed pup had passed for any breed the market might demand.

Sparrow had sold them, crossbred them, clipped their tails until each had emerged, no matter how many mongrel strains had brought him forth, a "pedigreed blood-typed turo-breed."

His masterpiece, the unholy freak now making circles in the hope of a short beer, was a cross between "an English sheepy 'n a Division Street beagle—only I call him a square-snapper for short. What he's best for is catchin' squirrels 'n shakin' the dirty walnuts out of 'em," the punk explained earnestly. "In his native hab'tat you got to have a dog like this if you're out to pick up a sack of walnuts. But the trouble is he's just trained to chase them one kind of squirrels 'n they're gettin' kind of rare over here account of the climate changin' so fast. So he don't have nothin' to do but hang around taverns 'n wait for the climate to change back a little."

Certainly Rumdum was the luckiest hound in Chicago. For he alone, of all the city's countless dogs, had received Professor Saltskin's postgraduate course in square-snapping. He had studied at the feet of the philosophers who lounged out their lives on the curb in front of the Tug & Maul waiting for a live one. He had earned his degree by snapping suspiciously at all uniformed toilers: mailmen, milkmen, Good Humor men on bicycles, streetcar conductors and anyone carrying a lunch bucket—everyone, indeed, who didn't smell of beer or unemployment. Rumdum could tell a square with nostrils so clogged he had once mistaken molasses for beer.

"He got a degree what I call D.D.S.—Doctor of Dirty Square-snapping," Sparrow liked to boast. "Here's a dog got a better start in life than most humans. I named him Rumdum when he was two mont's old 'n told him straight out, 'I ain't givin' you no water 'cause I don't want to raise you pre-j'diced against somethin' better.' Too many dogs get offsteered onto water right off, they don't get no chance to make up their own minds what they really like best, beer 'r water 'r just plain whisky. The people should let a helpless beast make up his own opinions, otherwise it's croolty to our weak-minded friends, like takin' advantage of little birds, they ain't even learned how to fly yet. Today you could put Rummy in the bat'tub 'n he keeps his dirty snout up so's he don't have to taste that other stuff.

"But he ain't the kind to just beg beers off you 'n then go to sleep on you. Rummy, he's a natural entertainer, he pays his own way—look—he's dizzy but he's still in there"—Sparrow reached over and set the hound to circling in the opposite direction, which for some reason caused the dog to begin breaking wind again.

"You wouldn't hire no M.C. if you was needin' a detective, would you? Well, Rumdum's field is strictly entertainment. He don't guard no cash register. He don't even howl when somebody's gonna croak. He just hiccups. He don't care whether his hair is smood down or not, he don't care how he looks or what becomes of him. He don't even bark. He just whines when the brew'ry truck guys come to take back the empties, account he don't know they're empty. He figures they're takin' away all the beer in the world 'n there won't be enough left for him. He sure looks sad when they do that on him. I tell him, 'Look the other way, Rummy,' when I see 'em comin'. But he peeks 'n then that tail droops."

"He don't bark is right," Frankie agreed. "He won't even bark at a cat. I seen Antek's deaf tom tree him wit' my own eyes."

"Let's face facts, Frankie," Sparrow protested. "It wasn't no tree. He just jumped up on the bar to avoid a disturbment was all. He knew it wouldn't look dignified, a big fat hound like him lickin' a poor skinny little old deaf-'n-dumb cat. That dog got real pride, Frankie. He won't fight out of his weight when there's no principle involved."

"If there's no bowl of beer involved, you mean. That's the only time I ever seen him show his teeth—when somebody took his dirty beer away."

He had met him before, that certain down-at-heel vet growing stooped from carrying a thirty-five-pound monkey on his back. Frankie remembered that face, ravaged by love of its own suffering as by some endless all-night orgy. A face forged out of his own wound fever in a windy ward tent on the narrow Meuse. He had met Private McGantic before: both had served their country well.

This was the fellow who looked somehow a little like everyone else in the world and was more real to a junkie than any real man could ever be. The projected image of one's own pain when that pain has become too great to be borne. The image of one hooked so hopelessly on morphine that there would be no getting the monkey off without another's help. There are so few ways to help old sad frayed and weary West Side junkies.

Frankie felt no pity for himself, yet felt compassion for this McGantic. He worried, as the sickness rose in himself, about what in God's name McGantic would do tomorrow when the money and the morphine both gave out. Where then, in that terrible hour, would Private M. find the strength to carry the monkey through one more endless day?

By the time Frankie got inside the room he was so weak Louie had to help him onto the army cot beside the oil stove. He lay on his back with one arm flung across his eyes as if in shame; and his lips were blue with cold. The pain had hit him with an icy fist in the groin's very pit, momentarily tapering off to a single probing finger touching the genitals to get the maximum of pain. He tried twisting to get away from the finger: the finger was worse than the fist. His throat was so dry that, though he spoke, the lips moved and made no sound. But Fomorowski read such lips well.

"Fix me. Make it stop. Fix me."

"I'll fix you, Dealer," Louie assured him softly.

Louie had his own bedside manner. He perched on the red leather and chrome bar stool borrowed from the Safari, with the amber toes of his two-tone shoes catching the light and the polo ponies galloping down his shirt. This was Nifty Louie's Hour. The time when he did the dealing and the dealer had to take what Louie chose to toss him in Louie's own good time.

He lit a match with his fingertip and held it away from the bottom of the tiny glass tube containing the fuzzy white cap of morphine, holding it just far enough away to keep the cap from being melted by the flame. There was time and time and lots of time for that. Let the dealer do a bit of melting first; the longer it took the higher the price. "You can pay me off when Zero pays you," he assured Frankie. There was no hurry. "You're good with me any time, Dealer."

Frankie moaned like an animal that cannot understand its own pain. His shirt had soaked through and the pain had frozen so deep in his bones nothing could make him warm again.

"Hit me, Fixer. Hit me."

A sievelike smile drained through Louie's teeth. This was his hour and this hour didn't come every day. He snuffed out the match's flame as it touched his fingers and snapped the head of another match into flame with his nail, letting its glow flicker one moment over that sievelike smile; then brought the tube down cautiously and watched it dissolve at the flame's fierce touch. When the stuff had melted he held both needle and tube in one hand, took the dealer's loose-hanging arm firmly with the other and pumped it in a long, loose arc. Frankie let him swing it as if it were attached to someone else. The cold was coming *up* from within now: a colorless cold spreading through stomach and liver and breathing across the heart like an odorless gas. To make the very brain tighten and congeal under its icy touch.

"Warm. Make me warm."

And still there was no rush, no hurry at all. Louie pressed the hypo down to the cotton; the stuff came too high these days to lose the fraction of a drop. "Don't vomit, student," he taunted Frankie to remind him of the first fix he'd had after his discharge—but it was too cold to answer. He was falling between glacial walls, he didn't know how anyone could fall so far away from everyone else in the world. So far to fall, so cold all the way, so steep and dark between those morphine-colored walls of Private McGantic's terrible pit.

He couldn't feel Louie probing into the dark red knot above his elbow at all. Nor see the way the first blood sprayed faintly up into the delicate hypo to tinge the melted morphine with blood as warm as the needle's heated point.

When Louie sensed the vein he pressed it down with the certainty of a good doctor's touch, let it linger a moment in the vein to give the heart what it needed and withdrew gently, daubed the blood with a piece of cotton, tenderly, and waited.

Louie waited. Waited to see it hit.

Louie liked to see the stuff hit. It meant a lot to Louie, seeing it hit.

"Sure I like to watch," he was ready to acknowledge any time. "Man, their *eyes* when that big drive hits 'n goes tinglin' down to the toes. They retch, they sweat, they itch—then the big drive hits 'n here they come out of it cryin' like a baby 'r laughin' like a loon. *Sure* I like to watch. *Sure* I like to see it hit. Heroin got the drive awright—but there's not a tingle to a ton—you got to get M to get that tingle-tingle."

It hit all right. It hit the heart like a runaway locomotive, it hit like a falling wall. Frankie's whole body lifted with that smashing surge, the very heart seemed to lift up-up-up—then rolled over and he slipped into a long warm bath with one long orgasmic sigh of relief. Frankie opened his eyes.

He was in a room. Somebody's dust-colored wavy-walled room and he wasn't quite dead after all. He had died, had felt himself fall away and die but now he wasn't dead any more. Just sick. But not too sick. He wasn't going to be really sick, he wasn't a student any more. Maybe he wasn't going to be sick at all, he was beginning to feel just right.

Then it went over him like a dream where everything is love and he wasn't even sweating. All he had to do the rest of his life was to lie right here feeling better and better with every beat of his heart till he'd never felt so good in all his life.

"Wow," he grinned gratefully at Louie, "that was one good *whan*."

"I seen it," Louie boasted smugly. "I seen it was one good *whan*"—and lapsed into the sort of impromptu jargon which pleases junkies for no reason they can say—"vraza-s'vraza-s'vraza—it was one good *whan-whan-whan*." He dabbed a silk handkerchief at a blob of blood oozing where the needle had entered Frankie's arm.

"There's a silver buck and a buck 'n a half in change in my jacket pocket," Frankie told him lazily. "I'm feelin' too good to get up 'n get it myself."

Louie reached in the pocket with the handkerchief bound about his palm and plucked the silver out. Two-fifty for a quarter grain wasn't too high. He gave Frankie the grin that drained through the teeth for a receipt. The dealer was coming along nicely these days, thank you.

The dealer didn't know that yet, of course. That first fix had only cost him a dollar, it had quieted the everlasting dull ache in his stomach and sent him coasting one whole week end. So what was the use of spending forty dollars in the bars when you could do better at home on one? That was how Frankie had it figured *that* week end. To Louie, listening close, he'd already talked like a twenty-dollar-a-day man.

Given a bit of time.

And wondered idly now where in the world the dealer would get that kind of money when the day came that he'd need half a C just to taper off. He'd get it all right. They always got it. He'd seen them coming in the rain, the unkjays with their peculiarly rigid, panicky walk, wearing some policeman's castoff rubbers, no socks at all, a pair of Salvation Army pants a size too small or a size too large and a pajama top for a shirt—but with twenty dollars clutched in the sweating palm for that big twenty-dollar fix.

"Nothing can take the place of junk—just junk"—the dealer would learn. As Louie himself had learned long ago.

Louie was the best fixer of them all because he knew what it was to need to get well. Louie had had a big habit—he was one man who could tell you you lied if you said no junkie could kick the habit once he was hooked. For Louie was the one junkie in ten thousand who'd kicked it and kicked it for keeps.

He'd taken the sweat cure in a little Milwaukee Avenue hotel room cutting himself down, as he put it, "from monkey to zero." From three full grains a day to one, then a half of that and a half of that straight down to zero, though he'd been half out of his mind with the pain two nights running and was so weak, for days after, that he could hardly tie his own shoelaces.

Back on the street at last, he'd gotten the chuck horrors: for two full days he'd eaten candy bars, sweet rolls and strawberry malteds. It had seemed that there would be no end to his hunger for sweets.

Louie never had the sweet-roll horrors any more. Yet sometimes himself sensed that something had twisted in his brain in those nights when he'd gotten the monkey off his back on Milwaukee Avenue.

"*Habit? Man,*" he liked to remember, "I had a great *big* habit. One time I knocked out one of my own teet' to get the gold for a fix. You call that bein' hooked or not? *Hooked?* Man, I wasn't hooked, I was *crucified.* The monkey got so big he was carryin' *me.* 'Cause the way it starts is like this, students: you let the habit feed you first 'n one mornin' you wake up 'n you're feedin' the habit.

"But don't tell *me* you can't kick it if you *want* to. When I hear a junkie tell me he wants to kick the habit but he just can't I know he lies even if *he* don't know he does. He *wants* to carry the monkey, he's punishin' hisself for somethin' 'n don't even know it. It's what I was doin' for six years, punishin' myself for things I'd done 'n thought I'd forgot. So I told myself how I wasn't to blame for what I done in the first place, I was only tryin' to live like everyone else 'n doin' them things was the only way I had of livin'. Then I got forty grains 'n went up to

the room 'n went from monkey to nothin' in twenny-eight days 'n that's nine-
ten years ago 'n the monkey's dead."

"The monkey's never dead, Fixer," Frankie told him knowingly.

Louie glanced at Frankie slyly. "You know that awready, Dealer? You know
how he don't die? It's what they say awright, the monkey never dies. When you
kick him off he just hops onto somebody else's back." Behind the film of glaze
that always veiled Louie's eyes Frankie saw the twisted look. "*You* got my monkey, Dealer? You take my nice old monkey away from me? Is that my monkey
ridin' your back these days, Dealer?"

The color had returned to Frankie's cheeks, he felt he could make it almost
any minute now. "No more for me, Fixer," he assured Louie confidently.
"Somebody else got to take your monkey. I had the Holy Jumped-up-Jesus
Horrors for real this time—'n I'm one guys knows when he got enough. I
learned my lesson but *good*. Fixer—you just give the boy with the golden arm
his very lastest fix."

"What time you have to be by Schwiefka?" Louie wanted to know.

Frankie brushed the hair, matted by drying sweat, off his forehead and
glanced at his watch. Sweat had steamed the crystal, he couldn't read the hands.
He dried it on the bedcover, for his shirt was still wringing damp. "Nine-
thirty—I got an hour and a half. I'll make it."

"Crawl your dirty gut over to the table," Louie advised him. "Can you take
coffee?"

Frankie thought it over carefully. "In a couple minutes," he decided. "Half a
cup anyhow."

"You better," Louie counseled him, "you're likely to get so hungry around
one o'clock you won't be able to steal enough for another fix."

Louie busied himself over the little gas plate in the corner and didn't look
around till he heard the dealer move. Frankie was swaying but he was on his
feet and he'd make it fine, all night. All night and maybe the whole week end.
It was hard to tell with these joy-poppers. "That stuff cost me more than the last
batch," he said indifferently.

"I know," Frankie grinned, "you told me," sounding bored while he used a dish
towel on his chest beneath the soiled undershirt. "Keeps goin' up all the time, like
a kite with the string broke off." His eyes were growing heavy, the towel slipped
out of his fingers and caught under his arm, hanging there like a flag at half-mast.
The junkies' flag of truce, to guard him as he slept. There beneath a single bulb,

flat on his feet, the knees bending a little, the slight body swaying a bit, the flat-bridged nose looking peaked. Hush: he is sleeping the strange light sleep.

"I can't help it when they up the price on me," Louie added. "They got me, Dealer, that's all."

"The way you got me," Frankie murmured knowingly. Then he smelled the coffee, got down to the table in front of a cup, took one sip and, smiling softly, started to let his head fall toward his chest. Louie got the cup out of the way of that blond mop before it bent to the table.

"Now look at him sleep, with all his woes," Louie teased him almost tenderly; and Frankie heard from a dream of falling snow.

The snow fell in a soft, suspended motion, as snow does in dreams alone. He coasted without effort around and around and down a bit and then up like that kite with the broken string and came coasting, where all winds were dying, back down to the table where Fixer sat waiting.

"I got no woes," he laughed among slow-falling flakes, seeing Louie smiling through the snow. "You got a woe, Fixer?" he asked. "It's what I been needin'— a couple good old secondhand woes."

"You'll have a couple dozen if you ain't boxin' that deck by Schwiefka's suckers in half an hour," Louie reminded him.

Frankie got the rest of the coffee down. "Squarin' up, Fixer," he assured Louie. He held the cup out at arm's length. "Look at that." Not a tremor from shoulder to fingertip. "The sheep 'r gonna get a fast shearin' t'night, Fixer," he boasted with a strange and steady calm.

"I think you're one of the weaker sheep yourself," Louie decided silently.

She remembered the years of their courtship like remembering an alien land. Years of the white wafer of friendship broken on *Boze Narodzenie* and its brittle fragments (that broke, like so many friendships, at the touch) being passed from hand to hand across the straw-strewn tablecloth. Years of the soft and wild ancestral songs: "*Chlopek*" sung in the evergreen's light. And on the tree's very top a single star to which all good children must say: "*Gwizadka tam na niebie.*" A starlet there on the heavens. Feasts of Epiphany, when she and Frankie together had marked neighbors' doorways with the letters that remembered ancestral kings, K, M, and B, with tiny crosses between; that neighbors on waking might remember how Kasper, Melchior and Balthasar had borne gifts to Bethlehem.

Years when everything was so well arranged. When people who did right were rewarded and those who did wrong were punished. When everyone, in the long run, got exactly what was coming to him, no more or no less. God weighed virtue and sin then to the fraction of the ounce, like Majurcek the Grocer weighing sugar.

Together she and Frankie had carried Easter lamb to Old St. Stephen's for Father Simon's blessing—could it really be so long? How had they both forgotten God so soon? Or had God forgotten them? Certainly God had gone somewhere far away at just the time when she'd needed Him most. Perhaps He too had volunteered and just hadn't gotten His discharge yet. Perhaps He had been a full colonel and still felt the need of keeping His distance. If He had been only a private, then He must have re-enlisted. Or else the world had gone wrong all by itself.

He had been closer on those far-gone forenoons when she and Frankie had followed the malt-hop trucks down the horse and-wagon alleys of home, each with a tin can to catch the malt-dripping. That was forbidden drink, the trucks hauled it out to the farmers for pig food. But one morning she and Frankie had drunk from the same can and gotten as stewed, all by themselves, as any two twelve-year-olds in a West Side horse-and-wagon alley can get.

Yet even then Frankie's indifference had tortured her. So free and easy he'd been, into their free-and-easy teens, in a way she herself could never be and not like a really decent fellow ought to be at all. As careless of her love as if it were something he could pick up in any old can just by following a malt-hop truck.

"I never run for streetcars," he'd had the brassbound nerve to tell her the year she was seventeen, after standing her up for half an hour in front of the Pulaski. "What's the use? There's always another big red rollin' along right behind. Just like you dames—soon as a guy misses with one all he has to do is look back over his shoulder 'n here comes another down the block pullin' up for a fast pickup."

"I just won't *stand* for that kind of talk," she'd told him flatly, stamping with rage. "I want you to be *where* you're supposed to be *when* you're supposed to be 'n dressed like you're goin' to the Aragon, not to shoot six-no-count pool by Wieczorek—that's what *I* want."

"There's people in hell want ice water too," he'd grinned at her. That unforgivable, careless grin that she couldn't get out of her system and had to have all for herself and couldn't ever quite seem to get all for her very own for keeps.

It had almost seemed at times that he didn't really care what she thought in those years. When she'd reproach him for going with other girls he'd confirm anything she chose to suspect with that quick, confident grin. How could any-one make a fellow like that ashamed of himself? She didn't know how. It hadn't seemed to make any difference to him whether he dated a schoolgirl, a nurse, a dimwit, a shimmy dancer, a hillbilly, a married woman, an aging whore, a divorcee or just some poor tired trampie: he dated everything he saw in skirts and gave each the same corny play.

One afternoon he'd been promenading down Augusta Boulevard with some good-natured piece of trade who liked to say, "I was a lily of the valley in my time, now I'm just Lily of the Alley. *Say*—didn't *I* turn out to be a beauty?"

Sophie had confronted him the very next morning with the fact that her very own father had seen him with the lily. For a moment Frankie hadn't even seemed to remember. "Oh yeh," he'd recalled at last, "you mean Lily Splits. Yeh, sure, we lifted a few, we always do. Splits likes me. Well, I like Splits. Poor kid was born with one foot in a cathouse, I knew her when she first stared travelin' the bars. But you know she's a funny little bum at that—they say she still won't do it with two guys in the same room. What she really likes best is just clownin' around."

"Is that all you were doin'—clownin' around?"

"Not just clownin'—Splits got her serious side too. Just like me. We were talkin' on that Chester Shudefski—Shudefski from Viaduct not Shudefski by Whisky Taverns—you know, the real muscle-built one, not Old Uncle. That Shudefski, that was Splits' fee-an-say, he was bartender by Widow Wieczorek then. When she went to see him she had to sit by the bar 'n have a double shot, all Widow served them days was doubles. Only Shudefski ratted on Splits, he went into the Marines. That wasn't so good for Splits."

"Is that why she been livin' off hard-boiled eggs 'n p'tato chips ever since?" Sophie had wanted to know in her politest, most contemptuous tone.

"That was it awright. She just kept comin' by the p'tato-chip bowl like Chester was still workin' there."

"She ain't come out yet."

"Oh yeh, she had to come out, her credit give out by Widow, she had to get on the wagon. She's gettin' on the wagon again one of these days."

"You think so? Wait till the first rainy day."

"Yeh," Frankie had conceded gloomily, "I think that's what lots of people are waitin' for: the first rainy day."

She would grasp his throat in exasperation after he'd strung her along awhile like that, pretending to choke him and really wanting to hurt him. Only when she played that way her fingers would touch the short hairs on the back of his neck and weaken till the weakness spread back to her shoulders; while his own hands would grow so firm on the slope of her hips.

"You're my honey, I wouldn't choke you really," she'd assure him weakly at last.

He had won every single one of those skirmishes though he'd been dead in the wrong every time. And each time she'd been so right, so terribly right. Till each defeat she suffered had aroused a secret need for the sort of vengeance that a certain sort of love requires.

For that had been the endless pity of it: she had loved the clown. She had loved him deep in that curtained corner of her mind where, unknown to herself, she had planned an ultimate reckoning.

It had been in that curtained corner, at last, that her mock pregnancy had been devised. Out of that false pregnancy their marriage had been forged.

Had it been because she had really wanted a baby so badly? Or had needed so to punish him? Her breasts had swollen, she had suffered morning sickness—and after five months had wound up the game by lying nine days with an icebag instead of a baby at her breast. Empty-breasted and empty-armed while other women nursed their young. And when he'd come to see her hadn't reproached him once. It wasn't necessary. She had read in his eyes the realization of what he'd done. "Don't look sorry, Frankie—it wasn't your fault," she'd told him. He had been too miserable to reply. He knew whose fault it had been all right.

That had been the first time she'd gotten underneath his indifference. The hook was in. She had never let go since. He had been sick with concern for her.

After that no one but her father had continued to remind her that Frankie really wasn't good enough for her. "A bad child often lies in a good mother's lap," was the way the old man had put it. And it was true that Frankie hadn't even finished grammar school while she'd gone on to almost a full year of high. "A girl like you with a good Polish education," the old man had sought to shame her, "goin' with a gambler—for shame, Zoshka. You tell him right out when he comes tonight he isn't good enough for you with his dice and cards and pool shooting all day—what kind of a husband is *that?*"

Yet all Frankie had done that night, when she'd told him, like a dutiful daughter, just what Papa had said, was to twiddle his thumb playfully in her ear till she'd protested, "Get out of my clean ear!" and the dice and card playing were forgotten. Between such idle play and her thousand superstitions—"Always hand beer to me wit' your right hand. A fallin' picture means deat' "——they had drifted at last, one windy Saturday morning, into marriage at Old St. Stephen's.

"He told me he loved me that night," she still liked to recall. "I remember. 'Cause I asked him."

"You would of kicked me out of bed if I hadn't said yes," Frankie Majcinek might have replied.

Because, right off, it hadn't felt like holy wedlock at all. He'd celebrated his wedding night by taking over the drums in a three-piece band hired for the occasion and getting blind drunk to follow. Wedlock hadn't changed a thing. His love-making was still maddeningly casual, a sort of routine which she couldn't feel was anything more than he'd had with too many lilies of the val-ley. Once he'd even had the brassbound nerve to ask her, "What'd you rather do—go to bed 'r listen to me keep time on the tubs to the radio?"

"Neither," she'd told him. But had chalked up one more in her book of grudges all the same. For when he gave her pride the back of his hand she no longer protested openly. After their marriage her anger raged silently.

If only he would have hit her so that they would have been able to make it all up in bed later. "If Jesus Christ treated me like you do I'd drive in the nails myself," she told him in her mind as, in a passion of frustration, she watched him dealing, eternally dealing.

She could draw neither anger nor hate from him—until the accident that had left her in the wheelchair.

"He nailed me to the wood that night," she told her friend Violet.

"We all got a cross to bear," Violet assured her, "I got Stash 'n you got Frankie."

"Wrong both times," Sophie contradicted her flatly. "My cross is this chair. I'm settin' on *my* cross. All you have to do is send yours to work 'n you're back on the ground. I'm *nailed* to mine."

"Sometimes I think them nails is in your head, honey," Violet decided, "you're drivin' 'em in yourself."

"A lot you got to holler anyhow," Sophie evaded the accusation, "callin' your meal ticket a cross—if you want to get rid of Stash all you have to do is go to work yourself."

"Don't say 'work,' "Violet reproached Sophie softly as though she'd heard an obscene word, "it's the nastiest word I know—'n I know 'em all."

So it was forever Frankie who drove in the nails and always her own palms, already bleeding, that must receive them. And all so matter-of-factly, like having some absent-minded carpenter about the house. Never once did he seem to see, even dimly, how inwardly she bled.

And you couldn't get him to Mass with wild horses any more. She even gave him his choice of even-hour or odd-hour Mass. But it seemed, either way, he still didn't have the time. He'd have to figure the Monday morning line instead.

"I'll make a man of him yet," she'd boasted to Violet shortly before the accident, "just like that Jane Wyman done that time with some goof battlin' the bottle worse'n Frankie. When I'm through wit' him he won't want to look at another deck 'r the inside of a whisky bar."

She hadn't made much of a job of it, she had to admit now. The only thing that had kept him near her had been the accident. The blessed, cursed, wonderful-terrible God's-own-accident that had truly married them at last. For where her love and the Church's ritual had failed to bind, guilt had now drawn the irrevocable knot so fiercely that she felt he could never be free of her again. Every time he came in stewed to the gills, with Sparrow holding him up by the belt, he'd mumble the minute he saw her waiting in the chair, "I'm no good. Here. Hit me." He would offer her his chin to hit. To make up for everything.

"The only time I get a decent word out of him is when he's stewed," she complained to Violet, "if he has to get stewed to realize what he done to me, let him get stewed every night."

"That goes to show his heart is right when he's sober," Violet assured her.

"I lost my taste for the booze the night Zosh got banged up," Frankie told the punk like confiding news of a secret disease.

A secret disease: the disease of his crippled joy. All those things which had once lent him pleasure were being soiled by a slow and cancerous guilt: the image of her waiting, night after night, who had so loved to dance and be with dancing people. He heard her lost laughter in that of any girl on the street below. "She don't even laugh like she used no more," he realized with a pang.

When she sat napping, one arm resting on the wheelchair's arm, he saw her index finger pointing its long red-tinted nail—even in sleep she accused him. And between the cards her eyes reproved him. All night long. Her face, as it once had been, returned to him like an extra queen packed into a fixed deck; with each new deal returning him, over and over and over again, to that August night when the photostated discharge in his pocket was only two months old.

In a week when every tavern radio was blaring triumphantly of what a single bomb had done on the other side of the world.

They had been drinking at the Tug & Maul that night, with Owner serving something he called Antek's A-Bomb Special, made simply by pouring triple shots instead of doubles into his glasses. It was almost time to go home and the barflies were pleading for just one more Special and just one more tune. Owner wouldn't serve another but let the juke play one last sad bar of the final song of a world that had known neither A-bombs nor A-Bomb Specials.

> *"There's nothing left for me*
> *Of days that used to be . . ."*

While Antek's own pallid eight-year-old scooped up the night's last crumbs out of the potato-chip bowl.

"Whose is *that?*" Antek wanted to know, impatiently suspecting a practical joke too late in the evening. Between the juke and the 7-Up sign someone had abandoned a cracked crutch. It had struck Sophie so funny she'd wanted to buy Antek a shot on it.

"Must be good whisky you're sellin', Owner," Frankie had flattered Antek. "They come in here on crutches 'n walk out by theirselves."

"Must be some guy got well on the horses," Antek decided, and bought both Frankie and Sophie a shot. So they bought him one back and by the time Antek went to turn off the back lights he was weaving so he could hardly find the switch and Frankie was so stiff he could hardly stay on the bar stool. Much too tight to worry about what fool or other had left a cracked crutch between a juke and a 7-Up sign. They were two doors down from their own doorway—but all of a sudden he had had to see "what the people 'r doin' on Milwaukee" and there was nothing to be done with him but to let him have his way.

So drunk that his head had fallen across the wheel in the late Ashland Avenue traffic—she grabbed once for the wheel and he shoved her off, mumbling some drunken singsong about "War's over, war's over, war's over for Frankie—drives like he deals, deals like he lives 'n he lives all the time—war's over, war's over—" Sophie cringed at the screech of metal upon metal as a northbound trolley pulled past and kicked his foot off the gas.

"Pull over, goof, you scraped the trolley." He'd stepped on the gas and wheeled around the corner.

There hadn't been any corner. They'd crashed into the light standard of the safety island, bounced over the broken base and slammed sidewise into a billboard offering everyone in Chicago a spanty-new paste-and-paper Nash.

In twenty seconds the abandoned Ashland Avenue midnight was thronging with sprouts who should have been in bed for hours and windows began blazing with light as if everyone had been sitting around in the dark just waiting for an accident to happen and here they came, lurching with age and skipping with youth, the lame, the sick and the lazy, the fearful, the cheerful and the tamed, recalling with laughter other local disasters—jostling, jumping and shoving with eagerness—all those for whom nothing had yet happened in the world shouting that it had happened at last, they'd always known it would happen sooner or later, that corner had always looked *so* unlucky.

Something had finally happened outside of the movies. Death in a blazing Chrysler or a blood-covered madman pinned to the pavement by a pair of poolroom bullies: madman, Chrysler, flash fire or a scoutmaster helping an old lady across the street, it was all one. Something had been made to happen in their lives at last.

Everything arrived in nothing flat. A fire-insurance patrol, the pulmotor squad, the hook-and-ladder boys—everything but an ambulance. Frankie and a nineteen-year-old in a staff sergeant's uniform took over, hauling Sophie between them up and down the curb to nowhere, neither being certain who was giving the orders, while the crowd looked on admiringly at the military in action.

"Artificial inspiration," Frankie explained to his audience and wouldn't let anyone but the sergeant help him haul her about; till a stray cop, wandering out of the Safari to clear his head, nabbed the sergeant on sheer blind impulse.

"Let's see your papers, Sergeant."

The soldier just didn't have any papers. He didn't even have a draft card.

"I tawt you looked like some kind of spy awright," the cop announced, ignoring the leaning light pole, the bleeding woman and the fire department. "I'm gonna put you under the authoriety of the F.B.I."

"I got a draft card at home," the sergeant offered meekly, chastened at finding himself so heavily outranked.

"Yeh—but where's your license to drag this woman around at t'ree A.M.?" He had spotted Sophie at last and could tell at a glance she was a woman. "You pushed her." The law had reached its verdict. The sergeant shook his head, No, No, he hadn't pushed a soul. But the law wasn't taking any such guff. "Who give you the right to shove a woman in front of a car anyhow—you *married* to her? Let's see your license for *that*."

"This is just her boy friend," a helpful bystander offered, "that's her husband settin' on the curb holdin' his dirty head. He tried to run the soldier down for datin' his wife. Looks like an internal triangle to me. If you ask me they're all three of them no good."

"Nobody asked you."

Yet the law could see there was something to the story all right. Frankie sat on the curb with his army shoes in the gutter and his combat jacket ripped below the shoulder halfway to the overseas stripes below the elbow. Dabbing at his forehead with a handkerchief and wondering how to get the booze off his breath in a hurry.

"You kids got a stick of gum?" he whispered to two ten-year-old girls studying him placidly, both of them chewing like twin calves side by side. One came up with a single dirty stick, its wrapper long unpeeled, and offered it just out of Frankie's reach.

"Joosy Froot. Only cost you a nickel." Her accomplice nodded approvingly. "That stuff is pretty hard to get these days, mister."

Frankie found a lone dime and when the girl had it safely in her hand she advised him further, in lieu of a nickel change, "You don't have to worry about that stupid bull, mister. He's as stiff as you are."

"He can fwisk you but he can't search you," the other told him softly, with the softest lisp possible. "Don't let him search you without a wawwant."

The corner pharmacist brought Sophie around and slapped a bandage above Frankie's right eye. When the wagon arrived to take the sergeant away for lack of papers Frankie was sober enough to get by by identifying himself and pleading the old tune: "Only two small beers, Officer, all I had. I'm a combat vet. Purple Heart. Good Conduct. Buddy of Captain Bednar by Saloon Street."

While they waited for the ambulance the cop walked about, a wadded *Tribune* jutting out of his hip pocket, with the deliberate gait of any stewed flatfoot, around and around the battered car, slapping his big feet righteously up and down while the crowd grew and some newspaper joker took a flash-bulb photo of Sophie, stretched out on the wrinkled running board with somebody's corduroy cap under her head, resting against the fender's slope. The bulb burst, splattering glass for a dozen feet around, so that the pharmacist had to run back for more bandage and the cop had to run the photographer off, press card or no press card.

Yet the photographer remained, a small man in a raincoat almost dragging the ground, shivering with either humiliation or the cold early morning air. Pretending, on the border of the crowd, that he'd abandoned the idea of getting a close-up shot while furtively preparing another bulb. When the cop regarded him suspiciously once more he spoke up humbly, "I just like to watch." And inched up ever so little. "I'm neurotic, I like to get up close to accidents."

A weak excuse.

It was half an hour before the ambulance arrived, the early morning trolleys were blocked halfway to North Avenue and everyone but Frankie and Sophie and the sergeant felt it had been well worth the trouble. The pharmacist and photographer, the cop, the audience, trolley conductors and motormen, all agreed tacitly that this had been a better summer night than most.

"Not a bone broken," an intern had assured Frankie of Sophie's condition. "Just shock." She was lying on the receiving-room table, eyes wide and pupils dilated. "Open the door," she asked in an oddly altered voice; the door to the long white corridor stood wide.

"It is open, Zosh," Frankie told her, stepping close to her.

"Open the door," she asked again, as though she had not heard and did not know who he was.

There was only one door to open. A closet door, and he opened it just to please her. Inside it, leaning against a wheel chair, stood a crutch with a cracked handle. He closed the door again softly. When the intern came in to look at her again she slept like one who hadn't slept in weeks, without help of any drug at all.

Four mornings later she was back home and no worse for wear, apparently, except for a bluish wound on her lip, where she had bitten herself through the force of the smashup into the light pole and a tiny cut over her ear where the flash bulb had burst above her. Yet she did not seem to share Frankie's elation at all. He'd gotten the super's man, Zygmunt the Prospector, on the job and felt confident of beating any drunken-driving charge with which the Traffic Bureau might confront him.

"You sore 'cause you didn't get your back broke?" he asked her. "You ought to be singin' 'n you're moonin'."

"I just don't feel like it's *over*, Frankie," she told him. "Last night I had a sleep warnin'—my leg jerked 'n woke me up, it was a pre-motion, what they call it."

"So long as you're feelin' awright, what you got to holler?" he wanted to know, and had hauled out the practice board against the time when he could afford a set of real traps of his own, quit Zero Schwiefka cold and go on the legit with a big-name band.

Listening to the light mechanical beat, it began to sound for the first time, to Sophie, like a hammer's rapid tapping. When she'd closed her eyes his hammer went tap-tap-tapping down a thousand little bent rusty nails. She had had to clench her palms tightly to fight off the panic rising within her and when he'd looked up at her her eyes had had the same immovable stare they'd had on the receiving-room table.

It wasn't till he'd stopped beating the board that that look had faded out and she had shuttered her eyes.

But he had known right then, however inadmissibly, that something had gone wrong with his Zosh.

Zygmunt, a man continually clutching, for one reason or another, at other men's sleeves, had attended so many night schools in his early manhood that now, in his bustling middle age, he retained the pallor of his Kent College nights: the look of the downtown pavements after the rush-hour window-shoppers are doing all their window-shopping through the bright interiors of dreams. The light on his glasses seemed a reflection of the light of law-school chandeliers in those desperate days when he felt that if he didn't pass the bar he'd be tending one the rest of his life. He looked like a man who had never seen a cloud.

He'd passed the bar, put out his shingle, won his first case in a blaze of patri-otic oratory—and had been disbarred for representing conflicting interests three months later. Now he called himself a claim adjuster and had been known to reach a hospital ahead of the ambulance. Railroad brakemen, switchmen, ambulance drivers, nurses and interns beheld him with cries of sheerest joy. Only insurance men felt pain. Each year he gave precisely one thousand dollars worth of Christmas presents to railroad men and hospital attendants while the sour-looking insurance adjusters sent greeting cards in unsealed envelopes bearing half-rate postage.

"Zygmunt does us poor people a big favor," one old contented cripple informed Frankie, "if it wasn't for him I would of settled for fifty dollars 'n I would of been screwed cold. Zygmunt got fifteen hundred out of court *'n five hundred of it was all my own!* It's what I call a deed for Justice, what Prospector done for me that time. If he ever runs for coroner he got my whole family's vote."

The bruised, the cut, the fractured, the shocked, the maimed and the slightly frayed, all loved the Prospector with a deep, calm love. He was their Division Street Jesse James boldly defying the impersonal giants of the insurance trusts.

Zygmunt, in turn, loved the bruised, the cut and the frayed. He loved each sweet sufferer of them for all they were worth. What was more, he loved his country and, yet more ardently, the city that had given him his chance to serve mankind. "I'll tell you what my ideal is," he told Frankie, "it's to make Chicago the personal injury capital of the United States of America."

He was well on his way toward achieving just that. Hustling down hospital corridors with a fountain pen at the ready and a legal retainer blank flying like the Stars and Bars at Bull Run, he brought news of new hope to those still under shock. It was those under shock, he had learned, in whom the true faith abided.

His tipsters gave him head starts to hospitals where doctors competed with nurses for the chance of making a ten-spot on the side. For it wasn't always the easiest thing in the world to visit a victim still too woozy to know what had hit him. Yet as often as not Zygmunt got past the reception desk and out again without any hospital official knowing, officially, that he'd been prospecting the wards at all.

For the reception desks regarded ambulance chasing as some sort of felony or other and Zygmunt himself, at certain moments, wasn't altogether too sure it might not turn out to be denounced as such on Judgment Day. Therefore he played it safe by hustling both sides of the street, the churches as well as the hospitals, and had more novenas to his credit than defrauded cripples. He kept the ledger balanced slightly in Heaven's favor.

In the instance of Francis Majcinek vs. a city light standard his earliest concern was, "How much disability you get, Dealer?"

"Twenty-five a month." Frankie had had the presence of mind to cut it down a bit.

"In six months you'll have me paid off. Sign here."

Six months was exactly what it had taken. It would have taken longer had Frankie admitted to his forty-a-month disability. But fifteen of that was already going to Louie Fomorowski and a man had to keep his nose above water one way or another.

"Just a couple lucky Polaks," Zygmunt congratulated Frankie and Sophie whenever he dropped in to collect his twenty-five and remind them that the drunken-driving charge had been dismissed and the light standard billed to the taxpayers at large. And clutched at Frankie's sleeve when Sophie wasn't looking.

"I'll say," Sophie would agree without heart. "If I get any luckier I'll be the luckiest woman in the cemetery."

For the second time Zygmunt collected she was in the chair.

On the night of V-J Day she had sat up in bed and shaken Frankie. "Wake up, honey. Somethin's goin' to happen." In the first faint light he had seen that her face was buttoned up like a locked purse—then something behind her eyes had shifted with fear as in those of a cornered cat's.

"It feels like air bubbles in my neck—*honey*, I feel so *queer*." She was trying to smile at him: an embarrassed, apologetic smile, not like her own smile at all. "I was dreamin' about the accident, like in the car when we started tippin'—"

"You must of been readin' about that couple in the paper, their car caught fire."

"What happened to *them?*" Her breath felt cut off. Her hands were crossed upon her throat and on the wall the luminous Christ glowed faintly above the clock. "I'm sweatin' on my palms." She put one fat damp hand upon his own.

"They were trapped, that's all."

"Oh." With relief. Things that happened out of town never seemed to have happened to real people somehow. "But *we* didn't," Frankie assured her hurriedly, turning toward her onto his side. That was the first time he had seen her breasts, full to the pink and rigid nipples, without feeling any attraction at all. "You got a headache?" he asked.

"I just feel sort of choky-like. Like I'm drinkin' ginger ale I can't taste."

"You want a real drink?"

"No. It's *somethin'*. Frankie"—she paused as if it were too foolish to say—"I can't get up."

She tried to smile but the lips froze with a rising fright. He touched her knee. "A little charley horse is all you got." And massaged her legs gently while she braced herself by her elbows against the pillow.

"I—I can't feel you rubbin' so good."

"Lay back 'n take it easy," he ordered her professionally, "your nerves is exhausted. I think that croaker missed a joint lookin' you over."

"Don't say 'croaker,' honey. Say 'Doctor.' " She lay wide-eyed, looking up at the shadowed ceiling for some friendlier shadow there. "Frankie, if it was just somethin' bust, wouldn't it hurt like *everythin'?*"

"Somethin's bust awright," he decided. Not knowing quite what he meant by that himself.

The analyst at the people's clinic was young, pure in heart, and dressed in theories as spotless as his own chaste white jacket.

"The name is Pasterzy," he introduced himself, gripping Frankie's hand in a med-school grip. "A good name for a doctor," Frankie told him, "this is my wife."

He had brought her in a borrowed wheelchair and she'd raised one hand listlessly to take the doctor's hand. Then had simply sat regarding them both with a sort of puffed-up hostility.

Young Dr. P. had immediately taken her by surprise with a needle jabbed into the tender back of her calf. Her eyelids had fluttered but she had not cried out.

"You felt that," he'd accused her gently.

"Of course I felt it, goldarn t'ing." She had turned to Frankie indignantly. "This dummy *pinched* me, Frankie—what's the big idea?" But all Frankie had done was to stand there like a goof watching another man stroking his wife's leg clear to the knee.

"You're lying to yourself, Mrs. Majcinek," Dr. P. had told her tactlessly and she'd turned in a flood of tears to Frankie. "Don't just *stand* there when he's talkin' like that—*gawpin'* while he calls your wife a liar 'n cops free feels—get me to a doc who *respects* people." She turned with condescension upon the doctor kneeling at her feet. "*Do* you mind?"

Dr. P. stood up and the two men had exchanged understanding glances. "Bring her back after she's better rested," he'd told Frankie.

Halfway through the door Sophie had grabbed the chair's wheels to keep from being pushed all the way through before taking one over-the-shoulder parting shot: "If you're so damned smart why ain't you a millionaire?"

That night she had dreamed that she was about to be jabbed by a flaming needle in Frankie's hand: she'd gotten out of bed, turned on the light and wakened screaming. Frankie had carried her back to the bed and she hadn't gotten out of bed unaided since. Living between the bed and the wheelchair, her arms had grown flabby while her legs had lost flesh from disuse. The skin had crowded pendulously upon itself beneath her chin to make her eyes mere pale gray slits reflecting her sick despair.

That Pasterzy had taken as much as any doctor could. Frankie would have to wait outside and when Sophie was returned to him she would look so careworn that Frankie would hardly have the heart to question her. Yet couldn't help wondering humbly.

"What he do, Zosh?"

"He took a sample of blood. He says I got real good blood. Wait till he takes a smear, see what he says then."

"He don't hurt you, does he?"

"It ain't hurtin' like *that,* Frankie, it's just he's such a squirrel. His roof is leakin'—he don't even *look* at the pins no more. He don't even touch me, he don't even taken my pullis, maybe I got a fever. He just asts them person'l questions. He's a stinkin' t'ing hisself, I think, 'cause I don't like how he talks. You should of heard what I told him when he started pikin' around to find out what you do for a livin', how much dough you make. I told him you're out of work 'n that stopped him cold."

"You done just right there," Frankie had conceded. They had to be pretty sharp to get around his Zosh, he knew. "Didn't he give you no perscription for medicine though?"

"He don't give me nuttin' but talk, talk, talk, that's what I'm tryin' to tell, he's one big stinkin' t'ing."

"Don't say 'stinkin' t'ing,' " Frankie had suggested, "say 'reekin'.' "

"He's a reekin' t'ing all right. He wears me down till I'm reeker'n he is. Tells me to go home 'n rest, get fresh air. Where the hell does he think I live—by the Humboldt Park lagoon? 'Get built up,' he says. 'Built up fer what?' I ast him. 'So's you can tear me down again?' He wants to know too much, why I said *that.*"

"What he say then?"

"He says he's a sort of siko-patic doctor, he got to find out *every*thin'—'Did I like to play wit' little girls 'r little boys when I was a little girl?' Is that *his* business, Frankie? I told him sure I liked the little boys, the nice ones anyhow, I liked the little girls too, if they just wasn't sheenies. Then I ast him a thing or two myself."

"What you ask him, Zosh?" Frankie sounded worried.

"I ast him why don't he wear boxin' gloves when he goes to bed. 'N you know what? He took off his glasses, blew on 'em, put 'em down 'n then starts walkin' around lookin' for 'em. I had to tell him where he just put 'em. Why do I have to have some popeye kike like that quackin' at me anyhow, Frankie? Ain't there no *real* doctors no more?"

"Don't say 'kike,' " Frankie protested mildly. "He's a Polak."

"Some Polak. He's a reekin' t'ing is all."

Frankie was relieved when she and Doc Pasterzy had at last washed their hands of each other. Those trips down Division, wheeling her in the chair, had left him feeling half crippled himself.

But she wouldn't go to County. "We give them my mother's heart there," she claimed, "they put a auto-topsy on her."

Eventually she had run through a whole series of quacks, faith healers and, for as long as Frankie's terminal-leave pay had lasted, an "electric blood reverser" manipulated by Old Doc Dominowski.

It didn't do any good to tell her what all the neighborhood hustlers knew: that old Doc Dominoes, as they called him, wasn't Doc Dominowski at all. The original Doc Dominowski had had a license. But after his passing his daughter had rented his office to this blood-reversing impostor who'd left the deceased doc's shingle up. A ruse as simple as that. Though in print he had never claimed to be anything but a wandering masseur.

The present Dr. D. had had a slogan stamped over his Damen Avenue door: *Ad Electrica Necessitas Vitae.* An inner legend announced *Big Boy Is In.*

A diploma in the waiting room revealed Big Boy to be a member of The American Association of Medical Hydrology, whatever that might be. Furthermore he was a deacon of the Royal Aryan Society for Positive Christianity and as such was privileged to throw in divine healing without extra charge. That went right along with the three-dollar treatment for a touch of the astral power and a short lecture on the latent powers possessed by all of us. "Pow-wers what vassly transent our normaller ones," was just how Big Boy put it. The whole trouble with Sophie, he saw as soon as he set eye on her, was that she hadn't been awakened; and had the brass to tell her husband so.

"God help me when she comes to then," Frankie sulked to himself. He knew a rogue when he saw one and this mild-looking, white-haired, stoop-shouldered coneroo with the flat pink snout, a toothpick stuck in one corner of his mouth and his initials embroidered in red upon the pocket of an army-surplus surgeon's smock, looked like an old hand to Frankie. He boasted that he was the most popular spine manipulator and ray caster on the Northwest Side. He still looked like the business end of a fugitive warrant to Frankie.

It was true. The diplomas hung about the waiting room, just high enough to make reading difficult, were mostly grammar-school graduation certificates.

The only course Big Boy had completed was the one offered by the House of Correction, where he'd done a stretch for prescribing cinchophen, a drug for which he'd once entertained such a fondness that he'd succeeded in tearing up some three dozen human livers before his supply had been cut off. He'd picked up his present racket in the bucket, as being safer than either peddling cinchophen or living on the curette.

Safer, more respectable and more profitable, what with red and green light rays, a bit of fancy bone snapping, neck twisting and pills of every hue, shade, shape and size. He liked to wet his fingertips from his lips, when he felt the psychic approach was required, place them tenderly upon the patient's forehead and gaze into her eyes steadily, seemingly entranced by something there. Then he'd come out of it, prescribe Holland gin, collect his three-fifty and send out for a pint of Cream of Kentucky for himself.

"I'm gettin' the astral pow-wer," he would confide in some matron who lay supine and stripped to the waist before him. "You got to relax, you got to tell yourself you're not afraid of *anything*." While his hands caressed her so warmly that she felt herself starting to burn with rare courage. He had found most matrons brave enough after a while.

He never made verbal propositions: those hot damp hands did his proposing. Proposed and fulfilled. For old Doc D. wasn't working for nothing. "We don't do business in an alley," he warned any woman wearing a fur coat; though his side entrance opened onto an alley all the same. He charged as much as the traffic would bear and when the payments began coming harder the patient was cured, he'd decide after a glance at a book in which no records were kept at all. "You've cured *me* all right," the patient would have to conclude. For by the time he was through with a woman he had more on her than she had on him; he himself never got out of line until the patient was so far off base she couldn't get back in a month of extra innings.

"I can see it now," he told Sophie, breathing heavily above her, "I can see the astral pow-wer." The sheet was covering her modestly from throat to knee, he hadn't yet been able to figure how much of a charge she'd stand.

"With some patients it is little white dots, with others colored dots. Each person has his own color."

This was true too. Big Boy's own special color was the hard cold green of ten-dollar bills.

"What's my color?" Sophie asked.

"Turk-woiz blue. You *can* feel *something,* can't you?"

"Yeh. I feel *some*thin'." It was his right hand growing moderately bold as his breath grew warmer and the astral power really began to *move.* "My husband takes care of that angle," Sophie told him quietly, wishing Frankie really did. For Frankie's physical interest in her, increasingly casual since their marriage, had passed altogether with the accident.

Old Doc D. immediately became professional. "You got the blood pressure of a five-mont'-old baby—but that's nothin' serious. Eat lots of hot t'ings—pepper 'n hot sauces. Drink a little wine before meals or a little whisky. But *never* mix them. And *believe* you're going to get well. Now turn over and we'll wibrate the wertebrays."

Big Boy loved to wibrate the wertebrays. When he'd wibrated each one he applied a grease to her back, sharpened a pencil and recorded, down the spinal column, the location of something he called "ligatites." They were the *real* cause of Sophie's trouble. He showed her a rough diagram of her spine. "You can see for yourself what shape you're in."

She saw. But he sensed her doubt and decided that the root of her difficulty was Lack of Faith—which was also curable. So she attended a meeting of the Royal Aryan Crusaders and the Aryans sold her so many varieties of pills, pamphlets, booklets, wormwood tea and senna leaves that she couldn't afford to have the wertebrays wibrated for three weeks following.

When she resumed treatments, largely because of Frankie's gloomy aversion to the doc, Big Boy introduced her to the electric blood reverser. This was simply a frosted twenty-five-watt bulb which glowed with a lavender light. He also had some pale green bulbs for the better-heeled clientele and if necessary he could, literally, make sparks fly. It was only by sheerest chance that he had as yet electrocuted no one.

"I'm talkin' cold turkey to you now," he warned Sophie. "How many treatments can you take a week? You ought to take them every day so the good effect don't wear off in between. But you got to come t'ree times a week or they won't do no good at all. It'll be the greatest investment you ever made. Have your husband wash your feet in ice water every night, don't drink no liquor except beer, no eggs in hot weat'er 'n come back T'ursday for wibrate the wertebrays."

Frankie knew he was being played for a mark but it took Violet to put her foot down. When she no longer had anyone to wheel her down Division to Big Boy's, Sophie finally resigned herself to forgoing his ministrations.

Thus Frankie had robbed her again, of course, of her one chance to get well. If he wouldn't let her go to Big Boy's she wouldn't go anywhere at all. For weeks she wouldn't let anyone help her upstairs but Frankie.

Even though Vi had helped her down the stairs it had to be on Frankie's shoulder she must now come up. Once, wearied like a child by hours of horror films and animated cartoons, she clung with all her weight to the banister, crying that no one must touch her any more but Frankie.

"Let me help you, Sissie," Violet urged her, wiping Sophie's forehead, "Frankie's gone to work."

"He ain't *suppose* to go so soon," she complained miserably in the darkening hall, "he's suppose to help me up, *he's* the one who done it, he's *suppose* to, he's *suppose* to——" She began beating the scarred newel post with both fat fists. "He went early just so's he wouldn't have to 'n I *told* him to wait—I *told* him, I *told* him——"

"He got to earn a livin' first, Sissie. He ain't even got the clinic paid off yet."

"You call this *livin'?*" Sophie wanted to know, and her voice rose into such a hysterical rattle that Violet slapped her cleanly across the cheek. For one moment Sophie's full-moon face stared out in white shock at Violet's impudence. "Now my best friend turns on me," she mourned, "he made me this way 'n you stick up fer him—you got a name like a flower but you're a devil all the same. Go *on,* get upstairs, the sheeny shoplifter is waitin' to give you some hot lovin', you'll just have time before Stash gets home—I'll get upstairs by myself 'r die right here in the hall." She was pale with sweat and leaned heavily upon the post for support. Violet waited, hands on hips, for the tantrum to pass.

But at last had turned slowly away, so sorry that Sophie, of all people, should talk like that. Violet had hardly felt the stairs beneath her feet. In the hall at the top of the flight a red light shone over the gas meter, among a dark maze of pipes, with the meter's single hand pointing to some midnight when no cripple would be crying below with her head on the dark newel post. Some midnight when neither Sparrow nor Frankie would be near at hand nor anyone at all, of all the friends she knew. She looked down over the banister. Sophie was in the middle of the first flight and coming on strong.

Stiffly, like a woman who has overslept, holding the banister with both hands, but still coming. "I knew all the time you could do it, honey!" Violet cried down and Sophie went down in a heap, her fingers clawing piteously at the rail. To hold herself there tensely, without a single cry, till Violet had hurried down and helped her all the way up.

"Did you see me?" Sophie asked like a child caught in mischief.

"You were comin' along somethin' wonderful, Sissie," Violet assured her, "you were climbin' as good as anybody—it shows you can do it if you just want."

"You saw what happened when I tried too hard, didn't you?"

"I shouldn't ought to of hollered," Violet realized too late. "I'm sorry about slappin' you, Sissie, it was just to keep you on the ground." She waited for Sophie to say she was sorry too.

"Am I gettin' *awful* fat, Vi? Is that why he won't help me upstairs no more? I just couldn't *stand* his not lovin' me like he used."

"Stop whimperin'," Violet scolded her, "of course he loves you like he used. He wouldn't be takin' care of you so good if he didn't." Which was true enough, Violet knew: he loved her as little as ever and took just as small care of her as before.

When he did help her up the stairs she needed his arm to lean on across the floor and, once in the chair, needed to be wheeled and, being wheeled, needed to be comforted. Till there was no end, no end to her asking at all.

When he refused to wheel her it was as if a priest had suddenly refused to confess her. "Tell me what *I* done to *you,* you can't even wheel me a little. You think I *want* to be laid up in a chair all my life? You remember me ever askin' you, 'Please smash me up?' "

Frankie would give in to her as he always gave in. As he gave in to Schwiefka in arguments over the take. As he gave in to Louie in arguments over the price of "God's medicine." As he gave in to Zygmunt and Antek and Schwabatski. "There's just one guy I don't give in to in this world," Frankie considered, "the punk got to take what the others hand to me."

And would hear an echo of Sparrow's protest: "It's just since you come back you're givin' me gas, Frankie. You never used to give me gas before."

"It's what I got you around for," Frankie would remind him brutally. Thus even Sparrow had to feel the edge of those fragments of jealousy into which Sophie's love, like her crockery, had been shattered.

Long, ugly fragments for Frankie and slenderer, more delicate ones for Violet and Violet's iron health. "If I go downtown 'n see somethin' I like I'll buy for you too," Violet would try to assuage her.

"You don't have to buy me nuttin'," Sophie would scorn everyone. "Just buy that Frankie a set of drums. He's gettin' a job wit' a big-name band one of these days—he ain't said which day. Just don't hold yer breath till then, that's my advice to all you Division Street hustlers."

For those nearest our hearts are the ones most likely to tread upon them. What she could not gain through love she sought to possess by mockery. He was too dear to her: into everything he did she must read some secret hatred of herself.

"Whyn't you come right out 'n say you wisht I'd got killed 'stead of crippled?" she accused him without warning.

"I didn't say nothin' like *that,* Zosh," he threshed about trying to clear himself. "All I said was I wish you'd just *try* to walk again."

Yet she had planted the doubt in his mind. "Of course I don't wish nothin' like *that,*" he would have to tell himself. With the pang of guilt in the very words.

Violet helped him. "I don't think you *want* to get well," she told Sophie. Then would wait for Sophie to stop whimpering so she could make it all up to her for saying that by wheeling her down the street to the Pulaski, chain the chair in the lobby, help her into a seat and call for her when the double feature was done.

"I could die listenin' to that Dick Haymes," Sophie would say while being wheeled home.

On days when the bill remained unchanged Violet would pop her hennaed head in the door and ask, "Zosh, you want to play checkerds?"

And all the while they were playing would keep up a stream of idle reminiscence calculated to keep Sophie's mind off Frankie and all the trouble he'd brought her just like her father had warned her.

"I've had trouble with my eyes lately," Vi would hint till Sophie would ask why she didn't get glasses.

"It's not that kind of trouble. It's from flirtin', that kind of trouble. Me 'n my bedroom eyes."

That was Violet's idea of high humor and Sophie's idea of nothing at all. "You ought to cut all that out, it just ain't right," Sophie would scold her, "bein' hooked to old Stash 'n flirtin' around with Sparrow."

It was true. Violet let the punk make hurried love to her on rainy afternoons—then rushed him out into the rain in time to have dinner on the stove by the time old Stash returned from work. When Stash wanted to know where she'd been all afternoon it was always "takin' Zosh to the movies, Old Man."

Only once had Old Husband taken the trouble to check with Sophie, and Sophie had been loyal enough to reply, "Vi was settin' by me all afternoon by the Pulaski, we set t'rough two stinky shows. One was white gorillas 'n the other was Carmen Bolero—he had two orchesters 'n did they make *glad*."

A girl like Violet, a warm one like that, to marry an old icicle like Stash Koskozka, whose need for her stopped when she'd finished warming up yesterday's *pierogi*.

"Still, if I'd hooked up with anyone but Old Man,"Violet tried consoling herself, "I wouldn't never have had the time to keep the punk out of jail. He couldn't stay out of jail a week without me. With me watchin' over him sometimes he stays out a whole month. Once he wasn't in for six, I was certainly proud of him *that* time. Then he went 'n spoiled it all, gettin' picked up twice the very next week—nothin' serious of course. I keep him out of serious trouble."

Stash's curiosity seldom went beyond a vague wonder that she could consume so much Polish sausage; no matter how much of the stuff he hauled home there was usually no more than a single dry butt end around when he went to the icebox.

Yet, after the manner of simple hearts, Violet was confident that her secret was buried as deep as God's toenails. Scarcely a living soul in the whole great gray frame hotel nor in the one long bar below knew, she was sure. Except, of course, Sparrow's buddy Frankie and her own best friend Sophie and trusty old Antek the Owner and one or two of the Tug & Maul's more reliable barflies. She could swear that scarcely anyone from the Safari knew a thing—and who cared what those swishes thought anyhow? Unless that long, lean, lanky, sidewinding Fomorowski had picked up a whisper. At any rate Stash never spent in either bar, so it made no difference at all. They were all good guys by Antek the Owner and wouldn't want to make trouble for a girl.

Though what in the world any redhead stacked like Vi could see in a shapeless bag of bones like the punk was one of those things those same good guys marveled upon. If one asked, Violet always made the same reply "What does any Division Street woman see in any Division Street punk?"

The fact was that to the Tug & Maul boys the punk sometimes seemed something clean off Division Street, if not out of the world. The only routine work he'd ever performed successfully was the window-peeping routine, conducted between 10 P.M. and midnight of midsummer evenings, which he'd called his "scraunching route."

The scraunching route had had seven stops, each timed for the most rewarding moment and requiring anywhere from ten minutes to half an hour of hanging from a limb, crouched on somebody's porch or leaning, with a telephone directory underfoot, against a pane whose shade reached only to two inches of the sash.

"I've seen a thing or two in my time," he still liked to boast, "that was how I found out the best place for wolfin' ain't the taverns. It ain't in dance halls 'r on North Clark on Saturday night. It's in the front row in Sunday school on Sunday mornin'. Oh yeh, I know a thing or two, I been around."

The punk knew a thing or two all right. He knew almost everything except how to stay out of jail. For jail was the one place he'd been most around. He'd been around jails so much that, as Violet never wearied of promising him, "someday you'll be in so long you'll get to thinkin' you're the warden."

It had been Violet who had first diverted him from the scraunching route. He had been boasting, to a small but select circle at the Tug & Maul, of what he'd seen the night before, when Violet, uninvited, had interrupted to observe that if she were his girl friend she'd be so ashamed she wouldn't be able to hold up her head on a lighted street.

"'Shamed 'cause a fellow like me is studyin' to be a Pinkerton?" He had feigned amazement. "Don't you think I want to *make* somethin' of myself? Don't you think there's big money in detectin' things people 'r doin' when they don't know any-body's lookin'? How you suppose Pinkies get trainin'—in classrooms?"

"I know you don't get detective trainin' doin' a dry waltz with yourself on somebody else's fire escape," she assured him. "If I was your girl friend 'n caught you on *my* fire escape I'd testify up against you myself, so help me."

"If you was my girl friend," he whispered in his special inside-info whisper, "I wouldn't be playin' Pinkie wit' myself."

It had begun as simply as that. He'd given up his scraunching route for her. He'd given up almost everything that makes life worth while, it seemed. Everything but stealing dogs and telling lies and keeping one eye peeled for stray change along bar rails.

The bigger the lies he told her the tenderer Violet had felt toward him. The dizzier he appeared the more deeply he'd endeared himself to her warm round arms. "He's not a Polak, he's not a Hebe, he's just nobody's poor sparrow at all—who's to take care of him if not me?" She really wondered who.

"I can't stand a liar myself," Sophie answered that one virtuously.

"Lies are just a poor man's pennies," Violet told her. "Fact is, that's just how he started out with me—tellin' lies. I didn't know him so good then, only from seein' him by Antek's 'r standin' on the corner of Damen 'n Division in them same old baggy pants 'n perfesser's glasses, holdin' a dog on a leash 'n both lookin' like they been in a battle. I didn't know about his window peepin' till he starts braggin' by Antek that time. He was just so afraid he wasn't good enough for me, that's all his braggin' was," Violet explained. "He didn't think he was good enough for *any*body, he was tryin' so hard to show he was *some*body. So it was up to me to show him he was somebody all by hisself—that's the first thing a woman got to do for a man. 'N of course there's no sense tryin' to prove somethin' like that standin' up. The least a girl owes to herself is to be comfortable about it."

"It's what they call syko-ology," Sophie informed her loftily.

"That ain't what *I* call it, Sissie. I just call it savin' poor man's pennies. 'Cause that's all his big lies are, Zosh. Just a poor punk's pennies."

"You leave me agasted," Sophie told her, knotting her babushka under chin with impatience in every fingertip, "I just don't see how some of you Division Street women live, that's *all*."

"Well," Violet reflected a long minute, "I guess it's like Frankie says: some cats just swing like that, Zosh."

It was Violet who'd gotten Sparrow right side up the time he was put on probation "just for settin' in a corner drinkin' a couple beers. Some fella come in pertendin' like he's drunk, buys me a couple cheap shots 'n says there's guys followin' him, they're after his watch, would I hold it for him. I got such a honest puss. So I done the guy the favor 'n sure enough, one more shot 'n the bum starts to holler somebody copped his watch.

"It all just goes to show you, don't try to do too much for people or you'll wind up in the short end of the funnel. It's my one big weakness, helpin' guys who can't help theirselves."

"Yeh," Violet reminded him dryly, "I guess you thrun the pop bottle through Widow Wieczorek's window that time just to let in a little air too. You know," she added before he could answer, "it ain't that I love you so much, it's more that I'm sorry for you because your mind is so weak."

"I see what you mean," Sparrow decided, "I'm the first person you ever met with a mind weaker than yours—is that it?"

"Not en*tire*ly. What I *really* like about you is you're so mercenary."

"And what I really like about you is that if you had a hummingbird's brains you'd fly backerds," the punk forgave her for everything she'd done for him.

She'd kept him out of trouble then until he'd slipped on the ice one January night and that had been the worst rap of all. The sidewalk was like the dance floor at Guyman's Paradise, anyone could have fallen. And have one elbow go through a window. A jewelry-store window. In the dark a thing like that could happen to a Park District policeman.

Frankie had gotten Zygmunt to put in the fix, the charge had been changed to drunk and disorderly, and Sparrow had gotten two years probation. But it had cost Violet one hundred silver dollars of old Stash's money. So the least the punk could do for her, he felt, was to stay out of further trouble.

The only time in those whole two years that the police had persecuted him was when he'd taken a short cut on his way to putting a potted geranium on his mother's grave.

He had to take a short cut through an alley toward the florist's when the squadrol slid up beside him. All they wanted to know, after he'd explained his business, was how he expected any florist to be open at 4 A.M.

"Why, that's the oney time to buy geran'ums—right before sunup. You see," he explained easily, "it's a night-bloomin' geran'um I got to have, it's what Mother always liked best."

That might have stopped them if it hadn't been for the bathtub on his back. Sure enough, they noticed it. Chicago cops are pretty sharp about bathtubs being carried through alleys piggyback at 4 A.M. Though the punk himself didn't see anything particularly out of the way. "A little clumsy for carryin' geran'ums," he conceded to the aces, setting the tub down to light the butt of a dead cigar with a borrowed match, "but when I seen it layin' there in the middle of the alley the first thing I tawt was somebody better get that tub out of the way before Szalapski the Milkman's horse breaks a leg over it in the dark. That's Szalapski from Nort'western Dairy—not that Szalapski I Fix Fenders—it ain't that the horse don't know the stops by hisself it's just that he don't see so good no more—not like that good old Rumdum the Pedigreed Square-snapper— that's my blood-type Polish Airedale, he don't get along so good wit' Owner's deafy-dumb cat—say, you fellows want to buy a dog?"

A few other items were missing from the plumber's. In fact the faster he talked the more the squad found missing. What worried them most was the flashlight and crowbar, they seemed to think the punk had something to do with those too. But the plumber dropped charges when Violet took care of him and Stash did without Polish sausage at all for a while.

The court put it down as malicious mischief and Sparrow had gone away for thirty days.

The day the wagon took Sparrow out to Twenty-eighth and California Violet got roaring drunk in the Tug & Maul. And, as always when she had too much, upbraided all the males in sight just for being males. She wasn't going to live with old Stash another day, she told the house. "Or any other of you godamned hairy-ass morphodyke booze bums who think a girl got to be grateful when her old man brings home bargains from Nostriewicz's Hi-Klass Bakery—they ain't even got good *freshy* stuff by Nostriewicz 'n here *he* comes bringin' me the day-olds that's a day old when they're freshy even 'n tells me I should sew buttons on his pants 'n sell the zippers to Efjievicz the Tailor because all the young guys are bringin' Efjievicz pants to take off the buttons 'n put on zippers 'n Efjievicz don't have enough zippers 'n Stash is too old for a zipper anyhow, it's just for young guys in a big hurry, he ain't never in a hurry for nothin' but bargains by Nostriewicz no more—*he's tellin' me.*"

The barflies applauded timidly, they felt she deserved applause.

"*He's* tellin' *me* he's not so young no more. Godamnit, *am* I married 'r ain't I?" she demanded to know, steadying herself against the bar.

"Don't sound like you are," Meter Reader, with the holes in his cap and whisky in his hand, felt obliged to reply.

"That's just *your* opinion," Violet almost blasted him off the stool. "Who ast *your* dirty opinion anyhow? Who you think *you're* tellin' what to do? Who *you* married to?" She sized him up with growing contempt. "Hell, you're in worse shape than my old man—you're married to your dirty fist, that's who *you're* married to—where you get off anyhow tellin' other people what to do 'n how to live? Ever try mindin' your own business, you moldy-lookin' sandlot spigotheaded bakebrain? I'll use your dirty skull for a bar towel, you tellin' *me* what to do 'n what not to do 'n all that *kapustka*—" Violet wasn't big, but she looked big enough to do it—at such moments the helmet of her hennaed hair and the wide-set gray eyes flared with a single flame. Meter Reader took up his glass quietly and retired to the rear of the bar. Meter Reader was saving himself for the exigencies of his coaching position with the Endless Belt & Leather Invincibles.

That thirty days had taught the punk a lesson. It had made him feel badly, costing Violet all that money. Every time she'd had enough saved to divorce Old Man she'd have to spend it putting in the fix for him. He'd brooded about it the whole thirty days, and made up his mind that the first thing he'd do when he got out would be to steal the divorce money for her.

He'd picked on Gold's Department Store when a goodly crowd was there.

Sparrow had been stealing odds and ends off Gold's counters since he was in short pants. He knew that the only gun in the store was an ancient cow pistol carried by the old man who runs the freight elevator. The elevator man is even older than old Gold; all he does is lean against the shaft, half asleep all day. It's like a pension.

Sparrow had felt that if he could get the gun off the old man without getting himself shot straight through the head the rest should be fairly easy. He began drinking on the notion next door to Gold's and, as the afternoon wore on, the more natural the notion had appeared. He wasn't able to understand why he hadn't thought of it long before.

But when he'd shuffled out of the bar and had seen how swiftly the long street was darkening, he'd gone cold sober with the recollection of his recent thirty-day stretch and had had to return, in a hurry, to the bar.

He'd gotten drunk all over again on Vi's credit, which was good so long as Stash held down his icehouse job. But by nine o'clock the credit gave out and he'd been brooding on the idea so long he couldn't back out. To falter would have been to reneg on Frankie as well as on Violet, he felt. Both had done so much for him—and what had he ever done for either? Nothing. Not a thing. He never did anything for his friends but use up their credit and get them in trouble. He'd do something big for them all. Right now.

So shuffled, cap yanked low, straight down the middle aisle—Ladies' Hose and Fancy Footwear—to the freight elevator where the ancient house dick lounged in dreams of long-lost daily doubles. Sparrow shoved his combination flashlight pencil into the small of the old man's back, grabbed the gun, shoved him into the lift and snarled just like Edward G. Robinson, "Into the basement wit' the rest of the rats—*copper*."

His glasses had clouded up, but he heard the door of the lift crash shut and the cables whining downward and the dozen-odd customers began turning slowly toward him like people in a slow-motion movie. In that moment he saw himself through all their eyes: a cardboard cowboy in horn-rimmed spectacles waving an oversized cow gun. He heard his own shrill voice carried away down endless nylon aisles on the scudding of the overhead fans.

"Face the waw-awls, every*body!*"

He saw them turning, by ones and twos, old Gold with a steel washboard under his arm and the cashier's face white as a split apple against the parched black line of her brows just as she took a header and he hollered, "Leave her lay! She oney fainted!"

Leaning across the counter he banged the cash drawer open and saw bills stacked there just for Sparrow. Tens and twenties and singles and fives rubbing rawly against the icy sweat of his palm—and the shining dimes and quarters in the last drawer over! He reached so far he tottered, the liquor came up in his throat and his lips moved with whisky or greed; heard a quarter go tinkling along the floor toward Fancy Footwear and followed it anxiously, a dozen pairs of eyes following it with him, to a rack bearing spring topcoats. Pocketed the lucky quarter, pulled the flashiest coat of all off the rack and was struggling into it when old Gold's nose appeared above the cosmetics counter between two jars of cold cream, the washboard glinted one moment as it trembled in his hand and the momentum of his swing carried him half across the counter, sent the cold cream jars and a stack of blue-boxed Kotex into the aisle as the board caught Sparrow spam behind the left ear.

He went down as if he'd been shot; the cow gun went clattering down those endless nylon aisles.

Half the crowd began shoving the other half aside for the distinction of being the first to sit on the gangster while others bound him with clotheslines and a couple cooler heads used the excitement to snatch such small items as happened to be lying loose and near at hand. In the haste of binding the punk old Gold became securely tied to him; the punk reared his head groggily to protest something or other and someone promptly banged him back to sleep with that same washboard. When the aces arrived old Gold was still trying to free himself.

In front of the store half the neighborhood waited to see who the cops would bring out this time. They came out carrying something that looked like a giant beehive with old Gold in tow. For all you could see of Sparrow in the yards of clothesline circling him from forehead to ankles was the point of his pale nose sticking out of the coils. The aces shoved old Gold into the wagon with him— if he wasn't an accomplice what was he doing tied up with a gangster?

Some gangster. At the Saloon Street Station it took the officers ten minutes to unwind the punk and ten more to loosen old Gold. Sparrow sat up blinking, looking for his glasses, and Sergeant Kvorka immediately poured a bucket of ice water on the punk's head so he could see more clearly.

The first person he'd recognized was Violet. He blinked up at her with his shortsighted eyes, waiting resignedly for her to explain *this* caper to him. "Well?" the punk demanded.

"Ask him what he thought he was trying to do," the bewildered aces urged her. They wanted to know too.

"I went in there to try on a topcoat," he explained haughtily, without taking those accusing eyes off her, "because I wanted to look nice just for *you*. I took the gun off that old man 'cause he got a old grudge against me. I was gonna give it back to him right after I paid for the coat. But when I had it on, all of a sudden they wouldn't give me a chance to pay for a thing, just like they been layin' for me all along. You know as well as I do, honey, I'm not the kind goes around tryin' to get somethin' fer nothin'."

The aces looked at Violet and Violet looked at the aces.

"We'll have to get another kind of lawyer now," she sighed. "Here goes the divorce again. It looks like the oney honeymoon you 'n me'll ever have'll be in the Bridewell."

"I'll defend myself," Sparrow announced, "it was self-defense. That makes it false arrest." He just couldn't get that false arrest notion out of his offbalanced skull.

"If you don't button up I'll sue you for breach of promise even if I *am* married," she threatened him, getting angry with him at last. "You're goin' to cop a plea 'n get paroled to me—if I ain't gonna be your wife I'll just be your dirty guardian." Abruptly her anger turned to tears and he'd never seen her cry before. "Then I can arrest you myself when you get out of line—I'll arrest you every night just to keep the aces from doin' it."

"I'll have to look up the law on that," he dismissed her. "I don't think they got me yet."

They hadn't. The two analysts who questioned him at Central Police turned in reports at such variance that Zygmunt was able to put in the fix with almost no trouble at all.

Violet had to pay Zygmunt off in installments, out of Stash's hoarded checks. Every time she'd get the Prospector paid off she'd have to start chiseling on Old Husband again. It made her pretty mad at Old Husband sometimes.

Just the way he kept hanging on, month after month, was enough to wear away any woman's patience. "I wouldn't mind his hangin' on to me if it *meant* anythin'," she complained to Sophie, "but I don't have to tell *you* it don't mean a thing, the shape he's in."

Old Husband, it seemed, had added one more trick to the repertoire of his senility. When he brought home his bargains of late he locked them up in the broom closet for fear Vi might throw them in the garbage can as she had so often threatened. He was getting so he locked up everything. He had a lock put on the pantry, leaving what he judged was just enough food for one healthy woman on the kitchen table before he left for work. Vi was embarrassed, when she went to get the punk a slab of Polish sausage, to find herself literally locked out of her own home while remaining inside it. She took a hammer to the lock and tossed the punk the entire sausage, not even salvaging the butt end for Stash. For two nights thereafter Stash slept, bargains and all, in the broom closet.

Strangely, he hadn't seemed to mind it there particularly. If it hadn't been for the Jailer's protest, because of the difficulty the situation gave him in getting to his mops and buckets, it might have developed into a permanent arrangement. As it was the Jailer drove the old man, in his long underwear and holding his pants in his hand, back to his proper home. "And keep door closed," was Jailer's final word. It had become an obsession to Schwabatski: before a tenant could step through his own doorway Jailer was telling him to close the door behind him.

Violet reported to Sophie, with a certain hopelessness, "He *liked* livin' in the broom closet wit' the rest of the mops."

Sometimes, watching unsmiling while Stash beat his gums around the evening pumpernickel, she would urge him to eat a bit faster; without adding that Sparrow waited for her in the bar below. The old man would pay no attention at all, his battle was with the dark and bitter bread as he sopped it about a beef stew that wasn't any fresher. For the address where the latter delicacy was available was a secret locked, as he'd locked the pantry door upon her, deep within the darkest recesses of his day-old, half-price soul.

His secondhand, rabbitty, battered, bruised and terribly defenseless soul.

"All bein' married to Old Man means is lettin' him tear the date off the calendar every night 'n lettin' him read the thermometer every morning," Violet explained to Sophie, "he gets a kick out of little things like that—it's like a thrill to him, sort of, to tell me what the temper'ture is outside. I got to pertend I didn't have no idea it was that hot 'r that cold. I'll tell you what, he leans out that window so far some mornings, just so's he can surprise me, it scares me. Then I got to pertend I'm sleepin' so's he can wake me up 'n tell. He don't

mean a bit of harm, that good old man. Just trusts me all down the line like a
baby. In a way it is like takin' care of a baby. 'Cause he don't come on wit' no lies
like that conniving punk."Violet sighed reminiscently. "*Such* big wonderful lies."

Up the stairwell they heard Blind Pig come tapping, tapping. Pausing only to
touch the latch of the dealer's narrow door as though accidentally and then pass
on and up two flights: tapping, tapping. All the way up to a curtainless, lightless,
windowless corner where he sat in the endless dark with his cane between his
knees and said softly over and over: "I'll take all I can get."

"He does that a-purpose to let us know he's upstairs," Sophie told Violet of
the light tap on the latch. "What the hell does he think Frankie'd want to see
him about?" she suddenly wondered aloud.

A cold wind followed the blind man up the stairs and Violet folded the blanket snugly about Sophie's legs. "That crummy deadpicker left the downstairs
door open again," she sympathized with Sophie as though the door had been
left wide just to make Sophie shiver a bit. "Now I got to go see what's goin' on
upstairs, what the people 'r up to."

Whether Violet returned to tell her or not, Sophie could usually tell what
the neighbors were up to: kissing or drinking or counting their money.
Sometimes there was an argument on the stairs between the Jailer and that one
who had thumbtacked his nickname so proudly upon his door: *Mr. & Mrs.
Drunky John.*

"You buy for booze and forget rent," the Jailer was scolding John right outside Sophie's door and a kind of cold glee seized her, she wheeled softly to the
keyhole to hear every single word.

"See my wife."

Sophie sniffled. Some wife. As if everyone didn't know what that Molly
Novotny was, hustling drinks and calling herself "a hostess." A hostess, mind
you. "I knew her when she was fourteen 'n goin' out with every Tom, Dick 'n
Harry who'd ask her." It served her right now, Sophie felt, if all the girl got out
of sharing a man's bed was light mockery and heavy blows.

"What Judge tell you last week," the Jailer demanded to know, "five or ten?"

"Seventeen—but I don't have to do 'em."

That was where the Jailer had him. "If I sign complaint you do 'em."

The Jailer was toughening up a bit, it sounded to Sophie.

Yet Drunkie John's chief skill was in using the affection others felt for Molly
to gain himself all manner of reprieves; reprieves of workhouse sentences,

reprieves of rent, reprieves to go on drinking. Nothing ever really happened, John had learned, when the rent was overdue. The Jailer always turned soft-hearted when it came to the actual signing of a complaint. He was altogether too fond of Molly to send her man to the workhouse. All he had ever yet extracted from John was a promise to stop kicking her.

A promise seldom kept. Sophie had heard John telling Molly, coming past the door late at night, "I'm not layin' you, sister—I'll never lay you. Just let me get in those kicks." They had passed to the sound of her crying, "All I want from you is to be left alone."

Once it had been Nifty Louie on the other side of the knob. Early morning, everyone from the first floor to the fourth up to do an honest day's hustling and Louie doing the talking for everyone. "My business is everybody's business—informin' is a racket like everythin' else. Anythin' that pays ain't nothin' to be ashamed of, one racket's as good as the next. A man who's ashamed of his racket is a man who's ashamed of his mother. The only thing a man got a right to be ashamed of these days is bein' broke. Get yours, Piggy-O. I'm gettin' mine. We'll go to town together."

And Piggy-O's flat half-lisp, like the voice of a man being willingly chloro-formed, "*They* ain't gettin' ahead of *me*. I'm goin' to town too."

Some mornings there were no voices but those of the air shaft, making kitchen sounds. To these Sophie listened, she heard a secret meaning there. A woman sorting knives and forks and spoons into separate drawers, tinkling the separate tenement seconds off. Then the beating of a heavy spoon, as the one task was done and a new one begun, into a platter or bowl. Homesick sounds that her mother once had made and now would make no more. Sounds out of a time of contentment that should have been her own; sounds that belonged to all women in the world save herself. A searing self-pity would seize her, that Sophie Majcinek of all women should be so punished. She would wheel away from the door and the air shaft's many voices.

To sit by the window, flyspecked since summer, where only the iron traf-fic's metallic cries could reach her heart.

Where only the carnival of the cars could please her eye. Blue, green and mud-splattered, Fourth of July red or funereal black, truck and trailer, roadster and sedan, low-slung coupé or pompous hearse: all day the city's varicolored traffic passed, paused, and rocked on again.

While the cry of a single record, always the same old cry, came to her down from the fourth floor rear where some old fool in pin curls fancied it was 1917 again.

"It all seems wrong somehow
That you're nobody's baby now . . ."

There through the starless night or the thunderous noon, sunlight or rain or windless cold, she would sit till the tenement's long shadows moved all the way down from the fourth floor rear, slid silently under her door and drifted across her lap. To tremble one moment at still finding her there and then lie comforted and still. While all the air hung wearily.

Long lonesome shadows of the December tenements that fled the neon carnival below to turn each night toward her for rest.

This was the shadow-gatherers' hour: the hour for those all over the earth who had rest neither in sleep nor waking. Some gathered their shadows like memories; but she gathered hers like unborn children to her pale and secret eyes.

She knew when the shadows waited to come by the way the luminous crucifix glowed a bit. They moved toward her then for warmth, they had been feeling unwanted all day. Like everyone else in the world for whom things had gone wrong. They knew that here they would come alive, for here they were loved and wanted at last. She alone knew how lost all shadows felt: it made them the dearer to her own unwanted heart.

To the heart weighed down by its own uselessness. What good is any unwanted heart?

That was why they must never forsake her and always be faithful and forever be kind. Here in the amber evening's light where all the air hung wearily.

"You bad little kittens, you've lost your mittens," she would scold them like storybook children. For everyone needed someone and everyone had to pretend a bit to be somebody. There was a boy for every girl in the world, it said in the old song.

And would not touch the shadows for one moment for fear her sweet half dream be lost.

For she, like the luminous Christ, had also been betrayed. She too had bled, and bled each day, for another's sin. Between herself and that tarnished crucifix a bond of blood and pain had grown. She had seen that it glowed out of love of everyone she herself wished to love and could not. How could she love who had never learned how?

Tonight, just as the wan winter-evening light fanned out into all the colors of the hustlers' night, God tossed a handful of city rain across the green and red tavern legends like tossing a handful of red and green confetti. Overhead the wavering warning lamps of the El began casting a blood-colored light down the rails to guide the empty cars of evening down all the nameless tunnels of the night.

Beneath the dresser the hound she had wanted so badly, and so soon had come to despise, slept with his great snout in a saucer wherein the drying dregs of another day's beer had left an unclean amber line. The last fly of autumn walked a lonely beat there, between the saucer's brim and the hound's nostrils: trapped, like the hound, in hustlers' territory with one conviction to go.

In the room's corners there remained fragments of the dish-breaking tournament of the night before. She remembered with something of pleasure; and something of sadness too. For it had been Frankie, on his knees, who'd cleaned up that mess when he'd come back from work. She had wakened to see him crawling.

Crawling. And hadn't made a sound lest he get to his feet in shame. She had just let him think she hadn't seen.

Then, when he'd climbed into bed with the floor quite clean, she'd laughed a little, softly, just to let him know she'd been awake and watching the whole time he'd been on his knees.

What was it the goof had said then? *"Please* don't, Zosh." How was that for a husband? *"Please* don't laugh at me, Zosh." A husband like *that.* "It's about time you done some crawlin' around her," she'd told him and had turned heavily onto her side to dream he was trying to crawl up a fire escape in the rain and could not tell her why.

In a rain, a freezing rain. Yet would not tell her why. Had dreamed with a certain pleasure; yet with something of sadness too.

Now he was gone once more, to deal till morning where the southwestern sky hung in cloudy amber folds, shielding a dull gray moon. A wind began parting them, like a curtain parting upon the opening act of a play staged just for her, to reveal a paper moon pasted stiffly—for as long as paste might hold—but one that did not weave with light as the real moon was supposed to do.

As the moon of her girlhood had woven all night: great copper strands through clouds of cloth upon the darkness's measureless loom.

These nights the moon wove neither copper nor gold, even the clouds were pasted there. Moonlight that had once revealed so many stars now showed her only how the city was bound, from southeast to the unknown west, steel upon steel upon steel: how all its rails held the city too tightly to the thousand-girdered El.

Some nights she could scarcely breathe for seeing the flat unerring line of cable and crosslight and lever, of signal tower and switch. For the endless humming of telephone wires murmuring insanely from street to street without ever saying a single word above a whisper that a really sensible person might understand.

For the city too was somehow crippled of late. The city too seemed a little insane. Crippled and caught and done for with everyone in it. No one else was really any better off than herself, she reflected with a child's satisfaction, they had all been twisted about a bit whether they sat in a wheelchair or not. She could tell just by the way once familiar doorways had come to look menacing in the morning light, ready to be slammed in the face of anyone who knocked at all. Nobody was at home to anyone else any more.

"They don't even act like they know what they're doin' no more," she decided, watching a couple moving aimlessly together down the long street below. "'N that Frankie Majcinek is the worst of all."

She heard the umbrella man with his bell, far away; and a hot-dog vendor's cart near at hand. Saw how the moon followed the hot-dog cart like a cripple left to follow alone, leaning, one bitter moment, upon the crutch of the signal tower. It had always gone its own brave way; now it followed lamely after every fool below. It too was somehow broken. It too now played the fool.

She grew tense to see how the nameless people were bound, as they went, to the streets as the streets seemed bound to the night and the night to the nameless day. And all days to a nameless remorse.

No one moved easily, freely and unafraid any longer, all hurried worriedly to work and anxiously by night returned; waited despairingly for traffic lights to change, forever fearing that the green light might change too soon and, when that warning yellow flashed, stormed through to beat the deadly red. Was there no time left for easy passages and casual pleasures down tree-lined boulevards? Her hours, that had begun so pleasantly, borne on a lake wind by morning and so certain then to blow off the lake every morning forever, now passed in a cold draft from a half-lit hall, rattling a loosened latch.

The wind, like the moon and Frankie Machine, all had turned secretly against her. One wind or another, one moon or the next, whether he returned by midnight or noon—all things recalled to her only that dead year's final midnight when the chairs had been stacked and some fool had left a cracked crutch between a juke and a 7-Up sign.

"It was mine 'n I didn't even know it," she felt a ceaseless wonder now. And a bottomless sorrowing: "I shouldn't ought to have laughed when I seen it."

For since that night everyone had become afraid of closing time everywhere, of having the lights go out in the middle of the dance while the chimes of all the churches mourned: a requiem for everyone trapped beneath the copper-colored sky of noon or the night-lit ties of the El. Faintly through the flooring, two flights below, she heard the fans in the Tug & Maul begin thudding, slowly yet with a gathering vibration, then settle down to a steady hum no heavier than that of a sewing machine being pedaled between narrow walls. It told her the smoke was getting heavy and the laughter louder there.

So took to weaving her hands in a slow fantasy, like a drugged hula dancer, watching the fingers flow like separate things before her eyes and singing in a voice so thin and off-key that the hound beneath the dresser opened one boozy eye in pain.

> *"I'm no millionaire*
> *But I'm not the type to care . . ."*

After she had sung all the songs she knew her hands went on weaving half-forgotten fairy tales.

"My name is Rumpelstiltskin," she told herself aloud, and laughed derisively at her own voice. "Who the hell is Rumpelstiltsky?" Till some forgotten fairy of her mind replied, "You can weave gold where there is no gold."

Sophie was always pleased to hear such words come to mind so easily, as if spoken by another: some happier, some might-have-been, some used-to-be or never-was Sophie. And listened to the glistening hum of the tracks, leveling dead away toward midnight after every El that passed; following faintly all the way to the Loop straight southeast into the metallic moonlight's mocking glow.

Tonight the moon held to the leaning ladders of the rain as it rose. She moved her chair with it till she could see where the flickering warning lamps burned, along the El's long boundaries, like vigil lamps guarding the constant boundaries of night. Could even see the passengers in the cars as the locals slowed toward the station.

All night, each night, waiting for Frankie in dry weather or wet, whether the moon held to the farther crosslights or to the near-at-hand signal tower, the vigil lights burned faithfully to guard a night gone false. They seemed so right, so dependable and true, in a world gone wrong, all wrong. It made her want to cry out for everyone locked in some tenement's pit on any long and littered street.

Till darkness brought her sleep on a weary handcar, switching her onto a nowhere train that curved and descended, softly and endlessly, out upon the vast roundhouse of old El dreams.

She was a girl again sitting on Frankie's doorstep watching the sluggish late-summer flies settling heavily against the screens. The last leaves of some sultry September hung stiffly, like leaves pressed between the pages of an old catechism. Along the arc-lit parks and playgrounds the trees were still as shadows of trees down some picture-postcard street.

She had come to borrow his roller skates and he was telling her, "You can only have one and you have to do what I do." Then rolling away on his single skate down the darkening boulevard the old terror that he was going away forever shook her and she had to follow—he was so far ahead, the night was so dark, the trees stood so stiffly and so tall while the arc lamps watched too steadily—yet somehow with light about him so that she could see every turn he made and did each one exactly as he'd said she must all the way up to that old leaf-covered porch of which he'd taught her to be afraid because no one lived there any more. She was careful to go through the broken latticework left leg first as he had done and down into the dangerous hide-out lit only by a single broken ray from the arc lamp's eye across a leaf-strewn darkness where other lovers had lain. Here, where the earth held like a pang the odor of dry leaves, night dew, and faintly the scent of sometime lovers' sweat, he had said, "Lie down, Zosh."

The yellow arc lamp's single eye found them out. To watch unwinking while the bells of Old St. Stephen's rang out a warning right overhead, shaking the picture-postcard trees till the brittle leaves fell stiffly down and flies fell off lattice, window and screen.

She wakened in the chair to hear the last echo of St. Stephen's fading across this present midnight's dreaming roofs. And her whole life, from her careless girlhood until this crippled night, seemed caught within that fading chime. For now, as though no time had passed but the time it had taken to dream it, the leaves were stiff with age again, sultry September had come and gone and the wind was blowing the flies away.

"God has forgotten us all," Sophie told herself quietly.

For the rain would come straight down forever and nothing would ever change at all. Save the picture on the calendar. And a long nerve in each thigh.

The mousetrap in the closet clicked. She felt it close as if it had shut within herself, hard and fast forever. Heard the tiny caught thing struggling, slowly tiring, and at last become still.

The wind was blowing the flies away. God was forgetting His own.

A single wire was strung tautly across the room, bearing a wooden marker for remembrance of a time when the place had been a poolroom. Beneath it a circle of red leather and chrome chairs, a splash of yellow ties and sallow faces wavered about a horseshoe-shaped table.

The evening's first cigar smoke moved below the single light like the opening shot of battle upon a long green meadowland. All the day's horses had made money or run out hours ago; there was nothing left on the wall, where they had drummed up the dust of Bowie and Tanforan, but tomorrow's possibilities:

TRACK: *Fast. Heavy. Muddy.*

The dealer placed a new deck in front of Schwiefka for cutting and, while Schwiefka cut, took time to wind his PX wrist watch carefully; as if setting it to keep time, this whole long night to come, to the players' troubled hearts.

No confedence games aloud

a red legend warned everyone above the dealer's head. Strung from that same taut wire that held the poolroom marker, it would waver a bit and darken as the smoke grew heavier. On the other side of the marker hung a meaningless little green invitation as dated as last year's calendar:

SHORT CARDS
60¢ per hour

No one had played short cards here since Pearl Harbor. Schwiefka, and Schwiefka's shills, killed the hours before the suckers' hours with call-rummy and no-peek between themselves while listening to each other's boasts and complaints.

"I went to five taverns 'n a guy bought me a drink in every one," Sparrow reported with real pride.

"The same guy?" Frankie asked, riffling the deck.

"Differ'nt guys," Sparrow explained indulgently. "Now I ain't even got for a bottle wine—'n you sayin' I ain't really broke."

"You're always broke," Nifty Louie observed, "I think when you were born your old man was out of work."

"If yours'd ever had a steady job you never would of been borned at all," Sparrow retorted.

"Trouble with both you guys is you spend your dough on foolish things," Frankie counseled them both in all seriousness and Louie, who had followed Frankie in tonight, asked too casually, "What you spend yours on, Dealer?"

Frankie dealt around for reply, skipping Sparrow, who professed to be too broke to play. When Drunkie John came up with an unlabeled half pint off the hip and offered it to the punk for consolation, Sparrow eyed it sadly and mourned, "Boy oh boy, the bottle wit' out a name." In a tone so melancholy it sounded like, "Boy oh boy, the Christ wit' out a cross." Drank without pleasure, handed it back to Drunkie John and sat back unhappily. "Borrow me a dirty sawbuck, I wanna play too," he asked the players on either side of him, twice each.

Each time each answered, looking straight ahead at the dealer's eyeshade, "Never play against my own money."

"Then borrow me a dirty deuce."

Sparrow was always careful to identify any money he was able to borrow as dirty, suspecting that he thus reduced the obligation slightly. It troubled him to see the cards going around, skipping only himself. Yet he didn't like to ask money of Frankie, it seemed like Frankie never had a dime any more. And looked so pale, so pale.

"Let me deal," he begged Frankie, "let me relieve you two bucks wort'—go pertend you got a date wit' a movie actress 'n don't come back till the marks start knockin'."

The dealer made no reply and didn't look as though he cared one way or another. If Schwiefka wanted to let the punk fool around for half an hour it was all right with Frankie.

But Schwiefka paid no heed and Sparrow waited miserably.

"Well, should I start washin' my hands to get ready?" he wanted to know after a minute.

"Yeh," Schweifka deigned to answer at last. "'N wash yer face too."

"Let him deal," Nifty Louie urged, "he can't steal no more than Machine."

Nifty Louie's roll carried weight with Schwiefka. He shrugged uncertainly. Sparrow nudged Frankie out of the slot and the players tossed in a nickel ante each.

"Look at the Jewish deal," Louie marveled, for the punk dealt left-handed.

Sparrow dealt swiftly, sometimes with the right hand and sometimes with the left, sometimes beginning with the player to his right and the next time to his left, it was all one to Sparrow. But all the while watching that pot like a mangy chicken hawk. There was four dollars and twenty cents in it for the winner—the player he'd just asked for the loan of a two-spot. The punk knew when he had a good thing. He shoved seventy-five cents of the four-twenty to the winner, put a single lonely dime in the big green bag and got the rest in his own shirt pocket all in a single scoop of those ragged little claws.

The winner looked down in cold horror: he'd spent over two dollars to win a four-dollar pot and had six bits of it in front of him. "Back off if you don't like how we deal here," Sparrow anticipated his protest. "Should I deal you out?"

The others cheered wildly, they hadn't lost a dime on the deal. "Ata-boy, Sparrow, you're in the driver's seat now."

They didn't cheer for long. The next pot held three dollars, of which the dealer got a dollar-forty for his trouble, the house earned thirty cents and the winner the crumbs.

Oddly, there weren't many players for the next hand. Only forty-five cents lay in the kitty and Sparrow got two bits of that before Schwiefka had him by the neck. Before the punk could squawk so much as once he was sitting on the other side of the table right where he'd started. Only this time with nearly five dollars before him and there wouldn't be any getting him out of the game till it was gone.

"I'm supposed to be dead in 1921," Louie began confiding in Drunkie John. "Here it is almost '47 'n I'm still pumpin' water."

Louie could never quite get over his feat of having pumped water so long. "The guys who were lookin' for me in the old days 'r gone: dead 'r drunk 'r dyin'. Them was the ones rubbed garlic on the shells—I'm suppose to have a garlic slug in my head twenny-six years 'n all I got was a toenail yanked off with a red-hot pintsers." Under the light, perspiration had dried the violet talc into the corners of his lips and the lips barely moved when he spoke. "Doin' time 'r lushin', dead 'r drunk 'r dyin'."

"I remember Frank the Enforcer," Drunkie John boasted, showing his blackened teeth, "he was the kind who'd blow half a hundred over the bar but wouldn't spend for a pack cigarettes. He'd smoke yours." And drank. From the bottle without a name. "Them was the good old days, when a guy got thirteen years for a misdemeanor. When you done somethin' then you paid for it," he mourned. "It ain't like now. It's too cheap now." The marks of debauchery were seamed across his face like a chronic disease.

The only one here who seemed to have no memories of torture, murder and grand larceny was Umbrella Man, who walked about the streets smiling gently, day after day, tinkling an old-fashioned school bell and bearing a battered umbrella strapped to his back. He could not look on violence without panic, so it was always told of him with surprise: "That fool with the umbrellas—you know who *he* is? He's the brother by the smartest cop on the street. You know Cousin Kvorka, the captain's man? He's everybody's cousin—for a double saw that is. He's over there shakin' down the greenhorns 'n the biggest greener on his beat is his own brother. The mutt is suppose to fix umbrellas but he ain't gonna fix mine. He don't act like he could heat water for a scab barber."

Beside Umbrellas, the one called Meter Reader had once played sandlot baseball and now coached his employers' team, the Endless Belt & Leather Invincibles, an aggregation that hadn't won a game since Meter Reader had taken it over.

"Next time you come up here after raidin' the five-'n-ten I'm gonna turn you in to Record Head myself," Louie warned Sparrow just to start the evening rolling.

"The day you turn him in I'll have *you* deported," Frankie put in quietly. "The dealer has got hold of hisself real fine," Louie thought just as softly.

"You can't do that to *him*, Frankie," the punk objected, "he ain't got a country."

Yet no one had to be a Pinkerton to tell that Sparrow had been raiding the five-and-ten again. He was wearing half a dozen red-white-and-blue mechanical pencils, each containing a tiny battery and having a tiny bulb at the point commonly occupied by an eraser. He had seen the one Sophie toyed with and had decided he needed a handful of them himself.

"What the hell good is a pencil with a flashlight on it?" Louie wanted to know. As Frankie's grip on himself tightened Louie felt increasingly restless.

"They're good for writin' in blackouts, brother," the punk explained.

"You hit him from this side, I'll hit him from this," Louie exclaimed in disgust at Sparrow's argument. "The war's over—'n don't call me 'brother.' "

"Still, they're good on dark nights to save 'lectricity," Sparrow persisted. "You could write all night 'n it's easier on the eyes too."

Louie rolled a quarter toward the punk, received one of the pencils and warned him, "You got to replace the battery when it burns out, for free."

"For a *quarter?*" Sparrow was indignant. "Don't you figure I got labor costs? Replacements is free just wit' the fifty-cent deal. You want another one 'n get free batt'ries the rest of yer life?"

"When the battery wears out you'll replace it—or eat the pencil," he advised Sparrow matter-of-factly.

"How can I refill it if the five-'n-dime puts somethin' else on the batt'ry counter?" Sparrow pleaded.

"Don't ask me how to run your business. This thing is guaranteed for life so far as I'm concerned."

"Here's yer two bits back," Sparrow offered to return the coin.

"Keep your money, Solly," Frankie suggested, "if that battery lasts three days it'll prob'ly outlive Louie." As though secretly convinced of Frankie's prophecy, Louie reached anxiously for the coin as if for his very own life being held, just out of reach, in a stranger's hand. Sparrow thrust it deep into his watch pocket. "I just realized how right Dealer could be," he told Louie, and saw the pallor of Louie's flesh under the violet talc. "You look like if the batt'ry lasts the night it's a lifetime guarantee in yer case."

"I'll die like Machine deals," Louie conceded, abandoning the argument in a surge of weariness—"fast."

"It's how you've lived," Schwiefka told him.

"It's how we've all lived," Drunkie John reminded them all, speaking as if it were over and done with for everyone. Everyone's chickens would be coming home to roost soon enough, John felt.

Sparrow, studying Louie's ravaged face in the greenish light, suddenly relented. "I'll refill it any time it goes dead, even if I have to sneak in the warehouse to do it."

"You keep hangin' around that warehouse after dark you'll end up on a slab before he will," Frankie put in nervously. But Sparrow shook off the warning.

"I'm a businessman," the punk explained with dignity. "I filfull my obligations even if I have to rob a warehouse to do it. You think I want my credit to lakse? That's the difference between a businessman like me 'n a cheap hustler like you—you hustlers got no credit."

Frankie shuffled the deck slowly, stalling in the hope that the suckers might start knocking to get the night over and done and forgotten. "That's the trouble with the whole country, all you businessmen cheatin' the peoples so fast 'n hard there's nothin' left for an honest hustler to steal."

"I'll tell you what I think for true," Sparrow offered seriously, "I don't think there's any difference: a businessman is a hustler with the dough to hustle on the legit 'n a hustler is a businessman who's either gone broke or never had it. Back me up with five grand tonight 'n tomorrow mornin' I get a invitation to join the Chamber of Commerce 'n no questions asked."

"Record Head'll get you first," Louie repeated his warning to Sparrow.

"Yeh," everyone agreed at once, their spirits improved by the punk's prospects for a long-term jacket, "by the time he gets out Kvorka's kid'll be wearin' the old man's badge."

"It's too cheap now," John renewed his ancient complaint, "when you done somethin' in the old days you paid for it."

"The hell with the old days," Sparrow protested, looking resentfully at John. "I hope your batt'ry goes dead too."

"His battery's been dead for twenty years," Frankie had to put in.

"That's all right," John pointed out, "the batt'ry may be dead but the brain is still workin'. What good is hot batt'ries when the radiator's leakin'? Look at this punk—his tubes is boilin' over but his connections is spillin' like a secondhand Essex."

"I'm still on the legit," Sparrow answered without glancing at Louie, "compared to some people anyhow. There ain't no joy-poppers waitin' for *me* down by the Safari."

It was the first time Frankie realized that the punk was on to Louie's racket and he felt an unreasoning resentment of that knowledge. How much did the punk know? It must be just some word he'd overheard and was tossing around with no real knowledge of the accusation he was making, Frankie decided uneasily.

Sparrow had pressed the game too far. With the ace of clubs in his hand Louie asked, "You want to die in an alley?" With all the jesting gone out of his voice.

Sparrow didn't have the courage to defy Louie when Louie talked business—but he had an ace in the hole himself. He could throw out the knuckles of the index finger of his left hand, broken in some childhood antic, bending it into a series of unnatural ridges which he could point at an opponent silently, thus avenging himself without risking provocative language.

"I'll make the ju-ju sign on you," he threatened Louie softly, and Louie overheard. "You point that freakin' finger at me 'n you're one dead pointer."

It was a challenge. Everyone had seen him challenged. So the moment Louie's eyes returned to his cards Sparrow pointed, swiftly and damningly— Louie heard the knuckles crack. Somebody laughed and Frankie felt his innards tighten with this night's first intimation that God's medicine might not choose to hold him together till morning.

"Was you pointin' that freakin' finger at *me?*" Louie just had to know.

"I don't point nobody but enemies," Sparrow appeased him hurriedly, "'n you 'n me 'r old buddies." And went lightly into some little nostalgic tune or other of his own.

> *"I used to work in Chicago*
> *In a big department store."*

"The telephone's goin' to ring," Blind Pig suddenly shushed everybody, and before he'd finished his warning it rang. A trick which, like his other rare assets, didn't mean much. Yet not even the punk could outguess a telephone. "Specially a phone wit' out a number," Pig boasted as if the fact that the phone had a blind number somehow made the trick tougher.

Its number was known only to the one who called, at the same hour, every Saturday night. Schwiefka would answer and his voice, slavish and greasy, had the politeness he reserved only for women of means. "Hold on good," he would be heard saying eagerly, "I'll call him." Louie would take the phone while Schwiefka returned to his seat beside Frankie. "You look like a cat eatin' hot horse manure on a frosty morning," Frankie would tell him then.

"I oney wisht I could get on a City Hall pay roll for tellin' when somebody's dirty phone is gonna ring," Pig lamented. "I hear it comin' over the wires. I hear things before a dog could hear 'em."

The allusion to a dog returned Frankie's mind to the room where the hound cowered beneath the dresser, waiting for his return. Rumdum had feared Sophie from the first.

And after Louie's return to the table all things began weighing namelessly upon the dealer till even the deck seemed heavy in his hand. For one moment that nerveless wrist trembled, then steadied for the rest of the night. Yet in that brief trembling Frankie knew what was wrong. He hadn't expected to need another fix this soon.

As the cards went around and around, as if being dealt out of a machine, he saw again the narrow, uncarpeted stair that climbed two flights to a single room where a scarred practice board stood jammed under a sink full of dirty dishes and an older deck lay on the shelf above; the shelf that never got cleaned because Sophie couldn't reach it from the chair.

"Still, whenever I leave a bottle up there, there's always a couple good nips gone out of it," he mused. "She can reach up high enough to get a bottle but not high enough to clean the shelf it's standin' on. She must use the pillow."

"Look at the mope—he's dreamin' he's marryin' a movie actress," Schwiefka said, and tossed the green silk bag to the dealer. The fun was over for the evening.

Now the suckers would start dropping in, look absently at the day-old *Racing Forms* for a minute pretending they'd just dropped in to get the results; then each would sit in for "just half an hour, to kill the time—this is the night I take the old lady out steppin'." It was a common device, calculated to leave an opening by which one might, in event of unusual early luck, go south gracefully with a small, but tidy, bundle.

In half an hour anybody's old lady was forgotten, the bets were up to a dollar and two, the cut was five per cent up to fifteen dollars and at the door Sparrow was letting the first live ones in. The five per cent went into the green silk bag and when one of the winners tossed the dealer a quarter for himself, Frankie rang it on the metal shade of the light above his head to indicate— whether Schwiefka was there to see or not—that it was his and not the house's.

If the punk was dubious of some stranger's face he opened the door only wide enough to say, "Nothin' like that goin' on in here, Mister. This is Endless Belt 'n Leat'er Specialties—you want to buy a endless belt?"

Thus to the man who sometimes called himself a "traveling dealer," whom others called Frankie Machine, life was pretty much of an all-night stud session. With himself in the dealer's slot and Zero Schwiefka getting the take.

Steps on the stairs and a light tapping at the door.

"It's a sucker, I can tell how he knocks, so light," Sparrow said, rising to let the mark in.

The only time Frankie saw Drunkie John of late was at Schwiefka's table. For the Jailer had gotten rid of him at last and Molly-O lived on alone in the room they once had shared.

Dark-haired Molly's little nest lay in the darkness of the first floor front, its only window opening out onto the unpaved tunnel below the cross-steeled El. Yet she kept the window's single curtain fresh, to hang as white and limply as a curtain overlooking a country lawn.

It never hung limply for long. When the Loopbound express was still a quarter of a mile away the curtain would stir uneasily with the rumor of its approach, flutter and billow tensely while the room shook a little and then a little more till the curtain bulged out in a rigid and frenzied whiteness, straining and beating furiously at the sill as the cars hurtled overhead; to flutter once and sink back limply at last.

Drunkie John had left her for his first and truest love: the bottle without a name. He would return when the bottle went dry, and if he came when the Jailer wasn't by to protect her she would give him a dollar or two. She drew a percentage of every forty-cent drink she hustled, there were nights when she made as much as ten dollars; and nights when she wound up without a dime and owing the house five dollars to boot. "I'd be cheaper off livin' somewheres where you couldn't find me," she had complained to John the last time he'd called.

"I'd find you all the same," he'd assured her.

She was happy to be rid of him at any cost. Now in the mornings she would waken, her head on the small red pillow, to see the curtain's whiteness veiling the room. Behind it the dresser would seem strangely unreal, as it might appear to a waking infant: veiled by light flowing from another world.

Veiled too by a new contentment in waking without John beside her; a contentment forever tinged by dread of his return.

Two lamps stood on the dresser, one with a red bulb and one with a blue. Between them, for some reason, a magazine cover had been thumbtacked to the wall bearing the momentous query: *Is Jazz Going Hibrow?*

The blue bulb burned, the red bulb burned: the curtain stirred and slow steps passed. It didn't look like much of a Christmas in dark-haired Molly's nest.

Nor any season for merrymaking in Frankie Machine's heart. On the night following the great dish-breaking on the second floor front he stood outside her door looking quietly down at Rumdum's equally quiet mug. About the dog's throat Sparrow had tied a blue ribbon bearing a red, heart-shaped tag with the simplest sort of appeal: *Have a Heart.*

"I'll take him here," Frankie told the punk. "Zosh is sleepin'. I'll see you at the joint around ten."

"I gotta go up to see Vi," Sparrow explained, moving toward the stairs, "Stash is hittin' the hay early these nights."

Without turning his head Frankie said, "Don't knock on my door. Zosh is sleepin' too."

"You told me that twice awready," Sparrow reminded Frankie. "She can sleep all night if she wants, I got nuttin' to bother your Zosh about." He sensed that Frankie was trying to tell him that no one had seen Frankie outside the door of the first floor front. What kind of bull was Frankie feeding Zosh now that she wasn't even supposed to know he was in the building? "Frankie's in the switches," the punk brooded, "it's like he wants to run somewheres 'n can't make up his mind which way to head."

As he passed the second flight he heard Sophie wheeling across the room. If it was just a matter of giving that Molly Novotny a play, Frankie ought to know by now he could trust a guy who'd never given him away yet. "You'd think it was a big deal, tryin' to make a chick, the way *he's* goin' about it," Sparrow decided with something of scorn; he'd always been a swifter and surer operator with women than Frankie.

Frankie waited till he heard Sparrow's steps fade out on the third floor, then touched the bottle on his hip and knocked lightly at the first floor front. He had to knock twice, he knocked so lightly, before she replied.

And managed to look just a little surprised when she did. "You knocked so light," she told him, and through his mind went Sparrow's warning: "It sounds like a sucker, he knocks so light."

"I wasn't sure it was *any*body." She looked from the tired-looking man to the demented-looking hound. This time she was protected against the light, standing in her fresh white dress and the little blood-red earrings against the sallow olive of her cheeks and the midnight darkness of her hair. The hair that swept down over her shoulders as if touched by the wind that drove the curtains aside when the long Els stormed overhead. She was looking less careworn since John had left her.

"I just thought you'd like to see a dog that drinks beer," Frankie apologized, "you told me to get one of my own to kick."

"I didn't say nothin' about a beer-drinkin' one, Frankie," she protested as gravely as a child. "But if you want we'll try him out." Rumdum, at first listening only listlessly, picked up suddenly and hauled Frankie forward into the room.

"The smell of Budweiser makes him powerful," Frankie explained. Before she could get the saucer filled Rumdum had licked the saucer dry and Frankie had to clamp his snout with both hands, the great hound whimpering broken-heartedly, till she could get it filled again without losing a finger.

"He ain't had a drink all day," Frankie sympathized with all dry throats. "Fact is, I ain't neither." He pulled the bottle off his hip with feigned surprise at find-ing it there. "Look what some guy stuck in my pocket!"

"I'll stick to beer," Molly told him cautiously. "I been on the wagon since John's gone." She turned to the little combination record player on the dresser while he drank.

> *"Everythin' is movin' too fast,"*

the record complained drowsily.

"I got Girlie tied up in the pantry," Molly reported. "I really don't have room for her in here but I can't find nobody to take her off my hands."

"I know a party might be some help that way," Frankie offered, while Rumdum's tongue lolled at the half-empty bottle on the table. Molly poured him another saucer and herself a glass—before the foam had settled he was lolling up at her for a refill. While from the pantry, muted and mis-erable, Girlie moaned a melancholy protest. Rumdum's left ear perked to half-mast.

"Don't let her loose," Frankie counseled Molly. "She might remember me 'n take a bite."

> *"Slow-ow down*
> *Slow-ow down,"*

the singer counseled both Frankie and Rumdum,

> *"'Cause everythin' is movin' too fast."*

"I just bought this one," Frankie indicated the half-perked ear with the point of his shoe, "to give Zosh somethin' to do beside stone me."

"I remember Zosh from the old days, Frankie. Remember the time you took me to the dance by St. Wenceslaus 'n she come right across the floor 'n slapped me a good one, right in front of everybody—you wasn't supposed to go dancin' with nobody but Zosh? 'N look at her now. Such a *shame*."

But couldn't keep the small note of triumph out of her tone. Frankie didn't have to have Molly Novotny remind him that Zosh didn't talk to just anybody in those years.

"She's still pretty, too," Molly added hurriedly, and picked up some song or other in her hoarse, wise, taunting voice, letting her eyes remember the one night they had danced together.

> *"This is a great big city,*
> *There's a million things to see,*
> *But the one I love is missing.*
> *Ain't no town big enough for me."*

Rumdum barked weakly, more like a dream than a dog, scratched himself feebly and folded up onto his forepaws to sleep the sleep of the just.

"A dog should have fleas once in a while," Molly told Frankie seriously. "He ain't a real dog if he don't. I don't know why."

"Them little fox terrors is good," Frankie informed her. "Out West they carry them on a saddle 'n when they see the fox the little terror leads all the other hounds to it."

Rumdum's paws waggled in sleep. He was a dream terrier running down a dream fox, leading all the other hounds to it. The fox changed into a great white merry-go-round steed, loping with infinite mechanical ease to some old merry-go-round tune and the dog scrambled, slipping and falling and barking, upon its terrible hooves; all down the weary merry-go-round of old-dog dreams.

"Dogs dream too," Molly added, from some authentic source she did not care to reveal, "they dream they're doin' what they like to do best. Just like people."

"That one don't," Frankie assured her, "or he'd be dreamin' he was drownin' in a beer barrel 'n wake up yipin'."

"I don't sleep good myself—I guess I'm just not used to sleepin' alone. I dream that John is back 'n wake up. Some nights I can't sleep at all, like my vitality is runnin' away with me. I'm too high-strung. You know what I am?" And before he could ask what—"Polish, Bohemian 'n Magyar."

"No wonder you can't sleep."

"All I do on rainy days here is play classical music," she informed him with a primness he thought she had long lost. "I try to stay out of the whisky taverns now that John's gone. You like classical music?"

"No."

"I do. Sometimes I hear a new word. Then I find a word to rhyme with it'n make up classical music to go with it. You read books?"

"No."

"I do. Sex books. *Intellectual* sex books like that *Strange Woman*. She has this guy, that's the sex. Then they get married, so that makes it intellectual."

Since he had nothing to add to that, and still didn't reach for her or move, she fell into one of her little singsong taunts:

> *"Let me be your little sweetheart,*
> *I'll be much obliged to you."*

Then, with a gesture Frankie never forgot, touched two fingertips lightly to her tongue, then touched the fingers to her breasts. "It's how the girls do at the Safari," she apologized—and actually blushed. "But all I do is get the suckers to drink."

"If people dream what they *want* to dream"—he came awake at last—"then I'll dream I'm gettin' a new girl on the first floor front—I think you're a *nice* girl, Molly-O."

"I know," she acknowledged readily, "I'm a *real* nice girl. 'N the bathroom's to the right."

"I mean it, Molly-O. You got the good kind of heart, the kind that melts a guy."

She studied him to see just what made him tick. Something had gone wrong with him, she sensed without being able to put a finger on it while her eyes moved from the shaggy tousle of his hair to the battered army brogans. "You don't keep yourself sharp like you used to," she decided. "When you gonna get that sleeve sewed up?" It was the sleeve that had been ripped in the accident, Sophie hadn't yet gotten around to patching it. Some days it was hooked together with a safety pin and some days wasn't hooked at all. "I remember you when your pants was so sharp they was jealous of your shoes," she teased him in a voice ready to break into laughter or tears without knowing which it wanted most to do. He came to her.

"Yeh. 'N I remember you when you had that profile that went all the way down."

"I *do* get lonely," she had to confess then, and her voice broke on his name. "Frankie."

A quarter of a mile away the Loopbound El sent the curtain stirring and as the cars clattered overhead it bloomed, passionately and white. Then slowly fell and went limp. With his face buried between her breasts he heard the city beyond the window stir like a sleeper with the first rumors of evening.

When evening came taxiing in under the arc lamps she rose, while he still slept, and sewed his sleeve with love. "I'm patchin' his heart," she told herself quietly.

She didn't sew well. By the time she was through, and pleased with her handiwork, it still looked as if it were hooked with a pin. She had been loved, before the world went wrong, and now was loved again.

All through that night, long after he had left for work, she remembered how he had been before and how he was now. And a tenderness mixed of pity and love shook her like the wind off the tracks at midnight.

Till tenderness turned into sleep; as night turned into morning.

Later on that Sunday forenoon Frankie lay again on his own bed up on the second floor front trying to believe that, if there had been no war at all, if he hadn't volunteered, if there had been no accident, if there hadn't been this and there hadn't been that, then everything would certainly have turned out a lot better for Frankie.

Violet had wheeled Sophie to Mass—if he could only believe that going to Mass might help undo what he had done he might even go himself. If only it might make a little bit of the might-have-been still come true perhaps it would be worth while to go sometime again. Maybe if he went along some Sunday, suddenly right there by the altar rail Sophie would get up on her feet and tell him, "Nobody'll have to wheel me here no more, Frankie. Let's go dancin' by Guyman's Paradise t'night."

But Sunday morning was always pretty rugged for anything but sleep. All the miracles were performed on Saturday night, it seemed. Down on the first floor front.

"I'll say one Hail Mary, one Our Father, 'n one Act of Contrition," he compromised with himself, "just as soon as Vi 'n Zosh get back."

So the first thing he did when they returned was to reach for the bottle on the shelf above the bed.

And the second thing he did was to go back to sleep.

Yet there was a difference now to the dealer's nights. He had found that, with Molly Novotny's arms around him, he could resist the sickness and the loneliness that drove him to the room above the Safari. He had confessed the whole business to her, she had half guessed the truth before he had told it.

"I could tell somethin' was wrong the minute you put your head in that door the other evening, Frankie. I said to myself, 'This guy got somethin' eatin' on him, he got that beat look them Safari junkies got.' Frankie—the next time you start gettin' sick you come to me instead of to Louie. I'm better for you. And I'll lock you in here if I have to but I'll get you off that dirty stuff.

"If I just knew you a couple days I wouldn't care, it wouldn't be none of my business. But I knew you when you were the best guy I ever knew 'n I want you to be the best guy again."

He had fought off the sickness four nights running and on the fifth it was no worse than being hungry all night. "I got one of that monkey's paws off my back," he bragged to Molly.

In the dealer's slot his old confidence ebbed back a bit, until he could again assure himself, "It's all in the wrist 'n I got the touch."

Only the blurred image of a woman in a wheelchair remained to darken his moods: that was the monkey's other paw.

Each night he slipped singles and fives and deuces into the green silk bag. Frankie dealt the fastest game in the Near Northwest Side when he was right, and he was more right now with every night; at moments it seemed to him he was faster and steadier than he had ever been. At any second, through all the hours, he knew to a nickel how the pot stood and controlled the players like the deck. They too were aces and deuces, they too were at his fingertips once more.

For like the deuces and aces they all came home to him toward closing time. Turned face up at last, their night-long secret bluffing was exposed at last: the fat florid kings, the lean and menacing black jacks and those sneaky little gray deuces, all betrayed the sucker by morning.

In the early light Schwiefka, with his fry-cook's complexion, called "Change it up!" to the steerer for the last time. And went south with the bundle.

There had been only one serious argument at Schwiefka's while Frankie was in the slot, for Frankie had the knack of anticipating funny business. He sensed the sort of desperation which would tempt a man to slip a single exposed ace around the hole card, flashing it so fast it gave the impression of a pair. It had been that one pulled, for the sake of caution, on the slow-witted umbrella man, in which Frankie had trapped Louie cold.

Everyone knew immediately what had happened—everyone but Umbrellas. All Umbrellas knew was that Louie had said "bullets" and reached for the pot.

Frankie had flipped Louie's cards open before the fixer had had time to get them back into the deck.

"I *swear* I seen bullets," Louie had pretended casually, and nobody told him he lied. But Umbrellas had gotten the pot and Louie had never quite forgiven the dealer for exposing him. "You'd think it was comin' out of his own pocket," he complained later of Frankie.

Since that time there came a moment every night, before the first suckers started knocking, when Frankie would look uneasily at Louie and say, "I call the hands. What I say goes. That's how it's always been 'n that's how it's gonna stay 'n nobody's gonna change it." He told Louie that exactly as some sergeant had once told it to him when he'd questioned an order. It had worked on Private Majcinek. So ex-Private Majcinek assumed it had an effect on the fixer's narrow head.

And studied each fresh sucker with a practiced eye. Schwiefka sent occasional stooges into the game to keep his dealer straight—usually one wearing a loudly flowered tie and sideburns; with a habit of finding the dealer's toe under the table to indicate that a bit of co-operation with that deck wouldn't go unappreciated. Good-time Charlies with the usual whisky glass in the middle of the forehead and that certain faraway look which never troubled to count a winning pot to see whether it was right. "*We* trust each other, Dealer," was the implication of that look.

The dealer trusted no man on the other side of the slot. He had outlasted forty such touts. They didn't call him Machine just because he was fast. They called him Machine because he was regular.

He couldn't risk being anything else; dealing was the sole skill he owned. "The day I get my musician's union card is the day I'll steal Schwiefka blind," he planned in his tough-skinned larcenous little heart. Until that day he would be as straight as one of Widow Wieczorek's ivory-tipped cues.

One by one Schwiefka's shills would give place, as the winter night wore on, the stakes would grow higher as the air grew heavier and the marks grew lighter; to be replaced, one by one, like so many sausages into the same sure grinder.

While at the door Sparrow urged losers and winners alike: "Tell 'em where you got it 'n how easy it was."

Till Frankie would sit back wearily, sick of seeing them come on begging to be hustled, wondering where in the world they all came from and how in the world they all earned it and what in the world they told their wives and what, especially, they told themselves and why in the world they always, always, always, always came back for more.

"More, more, I keep cryin' for more more—"

Some tattered walkathon tune of the early thirties went banging like a one-wheeled Good Humor cart of those same years through his head as the cards slipped mechanically about the board and his fingers went lightly dividing change in the middle, taking the house's percentage without making the winner too sharply aware of the cut. It was one thing for a player to understand he was bucking a percentage and quite another to see it taken before his eyes. To the mark it always seemed, vaguely, that the dealer might have overlooked the cut, just this once, out of sportsmanship. For when the sucker held a hot hand five per cent didn't trouble him—he'd be feeling too smug about having the case ace concealed while that chump across the board was pitching in his last desperate dollar in the hope of hooking that same ace. And when he wasn't involved in the pot the sucker didn't care if the dealer took ninety per cent. It wasn't any skin off his hide then, the sucker figured.

"I hope I break even tonight," was the sucker's philosophy, "I need the money so bad."

And always the same tune clanging like a driverless trolley down some darkened backstreet, past familiar yet nameless stops, through the besieged city of the dealer's brain.

"More, more, I keep cryin' for more more more—"

A tune he'd heard some afternoon when he and Sophie were first engaged and he'd liked taking her down Division because she dressed so sharp and had that haughty, hard-to-get stride that had had everyone fooled but himself: he'd solved it before she'd had a chance to develop adult defenses.

A stride somewhere between a henwalk shuffle and a Cuban grind, one of the boys had once described it. A walk as provocative as a strip teaser zipping down one black glove on the runway just to give the boys an idea of how much there was to zip before taking it all away again. And those silk-sheathed legs as proud-looking as a fawn's.

Once, when both were still in their teens, he'd ignored Sophie for a month just to show her he didn't care one way or another. Until she'd asked him straight out if they were still sleeping together on Saturday nights or not.

He'd fished a nickel out of his pocket and slipped it into her palm. "Here's a nickel, kid. Call me up when you're eighteen. Right now I got to do some shoppin' around."

She'd gone off in such a high-wheeled huff he'd thought that that was surely the end of *that*. But two days later she'd slipped him a note in front of the corner *apteka*. "I have to talk to you."

But in her own living room there really hadn't been anything to talk about after all. She'd come down off that high horse onto her knees. He'd brought her down till she'd never have her full height again. He'd broken her pride for keeps that afternoon.

Now for ten years she had held him in the hope of recovering that lost pride; till it had grown too late to loosen her grip upon him. If she let go of him now she let go of everything.

The old days, the old days, Frankie thought nostalgically. When every other door was a tavern and you had as much on the next guy as he had on you. When the worst thing the neighborhood bucks got pinched for was strongarming and no one fooled with anything deadlier than whisky. When there weren't any fixers strolling through the Safari with more dough tied up in a single brown drugstore bottle than in a case of the best bonded scotch behind the bar.

And the old days before the old days, when burlesque was still burlesque, Kenny Brenna was the funniest man in town and the street-car men got salt out of the box down on Augusta Boulevard to melt the ice in the switches. Down on Augusta where they'd played the same games other children played in less crowded neighborhoods—but had played them with little vicious twists unknown to luckier stubs. They'd played Let Her Fly simply by wrapping up garbage from the nearest can and sneaking up on a privately selected opponent with it: one who never knew he was anyone's opponent at all until the garbage hit him in the teeth. For the game's single rule had been that the player at bat was anyone with garbage in his hand who had voice enough to call out, "Let her fly!" before pitching it. The kid who didn't duck fast enough lost right there.

Rules had been added and the game extended but you still had to be ready to duck every second. "Jacks check, the bullets say a buck," he intoned unemphatically, hearing his own voice going on and on like a voice belonging to somebody else. "King sees, a buck to you Jacks, Jacks bump a buck, Big Ace sees 'n here we go, down 'n dirty, when you get a hunch bet a bunch, nothin' to it if you know how to do it—turn 'em over when you're down—man with the hammer bumps a buck, Jacks call——one bucket of paint all red——a winner every hand, hooked it in the dark he says well well, slip me a half 'n make me laugh, thank *you,* the more you bet the more you get——"

"More, more, I keep cryin' for more more more——"

The old days, the old ways, before all the stoplights turned to red and there was still time between deals for a laugh or two over a nickel beer.

"He ain't even got his first papers 'n he got a City Hall job," somebody complained of somebody else and the night was long, so long, and all night long the derisive little diamonds mocked the fat and happy-looking hearts. And the sour spades, that had seen too much of everything and had been disappointed in it all for so long, stood aside with cynical indifference while the murderous black clubs ambushed the hopeful four flushes and the foolishly faithful four-card straights; while the little old gray deuces died, heartbroken, by the way. Till the green silk bag was filled and emptied, half secretly, half guiltily, as a thousand green silk bags had been filled and emptied secretly before. And were always brought back for more more——

"I keep cryin' for more more
Give me more more more——"

As this night followed a thousand nights and these men followed a thousand hopers who had sat here before them to go down to their graves holding a four-card straight in one hand and would never be remembered at all. Their mouths were stuffed with race-track dust; and no one to remember at all.

Their sons had taken their places, passing the time, while waiting for death to deal one from the bottom, by drawing to aces and eights. Their hell was a full house that never won and their last hope of heaven a royal flush.

"He got a loaf of bread under his arm 'n he's cryin'," somebody said of somebody else. While the biggest sucker of them all sat in the dealer's slot till morning, getting relieved fifteen minutes every two hours, and thought and thought and thought. For every time he was relieved his newly recovered confidence slipped an inch. And the old regret, like the old wound fever, struggled in him to kindle fresh flames of guilt. Guilt that burned like so many small strange flowers putting out petals of fire in place of leaves. "I told her in the hospital I was gonna make it all up to her. I'm makin' it up to her awright. Just one flight down. Through a different door."

"What's it mean when a dealer's hand gets shaky?" Louie asked Schwiefka without looking at any dealer at all.

"That's the first sign of insanity," Schwiefka decided.

"Hell, it's the last sign," Frankie threw them both, out of sheer irritability. "I blew my stack a long time ago settin' right here watchin' tinhorn West Side gamblers tryin' to make a pair of bullets out of one little acey."

"Don't give *me* that old *kapustka*," Louie ordered him. "You ain't the guy to be rememberin' *anythin'*."

"Okay," Frankie conceded with his hand around the deck, "maybe it's time we both started forgettin', Louie."

Louie nodded and held his peace. "The price just went up on you, Dealer," he told himself confidently. "That stuff is gonna be awful hard to get around the middle of next week."

"Deal, deal," Schwiefka demanded uneasily, sensing something old, unspoken and violent in the air, and the players all began wheedling the dealer at once. "Give us somethin' to remember you by, Dealer—we're gettin' quartered to death here."

"Toward morning the farmer gets lucky," Frankie assured every farmer present. And the cards went around and around.

Thus in the narrowing hours of night the play became faster and steeper and an air of despair, like a sickroom odor where one lies who never can be well again, moved across the light green baize, touched each player ever so lightly and settled down in a tiny whiff of cigar smoke about the dealer's hands.

Now dealer and players alike united in an unspoken conspiracy to stave off morning forever. Each bet as if the loss of a hand meant death in prison or disease and when it was lost hurried the dealer on. *"Cards, cards."* For the cards kept the everlasting darkness off, the cards lent everlasting hope. The cards meant any man in the world might win back his long-lost life, gone somewhere far away.

"Don't take it hard, your life don't go with it," was the philosophy of the suckers' hour.

But each knew in his heart, when he said that, that he lied: each knew that his life was reshuffled here with every hand.

Till the last fat red ten had been dealt, the final black jack had fallen, the case deuce hadn't helped after all and the queen of spades had been hooked, by somebody, just one hand too late.

"If it hadn't been for me—if it hadn't been for me—"

And the last discouraged sucker had thrown in his cards to the biggest sucker of them all.

"What's right is right," Frankie decided as the last hand was dealt around, "you can't go smashin' up a woman 'n then make a fool of her on top of it with another woman. A guy got to draw the line somewheres on how bad he can treat somebody who can't help herself no more just account of him."

Walking home with Sparrow where the long arc-lamp shadows slanted across the snow-wet walk, as on any lost corner at 4 A.M., they heard a switch engine's burdened coughing.

"Trying to get up steam," Sparrow whispered as confidentially as if he had just had it straight from the engineer.

But to Frankie Machine it sounded more like a man trying to cough with a thirty-five-pound monkey on his back. One breath to the second, no more and no less, as the hairy little paws tightened about his shoulders to get set for just one more ride. Under the shoulders, deep in the stomach's pit, some tiny muscle like a small cold claw probed upward toward his heart, didn't quite reach it and contracted again, leaving the heart fluttering with anxiety for the whole stomach to turn over: he retched, wanted to vomit and had nothing to vomit at all. That small cold claw would reach again, in its own good time, as mechanically as he himself could shuffle a cold deck at will. It would reach. It would get there and he'd fight it down.

It was just so damned hard to fight alone, that was all, with so little to fight for. A half pint of good whisky would keep it down until he could get to sleep; but only for an hour. Then he'd waken and no whisky would do him good in that hour. He'd need Molly-O to hold him then. It would be Molly-O or a quarter-grain fix, he'd never make it alone.

Every time he got sick lately it seemed the damned punk was on his heels, staring at him through those foggy glasses, trying to pretend he didn't know a junkie when he saw one. Why didn't the little chiseler speak out?

At the corner of Damen and Division he turned abruptly on Sparrow. "Which way *you* goin'?" Just like that.

"Why—home, Frankie. Same as you."

"You tellin' me where I'm suppose to go now?"

Sparrow saw Frankie's face then, peaked with suffering in the arc lamp's feeble glow, and wanted to help and didn't know how and didn't want to understand.

"I got business." Frankie let him have the edge of the knife turning in his breast. "Case out."

Twice now within the week Frankie had turned on him like this, he was beginning almost to expect these sudden changes, meaningless and swift. With no further word the punk turned, feeling there was no place for him in any joint on Division Street, nor in the whole wide world, without Frankie Machine.

Shuffling down the shadowed street, Sparrow hoped a squadrol would pick him up just so that he could feel, for ten minutes, that he was going *somewhere*. He wanted to feel walls and safety about him, needed to be *inside* something. Frankie had been his wall and the wall was gone, leaving him as defenseless as he had been in the years before he'd hooked up with the dealer. When he reached Paulina he realized Frankie must be kidding, wanting to teach him a lesson for something, making him walk just to see how far he'd go before looking back—Frankie would be standing there waving to him to come back and get shoved around, pretending he was mad about something—Sparrow turned with swift hope.

But no one waved in the arc lamp's feeble glow for any punk's returning.

No one stood waiting under any arc lamp for any lost sparrow at all.

Something tugged just hard enough at her foot to waken her; the army blanket had fallen across her toes. Yet she sensed a secret message in being awakened so: someone was trying to tell her she must not sleep tonight.

Down both sides of Division Street the occasional arc lamps burned and it was late, so late, there should be a light step on the long dark stair and someone to cry out that the night was too long.

And come up to wheel her a little while.

Whatever time it was, he was long past due. Unless there were two kinds of time in the world these days: Gamblers' Time and Cripples' Time and cripples must now set their watches by gamblers.

All her life, it seemed in this winter hour, he'd been standing her up somewhere. This time would count against him like the others, not one time would be forgotten. He'd go to purgatory with what he had done to her on his soul and she'd sit there then just as she sat here now. He wouldn't be getting rid of her in the hereafter, if there were any sort of justice at all, any easier than he could get rid of her on West Division. And wondered cloudily how she'd get the chair

into purgatory. It would be shipped right along with her best clothes, she supposed, and the Special Dispensation showing she really didn't belong in purgatory herself, she was just there to make sure that that Frankie Majcinek paid off.

"He's fixed me so's I can't have no kid," she pitied herself for the thousandth
time, "that counts against him just as much as if he'd killed somebody. He *got* to
be fait'ful now 'r he won't even get as high as purgatory," she assured herself confidently, and a twinge of perverse pleasure took her, twisting her lips into a loose
and sensual line. "A man just *got* to stick by a wife who can't stand on her own two
feet five minutes at a time," she felt with the same sense of a long-stale triumph.

For if she'd made a secret bargain with herself, in that darkened corner of
the mind where all such bargains are made, she would stand by the deal. She
was bound now by it as irrevocably as Frankie was bound to her and she was
bound to the chair: she would not now return to that corner except in dreams.
Not to that curtained hide-out, not to that secret place. She had gone to that
bookie in the brain where hustlers' hearts pay off to win, place or show. She had
bet her health on a long one and waited each night to be paid off in her turn.

A door slammed downstairs and the Jailer's voice, heavy with sleep, called
down irritably, "No rooms! Too early! Go by Wieczorek and sleep on pool table!"

But still no hand on the door below. No step on the long dark stair.

Nor ever yet had wondered why she dreamed, so often with the same deep
dream, of a distant cousin, a girl of nineteen who had died in Sophie's childhood. She saw Olga in a nun's habit walking down a long white corridor. It was
night, the whole great hospital was still: only the faint sweet smell of anes-
thetics and the sound of the nun's slippered tread. Sophie saw the girl, all in
white and immeasurably far away, as though looking through a minifying lens.
The lens turned in her dreaming brain, a narrow dark door opened and her
own face, like a face seen under water, the eyes wide and brimming with joy:
"Olga! Honey! Look! I'm on my feet again!" She was crying for happiness in
that dark door and wakened with a sob breaking like a small bone in her throat.

Then the sense of loss that deepened as wakefulness widened, till the whole
world seemed one great room wherein she had lost something long ago, something so dear, so dear. "Why should I worry?" she asked herself suddenly, with
a certain self-derision. "I got mine."

That was, seemingly, true enough. She had got exactly what she had wanted
more than anything else in the world. Frankie Majcinek. Had him forever and
for keeps and all for her very own. For there was no other place in the world

for him, since the accident, save this one small furnished room. So now it was time to feel her victory in her heart, sweeter than all the dances she had missed through that perverted victory.

Then why did it feel as though the all-night movies had all been emptied, why did it feel they must be showing broken reels to empty rows and that the all-night bakery fires had gone out: that the loaves would grow cold and mold slowly to dust in ten thousand rusting stoves?

Why did it feel so late, so late that she would never get there in time after all?

"It's just the way things would be if that Nifty Louie was God 'n Blind Pig was Jesus Christ," she decided feverishly, "it's just about the way them two'd run things."

A trolley yammered past like a dog pursuing a rabbit and pulled up with a startled little yelp.

And heard his step on the long dark stair at last coming up just one step ahead of the first metallic cries of morning.

Until the night of the Great Sandwich Battle old Stash had only once given Violet concrete grounds for divorce. That had been the night he'd gone on what she still referred to as his "tandem." She had never let him forget that sorry occasion.

It was bad enough that a man of his years should come wheeling in at 2 A.M. of a summer night with his shirt ripped half off his back—but before she could rip the rest of it off him her breath was cut off by the spectacle of somebody's grandmother in nothing but a suit of long underwear, the high-heeled shoes once called "baby dolls" and one earring dangling like the final symbol of a misspent youth.

When Vi had recovered her breath all she could gasp was, "Lady, whoever you are, they're lookin' for you—but they ain't gonna find you *here*"—and rushed Grandma, drunk as a coot, down the hall and down the steps and out into the street with one good strong shove to get her going in somebody else's direction—then two steps at a time all the way back up to see what Old Husband was up to in that *unusual* condition.

A good thing she'd taken two at a time. He was tottering half out the window, trying to read the temperature on the thermometer nailed to the outside wall with his shoeless toes barely touching the floor. She hauled him back so hard he landed flat on his back in the middle of the bedroom floor, creaked over upon his side and went into a snoring sleep.

But who wants to sleep with a drunk beside the bed? She had rolled him, like a half-filled laundry bag, right under the springs. But he'd tossed and mumbled so restlessly there that at last she had hauled him out of it by the ankles, supported him down the hall with his head dangling like a Christmas rooster's, into the broom closet. Putting a pillow under his head, she'd locked him in with a reproach he never heard. "Just to teach you a lesson, Old Man."

After that the hall broom closet had been his punishment for almost any misdemeanor. The last stretch he'd spent in there had been for doing nothing worse than bringing home a loaf of day-old pumpernickel. She'd warned him that she wouldn't eat day-old food but yet he fancied, after fifteen months of married life, that she rejoiced secretly in all his bargains. He had a sneaking senile conviction that she'd married him because he knew where all the best bargains were to be had for just a little wheedling and the wearing of a tattered sweater. "Makin' poor mouth,"Violet called it. And for this reason kept his bargain-store addresses a secret from her, for fear that when she found them out she would leave him. What other reason could she have had for marrying him? he had asked himself in the cold white light of day. Old Husband wasn't just anybody's fool. He was everybody's in general andViolet's in particular.

She had tried to cure the bargain-store habit by dumping all his day's spoils into the container at the end of the hall. When he'd seen her do that he had retired to the closet voluntarily. Perched upon a bucket there, a frayed blanket clutched closely about him as the night wore on and the hall grew chill, he had worried most of all about whatever would the neighbors think.

Neighbors could think what they damned well pleased in Violet's book. Every hour on the hour she'd sallied forth to denounce him through the closet keyhole. *"Doopa!* Come out! I got to slug you!" Old Stash was too sly for that. He'd stayed where he was.

He never understood why such little things made her so hopping mad and it looked like he never would catch on this side of purgatory. Yet it was all for the best that he remain in the fog of cut-rate prices in which he wandered numbly between broom closet and icehouse and his own warm bed. For even though he did wise up there wasn't a thing, at Old Husband's age, to be done about it.

Sometimes she punished him by not letting him pull the date off the calendar for three or four days. Then, when he would hand her the Saturday night pay envelope, she'd reward him by letting him tear off all three days in a row—

she would have to watch him to see that he didn't go over into the coming week. Old Husband literally chortled with glee when he'd gotten all three off and in his hand, if those three had finished the month.

She had even caught him sneaking into the calendar at night to tear off a page while she slept. And once, in a panic of frustration, he had ruined an almost virginal calendar by ripping off sixteen weeks in a row; as though he could no longer wait for the endless weeks to pass. She had put him to bed with a fever, soothing him with a hot-water bag across his stomach.

It wasn't simply bad luck that the bag had leaked a bit. It too had been bought secondhand.

On the night of the Great Sandwich Battle Stash gave her, she felt, even further cause for separate maintenance.

Although, if the sausage hadn't slipped out of the sandwich, everything would have been fine and dandy, like sugar candy.

That was one accident that Violet couldn't blame the punk for. It was one time it was truly all her fault, for bringing him upstairs when she knew Old Husband was likely to wake up.

Still, it's not easy to blame Violet either. Maybe it was really Stash's fault for going to bed too early.

Unless it was Stash's boss's fault for working the old man so hard he couldn't stay awake after supper, just when Violet would start taking out the pin curls and getting ready to go places and see things.

"I used to cry sometimes when I first married Stash," she confessed to Sophie, "I didn't have no place to go. I used to shave him with a 'lectric razor then. He could shave hisself all right, but I liked the sound it makes. That's the oney pleasure that old man ever give me."

On the night of the Great Sandwich Battle she fixed him a glass of warm tomato juice with a raw egg floating in it—Widow Wieczorek had confided in her that it had worked wonders with the late Emil W. when he'd first started slipping. But Stash turned in half an hour earlier than usual; all it had done was to make him limper than ever.

"Next time I'll try goat's milk," Violet planned wistfully, watching him shuffling off toward the bedroom with the left-hand flap of his winter underwear dangling. "If that don't work I might as well be a widow too. Wonder if there's such a thing as a pension for icehouse widows. Them big ice blocks could be dangerous, all sorts of things could happen."

She just wasn't tired a bit. She hadn't done a thing all day except to wheel Sophie to the Pulaski, return to sweep Sophie's flat and wash up yesterday's dishes while Frankie snored on the bed, sluice the stairs for Schwabatski and sweep the water down four flights into the gutter, then clean up her own rooms and heat up some restaurant leftovers she'd decided were ripe enough for Old Husband's supper. He'd hauled the mess half a mile the evening before and had weighed it before leaving for work to be sure she didn't eat more than her share before he returned.

Vi didn't mind heating the moldy stuff so much as long as she wasn't expected to share it. "He don't care what he scoffs up," she marveled nightly, "so long as it's a big bargain is all that counts—'n both sides of the sandwich to match. Don't ask me why, he don't like it when one side of the sandwich is bigger than the other."

"Is all dirty, too t'in," Stash described an uneven sandwich. It affronted some deep and childish hope still living within him that everything in the world—even sandwiches—be turned out without rough edges that might hurt little boys.

The same sort of hope, perhaps, which led him to stop at the same currency exchange regularly to change dirty dollars for nice new clean crisp ones. "Cott this opp!" he would demand of the cashier, handing her a soiled ten-spot—when she had humored him and he was tucking away ten crisp new singles he would feel he'd driven the cleverest sort of bargain.

Even the weather must come out even for Old Husband. Hardly anything pleased him more than a nice even-numbered temperature, like 60 or 80 or 100. Just as the best days of the month seemed to him to be the 10th, the 20th and the 30th.

Yet now that it was time for him to go to bed, Violet was one wife who knew her duty. Stash sometimes couldn't get to sleep unless she was lying beside him. And you never could tell for sure, maybe that egg would have a delayed kick. But tonight he was drowsing by the time she had her skirt off and that's enough to discourage the willingest of brides. Particularly since she was wearing, for the very first time, a pair of lacy black Suspants the punk had stolen for her from Nieboldt's.

Who is supposed to appreciate a glamorous thing like that, a thing an actress might be wearing—skintight with garter tabs—if not a girl's husband? She sat admiring her legs, pointing the tinted toenails delicately to emphasize the long slimness of her calves and the full womanly bow of her thighs.

Violet was a good girl at heart. But even a nun needs the appreciation of others. For the tinted toenails and the fancy garter tabs there was no man near to so much as say "Wow!"

She looked at her watch. Ten o'clock and right on the hour the old man began snoring up a row that made her wonder what in the world had been in that egg after all. From below, between snores, rose the pre-Christmas revelry of the Tug & Maul. She pulled the shade like lowering a curtain upon temptation, turned on the shaded bed light and read *Steve Canyon* all the way through, she was that bored. Then just sat looking down at Stash's toothless maw, open and drooling a little, comparing it with the square and virile set of Canyon's jawbone. Even the punk had more jaw than old Stash—in some ways, she remembered with real warmth, the punk didn't have to give an inch to Canyon. She turned out the bed light and lay for a while remembering past laughter and wondering what she'd been thinking of in marrying the old man anyhow. Because she'd wanted to take care of somebody—or for his fifty a week?

A bit of both, she compromised anxiously. Then making no particular effort to keep from waking him, crawled over him, teasing the hairs sticking out of his nostrils with the nipple of her breast just for the hell of it, shoved her feet into slippers and tightened her winter coat modestly over her sheer nightdress.

"Go to sleep, Stash," she told him gently, "have a good dream you're winnin' a turkey raffle." Locked the door behind her and stepped softly down the stairwell into the murmurous corridors of night guarded so constantly, as on all winter nights, by Prager beer signs and the great Milwaukee Avenue moon.

Prager beer signs down one side and High-Life down the other, all the way down Milwaukee to the streets where the dark people live, drinking cheaper beer.

And who should be sitting at the bar, goofy and gay as always, but Solly Saltskin.

" 'D. 'n D.' don't mean 'drunk 'n disorderly' in my case," he was explaining to Antek the Owner. "In my case it means 'Damen 'n Division,' 'cause that's where I always wait when I want to get picked up."

"Just don't get picked up for anythin' worse'n D. 'n D.," Owner counseled him.

"That's where I got *them*," Sparrow whispered confidentially. "That Kvorka ain't got the heart to pinch me for nuttin' serious, he knows me too long. If he did Bednar'd fire him, Bednar likes me too."

In fact all our most ignorant people were there and the juke played on and on.

"Oh, my man he's six foot three,
He knows just what to do for me."

Well, little Solly S. wasn't any six foot three, but he knew how to treat a girl till she felt he must be five-ten at least. They had quite a few together, he'd taken the night off just to show Schwiefka how much the joint needed him at the door and had been waiting here in the hope she might come downstairs for a small beer after Old Husband was safely tucked in the sack. They teased each other and drank till closing time, when Sparrow said he was "hungry enough to eat little ginny pigs."

"I'm so hungry if I can't have a sandrich I got to have a pint," was just how the punk put it. "So now we'll get a bottle 'n go by your house."

"Stash wouldn't like," Vi explained sorrowfully, ordering that closing-time shot with which one defies all sorrowing.

"It'll be okay," Sparrow fixed everything, "we'll give him half the bottle. Then we'll turn on the radio 'n dance."

"Stash wouldn't like."

"Why not—the radio broke?"

"The radio's all right." Violet was weakening so fast that when he hooked her arm and said, "Let's go," she finished the shot that made everything seem just the way everything ought to have been long before this night.

Owner was putting the chairs up on the back bar and the lights in the big brass juke were running down like a rain-washed sunset. They steered each other outside and up the first flight to home in a weaving progress, each urging the other to walk more soberly.

"Watch how *I* do it," Violet commanded, going up four cautious steps and coming down a reckless five. "Now *you* try."

Sparrow made it fine, clear to the top of the first flight all by himself; and stood trying to focus his eyes behind the shell-rimmed glasses until she'd made it all the way too.

"Poor old Stash," she giggled, "he works too hard." That set them both to tittering as if it had been the funniest thing they'd heard in a month.

"You know what?" she asked.

"What?"

"Works too hard." This time it was even funnier, she had to hold the banister to keep from falling back downstairs.

As they wove past the second-floor desk Poor Peter Schwabatski looked upon them reverently from beneath half-lowered lids: he saw strange angels passing all night long. These two seemed holier, somehow, than any that yet had passed. The Jailer planted his horse-faced dimwit behind the desk each night in the hope he might be mistaken for a watchman; the boy passed the creaking midnight hours by planting paper daisies. Two of these grew out of a long crack in the desk to embroider the dusty old legend, *Quiet or Out You Go Too*. To which no guest had as yet offered the slightest deference.

Poor Peter's pious regard subdued Violet and on the final flight she shushed Sparrow though he was making no sound at all. "Hard-workin' people. Mustn't wake up hard-workin' people." So both felt very sad, all the way down the hall to her door, for hard-working people everywhere that mustn't be waked up in the middle of the night. They stood together one moment in the threatening dimness, like the dimness in which all their lives had been lived—and decided to laugh together like that just once more. He threw back his head like a demented spaniel and howled, "*Whaaaat?*"

"Works too hard."

Only this time it wasn't funny at all.

For all the doors belonged to hard-working people. All the doors of both their lives and nobody laughs at a thing very long when he's drunk out of bleakest loneliness. Behind her door yesterday's empties crouched beneath a single-faucet sink: they were lined up there like a scoreboard recording the emptiness of her hours. For in the room beside the sink an old man slept her sweetest hours away.

"Open the door, Richard," she giggled unhappily, handing him the key. He took it without putting it in the lock while she studied him. "Honey," she asked solemnly, "how come you never met Stash *form'lly?*"

"How come I'm s'pposed to—form'lly?"

"How come you ain't s'ppose to, what *I* want to know," she insisted, feeling the whisky move. When she put it that way Sparrow realized he was supposed to meet Old Husband all along. It seemed then that Old Husband had been waiting politely to meet Solly Saltskin a long time and now was his big chance to give the old man the break he deserved. Old Man worked too hard, he deserved something to happen to him in his declining years. All the people worked too hard, all the people deserved something nice in their declining years. He ought to do more for the people, they had such a hard way to go.

"That's right," he agreed at length, "form'l obligation."

"Shamed myself, you never met Old Man,"Vi confessed, taking the key and opening the door herself.

Inside she threw off her coat, unmindful that she wore only a sheer night-gown underneath; but then it was so warm and everyone was such old friends. From the bedroom came a low warning rumbling as if the Garfield Park Express were running straight through the house.

"Change cars in there!" she called good-naturedly. Yet something about Old Husband sleeping in there like a child, so alone, filled her with such a rush of tenderness for him as she had never before felt. As soon as she had finished making a sandwich for Sparrow she made one for Stash out of the crusts, so that it would look like a big bargain. He had to wake up pretty soon anyhow if he were ever to meet Sparrow.

"Look, it's Christmas awready!" she cheered Old Husband awake. "We got Sparrow for comp'ny 'stead of Santa Claus—ain't that *wonderful?*"

He wasn't yet sufficiently wide awake to tell how wonderful it all was. Just poked his frightened old eyes about the room, so suddenly filled with light and harsh cries that had been so dark and still with sleep but one moment before.

"Where you gone?" he asked at last.

"Ain't gone, been awready," she saw him start at something over her shoulder, then droop one eyelid to see the apparition better. "What *is?*" Old Husband wanted to know.

"That's *him,* that's *Sparrow,* honey—didn't I ever tell you about *Sparrow? Sparrow!* I never even to-old him a *thingg.*" Her giggle alone would have betrayed more than whisky to anyone but Old Creep Stash.

While Sparrow, with the light from the night-bulb against his glasses mak-ing his face strangely featureless, was saying something real nice, anyone could see. It wasn't clear just what because his mug was stuffed with Polish sausage and its string was dangling from the corner of his mouth. A fellow could choke that way, just saying something nice.

"Shall I make you another, lover?" Violet wanted to know.

Under the night light's pale green glow Lover nodded. "Yup. *Two* more. Wit' little ginny pigs 'n ketchup all togedder."

"Dronk t'ings," Old Creep disapproved, scraping his toes about the carpet in a vague hope of finding slippers there. "Is *bad,* not *drassed,*" he added, redden-ing at the spectacle of his own wife cavorting about before a stranger in noth-ing but a sheer nightgown. What kind of big bargain was *that?*

"You boys talk over old times together," Violet suggested lightly, making another dash for the kitchen.

Sparrow sat on the bed's edge beside this Stash, feeling remotely troubled. Then realized where his trouble lay and removed one slice of bread off the sandwich, wiped the mustard off carefully upon Stash's sheet, gave the opposing slice the same treatment and resumed chewing. "Don't like mustard," he explained.

"I got hard day," Stash asserted, eying the string dangling so unevenly from the corner of the punk's mouth; as if that held some solution for the peculiar way in which things were being run by Stash Koskozka's house this night.

"*You* like mustard?" Sparrow asked, to keep the conversation sprightly.

"Don't like mustard, don't like sandrich, don't like comp'ny," Stash challenged him boldly, "all too t'in."

Sparrow shifted the string a bit to show he was thinking that over. Then let it down and rolled it neatly back up to show he was shrugging, sustaining this yo-yo-like indifference until Violet returned with his second sandwich.

"Don't *want* sandrich," Stash persisted, growing petulant—then saw it hadn't ever been intended for him and, perversely as a child, just to keep Sparrow from having it, grabbed at it so abruptly that the sausage slid out and slipped down his winter underwear to lodge loosely into the top of his heavy winter socks, making a bulge there the size of an ankle and leaving a light trail, like an insect's trail, down the underwear.

"Goofy t'ing, you make clomsy by me," Stash scolded the spot Sparrow had left on the sheet. It was, he perceived, Polish sausage that was to blame for everything tonight.

"You shouldn't wear your underwear to bed anyhow," Violet reproached the old man, "you'd sleep better in pajamas."

"After all," Sparrow mocked him, "he ain't so young you should wake him four o'clock by morning, he should make glad for you because pretty soon is Christmas, ain't it?"

Stash chose to overlook the mockery. With unruffled poise he fitted his upper plate into place and shuffled it loosely about a moment to make it fit securely. The sucking sounds he made to get it into place irritated Violet like fingernails screeching down a blackboard.

"After all the work I went to," she mourned her marriage tardily now, "gettin' out of bed in the middle of the night to make my husband a snack 'n what does he do but slap it out of my hand 'n call me 'goofy t'ing'—I got a good

Polish education 'n I married the biggest dummy ever walked in shoe-leather"—she turned on Stash—"get up 'n wash the peanuts off! Get up 'n take last mont's bat'!"

Yes, it had been just about the finest sandwich a loyal little wife could make her man but instead of thanking a person he just sat sucking his teeth in front of the first real company she'd had in days.

"No-good t'ing," Stash insisted, distressed by the mild itching of the mustard drying between his toes, and brought his knee up to investigate that itch at the precise moment that Vi bent to retrieve the sandwich. The bone caught her over the eye.

That did it. That was all she had, subconsciously, been waiting for since her unconsummated honeymoon.

"You done that a-purpose!" she gasped, and cracked him across the upper plate with the flat of the carpet slipper. "Let's *see* who's the clumsy t'ing," she challenged him, feeling the whisky rise in her throat with her rage, and Sparrow shifted a bit to give Stash room enough to fling the retrieved sandwich, mustard, ketchup, pickles and all straight into Violet's face and down the shadowed hollow of her gown.

Sparrow looked *so* sorry. He didn't like to see food wasted that way. Before he could recover even a small section of the sausage Vi gave the old man the slipper again, the upper plate popped out and he yelped like a lashed pup expecting more. You could see Stash's lip beginning to swell, he put a hand to it tentatively but she slapped the hand down. He clasped the pillow about his ears protectively. You couldn't treat a hard-working man this way.

"Work *all* day, seven days, no days off, buy nize t'ings by howz," he sobbed brokenly, "pay *grocernia,* pay *buczernia,* pay mens I don't even know what's for, comes time to sleep everyt'ing all paid 'n nize clean howz so *ever'*body sleep—who comes by howz from whisky tavern?" A drop of blood mixed with sweat and tears dropped down the point of his tiny chin. "Mrs. No-good wit' dronk pocket-picker! Should be in bed by *hoos*band, hits by *hoos*band instead on head 'n makes funny: 'Is Christmas, now we fight all night!' Is somethin' got to happen, is *all.*"

He dropped the pillow, reached for the dresser drawer, came up with his .38 and banged Violet across her new permanent with the butt.

Sparrow watched the sausage slide at last out of the depths of the gown and saw, with a melancholy regard, a fine round piece roll beneath Stash's heel—a heel stained yellow with mustard or indignation where the sock was torn. Sparrow felt a twinge of disgust at the way everything in the joint, bedclothes, underwear, curtains and walls, was daubed with fresh mustard. One hell of a way to run a house.

"Bein' unsanit'ry is worse'n bein' goofy," he philosophized softly while recovering the remains. "Funny I done like mustard"—wiping the bread clean on a handy corner of the dresser scarf. Heard the bathroom door slam and glanced up to see why all these people were so excited. Stash was in a neutral corner, breathing hard and looking beat to the floor. Sparrow saw him lay the .38 back in the drawer, put his head between his hands and whimper.

Must be crying because he was so hungry, Sparrow reasoned. "You want a bite, Old Man?" he asked consolingly. "Anybody could have a appetite after all the exercise you just done. How come you don't take it easy nights after the way you work all day? You burnin' the handle at bot' ends? You like a nice piece sandrich?"

Stash shook his head; he was too miserable to raise it.

"You don't relax enough," Sparrow counseled him. "You're not so young like you think no more. If you don't take things a little easier you'll lose your stren't, you won't be able to do your fam'ly duty. You might even lose your job. After all you got responsibilities, Old Man."

"*How* can sleep?" Stash pleaded with a ptomaine eye. "Is too much gone on. I'm tellin'! Pretty soon h*oo*sband gone by brooms closet."

"Don't bother," Sparrow reassured him, "we still got two flutes from Old McCall left."

"Is not for drinkin', by brooms closet—is for *some place sleepin'! Sleepin'!*" His voice rose in a plaintive wail for peace and understanding, trying to make someone on Division Street remember what sleep was. Nobody seemed to need sleep any more on Division but poor old Stash Koskozka.

Sparrow studied him calmly, with a steerer's clammy eye. "What you hollerin' at me like I was a unnerground dog? You tryin' to make trouble for me?"

"All he is to *me* is trouble," Violet affirmed loudly from the bathroom.

"You must be siko-static, Old Man," Sparrow decided with his best bedside manner, "you should go by a siko-stat. He'll take yer temper'ture. He'll patch yer dirty roof where it's leakin' a little. You look like somethin' the cat never buried."

In the bathroom Violet studied her image with a rising dismay: a thin streak of drying blood soiled her ten-dollar one-day-old permanent. Her hair would have to be shampooed and hennaed and there went the sawbuck she'd been a full month chiseling off Old Husband. She strode back into the bedroom and jerked the old man's head up with a neat rap under the chin with the hairbrush.

"Look, you. You rurned my perm'nent. You gonna give me a tenner for another." She began hauling him by brute strength as if to the nearest cashier's window; at the bathroom door he broke free.

"I'm gone!" he shrieked, breaking blindly for cover down the hall, bumping from doorway to wall all the way down to the broom closet, pausing there to fumble down the sides of his long underwear. The closet key was in his pants, the pants were hanging on the bedpost and he couldn't understand why he couldn't find any pockets now.

For the closet was his sanctuary, where a chair and an army blanket, kept in reserve for storms like this, would lend him a brief security, if not sleep, before morning lighted the way toward his icehouse refuge. But something about his feeble fumbling at the closet door enraged her anew. "You ain't even man enough to get into a closet," she taunted him brutally.

Stash turned in the dim-lit hall in all the chaste white pride of his long drawers and told her, like a saucy child, "Who *wants? I'm* not tell Mrs. No-good where at is chippest restaurant-baker*ee* on *Di*vision. Ha! *Ha!*"

"Go *on!*" Violet commanded. "Get in there! Who wants you 'n your sec-ondhand pumpernickel? You're bot' dried up! Lock the door after you, go croak under the scrub pail, it's where you was born! You 'n the rest of the brooms!" Abruptly, inflamed by a memory of day old beef stew, she bore down upon him.

Stash wheeled and made for the fire escape, one side of the hall to the other like a rider on a trick bicycle, trying to ward off her blows with his thin little elbows. Down the hall a woman with her hair in crimpers opened her door just the tiniest crack.

"Don't excite yourself, honey," she advised Violet.

Immediately Vi raced back—for what she wasn't certain—till she saw the .38 lying where Stash had tossed it so wearily. Sparrow stepped lightly to one side to let her pass on the return trip. "Where'd that motherless animal go?" she wanted to know. Just like that: "Where's that motherless animal hiding?"

"Hoosband went that way," Sparrow informed her, pointing helpfully toward the fire escape, "only he got no pants. Ain't you gonna give yer old man his pants, honey?"

"What for? He ain't gonna have nothin' left to put into 'em. I'm gonna shoot it off."

"Wait," Sparrow cautioned her. "Don't plug him till I get the pants. I don't like seein' a man get shot wit'out pants on." His sausage string wandered up and down while he picked the pants off the bedpost, brushed them down with the butt of the sausage and wandered back down the passage, casually inspecting the names on the doors to see whether anyone he knew had moved into this particular goats' nest.

Poked his nose onto the fire escape to see if anything worth watching awhile was going on out there: not much doing there either. Just the white bottom of an old man's underwear shuddering wretchedly through the frost-covered crisscrossed ironwork in the winter dawn. Just an old man holding his head in his hands trying, somehow, sometime, to get to sleep for a little while.

It looked pretty cold to Sparrow, trying to sleep all scraunched up like that with Violet sneaking up underneath and the alley arc lamp's light shimmering down the barrel of the .38.

"I like to get up close to accidents," Sparrow recalled, switching the string in mild anticipation, and just as he switched it Violet pointed the barrel toward the arc lamp: in the shattering of the lamp the old man went forward with the blast as though catapulted by the Hindquarters of Destruction. To come up with his knees on the ironwork and his fingers clutching Violet's fluttering gown. "Stash give double sawbuck," he begged off. He sounded ready to cry, he was that crushed by fear.

"Then get your dirty wallet 'n start makin' good," she gave him his terms. "'N while you're gettin' it put water on the stove for dishes. You'll have just time to clean them up before you go by job. Jumped-up-Jesus-from-Joliet, Old Man, I got to get some sleep *sometime* tonight." She herded him down the hall before her. In the dimness Stash paused to plead over his shoulder, "You not shoot Old Man in ess, hoa-ney?"

"I just ain't made up my damned mind."

Then saw someone else in the hall and made her damned mind up in a hurry. Sparrow was leaning confidently against the wall, advising a shadow wearing a badge, "Here's your man, Sergeant, here's your man." Stash felt the .38 returned gently to his hand and held it in dull surprise.

It was just like one of those nosy neighbors, Vi reflected, to be minding other people's business when they ought to be in bed. Sparrow chewed on while the officer relieved Stash of the .38 and all three eyed Old Husband suspiciously while he struggled, first on one foot and then upon the other, into his greasy work pants. Nobody offered him an arm to lean upon, even when he went face forward and caught himself, by sheer luck, against the wall.

"Looks like one of them Berkshire cases to me," the law surmised. "If I hadn't happened along you'd be up on a murder rap—how many people you slaughtered with this thing lately, Old Man?"

"He sure has been terrerizin' *us* t'night," Sparrow put in. Stash gaped and looked to Violet for help. An odd place to look for it. "How about my ten bucks?" was what Violet wanted to know.

Stash turned hopefully to Sparrow.

"He buries his dead under his fingernails is what they tell me," Sparrow felt it his duty to inform the law. Stash shook his head in vague assent, sensing he had somebody on his side at last. "You good boy," he thanked Sparrow for everything. He could tell that Sparrow was going to make something nice happen for everybody now. So everyone could have secondhand twist bread and go back to bed.

"Maybe he oney fired to scare her," Sparrow suggested, not wanting to take any chances on having to sleep with Old Man rather than Violet. Over the officer's shoulder he saw Poor Peter's face, as white and long as the face of an Aberdeen rabbit, come peering. Sparrow waved once and the docile, dolorous mug disappeared once again into the dimness. The Jailer wouldn't be able to make much sense out of what Poor Peter would be trying to tell him, the things he had seen in the night, that was certain.

While all down the hall neighbors peeked out of darkened cracks just long enough to see what was going on without becoming involved. Every time the law eyed one of the slightly ajar doors it closed slowly and ever so softly; as though only the morning wind were shutting it.

"You ever confined to an institution?" the officer turned on Stash professionally.

"He means where you work, Old Man," Violet translated loosely.

"Sure, sure, worrrk ever' day, sixteen-eighteen hour, I'm not gone by yoo-nyun." Stash put a timid hand on Vi's broad shoulder. "My hoa-ney," he explained, feeling that the gesture would clear everything up. And shivered in the bitter tenement wind. "My hoa-ney, I'm still love her." Someone, he felt uneasily with that uneasy wind, was trying to take his hoa-ney away.

"You got a damned funny way of showing affection," the ace observed, playing a flashlight onto one of the slightly ajar doors. "I'll have to book this old sot for drunk 'n disorderly, creatin' a nuisance of hisself, malicious mischief 'n attemp' to do great bodily harm. Besides, who's going to pay for that arc lamp, cowboy?" He flashed the light briefly to surprise anyone reaching for a five-spot.

But caught no one reaching for a thing.

"The courts are very severe on these cases of late," the ace went on regretfully, "it might be assault wit' attemp' to tap a gas main for immoral purposes for all I know. Seems to me you answer the description of Firebox Phil, the fiend who's pullin' boxes for the purpose of pickin' the fire chief's pocket when he hangs his coat on the hook-'n-ladder."

The wind searched curiously all the way down to the end of the hall; yet no one reached for a fiver at all. It turned and jostled back between them, nudging each suggestively. Yet no one came up with a crying dime.

"You better look out or he'll try to buy you off," Sparrow warned the law.

"Where *you* work? You look *awful* familiar to me," the ace turned irritably upon the punk. "Let's see some eye-dintification."

Sparrow's wallet was in apple-pie order. It wasn't his, but it was all there: the photostated discharge stolen off a sleeping drunk on a Humboldt Park local and the Social Security card with the carelessly forged signature. He let the ace see there wasn't so much as a single loose deuce in the package.

"Now let's see *yours,* Scarface," he turned back to Stash, sensing easier game. He didn't want to fool with the one in glasses, he looked like some kind of crook.

"Worrrk by izehowz," Stash insisted, feeling the net beginning to close.

"He didn't even register for the Spanish-Americun War, I bet," Violet scoffed, while Old Husband hauled out his icehouse badge and his Christmas bonus check.

"'N you told me you were broke just last night!" Violet whooped in indignation. "Gimme that! A fine pervider *you* turned out to be, holdin' out on your own flesh 'n blood. Bringin' home stale pumpernickel with a uncashed check in your poke! I guess you figure you could take it with you 'r somethin'."

"If he can't he won't go," Sparrow put in, and apologized immediately. "I heard that on the radio."

The ace craned his neck, inwardly cursing his slowness in failing to grab the check first—not a loose fin among the three of them. Maybe he ought to make them take off their shoes; if he could just think of one good reason for the pair still wearing them. Well, he could always get a fin for the gun from any Division Street hood.

"Now I go by worrrk," Stash announced, hugging himself to keep warm while Violet, relenting at last, buttoned his fly. When the whisky ebbed she'd be half sorry for him.

"Now you go by station howz 'n get good lawyer," the officer corrected Stash. "Maybe you'll talk better English after you've slept a spell."

At mention of sleep Stash looked homesick for bed. Anybody's bed. Was there such a place left in the world where no one woke you up at a quarter to four, plastered you with mustard and ran you onto a fire escape in your underwear for neighbors to make bad scandals?

"We got a nice dry cell for you—or don't you think it's time for your fam'ly to get a little rest? You ought to be *ashamed,* a man of your age, 'n holdin' out on your kids on top of it." Apparently he'd concluded that Sparrow and Violet were brother and sister.

Old Husband hung his unhappy old head. He just hadn't known you could be arrested for holding out a pay check on your wife. Down the stairwell and by the ace's firm hand on the back of his belt, all the way down, he realized now it was a real bad thing he had done.

"Could sleep by station howz?" He wriggled a bit with hope.

"Yeh. 'N coffee 'n a sausage sandrich for you too."

Stash slid his dim eyes sidewise like a condemned rooster's. "Please—no sandrich."

Violet and Sparrow, standing with arms hooked about each other's waists as the first light began carpeting the ironwork of the fire escape and started down the hall, watched from the alley window while the law helped Stash into a squad car. They saw the little red taillight wink up at them once. To warn them to be good children so *they'd* never have to go to jail.

"That old man is certainly a lot of trouble to me," Violet sighed as the car pulled east out of the alley and wheeled south toward the station.

"I hope they take him to Racine Street better'n by Saloon Street—by Racine they got mattresses," Sparrow hoped wanly in the wan city dawn. While the light of Chicago's vast West Side, like the light of nowhere else in the world, crept softly, with its special Chicago softness, up a hundred thousand seamed city walls. "What makes that old man so mean in the first place?" Sparrow wondered. "Don't you treat him nice?"

The light filtered down from a hundred thousand roofs and across the floor just as it had filtered across the Humboldt Park lagoon on their first mornings together, when the lagoon was the thrill of a clandestine honeymoon month, before the whole world started acting clandestinely.

Violet shrugged. "They all get that way when they get old," she advised him like a grandmother.

"I'm not so hungry no more," Sparrow decided, "one more sandrich is all I could eat."

"Just the same, it was mighty sweet of you to pick up the sandrich when he slugged me wit' it—did you see him *hit* me?" For one moment he felt she was going to get mad all over again. Then she added: "The poor old man," and Sparrow knew she was almost sober.

"Don't worry about your perm'nent," he flattered her, "spendin' on hair like yours is just tarnishin' the lily. With hair like yours you could be a model 'n pose."

"Yeh," she laughed off his praise, "under the arms maybe." She raised her arms elegantly, like a real lady in a deodorant ad, high over her head. "Anyhow it ain't red, it's just awe-burn. Would you like me wit' red hair all over?"

"I like redheads of any color—oney first fix the sandrich 'n get some clean sheets on the bed. Old men 'r kind of moldy, you know. 'N leave the dirty mustard off. Off the sandrich, I mean. It got on the sheet awready, somehow. You know what I mean?"

"I know what you mean," she replied, and went to the bedroom to change the sheets and stash Stash's upper plate in the drawer on top of the .38, wondering casually how in the world that poor old man was ever going to eat without his plate. There was a daub of blood on her slip and she was examining it when the punk shambled in and said, "Let's see."

"No," she told him firmly, "there's blood on it. I don't think a man should look at blood on a woman. I don't like the sort of man that would."

So Sparrow ignored the slip, he was accustomed to her superstitions "I hope Old Man gets a *good* lawyer," he hoped.

"Yeh," Violet repented, "I'd hate to see him lose that job. But maybe this'll teach him to quit dictatin' everybody. Honey, that string is *ticklin'* me."

Sparrow generously switched the string to the other corner.

It was better than no love at all.

He hadn't stopped by Molly Novotny's door for three nights and three days. But for the second time in the week he had had his last, final and never-again fix. This time he was through and meant it. So he wanted to tell Molly how she had helped him to beat the stuff just in time.

He came down the stairs with Rumdum plowing on a leash before him and his mind went down the stairs one bound ahead of the hound. Frankie had dark-haired Molly on his mind as well as the needle and he couldn't get either off. His eyes had a curtained look; to hide the need of both from himself. But Rumdum's were hotly eager for everything.

For Rumdum had good beer and Girlie on his mind and he and Frankie were going calling together.

Within Frankie heard the phonograph's sleepy murmur, but he did not knock. Some aversion to knocking at this door still held him, it must always be somehow accidental and nobody's responsibility; he kicked Rumdum in an oblique hope that the dog might protest loudly enough to get Molly's attention. But the hound only slid one cold eye sidewise. When the murmuring paused Frankie stepped, gently but firmly, on the dog's tail. Rumdum put it between his legs and sat down heavily upon it, looking as wronged as a hound could look: he didn't want to take responsibility either.

Frankie stood looking down at the ravenous-looking freak at his feet and saw a shiver, as of returning life, run through that mangy and bloated form: the beer-clogged nostrils had picked up, faintly, Girlie's special scent. A scent, for Rumdum, like that of no other bitch the whole endless length of Division Street. He bristled and forgot himself long enough to give forth with a low, menacing, masculine growl, reserved strictly for occasions when no opponent was in sight. Molly heard that boastful rumble and opened the door just a crack.

"He stopped dead here 'n I couldn't get him a step farther," Frankie explained casually. "I think he got a crush on Girlie."

"He sounds mad at somebody."

"He's just puttin' that on. All he is is thirsty again 'n he knows the place he gets took care of. Say, I'm sort of dry myself. How about a little Christmas cheer? You dry?" And fetched Rumdum a sharp kick to make him leave off growling long enough so a person could make himself heard. "I guess he's likely to go on like that till he gets some beer in him."

She opened the door just wide enough so that he could brush past, if he pleased to, or stay where he was. Yet gave him the benefit of both breasts against his arm as he passed.

He sat down in the big red upholstered chair in the corner, looking shab-
bier than ever in his stained field jacket. While Rumdum swished about his legs,
suddenly coy after all his growling threats about what was going to happen to
her if he ever got within paws' reach of her lovely flanks.

Girlie, snarling defensively down at the oversized mongrel from her sanctuary in Molly's arms, seemed to share some of those reservations about
Rumdum which Molly held for Frankie. Whose big dog had *he* been lately?

"I'll tie her up," Molly announced, and when she returned to her guests: "I
left her a saucer of milk. She isn't old enough for beer."

"If she hangs around this one she won't drink nothin' else," Frankie bragged
when Molly came to sit beside him on the chair's broad arm. To study him with
her direct child's gaze.

"You didn't come back," she reminded him. "You went 'n got fixed again 'n
was too ashamed to come back."

Her directness shook him, he hadn't had time to lie.

"It was the last one, Molly-O."

She'd been planning for three days to give him the sharpest dressing down
she'd ever given anyone. Yet now that he was here, with the tired look under his
eyes, all she could think of was, "I threw myself away on a man worth nothing
at all. I can't lose now by going along with one that's worth something." And
took his head to her breast.

"You don't know what it's like," he told her without raising his head from
the clean milk-and-fur odor of her. "All I hear up there is how I smashed her up
a-purpose. If just she didn't think *that*."

"She's got you thinkin' you done it a-purpose, is that it?"

"All I know is she got me stonin' myself. How does a guy know what he was
really thinkin' when he was stewed?"

"You can't take what she says now like it's somethin' real, Frankie—Sophie
ain't been right in the head since the accident, everybody knows that."

"But it was me made her wrong in the head then, 'n everythin' I do since
makes it worse for her, I don't know why. What if one of them pin-curl biddies
upstairs seen me come in here?"

Molly lifted his chin until his eyes were forced to meet her own. He read
an ancient anger there. "I ain't forgot the time I was just a kid 'n she cracked me
in front of everybody—'n you backed off 'n let me go bawlin' home by myself.
You was that scared of her even then. 'Cause you didn't want to go home with

her that night. You wanted to go home with me. It was how I wanted it too—things would have been better for me since then if you'd done like you felt instead of like other people told you you got to."

He pressed her hands to his shoulders and turned his eyes away; but she brought him back.

"You know why Zosh slapped me that night? 'Cause she was wrong in the head awready, that was why. She was evenin' up on you way back then. You wouldn't fall in love with her the way she wanted you to, the way she was in love, she had to get even with you for that. She never got another chance till the accident. That was her one big chance 'n she took it without even carin' what she was doin' to herself. It's all she ever tried to do for you was to get even. 'N you're lettin' her do it every time you knock on that Fomorowski's door or sneak up to see Blind Pig. You know it in your heart 'n you're backin' down from admittin' it to yourself just like you backed down that other night."

Rumdum, jealous of Molly's arms about Frankie, padded up and put his head on Frankie's knee and Frankie caressed the big ugly muzzle absent-mindedly.

Molly wouldn't let him go.

"If you want that girl to get well you ain't going to do it by gettin' as sick in the head as she is. It's what you're doin' every single time you pay off Louie to use that dirty hypo on you—"

"It ain't just that, Molly, it's that lead I got in my gut, it still hurts sometimes."

She shoved him away from her. "Don't give me that Purple Heart romance. It's nothin' of the kind 'n you know it. If things were right with you you wouldn't be runnin' to Louie because you got a pain in the belly. You're runnin' over there because you get to thinkin' the whole thing is all your fault, that you smashed her up on purpose. She's got you lyin' to *yourself,* Frankie. You *got* to believe that that girl was wrong before the accident and the accident was just somethin' that could have happened to anybody who'd had one too many.

"It happens every day, there wasn't anythin' special about yours—you think your accident was like made in heaven? Can that bull. It was made right down at the Tug & Maul at the bottom of a whisky glass 'n you better start pickin' up the pieces 'n start livin' again with what's left over. If she don't want to put the pieces together for herself you got to do it for yourself."

Her hand, with its wrist as thin as a child's, lay firmly upon his own.

"Things have sure went to hell on a handcar since the accident," he acknowledged.

"Were they ever the way they should be between you 'n Zosh? Before the accident, Frankie. That's somethin' I got to know."

He shook his head. No. It never had been. It hadn't ever been right. "She never trusted me." He'd brought it out at last, avoiding Molly's eyes.

"Look at me. You think *I* can?"

It had been a long time since Frankie had looked at anyone steadily. How could he expect anyone to trust him who could not trust himself?

"I always trusted you, Frankie, from way back. I trust you now."

"I trust you too, Molly-O," he said mechanically, and she let his eyes go at last. She unbuttoned his field jacket, he looked so warm, and tripped the knot of the little blue jazzbow about his throat like tripping the knot which held his innards so tightly of late. He felt the knot within loosen with the realization that he could talk straight to somebody at last.

For how does any man keep straight with himself if he has no one with whom to be straight? He had never fully trusted Sparrow, the punk thought too fast for him. In their world of petty cheats, phony braggarts, double clockers, elbow sneaks, small-time chiselers, touts and stooges and glad-hand-shakers, one had always to be on guard. He had been on his guard since the day he'd been chiseled out of two steel aggies back of the McAndrew School, when he was nine. He had been on guard with everyone since and with Sophie most of all. He had a blurred, reasonless conviction now that, somehow, it had been she who had stolen his two steel aggies, never to be replaced.

She'd never given his aggies back. He lost them anew to her every day. Well, let her keep them then, let her keep everything. Let it be as she said, all his fault, and let him go at last. He felt an almost animal-like yearning to let his guard down and take all the blows there were in the world till there were no blows left: to sink under them in utter weariness into sleep and wake up being the real Frankie Majcinek. The Frankie who was straight with himself as he was with the world. The Frankie he had never been.

To sleep a bit in this small room and waken to see the curtain flutter and feel a trust of all things near. To sleep so long, on this small woman's olive breast, feeling her trust of him binding him like her arms, that he would waken to become what Molly once had glimpsed in him. What she knew he yet might be.

He had never been trusted. He had never trusted himself. The thought of being trusted hit him like a double shot on an empty stomach. He wasn't ready for anyone's trust. He had been too long trained in wariness to drop his guard that low. That low, and that fast.

Wary of all straight answers. On all the backstreets of home he had learned how a straight answer could land a man in the lockup while the boy with the quickest lie stayed on the street. Yet—if there were just one person to whom one's answers were always straight, just that might make the whole twisted world come straight—he looked up to see Molly reading him like reading yesterday's race results.

"All we done, from the first time we went roller skatin' together, was fight," he told her. "We battled all the time we went steady, we battled the weddin' night till 4 A.M., we started in again when we woke up 'n kept it up till I went in the army 'n started all over the day I got discharged. We kept it up till the night of the accident 'n we ain't quit yet."

The naked bulb that burned overhead, by night, by noon, by twilit hours, hung like a little bald yellow skull on a chain like a twisted rope. Below it she had a candle burning, a candle red as wine. It's tiny flame pointed, upon the yellow wall, to the skull burning overhead: it glinted a bit on the bottle of cheap cologne and in the depths of dark-haired Molly's eyes. On the other side of the window a prairie snow fell across backstreet and tenement, looking for dry leaves upon which to rest and finding only concrete and steel.

"I know," Molly laughed with that laugh so soft one hardly heard the small rasp in it. "I heard you two goin' at it one night, it sounded like all the dishes in the place gettin' bust. I had to hold my ears. What went on?"

" 'What went on?' Why, that's just *what* went on: all the dishes in the joint gettin' bust. She started it just to show me she didn't care one way or another, for dishes 'r me 'r anythin' no more. So I helped her out to show her I didn't neither. I don't."

"You just think you don't," Molly decided. "So now you're eatin' out of paper plates?"

"*I* ain't eatin' up there at all. Vi brings her soup in a bowl 'n I eat by Messinger's on Milwaukee, it's where you can lay your dirty head right down on the table 'n go to sleep 'n they don't bother you if they seen you spent for coffee."

"I like Violet," Molly told him as if thinking of something else, then said what she was trying to say. "Don't go by Messinger's no more when you want to put your dirty head down somewheres. I got a table 'n you don't have to buy coffee to put it there. I'm settin' here three days now waitin' for you, listenin' to the Els go by, countin' how many cars it sounds like. You don't know how lonely it gets, waitin' for El cars. Frankie, let's *both* quit stonin' ourselves."

He didn't know she was crying till her tears touched his lips.

"I know how lonely it gets waitin' for Els," Frankie Machine told dark-haired Molly.

Frankie sat in the dealer's slot but he did not see the players. He saw only their shadows along the pale green baize and he dealt only to shadows.

For each sat in the same seat every night and he knew each shadow well. The heavily crouching one to his left was Schwiefka's, the trembling, pinheaded one was Sparrow's; the humble, headless and hunched-up one was Umbrellas', bent as though still carrying his daytime burden. And the ever-shifting, wavering one, that seemed to change shape as its owner reached in a shadow pocket for the shadow of a single cigarette, was the tallest, leanest shadow of all.

"Louie's all dressed up tonight," Sparrow feigned admiration of Louie's soft green fedora with the red feather in the brim and his polopony shirt. "You goin' cabaretin' for Christmas Eve, Louie?"

"No, I just got tired of winnin' in my old clothes," Louie explained confidently, and shifted the fedora onto the back of his head so that everyone might see he had just had two bits worth of Division Street sun tan and a Paradise Ballroom haircut. The man would never see fifty again, yet dandied about as if he were twenty-two, whistling at the girls and fingering his American Legion button—a habit derived after six months spent in Stateside army camps in 1918.

"I could of got ten to one in 1924," he announced. But no one asked him ten to one on what. Everyone knew. They'd heard it all before.

"Ten to one I wouldn't live out the year 'n that was only May," he answered himself as though someone had asked, as if anyone cared. "Standin' right there by the Four-Corner Tap I told Red Laflin he'd be dead before I was 'n he lived twenny years 'n his best rod man is buyin' me a shot every time I stop by the Four-Corner just to say hello, just for old time's sake. 'You was Red's best friend,' he tells me, 'n puts the bottle on the bar."

"'N you're just the *schleck* to kill the bottle wit'out layin' out a dime, too," Sparrow observed. "Red must be turnin' over when he sees his best rod man settin' that big free bottle down."

"I mix it wit' lemon," Louie explained smugly, "it don't burn up your insides that way."

"I always wondered who burned down Laflin's joint," Sparrow wondered idly, and added hurriedly, "I know it wasn't no guy from around *here*."

"Back off, Jewboy," Louie told him, sounding bored, "your job is by the door."

"Zero'll tell the steerer when to get by the door," Frankie put in quietly.

And the cards went around and around.

"He's just afraid I'll win his dollar-twenny before the suckers start comin'," Sparrow explained of Louie.

"Quit waspin' him," Frankie ordered.

But Louie opened his wallet and started counting just to show how many "dollar-twennies" he was holding. There was a c-note right on top, then a couple fifties, then so many twenties and tens that Sparrow figured it, just offhand, at better than half a grand.

"Thanks, Louie," he offered, "I was just wonderin' what you were holdin'— which alley you go home by? I'll walk you down."

"I could buy a hundred Jewboys," Louie told no one in particular, and returned the bills to his poke.

"We know where you get it, too," Frankie said boldly, seeing nobody's shadow at all.

"We give the public what it asks for," Louie smirked.

"Be careful the public don't give you what you're askin' for," Frankie told him. And thought to himself, "This joker thinks he still got me on the hook, he'll find out nobody needs him."

And the cards went around and around.

There came a scratching like a cat's scratching at the metal door, but Sparrow did not rise.

"It's just that blind hyena again," he said, "let him wait."

"Let him in," Frankie asked, "I need coffee."

Sparrow rose, and a moment later the greasy white cane and the gamy odor of the peddler moved across the table like a cloud off the canal.

"Sit next to me, *prosiak*," Nifty Louie ordered, pulling the peddler around into the empty chair beside him. "You want a hand of no-peek? I heard you was pretty good at it."

"Can't deal no blind guy," Frankie protested, "I'll do everythin' but that."

"Blind guys are the *betht* to deal," Pig himself pointed out politely, "they can't tell what they're holdin'."

"I'll read his hand," Louie explained.

"Blind, bummy 'r beggars," Frankie insisted, "no two guys holdin' one hand."

"I'm goin' to Stickney to play," Louie announced, "this is Clark Street poker—hobo gamblers, hobo steerer, hobo dealer."

"If he stands behind Pig it's awright, Frankie," Schwiefka compromised anxiously, "it'll be Louie's hand, only Piggy-O holdin' it. Be sociable."

"Why can't he play it hisself?"

"I believe in blind man's luck is why," Louie told everyone, fingering the yellowed Legion button. And placed a silver dollar in front of Pig.

Frankie reached over, tested the dollar against the metal shade of the night light, then peered more closely at its stain.

"I seen that dirty buck somewheres before," he decided, returning it to begin boxing the cards. "Somewheres before. That's bloodstains on that dirty buck."

"The bank'll cash it," Schwiefka put in, "deal us a round of blackjack, make everybody happy."

"It's my good-luck piece," Louie told them all, "I'm always superstitious as a whorehouse rat toward Christmas."

Umbrella Man rose uneasily and shuffled, still half crouching, into his coat, fearing the air of challenge going around the board. When Sparrow returned, after letting him out, the soiled dollar lay in front of Frankie: he had dealt himself a winner.

"Gimme back the silver." Louie was laying down a crisp new single in exchange. "I wasn't bettin' the silver one, it was just to bring the old luck around."

"It's *my* good-luck piece now," Frankie said, with a low, soft malice in his voice, "I get superstitious myself around New Year's."

"Change it for him," Schwiefka ordered his dealer.

"Keep your muscles in your pockets, bakebrain," Frankie answered, "I make the change around here."

Louie rose. "If I once quit a joint I never come back in it 'n neither do my friends," he threatened Schwiefka's purse.

"Nobody sent for you in the first place," Frankie assured him.

"*I* sent for him," Schwiefka decided, and reached for the blood-stained buck.

Sparrow's narrow hand got it first and had it pocketed by the time Frankie had pushed back his chair. "If you sent for him you deal to him," and sent the deck flying across the board, aces and kings and deuces scattering across the floor. Schwiefka, bending heavily, went in pursuit of his sixty-

cent deck while Frankie followed Sparrow down the steep stairwell to the
street.

"He's gettin' too big for his britches," Schwiefka complained peevishly to Louie
when he'd gotten his deck together again. "In the old days for a dealer to walk out
on me like that, he wouldn't be dealin' no place for life. He'd be spottin' pins in
a bowlin' alley 'n lucky to get that, it'd be just 'cause I was sorry for him."

Louie wasn't hearing Schwiefka. He was hearing only the dealer's footsteps
walking away with Louie's special luck. With the dealer's every step Louie felt
one step unluckier. He had never felt so unlucky so fast in all his life.

It was the sort of night he went to a dance or stuck close to the bars and
wouldn't let himself glance at a deck or a pair of dice or a cue. Just like that, only
worse. All his luck stepping down a staircase inside of the luckiest buck in the
world. "I got careless, teasin' him wit' that dirty buck," he realized with a strange
despair. Then slapped his fedora forward onto his skull and hurried after his dollar.

At the top of the stairs Schwiefka heard him call down; they all heard him
call down.

"Dealer! I want to talk to you!"

Everyone there heard Louie ask that. But not one heard the dealer reply.
Then the upstairs door closed behind Louie; and none had heard the door
downstairs open at all.

All heard a long, steep, waiting silence there, where the dealer and the
steerer waited within the stairwell's high-walled pit, for someone coming
down to them from above.

The dealer and the steerer heard the upstairs door open and close; like a
door shutting upon some long-lost argument. Both watched Louie's lean dark
figure coming down, the sparkler in his tie glinting like a one-eyed cat, one
step down and one step down. He was a long dark time coming down.

Laughing nervously to himself as he came. "I'm givin' you a buck fer a buck,"
he repeated his offer, sticking a folded single into Frankie's jacket pocket. "No
more 'n no less."

"Don't buckle, Frankie," Sparrow encouraged him. If Frankie buckled now
he'd buckle for keeps, he'd buckle in everything, the punk sensed.

"I don't want trouble, I got enough," Frankie mumbled his apologies with all his
defiance swept under. "Give him his dirty buck back, Solly. He worked for it."

Sparrow stalled, fishing for it in all the wrong pockets at once. Frankie
unfolded the single just to be sure it wasn't a phony.

"It's good awright," Louie laughed, "it come from the same place as the silver buck. You give it to me yerself last week—remember?"

"I remember—'cause it was the last one you're gettin' *that* way off me."

"Wrong again, Dealer. You'll look me up ten thousand times to come. 'N on yer knees to beg me to take your money too."

"*What* way, Frankie?" Sparrow put in innocently, pretending to forget all about the silver in his watch pocket.

"None of yer sheenie business," Louie told him. "Come up, Jewboy—the buck, the lucky buck."

Sparrow offered it to Louie's reaching hand, then let it slip through his fingers deliberately and stepped back just in time to let the back of Louie's hand whizz past his lips.

"A Jew trick," Louie laughed derisively, and the odor of violet talc touched the air. Sparrow opened the door to the alley so that he could kick the coin out into the alley's darkness if he spotted it first; and retrieve it in the morning. Through the open door the arc lamp's light fell across Louie's face.

Frankie felt his own back pressed hard against the hallway wall knowing neither God nor Molly-O could save him from going to Louie on his knees with ten dirty thousand more. "There's people ought to be knocked on the head," he told Louie without hearing his own voice at all. "I want people like you knocked on the head."

"You couldn't knock nobody's head," Louie laughed at him, "all you can knock around is that beat-out hustler John brushed off, the piece of trade with the pinned-up skirt." Then spotted the buck, trapped upright under the door's lower hinge, and bent swiftly for it.

Frankie locked his fingers to stop their shaking. If the shaking didn't stop he was going to cry in front of the punk and a flame of cold shame for having lain in a cold and secret sweat begging for morphine charged the fingers with a pride of their own. He rose on the balls of his toes and came down with all his weight full upon that white defenseless nape.

The throat made a single startled gurgle.

Then the neck flopped forward like a hen's with the ax half through it.

An irregular thunder beat in his ears and a whitish lightning hurt his eyes till he felt Sparrow's hand on his arm and Sparrow's inside-info voice near at hand. "Take it easy, Frankie, we're in the clear." The irregular thunder became a bowling alley's harmless roar and the lightning steadied to the alley's unquestioning glare. "I didn't even hear him fall," he heard his own voice returning.

"You keep sayin' that, Frankie. Quit sayin' that. We got to be upstairs before the aces pick him up."

"Did you run too?" Frankie asked, feeling the first recession of the shock that had blacked him out.

"Sure I run," Sparrow reported with pride, "after I hauled him out of the hall. He's behind Schwiefka's woodshed, it'll be morning before anybody spots him—can you handle the deck?"

"I can do anythin'," Frankie decided firmly. "All I need is one quick one. You think maybe it was just his ticker give out?"

"His ticker give out awright"—Sparrow gave a little chortle of hoarse glee—"whose ticker wouldn't give out when a boxcar lands on the back of his neck?"

At the bowling-alley bar Sparrow surveyed the dealer from behind his great glasses, trying to hurry him without rushing him back into panic. "He hit the floor like Levinsky," Sparrow told him, covering Frankie's glass with his palm. "You got to get back to the slot, Dealer."

At the prospect of returning Frankie felt something that had been holding him together open and let his stomach slip through. Sparrow saw him pale, yet kept the glass covered.

"You *got* to make it, Frankie."

"I can make it. One more and I make it."

"One more and you'll never make it." Sparrow was firm. He saw Frankie's hand tremble as he lifted the empty glass to his lips in the hope of finding one last small drop. "Steady hand 'n steady eye," Sparrow told him.

But what was it Louie had told Frankie? "You'll come beggin' on your knees."

That was it then. The fast shuffle-off on Damen and Division and the sudden turn of mood in the back booth at Antek's. A guy as right as Frankie letting himself get hooked on a kick as wrong as that. It was Sparrow's turn to feel a little sick.

"Stick by me, Solly," Frankie pleaded exactly as if Sparrow had spoken aloud.

"I'm stickin', Frankie."

Neither looked toward the woodshed shadowed by the wall of the Endless Belt & Leather Works as they returned down the alley through which they'd fled. A couple of Schwiefka's dated racing forms scurried down the alley before them, pursued by a bitter wind; whipped past the woodshed's corner and banked against the wood as though sent by the wind to cover something there. Neither spoke till they came to the darkened alley hall.

"I hope you had sense enough to get our lucky buck back," Frankie remembered suddenly with a real sense of loss.

"There wasn't time for that, Frankie—it was pitch him by his ankles 'n run, you ought to be glad I didn't just let him lay. You weren't easy to catch. I still don't know where you were headin'."

"I had a place all right, don't worry," Frankie lied firmly. "Where the hell *was* I goin'?" he had to ask himself. Then, begrudgingly: "You done awright for once."

Outside the alley door Sparrow whispered pointedly. "I'm glad we were havin' coffee when that guy Fomorowski Whatever His Name Is got slugged next door." He stooped, picked up a handful of Christmas Eve snow. When they walked in on the shills he shambled to the table, goggling dizzily, extending the snow and asking, "Who wants ice cream? Awready it's t'ree inches deep!"

"If Louie don't come back it's you guys' fault," Schwiefka grumbled while Frankie, pale but steady, slid into the dealer's slot. "You two guys gonna find yourselfs out of a good job one of these nights, treatin' the customers like they was underground dogs."

"We'd be cheaper off wit' out this one," Sparrow told him.

"Yeh," Frankie backed up the punk, "this is gettin' to be a good place to hang away from, there's too many arguments goin' on."

He looked around for Blind Pig as he riffled the deck.

But the peddler had left in the wind and the snow.

As the cards went around and around.

Stash was out of the bucket and all was forgiven. There would be a dance in the hall that stood in the shadow of Endless Belt & Leather and everyone would be there.

But right from his first hour back home he began giving Violet trouble again. Something had happened to the old man in his five days at Twenty-eighth and California, he'd gone a bit stir-crazy it began to appear.

First thing he shakes his head, No, to washing dishes after Violet had finished eating. So she cleaned them up herself and sent him down for a half gallon of beer—and here he comes back upstairs with nothing in his hand but five two-bit cigars and a dollar-fifty lighter. "Where's my beer, Old Man?" she wanted to know. But all Stash does is look about dreamily, like he thinks maybe he heard somebody ask him something, and lights up a fresh cigar.

"No more day-old pompernickel," he gave her a reply at last and before she could realize just what he meant by that there was a tap-tapping at the door and there was Sparrow with a blue-and-white pencil-striped mattress on his back.

"Got it in the section next to the 'lectric eye-rons," Sparrow boasted, dumping the mattress right in the middle of the floor, "just picked out the prettiest one, hauled it off the pile, told the girl I was from the basement, they got to have six down there right away to ship to the South Side store, special order, they got up here by mistake. She's still waitin' for me to come back 'n get the other five."

"Don't tell Zosh how you got it," was Violet's thought, "she'd be so ashamed."

"Yeh. But think how proud Frankie's gonna be," Sparrow pointed out and turned to Old Husband. "I bought it for you, Old Man, it's your comin'-home present to sleep on when I got to sleep in the bedroom. I don't want you bein' uncomfortable on the front-room couch."

"Don't want." Stash kicked at the mattress petulantly.

"*What* don't you want, Old Man?" Sparrow demanded to know. "You'd rather sleep on the couch wit' out no mattress, you mean?"

"You pay *board,* what *I* want."

So that was it. Just like somebody owed him something. For a moment Sparrow was so hurt he thought of walking right out and leaving Stash to try to handle Violet himself awhile. It took more than a new mattress for that. He himself was being extended beyond his own powers, he knew. "You talk like a bolt from the blue, Stash," he counseled Old Husband, "you don't get the idea at all. Times have changed. I *live* here now. You're the boarder these days. It's why you got to pay the rent."

Stash grappled with his truss over the heavy, bleached-out underwear, got it straight all around at last and announced firmly: "Am h*oo*sband. *You* pay rent."

Violet, sprawled out on the mattress, her hands beneath her hennaed head and her legs spread a bit to explore its possibilities, rolled over and buried her face in her hands, laughter shaking her shoulders. "He says he's my *husband,*" she managed to gasp, then dried tears of laughter out of her eyes, gathered the mattress in her arms and marched off to the bedroom with a low word to the punk: "I'll be waiting, lover."

In a minute she was back: "It's too small for a double bed so I put it on *your* side—I got so much meat on me I could sleep on the floor 'n it'd feel like plush—but your poor little bones, the way they stick out—"

"Ess," Old Man agreed with a malicious glee, "is good enough for Mrs. No-good, on floor." He pointed commandingly to the sports section wadded into a hole in the battered couch. "*Mr.* No-good *there.*" He got a good grip on the truss and stood right up to Sparrow. "Stash boss by howz now. Stash sleep on *bed.*"

"If you don't stop tryin' to make trouble around here you can't tear no more days off my calendar," Violet told him, and went into the kitchen to see to the one small bottle of beer remaining there. Sparrow heard the tinkle of glass against the icebox door and followed. "We can't afford to have you drinkin' up our good beer on us, the way you're actin'," he warned Stash, "you stay out."

When Sparrow passed the bedroom door on the way downstairs for more beer he saw Stash stretched comfortably on the new mattress, working on a fresh cigar and with a half gallon all his own beside the bed. There was something wrong, Sparrow sensed, in the old man's very posture. If he felt that relaxed today how could anyone be sure he'd feel like getting up at 5 A.M. to go to work tomorrow?

Stash got up in time to go to work the next morning—but Vi had to roll out first and get the coffee perking before he did it. "We can't go on this way," Violet told him in the cold little kitchen, afraid to return to bed lest he return there too. "There got to be some changes made."

"Is right," Old Man agreed. "You go by job instead."

Sure enough, he returned that same afternoon with his rusted ice tongs over his shoulder.

"Did you quit or was you fired?" she wanted to know before he had hung up his coat.

Stash made no reply. But he stayed home drinking beer the whole afternoon and in the evening Violet and Sparrow held an anxious conference in the kitchen.

"He says he ain't gonna do nothin' but set around 'n read the temper'ture the rest of his life. Then he looks at the calendar like he wishes it was time awready to pull the date off for tomorrow."

"He'll get tired of settin' 'n settin'. He'll go back to work just to have somethin' to do," Sparrow hoped vaguely.

Old Man never wore pants or shoes or shirt about the house. When ready to eat he simply thrust knife and fork into the truss and sat wiggling his toes, in their heavy socks, till food was put before him. He broke in upon the conference, shuffled his upper plate into position and said, "Ready."

"Ready for *what?*"Violet wanted to know in alarm. She had set plates for only two. Stash reached over and placed Sparrow's plate in front of himself.

"This stuff ain't for you, Old Man," Sparrow pointed out, "this is *fresh* stuff. You couldn't digest it. It'll be ripe for you tomorrow, there'll be lots left over."

"I digest awright," Stash assured him. "*Now* I'm eat. Ever'tin' frash. Tomorrow you eat, little bits left all over."

Sparrow and Violet watched the old man spreading creamery butter upon fresh rolls with something akin to horror. He helped himself to her dollar-twenty-a-pound ham.

"Pick the strorberries," she commanded Sparrow, "I got to see how far this thing is going to go." But her voice faltered.

It went as far as the "strorberries." Stash poured half a pint of whipping cream over them and lit a tailor-made cigarette out of Sparrow's pack, left lying carelessly beside the sugar bowl.

"Why don't you finish the cream, Old Man?" Sparrow asked. "It might go sour."

"Is for coffee," Stash explained regally, shoving his cup toward the perking Silex. Violet filled it with a strange docility.

"Now Stash gone by bed some more—*ever*'tin' be nice, quiet," he warned them both after the very last of the cream had gone into his coffee and the last of the coffee had gone down his throat.

The fact that the right-hand button of the underwear's trap had now loosened didn't in the least detract from the dignity of the old man's exit. They heard the closing of the bedroom door, the sighing of the new mattress giving surcease to his brittle old bones and the first gentle snore before either dared to speak.

"It looks like our move,"Violet said dismally, after the dishes were washed and they had returned to the front-room couch; there was scarcely room for both of them to lie comfortably on its worn springs.

"Don't say 'our,' " Sparrow reminded her, "say 'yours.' *You* married him."

"Yeh, but I wouldn't have had to hang onto him this long if you went out 'n got a steady job," she pointed out. "You could make it on the legit if you really wanted."

"Sure. I could get a Number Two shovel 'n get on a blast-furnace shift in Indiana Harbor 'n come home nights in the same shape as Stash is now 'n be snorin' here on the front-room couch while you're—" He stopped himself.

"Go ahead—finish what you started to say." Her eyes had darkened danger-ously. "I s'ppose I'm in heat every time I see a pair of pants hangin' on the line? All I think about, I guess, is that velvet-lined meat grinder?"

"That about sizes it up," Sparrow thought discreetly. But all he said aloud was, "All I meant was if I had a full-time job I couldn't do my fam'ly duty so good."

"You're not breakin' no records as it is," she assured him, "'n anyhow I'm not tellin' you to start swingin' no shovel. You could be a Western Union mes-senger 'n drop in to see me between messages."

"I'd never get back to the office on time," he predicted, "I'd be fallin' off the bike. Why don't you go by Western Union yourself?" And added silently, "Then I could rest up between messages."

"Fat chance *I* got of goin' to work," Violet complained as might anyone unjustly deprived of the inalienable right to work for a living. "Who'd take care of Zosh 'n that oversize fart hound you palmed off on Frankie? If I didn't get down there 'n sweep the floor the bottles'd be overflowin', they'd be up to the sink."

"So long as they don't go no higher," Sparrow philosophized, "if they did they'd get in the way of the dishes."

"Frankie's got her so spoiled she won't even put the dishes on the sink, she waits for me to pick them up now, just like she's tryin' to see how much I can take off her. I'm glad they only got one room 'cause she eats all over the place. I find dishes in the drawer, they must of been there since Frankie was in the army."

"It don't look like you'll have time to be cleanin' up down there any more," Sparrow reminded her, "the way Old Man is actin' you'll have to start in up here first."

"He'll come to his senses when I won't let him tear the days off the calendar 'r read the temper'ture."

"How you gonna stop him?"

"I'll put the calendar up where he can't reach it 'n lock the window so he can't lean out. He can't open it by hisself, the lock gets stuck. He has to holler for me to come unlock it."

"Don't let him lean out too far."

"That's what scares me, he leans out too *damned* far."

"Hold his legs."

"*That's* the part that scares me, it's when I'm holdin' his legs. What if I let go?"

"You won't let go."

"I know I won't."

"But you might forget to lock the window—well, I'm glad tearin' days off the calendar is all he wants to tear off." Sparrow spoke with an uneasy gratitude. He wasn't as certain, as he once had been, that Violet was an unmixed blessing.

"Hurry up, honey," she panted in his ear, "we got to get dressed pretty soon 'n get down to the hall. I got to get Old Man dressed 'n shaved 'n clean socks on him. After all, the New Year's party is for him."

"*This* one ain't," Sparrow commanded her, "quit quackin' 'n get to to work."

That was as far as Violet and the punk ever did get in resolving the problem of having a husband in the home. Had it not been for chance and an icy pane, old Stash might in time have driven them both to carrying messages for Western Union.

The first guest to arrive at the New Year's Eve ball was Umbrella Man and as soon as he came in it was apparent that the occasion had been misunderstood. He carried a rebuilt umbrella "for bride-lady" under his arm, his pants were pressed and no one could convince him that it was just a coming-out party for Old Husband because Old Husband had just come out.

Then Meter Reader the Baseball Coach came bringing a third baseman's mitt with the signature of Stanley Hack autographed into the leather for Sparrow; and a book on how to throw your voice for Violet. He pretended never to have heard of anyone called Old Husband at all and had just dropped in to kiss the bride. So all he'd do when they tried to explain things to him was to say, "Don't thank *me,* thank my boys."

So they guessed somebody had been going around saying Violet had finally divorced Old Husband at last and was getting hitched to the punk. Which, with all the presents the rumor had brought in, didn't do any particular harm. So everyone had a long pull of *wiśniowa* on it while Stash went about showing his clean socks to everyone and pointing with pride toward Violet, to show it was Mrs. Him had given them to him.

Then Antek the Owner arrived with a bruised cheek. He'd been drinking his own whisky all day, till Mrs. Owner had locked him out in order to have something left for Monday's customers. Owner was on the verge of tears. "Married fourteen years 'n never a harsh word—now she bats me with the mattress board 'n locks me out of my own home. I got no home no more, fellas. I got nothin', it's all in her name. Owner's out in the cold world all alone, can't even get in to see his own little girl—isn't that a *shame,* fellas?"

He didn't draw a tear. Everyone knew he got maudlin as regularly as he had a good week and was locked out till he sobered up. Locking him out, after a good week, was the only thing that sobered him. He had a crying need for pity and could never understand why no one sympathized with a man robbed, overnight, of wife, home, family, honor and his lifetime savings.

When Owner wanted to cry, he cried, and anything at all did for an excuse. What really mattered with Owner wasn't on the tongue but in the heart; since he had no words for his heart, he wept.

"I'm not cryin' for my own trouble," he confided in Frankie, leaning so heavily across the wheelchair's arm that Frankie had to brace it with his foot to keep it from being rolled backward, "I'm cryin' for everybody's." He took off his glasses to cry the better for everyone; for the lenses were so splashed with tears they were indistinguishable from the beads of sweat about his round bald brow.

"You're cryin' from the skull now, Owner," Frankie informed him. "When it starts comin' out of your ears it's time to use the handkerchief." And assured Sophie from where he stood behind her, "He'll be back behind his bar Monday morning."

They wandered in from all over the ward, the invited and the uninvited, the wary and the seeking, the strayed, the frayed, the happy and the hapless, the lost, the luckless, the lucky and the doomed. Some, on the assumption that if anyone were getting out of jail it must be the punk again, to congratulate Sparrow; only to find all the more reason for celebration when they learned that, just for this once, it wasn't the punk at all.

Everyone got congratulated for something or other whether he deserved it or not. Everyone but Old Man, who couldn't even get congratulated on his new socks. So he tried going about announcing "Stash boss by howz" while clutching a week's worth of calendar dates; and still no one paid him any mind.

And some came just to celebrate the season with Frankie Machine.

Yes, and one blind peddler so drunk he merely sat in a corner and called out, from time to time, that he, alone of all good hustlers, had come to mourn a hustler.

To mourn for Fomorowski, Blind Pig defied them all.

While the whole long hall rejoiced.

And Violet, finding pity at the bottom of a whisky glass, began making every stewbum, who came up to kiss her, shake hands with Old Husband first and admire his socks. Till the old man, clutching his calendar dates like so many retrieved hours, felt the party must really be for him after all.

Meter Reader kept running back and forth in the center of the floor scooping up an imaginary grounder he'd missed in some long-gone summer's double header. For Meter Reader didn't know a meter from an egg beater: it was only that long ago he had come into a meter reader's cap. It had lost the insignia above the peak, but still served when he coached the Endless Belt & Leather Invincibles. He was still trying to explain Endless Belt's 19–1 loss to Lefkowicz Fast Freight and the boys were egging him on.

"I'm *proud* of my boys," Meter Reader insisted, "proud of every man of them." He still lived over that overwhelming defeat though it had been achieved on the Fourth of July and the year was running out with the hour. He still had to establish that he felt no shame in that defeat. When Meter Reader grew excited he couldn't see he was being jived a bit.

The phone rang and someone said it was Owner Budzban of Endless Belt wanting to talk to his coach about spring training. Of course it was only Sparrow phoning from across the street, but the hall grew quiet so Meter Reader could hear the message better. Out of the corner of the eye everyone watched him listening so humbly, head sinking slowly in despair while the punk told him he was through at Endless Belt—his check would be mailed to him Monday morning. No, there was nothing wrong with his work at Endless Belt, it was just that the company couldn't afford to back a losing team any longer. Feeling was running pretty strong, the boys wanted a winner this year so it had been decided to let Coach go with the best of New Year's wishes.

Meter Reader came out of the booth looking brokenhearted. Losing the job was nothing, he had held onto it only because it had made a coach of him with each returning spring. "One hell of a New Year's resolution they made *there,* it's all I got to say," he mourned. "But I seen it coming since July. Well, I'll find something else"—then as if suddenly jolted by the full truth of what had happened to him he seized Frankie by the sleeve and shouted right in his ear, "I'm *proud* of my boys! Every fool man of them!"

"Meter Reader!" someone called, "there's a Mexican out here wants you to coach for Vera Cruz next season—can you talk Mex? What should we tell him?"

Meter Reader, to whom all things were possible, waddled out to see what kind of offer Vera Cruz had for him. Before he reached the door the phone rang for him once more and the same voice came on again: "Is Owner Budzban. You could have job back but we got to get new coach. Is okay?"

So he smelled the punk at last and came out of the booth this time refusing to talk to anyone. He got a good hold of the bar and wouldn't let go. It took Meter Reader some time to grow suspicious—but once he became so he over-did it. When the phone rang and he was told his girl was on the line he refused unconditionally to answer. For a week now he wouldn't be believing the sim-plest sort of neighborhood gossip.

While Sophie sat so flushed with excitement that she looked ready to get up and start dancing herself any minute. Sparrow wheeled her under the mistletoe and kissed her, and all the boys kissed her, till it hardly felt that she was just somebody in a wheelchair at all.

High atop the Christmas tree a single tinsel star looked down and Old Husband, weaving a little in the middle of the floor, pointed the neck of an empty whisky bottle at it and shouted, "*Aj Za stary jestem popatrzýc na gwiazdyck.*" He had grown too old to look at stars. And fell back, exhausted, into many waiting arms.

With Blind Pig looking up at the great load of silver icicles and artificial snow borne by the tree just as if he could see it all; and his eyes still red from weeping.

For everyone who really mattered had come by now. Chester from Conveyor, Chester from Viaduct, Oseltski from Post Office, Shudefski from Poolroom, Shudefski from Marines, Szalapski from Dairy, Widow Wieczorek and Umbrella Man's brother, Kvorka from Saloon Street. And Sophie's own bright little grandmother with a bottle all her very own. Everybody who counted, a few who just imagined they counted, and a couple dozen more who knew well they never had, never would, never could and had never been intended to count at all.

Now began the midnight uproar to welcome the new year in. In the middle of the *Swiateczyna Polka* the younger couples began jitterbugging, and Sophie's grandmother shook her wise old head to see. She liked all things young people did, so long as it wasn't something old people did better, like counting their money. She liked it so well that she shook Umbrella Man awake, where he slept a drunken sleep in the chair beside her own, till he sat up and asked, "How far are we?" And promptly returned to sleep.

Violet, pickled to the point of elegance, strolled like a lady in her fancy, fancy gown, dragging cigarette butts in her train, gesturing artistically and asking everyone, "I *do* carry myself nice—don't you really think?" Right up to Sparrow to take him dancing around, singing hoarsely into his ear at every turn.

> *"Let me tell you, laddy,*
> *Though I think you're perfectly swell*
> *My heart belongs to Daddy,*
> *Da-a-dee, Da-a-dee, Da-a-dee—"*

At the bar there was such a crush that the liquor ran out three times and emergency rations had to be rushed in by a squad of four flying lushes. It was one of those nights when everyone felt, for some reason, he really never had to go to work again at all.

In one moment everyone had to have a drink on everyone else. Men who wouldn't loan their mothers three dollars without an I.O.U. heard themselves telling ancestral foes, "Keep your money, Emil. Spend mine. I got too much." The orchestra got tight to a man so that the drummer stood up on his traps, alleged he was Gene Krupa and wanted to buy some cigarettes, then toppled into the sax man's lap. Immediately the sax man began taking a collection for the drummer and turned it over to the pianist. Who promptly rose to spend every dime of it back on the dancers.

Frankie took over the drums. For half an hour, while everyone was helping to bring the drummer around, the dealer was a man in a dream: he was Dave Tough, he was Krupa, then he was Dave Tough again without missing a beat. "The kid can do it when he feels like it," somebody said, and everyone shook his hand to tell him he was as much in the slot with the traps as he was with a deck.

Cousin Kvorka held his hand last and longer than anyone. "You can do it when you want to, Dealer," Cousin told him.

"Don't call me 'Dealer,' call me 'Drummer,' " Frankie asked: he never had it in him to answer Cousin in a really friendly way at all. He turned toward the bar. Cousin turned him back.

"Before you start hittin' the bottle over there I want to do you a small favor, if you'll let me," the leathery little man asked Frankie with real humility, "for the way you've kept the wolves off Umbrellas at Schwiefka's," he explained with the embarrassment of a man more accustomed to denying a favor than to be asking the privilege of doing one.

"You don't owe me no favors, Cousin," Frankie told him with a sullenness he could not keep out of his voice, "it's my job to keep the game straight, it's what Zero pays me to do. Umbrellas gets the same deal as everyone else."

Cousin had maneuvered him into the corner of the men's wardrobe within a few steps of a couple bucks trying to start a crap game. "I wouldn't sleep tonight if I didn't tip you, Frankie."

Frankie had the feeling, cold and swift, that the party was over and the new year well begun. Through the hubbub and the laughter, the smoke, the music and the stomp of dancing feet, he sensed, for one moment, that 1947 was going to be a long, long year for Frankie Majcinek.

"Spill it," he told Cousin Kvorka.

"When we picked up Fomorowski he been layin' there two days 'n if some potato peddler hadn't stopped by the shed to pee he might be layin' there yet. The guy was *covered up.*"

"You should of buried him deeper then," Frankie suggested without troubling to feign surprise. "Why you tellin' *me?*"

Kvorka bridled a bit. "He didn't freeze to death, Dealer."

Frankie waited.

"I ain't tryin' to make no pinch, Frankie," Cousin assured him earnestly. "I ain't even tryin' to give you advice. But it would do you some good to know what the score is on Louie now."

"Sounds like the game's over for Louie," was all Frankie had to say.

"He's at the morgue 'n there'll be a coroner's inquest. I can tell you the verdict now 'cause I tossed him in the wagon myself."

It was Kvorka's turn to wait. Either the dealer needed to know or he didn't.

"What's the story, Cousin?"

" 'Death due to assault, assailant unknown.' His neck was broke, Frankie."

"It you ask me that's a damned good thing 'n I'm happy to hear it," Frankie told him steadily.

The crap game was getting well started. "Only tryin' to square a favor," Kvorka told him.

"What do I need favors for?" Frankie turned on his heel. What did the guy take him for? Some high school stub who'd break down 'n say, "Please don't arrest me, Mister, I won't do it again"? It would be a cold day in hell before Bednar would pin a rap like *that* on Frankie Machine. He stood watching the crapshooters until he saw Kvorka get his hat and overcoat out of the wardrobe and leave. "He could save his favors," Frankie repeated. Machine didn't scare as easy as some aces might think, he told himself.

But when somebody offered him the dice he shook his head, No, and wandered off looking for Sparrow. He went around the hall twice and couldn't spot him.

Wandered without noticing that everything everyone was doing around him was the funniest sort of thing anyone had ever yet done. The hall was jumping with comical fellows wearing their girls' best hats and every man of them doing it like he was born for the stage.

Best of all, no one seemed to mind being outdone in anything. Though each tried to outsing, outdrink and outdance the next fellow, yet between the singing and the dancing and the drinking each conceded readily he didn't do nearly as well as anyone else in the place might have. Each exhibited his humility and trust by offering his whisky, his counsel and his girl to whoever stood nearest.

"Just *everybody* is feelin' good tonight," Sophie laughed, and felt just as good as anybody. Following Frankie's circuit of the floor, she wondered who he was looking for. If it was for whom she suspected, she determined, someone would learn that it was as easy to slap a face from a wheelchair as from a standing position. Her suspicion trailed along behind Frankie as she watched him, hatless, leave the hall.

For he knew where dark-haired Molly sat by herself, in the nest on the first floor front, and it wasn't Sparrow he had to see most of all. Remembered where she sat counting the Els that passed in the night.

It was New Year's Eve on the El, it was New Year's Eve down Division Street, it was Happy New Year's Eve for the boys from the Tug & Maul and the girls hustling drinks at the Safari. It was Happy New Year in Junkie Row at Twenty-sixth and California and Happy New Year for the Endless Belt & Leather Invincibles.

It was Happy New Year everywhere except in Molly Novotny's heart; neither her heart nor her nest gave sign of the season. The stove was smoking again and she thought carelessly, "We get the ones the landlords buy up for old iron," of both the stove and her heart. The day comes when both feel past throwing heat.

It's like that for all hustlers' hearts: to pay the most and get the worst. The only thing a hustling girl has that doesn't get stopped up is her purse. And that's as full of holes as a married man's promises.

Yet, when the El passed overhead, it drew the curtain up in that same passionate fluttering that had touched her heart so strangely the first night he'd come by—then died, as she felt her heart had died; and dwindled like any dying heart away. He would not be by again.

She tried to rouse herself, saying it would never do, letting herself feel so useless again. She had never understood why she had lived with a man like Drunkie John, for whom she had cared nothing at all, and found the answer now: when a woman feels useless she doesn't think anything of throwing herself away. One way of doing it, with one man or another, was as good a way as any other then. She ought to be hustling drinks across the street this minute instead of letting herself feel that, unless one certain clown knocked soon, she would be useless all her life.

It seemed to her now that all she had ever wanted, with one man or another, one street or another or under any old moon at all, was simply this: a man to care for, and a child of her own. To nurse in the silver evening light and tend in the gilded morning. That was all she had ever wanted.

Or ever could want again.

As the party down the street grew gayer and the revelry in all the bars increased, she sank into a pleasant sleep and dreamed she held somebody else's baby to her naked breast while someone knocked and knocked at some far door and she could not answer without letting the baby go.

"John is drunk and back at the door," she counseled herself in sleep, "come to take my baby away." She wakened in a dead-cold fright, the fire had gone out and yet the knocker rapped on through her dream.

"It's me, Molly-O," Frankie's unemphatic voice. "I know you're there. I asked at the club and they said you hadn't showed up. You sick, Molly? You mad at me?"

She watched the knob turning, he was trying to see whether it had been locked against him. Then rose at last and let him in.

"He's scared," she thought the second she saw his face. "I'm the girl he comes to when he's scared."

He stood with his back against the door and he was sweating across the hair line, there were flakes of snow on the hair.

"Who's chasin' you, Frankie?"

"The aces. They're goin' to pin the sluggin' on me."

"Are you clean?" she asked and before he had time to fashion the lie, "Don't tell me you weren't in on sluggin' Louie. It'd spoil just everythin' if you did. We been straight with each other so far—let's keep it straight. The way it is with you 'n me, when it ain't straight no more it's over. There ain't six barflies between Antek's and the Safari who can't take one good guess about who got Louie that night. It ain't that hard to guess with your buddy spendin' like crazy."

"The punk ain't had two bucks all his own to spend in a month," Frankie reproved her. "What *you* tryin' to hand me?"

"Just what the people are sayin'. Buyin' drinks by Antek like he owns the joint all yesterday afternoon."

Frankie laughed uneasily. "You didn't see no cash go over the bar, did you?"

"I wasn't there, Frankie, I just *heard*. They don't like it at the Safari if I hang around Antek's too much. Where I make my livin' is where I should spend, they think."

"Then I'll tell you this: either the punk is spendin' Stash's Christmas bonus money or he's runnin' up a tab on Antek. Stop worryin'."

"I ain't worryin' about the punk," Molly told him gravely, "it's you I'm worryin' about."

He went to the window. Between the girders of the El the snow was freezing fast. "No, I ain't clean," he answered with an ice-cold bitterness. "I ain't got enough blood on my hands, I got to pull somethin' like *that*."

It wasn't till he'd told her that she came to him, to link one arm into his own. "Don't torture yourself. It's a good thing he's gone. I seen the way he hooked a couple of them Safari kids onto the needle."

"I don't feel proud, like I done somethin' so great," Frankie told her with a grin at once both grateful and heartsore.

Seeing the defeat in that smile, Molly thought, He's going to have to run for it all right. "When you're ready to take off I'll take off with you," she told him matter-of-factly. "But let's not start runnin' till we're chased, Frankie. We run now we give the game away. Let's tough it out till it blows over a little. If we run we split it wide. Give it a chance to heal. Let them pick you up 'n haul you down to Record Head, there's nobody around here who'll testify up against you 'n nobody who can prove anythin' if they did. Tough it out, Frankie. I'll tough it with you. We'll tough it together." And took his tough little mug in her hands, gave him one small tough kiss and held it for luck. When she released him he grinned in the way she remembered best, with something of the old hope in his eyes.

"I took over the traps for the drummer tonight," he told her as proudly as a boy, "I didn't miss a beat the whole time."

"Where'd you disappear to?" Sophie was parked in the dance hall's vestibule and the party was over for her too.

The party was over for everyone. The crap game was over, losers and winners alike had left, the orchestra was packing its instruments and a janitor was pushing a broom down one side of the floor. All that remained of the night's many dancers were the shadows of two drunks on the walls, clinging to each other in a freakish caricature of a dance like a couple drunken bears: Meter Reader hauling Umbrella Man around and around the hall for no reason anyone could see at all. Their shadows fell across the wheelchair's arm like a derisive memory of all the boys she had danced with and now would dance with no more. He hadn't thought she'd noticed him slip away.

"I had to see a clocker. He give me a good thing for Tropical tomorrow."

An anxious wind hurried past them like the old year's last latecomer, Umbrella Man fell to his knees within as though to beg or pray and Meter Reader hauled him across the floor by the collar with the janitor nudging both playfully at the heels across the floor and out of sight while the wind went seeking someone in all the littered corners.

"It wasn't so good as the dances we used to go to, was it, Frankie?" she asked, hoping for some reason it hadn't been.

He tucked the blanket in about her feet without reply and wheeled her out onto the street, the chair making a tiny trail in the light new snow all the way down to Division. To be blown, as soon as they passed, into the footsteps of the night's thousand revelers. And into their own dim hall. He shoved the chair into the alcove below the staircase and she leaned her full weight upon him for the climb. He had to hold to the railing, she had never leaned so heavily upon him. The steps rose, into a wan yellow light, more steeply for him than ever before.

"Don't lean so hard, Zosh. I can't hardly make it."

She lightened her weight a bit up to the second flight.

There, across the hallway window, the Division Street Station's signal tower stood out clearly and abruptly, its red and green ornamentation glowing down the tracks like an iron caricature of the Christmas tree they had left behind in a half-lighted hall.

With his arm about her they paused to see the snow falling aslant the crosslights as far as the night would let them see.

To Frankie that quarter-moon sky looked darker and all the iron apparatus of the El taller then ever. The artificial tenement light seeping across the tracks made even the snow seem artificial, like snow off a dime-store counter. Only the rails seemed real and to move a bit with some terrible intent. "Your hands 'r so cold I can feel the ice t'rough my mittens," Sophie told him, thrusting her damp, mittened hand out of his in a child's sudden displeasure.

So cold, so cold, hands, wrists and hearts: the old quarter-moon of the tenements shone no colder tonight than the blood crying for warmth in his wrists.

And though her eyes were still bloodshot from crying Sophie suddenly sang to him with a certain phony gaiety, "*You're gonna miss your big fat mamma one of these days*—you know why I like that song? 'Cause it reminds me of one I *really* like."

In the icy dark the street lamp's frosty glow lay like hoar across dresser and wheelchair and bed. The clock was beating out its heart on the wall in a freezing pain and the luminous Christ gleamed all around with an icy, creaking mystery. Below the crucifix Rumdum whimpered, shaking in all his limbs and pounding the floor with his whiskbroom tail in hope of some ultimate warmth.

"That sneak of a hound been curlin' up on the chair again," she snitched on Rumdum, he had so often been warned against shedding hair anywhere in the room except on the floor. The floor was all right because there Violet would sweep it up sooner or later.

"He was just tryin' to get warm," Frankie told her in the darkness, fumbling about the gas plate in the corner.

"Then why does he have to *sneak* about it, jumpin' off 'n pertendin' he been under the dresser the whole time we was gone?"

"'Cause he's scared he'll get rapped in the snout with the hair curler like the other time he tried it," he reminded her.

"I'll rap him wit' somethin' more than a hair curler," she warned them both, "if he got rapped wit' a little rat poison in his dirty beer we'd see how much sneakin' he'd do then."

A little blue flame spurted upward in the dark beneath Frankie's hand.

"You wanted a dog," he told her, "you got one." He sat on the bed's edge and smoked a cigarette while Rumdum nuzzled between his knees. Once the latch rattled suddenly and he wondered why he could never get used to the way the El rattled it.

"Wheel me a little, Frankie."

That meant she would sleep in the chair tonight, and he wheeled her till her head slipped onto her shoulder in a light doze. Beside the gas plate's feeble warmth she napped lightly, with the little blue flames playing on her nodding head; beneath the chair Rumdum shivered. The overhanging blankets kept the cold off his hide a bit down there.

From under the heaped army blankets on the bed—blankets stolen from army camps all the way from Fort Bragg to Camp Maxey—Frankie peered out, with one limp eye, upon the new year's calendar: January 1, 1947. Outside the pane the year's first snow turned into the year's first rain.

Time, Frankie saw by that calendar, was some old man with a scythe. Time was always an old man with a scythe, for some reason. Yet as he drifted toward sleep it seemed that Time was really Antek the Owner's great gray deaf-and-dumb cat, that simply sat all day on the bar and studied the barflies with such unwavering tolerance.

Everyone said the cat was dumb, all insisted he had never even been heard to purr. Antek alone knew differently; he alone had heard the old cat purr. "'N when you hear *that* one purr you're through," Antek was convinced. "That one keeps track of how many shots you put down every day. So long as you're just a sociable drinker he don't purr. But when you take the one that puts you on the lush for keeps, then he knows you'll never get off the bottle all your life, 'n he purrs once at you. He purred at me 'n he'll purr at you 'n with my own ears I heard him purr at Rumdum."

The old cat knew, Frankie realized dreamily, only the old cat knew. Watching and waiting for the finishing shot that each hustler came to with the cat-gray stroke of the years.

Dreamed he heard Molly-O cry out only one flight down; in a voice made remote by many walls. And muffled by a slow slant rain.

By walls, by rain and by years to be when he would hear no voice at all; muffled by the slow slant rain of a night he would never know.

Some rain that beat, like forgotten tears, against some other room's single pane: the rain of that far-off night when his name would be the name of nobody at all, as the name of one who had never lived. Save in the memory of Molly-O, grown too old to remember.

Caught between the dealer's slot and the cat-gray stroke of the years, Frankie saw a line of endless girders wet with the rain of those years to be. Where all night long, in that far time, the same all-night salamanders burned. Burned just as they had so long ago. Before the world went wrong. And any gray cat had purred at all.

The cold rain ran with the red-lit rain. Like years beating by on the wheels of an empty Loopbound El. Till his heart, that cried for a greater rest even in sleep, felt tattooed by that long rain's beating. Why was it that within the voice of any woman crying at night he always heard an infant's gasping cry?

As the first light began enfolding the signal towers with tourniquets of fog, a sounder sleep finally folded a tourniquet about the fever in Frankie's brain. The slow heart stanched itself at last; though the rain ran on forever. And Molly-O, so far below, had yet such a long hard way to go.

"Sophie knows," he mumbled in sleep, "she knows about Molly-O, but she don't know about everything. 'Cause the cat won't purr, the cat won't tell. Nobody can tell which way the old cat'll jump."

And a dream cat leaped, in a slow and stiff-legged tableau, down a steep dark stair where paper daisies bloomed in an unabating rain.

Two hours later he felt himself being shaken awake by Record Head Bednar's hand on his shoulder. He opened his eyes to see only Sophie shaking him. "What's the matter? What's up?" he wanted to know irritably; yet relieved that it had only been Zosh after all.

"Nuttin', dummy," she scolded him. "You just look too lonesome when you sleep. I don't like it when you look so lonesome, it makes me feel lonesome too—*I'm* here, ain't I? If you got to sleep lookin' like that get up 'n get dressed, it means you need a drink." Then, curiously, almost gently: "Why you look like that when you sleep, Frankie?"

"Some cats just sleep like that," he told her without hearing his own voice. He was already purring, back in dreams, among all manner of other strange lost strays.

Time may well redeem the forger while leaving the bad checks unredeemed was how Antek Witwicki looked at it. And just to show how little trust he had in Time had had a fresh challenge painted above his register for all Tug & Maul employees to heed:

> I'll cash the checks here—Owner

Then, reminding himself that the only other employee of the place was Mrs. Witwicki, had softened the alarm with a gentler admonition:

> He who drinks and drinks with grace
> Is ever welcome to this place
> But he who drinks and starts to swear
> Is never welcome anywhere.

Antek also expressed his faith in the high art of graceful drinking by sternly forbidding all strong-arming upon the immediate premises. "Take him out on the street," Owner would insist, "and I don't mean in front of my doorway neither. The city put up a billboard for that purpose around the corner."

His sense of justice was as decided as his love of graceful living. He backed up law and order with a wooden-handled plunger originally designed for the flushing of basement sewers. By reaching over the bar with the business end, to conk guilty and innocent alike, whichever happened to be nearest, he accounted for all sorts of unpaid sins. Although not so damaging as a blackjack or a rubber-handled gearshift, it was certainly more humiliating to be conked out of a tavern with a plumber's plunger: there is scarcely more dignity to that than to being *swept* out, like a gum wrapper or a cigar band, in front of a janitor's broom.

For the more serious brawls he went for a half-filled water bucket kept below the bar with a bottle of ammonia waiting beside it. A dash of ammonia in the water and a heave of the bucket over the bar would break up anything from bulldogs to men. He had used it with savage success on cats, bulldogs, torpedoes, ex-pugs, drunken paratroopers and cuckolds demanding satisfaction from their wives' consorts. It had worked every time.

"The only thing it ain't worth a damn on is a woman under sixty or a girl over twelve," he conceded with some bewilderment. "We had a pair of biddies go after each other here one Easter morning—the one on top had her slipper off and was trying to get the other one's eye out with the heel—but *that* one got her teeth through the cheek 'n both 'em with their Easter dresses half ripped off. The toot'-holt one kept the shoe-holt one from gougin' her but the shoe's boy friend hollered somethin' so she started rammin' the slipper up between the toot'-holt's legs—you ought to have heard the bloody screamin' then—I figured it had gone far enough 'n went for the bucket 'n ammonia but it didn't help a thing. I had to cold-caulk that one wit' the slipper. What would *you* have done, you was me?"

The Tug & Maul, this winter noon, looked much as it had that Easter dawn. Frost had gathered on the windows and by night there would be neon rainbows in the snow. But, behind the piled beer cases, the same old mural took up the wall to the roof: a great spread-winged hawk painted there in descent upon one stuffed and helpless Christmas duck. The stuffing had been packed into the poor bird to the bursting point, it hung upon invisible wires. How it had ever gotten off the ground in that shape the artist had not so much as by a footnote indicated. While over the unhappy fowl's head hung, forever, the great obscene claws of the descending killer. It too seemed suspended upon invisible wires.

Frankie Machine sat on a beer case listening to Meter Reader trying to establish credit with Antek without first settling his Christmas-week tab. "I never let the same guy hook me twice," Antek explained. "I'll take it once. That's all."

"You're a better man then than Jesus Christ, to hear you talk," Meter Reader reproved Antek irritably. "*He* turned the other cheek, but that ain't good enough for *you*."

"He didn't turn it, that's where you're wrong," Antek informed Meter Reader. "He run the bankers out of the temple with a *whip*—you call that turnin' the other cheek?"

"That was different, they was Jews." Meter Reader was growing excited with his need of a double shot. "'N I'm the guy who can tell you about the Jews. You know what one told me once? He told me, 'Your best friend is the dollar.' What do you think of *that*?"

"It was a Polak told *me* that," Antek differed calmly. "My old lady, in fact. 'N she didn't turn the other cheek neither."

Frankie Machine witnessed Meter Reader's defeat without interest: he was feeling like the duck on the wall overhead. A half gallon of Schlitz stood between his knees, it was nearly noon and he'd been waiting for the punk almost an hour and no sign of him yet. The punk was getting too independent, for some reason.

Antek ambled over to where a girl, with a bottle of cream soda on the table before her and a shopping bag in her hand, sat waiting for some drunk with his head on the table. Husband, brother, father or friend, she was waiting for him to come to his senses and it looked like a long, long wait. Antek shook the fellow but all he got was a cockeyed leer and a sickly grin for reply; the fellow seemed hopelessly drunk.

"Get him out of here," Owner ordered the girl.

"Why pick on *us* all the time?" she wanted to know. For there were equally hopeless drunks sleeping it off on either side of her.

"Because he didn't get it in here is why," Antek explained. "I take care of my own customers. They could sleep here all day 'n half the night if they want. But I ain't in the samarathon business, takin' care of stiffs who get it somewheres else. Leave him sleep it off where he bought it."

Recognizing the essential morality of this point of view, she bent forward and with a single finger tapped her companion below the elbow. Though he had hardly sensed Owner's heavy-handed treatment at all, he rose automatically at that light touch, wiped his nose on his sleeve and told himself thoughtfully aloud: "The question got to be settled this Sunday. Father Bzozowy keeps Belgian hares. Somebody stole all four valve caps on me again. Why do they keep playing the same record all the time?" And went for the door like a sleepwalker without even pausing to see whether the girl, whatever she was to him, was still with him or not.

How any man could find any door in such a stupor there was no way of telling—but he made it with the girl on his heels and right there she turned, stuck out her tongue at Antek and told him obscurely: "That's for short measurement," and was gone, shopping bag, cream soda, zombie and all, to the very first bar that would let the pair of them sit around out of the cold and the wind and the wet for a little half hour or two.

Frankie watched Antek's second triumph in as many minutes with an eye turned inward upon a sea of faces, like faces borne on a shoreward tide. Cousin Kvorka's moonlike mug, full of a clumsy yet gentle anxiety, for he had something of Umbrella Man's native gentleness; Record Head Bednar's harassed face, brooding under its shaggy brows, looking like that of a man who has acted so heroically all the days of his life that he no longer has enough courage left to get him through the nights; Sophie's eyes, full of a pale suspicion; Sparrow's intense, peaked and eager look wanting to tell him something and being somehow afraid to say it and then smiling with Nifty Louie's thin, disdainful smile as though to say, "You don't have the whole story yet, Dealer."

Molly Novotny's face, full of a dark and steady appeal, upthrust trustingly to his own.

There was something had to be straightened out with the punk before he could take off with Molly. That punk wasn't helping matters much, if what Molly said was true, buying people drinks and everyone knowing the kind of wad Louie had carried. How many people had Louie counted out his money for before he'd counted it out for the punk? There wouldn't be one who remembered seeing another man's money that night.

"How come I'm never around when he's doin' the buyin'?" Frankie asked himself broodingly. The punk was going to have to be straightened out all right, this business about Louie looked like it might not blow over for three weeks yet.

So first of all he'd have to get straight himself. He motioned to Antek for a double shot to start getting straight on right away.

For way down there, in a shot glass's false bottom, everything was bound to turn out fine after all. Bednar was certain to find that death at the hands of person or persons unknown actually meant death due to causes unknown; so that it didn't really matter after all. Any more than it would matter after he and Molly Novotny had gone away together. Vi would take good care of Zosh then, till Zosh was back on her feet again and married to some fellow, some sort of doctor, who'd take better care of her than Frankie ever had. So that after a while there'd be hardly any hard feelings left at all and he and Molly would go to visit Soph and this real good guy she'd married and they'd all wish each other good luck and really mean it.

He finished the shot and tried to remember: What was it he had had to worry about? He had the situation beat and it hadn't been as tough as he'd thought it was going to be. He motioned to Antek with the shot glass and Antek brought over the bottle to save shoe leather.

Sparrow shuffled in and stood in the doorway trying to locate someone in the dimness. Frankie could see him clearly against the light from the street but did not call out. He sat and studied, one minute, this alley nomad with the forehead so high it looked capable of holding everything while all that ever actually sank into it were blows. It was time to check up on the punk.

As he came toward the back Sparrow's eyes searched furtively along the bar rail as though he'd lost something there.

"I think you're still in the junkin' stage," Frankie greeted him with a calculated scorn, "spyin' for dimes along the bar rail, you must be down to your last nickel."

"Who wants to be rich?" the punk evaded him. "You think I want to be the richest guy in the cemetery?"

"How come when you're with me you're always broke 'n the other times you're buyin' the drinks?" Frankie put it bluntly.

"It ain't just when I'm wit' you I'm broke," the punk assured him lightly, squatting down across the table from the dealer, "it's all the time."

"That ain't the way I heard it. They tell me you're spendin' awful easy these last couple days. Did one of them easy bucks have a little blood on it, Solly?"

For one moment Sparrow didn't really seem to get it: his jaw hung slack. Then his eyes sought something along the floor and he answered in a mumble without meeting Frankie's eyes at all. "I had a couple bills Wednesday night but you wasn't around. It was Stash's Christmas bonus check 'n me 'n Vi was lookin' for you to help us tear a hole in it. We come in here lookin' for you 'n we drank half of it up waitin' for you. You think I'd be drinkin' Louie's bloody bucks up in *here?*" His eyes met Frankie's at last. And demanded an answer in turn.

"I'm just askin' whose dough you're spendin'," Frankie heard himself apologizing and felt dismayed: he'd backtracked to everybody for years but never before to the punk.

"Whose dough you *think* I was spendin'?" Sparrow had the offensive at last. Everyone else made Frankie buckle—why shouldn't he? Sparrow thought excitedly.

"I thought maybe Antek was givin' you credit again," Frankie said weakly.

"You're the only guy can run a tab on Owner these days," Sparrow pursued his victory. "You want to start a new one wit' him now? I'll call him over."

It looked like Frankie had not only been outmaneuvered but was going to buy the drinks to boot. He pushed the bottle toward Sparrow and while the punk drank alone the dull drums of suspicion began beating another tune. Between the fumes of whisky there he began probing into darkened corners, like a man looking for a lost coin in an unlit steam room with the heat on full. Yet couldn't quite touch anything that felt real for all his probing.

"I'll tell *you* somethin' now," Sparrow decided after finishing a second shot, apparently not even noticing that he was drinking alone. "Pig is settin' by the Safari in a new suit 'n *really* buyin'—how come he couldn't even get in there by the front door before 'n now it's like he owns the joint?"

"What good would it do Pig to strongarm Louie?" Frankie asked foggily. "Who'd give him a square count? He wouldn't know if he had forty bucks 'r four hundred."

"Owner'd give him some kind of count, Frankie," Sparrow decided. "You want to ask Owner if he give Pig a square count?"

"Don't pertend to be *that* dizzy," Frankie scolded him hotly. "Don't think that dizzy act can get you out of *every*thin'. I know you better than you know yourself."

"All *I* want to know is this," Sparrow asked quietly, with no further dizziness at all. "Who's wearin' the new suit—me or Piggy-O?"

"That doesn't prove much," Frankie grumbled; but this time he filled both glasses. Then shifted his cigarette to the corner of his mouth till it dangled and Sparrow realized swiftly, "Now he's gettin' set to pull one of his corny movie acts on me."

Frankie passed his hand ruminatively across his cheek just the way that Bogart did it when they were hunting him down and he needed a shave. Somebody had squealed, that was it, it was between himself and Edward G. Robinson now.

"We could go look for Pig in the Coney Island Diner," Sparrow suggested, for he dearly loved this movie game. Like the reading of serial numbers on streetcar transfers, it was one game he played faster than Frankie.

"What's the use of goin' to the Coney? You said he was at the Safari."

"That's just why we should go to the Coney, 'cause he won't be there. We just come in 'n look around at the menu 'n when the counter guy asks what do we want we tell him somethin' that's crossed out."

"I don't get it."

"You just don't see the right movies then. We ask the counter guy what people do in this town 'n then you say, 'They come in here to order the crossed-out dinner—ain't that right, smart boy?' "

"Does Pig eat *there* now?" Frankie was at sea and not even drifting.

"Forget it," Sparrow told him, "I'm just too educated for you. We can pick up Pig at the Safari if there's somethin' you want to see him about. You sure you want me along?"

"You're just the guy I want along," Frankie assured him.

"I'd like to have a cam'ra 'n just go around gettin' pictures when somethin' big happens," Sparrow began daydreaming innocently as they came out on the street, but Frankie dismissed his innocence. "You may be the richest guy in the cemetery yet," he warned Sparrow.

They found Pig at the Safari with his face shaved and washed, a new haircut and wearing a new suit and new shoes. The suit was already crumpled about the thighs and the shoes were two-tone jobs such as Louie once had worn; but it was still Pig inside the glad rags all the same.

Pig smoking a cigarette through a holder.

"Waitin' for a live one, Pig?"

Pig smiled straight ahead with nothing abject in his smile at all. "Yeh. Who you guys waitin' for? A dead one?" His humility was gone with his half lisp. He talked like a man in the driver's seat with one foot on the brake.

"Bring it to the table," Sparrow told the bartender, preceding the peddler to the rear with Frankie following. In the corner, beneath a frosted bulb, Pig sat looking out upon that dark and wavering shore which only the eyeless may see and only the dead may wander.

"They tell me you're in the bucks these days, Peddler," Frankie attacked him directly.

"I know who you guys are," Pig informed them in a dead-level tone.

"Of course you do," Sparrow agreed. "I'm the steerer 'n my buddy's the dealer, he got somethin' he wants to find out."

"You're the guys awright," Pig told them both in that same flat knowing voice.

Now it was time to say: "You heard Louie get slugged. Heard us run and tapped down the alley till the odor of violet after-shave talc hit you. You touched him where he lay, bent above him and found the heavy roll you'd heard him bragging about half an hour before. Then pushed a few papers above him and tapped away to someone who'd give you a square count."

But there was no way of asking a thing, it dawned on Frankie at last, without betraying himself. As if sensing Frankie's thought the blind man told him, "I believe in live 'n let live, Dealer. Nobody asks me questions, I don't ask nobody questions. I got to live too."

His fingers found Frankie's knuckles and touched a ring, of heavy German gold, that Frankie had worn since returning from overseas. "I ain't no big snitch, I ain't puttin' no finger on guys who don't put no finger on me. It's just live 'n let live, how I look at it."

"I think you got a good sense of direction some nights all the same," Frankie told him, but Pig didn't seem to hear. "I'm just one more poor blind bummy peddlin' pencils," he mourned, "just a poor old down-'n-out bummy 'n you two guys muscle me back in some corner 'n talk like I got to watch my step, like I'm some guy killed some guy 'r somethin'. A blind guy couldn't even rob nobody, he wouldn't know who was a-watchin'."

Suddenly he lolled his tongue at them both: he'd been laughing at them the whole time he'd been pleading.

Noiseless laughter. Yet he laughed long. While Frankie watched, unable to move. Spittle flecked Pig's lips. And still he had not finished.

"You guys," he regained his breath at last, almost helpless with soundless glee, "you guys can't fool me, I'm too ignorant. You gonna break my neck too, you guys? It hurts my feelin's, how you talk to me. Why don't you buy me a drink 'n talk *nice*—a *good* drink—'n then let me alone. Ain't I lettin' you guys alone? Okay, you guys?"

He thrust one hand before him, knowing it would not be shaken. That was like him: to seek some humiliation that flicked the long-dying membrane of his eyes and so pleased the twisted spirit. To feel that inner vindication, as of insult upon injury. Sparrow tapped Frankie's shoulder and nodded toward the door. "We can't set here all day wit' out buyin' the bummy a drink, Frankie."

Pig heard them leaving and called out eagerly, knowing his voice would be ignored as surely as his hand, "You guys! Buy a drink! I'm waitin' for that live one!"

At the door Frankie blinked out into the winter sunlight. Slanting toward them across the street a well-dressed matron minced through the sunlit traffic's wintry bustle. "I'd like to be a tradewind 'n blow down *there*." Sparrow watched her with his lewd little eyes while a lewd wind whipped her skirt. "You see her give me the eye? I bet if a guy had a Lincoln Park yacht 'n a captain's outfit he'd get all he wanted."

Frankie spun him about with both hands. "If I was sure it wasn't Pig that rolled Louie you'd get all you wanted awright. If it wasn't him it was you 'n that's a lead-pipe cinch." He shoved Sparrow away from him. "God help you, punk, if it was."

"I'd be the richest guy in the cemetery then for sure, eh, Frankie?"

Sparrow goggled up at Frankie dizzily.

That was the last sad afternoon that the dealer and the steerer sat together to pretend things were as they once had been between them. While the troubled light first wavered, then slanted and darkened across the floor and right outside the ice creaked once, for the puddles were freezing over in alley and street again and Frankie himself felt half frozen. He always felt half frozen of late.

Sparrow leaned across the same table at which they'd begun the afternoon, trying to beguile Frankie away from his concern for a dead man's bankroll.

"Wolfin' is just like dog stealin', Frankie," he confided earnestly the minute they had returned to the Tug & Maul. "You find out where they live 'n wait till they're on the loose in the back yard."

"I like a dame with them glasses with the string on," Frankie conceded reluctantly, "it's dainty-like."

"You know the kind *I* like, Frankie? The Bette Davis kind—you know, with them real poppy eyes."

"What's so hot about poppy eyes?" Frankie felt irritable. "I know one with poppy eyes 'n a goiter too—you want a introduction to one with a goiter the size of this bottle?"

"I don't mind poppy-eye goiters, Frankie." Sparrow's enthusiasm picked up a phony momentum. "I'd like a poppy-eye on that Lincoln Park yacht—it don't even have to have no engine, just have it settin' there to point out to the chicks we're walkin' through the park, accidental-like—'Oh, there's our yacht, the crew must of brought her in from Belmont Harbor'—'n when they don't believe it we walk 'em right on board."

"You take the one with the goiter," Frankie decided firmly, going up the gangplank without looking back.

"Once they're on board they got to stay all night," Sparrow revealed. So Frankie drifted with him, borne by Old Forester, out of the Lincoln Park lagoon onto shoreless waters while Sparrow gestured unobtrusively for two more beers. "We'll drift right out into the lake," the punk murmured dreamily, his eyes half curtained by the small waves' dreaming motion; for one moment, behind that curtain, his eyes surveyed Frankie with the hard cold gleam of understanding. Only to soften as the glasses were refilled. "Maybe we better stay in the lagoon," Frankie cautioned himself in a faraway voice, "account of havin' no motor we might not get back to shore in time."

"In time for what, Frankie?"

"In time for everythin'—I don't know—somethin' might be goin' on on land, events might be happenin' 'n we'd be elsewhere."

"We could tell the chicks we're offshore anyhow, Frankie."

"That's right. 'Cause it's dark 'n they got to take our word. I point to the lights along the drive 'n tell 'em: 'Now we're passin' Michigan City.' 'N when we pull past the pier I say, 'Look, you—Du*loot!*' 'N all the while we're driftin' we're savin' oil 'cause it's just the little waves lappin', we're only two blocks away from the zoo so's we can always get back in time."

"In time for what, Frankie?"

"I don't know. In time to see 'em feed the lions, I guess." He had drifted so far out Sparrow saw it was time to tow him in.

"What if they hear them lions roarin' for their breakfast?" he asked. "Don't they know it ain't Duloot we're passin' then?"

"Tell 'em they're sea lions. It's time for breakfast anyhow, so we got to get rid of 'em. We say we're back in port 'n got to turn the boat over to the crew to get it remodeled right away, the engine's missin'. We duck the chicks through the underpass."

"How many chicks, Frankie?" The punk felt reluctant to duck so fast.

"Just two is enough. Rye-awlto chorus girls you—one a blondie 'n one kind of redheaded."

"Who's the blondie for, Frankie?"

"For you. One more redhead'd kill you. 'R maybe she's dark, one of them with one of them real nice protudering Hottentot behinds."

"Not all them dark ones got protudering behinds," Sparrow put in cunningly, "look at that little Molly-O, she's trim as a policeman's whistle."

Frankie pushed his glass away for reply. He wanted that same Molly so badly his throat felt parched. But if the punk thought he was getting anybody's goat he'd find Frankie didn't bite that easy. "I'm through lushin' for today," he announced.

"You want to go by Thompson's 'n get two meals on one ticket, Frankie?"

"I ain't hungry."

"How about a show then? We got to do somethin' if we ain't gonna set here 'n just get tanked. You want to go by the Pilsudski?"

"The Pilsudski smells of sheenies 'n the Pulaski smells of Polaks," Frankie complained, trying not to see the terrible emptiness of the glass in front of him. "Excuse me," Frankie begged the punk's pardon, "I didn't know there was a sheenie in the house."

"Excuse *me,*" Sparrow begged politely in turn, "I didn't know there was a Polak. You want to go dog-stealin', Frankie?"

"You *that* broke?"

"Just to *do* somethin', Frankie. Just to pacify the time. If we don't we'll get stiff, it wouldn't be no good if Kvork had to pick us up when we were stiff. By the time we got sober we'd be puttin' the finger on ourselves."

"That's all blowed over," Frankie decided. "The cops pick up stiffs like Louie every day. Their tickers go bad is what happens. A guy like Louie, he didn't have a relative in the world. He just clunked out. It's all in the day's work for Record Head."

"He didn't have a relative to claim him is right, Frankie," Sparrow counseled Frankie, "but he owed more guys money than there are bottles on that bar. 'N every one of 'em plays ball with the super." Sparrow looked disconsolately into his glass and whimpered, "I wisht you hadn't slugged nobody, Frankie."

"'N I wish you'd of had the brains to grab the roll when I did 'stead of leavin' it to Pig to tap out." Keeping his eyes on the punk.

The punk's eyes never wavered. "If I had we'd both we wearin' new suits now, Frankie." He wasn't being caught off base that easily.

The punk was getting too smart these days, that was all there was to it.

Another week and he'd be as smart as Frankie Machine. "Let's go dog-stealin',
Frankie," he begged. "Just for the old fun."

Frankie was firm. "No percentage. I don't want no janitor takin' potshots at
me. Where's the payoff?"

"Then let's put on our ties 'n go down to the Rye-awlto."

Frankie tapped his glass. He couldn't get it filled at the Rye-awlto.

"You want to go plain-stealin' then, Frankie?"

"Why you always so hungry to latch onto somebody else's gold? Stealin'
what?"

"'Lectric eye-rons by Nieboldt's, it's where they're makin' profits to galore
these days, they'll never miss a couple eye-rons more 'r less. 'N there's nobody
around on the third floor, it's what they call the honor system so they don't have
to hire no help. That's the beauty part, you just help yourself, it's better'n
boozin' 'r wolfin' in hallways even."

"I'd do better to go to theY. 'n take my belly off," Frankie murmured, with no
intention of working off his beer paunch at all. "What you get for them eye-rons?"

"A fin apiece anywheres. It'll kill the old monotony. After all, God hates a
coward."

"Well," Frankie conceded, "God hates a coward awright—but empty your
pockets all the same. The only way I go boostin' is empty-handed." And thought,
"If God hates a coward that much he must be workin' up one terrible grudge
against me—I'm gettin' so I'm afraid to be alone with a bottle." He finished the
beer before him, wavered one moment on the Nieboldt plan—then the booze
left in the bottle felt riskier to him than electric irons. "Let's go, punk."

He was mildly surprised to see that, out of nowhere, the punk was suddenly
carrying a shopping bag; it hadn't been in view the whole afternoon.

"What makes you so roundabout when you want help?" Frankie scolded him.

"I always carry a shoppin' bag," Sparrow assured him brazenly, "in case I run
into some guy who wants to go 'lectric-eye-ron-stealin' by Nieboldt's."

The after-Christmas remnants had been piled in disarray upon every counter.
The tidy little beribboned gift packages were all gone and in their places were
hastily stamped placards: Marked Down for January Clearance. And in the aisles
half the women of the Near Northwest Side jostled one another just to see how
much they would have saved if they hadn't done their Christmas shopping
till now.

Slips, bras and pajamas were heaped as if ready to be swept into the alley if not sold before closing time.

Frankie and Sparrow took the faintly murmuring escalator up to the third floor, where the punk became diverted by some marked-down toy automobiles. Frankie hauled him forward. "Let's pick up them eye-rons."

The punk led the way a few yards, pausing only to inspect a vegetable bin at the base of an electric refrigerator. Frankie lugged him on past hardware and kitchenware, crockery and paints; till they came to an oasis of fluorescent light wherein, it appeared, the store had forbidden all its help to enter. Not a salesgirl in sight.

"It's 'Everybody's on His Honor System,' Frankie," the punk felt obliged to explain the miracle, "even me 'n you."

Frankie covered, holding the handle of the bag, while Sparrow lowered half a dozen irons into it. When Frankie felt their weight pull on the handle he turned away, leaving the punk standing with an iron in each hand—he got rid of them as suddenly as though they were heated. "We'll take the elevator down," Sparrow urged him, "it looks so innocent-like."

"Escalator is the best," Frankie decided, and Frankie always decided right. You couldn't get out of an elevator fast.

He looked around and saw Sparrow back at the refrigerator, examining the vegetable bin; the punk caught up with him at the head of the stairs. "My roof always leaks a little faster in January," he apologized, before Frankie could start scolding, "that's the time of year I first started gettin' dizzy when I was a sprout."

At the top of the second flight the bottom dropped out of the bag.

Frankie watched them tumbling down the narrow escalator stairs as if they were on rollers and wanted to laugh when one barely missed a salesgirl's ankle—the bag slipped from his hand, he shouldered the girl to one side, saw her mouth widen with indignation and then knew it was no use running, no use at all: two floorwalkers, a house dick and a dozen bosomy saleswomen clamored around, pecking at him like overfed hens.

"They had an ace hidin' in the drapes," Frankie realized wryly, "the punk caught somebody's eye foolin' wit' that vegetable bin." And told the house dick quietly, "Let's go where we're goin'."

They came down that littered aisle in a sort of carnival with the house dick holding his belt from behind and a floorwalker on either side holding his arms and the bosomy biddies following behind, cackling as they came. Under their feigned horror Frankie heard their easy laughter. He caught a glimpse of a butcher holding a broken-necked rooster, both butcher and rooster sliding one limp dark eye sidewise at him as he passed.

He felt the patrol car wheel out from the curb and saw the wan early January sun lying in a checkered pattern across the car's scarred floor. It was evening, the snow was drifting a bit toward the curbs and when the car stopped for the lights he heard the wind getting up all down the trolley tracks trying to hurry the patrol along a bit: it would be long melted before he saw any trolley run again.

"The punk saw that ace 'n ducked without givin' me the word," Frankie decided bitterly. "If I ever find out for sure it was him rolled Louie—" He touched his left hand to his shoulder: in the excitement one of the biddies had torn the sleeve again.

The young men had engraved their bitterest disappointments upon the walls beside their fondest hopes. They had exposed their betrayers there, mocked their lawyers and doubted their wives. One had assured his sainted mother he was going straight the moment he could make bail and with the same stub end planned straight mayhem, the moment bail was made, upon one Crash Kolkowski. No reason was offered; yet the emergency stood plain:

> If it wasn't for Crash Kolkowski I wouldn't be in here and where he should
> be is in hell with his back broke. Every time he comes around shooting off
> that big flannel mouth us good guys should get together and break his back
> five or six times. Nobody should even buy him a shot.

The prospect of Kolkowski sweating out an eternity with his spine in a cast while all the good guys in purgatory stood around refusing him just one small snort was sufficiently dismal. Yet even sadder, it seemed to Frankie Machine, was another second guesser's plea:

> Don't go by Dago Mary she give bad drink

Had Dago Mary prepared the sodium amytal the night before? Or was it only that the coils hadn't been cleaned? A deed premeditated by midnight and executed with deadpan deliberation in the dangerous noon? Or some casual midweek evening's error achieved in innocent merriment? Upon the gray confessional of the walls Frankie Machine found no answer at all.

With tedious attention to detail someone had illustrated precisely how a certain aging judge would look, gavel in hand, wearing nothing but high-button shoes and a flowered cravat, while sentencing a sensibly clothed civilian to the electric chair for indecent exposure: a single button had been found loose upon the offender's fly.

To leave nothing to the imagination the chair, sizzling invitingly, had been sketched in beside his honor. To show how no time was lost, locally, in appeals for pardon, parole or probation, the judge had his hand in reaching distance of the switch and was sweating with impatience to fry this miserable joker personally. There would be no commutation of sentence here.

Chicago justice was in a bad way all right. One could see that at a glance: not a single finger of scorn was pointed at the judge for his own nakedness.

Indeed the Irony of It All had inspired another amateur to scratch a second portrait: a beat-out, tattered, crooked-limbed wreck, groping in two directions at once and captioned *Chicago Justice Deaf Dumb Blind and Falling Apart.*

In for a bum rap, one hand explained, *I never rolled a drunk in my life.*

While another commented knowingly: *In for a bum rap too I never rolled a sober one.*

That's how it is, another had confided, *when you hit some lousy bum the dough falls out of his pocket and you get the blame.*

By the yellow night light's glow Frankie saw how the four walls, as well as the floor—and by some frenzied acrobatics the very ceiling—recorded with equal fame the damned and the saved: those who would surely ascend the golden escalator reserved for good guys and their trueblue pals, the real sports and square johns capable of breaking any Kolkowski's back; while upon the rusty freight elevator clanking miserably downward forever would go all copper johns, double clockers, lush workers and mush workers, deadpickers and turncoats, rats, pigeons, stooges, short faders and crap catchers, deadheads and deadbeats who had ever stood drinks for Kolkowski, loaned him a dollar or applauded that big flannel mouth.

Frankie could smell the walls. They were closer now than they had ever been; they bent together above him till the door seemed a part of the walls.

Walls which revealed that, by and large, the young men preferred the simple, straight-from-the-shoulder take-it-or-leave-it sort of warning:

All cops are stooges

Never rat on a pal

Get a steady job and stay home nights and keep off N. Clark.

While at the very bottom of the cell some latter-day Moses had written off all preceding commandments: *Everybody shut up. If you were any good you wouldn't be in here.*

In the growing light the wall legends continued like the continuation of a dream begun in another place: the legends that follow upon each other in all the tongues of man, from cell to cell and jail to jail, linking seas to cities and cities to plains, down the streets of all the world wherever a thief stands waiting behind steel bars and a turnkey waits by the wall.

In one corner some repentant bravo had inscribed a prayer for the salvation of all such sinners as himself, recommending them to John 3:7, and adding piously that he'd leave his body to the Board of Health and his ivory-tipped cue, locked in the middle rack at Spongy Kaplan's Snooker Palace and Pool Parlor, to Hines Memorial Hospital, providing such sacrifice would bring just a bit more sunshine into the lives of his fellow men.

Have Doc Bunson call for my body personlly, this soldier of the Lord had directed in a testament above the water bucket, *He is a personl friend of mine and no auto-topsy is necessry.*

While dated in the same week some revived will to live and still to do great deeds had come into the same wavering hand. Couched there in formidable obscenities the repentant bravo promised that same Lord he'd burn his old man's house to the ground within the hour he made the street and found the matches; adding an invitation to all rogue males within the city limits to enjoy his wife's favors on their first night out of the clink.

> My wife only sleeps with her friends and she don't have a enmy in the
> world. Call her at Madison 1-6971 and have yourselfs one hell of a time.
> The tramp married me for my alotment and my old man and her played
> the horses on my cash 19 months while I got scabies for my country over-
> seas. Now I'm headed for almoney row my old man & that tramp still
> playing them on my dough I can't even get a winner off her she just gives
> them to the old man I can go scratch my dirty scabies and she says thats
> my todays hot tip for you soldier—How you like them onions?

Whether anyone like them onions or not, there they were, all ready for peeling.

Frankie rolled over onto his side to examine the opposite wall in a sluggish hope that there might be some drawings of women there.

But any one side of any jailhouse wall is never much different than any other side. There are only the same old threadbare variations on the same age-old warnings against all the well-tried ancestral foes: whisky and women, sin and cigarettes, marijuana and morphine, marked cards and capped cocaine, dirty laughter and easy tears, engineered dice and casual disease, bad luck and adultery, old age and shyster lawyers, quack doctors and ambitious cops, crooked priests and honest burglars, lack of money and hard work.

Girls who would and girls who wouldn't. If they did they were no good and if they didn't what good were they? One biographer wanted to know and another replied smugly:

> All women are deseased

Yet went on to offer consolation for this blow:

> We're all victims of circumstance

And for further consolation to all of Circumstances' victims:

> Drink Dr. Jesse Blue's bay rum and get six months

While another hand countermanded all preceding instructions by commanding everyone, simply and to the point:

DRINK DERAIL

I'm just a jailbird, one bird of passage mourned, *Give me wings 'n I'll fly out.*
The only bird that flies out of here is a pigeon, another pointed out.
Held Fri. 9 pm to Tuesday showup 96 hours, some green youth protested.
This place gives me the baloney blues, yet another complained.
America the Anti-Christ Nation, one announced obscurely.
Never again, one promised forever.

Frankie examined the myriad dates, initials, and hearts pierced by a hundred unkept vows. Melancholy memories of men who had since gone down the city's thousand ways like sparks off a State Street trolley, leaving only these few poor scribblings to prove it had not been, after all, but a nightmare within a nightmare.

Frankie searched carefully, hoping to find the name or initials of someone he knew or fancied he once had known. But the single arresting detail he discovered was a woman's scratching, accomplished with a hairpin or barrette and almost obliterated with time, from years when the tier had been used for women.

> *A whore's life is always hell*
> *She's always living in a cell*

Signed, one could see through the grime, painstakingly; certain that this inscription was all she would ever have to bequeath to all good hustlers who were to follow:

> Lucille just a hard-luck bitch

What had become of sweet Lucille? Frankie wondered wistfully. And what was to become of Frankie Machine? Had unbearable bad luck taken her, as it seemed by way of taking him, for a long slow walk down a short and downhill pier? Or had it changed strangely, as his own was bound soon to change, just in the nick of time, on the night she'd met the Salvation Army drummer whose old man owned a Florida dog track? Had they truly reformed each other then? Had they, too, found, like Mr. and Mrs. Francis Majcinek would someday find, that everything turns out right after all? As everything always does? Had the dream man found his dream woman hadn't, somehow, been soiled by a thousand and one nights on North Clark Street after all? Did they find that a million dollars really made a difference in the end? Had it really ended like all good double features ought?

Good luck or bad, faithless or true, Lucille was gone with the Pulaski's tenderest close-ups, accompanied only by last night's slenderest shadows. And the dead-cold fog of North Clark Street through which she tapped on through the mists of nights no man remembered.

Along the tier a hundred thieves argued in sleep with unseen turnkeys: the unseen pokies of all thieves' dreams who stride, jangling the special keys to each thief's private nightmare, down all the lonely corridors of despair. There was no delivery from the dead end of lost chance. No escape from the blue steel bars of guilt.

Somewhere far above a steel moon shone, with equal grandeur, upon boulevard, alley and park; flophouse and penthouse, apartment hotel and tenement. Shone with that sort of wintry light that makes every city chimney, standing out against it in the cold, seem a sort of altar against a driving sky.

Beyond the bars light and shadow played ceaselessly, as it had played beneath so many long-set moons, for so many that had lain here before Frankie: the carefree and the careful ones, the crippled and the maimed, the foolhardy phonies and the bitter rebels; each to go his separate way, under his own private moon. Against a driving sky.

Upon the walls, as morning moved from the women's tiers down to where he lay, Frankie fancied many shadows: of Blind Pig with his cane stuck under his armpit; of Sparrow shuffling along with a shopping bag in his hand; of Sophie wheeling toward him and Nifty Louie, head hanging loosely, walking in sorrow away from everyone. Antek the Owner bent over his bar as if in prayer; Zygmunt the Prospector counting all his money; and Record Head Bednar studying two strays across his desk as if to say: "I figured you two'd be back."

Saw again the green baize table as it had been the night of the argument over the soiled silver dollar: Schwiefka looking down at him with the green silk bag in one hand and the other extended toward Frankie for his take. Yes, and behind Schwiefka, Bednar's shadow waiting forever for his take of Schwiefka's take.

Frankie Machine wasn't happy; yet Frankie wasn't too sad. He felt oddly relieved now that, for a while at least, all things would be solved for him. There was nothing he could do now about Sophie, nothing he could do about Molly, nothing he could do about boozing. Not a thing he could do about hitching up the reindeers for a sleigh ride through drifting snow.

"It'll be my chance to kick the habit for keeps," he realized. Caught between the wheelchair and the first floor front, between Old Crow and a little brown drugstore bottle, between his need for Molly Novotny and his need for the man with the thirty-five-pound monkey on his back, the dealer had found an iron sanctuary.

"When I get out I'll be straight as a cue, 'n Molly-O'll be so proud we'll stick together the rest of our lives 'n everythin' on the legit," Frankie assured himself.

And meant every word of it, too.

It was during that loneliest of all jailhouse hours, the hour between chow time and Lights-On, when empty pie plates stand in a double row, one or two before each cell waiting for a trusty to return them to the kitchen. Those within the cells slept the uneasy evening sleep till a buzzer sounded a measured warning and the sleepers wakened. Then all said at once that there, out there, just the other side of the green steel door, the snickerers were coming in. To accuse someone of everything and almost everyone of something and snicker at everyone in between.

A holiday air seemed suddenly to festoon the tier, as if a play for which all had rehearsed many times was to have an audience on the other side of the footlights at last. No one seemed worried about catching a finger out there. Everybody was in on a bad rap so how could anyone get fingered?

Already the snickerers were waiting restlessly, in darkened rows, to identify the man who'd slugged the night watchman and the one who'd snatched the purse through the window of the moving El; for he who'd chased somebody's virgin daughter down a blind alley or forged her daddy's signature; tapped a gas main or pulled a firebox; slit the janitor's throat in the coalbin or performed a casual abortion on the landlord's wife in lieu of paying the rent. All the things that had to be done to help someone else out of a jam. The little things done in simple fun and the big things done for love.

The snickerers were really too serious-minded. They suspected everybody and helped no one; they were afraid of one another and had almost no fun at all.

Frankie, offstage among other bit players, heard the voice of the evening's star and caught glimpses of that noble brow whenever the door opened and shut: Record Head Bednar lowering the mike to question a cap the color of any district-station corridor above a shirt broken out with blood spots.

"What you cuffed for?" Record Head longed to know.

"Took a cab home was all," Frankie heard Blood-Spots explain.

"That's no crime. Did you pay the driver?"

"I couldn't."

"Why not?"

"He wasn't in the cab."

"That's the chances you take. Next man."

The mike was moved before an old hallroom boy who stepped forward as proudly as a newly appointed ward committeeman at a politician's banquet, quavering importantly.

"Now I realize the true wort' of friendship—if a man has friends that's all he needs."

"You weren't looking for friends with a nine-inch file in a dentist's office. You were prospecting."

"I'm a maintenance engineer at Thompson's." As if that explained the file.

"You mean you have charge of the doughnuts?"

"I got a good record there."

"You got a good one here too." The captain waved the charge sheet before the mike and passed on to the next funny fellow.

"Back so soon, Julius?"

"*Back?* I ain't even been *gone.*"

"Silly Willie here hustles schoolboys out of their lunch money with phony dice," Record Head explained and returned his attention to Julius. "What were you carrying a pistol for?"

"For pertection."

"Protection from who? Those seventh-graders?"

"I brought it back from the service."

"How long were you in?"

"Thirty-eight days."

"How many times were you wounded?"

Julius permitted himself a derisive little one-sided smile, faintly contemptuous of all non-combatants, and let the listeners wait.

"Okay," Record Head forgave him impulsively, "we'll lock up the officer who pinched you. Okay?"

"Okay."

"Then we'll give you back the gun and an extra box of shells if you promise not to sue the city. Promise?"

"Suits me fine."

It suited Julius fine.

As the first line was led off the line behind the green steel door inched up a few feet and Frankie stood with a backstage view of the rows where, here and there among the listeners, a police badge glistened and all faces were dark and featureless. While upon the stage all faces were lined up under a glare that brought out every wrinkle, pimple and scar. A girl in plaid slacks was being urged forward by a police matron. Casting her eyes downward, the black arrows of the girl's lashes became dipped in two great tears.

"Save it for the jury, Betty Lou," the captain counseled her and turned to the listeners. "This is the slickest little knockout broad in seventeen states. How come you always pick on married men, Betty Lou?"

Betty Lou lifted the long damp lashes: the eyes held a wry and mocking light.

"They're the ones who don't sign complaints," she explained softly. And gave the audience a hard profile.

So the men came on again: the ragged, crouching, slouching, buoyant, blinking, belligerent, nameless, useless supermen from nowhere. "For climbin' a telephone pole at t'ree A.M. wit' a peanuts machine on my back." "For makin' anon'mous phone calls to call my wife dirty names." "Twice as big a crowd as here 'n a woman picked on me." "Went upstairs with a girl 'n came down with a cop."

A shock-haired razorback with a bright Bull Durham string hanging over his shirt pocket's edge: "Just throwed a rock at a wall 'n it happened to go through a window instead. So I followed through. But I didn't have no *intent* of stealing."

"You never have. But you're in and out like a fiddler's elbow all the same. What was the stretch in the Brushy Mountain pen for?"

"I got the wrong number was all."

"I think you did. The wrong house number."

"That's right. The people were home. I was drinking pretty heavy."

"What do you do when you're drinking light?"

"Mind my own business."

"You haven't got any business. For a quarter you'd steal the straw out of your mother's kennel."

The razorback tossed his tawny shock and his face in that light looked tawny too. "What I'd do for a quarter you'd do for a dime." And held the captain's gaze to prove it.

Record Head's heart felt suddenly as if it were beating without love for any man at all. The finger of accusation leveled at him so steadily by a shock-haired boy revived in him the dream in which he was the pursued.

"How'd you like it in the pen?" he asked in old routine.

"I didn't."

"Why not? Wouldn't the warden give you his job?" That was always the answer to *that* one. They always stepped into it the same way.

Yet the light titter of lip laughter that followed, as it was always so sure to follow, didn't fill the emptiness down the dry well of the captain's heart. He listened to the next youth, an epileptic in a dark green wool sweater and a stocking cap, without really hearing the boy's words at all.

"Just havin' fun with a little girl—I was in Dixon but my old man got me out, I was gettin' worse. When I fool around a little I get better."

"Well," the captain thought absently, "we all feel better if we fool around a little"—and caught himself up sharply. "I need a rest is all," he decided, and forgave himself uneasily.

As he could not forgive one of those up there under the lights.

"A friend of mine went to sleep and I took his money before somebody else did." "For unbecoming words to a lady, I think it's called." "For tryin' to talk a friend out of trouble—he was settin' in a patrol wagon, I told him to come out of there, so they put me in with him." "Went down to the West Side to round up bums for a labor gang 'n got picked up for one myself." "Picked up at an unreasonable hour."

Of late all hours to the captain seemed unreasonable. "I know you," he thought cunningly of all outlaws. "I know you. I know you all."

Till the next line's shadows came on, and the outlaws followed their shadows.

Followed their shadows into the glare; and left the glare once more to shadows.

It made the captain want to shield his own eyes; for a moment he looked ready to cup his head in his hands. "The old boy is drivin' himself as hard as he's drivin' the bums," Frankie thought with a certain malice. Then the glare hit his own eyes.

A glare that made any man look like a plastic job with a prefabricated expression grafted on, according to some criminologist's graph or other, to fit the crime of which the captain's charge sheet had him accused: here was a pickpocket's deadpan mask and here a shoplifter's measured manner. Here the brutal lines of the paid-in-full premeditated murderer and there the coneroo's cynical leer.

Yet the man behind the murderer's mask was under the lights for stealing a bushel of mustard greens and the coneroo's leer had been picked up for oversleeping in a Halsted Street hallway.

"Why you living on Skid Row?"

"'Cause I'm on the skids. That's plain enough."

And the black and bitter orange of the brownskin buck's sweater standing out so strongly and strangely against the fluffy white and pale blue of the aging white beside him.

The listeners watched the captain survey the next man, up and down, head to toe and back again, to ask at last: "Where's your shoes, boy?"

"Left 'em in the tavern."

"Hadn't there been a fight in there?"

"Lord, there's always a fight in *there*."

"Then you know the place."

"Sure. I hang in there."

"Where? On a hook?"

"No. By the bar. I preach salvation there."

"Where were you ordained?"

"I just have a local preacher's license."

"How do you get one of those?"

"You have to see the pastor and the deacon."

"How about the precinct captain?"

"He's in jail."

"I think that's where you get most of your philosophy yourself."

"That's where I took up the ministry all right."

"Can't you preach salvation with your shoes on? Is that some Hindu cult out there says you have to take off your shoes?"

"No, sir. I was collectin'."

"But couldn't you collect with your shoes *on?*" The captain sounded determined.

"It was my shoes I was trying to collect."

The captain leaned forward, steadied his head with both hands and pleaded as if already fearing the reply: "Just tell me one thing—*who* had your shoes?"

"Why, the precinct captain, of course. That's what I been tryin' to tell you."

The captain shook his head with the melancholy manner of any man who knows he can't win and motioned wearily for the mike to be moved on.

"Next man, what for?"

"For standin' by watchin'."

"Watchin' *what?*"

"The officers linin' up the boys on Thirty-first Street."

Bednar took a moment to raise himself slowly onto his toes to make certain that this one was wearing sandals or any sort of footwear at all. "I don't want to go through *that* again," he cautioned himself aloud. "They lined you up too?"

"One of the officers called me 'boy' and I told him I was a man so I had to come along."

"The milk's still wet behind your ears, a boy is all you are. But you'll be Joliet-bound before they're dry 'n they'll make a man of you there. Next."

"I'm accused of rape."

"How old was that child?"

"Thirty-seven. She volunteered her services."

"She volunteer her ring and watch too?"

"Yes, sir."

"What a man. Weren't you the one who was in here last August for assault-ing your baby?"

"That's some misidentity. All that happened was I dropped the lid when the Mrs. slugged me with the fuel-oil can."

"What about that gun charge in 1944? Was that 'some misidentity'?"

"I was a janitor then 'n had to protect myself from tenants."

"Making you a janitor is like putting an automobile thief in charge of a park-ing lot. You're the biggest misidentity ever walked in shoe leather."

The captain's eyes went down the line. The masks were managing to change, slowly and ever so slyly, to look less like plastic men and more like some plas-tic zoo: animals stuffed for some State Street Toyland the week before Christmas. Here was the toothless tiger and here the timid lion, here the bull that loved flowers and there some lovelorn moose.

The toothless tiger stood in a faded yellow hat from some long-faded sum-mer, his stripes blurred by the city jungle's dust and sprayed blood dried on the hat's stiff brim: but still trying to look like a tiger. It always seemed some long-faded summer for those who lived in that feral glare under one hard straw kelly or another; or any old hat at all.

"My buddy hit me wit' a Coca-Cola bottle," the toothless tiger explained, "so I bust his plate-glass window."

"You're mixed up with so many busted windows you ought to join the fire department. Ever do time?"

"Just a week once, for robbery."

"Only a *week?*"

Frankie had to crane his head to get a glimpse of this one. For every time the audience snickered Frankie snickered too. He'd have to remember all the things these fools said to tell Molly-O some day.

"It was just a small robbery."

The captain's eyes besought the darkened rows for help but the rows only looked back at him bleakly. Till the next odd fish stood forth.

"Officers don't like my looks is all. I sell strictly American merchandise and don't have no complaints."

"If they don't complain it's because they're ashamed to admit buying the stuff. You sneak up and offer them phony jewelry as if it were hot stuff," the captain accused him.

"It ain't phony, it's American-made," the coneroo begged off.

"Well," the captain pondered, "you been acting funny since 1919 and most of the cops who used to arrest you are dead. How'd you beat that federal rap? You must have had a good lawyer."

"No lawyer at all."

"Who prepared the writ?"

"Another con. He shuffled off a little time for me."

A nerve tugged suddenly at the captain's left wrist as if someone unseen were trying to cuff it to the mike. "You another one of them window smashers?" he asked the boy in the black-and-white lumberjack.

"No, sir. I'm a seaman."

"Then how'd the window get broken?"

"Knocked my old man through it."

"You're a seaman all right. On the Humboldt Park lagoon."

The Humboldt Park salt snickered. "Very funny," he observed. "Captain, you're killing me."

The flat-nosed, square-faced, tousled blond with the dark lines under the eyes was next. With his left sleeve slit to the shoulder. As if his life, like his knife, had been turned upon himself at last.

"Francis Majcinek, *Divi*sion Arms *Hotel*," and added indulgently: "That's on *Divi*sion."

"Thank you. I always thought it was on Eighth and Wabash—where's the punk?"

"Wasn't picked up with no punk."

"Talk into the mike, not at me. And get off that back rail. What were you up to with the shopping bag at Nieboldt's, Dealer?"

"Went to buy an eye-ron."

"With a shopping bag?"

"Had to stop by the butcher's on the first floor."

"You should of stayed on the first floor. Those weren't lamb chops fell out of the bag."

Frankie grinned. He could still see those damned irons bouncing.

"Get that grin off your puss—what else did you boost over the holidays?"

Frankie managed a look of blandest innocence. "You got me wrong, Captain. I was lookin' around for the cashier—"

"When the bag broke," the captain finished for him. And eyed him broodingly. "I like liars," he decided at last, "but you suit me too well. What did you need *six* irons for? I don't suppose you were planning on *selling* them?"

"No, nothing like that, Captain," Frankie assured Bednar earnestly, "I needed one for the wife 'n the others were for when that one wore out. They make things so *cheap* these days."

"I don't know who you think you're kidding or whether you're trying to be funny," Bednar told him, studying him to find out what was really the matter. There was something wrong all right, the dealer really wasn't trying to be funny at all; his face had somehow altered in the past month. At the moment it looked both pious and weak. "Come down off that cross 'n give me a straight story," the captain pleaded—and as he asked it he got it—in one moment he knew beyond any doubt at all. "How long you been on the stuff, Frankie?"

Frankie heard the small, reluctant note of surprised sympathy under Record Head's voice.

"Not too long," he acknowledged easily, coming down off the cross in return for that small reluctant note. "I've kicked it."

"Where you're going you'll have to kick it. You think you can straighten up out there?"

"I'm straight now."

"And you won't go right back on it when you make the street again?"

"I've learned my lesson, Captain."

"I hope to God you have."

The captain took off his glasses and covered his eyes, to rest them from the light a moment. When he replaced them he studied Frankie's charge sheet a long minute, while Frankie shifted restlessly in the glare and wished they'd move the damned mike away from his chin. When he heard the captain's voice again he turned his head attentively toward the shadow out of which the voice came at him.

"Here's a man with thirty-six months service and the Purple Heart," he heard Bednar telling the listeners, "he was a fast hustler with a deck when he went in the service and he's probably faster now. Are you one of Kippel's torpedoes now, Frankie?"

"All I do is deal, Captain."

"How long you been out of the army?"

"Over a year."

"And Louie Fomorowski been dead how long?"

"I didn't even know the fellow was sick, Captain."

"Then you did know the man?"

"Heard of him."

"Seen him on your bedpost lately?"

"I sleep pretty sound."

"You don't look it. Frankie, you don't look like you slept in a month." And never took his eyes off Frankie all the while the mike was being moved. While Frankie looked straight ahead.

"Not a nerve in his body," the wondering listeners heard the captain murmur at last.

In the brief interval between the departure of one line and the arrival of the next the captain leaned forward on his elbows and spread his fingers gently across his temples; the light kept hurting his eyes. And didn't feel he had heart enough left to face one more man manacled by steel or circumstance until his own heart should stop hurting.

Yet they come on and come on, and where they come from no captain knows and where they go no captain goes: mush workers and lush workers, catamites and sodomites, bucket workers and bail jumpers, till tappers and assistant pickpockets, square johns and copper johns; lamisters and hallroom boys, ancient pious perverts and old blown parolees, rapoes and record-men; the damned and the undaunted, the jaunty and condemned.

Heartbroken bummies and the bitter rebels: afternoon prowlers and midnight creepers. Peeping Toms and firebox pullers. The old cold-deckers and the young torpedoes coming on faster than the law can pick them up.

The unlucky brothers with the hustlers' hearts.

"It says here you were annoying a ten-year-old girl."

"I beg your *par*don."

"Beg my pardon for *what?*"

"It was a ten-year-old boy."

The captain crossed himself. "I beg *your* pardon," he apologized, adding under his breath, "through your jugular vein." The captain felt ready for almost anything tonight, in the weariest sort of way. For knowing the answers to every alibi and having a tailor-made quip ready for every answer only seemed to make him wearier than ever of late.

"Snatched a purse where Sinatra was singing."

"Do you swoon too?" The captain was weary tonight all right.

Worst of all were the witnesses who snickered after every questioning. If only, just once, one of them would laugh out from the heart.

And felt the finger of guilt again tap his forehead and the need of confession touch his heart like touching a stranger's heart. A voice like his own voice, confident and accusing: "That's your man, Captain. That's your man." A voice like his own voice. Yet a heart like a hustler's heart.

"I'm affiliated with two bolts of poster paper," the odd fish near the end of the line announced before he was asked.

"Are you sure you're not incorporated?" the captain wanted to know.

"Put a cigar in my pocket 'n set my coat on fire," the next youth offered cheerfully.

"Why didn't you pull the firebox?"

"What do you think I'm here for?"

"I picked up a drunk," a South State Street strongarmer explained.

"I'll say you did. By the pockets."

"I got a perforated eardrum," the next pointed out as though that condition justified all felonies under ten thousand dollars.

"You must have got it crawling in 'n out of transoms," the captain diagnosed him, "you can still hear a squad car coming, can't you?"

"If I could I wouldn't be here."

"How long were you in Leavenworth?"

"Five years eight months twenny-eight days."

"How many minutes?"

"Next time I'll take a watch."

"Next time you won't need one. You're a habitual." Just as the captain said that his mind jumped to a conviction as automatic as it was without basis in the charge sheet: the dealer had had the punk with him.

Out of the file he kept in his head Bednar slipped a certain arrest slip. Then slipped it back feeling pleased with Mr. Schnackenberg's bill that made two felonies, of the same nature, add up to recidivism. The punk must have had a quicker eye for that ace in the draperies.

"Not off one conviction I ain't no habitual," the ex-con on the platform answered the captain's accusation at last.

"You'll have your day in court," the captain assured him. "Tell the court that Belgian .22 was to pick your teeth with. Maybe they'll believe you. I don't."

The man with the Southern Comfort accent and the true assassin's mug complained sullenly, "I ain't been in trouble in eleven years. They made a believer of me on Governor's Island. When I got out I got a lunch pail."

"Next time get a transparent one so the officers can see what's in it."

The captain had an answer for everything tonight. He hadn't been listening to their lies for twenty-odd years for nothing.

"I cook on the Santa Fe."

"Glad to know it. After this I'll ride the Southern Pacific." He dismissed the cook for some gaunt wreck in a smudged clerical collar. "Are you a preacher?" The captain sounded puzzled.

"I've been defrocked."

"You still preach pretty good when it comes to cashing phony checks. What were you defrocked for?"

"Because I believe we are all members of one another."

That one stopped the captain cold. He studied the wreck as if suddenly so uncertain of himself that he was afraid to ask him what he had meant by that. "I don't get it," he acknowledged at last, and passed on, with greater confidence, to a little heroin-head batting his eyes and coughing the little dry addict's cough politely into his palm.

"I ain't used the stuff for fourteen years," he lied right into the mike the moment it was moved to his lips.

"Then how come you were shooting that girl in the arm when the cops come in? You were putting her on it too, you Fagin."

"How *could* I? She been on it longer than I have."

"Tell that to a mule and he'll kick your head off. The girl is nineteen and you're forty-four and on top of that you had her so drunk she didn't even know her own name."

"Well, she acts older. 'N I ain't forty-four. I'm thirty-nine 'n that chick is twenty if she's a month."

The heroin head smiled virtuously at having established his innocence so irreproachably.

As the final line shuffled off the listeners rose in the rows as though to wish all such irreproachable innocents long life and good health on the way. Under the dimming lights the innocents filed through a green steel doorway into a deepening darkness.

But the listeners straightened their trousers and smoothed their dresses down and one by one, by twos and threes, by smiling threes and laughing fours, all left through a well-lighted door onto a clean well-lighted street.

With nothing, it seemed, to fear in the world at all.

Only the captain, trapped between the hunters and the hunted, looked mournfully through that green steel door as though yearning to follow his innocents there.

To follow each man to a cell all his own, there to confess the thousand sins he had committed in his heart.

For he seemed to see them still, each with the left hand manacled and the right thrown protectively across the eyes.

As his own left hand, in dreams, seemed cuffed, of late, to smooth cold steel. As he had one morning wakened to find his own right hand flung across his eyes. "I'll get dark shades for the bedroom," Record Head decided restlessly, "the light is wakin' me up too early."

For there was no priest to wash clean the guilt of the captain's darkening spirit nor any judge to hear his accusing heart. The court forbade him entrance to that narrow green steel door. Justice had been done; his case was closed. He could not even tell the names of those who'd taken the rap for him.

To leave him, of all men most alone, of all men most guilty of all the lusts he had ever condemned in others.

What was it that the defrocked priest had said? "We are all members of one another." What had the holy-sounding fraud meant by *that*? Why had several snickered then and not one had laughed out from the heart? Bednar hadn't understood then and could not let himself understand now. It had been too long since he himself had laughed from the heart.

Yet the words had left him with a secret and wishful envy of every man with a sentence hanging over his head like the very promise of salvation. Leaving him with no recourse save to swallow his own dark guilt, like a piece of spoiled meat in the throat, and turn out the chargesheet lamp.

"Come down off that cross yourself," he counseled himself sternly, like warning another.

But the captain couldn't come down.

The captain was impaled.

II

ACT OF CONTRITION

F. SCOTT FITZGERALD *In the real dark night of the soul it is always three o'clock in the morning, day after day.*

Frankie lived by day beside the ceaseless, dumping shuffle of the three-legged elephant which was the laundry's sheet-rolling machine. When he piled onto his narrow pad in the long dim-lit dorm at night and turned his face to the white-washed wall, the three-legged elephant of the mangle roller followed, galumphing, through dreams wherein he dealt Record Head Bednar hand after hand while Louie Fomorowski watched from behind the captain's chair. Night after night.

When the lights were down all voices were subdued. Down the long and low-roofed hall the good boys slept: the laundry and the bakery workers, the printshop typesetters and the boys who sat in classrooms and accepted their sentences with the dry, hard-bitten humor of old contented soldiers. These were the ones who had convinced the chaplain that they were really going straight this time. Frankie too had convinced the chaplain.

It had been harder to convince a certain ex-army major. "That vein been injured," he'd told Frankie in the infirmary on Frankie's very first morning. "How long you been punchin' holes in it?"

"I been on the sleeve since I got out of the army, Doc," Frankie told him.

"How big a habit you got, son?"

"Not too big. I go for a quarter grain a day."

"Big enough. But I've seen them come in here hooked worse than that 'n still kick it. In here you got to kick it. When you get sick I'll taper you off and if you behave yourself you'll be out for Thanksgiving and have it kicked for keeps. Still, there's boys in here who'll tell you they can get you anything from heroin to gage for a price—forget it. Capone couldn't afford the price. But if you get out of line any time you're in here—remember that you're on the books as a user. I'll get you shipped to Lexington 'n that won't be for a week end the way it used to be. That'll be six months added. I tell you now for your own good and I won't tell you again."

Frankie gave him the grin. "I'll tough it out, Doc."

After that Frankie slipped into a life like the life of the barracks he had known for three years. Orders were given matter-of-factly without threats; and were obeyed complacently. Most of the men kept themselves as clean as if preparing for retreat each evening and most, out of sheer boredom, attended services in the pink-and-white chapel on Sunday morning. And each good soldier counted his two days off a month, for good behavior, like money in the bank and well earned.

All but Applejack Katz, with a long-term lease on the cot next to Frankie's own: a man who daily risked his good-conduct time for the sake of a certain jar fermenting under the ventilator. He'd bought cider from one of the kitchen workers and, at every meal where boiled potatoes were served, stole the skins and made Frankie steal them too. He added the potato skins to the cider after lights out and was only waiting for a chance to snatch a few white-bread crusts. "When we get them crusts it'll only take a week after that," he promised Frankie. He leaned across the cot to add a low warning word:

"I seen you come out of the infirmary your first morning, Dealer. My advice to you is look out for the major. He's a psycho. What he'll do to you is to get you so square you'll never have another day's pleasure in your life."

Katz glanced about the dormitory with a look so swift and furtive Frankie was reminded, with a troubling pang, of Sparrow Saltskin.

"Listen. They sent *me* to a psycho eight years ago. I was forty-five then 'n if I'd worked two full weeks in my life I don't remember where. If anyone had told me, eight years ago, I'd go to work for eight hours a day six days a week and stick at it over two years I would of give him hundred to one against it. 'N I would of lost. 'Cause that's just how square I got.

"For two years I was off the booze, off the women, off the horses, off the dice. I even got engaged to get married in a church. All I done that whole time was run a freight elevator up 'n down, up 'n down. It scares me when I think of it now: I come near losin' everything."

Applejack lay back in the very real relief of one snatched from the eternal fires, at the last possible moment, straight up into Salvation Everlasting. He gave a low laugh, mocking and wise.

"Now they're after me to go back to that same psycho. 'He done me so much good that other time,' they try to tell me, 'he almost cured my new-rosis.' Sure the fool almost cured my 'new-rosis.' If I went back he might cure it alto-gether—and what would I have left? All the good times I ever had in my life was what my little old new-rosis *made* me have. Them whole two years on the square I didn't have one good time. I *like* my little old new-rosis. It's all I got 'n I'm holdin' onto it hard. My advice to you is hold onto yours: lay off them psy-chos. Look out for the major. When guys like you 'n me get square we're dead."

Katz had a record that read like a Southern Pacific Railroad schedule. He'd made every stop between Jeff City and Fort Worth and had fashioned applejack out of white-bread crusts and potato skins in every one. Of his fifty-odd years fifteen had been spent between walls and he recounted each one in terms of applejack. Sometimes it had been hard to make and had turned out badly, in other places it had been easy and had turned out fine: his life was the definitive work on the science of making applejack under the eyes of prison guards.

He remembered certain jugs as if remembering certain people: the El Paso County Jug, recalled with joy and a certain tenderness, that he had kept filled, through a kitchen connection, night and day for six blissful months. The Grant's Pass Jug, recalled with bitterness and doubt, that had been spirited out of his cell in the night and never seen again.

But applejack wasn't Katz's only interest. He had half a dozen minor pro-jects going, involving the bartering of nutmeg for Bull Durham, of Bull Durham for nutmeg and of emory for the manufacture of something he called a "glin wheel," a sort of homemade cigarette lighter. It was also his daily con-cern, while working beside Frankie on the mangle roller, to steal the paraffin wax off the rollers for the making of candles, which he sold clandestinely to the harder cons upstairs.

The cons up there were either in bug cells or deadlock. They were the pri-vates who went for stronger brew than applejack. These no longer cared: these

were the truly unsaved. Over the hump for redemption and the hour for turning back lost forever: too late, forever too late. So they hurried forward all the
faster into the darkness.

They talked in terms of police administrations and remembered in terms
of police cars. "That was the year the aces had black Cadillacs with a bell on
the side—or was that the year they had them speedy orange Fords?"

One night some pale castoff, a twenty-year-old so far gone in narcoticism
that nothing but the one big bitter fix of death could cure him, was placed
among the good soldiers either by error or just to see how long he could stand
it there.

It didn't take long for the panic to start. One look at the stolid faces about
him, he knew he was in the wrong tier and the horrors shook him like an icy
wind.

"Bond me out! Don't touch me!"

The junkie wants a bondsman though he doesn't own a dime. His life is
down to a tight pin point and the pupils of his eyes drawn even tighter: nothing is reflected in them except a capsule of light the size of a single quarter
grain of morphine. He has mounted the walls of all his troubles with no other
help than that offered by the snow-white caps in the brown drugstore bottle.
A self-made man.

But all the drugstores are closed tonight.

"Bond me out! Bond me out!"

And the flood of shameless tears. By the time the major shuffled in, yawning, with the hypo, the junkie was throwing a regular circus for the boys, tossing himself about on the floor. It took four men to hold him down to give him
his charge at last.

"I think he ate somethin' didn't agree with him," Applejack observed after
the youth was carried out. Such exhibitions seemingly required this flat, cold
sort of mirth. The only laughter that broke the monotony here was that same
hard-bitten glee: "The service is gettin' pretty bad when a man has to knock
his skull on the floor to get a charge of M. I remember a time when all you had
to do was hold your breath for half an hour."

Yet such pale youths felt as devout about their addiction as others might of
some crotchety religious conviction or other. "I'm just the type *got* to have it,
that's all. It's how I'm built. Don't ask me *why*—how do *I* know? It's just *something*, cousin. It's *there*."

Frankie Machine understood too well. Standing at the sheet roller on his eleventh morning, it hit him so hard and so fast he went down beside the machine while the sheets, unguided, twisted and tore themselves to shreds at the very moment that his own entrails were tearing at his throat and his very bones were twisting. He heard his own voice crying as shrill as a wounded tom-cat's down the icy corridors of his anguish.

He lay eight hours in a 104 fever before the major pulled him out of it with dolaphine.

"If you get sick on me like that again you won't even get paregoric off me," were the first words he could distinguish, and blinked the sweat out of his eyes to see the major studying him. "Next time I'm lettin' you sweat it out, soldier."

Back at the sheet roller two mornings later, Frankie felt he'd already sweated it out. All that remained of his sickness was a couple days of the chuck horrors, of which Nifty Louie once had told. "It feels like I got a tape snake or some-thin'," he complained to Applejack Katz, "every two hours the bottom falls out of my gut 'n I feel like I could eat myself through a cow on the hoof."

Katz traded off his "glin wheel" to a kitchen connection for a pound of lump sugar and gave it to Frankie. Frankie consumed it in a single day.

"Wait till the applejack is ready," Applejack immediately promised him, "that'll kill the chucks every time."

"Ain't it ready yet?" Frankie pleaded a little, he still felt so weak.

"Give it just one more day," Applejack promised.

Katz could give anything he owned to anyone but the warden. Except that applejack. He was no more able to give that away than to give away his blood.

When the horrors had passed at last Frankie felt himself beginning to want Molly-O again. He hadn't had one visitor, not so much as a letter or a card, in all those hard first two weeks.

But he'd gotten to know some of the boys who were neither trying to be good soldiers, like himself, nor bad ones like those upstairs.

These were the ones who just wouldn't work. Yardbirds who couldn't quite be trusted in a bakery or a laundry. They never disobeyed an order directly nor made trouble nor talked back. But time off for good conduct means little to men with no place to go and nothing in particular to do when they get there. They were men and youths who had never picked up any sort of craft—though most of them could learn anything requiring a mechanical turn with ease. It wasn't so much lack of aptitude as it was simply the feeling that no work had any point to it. They lived in prison much as they had lived out of it, vaguely contented most of the time, neither hoping nor despairing, wanting nothing but a place to sleep and a tin pie plate with some sort of slop or other on it a couple times a day. They neither worried about the future, regretted the past nor felt concern for the present.

They were the ones who had never learned to want. For they were secretly afraid of being alive and the less they desired the closer they came to death. They had never been given one good reason for applying their strength. So now they disavowed their strength by all sorts of self-deceptions.

They gave nothing because nothing had been given them. If they lost their privileges they shrugged it off, they had lost certain privileges before; one way or another they had had always to forfeit any small advantage gained by luck, chance or stealth.

Some slept at the race-track barns all summer and crashed County in the winter, year after year. Getting back to the barns a week sooner or later didn't mean much, it would probably be raining that week anyhow. So why get all steamed up in a laundry all winter for nothing? Where was the payoff?

They didn't even read comic books. They had been bored to death by all that the day before they were born. The whole business between birth and death was a sort of inverted comic strip, too dull to read even if set right. So what was the difference whether a man slept on wood or hay?

"Rubber heels 'n fisheyes again" was the word on the meatloaf and tapioca, "but wait till we get that mountain goat"—warless soldiers as indifferent to Sunday mutton as the walls were indifferent to themselves; yet feigning to look forward to a Sunday dinner as tasteless in the mouth as life was in their hearts.

Sometimes something wakened and flared feebly in one of these: he talked back and got to think it over in deadlock.

Deadlock was any cell with a red metal tag locked onto the bars to indicate the man was either a junkie or just out of line. As long as the tag stayed there it meant no yard privileges, no cigarettes, no newspapers and no mail; no candy, no card playing and the next time maybe you'll keep that big trap buttoned.

Deadlock meant a monotony more deadly even than the regular abnormal monotony of jailhouse days and nights. For no one can sleep all the time and deadlock brought hours when memory caught up with a man at last. Hours in which to sit and remember that willing long-ago lovely who'd married some square after all; or a family that cared less than ever. Or how suddenly the rain had come one blue-and-gold Easter Sunday a dozen blue-gold Easters ago.

Thinking of release only slowed the hours down to the deadliest crawl of all—yet of what else was there to think? And what could freedom mean except a chance to get out of the state with one clean shirt on your back and jump back on the con the day it got dirty? You had to get across the state line to promote some decent clothes and enough change in the poke to take a woman to a movie or a bar.

So the deadlockers walked up and down till they grew weak at the knees, slept and rose to walk again till night and day and the weariness in the knees and the weariness of the mind all rolled together into one big cell-sized, life-sized weariness.

"The day after I come out of deadlock the first time," Applejack Katz told Frankie, "I seen how they got all the clocks stopped at twelve o'clock 'n I realized I was in deadlock whether I was in a cell with a red tag on it or not."

Till night and day were one and the heart itself felt like a clock stopped cold on a dead-cold hour.

The very hour that life was to begin; and would not tick again.

Yet even a stopped clock can be right for a while. If time moves slowly enough. And Frankie lived in a deadlock only somewhat darker and narrower than that deadlock in which all his days had been spent.

Just one bit lighter than the deadlock of the cells with the red metal tag.

To the tune of some old frayed song, offered over and over again by Applejack Katz in his horrible fifty-four-year-old squawk.

> *"I'm a ding-dong daddy from Duma*
> *'N you oughta see me do my stuff."*

Till all the other cots would howl him down.

"That stuff ought to be about ready," Frankie hinted.

Applejack felt it wasn't yet sufficiently fermented.

Though Frankie would hear him rise in the night, fumble about under the ventilator, hear the secret gulping in the dark and the sound of the cork being carefully replaced; and once, long after lights out, that querulous, quavering squawk.

> *"I'd feel bad if you'd kissed too many*
> *But I'd feel worse if you hadn't kissed any."*

All the next day, working beside Frankie at the mangle roller, Katz murmured songs as frayed as his voice. There was a certain sly merriment about old Applejack. One felt that, secretly, he was convinced he'd already beaten the state on so many charges that there was no chance at all of the state getting it back in terms of timeserving. He could be in the rest of his life, he knew, and still end up far ahead of the game.

Down in the G-H blocks the punks from eighteen to twenty lived in shifts more sullen than that which Frankie shared with Katz. G was for the black punks and H for the whites. The whites went to school in the mornings and blacks in the afternoons. The sign in the mess-hall library said:

THINK
Read a good book

Which didn't at all mean that a black punk should be caught reading a good book at the same time as a white punk; and didn't say just what book. Each went to think separately, for the thinking of separate thoughts. For the black con's brain, it appeared, was darker than the white con's and therefore required the afternoon sunlight to assist the thinking of certain scheduled thoughts.

Yet, strangely enough, the chair in the basement accepted any color at all. Indeed, it was painted black just to show how little race feeling there was down there in the basement where the afternoon sunlight didn't shine at all.

Nor did the big black sheriff's wagon that pulled up for the haul to Stateville, St. Charles, Dixon and Menard draw any particular color line.

The punks piled in it, leaping over each other as if going on a picnic, filled with a sudden brainless, coltish joy to be out of the cells and riding in the open air for the hour that took them down Route 66. One hour. The years to follow were forgotten in the brightness of the immediate sun.

Screwy punks and tough punks, wise punks and dumb punks, dirty punks and clean punks, little punks and big punks, skinny punks and fat punks: here comes the wagon and we'll all take a ride.

Here comes the sheriff's wagon, punks, and you'll be a long time gone.

While all clocks will remain forever, however long you serve, precisely at twelve o'clock.

"A.M. or P.M.?" Frankie Machine wondered idly, as if it really made some difference. If you wanted to know the time you asked the screw and were told, inevitably: "Forget it. You ain't goin' nowheres."

The time the clockmakers had locked into the stopped clocks of these corridors was a different kind of time, Frankie felt, than that they had put into the
clocks outside. Just as there was a different sort of time for cripples than for
junkies, and a different kind of time than either for dealers, there was a special
kind of time for convicts too.

On Sundays he went to Mass, in the pink-and-white chapel lined with por-
trayals of the Stations of the Cross, fashioned by some forgotten felon. He
always knelt beneath one labeled *Jesus Falls the First Time,* he didn't know why.
Yet that one touched him most.

He would cross himself, genuflect and assure himself mystically, "Zosh'll be
so much better when I get out I'll be able to tell her about me 'n Molly-O
myself, I won't have to let Vi do the dirty job for me." On some Sunday morning dream train with the incense in his nose.

When his next ten days had passed without any recurrence of the sickness he
began drawing fresh courage with the passing of each new day. "The hell with Nifty
Louie 'n Private McGantic, too," he told himself one night, refusing either to see
Louie "on his bedpost" as Bednar had put it or to worry about McGantic's terrible
monkey. "Louie was a long time livin' and he'll be a long time dead and there's
more people better off for his bein' out of the way than not." And the memory of
that hallway blow returned to him like the memory of a blow by which he had
freed himself from McGantic's monkey. He felt not the faintest flutter of remorse
for his part in the passing of Louie F. Remorse touched his memory of the fixer
only when he recalled that, by losing his head, he had lost the fixer's big fat roll.

From the passage of the nights now he gained more strength than he had
ever gained from a hypo. He felt himself getting over the roughest point of the
hump without so much as a quarter grain to help him over. And knowing how
proud Molly-O was going to be for him, felt proud of himself.

The pride he'd abandoned in the ward tent on the narrow Meuse. Through
the open laundry window the first cold hint of spring touched him as had that
other spring on that cold and alien river.

"I got the second paw off," he confided to Katz; like a man who'd seen a fes-
tering wound in his flesh dry before his eyes and slowly start to heal.

For now all things healed strangely well within him, as though by grace of his
punishment. He was paying off for smashing up Sophie, the irons had only been
God's means to let him, a priest told him; so that when he was released everything he'd done would be paid for and he'd be truly free at last.

"I feel like, someday, I'm gonna shine again," he told old Applejack.

And heard, through walls as high as tenement walls, a long, slow, dull whirr-whirr.

As of a heavy sewing machine being pedaled by some lame and sweating con.

Ten o'clock in the morning. Above the visitors' cage burned one small dull red bulb and right below it, peering through the glass with the prison pallor on his face but the shadows gone from under his eyes, Frankie Machine waited for his first visitor; though they hadn't told him who it was. Certainly the punk wouldn't have the nerve to come around after the way he'd pulled out of the deal with the irons, ducking without a warning word so that Frankie might have gotten rid of that damned bag.

Then spotted Molly Novotny far down the line, trying to see over the heads of the other visitors like a child trying to see the animals in the zoo over the heads of the adults and saw him at last.

She took his breath away with her pertness: a neat dark suit and little silver-heeled slippers that tap-tapped right on up to him just as she'd tapped into his arms on the first floor front.

They had only fifteen minutes and he didn't know what to ask first. There was so much he had to know and she had so much to tell.

"That poor old man of Vi's is gone," was the first thing she reported. "He leaned out the window too far."

"So long as he wasn't pushed," Frankie told her.

"No, Vi just forgot to lock the window."

And they passed over Poor Old Husband as indifferently as life itself had passed Poor Husband by. "How's Zosh?" he wanted to know.

"Gettin' fatter than ever, Frankie," and heard the ancient malice in her voice.

"How are things going at the Safari?" As soon as he asked that he knew he shouldn't have. For she didn't lower her eyes, she simply curtained them from him and he'd never seen her look so hard.

"I ain't there no more, Frankie," she told him defensively. "I don't live downstairs no more."

"Where you livin', Molly?" A leaden fear had him. He had to ask her twice before she could hear through the glass. Or just didn't want to hear.

"Just around, Frankie. I'm just livin' around. You know."

The red bulb winked, the whistle blew, Visitors' Day was over.

And knew in his bones she wouldn't return on any Visitors' Day to come.

"Little Lester," he called himself. "Little Lester the Money Waster and Woman Chaser" and he lived up there in the bug cells with all appeals but the last one gone.

Down where Frankie lived below rumors came each night of Little Lester's latest piece of arrogance in the very face of the big black chair. But Frankie never got to lay eye on the fellow till, on the Saturday afternoon of Frankie's sixth week, he caught a detail with Katz.

"You two get the Susie-Q wagon 'n get up there to the fourth floor," Screw told them, "there's a ticket on both of you for talkin' in line."

There wasn't much to the detail. The Susie-Q wagon was the little white cart on which mops and buckets were borne. The fourth-floor boys themselves couldn't be trusted with buckets and mops. Half of them were in deadlock and those that weren't never moved without a screw's eyes following. They were the sullen jug-heavies and the loudmouthed torpedoes, the gaunt jungle buzzards and the true assassins.

"Me 'n you 'r just punks up against some of these birds," Applejack reminded Frankie in secret admiration of all assassins and Frankie was glad, in that moment, to be on the books as only one more jerk who'd tried to cop a piece of tin out of a West Side department store. He felt a clandestine thrill at recalling the thinness of the hair which had kept him out of the bug cells. "I almost made it up here myself," he boasted to Applejack, "when I was on the junk I pulled lots of jobs." And hastened to add, "I got it kicked for keeps now."

"It's what they all say," Applejack answered skeptically, and Frankie was too superstitious to boast further. "The smarter a guy is the harder he gets hooked," Katz observed, "I've seen 'em hittin' C, I've seen 'em hittin' M, I've seen 'em hittin' the H 'n I've seen 'em shootin' speedballs—half a cap of C 'n half a cap of H together. C is the fastest, it's what they start on when they're after a gentleman's kick. M is slower 'n H is the slowest 'n cheapest of all, it's what they wind up on when they're just bummies tryin' to knock theirselves out without no kick at all. But I'll tell you one kick to lay off 'n that's nembutal. If you miss the vein you get an abscess 'n the shade comes down. Lay off the nembie is my advice to you, Polak."

Just as if he hadn't heard Frankie tell him he'd kicked all that stuff.

"Another thing works funny is gage," Applejack resumed his report while dragging the little white wagon behind him. "One day you'll pay two bucks for a single stick 'n the next day some guy says, 'Gimme twelve cents 'n a pack of butts for a stick,' 'n you pass him up. It don't make sense to me neither the way they always say a guy gets 'high' on it. My cell buddy at Grant's Pass worked twenty years in mines around Scranton before he threw his shovel away 'n started eatin' a little higher up on the hog. The gage never lifted him up, it sent him down. When it was hittin' real good he'd get to thinkin' he was twelve miles underground. He never said he was 'coastin' in.' He always said, 'I think I'm comin' up.' Say, if you get detailed down to the kitchen sneak me a fistful of nutmeg, I know a fool who'll give a pack of butts for a sack of that stuff. I wonder what he does with it."

"Maybe he puts it in applejack," Frankie hazarded a guess.

"You guys laugh at my applejack," Katz told him, "but a guy got to do somethin' to keep his mind occupied. Otherwise I'd be thinkin' how it used to be outside."

"When will you make the street again?" Frankie asked him.

"Never, soldier," Katz told him without regret, almost with contentment. "When I finish here the feds pick me 'n I start a twenty-year rap—when I finish that one they can come 'n cremate me: I been caged up all my life, I don't want even my bones to be cooped up in some hole in the ground," he confided cheerfully to Frankie. "What can a guy like me do on the outside anyhow? I'm so used to holdin' up my hand when I want another piece of bread 'n dumpin' the silver in the wire basket on the way out from chow I wouldn't know how to do for myself on the outside no more."

A guard, eating off one of the same tin pie plates that the deadlockers used, in an empty cell with the door ajar, looked up at the pair as they passed and motioned them silently down the half-lit corridor toward the cell where Little Lester leered lewdly through the bars.

All day Little Lester stood waiting for someone to pass whom he could bait for a moment. He liked to be looked upon pityingly in order that he might catch the pity coming at him on the fly and hurl it back between the eyes—to see pity replaced there first by shock, then by real hatred. Little Lester had long suspected that everyone in the world hated him, on sight and from the heart; that all, without exception, had wished him to be dead since the morning he'd been born. So it pleased him to prove to himself that he'd been right in this suspicion all along, that everything the priests had told him since he'd been so high had been wrong.

Pity was the thing people used to conceal their hatred, Lester had decided, for the chaplain himself came now only out of a sense of duty. Lester had had trouble turning the chaplain against him but he had done it at last and now the chaplain hated him as cordially as did the screws, the warden, the sheriff, his attorney, his mother and sisters, his father and his old girl friend.

"You guys want a pack of Bull Durham wit' two papers for thirty-five cents?" he began on them hurriedly, the moment he heard the cart roll up. Though he knew every con was forbidden to talk to him while he was in the cell. "You guys want to change jobs? Look, you two first-floor marks, all I do is play solitary 'n chew the fat with the screws all day. How'd you like that awhile, marks?"

The marks didn't care to switch jobs at the moment, they had to keep the mops moving down the tier.

"Hey!" he called after them. "You the guys gonna split my pants 'n shave my little pointy head?"

"He's just tryin' to get a rise out of us," Katz cautioned Frankie, "he wants to see if he can get us in a little trouble, arguin' with him about somethin'. One of the screws asked his lawyer to make the guy lay off him, he kept askin' things like is them fuses all screwed in good 'n tight, he don't want no slip-ups 'cause he's invited his folks as witnesses—it's how he gets people's nerves jumpin'. If you ask me the guy is suck-silly."

"If you ask me it's his nerves is jumpin' the highest," Frankie surmised.

Applejack and Frankie stalled around at the far end of the block, for two soft-clothes men were coming up on either side of a little man with a bandaged eye and all three tagged by some joker in a spring topcoat, wearing the coat with the sleeves hanging emptily, like a woman's cape.

"That's a newspaper joker," Applejack assured Frankie, "I don't know who the bandage is but only newspaper guys drape a coat on them like that. You know why?"

Frankie didn't have the faintest idea.

"He ain't got time to button it 'cause he gotta keep his hands free of his sleeves to take notes, in case somethin' big happens real fast. If he takes time to get his hands out of his sleeves some other guy'll beat him to the phone 'n get a scoop on him. I saw all about it in a movie at Jeff City." Old Katz was proud of his knowledge.

Frankie understood. "You're right. I seen one come into the Victory on North Clark one night 'n set down with one bottle of beer 'n wrote in a little book-like, everythin' that was goin' on, what the people said. Then he picked up 'n didn't even touch his beer. He didn't touch his beer was how I knew there was somethin' wrong with him."

"It's sort of a club," Applejack explained, "they all get together 'n write a book." Though neither he nor Frankie could hear what either the bandage or the draped topcoat said to Little Lester, there was no difficulty at all in hearing the punk's jeering reply.

"Sure, ya stinkin' squeala, I'm the guy shot out ya eye. It was easy as eatin' a ice-cream comb. So what? Prove I'm nuts I go to the buggy bin—they feed you there, don't they? 'N if I ain't nuts I get the seat—so what? Then I don't have to bother with stinkin' squealas no more. It don't make *me* no difference.

"Naw, I don't feel nuttin' good 'r bad. Good 'n bad is strictly for stinkin' squealas. You know what? I chew t'ree packs of gum a day but I don't smoke. I don't even eat much. I don't even play ball. Movies I like better'n anythin'.

"But what I really like is mechanics. I don't like readin' about crime stuff, they don't put it down how it really is. What I really like is readin' about takin' t'ings apart 'n puttin' 'em togedder so they stay, like in airplanes. I used to go out to the airport just to watch, I seen them fancy squares all come down the gangplank like in them square movie pictures.

"But what I really like is gym-a-nastics. That's for me, it's what I took up in the neighborhood. I crooked four days a week from school—you know what I was doin'? I was workin' on the parallela bars."

Abruptly his mind returned to the point of the interview. "You know what made me sore?" Nodding toward the bandaged eye. "It wasn't when that pig of his scratched me, what really got me was when I shoot his dirty eye out 'n he says, 'Don't shoot me.' *After* I done it he comes on wit' a pitch like *that*." He imitated a high-pitched squeal: " 'Don't shoot me, *please* don't shoot me'— boy, I would of let the stinkin' squeala have it for real then only the dirty gun jammed on me, I should of cleaned it wit' somethin' good first.

"Naw, I never went for playin' wit' other kids, all they do is jump up 'n down. Girls 'r poison. Once though I had one of 'em 'I-got-to-get-in-tonight' romantic deals, we went down to Hubbard Street 'n got a free blood test. She was on one side of the screen 'n I was on the other 'n we hollered over to each other. A *real* romantic deal.

"My old man? His one big trouble is he's always a pallbearer 'n never a corpse. He'd look better to me wit' his dirty head off five inches beneat' the shoulders. You know what I told him that time he called the aces on me for sellin' the icebox while he was out stiffin' some piece of trade? I told him, 'Daddy darlin', you been workin' for me for twenny-two years. Now go out 'n get a job fer yourself.' It's what I told him, he's a stinkin' squeala too."

Applejack Katz looked at Frankie Machine and Frankie Machine looked at Applejack Katz. "Let's get the detail done," Applejack urged, "I got a deal on with a guy who got his hands on six bennies."

"*What* a loudmouth," Frankie whispered of Little Lester.

That was the name by which the screws knew Lester too.

Yet, when on the last Saturday afternoon in April Frankie sat for an hour at the same dayroom table where Little Lester sat, the punk spoke softly all the while. This was an assigned group permitted to write letters or play cards under the eyes of two screws, between four and five o'clock. If you didn't have a letter to write and didn't care for cards you went all the same. Neither Frankie nor Lester wrote letters. They sat across from each other with a soiled deck between them while Frankie showed him some of the tricks which had once seemingly confounded Sparrow.

"It took me ten years to learn this one," Frankie explained, "pick a card."

"Show me one that don't take so long," Lester reminded him humbly. Once away from his cell bars, he abandoned his tough-guy act; exactly as if he needed it only when locked behind steel for others to stare at and question.

He was only days from the chair if his last appeal were denied, yet slept and ate much as Frankie slept and ate. Therein lay a horror and a marvel for Frankie. Each saw the same gray corridors all night, each night, with the same yellowish fog wadded about the night lights. Each wakened from dreams of lifelong deadlock to the same muffled sounds: down the tier the long day was beginning.

Something of this awe was in Frankie's eyes when he noticed how neatly combed and oiled Lester's dark hair looked, and Lester caught Frankie's glance. "I'll have to wash the oil out the night before," he explained earnestly, not even in the same voice he had used for the reporters at all. "Oil leaves a burn 'n they don't like to leave a man burned even from sweat."

He spoke without any challenge to the world beyond the bars. "Here," Frankie insisted, wanting to do something for Lester, "here's one it only takes two weeks to learn. Pick a card."

But Little Lester had lost interest in cards and without a word picked up a book in which he sat immersed, not once raising his eyes till their hour was done. A book called *How to Write Better Business Letters*.

Frankie didn't see Lester again for several weeks, though he once or twice saw the boy's lawyer swinging down the corridor on that business of the last appeal.

Then, on a morning early in April, Frankie came out of the laundry with Applejack Katz to see two guards bringing Lester, uncuffed, to some unknown destination. He turned cheerfully toward Frankie as he passed.

"Hi, Dealer!" he greeted Frankie. "Take a look at a man on his way to the chair!" and sounded really deeply relieved.

A face like any stranger's face, slightly slant-eyed in the Slavic way. A face at once as old as the moons of Genghis Khan and as youthful as a child's playground in May. He seemed smaller than Frankie had remembered him. It had seemed, in the weeks since, that he was a big man. Small but rugged and built all in one piece, with a heavy-legged stride, a little bowlegged as if he had learned to walk too early about the West Side's broken walks.

Frankie noticed that he was wearing bowling shoes with both laces neatly tied.

"They ain't takin' him no place but the dentist's chair," Applejack grumbled irritably at Frankie's side.

Yet Frankie was to recall with awe, months later, those neatly tied bowling-league shoes still faintly touched with chalk.

"A guy got somethin' like *that* on his mind 'n he jokes about goin' to the chair 'n ties his laces like he had a big-league bowlin' match comin' up," Frankie complained to Katz.

"He has," Applejack decided dryly, "he got to bowl over six thousand volts from a settin' position. They're puttin' him down in the deadhouse Monday week."

Little Lester's last appeal had been denied.

When, two days later, Lester was taken into the prison yard for a workout Frankie and Applejack watched, from the ground-level laundry window. Lester and three others were being marched out there like stock. It was strange that the other three, though only small-time thieves, would draw a certain prestige about the prison for having been exercised beside the condemned youth.

It was three o'clock of a May afternoon, the hour when school doors open and the city's children ramble home down a thousand walks with books and crayons under their arms and their shoelaces tied into small, neat bows. A few

more days till summer vacation and out in the prison yard a great crane, straining skyward to see the first sign of summer, caught only a glint of rusted iron
sunlight instead. These were days of clouds swollen gray with promise of rain—
only to burst emptily and reveal the deepest sort of blue drifting there all the
time. Against the concrete wall Frankie saw a single con sitting on an upturned
orange crate looking, under his winter pallor, like someone who'd seen all
there was to see of grief, in prison or out.

That yard is laid out like somebody's country garden; there's a duck pond
and a chicken house and a pale blue birdhouse. Beyond the wall rises a two-
story-high legend:

BUDINTZ COAL
One Price to All

While directly across the way from Budintz that company's chief competi-
tor offers its own appeal:

RUSHMOORE COAL
Fastest Delivery
Cheapest in Years

Along rows where, in summer, vegetables would grow, the four cons stood
under the eyes of four guards. Behind them a machine gun's eyes peered from
the sentry's tower.

Without uniformity the cons touched their toes with their fingertips, bending awkwardly from the waist. Three of them had to stand spreadlegged to do
so. Lester, Frankie saw with an odd pride, touched the toes without either
bending the knees or spread-legging. Touched the tips of the shoes' neat bows
with the condemned tips of condemned wrists.

A man no taller, not so old, neither uglier nor handsomer than himself. A
man like any man, with a bit less luck than most. A punk like any punk. Clean-
shaven, vain of his heavy head of hair. A youth much like any youth who has
seen night games at Comiskey Park, shot six-no-count pool, applauded a strip
tease on South State, played nickel-and-dime poker in the back of a neighborhood bar, crapped out on an eight-dollar pass or carried a girl's photograph in his wallet one whole spring. Who perhaps had had a drink on the
house from time to time and worn bright new swimming trunks to the Oak
Street Beach some summer afternoon when he'd owned lake, water, sky,

beach, sand, sun, the bright blue weather and every girl of all the girls that had passed so yearningly by.

"He just does caliskonectics is all," Applejack informed Frankie. "Don't worry, they ain't gonna let him climb the horizontal bars. He might get too good at it."

"If it was me I'd tell 'em to let me skip the rope," Frankie said, because he wanted to say something funny too. Only Applejack didn't see anything funny. "What good would *that* do?" he demanded to know. "You'd still have to beat the chair. Nobody gets the rope in Illinois any more."

Yet Frankie wasn't quite as wrong as Applejack Katz thought. There was still one fugitive on Illinois's books that would die by the rope when he was caught. Down in the sheriff's basement, among slot machines confiscated from half a hundred roadhouses and roulette wheels that once had whirled for Guzik, Nitti and Three-Fingered White, stood the gallows that waited, year in and year out, for Terrible Tommy O'Connor's return.

Not many knew that still, behind the Board of Health Building, where once the County Jail had stood, the death house from which Terrible Tommy had escaped remained. Though the building about it had long been demolished, the little brick room waited, in the middle of a parking lot, for Tommy to come back. The law forbade the room, as it forbade the gallows, to be demolished until O'Connor was hanged. It looked like a long wait.

For it well might be that the little room would be the great city's most immemorial monument, more lasting than the Art Institute lions on the boulevard, Bushman in his cage near the Lincoln Park Lagoon or Colonel McCormick in his bomb shelter below the river.

"Just tryin' to make a little joke," Frankie apologized for his reference to skipping the rope. And the pale gray laundried light wavered, with an unwavering wonder, along the laundered walls.

"I think the stuff is almost done," Applejack confided that night to Frankie after a long visit to the ventilator. "Give it one more day."

With the pungent reek of the stuff on his breath as he spoke.

Each man knew the hour. Each man knew the day. Lester had not slept well the night before, the word was going about. He had wakened and played casino with the night screw through the bars. The night screw had taught him the game, the punk had grown to like it. Somebody who had it right from the night screw himself said that Lester had had one good last laugh at some misplay the guard had made. He'd been happy because he'd beaten the guard at the guard's own game.

Yet when the warden had gone to the death cell, the word went around, to read the death warrant, Lester had looked at him without fear and said, "Wait a minute, Frank, I want to finish this cup of coffee."

Such calmness seemed somehow more terrible to Frankie than if they'd said Lester was lying on his bunk in a dead-cold nightmare sweating out the hours. Instead he was sitting there killing the hours with cards just as Frankie had killed so many; while a clock had ticked away below a luminous crucifix.

There were no luminous Christs for Lester. Neither Christs nor clocks nor calendars.

Yet each man knew the hour. As each man knew the day.

But what if the laces broke on the way? Would he stop to tie them—or demand a new pair before he took another step? It seemed so wrong to trouble tying laces at such an hour, to comb and oil your hair and make corny jokes about going to the dentist's chair. It seemed so wrong to laugh because you caught a winning deuce against one of the men who was going to help strip you for the cold white slab. To brush your teeth or write a letter to your mother in California.

"If that letter goes out tonight," Frankie reckoned, "he'll be buried by the time his old lady reads it 'n he *knows* that when he's writin' it 'n when he tells the screw to send it air mail 'n seal it good—'it's somethin' *personal*.' "

Would he have to add that same old crack, used twice already in that same cell, "This is certainly going to be a good lesson to me"?

"One more white shirt is all you'll wear," Frankie told Lester, though Lester lay many cells away. "Shine your shoes like you're goin' to get married. Five'll get you ten you forget your act when they fit you into them tight black tights."

Frankie lay on his cot half fevered with the idea of Lester's trip to the chair, suddenly uncertain that he himself had really missed it after all. In his mind Little Lester and himself had merged.

"Let's see you trot through the little white door," he challenged this Frankie-Lester: "Three steps to the right 'n now take a load off your feet and don't let the smell of vinegar bother you either. That's only a couple drops on the sponge that fits between the voltage ankle and the clamp to keep the sponge from burning— all for your own good you know. Now just put your nose through the little black helmet. That's right—*now* let's hear you wisecrack, wise guy."

The wise guy of Frankie's fantasy had no word that one could hear through that dead-black hood.

Some other con, with his own private burden of guilt, cried out, in sleep or waking, and the lights in the corridor seemed to flicker a moment. The sleepers wakened, a long murmur went like a wave from wall to wall. It was that hour when men cried out in voices not their own.

For each man knew the hour. As each man knew the day.

They said, between the bakery, the laundry and the mess, between the printshop, the library and the little white infirmary, they said he'd come out of the death cell hooded all in black. The black tights shimmering under the lights, that final white shirt buttoned over one shoulder like a fencing master's, he had stepped forth into that hooded hour. They said it had taken a full minute and a half, from the moment he'd stepped into the big glass cage to the moment the switch had been pulled.

Some said it had taken nearer two. The voltage clamp had required adjustment after he was in the chair and there had been no smell of vinegar after all. They told just how it had been.

Between the darkened infirmary and the clean, well-lighted mess, between the sweating boiler room and the cool dry dorm—"the left knee kicked up, just once, after the switch was thrown." The voltage clamp behind the neck had fitted nicely on the very first try—only the one on the pale right ankle had seemed a trifle loose—but the *laces, the laces*—Frankie had to know—had he tied them up first or had he just let them loose? Did one of the screws tie them for him so that he wouldn't trip and skin his knee? The *laces, the laces*—

But no one had noticed if the laces were tied at all.

The single shoulder button had been stripped off when the shirt had been ripped down to expose the flesh above the poor seared heart. Five doctors— which one had pulled the button off? No—it certainly had been six—had pronounced the heart as dead as any hustler's heart can get: a charred lump of ashy flesh that sagged where the living heart had burned.

There had been one hundred and twenty men and two women on the witness benches, they said. It had all been spick and span behind the glass, everything had gone off in tiptop order, there had been not even the telltale flickering of the lights throughout the building.

Four buttons had been pushed by four unnamed men. They said. Yet only one of these had pushed the live one. None would ever have to think it was himself had sparked the living flame.

But the *laces,* the *laces*—

They had used an amperage of eight, everyone knew, because that was the usual amperage for a white man. Everyone said. Just as the usual amperage for a Negro was seven and a half.

Everyone knew.

Then they'd thrown him nine hundred extra volts just to make certain. Everyone knew about that too. Everyone told everyone else just how it had gone off. Everyone but Frankie had been there it seemed.

But the laces—

What laces? You think they let him walk in there with *shoes* on? Those tights cover your feet like an acrobat's tights, there aren't any shoes to it. Just a strip of black cloth sheared neatly halfway around the right ankle.

It wasn't until weeks after he'd been released that Frankie learned Little Lester had died on his bunk with eleven hours yet to live.

A heart attack, the warden had concluded.

Arsenic, the coroner's physician had insisted.

His heart had stopped beating too soon, the afternoon papers had reported.

And neither the evening nor the morning press would ever be able to prove a thing, one way or another, under any old buffalo of a moon, by flat-nosed, buffalo-eyed Frankie Machine.

Now, as the moon of other nights mounted the arch of June, he felt the touch of other Junes along the bars. Remembered how the orange Blatz signs of Wolcott Street would be glowing now each night more softly as the brief month passed trailing smoke, and July came on in a haze. And every arc lamp's reflection along the rain-wet, moon-wet, sun-wet, and summer-dusted walks would burn more deeply as the days burned longer.

Frankie could tell himself at last that he had buried his monkey as deeply as the county had buried Little Lester.

Each Saturday afternoon now the good soldiers were led into the yard for a game of softball. Whenever he found himself out there in the open, after the long week in the laundry, he was seized with the need of hearing Molly Novotny's teasing voice and a longing for the dark appeal of her eyes. He felt he didn't care whether he dealt another hand of stud in his life or not.

Playing first base on the last Saturday in August, he took off his shirt in the fading West Side sunlight and a swift squall, as if waiting all the bright afternoon behind the sentry box for some fool to do just that, swept the field in chilling gusts. By the time they'd played out the inning he was sneezing and by the time he got back to his cot he was in a wringing sweat. The laundry had weakened his resistance more than he'd known.

By chow time he was rocking down Fever Street in a sidecar attached to some Good Humor vendor's bicycle, racing east down Division with little pennants whirling in the white-walled wheels and the vendor, wearing a meter reader's cap and waggling a finger at Frankie to sentence him to life imprisonment in a broom closet for stealing Captain Bednar's only electric iron.

Sitting upright there among the brooms was good old McGantic wearing a sergeant's stripes on his sleeve, dead as a doornail in line of duty. Dead for days. The face had withered to a monkey's face, one dead brown paw pointed to where, upon an empty beer case, lay the same old hypo and two new quarter grains.

"If he wants water give him water," the major was telling Applejack, "and water is all he gets. He's still tryin' to kick the habit. Let him sweat it out. If his ticker ain't bad he'll make it."

Intern Katz understood. He knew how to get a half a cap of morphine out of the infirmary as well as how to fashion a needle out of a common pin. But he believed in Frankie Machine as he believed in his own applejack. "It won't be me to put him back on, Major," he promised. Then he was left to watch alone beside the narrow cot in the narrow little infirmary. Because its looseness seemed to be causing Frankie distress, Katz rolled up the nightshirt's sleeve.

Frankie felt McGantic rolling his sleeve to give him the one big fix that would fix him forever and for keeps. With all his remaining strength he pried at those fingers to get them off his precious arm. But the fingers had no strength left at all, something that was surely a hypo glinted in the light and in an access of hopeless dread Frankie cried like a sick baby for help: "Molly! Molly!"

But no Molly was near to reply. Only the sheet roller rumbling down the tier to punish him for what he'd done to Zosh. He ducked down Schwiefka's alley and around the shed to pick up an armful of kindling for Jailer. Deep under the wood lay a soft green hat with a small red feather in its brim.

Strong hands held him down while others fastened the voltage clamp to the back of his neck but he was too smart for all of them—he rested one moment to make them think he had really given in at last and then shouted out of his very bones, "A Polak never gives in!"—and kicked off all the hands at once. But it was all up with Frankie—the sponge was pressing his forehead and a voice was warning him through glass—"Don't let your life go with it, Dealer."

He opened his eyes and through the sweat saw Applejack Katz's good tough mug studying him gravely. And Applejack's long, hard hand drying the tears, fears and sweat away.

"You're toughin' it through the hardest sort of way, Dealer," he heard Katz telling him. "Quit stonin' yourself. You ain't *that* sick. How many guys you fightin' anyhow? Be yourself, Dealer. Be yourself."

"That's not so easy," Frankie whispered weakly. "I got to get straight first."

"It's the same thing," Katz told him quietly.

At Applejack's feet Frankie saw the infirmary's gray cat sitting upon its haunches. It purred, just once, to affirm Applejack's counsel.

As the fever lowered Frankie dreamed of someone folding and refolding bundles of newspapers right beside his cot and forced himself awake to see who it was this time.

Only the old woman of the wind, there on the other side of the pane, wrapping the great sheets of the rain.

Indian summer came and September drew toward its close. It closed in a green half-twilight, like the half-twilight of the heart. In this green-gray late September light the Prager beer signs gleamed redly as soon as the arc lamps gleamed yellow. Then the arrows of all the Old Style Lager signs began working anxiously back and forth till the yellow arc lamps dimmed and died, the scarlet Prager bulbs signed off and the overworked Lager arrows went to bed. Only the green-gray light was left, like a light left burning in a hallway entrance all night long. To light the morning's earliest peddler waking the tenements with one clear call: "Kartofflee! Kartofflee!"

Then the trolleys, like mild-tempered elephants, approached each other slowly and paused, with a primitive graciousness, to let each other pass; and went shambling forward once more upon their predestined jungleways as though the pause had lent each a greater understanding of all things.

Frankie came down Division Street, where only arc lamps and fire hydrants grow, wearing the same woolen army trousers and the combat jacket—its sleeve patched so neatly, by a county sewing machine, the old tear was scarcely

detectable. With a new checkered cap on his head and feeling as if some tightly
wound spring within himself had slackened, never to stand taut winding again.

Back in the city's littered bivouac he walked among the tenements of home
like an awol private returning to barracks from which his old outfit had long
ago convoyed and scattered for keeps. He felt both weakened and strengthened by his stretch. His hands hung heavily, the fingers felt like thumbs for lack
of use with deck, cue, dice or drum. But he'd beaten McGantic and McGantic's
terrible monkey.

He'd paid in full. He didn't have to punish the blood and bone any longer.
Molly-O had shown him what was gnawing at his heart and the long stretch
had forced him to the fight.

"Once you got the touch it's always with you," he remembered, and passed the
Safari without looking in. There was no longer anyone there he needed to see.

"When a cripple leads a cripple it doesn't amount to much," he recalled
someone telling him as he turned into his own dark hall.

In the dimness someone was shouting threats to someone far above. Halfway
up the first flight he made out the hulking raincoated figure of Poor Peter
Schwabatski pushing an artificial daisy into a crack of the stair. How long was
it now he'd been trying to make them grow there? Since before that middle
tread had come loose, Frankie remembered. When the dimwit had once asked
his papa why his flowers never grew, Frankie remembered the Jailer saying,
"Because it never rains indoors."

That was a hard thing for Peter to understand. It seemed to him it rained
all day indoors. All day it rained in Poor Peter's mind upon the paper daisies of
his brain: a paper garden in a paper rain. It was the reason he always wore a
raincoat, sun or rain; dust storm, blizzard or summer hail.

It was of this same Poor Peter Frankie had heard the Jailer speak mournfully once, after the Jailer had been openly boasting to Violet, "I know how to
hit them ovalries: the right one makes a boy, the left one a girl, right square in
the middle is what we call a murphydyke."

Where'd *you* hit it?" Violet had asked.

"I missed altogether, I guess," Jailer had acknowledged then with a smile so
wan Frankie had wished Vi hadn't asked that that time.

For the boy had been sitting then where he sat now, moving humbly aside as
always for traffic, too absorbed in his dusty flowers to lift his half-bald head. He
was not more than twenty but had been losing his hair since he'd been twelve.

As he stepped past Peter Frankie heard Violet and the Jailer really going at it.

"No hammering on Sunday!" Violet was demanding. "Go to sleep, drunk! Get a wife and hammer in bed!"

"One I had said no hammering on Sunday too," the Jailer reproved Violet, "she said I hammered enough all week!"

"You've hammered enough around here too—and you ain't hit a nail yet," she chided him. "Two years fixing one board!"

"You want to come down and try my board for size now?" he invited her. "You won't mind my hammering after *that!*" He sounded a trifle tight all right.

"Shame, Schwabatski," Vi teased him softly, "drinkin' up that boy's milk at the bars."

"Leave the helpless children out of this!" He waved the hammer, pretending to be ready to come up after her.

Frankie leaned heavily on the rail, waiting for he didn't know what. For some reason the twenty-watt bulb of the hallway had been painted a dull red, the same as that over the visitors' cage. As he passed the Jailer the old man's hammer caught him by the claw and hauled him back.

"It served that one right, Dealer—he went into that business in the wrong neighborhood—Polaks don't need what he was selling. You see: it didn't help him after all to have the devil for a father."

Frankie freed himself and went on up the stairs, but the old man shambled right on up behind him, babbling away till Frankie had to turn on him to get him back to his stairs, his son and his whisky.

"You'll never finish that step runnin' off at the mouth all day, Jailer," he urged without anger.

The old man took him by the jacket's sleeve and Frankie looked down into the grizzled, grayish, boozed and wrinkled mug, always so intent on giving fresh heart to all those who seemed to be in need of it.

"People like that *ought* to be knocked on the head!" he whispered as though he'd overheard Frankie's threat to Louie one night. "Don't torture yourself! Myself would of give you this hammer! Myself would have done it! Don't torture! Don't suffer!" The old man was pleading so, two steps there below, he seemed to be pleading on his knees. Frankie took the big veined hand and felt his own fingers' weakness in the old man's grip.

"All I done was a little stealin', Jailer," he told the old man softly. "Now I done my time for that, so let's forget what can't be helped no more. All sorts of things happen and then it's done and the less we talk about it now the better for me 'n everybody."

It was the assurance the old man needed, he sensed Frankie had found some degree of peace and let him go at last. Frankie saw him return, with a pencil behind his ear and a ruler sticking out of the back overall pocket, to his work among the paper daisies.

Overhead he heard Violet return back down the hall without a greeting. That wasn't like Vi at all. "She's gone to tell the punk I'm back," he guessed.

"You heard what I said all the same," the old man mumbled, through two nails clenched in his teeth as he squatted on the step. "Knocked on the head! With this same hammer!" Then the hammer's rapid tapping, light and sane and calm, a good carpenter's hammering, like the beat of a lightened heart. The Jailer felt better for having unburdened himself. Frankie could tell. But how long it had been since the old man had first wished to speak out Frankie could only surmise.

"The old man got good heart," Frankie told himself. Everyone, even those who left doors ajar just to bait him a bit, knew the old man had the truest sort of heart.

It was only that there was so little demand for the truer sort of heart of late.

Hearts shaped like valentines aren't at all the fashion. What is more in demand are hearts with a bit of iron—and a twist to the iron at that. A streamlined heart, say, with a claw like a hammer's claw, better used for ripping than for tapping at old repairs—that's what's needed to get by these days. It's the new style in hearts. The non-corrugated kind don't wear well any longer.

Hearts with a twist to the iron—that's what makes a good hustler's heart.

Behind the narrow yellow door bearing the red tin 29 he himself had nailed there, Frankie heard the old clock below the crucifix tick once—warningly—and pushed in without knocking.

Sophie sat with her head thrown back and eyes closed, looking debauched in the dim tenement light. Apparently assuming it was only that nosy Violet again, she said tonelessly, "You come in yourself this morning, did you? You only sent things yesterday."

The room certainly looked as though Violet only sent things these days. It didn't look as if it had been swept in a month; cigarette butts, Kleenex, bottles and hairpins littered the floor. The walls had grown darker.

Her scrapbook lay on her lap. "You pastin' pictures, Zosh?" he asked.

She opened her eyes, smiled wanly and lifted her hands listlessly toward him.

The gesture told him she had known it was himself in the doorway all the time, that she had been playing some strange game with herself after hearing his voice on the stairs, pretending she had not heard anyone at all. Yet he held both her hands in his. He had seen so many weary homecomings at the Pulaski. Till her fingers began to work like small claws upon his palms.

"You're stronger than you were," he told her. For her hands seemed to have gained a chily ferocity all their own. They felt so cold, so cold. He dropped them gently and went behind her chair to rock her shoulders awhile.

"That's *nice,* Frankie," she told him thinly, "you learned your lesson. God punished you. Always be nice after this fer what you done."

Violet's voice at the open door: "When did *that* sonofabitch break out?"

Frankie saluted her from where he stood. "Hi, Sergeant—come on in—but don't bring your army."

For the punk's shadow fell behind her.

"He didn't mean no harm, Frankie," Violet pleaded for him like a mother for a wayward child, "he just got scared 'n run."

"Then he can keep on running—right back up them steps. He's got somebody's nice fat bankroll up there to count and he's gonna get plenty of time to count it. I'm goin' back to work by Schwiefka tonight 'n that mocky ain't workin' no door where I'm dealin'. I'm the guy who got him the job 'n I'm the guy who's visin' him off it. That's the first thing I'm doin' t'night, it'll be my first good deed for society."

He heard Sparrow retreat as softly as he had come. As though knowing for months that that would be Frankie's answer. He'd run like a scalded dog all right, no two ways about it.

"What makes him so brave?" Frankie asked Vi with heavy irony. "He ain't got a bad conscience about anythin', has he?"

But Violet was gone, to console or upbraid her sparrow, and Zosh was waiting for him to turn toward her so that everything could begin again, just like it used to be.

"Your bonus dough is gone, Frankie," was her opening shot. "I tried to make it last. The last two mont's I been livin' off yer disability dough—'n even then I had to borrow a double sawbuck off Vi I ain't been able to pay back."

"You don't have to pay it back," Frankie assured her, "if it come from where I think it come from."

"She said it was Old Man's insurance dough," Zosh told him, "but the way she's actin' I don't care if I pay her back either. You really goin' back to work so soon, Frankie?"

"Just till I get back on my feet," he assured her. "I'm out for a real job, Zosh. Beatin' them tubs. I'm gonna be a drummer just like I always said." Then he noticed that no Rumdum crouched beneath the dresser. "Where's the hound?" he wanted to know.

"Vi took him, she got more room. How could I take care of him all day here by myself? He didn't like me anyhow. Why don't you get me a nice little puppy-pup, Frankie? You said you would. You *promised*."

So nothing had really changed after all. She would own a dog and he would be a big-name drummer. He would practice every night.

But she'd seen spurts of golden hope in him before. It would wear off now as it always had. He'd be back dealing where he ought to be and she'd be sitting where she ought to be and everything would be just the way it had been, just as it ought always to be.

He was pulling the practice board out from under the sink and brushing the months of dust off its scars and dents and picking up the sticks to get the feel of them again. Then put them down gently, for he saw she was nodding where she sat, the brief half sleep of invalidism.

"Let's do like regular people now," she murmured, as though in sleep. "Like regular people 'n go by the Aragon."

He stood behind her chair with his hands on the wood, ready to wheel her if she wakened. Then, as her head nodded, told her softly: "Have a good dream, Zoschka. Have a good dream you're dancin' again."

He could not see the trace of a smile that strayed so knowingly across her lips.

Neither the Tug & Maul nor the Safari saw Molly Novotny any more. She had drifted into the vast web of backstreet and alleyway, crosslight and traffic warning, of the overnight hotels and those little nameless restaurants that burn all night under the single sign: good eats.

"She's workin' in some boog honky-tonk," Antek told Frankie. "Ask Meter Reader, he's the guy who goes out scoutin'."

Frankie waited half a day for Meter Reader to show up, and got only the vaguest sort of information for his patience. "All I remember is a cat settin' on a piano. I was so boiled I don't know *where* I was. But I remember talkin' to Drunk John's girl. She was a little boiled herself."

So all nights ended for Frankie now with a firm resolution, renewed each morning, to scout around Lake and Paulina before the day was over. But 10 P.M. found him in the dealer's slot and he couldn't afford to miss a single night: he had to get a small stake together. He couldn't come to Molly broke and begging.

Yet the week ran out on Saturday night and he was no richer than he'd been on Monday morning. The old merry-go-round was rolling again and he had to ride as hard as any.

Once more the yellow arc lamps bloomed in the shadow of the El. Pumpkin-colored posters appeared in the bakers' windows among the round brown loaves of morning, announcing that Mickey Michaels' Melody Masters would play at St. Wenceslaus Kostka Saturday evening for the Endless Belt Invincibles S.A.C.

In front of Piechota's Poultry & Fresh Eggs Market a single gander stood gawking between its legs at a cord that forever held it fast.

Umbrella Man came in to Schwiefka's every noon with the *Times* morning line crumpled in his pocket, the daily double checked off and fifty cents in his hand. He never won and never complained. He came in with a bottle on his hip, made his bets like a man paying a bill, and left with the relieved air of one who has settled a long-overdue debt. The only return he seemed to expect was the privilege of climbing the same stairs and trying again another day.

He wasn't permitted to climb those stairs after the last race had been run. Since Frankie had been gone Cousin Kvorka had forbade him to sit in any poker game. So that, after his fifty-cent bet was made, Umbrella Man spent the evening drinking instead of playing poker. By the next noon, as often as not, he would still be weaving a bit.

It was said that he had taken to begging secretly for drinks at Widow Wieczorek's. That though he never begged anywhere with his lips, for fear of Cousin Kvorka, he managed to pick up a beer or two at the Widow's simply by using his eyes to express his need.

"The gray cat's purred for Umbrellas," Frankie heard Antek say.

All things remained the same; yet all things had changed. No one sat under the short-card sign waiting to bring up coffee and cigarettes for the players. Blind Pig spent his nights in the Safari now and lived in the room where Louie had lived, among Louie's abandoned possessions. "I'm takin' all I can get," Pig reassured the troubled ghost of Louie Fomorowski.

For Louie's old customers still found their way: they came now with cold, hard silver. Pig wouldn't touch folding money. "I can't get nobody to give me a square count," he complained of everybody.

The Prager legend above the Tug & Maul still came on at the same moment every night. Above the bar mirror, and all down Owner's wall, hung fresh ads for Budweiser, Chevalier, Nectar and Schlitz. As if in honor of Frankie's return.

And why was it, Frankie wondered, getting his own little beer paunch back, that the faces in Owner's ads were always so clean and healthy and wholesome and glad? There was the freshly scrubbed young housewife winking broadly at her own cleverness in having kept two bottles of some green offgrade brew in the icebox in event of company: evidently she was one of the few women in Cook County who had heard of beer. For her husband's enthusiasm over such foresight scarcely knew bounds.

Beside her was some usurer togged out in woodsman's gear, preparing an enormous t-bone—where had *that* come from?—over a smokeless fire in a clean green land of night-blue lakes and birch trees so straight and tall they looked like ivory-tipped cues. "He must of gone up there 'n shot it hisself," Frankie decided, missing the entire point of the ad, which was simply to take note of the cold beer mug waiting in the blanket-roll by that smokeless fire.

Down the line a pink-cheeked, overstuffed illiterate with a shot glass at his side looked benignly down, over volumes heaped by a cynical photographer, upon the barflies of the Tug & Maul who actually drank the stuff.

The barflies returned his gaze, from time to time. But a slight glaze so commonly clouded their sight that they thought, as often as not, that the man in the private library was Errol Flynn.

This freshly blooded race bred by the better advertising agencies looked down upon the barflies of the Tug & Maul, trying to understand how it was that these battered wrecks could look as though not one of them had ever seen a land of night-blue lakes with poolroom cues for trees. Nor any man's private library at all. They appeared not even to have discovered the public ones.

There were only boys with bad teeth, wives with faces still dented from last night's blows and girls whose hair was set so stiffly it looked metallic. There were only old drooling lushbums with faces like emptied goboons. There was only a long line of faces that had passed straight from the noseless embryo into the running nose of senility. And had seen no birch tree at all.

"I got to get a lib'ry card myself," Frankie determined.

That was only one of several matters he had to tend to right away. Another was the business of getting a job on the legit so that he could break clean with Zosh instead of running off like some sneaking punk. He was going to start on that the minute he finished his shot—he finished it. And was right on the verge of getting up to look up a certain name in the telephone directory five feet from where he sat—a name that had been told to him once, right in here, of a party who could put a man to work on the drums with or without a union card. But just at that moment he noticed that Antek's glasses had been broken while he'd been gone. "What happened to the goggles, Owner?" he asked urgently, needing to know the answer right away.

Antek made no reply. He felt he was being razzed and walked off with the string tied over one ear and knotted to the stump of the glasses' frame. Antek suffered occasional defeats, and these humiliated him more deeply than blows.

His deaf-and-dumb cat had also, it seemed, come under fire. She came gimping across the floor on three legs and somebody's hound, on a leash, made a run for her. Antek's wife, holding the leash, let the hound go just far enough to make the old cat scramble for it on all threes.

"The old cat's no good," Mrs. Owner explained herself righteously, "she's the one what trampled her young ones to deat'—somebody ought to give it to her good for that."

A dull compassion for all old cats hit Frankie. "She did it to make room for her next litter," he told the woman. So just to show everyone how she felt she hollered, "Get her, Bummy!" and let the leash go altogether. The old cat barely made it, half crawling and half slipping up the piled beer cases to safety.

And the old bums drooled and drooled.

Frankie turned away. It seemed that everything that ever happened to him had begun with some hound or other's aimless yapping.

Outside the traffic warnings flashed from red to green and back again. In the bar mirror he saw the door open and Sparrow wander in pretending he wasn't looking for anyone in particular. Then just happen to spot an old buddy who hadn't been around for a while.

"Hi, Dealer," he sounded Frankie out from the front of the bar, signaling to Antek for two shots. Frankie let his shot stand before him without even acknowledging that he'd seen anyone come in.

But out of the corner of his eye, turned toward the mirror, he studied the punk as never before. So this was the joker for whom he'd done nine months

in County. "He left me holdin' the bag for sure that time," Frankie reminded
himself firmly; so that he'd never, never weaken.

Sparrow leaned over the bar to Antek, whispered confidentially, and a
minute later Antek ambled down toward Frankie with a far too casual air.

"He wants to talk to you," Antek reported, "somethin' about gettin' back on
the door by Schwiefka. Says you got him awfully wrong about somethin'."

"If a guy wants a job by Schwiefka," Frankie said loudly enough for the punk
to hear, "let him go by Schwiefka. I don't run no joint, I'm just dealin'."

Antek, duty done, reported back to Sparrow and the punk picked up his
courage at last. Catching Frankie's eye in the mirror, he asked, in a small peaked
voice, "You still got them hard feelin's, Dealer?"

"I got no kind of feelin's."

"It wasn't no sense *bot'* of us gettin' busted, Frankie."

"No sense at all," Frankie agreed readily. "Who's arguin'?" Frankie certainly
wasn't. It was all over and done so far as Dealer was concerned. He turned on
the stool, leaving the shot the punk had bought him with his last two bits, and
brushed past him to the door.

Sparrow plucked pleadingly at Frankie's sleeve. "Let me talk to you,
Frankie."

Frankie looked down at him. The punk was looking shabby all right. And a bad
time of year for dog stealing. "There's lots of things I got wrong awright," he told
the punk, "but you ain't one of 'em. You're the one thing I'm real right about."

He turned up his jacket against the evening cold and left without looking back.

Each morning now the tide of his loneliness rose, to ebb only when he took
his evening place in the slot. To rise a bit higher, by the following morning, than
it had the morning before. If it hadn't been for the punk, it somehow seemed,
he'd be on the legit now somewhere with Molly instead of still hustling suckers all night long. His eyes, under the nightlight, no longer reflected the light.

It's all in the wrist, with a deck or a cue; yet the fingers had lost the touch.
The feel of the deck wasn't there any more. And it had all been better before.

He practiced squeezing a sponge ball one evening. "Tunney stren'thened his
hands like this," he explained to Sophie. And fancied the fingers felt stronger.

He gave the sports a shaky deal three nights running. On the fourth he settled
down. Till, toward morning, one sport sat with a low straight and three others
drew to two pairs. The second player's final card slipped face upward, matching

the pair of sixes already showing on the board. Frankie reddened and gave the others theirs face upward too, with a mumbled "sorry" to the one whose hand he had so clumsily betrayed, a youth known to him only as Bird Dog.

Four players turned up their cards with real relief; the dealer had saved them money from home. But Bird Dog shoved the pot toward Frankie.

"You won this one, Dealer," Bird Dog assured him, slapping his corduroy hat against the flat of his hand to indicate he was casing out, and tossed two bits of his own into the pot. "You win that too."

"Take your money, Bird Dog," Frankie begged off, "it's yours."

"No hard feelings," the boy assured him with a flat little laugh. Everyone watched him leave while Frankie boxed the deck, pretending it had all been the fault of the cards, and opened a fresh deck. The pot stayed in the middle for the next hand's winner.

His palms were sweating and the deck, that had always slipped so lightly, seemed half glued to them. On the very first go-round with the fresh deck he dealt a card to the missing player's empty seat and the cards had to be shifted all around the board. Schwiefka put his hand on Frankie's arm with a meaningful touch.

"Go down 'n get a drink, Dealer. You're dealin' like you got hairs in your teet'. I fired one guy awready who could deal that good."

Frankie shoved back the chair, slapped on his cap, and all the way to the door fancied small laughter behind him.

And right in the downstairs doorway, just as though he didn't know he'd ever been fired, the punk was waiting again. "How long you been waitin' for nothin'?" Frankie wanted to know. A cold wind came down the alley and the punk blew on his hands.

"A long time, Frankie. Get me my job back. I'm broke."

"You always were," Frankie reminded him.

When he reached the Tug & Maul Sparrow hustled in right behind him and stood watching while Frankie ordered a double shot for himself. His right hand was shaking so that he had to lift the glass with his left. Anybody's hand would shake, having a punk shadow him all night. The punk must be practicing to be a Pinkie again. He kept the hand in his pocket. He had two doubles before it stopped trembling.

"You got a loose crowd up there tonight, Frankie?" The punk sounded homesick all right. "You got to get back up there right away?"

"I don't *got* to go nowheres right away."

When Frankie ordered a third double shot Sparrow sensed that something had gone wrong in the slot. Frankie stuck to coffee between shifts when things were going as they should.

"Ain't you goin' back upstairs all night, Frankie?" And felt a faint little twinge of hope that, just maybe, Frankie had been fired too.

"Not tonight 'r any night. Nobody's stairs. I'm gonna try downstairs awhile." The hand was fine now, steady as a die. "I'm gonna find out what's doin' in the basement."

"You still got rent to pay," Sparrow reminded him meekly.

Frankie turned on him. "It looks to me like you're fallin' behind in yours," he accused the punk, looking him up and down from the worn shoes and the pants so thin at the knees to the coat that had once been old Stash's: it still bore the marks of an ice tongs faintly visible across the left shoulder. "You look like Vi has fired you too," he threw in.

"I'll get my own racket." Sparrow tried, at the last possible moment, to salvage something of his pride.

"It's pretty cold for rollin' stiffs," Frankie observed.

Sparrow saw then it was no use; no use at all. He wasn't even good for a shot with Frankie any more.

"What's yours?" Sparrow really wanted to know. "What's yours?"

And didn't stay for an answer.

Frankie saw his tattered coat catch in the door as it closed behind him, then the punk extricated himself and was gone into the November night. "It was toward this time of year I first hooked up with him," Frankie remembered with a heart homesick for many Novembers.

Owner came up with the bottle. "On the house," he told Frankie, and poured evenly for both the dealer and himself. Frankie shoved a half dollar toward Antek. He wasn't so hard up as some people seemed to think.

"See that sign of yours?" he asked, pointing to one of the bar legends:

> Our cow is dead
> We don't need your bull

"Well," Frankie told Owner, "my cow's dead too. So don't gimme none of *your* bull. Just give me a square count on *my* change." And spat, slowly and provocatively, making a great show of the act, between his knees and down to the floor at his feet.

Antek was hurt. He'd only been trying to patch things up between a couple old buddies and this was what he got. He withdrew the bottle and his own glass, returned with change for the half dollar and said, "Suit yourself, Dealer."

Then spat, just as slowly, just as provocatively, between his own feet.

"You call *that* spittin'?" Frankie laughed with a huge contempt, hawked once and blew a beautiful round gob straight over the bar to splash across the mirror where the photographs of Antek's wife and daughter hung in gilt-edged frames. Antek picked up a sodden bar towel and slung it straight into Frankie's face.

Frankie wiped his face absent-mindedly with the rag precisely as though it had been handed to him politely for just that purpose.

"After all, Frankie," Antek apologized in all humility, "a bartender got feelin's too." Then saw that Frankie was crying.

Antek watched this spectacle a minute, figuring something slowly to himself. Frankie handed him back the towel.

"I'll say this much about somethin' that's none of my business at all," Antek told him, measuring each word as though fearing to say one word too many. "I think you're dead wrong about the punk. That's all." And turned away.

So it really had been Pig—and the punk had been right in guessing that it had been Owner who'd given Pig "some kind of count" on Louie's roll. Then his pride came up to deny flatly what all his senses had told him at last. If he'd been wrong this long he'd just stay wrong. If the punk had gone, let him go. Let everyone, let all of them go.

It was too hard to get slapped in the teeth with a wet bar towel twice in a row.

He didn't tell Sophie of his determination to quit Schwiefka. Why hang on? He didn't even tell Schwiefka. The whole day following the night of the shaky deal he lay on the bed waiting for the old strength to return, in a single jump, to his wrists. He lay fully clothed, with his cap in easy reach of his hand; as though in order to be ready to go back to work the moment the touch returned.

But the feel of the deck had died with the light that had died in his eyes, leaving only a loneliness that was a loneliness for more than any lost skill.

More than a loneliness for careless nights when he and the punk had first gone on drunks together. More even than the gnawing need for Molly-O.

A loneliness that took on substance and form, like a crouching man wearing some sort of faded, outworn uniform.

He was lonely all right. He was lonely for his old buddy with the thirty-five-pound monkey on his back.

Neither Sophie nor Sergeant McGantic wanted him to practice at the board any more. She sat by the window and McGantic roamed the long, cold hall. It had been some hours since she had spoken. It had been some time since McGantic had called.

But toward the end of the afternoon she began telling him of all the things he had missed when he'd been gone. She had seen a movie about "Jack London in the Klondikes" and another wherein Joan Crawford had changed hats without a change of scene. "I'm gonna write to *Screenland* about that," she threatened to snitch on Joan, "they pay five bucks fer movie boners they call them."

She never wrote. But had added several morbid memories to the five-and-dime loose-leaf volume, her *Scrapbook of Fatal Accidence*. Yet there were long hours between them now when the book lay open on her lap and she had no word to say.

As if realizing at last that there was really nothing for her to do in the world. No true place of her own at all. Nothing to do but to wait. For what? For the booby hatch or a miracle, she didn't much care which.

"Why don't Vi come to see me no more, just to say, 'How you feelin'?' like she used?" she suddenly demanded to know.

"She's havin' trouble with the punk is why," he answered, not knowing himself just what he meant. "Vi is up to somethin'," he guessed indifferently and let it go at that.

Thus Sophie knew, more clearly with each hour, what she had so long suspected: that they were all in secret league against her. Violet and Frankie, Owner and Jailer, just the same as they'd been before Frankie had gone away; the overnight guests and creaky old Pin Curls down the fourth floor rear who played, over and over, just to get Sophie's goat, the same old creaking tune:

> *"Painted lips, painted eyes,*
> *Wearing a Bird-of-Paradise . . ."*

"You only make the same mistake once," she advised him abruptly.

"Whatever that means," he answered mechanically.

"Oh, don't always pertend you don't know what I'm talkin' about," she persisted, "a woman is the downfall of every man 'n a man is the downfall of every woman. You're my downfall 'n I'm yours."

"Quit fallin' down 'n say what you're tryin' to say," he urged her irritably, "quit beatin' around the bushes."

"What I mean is there's nuttin' deader'n a dead love," she told him sternly, "nuttin' deader."

"Sure there is," he assured her lightly, "dead people. They're deader'n anybody."

Her reply was simply to weave her hands in front of her face like a Hawaiian dancer and to sing saucily:

> *"Hello, Aloha, how are you?*
> *I'm bringin' you kisses*
> *From over the sea."*

She watched him slyly while they ate a cold-cut supper out of paper plates. There wasn't enough strength left in her wrists, she claimed, to slice bread or cut sausage. She watched while he cut everything into small cubes for her and then sat weaving her hands instead of eating.

> *"Others you've met*
> *May call you coquette . . ."*

"Quit yawpin' 'n scoff," he told her, "you sound like a lost orphan in a rain barrel."

For now she fancied herself a vocalist with an all-girl band. Over the sausage she smiled faintly at the unseen players, encouraging one with a nod here and another with a nod there. There was something really distracted about her smile.

"What the hell are you—a bird?" But his eyes were clouded with concern for her.

"Evelyn 'n her magic violin," Sophie explained easily. "I can do magic too."

"Well," he sighed, realizing he was in for a long, long night, "here we go again."

> *". . . mean to me"*

she sang,

> *"Why must you be mean to me?"*

and broke off abruptly to ask directly, "What do you think of the A. F. of L.?"

Frankie looked up, genuinely startled. "What the hell—you don't even know what the A. F. of L. is. I think you're tryin' to act crazier just 'cause I'm back. If nobody was here you'd have more sense. Quit disguisin' your eyes. Quit showin' off."

But whether she was just showing off or not he couldn't be certain. Half an hour later she overdid herself. He was dozing and wakened to see her tracing, with one forefinger upon the dust of the unwashed pane, the single word: *Perdition.* Just as she finished tracing it the sirens sounded, the hook-and-ladder pulled past and patrol cars, insurance cars and all the frantic traffic of a 4-11 alarm came crashing by with a sense of imminent doom. She wheeled to the door and shrieked up the stairwell to Violet, "It's goin' up! Loop 'n all! It's all goin' up!"

Violet came down the stairs at a gallop; she had to phone the papers to learn what was burning, how far it was spreading, and a kind of elation seized Sophie while Vi was at the phone behind Jailer's desk.

"It's just a short circuit by Fish Furniture's basement,"Vi reported dryly from the doorway. "All under control."

But Sophie herself stayed out of control the rest of the evening. Neither magazines nor scrapbook nor the promise of beer could give her consolation. Just to realize that that was all it had come to, that that was all anything could ever come to. Just the way Vi had said that—it made a person want to cry, that was all.

"The whole fire was in my head," she mourned.

He left for Schwiefka's toward eleven o'clock. There was no other way to make the long night pass.

And wondering, the minute he sat down in the slot, how in the name of sweet Jesus Christ he was going to make it without a charge till morning.

Solly Saltskin wasn't as happy, sleeping in the late Stash Koskozka's bed, as he'd once thought he'd be. If he could, occasionally, have slept there alone it might have been endurable. Sneaking in for an hour of fast woo a couple times a week when Old Husband had still been padding about had been one thing: being tied down to these same four bedposts all night long, night after night, was strictly something else. Of late the bedposts had taken to leaning together with a faintly disapproving air. They'd seen them come and they'd seen them go: this one wouldn't last as long as some of the others, they calculated, the reckless way he was going about things. A cooler head was what was needed; a cooler head, an older hand, a bit more restraint and snatches of sleep between rounds.

But Vi was so hothanded he didn't get a chance either to sleep or even to cool off between rounds. Once he evaded her senseless stroking with some such thin excuse as, "I'm just gonna have a fast cup of coffee in the kitchen—you go to sleep, you need your rest, you're gettin' to look like a wornout movie actor."

But just as he was putting the cup to his lips her fingers encompassed his throat from behind and he squawked like a strangling duck.

"Don't *do* that when you see I'm swallerin'," he protested.

"That's when it's most fun, when you're not expectin'—you didn't even hear me creepin' up, did you, Goosey? Still love me, Goosey-Goo?"

And crushed down upon his lap to feed him coffee from a Pixley & Ehlers spoon, howling with joy at his every wretched gulp.

"You look *so* unhappy, Goosey." She never ran out of new nicknames for him, each more revolting than the last. "Ain't there enough sugar in it? Now tell me I'm sweet enough for you, you don't need sugar with me settin' here."

All Sparrow had heart enough left to say was, "Let me up, Vi. I don't know what's gettin' into you lately, you didn't use to be like this *all* the time."

She didn't give him time to figure out a thing. She chirped kisses upon him instead. In time to the coffee's steady perking.

"The coffee's perkin' *over*, Vi."

He never remembered for a moment that the Jailer had never once scolded Widow Koskozka for leaving *her* door a bit ajar.

She let him up at last and, as he turned, shaken, to the percolator, goosed him with a single loonlike warning—*whoop!* He went clean off the floor on the point of her thumb, half a foot into the air, staggered hysterically into the wall and wheeled like a wounded rabbit to get his back up against something solid and looked at her in a panting despair, awaiting some final blow.

"*Never* do that," he warned her weakly, hysteria darkening his eyes. "*Never* do that 'n never *call* me that."

"Wait'll I get you in bed," she consoled him. "I'll make it all up to you, Goosey-joosey." And followed him mercilessly all the way back to the bedroom, breathing on his neck and tossing her flaming henna helmet about like a conquering lion's mane. He had been an entertaining toy in his time—but how could a girl afford a toy that never brought in a dime and drank up every stray nickel left lying loosely about? He wasn't weakening nearly as fast as had Old Husband, who'd given out entirely at the end of the first week. Sparrow only seemed to be a bit frayed around the edges. And the rent three weeks overdue.

Somebody had to go.

And she didn't mean Rumdum.

"You don't know how I miss Old Man, now he's gone," she tried for some reason to convince the punk, "you don't have no idea how sweet that old man could be when he wanted."

"Don't come on with the cheap romance," the punk scolded her. "You married him for his fifty a week 'n all you miss is that fifty."

"Well," she admitted, "he wasn't as much *fun* as you. You're the most fun I ever had with pants on," she flattered him with a knowing nudge. "You 'n your bedroom eyes."

"I think I'm the most fun you ever had with 'em off," he agreed dismally.

"'N just to think," she went on breathlessly, "I'm *all* yours, Goosey Lover."

"Don't *call* me that, it sounds like goosey liver." But what he really felt was that she wasn't all his so much as he was all hers and that there was no rest for the weary. It wasn't just coincidence that her favorite tune about the house, day after day, began to be:

> *"All of me,*
> *Why not take all of me?"*

He devised a more subtle means of evading her than that of the midnight snack. It was too easy for her to seduce him right there on the kitchen floor to the tune of the percolator's perking. He took to heading for the bathroom.

"Don't, Vi," he'd plead, as she'd drag him off the bed's edge down into the sweaty sheets. "*Don't*—I got to go by the bat'room." From beneath the bed Rumdum listened with sympathy; and a dull foreboding.

She'd relent then. For five minutes. Then he'd hear her making for the bathroom door; he'd grasp the knob firmly—there was no lock—and haul back like a crazed paralytic while she'd pull, shrieking at her discovery of this new game, on the other side of the knob.

Once, drowsing contentedly on the can beside the little five-watt bulb glimmering above the paper holder in the tiny darkened cavern, he understood, dreamily, Old Husband's love of the broom closet and failed to hear her tiptoed approach—when she rattled the board above his head he almost went into shock.

"Go back to bed," he begged, "for *God's* sake," but she fetched him in an iron grip, pants dragging and the plumbing's antique roar in his ears, flat down upon the cold linoleum.

While Rumdum galloped excitedly about them, nipping their heels.

Ten minutes later he rolled over, panting, wishing he had a pillow under his head. "Pull up the shade, Goosey," she ordered him, "let's see if it's gettin' light."

"If I pull up the shade I'll go up with it," he recalled the ancestral burlesque retort without humor. "I know now what they mean by 'mortal coil,' " he decided to himself, "'cause I got one I got to shuffle off before they haul me out of here with my toes turned up."

Twelve weeks of their hot-breathed union and the mornings were finding him faint. The punk woke to his ninetieth common-law dawn, on the first day of December, feeling he'd never make the ninety-first. He rose like a haunted ghost, washed in cold water and took one last fond look at the friendly percolator: that had revived him many an ardent midnight and now would revive him no more.

Beneath the sink Rumdum slept with one ear alert for the coffeepot's first perk. Vi was trying to wean him off beer with coffee.

Sparrow couldn't take the chance, even now, of putting the pot on the stove. She wakened to its contented perking as to some slow aphrodisiac and the time was come to go. He found three halves, wrapped in a ten-dollar bill, in her apron. The last of Old Husband's insurance money, and a pang of conscience flicked him. "So long as she don't shoot herself when she finds out I ducked on her," he hoped anxiously. "Maybe she'll get over the shock some day." And left as if it had been the percolator he had loved here so long and so well; it was all he truly regretted leaving.

He could not know that even then Violet lay wide awake and listening to his every secret move, scarcely daring to breathe for fear he might change his mind. "If he decides to hang on any longer I'll have to hurt his feelin's, that's all," she determined firmly. "I'll have to tell him right out I can't afford him no more."

She heard the door shut ever so softly and turned over on her side with the sighing relief of a job well done.

"I always wanted to get out of this crummy neighborhood anyhow," Sparrow rationalized going downstairs. "One more winter with Vi 'n I'd be tearin' all my pieces off the calendar too."

He went past Frankie's door noiselessly these days; there was no use trying to talk to the dealer any more. "When a Polak gets an idea in his head you can't get it out wit' a crowbar," Sparrow decided ruefully.

And so returned, with the city a golden roar in his ears, to the horse-and-wagon alleys of his childhood; with a rueful renascence in his heart.

For the alleys never changed. It was as though no time had passed since he had first escaped down them: playing hooky from that first truant officer as he was on the hook from Violet now. It seemed the same morning of golden escape.

The alleys had always been his sanctuary; they had been kinder to him than the streets. He had spent those long-ago days searching the ashcans for the tinfoil in discarded cigarette packs. Though the boulevard gutters had been better for tinfoil prospecting, the alleys had always been safer.

The tinfoil racket had been abandoned for the pursuit of beer corks. A still on Blackhawk Street had paid a dime a hundred for them in those days.

Beer corks were money: they were lagged, in lieu of pennies, along the sidewalk cracks. One red beer cork was worth five of the common brown-and-white rootbeer variety, and once Sparrow had hoarded a pearl beyond price: an orange-and-green job with an owl engraved upon it. No one in the neighborhood had ever seen one like it, he was offered as high as a hundred to one, in rootbeer tops, for it. Then he'd lost it out of a hole in his pocket and it had left a ragged little hole in his heart.

"Five up!" He recalled how the lagger's single toss had represented a gamble of five corks and the lagger nearest the line had gotten first toss—five from each player—and could keep all that turned up heads. He could then toss them one at a time or all at once just as the whim took him. Then the runner-up got second toss and by the time tossings came around to Solly Saltskin there was usually only one left anyhow and that his by default, there were no other tossers. But he'd toss it anyhow, just because the others had; it wasn't often there was anyone farther off the line than Solly.

Even then he had always been last. The decisive crack in the sidewalk had always, somehow, seemed farther away to him than it had to the other alley stubs. Even then he had blinked and goggled and furrowed his forehead and bit his tongue in tossing while those who lagged easily did the winning. Twenty years—and he still put his face too close to others when he spoke, still peered hopefully through double-lensed glasses as if trying to see whether there'd be a beer cork or two left for Solly.

Still sauntered down the one-way alleys between Division Street and the Armitage Avenue carbarns with some forgotten eye of childhood alert for anything that might be turned into a spot of cash.

The sights and sounds of the alleyways by morning were different for Sparrow than those of the boulevards and the car lines. He heard them as famil-

iarly as a nature lover hears murmurs of a forest morning. The clomp-clomp of
Western Dairy steeds and the clatter of tardy milkmen up back stairs and down
two steps at a time, the newsboy wheeling down a gangway on a bicycle and the
morning greeting of the rolled paper thudding neatly and accurately against
the wrong door, the odor of fresh rolls off the bakery truck—home sights,
home sounds and home smells for Solly Saltskin.

He stole a copy of the *Tribune* off some newsboy's two-wheeled cart and two
chocolate-covered bismarcks off a bakery truck, just to feel freedom returning
to his shaken spirit.

"I may die poor," he felt with his returning strength, "but I won't die tied. It's
not for me, the common-law life." And fed the second doughnut to Bogacz the
Milkman's horse. "You married, horse?" Sparrow asked in his rasping whisper.

The old stallion rolled one white, derisive eye: he saw so many of this aimless
order of alley wanderers, forever emerging out of the shadows to feed him stolen
restaurant sugar or doughnuts or salt he didn't really want. He took them only
because he sometimes got lonely himself over the week ends. Though knowing
there are worse things than loneliness along the long hard road to the glue works.

Sparrow heard the milkman's container tinkling somewhere behind him and
a hangover of guilt, from some half-forgotten caper among some other milkie's
quarts and pints, caught him and he crossed the avenue to scurry down the
opposite alley.

Toward noon he spotted a likely-looking terrier frolicking by itself in a yard
behind a chili parlor. He had it wagging its stump of a tail, his hand on its collar—
worth a dollar-fifty itself—when he glanced over his shoulder and saw an overweight gorilla in an apron stained with chili like freshly spattered blood and a meat
cleaver in one paw, surveying him silently from behind the screened doorway.

Sparrow cooed swift love words at the pup and fed it an invisible dog biscuit—the screen door opened and again he ran for it. When he glanced back
the cook was leaning over the fence, cleaver dangling and the whole man measuring him for future decapitation.

Sparrow didn't linger: the incident had proven to him that the heyday of dog
stealing was gone with the miniature golf courses and Star and Garter burlesque. There was no sort of living left in the alleys, it seemed. It was all on the
streets nowadays.

He had been dependent upon Frankie and Violet too long. Where would he
go when the sawbuck out of Vi's apron was gone? he wondered uneasily. It
looked like a long cold winter for Solly Saltskin.

He caught up on his sleep curled up on the Widow Wieczorek's pool table, curtained off from her bar, using a rack wrapped in his baseball cap for a pillow. The Widow had been widowed so long she'd cut her hair short and grown a mustache. She didn't mind one of the boys sleeping on the table if he lifted a couple with her first. She shook him awake toward two o'clock and he idled the rest of that bright afternoon away watching *Gringo Guns* in the roaring darkness of the Pulaski.

When he came out the evening light lay like a dreamer with sunburned flanks across the dreaming city: water towers, steeples and rooftops, all lay adrift in an amber sea; till the wind below began to search, in hallway and alley and yard, for the place where pale night was hiding.

A wind that stirred nothing else than a kite caught on a telephone wire. A kite of such a darkling red, with that lowering orange sun behind it flooding the heart-shaped wound where the wires ran it through, that it looked to be bleeding. The merciless city wires, upon which it tried to turn a bit, first this way and then that so helplessly, were tinted red from that enormous wound. Sparrow watched it flutter up there with the first rumors of evening, and his own heart pinked with the wind. The frail cross of the kite's frame hung as piteously as his own heart had hung, since Frankie had gone to jail, to the taut and insulated steel. Goggling upward at it, shivering a bit in the shabby coat, he felt for a moment as if he too were something impaled on city wires for only tenement winds to touch.

He had nine dollars left in his pocket and knew just the place to build it up to forty. All you needed to sit in on a stud session at Kippel's was a five-dollar bill on the board before you. "I could lick them rag sheenies every day 'n twice on Yom Kippur," he decided, taking the alleys toward Damen and Division.

He took a seat at the corner table, folding his nine singles to look like eighteen and declared himself casually—"from the pocket"—to indicate he reserved the privilege of reaching for his empty wallet. It was seven-card, two down, four open and the last one closed and he didn't glance at the closed pair till the first open card hit him: two blood-red jacks hiding just as the third jack slid in face up to meet its relations. Three J-boys wired, this was Solly Saltskin's night. He glanced one suspicious second at the dealer, saw he was just some run-of-the-mill houseman and that three jacks were just luck for one punk whose luck, God knew, was long overdue for a change. All he had to do was to suck the mockies in softly.

The mockies were wary of the new hand: he looked too simple to be quite true. Each felt he had seen the punk around before; but none could give him a name or place him. Kippel's players were Jews and this was a Jew—yet one who didn't somehow belong. They sensed a renegade.

They sensed it in the first-generation Polish inflection which association with Frankie Machine had lent him. They sensed it in the baseball cap, tilted at the jaunty Polish angle, instead of a conservative felt pulled down a bit over the ears. Kippel's customers wore white shirts and dark jazzbows and not one tie in that whole circle gave promise of lighting up even for a moment. "What's the matter—no gamblers in the house?" Sparrow asked with real resentment as, one by one, they dropped off from the challenge of the hidden jacks.

For, like the Jewish fighters, the Jewish gamblers were counterpunchers. They could wait on the defensive forever, hoarding their strength, their cunning and their cards for the single opening as though one opening were all that were granted a man in one lifetime.

They had learned that the one blow, the one ace, the single chance had to be the decisive one. They knew that for them there would be no consolation honors and no second chance. There was the knowledge of the long-hunted: to turn swiftly, with open claws at the very moment of disaster, upon the undefeated hunter.

For the hunter there was always another day. When the hunted lost they lost for keeps.

Therefore they had to win every day, they had to win tonight, tomorrow and forever. The long chance was the pursuer's luxury, the short one the necessity of the pursued. The pursued had to be certain beforehand, make no mistake in timing and do it all within rules laid down long ago by the hunter.

"If this was a Polak game nobody'd drop," Sparrow decided.

For the Poles shoved the law of averages off the table and chased the longest possible chance down fantastic myriad ways. With three kings face up about the board and not enough in the pot to warrant a 5–1 risk, they took the 52–1 chance without hesitation and went for the case king as if it were a hope of heaven. If they did hit it the very idea of having had the brassbound nerve to play a chance that long was as exciting a reward to them as the money it had won.

So long as they could still borrow from the bartender they played like men who never lost a round; though they might have been losing steadily for a month. The Jews recalled last year's losses and forgot this hand's winnings. The

Poles played the game for its own sake, to kill the monotony of their lives. The
Jews played to make the hours return to them of what other hours, in other
cities, had robbed their fathers; their lives were less boring away from the board
than at it. The Pole, even when playing on borrowed money and the rent overdue, still felt, somehow, that he could afford to lose all night because he was so
sure to win everything in the end. The Jew knew that the moment he felt he
could afford to lose he would begin losing till the bottom of the world fell
through and he himself went through the hole. It was more fun being a Polish
gambler; it was safer to be a Jewish one.

Now, after he had raised the bet to a dollar on his three jacks, only two players
came along with Sparrow. He hadn't yet filled but had an open six and an open
deuce to draw to and on the sixth card the player to his left suddenly bet into him.
Sparrow raised it a dollar without faltering and the third hand dropped. The final
card was down and the man who'd taken over the driver's seat checked. Sparrow
sensed him to be hiding. With only a single left in front of him he said, "Two in the
dark—one buck light." He was that certain his card was there. It *had* to be there.

"Owes the pot a buck," the dealer announced and Sparrow caught High
Man's eyes measuring him as if he were a badly marinated herring and shoved
two singles and a silver trail of quarters into the pot. "Two and two better." The
dealer counted swiftly—"but not so fast as Frankie"—Sparrow thought loy-
ally. Then lost courage and said, "I see."

"Three bucks light," the dealer warned him, and the punk's greedy little
heart fluttered weakly.

"Turn 'em over."

High Man flipped his hand: two little deucies and three little treys. He'd
caught. Sparrow revealed his three jacks wired. Beside a six, a deuce and a
queen. All the closed card had to be was a deuce—but the deuces were dead—
a trey—but the treys were dead—a queen then or the case jack—the dealer
flipped the card for him.

Nine of clubs.

"That nine of clubs is the devil card every time," somebody sympathized.

"I owe you t'ree, friend," Sparrow assured High Man. "Be right back with
the bundle—save my seat, Dealer."

"It's a long night till morning," someone surmised dryly. But Sparrow was
almost to the door before the bouncer collared him. "You owe the gentmuns
some money over there."

"Holy Jumped-up Jesus," Sparrow protested with real indignation, "I just told the man what I owed him myself—it's where I'm goin' now, to get it. Where the hell you *think* I'm goin'?"

"Out to steal it for all I know—but the gentmuns can't wait."

"If he can't wait let the house pay him off." Sparrow faltered then and he whispered in strict confidence, "I'm a steerer myself, friend. Us steerers got to stick together."

"Let him go, Ju-ju," someone said behind the bouncer. It was old man Kippel, looking as professionally tolerant as a Southern senator. Old man Kippel didn't go for rough stuff for sums under five c's. "Just see the lad don't sit in the dollar game no more."

"I'll remember you all the same, sheenie," Ju-ju told Sparrow, to let his boss know that his heart was in his work. But the punk had fled pockets empty and feelings wounded savagely. "Callin' *me* a sheenie, him the biggest rag sheenie on *Division*—he couldn't get no job except in a rag-sheenie joint."

And wondered whether that kite was still caught up there, so high on the city wires.

That was how Sparrow was still feeling when he wandered back into the Tug & Maul hoping that his credit might still somehow rate a shot and a beer. His rating had slipped badly with Antek since Old Husband had checked out. A new sign above the register apprised him that it was lower than ever today:

> I think you think you think you know what I'm thinking but
> I'm not thinking what I think you think I think: Credit.

While in the place of the *Our cow is dead* legend a more forceful one expressed Owner's current attitude toward everyone:

> Once a rat always a rat

And who, standing up to be counted, can say that not once has he played the rat?

So there wasn't any use reminding Owner how freely he had spent Old Husband's Christmas bonus and then had gone right on through the old man's insurance money while Frankie was sitting in the bucket. Owner had a bad memory for long-spent rolls. It hadn't even been a good idea to spend it with Owner, Sparrow realized regretfully now. "It seemed like I was buildin' up my credit then. But I was oney tearin' it down," he was forced to conclude these

many months after. "All the good I done was to get Frankie saltyback at me."
While the big bass juke mocked his present poverty.

"Wrap your troubles in dreams
And dream your troubles away . . ."

In the back booth, where he and Frankie had so often drunk together,
Umbrella Man sat with his great unskilled hands folded gently over his bell and
his head lying sidewise upon his hands, so that the bell's rain-rusted handle
made a long crease in his unshaven cheek. The bottom had pretty well fallen
out of things for Umbrellas when Frankie had taken the ride to Twenty-sixth
and California. He had been drunk most of the time since. His credit had fallen
to a state even lower than Sparrow's.

Once Cousin Kvorka had had him locked up overnight to keep him from
gambling and had then told him he was only out on parole. Umbrellas had
believed, ever since, that if he should ever be caught gambling, at any table
where anyone but Frankie Machine was dealing, he too would be sent out to
Twenty-sixth and California.

Now he raised his battered brow, called to some dealer of his dreams for
the one card that could save his life and waited, with a dull glaze over his eyes,
till it seemed to fall right in front of him. He studied the hypothetical card,
turning it over and over with fingers that seemed to feel it and read with heavy
lids: "Fulled up. Aces." Then boggled his eyes about at the hypothetical players
with whom he played so often of late: now one of them would have to buy him
a drink. And fell forward across his bell as though he'd been struck from behind
with the handle of his own umbrella.

They say it's hard enough to find a needle in a haystack. Sometimes it's even
harder to find five dollars in a city of four million people, most of them mil-
lionaires. So that when Sparrow heard a familiar shuffle behind him he turned
on the stool and said, "I want to talk to you, Piggy-O."

Pig, wearing his everlasting smirk with that same air of fresh prosperity he'd
worn ever since Nifty Louie had checked out, tapped on toward the eyeless
juke without hearing a word, leaving behind the same old smell of unwashed
underwear.

Tapped on more softly than before. Sparrow looked down. The big flat feet
had been squeezed into a pair of long, narrow, two-tone jobs more fit for a race
track in August than a bar in December. Nifty Louie's very shoes: Sparrow

could still see them coming down that long dark stair. "My God," he thought with something of awe, "I don't think he even left Louie his socks."

At the juke Pig turned his black snout up as if to identify the numbers on the box by smell; the very hairs within the nostrils seemed to quiver. And though his hands were as grimy as ever Sparrow saw that the nails had been manicured; to go with the suit that fitted him like a hide. He lifted the cane's begrimed tip till it touched the lowest of the box's numbers, then moved upward, exactly like a nervous spider, in little leaps from one number to that above till it attained the top row and punched his favorite number at last.

> *"O tidings of comfort and joy,*
> *Comfort and joy . . ."*

Sparrow waited till the juke had finished, then moved swiftly up to Pig's ear: "Borrow me a dirty sawbuck, Piggy-O."

Pig looked down at his hand, lying flat on the bar, just as though he could see the soot imbedded in the wrinkles there. Slowly it began to crawl with desires all its own, one manicured finger at a time, one inch at a time, to rest till the next finger caught up; then all went on together, in a miniature burlesque, till the bar's very edge was reached, and returned to the exact spot from which they'd begun that neurotic carnival.

"You made me dance to your music, brother—now you dance to mine," he told the punk at last.

"I was just a guilty culprit them days, Piggy-O. Times is different now. I'm not takin' no more gas off the dealer. Account of him I got the gate by Schwiefka. Hinges 'n all. What you think of a buddy who'll turn on a fellow like that?"

Pig looked over Sparrow's shoulder with a certain pursued look. "Schwiefka's is a good place to hang away from these days anyhow," he confided in Sparrow.

"You don't look like you need to shag coffee 'n cigarettes for him no more." Sparrow admired Pig's new look. "You look like you're doin' awright, Piggy-O."

"Even a blind guy can see an openin' sometimes," Pig boasted a bit.

Louie must have left an opening big enough to shove a suitcase full of little brown drugstore bottles through, Sparrow decided to himself. "Blind guys can hear real good sometimes too," he ventured, studying Pig's fat face. And saw the faintest sort of flattered smile stray a moment over those bloodless lips.

"The dealer off you?" Pig asked at last.

"Like a filthy shirt," Sparrow assured him. "He makes me feel like a heel. Not even a heavy heel. Just a light heel."

"Why don't you try steerin' by Kippel's, Steerer?"

"By *Kippel's?*" Sparrow felt shocked at the idea. "Not for me, Piggy-O. That's the sheenie cheaters' joint. I'll go on the legit before I go to work for sheenie cheaters."

"A guy workin' for me gets his dough in advance—he can't get cheated *that* way, can he?"

Sparrow's heart took a small, tight stitch. "Couldn't you just *borrow* me a sawbuck? It ain't my line of work, what you got in mind."

"It's up to you, Steerer," Pig told him coldly and turned to go. Sparrow caught the cane with real despair.

"I got no place to sleep tonight, Piggy." And sensed, even as he held the cane and would not let it go, that Pig had come into the Tug & Maul looking for him. That he'd simply let the talk run on until it had been Sparrow doing the seeking. He should never have talked that hard about Frankie.

"It's two bucks a delivery, Steerer. All I can afford." Then hearing no reply other than that despairing grasp on his cane, brought out a tiny package, wrapped by cleaner hands, out of an unclean vest. "I got friends who get sick. It's a good deed, deliverin' medicine to sick people."

"Bringing tidings of comfort and joy,"

the big brass juke agreed.

Sparrow needed a shot and a beer. But Pig let him sit feeling that his tongue was drying onto the roof of his mouth.

"This one needs it real bad, and a hot little piece, I heard—if she wants to show you she's grateful it's awright—but get the sawbuck first—bring it back 'n you get the deuce for delivery—Antek'll break the ten for me awright, he gives a guy a square count 'n don't ask questions neither. Yeh, 'n I'll buy you a double shot too. You stick with me you'll have your own sawbuck by twelve o'clock."

"Is it real far, Piggy-O?" It felt very far indeed.

And yet—how unlucky could one punk get in just one night? He'd had all the bad luck there was already and enough left over for a month to come. The image of the kite caught on the wires returned.

"It's a couple dirty miles for me but it's only around the corner for a guy with eyes. Kosciusko Hotel. I'll wait in the back boot'."

And the little drugstore package lay on the scarred bar between them. Pig moved it with the cane's curved handle toward Sparrow. If that Frankie wasn't so stubborn, it was all that Frankie's fault. As it moved toward him Sparrow saw, irrelevantly, that for some reason Pig had wrapped the cane's handle in tinfoil. When Frankie found out how mean he'd been he'd be real sorry.

The cane's bright silver luster had been stained, by those same hot blind hands, into a gutter-colored gray. "The dealer was laughin' in here today," Pig reminisced, "he was tellin' Owner how you couldn't pick up a dime no more 'cause you lost his backin'. He said it was gonna get pretty rough for you when the Jailer moved in by Violet. He said—"

"Don't tell me what nobody said," Sparrow interrupted him, "let's have the dirty bottle."

"T'ree-fifteen B," Blind Pig directed. "Go around the side door 'n use the elevator."

Sparrow yanked the baseball cap down over his eyes—it would be just his hundred-to-one luck to have Cousin Kvorka pick him up on general principles at the corner.

But at the corner there was only the amputee who sold papers there, his cap wrapped in the *Daily News* and folded into his crutch's handle to rest his armpit while he whooped, "Graziano suspended!"

Somebody was always suspending somebody, the punk reflected moodily. And the way the arc lamp swung one moment over newsstand and car line and curb gave a lilt of fear to his heart.

The lights were against him crossing Ashland but he wove in and out till he gained the opposite curb, keeping close to the store windows down to Cortez, and turned down a gangway where half-soled poverty has so long sought hotel side doors that Sparrow could feel, beneath his own thin uppers, the worn places in the walk's cold stone. He remembered it was the hotel at which he had first registered with Violet as man and wife and no more luggage between them than that carried by the pigeons drowsing in the eaves.

Now the first full moon of December burned with a steady yellow fury, the way a night light once had burned above the dealer's head. A pang of regret caught the punk unaware: that such nights could not come again.

Pausing to light a cigarette, the pang clung to his heart like the mist about the bulb at the gangway's end. "I must be cheatin' on somebody," he told himself uneasily, "I got that guilty-culprit feelin', like somethin's goin' to happen."

As he stepped inside the side door of the bright little lobby the elevator starter beckoned to him.

Sparrow didn't name the floor: he simply stood eying that starter until the cage paused on the third level and the fellow slammed the door open with confidence that it was the third floor the shabby little man in the baseball cap wanted. It came on Sparrow like a voice. "Go back, Solly. Go back or you'll never get back." But there was no place to go but out of the cage and into the long red-carpeted lobby.

He walked slowly, pretending to look for a certain door but only listening for the shutting of the cage behind him so that he could get rid of the bottle in his pocket anywhere at all. When he turned to see what was keeping the cage on the third-floor level that fishy-eyed starter pointed to 315B and called out in a soft-clothes man's command: "*Knock!*"

In a kind of paralysis, afraid to knock and afraid not to, fearing the ones who'd open the door when he did and fearing fast footsteps down the carpet behind him and the flash of a badge, he raised his ragged little claws to the indifferent wood.

And never knocked at all. The door opened to him.

Frankie.

With a line of sweat under his hair line and looking so sick Sparrow could only stammer, "I didn't know who I was comin' to." Frankie yanked him inside, slammed the door, took the bottle out of the punk's pocket and unwrapped it with fumbling fingers while Sparrow protested his innocence. "Honest to Jesus, Frankie, I didn't know it was fer you 'n it begun to feel like a dirty frame 'n I got scared."

"You always get scared too soon. You got the bull horrors. Hand me the hypo, I'm hitchin' up the reindeers."

The needle lay in a cigar box above the radiator and Sparrow brought it over box and all as if fearing to touch the needle itself. Frankie was swinging his arm to get the blood moving, but his legs went weak and he had to sit on the bed's very edge. His fingers faltered on his sleeve and then pointed. "Roll it up, Solly. I'm in a deadly spin."

Sparrow rolled the sleeve neatly and backed off. He wanted to go now. There was an odor near Frankie he couldn't name. Frankie smelled *green*. And he didn't want to see Frankie using that dirty stuff.

"I don't know if I can make it by myself," Frankie pleaded. "Don't chill on me. Stick with me just this one time."

But somehow had still enough toughness left to grin weakly at the fright in Sparrow's eyes. "You look as sick I feel," he teased Sparrow. "Maybe you need a charge yourself. There's enough for us both—we'll jump together."

"I ain't jumpin' nowheres but home, Frankie," Sparrow told him just as if he had one.

Frankie sucked the air out of the medicine dropper, then held a match to the morphine in the tiny glass tube. But his hand shook so that he couldn't steady the flame. "Melt it," he pleaded with the punk, "melt me God's medicine," and lay back with the one bared arm upflung and the light overhead making hollows of anguish under his eyes. His whole broad forehead glistened whitely with sweat and the throat so stretched with suffering that it shone bloodlessly.

A dead man's throat.

When the cap had melted Sparrow asked, "What do I do now, Frankie?" Frankie put a hand to his mouth, coughed the little dry addict's cough and pointed to his arm. "Tie it."

Sparrow took the tie off the bedpost and bound it about the naked biceps.

"Tighter," Frankie begged. "Tight as you can pull it."

When it was tight as a vise Sparrow took the tie's dangling end and, involuntarily, daubed the tears out of Frankie's eyes. "You're sweatin' awful hard," he pretended.

Frankie sniffled. Sweat or tears, it made no difference, all that mattered was to make the sickness stop.

"It kills me in the heart, how you are now," Sparrow couldn't keep from saying. "It just ain't like bein' Frankie no more."

"That's the hardest thing of all for me to be, Solly," Frankie told him with a strange gentleness. "I'm gettin' farther away from myself all the time. It's why I have to have a charge so bad, so I can come back 'n be myself a little while again. But it's a longer way to go every time. It keeps gettin' harder 'n harder. It's gettin' so hard I can't hardly afford it." He laughed thinly. "I can't hardly afford to be myself no more, Solly, with the way Piggy-O is peggin' the price up on me. I got to economize 'n be just Mr. Nobody, I guess." He looked at Sparrow curiously. "Who *am* I anyhow, Solly?"

He really didn't know any longer. From one day to the next, he no longer knew. For he answered himself in an oddly altered little voice, a voice Sparrow had never before heard. "Meet Sergeant McGantic, Solly—the guy they give the stripes to 'cause he got the golden arm. It's all in the wrist 'n he got the touch, it's why they had to give him the stripes. See them little red pinholes, Solly—it's the new kind of stripes us sergeants are pinnin' on the arm these days. The new way of doin' things we got, you might call it. You know who I am? You know who you are? You know who *anybody* is any more?"

"I don't know, Frankie."

"Tell me just one thing you do know then."

Sparrow watched closely to see whether Frankie were putting on a bit of an act, to get at something he still wanted to find out. It was hard to tell. "I'll tell you if I know, Frankie," he offered.

"Then tell me just this—why do some cats swing like this?"

Solly didn't know that either. He didn't know what to make of the answer any more than he'd known what to make of the question. Yet Frankie was laughing, weakly on and on, just as if he'd said something funny. While that naked arm looked far too white to have any gold left in its veins.

"You know the heartaches, Solly, I'll say that for you," Frankie took breath long enough to say. "You always knew the heartaches. Why don't you learn the good kicks too?" Then the weak laughter began again, with something almost convulsive in it now, as though he lacked the strength to laugh but somehow felt he had to—till it ran into tears of such a barbed despair that Sparrow called to him like calling to someone far away, "Be yourself, Frankie!" For a second he thought he was going to have to slap him to bring him back.

Frankie came back to himself, brushed the sweat off his forehead with the back of his arm and began flattering Sparrow. The punk heard the false note clearly now. "It ain't just knowin' the heartaches you're good for, Solly. You know how to do a thing, too. I'll say that much for a kid like you. 'Cause you're the one kid knows how to fix the old junkie when Old Junkie needs a little fix." He shook his head like a drunk. "Whoof! Old Junkie's spinnin' like never before. Hit the main stem 'n make me right."

Across the disheveled bed a new deck lay scattered. "He must of been shufflin' a few hands to hisself just to keep in shape," Sparrow deduced and told Frankie, "I don't know if I can find it, Frankie, it ain't my line of work." But felt Frankie's hand, cold as a surgeon's glove, guiding his fingers. "There. Press. Slow. *Now.*"

Frankie clenched his fist tightly to bring out the vein. Above the elbow a little inflamed knot began to point right at the needle. "Operation McGantic," Sparrow heard him murmur.

Sparrow saw the blood spray faintly, tingeing the morphine pink—and pressed while his own eyes went blind. "It feels like I'm puttin' it right into your poor heart," he thought. As the needle came out a slow trickle of blood followed halfway to the elbow.

Frankie lay sprawled loosely with his eyes shuttered; but with the first faint flush touching the pallor of his cheeks. As the pale morphine had been tinged by the suffering blood.

"How's my complexion?" he asked teasingly, without opening his eyes at all.

"Your complexion's awright, Frankie. But you can't deal on that stuff. Remember 'Steady hand 'n steady eye. It's all in the wrist 'n you got the touch'? Remember, Frankie?"

"It's all above the elbow now," Frankie answered, scratching his calf indolently. "I'm out of the slot," he assured Sparrow with a fresh confidence in his voice. The stuff was starting to hit, his eyes were dew-bright and the glow of health was on his cheeks. "Didn't I tell you I got a chance to start beatin' the tubs at a hundred-fifty a week? Krupa been askin' around at the Musicians' Club where can he get in touch with me, I guess some guys told him about that night at St. Wenceslaus when I got everybody goin' like fools the way I was in the groove. I may take it, I'll have to see what he got." He went right into some little old tune or other, rapping his knees with his knuckles, tongue between his teeth and his neck waggling an imagined rhythm.

> *"You got to gimme whatcha got,*
> *You got to gimme whatcha got . . ."*

"That's the best way to do, Frankie," Sparrow agreed earnestly. "Don't let them get you cheap." After all it's quite a trick to lose your strength and get a better job into the bargain. "Maybe you could get me somethin' to do with one of them orchester leaders," Sparrow offered his services as innocently as he was able. "It sort of looks like I'm in that line now anyhow."

Frankie yawned hugely. "Come here 'n scratch my back." And while Sparrow scratched his back he turned and twisted, with an animal's ice-cold joy. "I've said it a hundred times," he told Sparrow after the punk had been permitted to leave off scratching at last, "this one time and I'll kick it for keeps." He bent over to scratch his ankles and toes right to the nails.

"And?" Sparrow wanted to know.

Frankie looked up at him from where he bent his head over his shoeless feet. "I'm hooked, ain't I?"

He sat up then, making a deck of the scattered cards in complete absent-mindedness, his hands straying blindly for the cards while his eyes searched, on the other side of the pane, for something far out upon the shoreless waters of the night.

"I can't do much for you in that line, Solly," he decided, still riffling the deck idly. "About the only thing I have open is a watcher's job."

"A lookout, you mean, Frankie?" It was time to start taking Frankie seriously again, he was coming down out of the clouds. "I'd sure like steerin' better'n what I'm doin' tonight. I'd rather have a square job than what I'm doin' tonight."

"It's not steerin' exactly. It's watchin'. Indian-watchin', I think they call it. A little different but you'll pick it up. It's a new angle that's just comin' on."

"I'll take anythin', Frankie. Me 'n Vi 'r quits. Who'll tell me what to do?"

"Nothin' to it, Solly. All you do is, first thing you get up tomorrow morning you climb that big hill they have out there 'n when you see the Indians comin' you run right back down 'n tell the settlers. Nothin' to it so long as you don't fall asleep on the job."

The light broke over Sparrow as the cheap gag was driven home. "I know," he admitted forlornly, "I listen to the radio sometimes myself." His face was peaked with disappointment as he waited now only for Frankie to pay him off for the delivery.

"It's your chance to tell him who rolled Louie that night," he told himself— and let the chance pass. What was the difference what Frankie thought any more? He rose to go.

"Don't go," Frankie begged him.

"I got to," Sparrow realized, "I'm gettin' that guilty feelin' again, like the aces 'r gonna bust down the door."

Without a warning Frankie leaned forward and slapped the punk squarely across the nose with the flat of the deck. The punk sat down. "What the hell *is* gettin' into you, Frankie? I don't have to take *that* off you."

"You got that comin' for a long time, Solly."

"I tried to tell you once you got me wrong about Louie, Frankie. You wouldn't listen. I wasn't the guy got his roll. If I had we would of split like always. You can believe me 'r not."

"I know who got the roll now awright. But you still had it comin'."

"Awright—I ran 'n you got busted. I know I done bad then—but can't you figure I got scared just like you done the night by Schwiefka's hall? Can't you figure what another department-store rap'd do to me, Frankie? I couldn't even get paroled. Don't that give me the right to get scared too?"

Frankie listened with his head moving a bit from side to side, unable to decide whether to listen a while longer or just to use the deck again. It had felt pretty good for a minute there. "It ain't for that neither," he cut Sparrow short.

Sparrow watched the hand on the deck. "I won't take another crack off you," he told Frankie quietly.

The hand drummed the deck a moment, thinking that over, then moved off the cards. "You want to *know* what for?" Frankie demanded. And answered himself, "I'll tell you what for."

Sparrow waited. He wanted to know all right. "I don't know why you done that to me, Frankie."

"'Cause you double-crossed me on the streetcar the time Cousin Kvork picked us up on Damen 'n Division for nothin' 'n Schwiefka sprung us the next day. You didn't have no two pair on that transfer. So I owe you nineteen more."

Sparrow goggled, he was really stunned. He couldn't remember the game played in the cell nor how he'd evened the score on the trolley.

"Don't give *me* the goof act," Frankie threatened him, "hearts for noses—'n you lost both games."

Sparrow got it then all right. "I don't remember what I had 'r what you had, Frankie," he answered honestly. "But if you think I'm settin' here while you try knockin' my nose off you're gonna get your own bust in a brand-new place." His hand touched the glass ash tray on the arm of his chair.

And felt hardly afraid at all. For the first time in his life he looked at Frankie with the knowledge that it wasn't himself who would have to back down. "It's the new way of doin' things, you might call it," he explained.

Frankie tried to grin but the grin was weak. He scattered the deck across the bed in a gesture of surrender. "Maybe you won anyhow, I don't know," he confessed. "I don't even know what put it in my head. All kinds of things go through my head these days, how they get in there there's no tellin' any more. It's just the way everythin' is, I guess—you know how everythin' is, Solly? Let me tell you how everythin' is." He sounded like a man talking on and on for dread of something that will move through his brain the moment the tongue ceases its babble.

"I can see how everythin' is awright," Sparrow assured him.

"No, you can't see. Nobody can. Nobody knows, just junkies. Just junkies know how everythin' is. Sit down, Solly—*please*."

The light was fading in his eyes now, they were sinking into his head and the freshness the drug had brought to his cheeks had turned into a dull putty-gray. He said "please" like a man begging for a dime and just the way he said it left Sparrow feeling that he himself had just swallowed a mouthful of dust. "If it'll do you good to talk," he thought with the taste of dust on his tongue, "I'll listen this one time. Because I knew you when you were the best sport I knew my whole life. What's your story, cousin?" he offered aloud.

Frankie coughed into his palm. "It's like this, Solly. You put it down for months 'n months, you work yourself down from monkey to zero. You beat it. You got it beat at last." He was talking low and breathlessly, like one who fears that, if he doesn't get his story told quickly it will never be told at all; like one who believes he is the only one who knows. Really knows. "You *know* you got it beat. You got it beat so stiff when the fixer says, 'It ain't gonna cost you a dime this time, I got some new stuff I just want to try,' you tell him, 'Try it yourself,' 'n give him the laugh. When he tells you, innocent-like, 'The hypo is in the top drawer over there, help yourself any time,' just to put it in your head how easy it'd be, you turn him down flat. Because gettin' fixed is the one thing you'll never need again all your life.

"Three weeks later you wake up, it's dark out but not like night 'n it ain't morning neither—it's just Fix Time. It's comin' on like a wave way out there, bigger 'n bigger 'n comin' right at you till it's big as this hotel, it hits you 'n you're gone. You're so sick you're just turnin' around down there under that wave not carin' who knows, your mother 'r your sister 'r your buddy 'r your wife—anythin' just so's you can stop drowin' for a minute.

"Nobody can stand gettin' that sick 'n live, Solly. You have to puke 'n you can't. You just heave 'n heave 'n sweat 'n heave 'n still nothin' happens—then somebody turns on the faucet in the sink or the bathtub down the hall 'n just the sound of water runnin' rolls your whole stomach over on top of itself 'n you got to puke 'r die.

"Then you don't even know no more *where* you're sick—if you think just for one second, 'It's my poor gut'—it starts bustin' your brains out the back of your head just to show you. So you think it's your head 'n it slams you a dirty one in the stones—it's here 'n it's there 'n you're shaggin' it in a dream, tryin' to pin it down to some place you can feel it so you can fight it.

"But it won't stay still 'n you can't get hold 'n if you don't pin it in a minute you're dead"—he brushed the buffalo-colored shag of hair out of his eyes—"that's all. There ain't no 'will power' to it like squares like to say. There ain't that much will power on God's green earth. If you had that much will power you wouldn't be a man, you'd be Jesus Christ." He began drying the sweat out of his armpits with the pillowcase. "You know what you brought me in that little bottle, Solly?"

Sparrow didn't know. Frankie knew he didn't know. He wanted to tell Sparrow so that the punk would never forget. So that everyone in the world who didn't know would know forever and always what Solly had brought him in the little brown bottle.

"I knew, Frankie," Solly admitted. "I knew what was in the dirty bottle awright. I guessed when Pig asked me—"

"You didn't know a thing. You didn't have no idea at all. You still don't know. You just think you know. You think you know everything."

Sparrow wanted to go now, he could scarcely sit still for restlessness. And yet it was so hard, it was just too damned hard, to leave Frankie talking to himself all alone up here like this. "What was in it, Frankie?" he humored the man on the bed while watching him hopefully for signs of sleepiness. He could get Frankie's shoes off if he'd just drowse a bit, then turn off the light and by morning they'd both feel better.

But Frankie didn't look sleepy at all. A smile both benign and wan wandered across his lips and a look of childlike wisdom entered his eyes. "I'll tell you what was in the bottle, Solly." He looked demure, he looked so sly, his eyes sought the floor in a womanish sort of coyness completely strange to Sparrow.

"A itty-bittsy little old monkey, Solly, that's what you brought me in the bottle. Such a little feller he can hide hisself right inside there. You know where my itsy-monkey is now, Solly?"

These changes in mood, so swift and strange in one always so slow in all moods, brought a cold tug of fear to Sparrow's heart.

"I guess he was just too little for me to see then," he humored Frankie again.

"It's just what I thought you'd say"—Frankie looked triumphant—"'cause he ain't little at *all* no more. He's growed up into a real great big feller just since you been settin' there, Solly. He weighs thirty-five pounds 'n he's settin' right here on my back usin' all his weight 'cause he knows I got to carry him around wherever I go so's I don't get lonesome for nobody no more. Can *you* see him, Solly?"

"Why don't you try to sleep awhile, Frankie?"

But Frankie was wound up like a clock and there was nothing to do but listen to him till he ran down.

"Some weeks he only weighs twenty-six pounds, that's when I cut him down a little. Once I cut him down to zero, I starved the poor little feller to death. They buried him out at Twenty-sixth 'n Cal. 'N *that's* a funny thing right there."

"It don't seem so funny to me, Frankie."

"What I mean is so funny is when he come back to me last week he weighed forty-four pounds—where'd he put on all that weight, Solly?"

"It must of been another monkey, Frankie."

"Can you see him yet, Solly?"

"I think I can see him a little now, Frankie."

Frankie grew cunning. "Want to take him a little walk yourself, Solly? There's still two quarter grains in the bottle—you fixed me so I'll fix you 'n then we'll be buddies again like we used, helpin' each other out 'n hustlin' some mark so fast he can't figure which one of us hustled him 'n then we get together afters in the back booth by Antek 'n nobody knows what we're laughin' about, just you 'n me, the good old buddies again 'cause bygones is bygones. What you say, Solly? A free pop on me? Just to see what it *really* feels like? Then you'll know, you'll be more broadminded like."

"I got enough worries without that, Frankie."

"That's just the point, buddy." His voice began drifting somewhere the other side of the room, the other side of the curtained window, the other side of the street and the other side of the world. "There's so many little worries floatin' around 'n floatin' around, why not roll 'em all up into one big worry? Just like goin' by the loan shark 'n gettin' enough to pay off all the little debts with one big one? That's where I'm bein' smarter than you, it shows I'm gettin' out of the hole, it's what you ought to do too so's we can be buddies again: roll 'em all up into one big one like me, Solly."

"I don't have that many, Frankie."

Frankie laughed derisively, with a sort of loose contempt for himself and Sparrow and everyone. The only man Sparrow had ever heard laugh like that had been Louie Fomorowski. "You got more worries than you think, punk," Frankie told him. "You got more worries than Dick Tracy. Compared to you I'm little Orphan Annie. 'Cause my little worries 'r almost over but yours 'r just beginnin'."

His voice returned from the other side of the world to stir the curtain a moment and came right up to Sparrow. "Why you think Pig sent *you?*" Frankie pressed both hands to his temples as if trying to hold his mind onto a single big idea. "Get out of here, punk. I had it figured the minute you walked in that door, I just been tryin' to hold you to see if I was right. Now I don't care if I'm wrong 'r right no more—"

Sparrow didn't figure it—he only felt it. He was at the door and the knob was in his hand—it was turned for him from the other side and he had to step back to keep from getting banged by the door, they came in that fast, and he hadn't even heard a house key in the lock.

Bednar behind Kvorka. Both in citizen dress and their hats on their heads. With nothing in their hands.

Bednar put his back to the door. "Get the hypo, Sergeant," he told Kvorka.

"Now you know why Pig sent you?" Frankie taunted everyone. "This time you're comin' with me, punk."

"'N we hope you'll stay longer this time than the last," Bednar assured Sparrow with one hand in the punk's narrow belt.

Frankie rose, forever yawning, and studied Kvorka tearing up the bedclothes. "Holy Mother, look at that cop go," he laughed shrilly. "They still payin' sixteen bucks for turnin' in a hypo, Cousin? Make the cap split it with you—it's in the cigar box on the radiator, right there under your nose, it ain't even dry yet."

"On your feet, Dealer," Bednar scolded him. "We're takin' a little ride."

Some poolroom sharpie lounging in the lobby came to a sitting position when he spotted two hustlers being pulled in by a couple softclothes dicks and looked like he wanted to help get them to the station. But Bednar guided his little caravan unobtrusively out the side entrance and into the panel wagon waiting in the alley and wheeled away without a witness. It wasn't the sort of pinch to which Bednar wanted a witness.

As the wagon wheeled around the corner newsstand Sparrow heard the amputee, still pushing his papers there, call into him confidentially: "Graziano reinstated!"

Someone was always reinstating somebody. And all the way to the station listened to Frankie, still jabbering away, catching at all sorts of ragtags as if the stuff had given him some kind of delayed kick or other. He was going to beat the tubs with a big-time band, he was on his way now to the LaSalle Street Station to catch "the fastest flier they got there, I ride it lots of times, they call it the Twentieth-Century Note, somethin' 'r other." Then he had just bought out Schwiefka and was adding four tables and a line direct from the track— "Now's your chance to talk payoff," he told Bednar and when Cousin Kvorka urged him, "Take it easy, Dealer, we're still for you," he answered Cousin quickly: "How'd you like to transfer up to Evanston, Cousin? Just say the word."

He was buying a new Nash, he was getting divorced, he was sending Sophie to "Myer brothers," and he was getting married as soon as "all the dough I got outstandin' starts comin' in."

"Outstandin' is right," Sparrow put in. "Standin' out in the alley, you mean."

"Yeh," Frankie agreed strangely, "'n then I wonder why I feel so cold the next day."

Whatever he meant by that, his tongue had ceased to rattle. The rest of the way to the station he diverted himself simply by rapping the bench between his knees with his knuckles and humming idly.

> "I'm a ding-dong daddy from Duma
> 'N you oughta see me do my stuff—"

till he sensed just by the way Sparrow sat so stiffly across from him that the punk was freezing with fear.

"Looks like you're goin' to move out of this crummy neighborhood just like you always said you was goin' to," Frankie mocked him.

"I always try to keep my word, Frankie," Sparrow told him miserably.

Zygmunt the Prospector's full-moon face and Zygmunt the Prospector's full-moon smile lit up the query room for Frankie Machine without letting its mellow glow waste itself on Sparrow Saltskin. He took Frankie firmly right below the elbow; for a second Frankie fancied the other hand was trying for the pocket.

"Could you set bond for our friend here tonight, Captain?" Zygmunt had his hand around Frankie's shoulder now and Frankie felt himself coasting in at last.

"I'll set his bond at a hundred bucks right now," Bednar replied before Zygmunt had finished asking. "I'll let the court set bond for the guy who peddled it to him."

"Sounds like it was the punk Bednar was really layin' for," Frankie figured foggily. Something was awfully wrong, Bednar sticking it to Solly that hard. Bond in court would be a grand and a half if it were a dime.

"We're not interested in anyone but Mr. Majcinek," Zygmunt informed the captain blandly, clutching furtively at Frankie's sleeve. Frankie shook his head to clear it. *Whoof.* And just that fast felt someone had winked.

"Don't worry about a thing," Zygmunt confided in Frankie on their way back to West Division. "I signed for you on the super's orders. He takes care of his kids in the clutch."

"I didn't know I was one of the kids any more," Frankie confessed in real bewilderment. "How can I be when I ain't even workin' nowheres?" He was filled with an aching drowsiness, but he was back on the ground.

"You ain't said nothin' about wantin' a job," Zygmunt decided, "Schwiefka says you walked out on him. But if you want to go back dealin' Super'll find you a loose slot to fill in."

"How can I be settin' in a slot 'n settin' in the bucket too?" Frankie wanted to know.

"You ain't gonna be settin' in the bucket," Zygmunt told him firmly, "you're gonna cop out for this deal tonight. You're gonna tell the judge you're a user but it's the first time. It's no felony, Frankie. Not the first time. It's a misdemeanor is all. Super'll take care of that."

"Will Super take care of Solly too?" Frankie asked with a long sense of regret. He'd given the punk a bad time all right.

"The punk is a different case," Zygmunt advised his client sternly.

"Maybe it's none of my business," Frankie told Zygmunt when they paused on Ashland for the lights to change, "but I can tell Bednar if it's the guy who pushes the junk around a certain corner he's lookin' for, he ain't got him. All the punk ever done, since he took that bad fall by Gold's, is steer guys into Schwiefka's."

There was a queer little silence. Zygmunt seemed to be trying to swallow something that wouldn't quite go down.

Whatever it was, he got it down. Zygmunt could put anything down. "He delivered the stuff, that's all the captain needs. He been waitin' to get it on the punk a long time now."

"He certainly picked a funny night for it," Frankie brooded, dissatisfied with Zygmunt without knowing why. "Seems like he didn't want to pinch the true peddler at all." He was groping through an uphill darkness toward some door that *must* be there; yet with an increasing feeling, the closer he came to it, of being hopelessly trapped. "Seems like what he wanted was the punk—with

somethin' that can't be cut down to a misdemeanor. 'Cause if it was Pig he
wanted all he had to do was pick him up, Bednar knows who the peddler is as
well as you 'r me."

"You're cuttin' in too close, Dealer," Zygmunt warned him softly. "Why
don't you try to get some sleep? We'll talk it all out in the morning. You ain't
yourself tonight." Frankie felt a touch at his sleeve so light he wasn't sure
whether it was the Prospector or the wind.

In front of the yellow door with the red tin 29 nailed to the wood, Zygmunt
shook Frankie's hand and counseled him warmly, "Don't worry, Dealer. You
still got friends."

He had said something true at last. In his heart Frankie knew he still had
friends. Two of them.

One who was lost somewhere beneath the web of the Lake Street El; and
another lost behind bars.

Sophie was sleeping in the chair beside the window. The clock's hands lay
like a single horizontal cue across its face: a quarter to three. He fell across the
bed without waking her.

He had been sleeping scarcely an hour when he sensed someone had just called
up to him from the hall. But all the familiar sounds of night were missing below.
He lay listening for the beating of the clock beside the cross.

The clock had stopped, he read its hands in the phosphorescent crucifix's glow,
right-angled now precisely upon the hour: three o'clock in the morning.

With no child's voice down the steep dark stair nor one lonesome drunk
singing out from the one long bar below.

By the glare of the great double-globed arc lamp filtering through the dark
and battered shade he saw that Sophie had left the chair at last and in its place
had left a doll, some sort of mangy-looking straw-stuffed monkey of the kind
that is won at street carnivals. Over its eyes and below them some mimic had
painted in shadows of a purple harlotry with lipstick or rouge: the eyes surveyed the room gravely through its livid yet somehow dignified little mask.
Like those of a child whose face, seared by disease, accepts the horror it reads
in the eyes of others as its rightful heritage.

Pretending unconcern for its unwavering regard, he pulled the combat
jacket's collar up about his neck—and saw of what it was so terribly ashamed:
the rip in his sleeve was still torn. Molly had broken her promise to sew it after

all. Even the stripes on the sleeve seemed tattered. For he himself felt so frayed. Small wonder the thing in the chair felt ashamed of him. It wished him to be better dressed hereafter, always to be on time everywhere and not to be seen talking on corners at all hours of the night to people others didn't even recognize at high noon.

"I'm going to Stash's New Year's party," he apologized.

Of course everyone had already left the hall. Except a woman sleeping, head heavily upon her hands, below the sign that read NO REFUNDS. When she raised her head he saw it was Molly, drunk as always. Drinking all day and drunk once more.

She must be back with John, he heard the wind pick up in the street. Heard himself call some name in sleep and across his brain the dream flowed back like the flow of a wide wave over sand.

A faded trinket of a hat, topped by two paper daisies and soiled by a decade of free beers and dollar-a-minute love, lay beneath Molly's soiled hand: the hand of an aging woman. Someone had scattered a handful of change, halves and quarters and dimes and one silver dollar, beside the hat. Louie had forgotten his change—the hat, the hand, the daisies and the dollar were all so darkly soiled.

So knew she had been waiting for him here for ever so long. For news of some new hope. And he had come to her, as always, broke and hunted. Broke, beat and hunted, needing her help. So touched the paper daisies just to please her.

When she raised her eyes he hardly knew her, so careworn had she become, and a nameless regret touched him because she followed his fingers with her own with such ineffable tenderness, not blaming him, even now, for the way he'd made everything turn out for her after all.

"Them flowers been beat out for some time," she apologized for the daisies.

"You been a beat-out flower yourself awhile, looks like, Molly-O," he told her gently so that by his tone she would understand it made no real difference: she would always be a flower to him.

"We only bloom once," she told him in a voice that sorrowed because it wished for nothing any more except that she might bloom just once for him again.

Then tapped his fingers too familiarly. "Buy me one short beer, sport, I'm on my final uppers." And lifted the sole of her shoe to show him she wore only a pair of bowling shoes, still marked, in chalk, with the price it had once cost to rent them for a single hour: 10¢. With both bows so neatly tied, though the soles were worn to the ball of the foot and a line of dirt encircled the naked ankle like a chain.

"I think you turned out to be one of them kind after all," he reproved her.

"I always was one of them kind except with you," she admitted cheerfully and from somewhere the other side of the wall a low, agonized laugh, hoarse and significant, made him feel that some young girl was being either transported with rapture or murderously beaten in there.

"That's the other side of the wall, poor thing," he heard Molly telling him, "he does that to her every night, some nights it's worse'n others. Some nights, though, there ain't a sound—that's when it's worst of all."

"Does *what* to her?" Frankie asked with a certain fear.

Molly looked up at him with a dumb appeal, like a beaten animal's. "There ain't words for some things any more, Frankie," she told him with an effort. "There ain't no key to *that* room and all sorts hear about it. They come in at any hour at all 'n do whatever they want with her—she don't seem to care for nothin' since you went away like that." The fingers upon his own were chilled. It must take a whole lifetime for a woman's fingers to grow that cold, he thought as they listened together to the silence from the other side of the wall.

There that tortured laugh had rung. And Frankie understood slowly. "It's true. It's worse now when it's still."

So wakened to the silence on his own dark walls and Sophie's chill fat hand flat upon his own.

His own dark walls where a battered clock still beat the listening hours out. And an empty wheelchair stood beside a dark and battered shade. "It's worse when it's still," he repeated, wading heavily toward shore through the ebbing shallows of sleep.

The radiator began squealing as the heat strove to drive the night air out of the coils, like an uncovered child crying with sudden cold.

Coming out of the coils of his dream, with only a faint trace of morphine lingering along the edges of the brain, Frankie dismissed his nightmare for the more imminent one being woven, by hands as hard to grasp as those of any dream, about his waking hours.

He wrapped his shoulders in a blanket and sat by the window overlooking the abandoned tracks. "It's Louie that Record Head got on his mind awright," he decided with an odd lack of dread at the realization.

Somewhere a single warning bell, by dock or crosslight or bridge, yapped like a farm dog far away and went yammering into nothingness till the velvet dark surged back.

No, it hadn't been any accident that it had been the punk to whom Pig had passed the bottle. No accident, either, that Bednar had let him walk out of the station so easily while holding the punk so hard.

"It ain't the punk he wants, that's plain enough." Nobody needed any punk that badly. "All Record Head needs him for is to testify up on who slugged Louie. Clearin' that one up'll get Super off Record Head's neck." But how much pressure could the punk stand? How long would he be able to stand being wakened in the middle of the night and wheeled to a different station two nights a week without being booked in any?

"He either got to take a rap for peddlin' or finger me. He got to see it's his turn to take a rap for me like I took one for him. Or he got to cry off."

"Solly said he run from those irons before he had a chance to think," Frankie brooded. Well, now the kid was going to get all the time in the world to get things clear in his head. He would have to see it, Bednar wouldn't be able to move until Solly saw it as clearly as the captain. As clearly as Frankie himself saw it now.

"I got to sweat it out till I hear what the punk does," Frankie cautioned himself. "Settin' my bond at a hundred bucks—it's almost like the man *wants* me to jump bond."

There'd always be time to jump it. If he ran now, leaving Zygmunt to forfeit the hundred, he'd have to stay on the run. It would be the super's c-note Zygmunt had put up, he wouldn't be able to go back to work on Division Street till he'd squared that hundred.

While Bednar would have captain's men looking in every back-room slot on the Near Northwest Side for a dealer with needle marks on his arm and a slight squint in his eye.

He caught a picture of himself, wearing a little blond mustache and evening clothes, beating the drums with a big-name band on one of the revolving stages he'd seen in short features at the Pulaski—taking the bobby soxers' applause with Carmen Bolero. "I'll call myself Jack Duval 'r somethin'"—the fantasy collapsed of its own weight and he straightened himself out with bitter counsel. "A better name'd be Jack McGantic."

Someone turned on the water down the hall and all the second-floor faucets chirped at once, like so many crickets in a row.

It was too soon to run. For if the punk could take the punch there would be no need of running at all. He'd be clean of everything but possession of a hypo and it would be up to Zygmunt to put in the fix for that. If he ran too soon the game was lost before that last card had been dealt. "It's that last card that counts," he recalled.

Yet his heart was running already.

Down some rickety backstreet fire escape, his feet in heavy army brogans feeling, step by step, for the iron leading downward into some basement door-way, down any old dead-end alley at all. Headlong and heartsick down into any dark-curtained sanctuary where no one could find him at all.

No one but Sergeant McGantic.

It was always December in the query room. A light like a mustiness left over from another century filtered through the single window, far above, too high for anyone but a fireman to wash. It had been so long since it had been cleaned that, even on summer noons with the sun like a brass bell across pavement and rooftop and wall, the light sifted down here with a chill autumnal hue. It was always December in the query room.

When someone yanked the cord of the unshaded night bulb suspended from the ceiling like an inverted question mark—it had once held a gas flare instead of a Mazda—shadows would leap from the corners in a single do-or-die try for the window; only to subside and swing awhile with the bulb's slow swinging.

Then the wooden benches along the walls, where so many outcasts had slept, would be lit by a sort of slow, clocked lightning till the bulb steadied and fastened its tiny feral fury upon the center of the room like a single sullen and manic eye. To burn on there with a steady hate. Till morning wearied and dimmed it away to nothing more than some sort of little old lost gray child of a district-station moon, all its hatred spent.

It was not so much a room as a passage wherein were conveyed the pursued, by squadrol, panel wagon and Black Maria, out of the taverns, into the cells and thence swiftly down all the narrowing corridors of tomorrow.

Belonging, as it did, to no one and everyone, a place through which all passed and not one stayed, no one knew what it really looked like. Not even Record Head could have told its color, not even men who had confessed premeditated murder in it could have said whether its ceiling was low or high. Yet exactly as in the cells below, idlers wrote upon its walls: *This is my first affair. So please be kind.* Never once seeing how the walls upon which they wrote had been hallowed by pain. Only that bleak autumnal light, that had drifted down on so much anguish, told how these walls had been thus made holy.

For these were the very walls men meant when they said of another that he had his back to the wall. Here it was that they put their stubborn necks hard up against the naked brick, lied first to the right and then to the left, denying everything, explaining with scorn, swearing truth was truth and all falsehood wicked: and every word, from the very first burning oath, one long burning lie.

Indeed your query room is your only house of true worship, for it is here that men are brought to their deepest confessions. The more false and far-fetched their lies, the deeper and truer the final passion of their admission.

It was here that the truth, so calmly concealed from priest, mother, lawyer, doctor, friend and judge—from their very selves indeed—rose with such revealing fury at last to the tongue. It was here that certain couples, after sleeping beside each other for a decade, came to know one another at last: here the hardened tissue of lies was slit to expose the secret disease. Here the confession which salvages whatever love may remain was brought forth.

As well as the one word spoken too late. Sometimes penitently, sometimes triumphantly, sometimes shamefaced or feigning cynicism, the one word was spoken within this gutter-colored gloom. Too late.

That could, but for pride or fear, have been spoken in daylight and ease only a few hours before.

It was also the place to which they brought those for whom all was over and done, the final hope wrung out like last year's dishrag and washed down the Drainage Canal. Out to where the walleyed sturgeons roll.

Here too guilt was fashioned, like a homemade church-bazaar cross, out of those materials handiest to the law: a pack of greasy cards, a shopping bag with its bottom ripped out; or a little brown drugstore bottle.

It was here they brought Sparrow Saltskin, a baseball cap clutched in his hand, to sit in a cell by himself and think with a pang: "I'm in for it now."

All day long the voices of women came down to him. Sisters, sweethearts, mothers and wives bringing packages and messages, arguments and pleas. Money and tears and light, forced laughter.

Or just hope wrapped in an old comic strip.

The packages had to be left at the desk but fresh hope could be carried all the way down to the very last cell. Where some poor mutt of a cabbie, his tongue still burdened by a dying jag, kept boasting that his Gracie had actually come to see him. Just as if Solly Saltskin had ever said she wouldn't.

"Gracie came. Like she said she would. They wouldn't let her past the desk but she hollered down at me, 'Still wit' you, DeWitt!' "—all his worries solved because some dowdy old doll with a double chin and hair cascading down to her ears had hollered down to him through the concrete, the steel and the stone. He could face one to fourteen now with a splitting headache and a double-crossing lawyer because some Gracie or other had called some nonsense to him. Hope, tears and nonsense.

Borne on the FM waves of the heart.

There was neither sister, mother, wife nor any Gracie at all to call nonsense down to Solly Saltskin. Only Pokey, one button off his fly and one button on, pouring fuel oil from a rusty little tin can about the legs of the stool where he would keep an all-night vigil. The oil kept the bugs from crawling up his legs and the stool kept his elephantine bottom off the floor.

Only some muttonheaded Pokey. And Record Head Bednar.

The captain kept the punk waiting for him in the query room so long that, when he entered at last he saw, with an inner gratification, that the punk started to his feet—then changed his mind merely to sit looking bleakly anxious.

With the light from some long-dead December filtering down from that one window so far above that even the tireless last leap of the evening shadows could not reach it.

It was always December in the query room.

"Cards on the table, Steerer," Record Head told Sparrow right off, with no intention of revealing his own hand at all. The punk sat with his cap in his hand as if he'd just dropped in for a bit of a chat and would take off as soon as Bednar began to bore him. "We got a jacket for you that'll fit as close as nineteen does to twenty," Bednar told him. "This ain't malicious mischief or tampering, that you can get cut down to thirty days, Solly. We can call it the Harrison Act this time. Then it's the government holdin' the hammer."

"Don't start the heavy stuff till you feed me," Sparrow protested. "I was the oney one in the block didn't get coffee this morning."

"It's the new way we have of doin' things these days," Record Head explained. "First you answer the questions, then you eat. You know how long you're going to fall this time?"

"I was under the influence of a dramshop, somethin' legal like that, I didn't know what I was doin'," was the best the punk had for reply. "Anyhow you're s'pposed to feed me just like anybody. I was the oney one in the block didn't get coffee this morning."

"If you didn't know what you were doing you were out of your mind 'n we'll put you away in a room of your own. Is that what you're drivin' at, Solly?"

"What I'm drivin' at is somethin' to eat."

"In the booby house you eat every day."

"Well, I'll tell you," Sparrow answered earnestly. "You're not allowed to do that because I just ain't that crazy. I don't have all my marbles so I ain't responsible for no Harrison Act. But I got too many marbles to get put away. I was the oney one in the block this morning—"

"I don't want to hear about your diet. I want to know about them marbles."

"Well, if a guy got twenny-one he's all there, so you can give him time. 'N if a guy got only eleven you can put him in the booby house. But I'm right in between, I got nineteen, it's not enough to give me time 'n too many for the loony roost. It puts you on the spot, Captain, you can't do nuttin' wit'out two sikology doctors 'n they'll never get together on me, it'll end in a draw like the other time. They'll be up there testifyin' against each other about what is it goes on in my ubconshus till they testify me right back onto the street—'n the first thing I'm gonna do when I get there is to walk right into a hamburger stand 'n get somethin' to eat."

"Don't stop," the captain urged Sparrow to let his tongue run on a bit more. "I want to hear it all."

"You just heard it all," Sparrow acknowledged weakly. "I'm not a *legal* goof, I'm just a *street* goof, you got to find a guy like that a guard-yun 'n turn him loose. We eat real soon, Captain?"

"Maybe never," the captain cheered him, "your logic is too much on the side of what the courts call 'ten-you-us.' It means you been walkin' the same hairline too long 'n now we're yankin' it out from under you like an old rag carpet."

Sparrow sat with the cap dangling uselessly from his fingers: his hands felt as useless as a paralytic's. They'd made so much trouble for everyone he hoped they wouldn't make any more.

"Sure we give you the breaks because you're a little retarded," the captain went on. "You hand the boys a laugh so they go easy. But all the time we know you really ain't that retarded. We know it's just your act. But it's a good act, it's different, and we don't get many good acts around here any more." He paused to imply that the old days were gone for everyone. "Now you've worked the act straight into the ground. It was all right for dog stealin' 'n drunk 'n disorderly 'n Prospector got you off light for that cowboy caper at Gold's——who wants to rap a punk for a caper as goofy as *that?* But now you've pulled Uncle Sam's whiskers 'n Uncle ain't gonna care whether you talk goofy 'r straight. When you pull Uncle's whiskers, you go."

"I don't want to go."

"No, and I don't want to send you. What good would that do *me?* What good would it do me to add up a man's convictions 'n then have to tell him, 'Now you're a habitual. Good-by'?"

"I ain't," Sparrow corrected Bednar.

"This one'll make just enough," Bednar assured him.

"This one don't count toward the habitch act," Sparrow spoke up confidently. "This is a G offense, you just got t'rough sayin' it yourself. It got to be state 'n it got to be a crime of the same nature for you to call me habitual. What's more, usin' that stuff in the bottle is a misdemeanor the first time, that's all. Don't you figure I know *anythin',* Captain?"

"You weren't using. You were peddling," the captain pointed out.

"Well," Sparrow reflected aloud, "everybody's a habitual in his heart. I'm no worse'n anyone else."

The captain put both his elbows upon the table, leaned heavily upon them and studied Sparrow through fingers crossed before his eyes. Sparrow thought for one second that Bednar was smiling at him behind those great hands and a kind of panic took him to get this thing over one way or another, any way at all and the faster the better. When Bednar looked up there was no trace of a smile on his lips: he wore a certain fixed look. "Now it's comin'," Sparrow thought shakily, trying to hold that heavy gaze.

"You should of been a lawyer, Solly," the captain told him at last. "You know somethin' all right. The dealer knows somethin' too. You know who slugged Fomorowski and he knows who left him holdin' the bag at Nieboldt's. *There's* your crime of the same nature, Solly. You try beatin' Gold's 'n come right back tryin' Nieboldt's."

"I wasn't there."

"Frankie says you was. Frankie says it was your idea. Frankie says he done one stretch for you, now it's your turn to do one for him."

Sparrow stretched his narrow neck in his oversized collar. The cap dropped to the floor. He didn't feel it drop. Bednar waited.

"When did Frankie say it?"

"He ain't said it yet, Solly. He won't say it till we pick him up 'n ask him. What do *you* think he'd say, sittin' where you are? It's your skin or his, Solly."

"I don't know who slugged Fomorowski."

The captain sighed heavily. It was all to do again. He'd almost had it driven home into that narrow forehead; then somehow it had slipped off the skull.

"Look at it this way, Solly. You got two felonies against you—both state offenses so it works automatic: you're busted for life 'n no parole. You know the habitch act as well as myself. You can take that and we'll still get your buddy, sooner or later, for manslaughter. But we'd rather get him sooner. Later on it doesn't do anybody any good. Right now it helps some people a lot to get that Fomorowski thing cleaned up. So we give you a chance. You help us and you don't even get booked for peddling, you get booked for nothin' except maybe creatin' a public nuisance, just somethin' to cover the deal. Then you're back on the street 'n you've learned your lesson."

"Where's Frankie when I'm back on the street?"

"He'll be back on the street with you in eighteen months, you can take my word. The longer it takes to bust him the tougher we're going to make it on him—you'll be doin' him the biggest favor of his life by coming clean." But he seemed to be looking over Sparrow's head. The punk sensed that that was going to be a mighty long eighteen months.

"I don't want to do Frankie no favors," he told Bednar, "he's mad at me for somethin'."

"Then this is your big chance to patch things up with him. Who got Louie's roll, Solly?"

"They said Louie died from a hit on the head," Sparrow answered foggily. "Can I have a cup of coffee now, Captain?"

"You didn't have to have nobody tell you, Solly. You were there."

"I was by Schwiefka's that's where *I* was. I went out fer coffee 'n that's when it must of happened, when I was stirrin' the spoon. Why don't you talk to Schwiefka, Captain?"

"Schwiefka's clean 'n you know it. Tell us how Louie got it 'n walk out of here clean too. I'll see you go back to work by Zero's. A deal is a deal."

"The blood ain't on *my* paws," Sparrow said ever so quietly.

"You got no idea how bad unsolved murder looks on the books in an election year," the captain began from a new flank, feeling he was hitting the proper tone at last: one of confidential reasonableness between two practical politicians. "The Republican precinct captains are handin' out handbills rappin' the super—they're tellin' the people if it wasn't one of Super's boys done it why don't he put a finger on who really done it then? Louie owed too much, Solly. His connections were too good. That's where the pressure's on Super 'n that's where I put it on you. Louie owed more dough than you 'n me could count if we set here together countin' all night. Who got the roll, Solly?"

Sparrow looked at his hands, saw his cap was gone but his eyes didn't seek for it. Instead they stayed fixed on his hands, as though unsure whether he might not yet find a spot of somebody's blood there.

"They're pointin' your way, Solly. Louie had a roll on him that wasn't his own. Who got it?"

"They ain't pointin' me, Captain."

"I didn't say they was pointin' you. I said they're pointin' your direction. You were there, Steerer." The captain rose, came behind Sparrow's chair and put both hands on the punk's thin shoulders to steady him. "You go along with me 'n Super," Sparrow heard that confident voice so low and reassuring, "'n you'll be runnin' a game of your own. Some nice quiet back room 'n no trouble at all 'cause you'll have me 'n Super givin' you the protection. You could live by Kosciusko Hotel in a room of your own, when you want a girl you just pick up the phone 'n they send up two, you should take your pick. You don't even bother goin' out to eat, you just pick up the phone 'n tell 'em to send up an order of *shashlyk*."

"Don't like *shashlyk*."

The captain didn't press the point. He watched the punk wipe sweat off his glasses. The punk looked sick to death. He felt the shoulders tremble under his hands and took his hands away—the captain didn't like the feel of a trembling man.

Then looked at the punk just as at some sort of thing, and his tone came as hard as newly forged manacles. "Pick up your cap. Either you'll play ball or I'll give you to Mr. Schnackenberg. I'll be in court myself to make it stick."

Just outside the room someone was trying to strike a bargain with a couple arresting officers. "You let me alone 'n I'll let you alone." In that moment the captain saw the punk more clearly than he had ever seen him before: a sharp little alley terrier driven to the wall, trying to understand, out of cunning and unmixed fright, what his pursuer's next move would be.

"You're nailin' me to the cross, Captain," Sparrow pleaded.

The captain started, he hadn't really seen it in that light at all. "*I'm* nailin' *you?*" he wanted to know with genuine indignation. "What the hell you think they're doin' to *me?*"

"I'll take the rap first myself," Sparrow told him with something like finality.

For that was just how that Chester Morris had said it that time he was Boston Blackie at the Pulaski. Yet a tiny bubble swelled in his throat and could not burst. "You must think you're talkin' to some kind of stool pigeon 'r somethin'," he challenged the captain. Just as if Bednar had seen *Boston Blackie* that time too and knew his own part, he leaned over and touched Sparrow's shoulder paternally.

"Get a lawyer, lad," he counseled the punk gently. "Get a *good* lawyer. I want to see you get every break you got comin'. You're going to need every one of them."

"Can I have coffee now, Captain?" Sparrow asked wistfully.

But the captain had put his head upon his hands as if he were the one in need of confession. Sparrow leaned forward and saw, with a strange uneasiness, that the captain was feigning sleep.

They didn't call him Machine any more. The marks didn't want a junkie dealing to them. He didn't look regular to them any longer, they were not certain why. They sensed something had gone wrong, he looked so like a stranger at times. He saw this in their eyes and felt it in their voices; and somehow didn't care at all. He had the feeling he wouldn't be hanging around Schwiefka's long enough for it to matter.

Bednar was working on the punk was the word at Schwiefka's. There was no word that Bednar had broken him down. Frankie saw a small bet made, between meter Reader and Schwiefka, that the punk wouldn't break at all. But it was Meter Reader who believed in Sparrow—and who had ever heard of Meter Reader winning a bet on anything? "I'll wait till I see Umbrellas backin' the kid," Frankie thought wryly, "when I see that I'll *know* it's time to run."

Meanwhile he wandered restlessly between the room, the Tug & Maul, and Schwiefka's. He couldn't stand the room and he couldn't afford to drink all day with Antek and he no longer belonged at Schwiefka's.

"The dealer's on the needle," was the whisper, and overnight he was an outcast of outcasts and a new dealer—that very Bird Dog to whom Frankie had misdealt—sat in the slot. If Frankie wanted to take a hand the boys made room for him. Just a bit too much room, he fancied; the way they'd make room for a syphilitic. For the man on the needle, though he be your brother, is a stranger to every human who lives without morphine.

He sensed pity mixed with fear in the voices of those who spoke to him now. Yet Schwiefka let him take care of the door that Sparrow had so long and so faithfully guarded. He drew five dollars a night and tips, the same wage Sparrow had drawn. And each night, when he paid Frankie off, Schwiefka averted his eyes and asked, "You tried Kippel's, Frankie?" Frankie would shrug, he understood well enough. Schwiefka wanted him to be working for somebody else if the punk should start pointing.

Frankie would try to look as though he didn't know he were hot at all. He needed that fiver too badly. Each night now, after closing time, he spent half of it for a quarter-grain fix in Louie's old room. He paid Blind Pig the two-fifty in quarters and halves and fixed himself with the help of one of Louie's flashy ties and that same hypo he'd stolen overseas. "Just enough to put me to sleep," he would tell Blind Pig, "I ain't doin' no joy-poppin' these days. All I want is enough to keep from gettin' sick."

"Thought you was off the stuff, Dealer." Pig would feign surprise that anyone who wanted to be off it should go on feeding the habit all the same.

"When you come to the end it's the end, that's all." Frankie acknowledged his defeat in the wan winter light.

Each night at Schwiefka's felt like the last night of guarding any man's door: as each day seemed now it must surely be the last of all with Sophie. Sometimes he wondered idly how long it could be before she caught on to what was wrong. Then it would come over him that she had known from the day he'd come back and every day since. "She don't say nothin' because it's her one big kick. Like watchin' me crawl around the floor pickin' up the dishes that time." An hour later, recalling that he had entertained such a suspicion, would reproach himself. "I ought to be ashamed of myself, thinkin' of Zosh like that— how could she know about me when all I'm ever doin', when we're in the room together, is layin' on the bed?" He would make up his mind, there and then, to run for it. If she knew it was time to run and if she didn't know it was time to run before she found out.

Yet each night found him back at the door trying to overhear some mention of Solly Saltskin's name. Though he listened every night for word of the punk all he could learn was that the punk was still being held in one station or another. And would try in his heart to believe that Sparrow wouldn't finger him in any station at all.

The dread stirred with his every waking. "This is the day Bednar busts the kid." Then the need of the quarter-grain charge would start coming on so strong he would have to admit, even to himself, that the reason he hadn't yet run, in the very teeth of arrest, was that he feared to go far from the room above the Safari. "That's just what Bednar's bankin' on too," he felt.

One night when the table was filled and Schwiefka didn't want the door opened for anyone for a while, Frankie stood on the fire escape and saw how the unseen lights of the Loop were reflected in the sky like light from some gigantic forge beating in the pit of the city's enormous heart. A heart seeming now to beat in suppressed panic. A panic lying in wait, each midnight hour, at his own heart's forge.

Night of the All Nite restaurants, the yellow-windowed machine-shop night where daylight was being prepared on lathes. Night of the thunderous anvils preparing the city's iron heart for tomorrow's iron traffic. Night of the city lovers, the Saturday Night till Sunday Morning lovers, making love on rented beds with the rent not due till Monday.

Night of iron and lovers' laughter: night without mercy. Into a morning without tears.

From where the narrow alley ran a child's cry, high-pitched, brief and cut off sharply, came up to him like the cry of a child run down in the dark by a drunken driver. A cry that held no hope of help at all, a cry that pitched the very darkness down. Tautly, as he himself had pitched his tent that winter on the Meuse, with the stakes driven through the cloth like the cloth of the heart, the way darkness pinned any child down between tavern and trolley and tenement.

The darkness through which all such children of the broken sky line moved, their small white faces guided only by a swinging arc lamp's gleam and the swift-changing neon guide lights of the city's thousand bars. Till the difference between daylight and darkness seemed to them only the difference between the light of the alleyways under the El and the light down any gin-mill basement.

That was why, Frankie guessed, everyone from the neighborhood he knew, from the punk to himself, tried to be something different than what he was. The minute some kid with an accordion began playing for pennies in the corner bars he fancied himself a musical-comedy star. If a neighborhood girl got a Loop switchboard job she considered herself a career woman. Nobody bred

around Division Street ever turned out to be a cheap crook: they were all
Dillingers or Yellow Kid Weils to hear them tell it. Just as though the dead
wagon didn't cart off the international embezzler as surely as it bore off the
musical-comedy headliner and the crummiest stewbum who ever turned up
his toes between Goose Island and the carbarns.

Sometimes, as Frankie walked to the Safari in the earliest morning light,
after the night's last deck had been boxed, Division Street was deserted from
the *Dziennik Chicagoski* to the El. Then the changing traffic lights seemed to
warn no one but himself: STOP.

And so waited prudently, though there was no traffic in sight and the wind
so bitter, till the amber light counseled him to look both ways, for enemy and
friend alike, before crossing carefully.

Until the green told him to pull up his collar and keep moving straight
ahead, warning him it was just as dangerous to stand in one spot too long as it
was to try to beat the lights. That it was more dangerous now, with every hour,
to stand unmoving in a bitter wind; that it was his one chance to plunge blindly
ahead looking neither this way nor that.

For now, in this season of caroling, when fir trees were sold in every corner
lot, no morning brought tidings of comfort and joy.

Morning brought only church bells and dock bells, river bells and barge
bells, freight bells and fire bells—and the ceaseless charging of the westbound,
southbound, northbound, Loopbound Els.

The green light itself had turned informer.

It grew pretty lonely without Frankie. No fun like the other times at all. Only
the lost cabbie, one cell down, by turn boasting of his Gracie and repenting of
his own manifold weaknesses.

"Ask fer me on Wabash 'n Harrison," he began inviting everyone late one
night, his tongue still sounding burdened to Sparrow. "I'm the guy wit' the right
connections. Ask fer me on the hotel corner, I wheel the GI Joe cab there.
Gracie brings me sandriches but I got no damned matches. Pokey'd gimme
some but I don't want to wake him up. He let me make a phone call fer free
when I told him I was crashed but the morning guy is no good, he wants a buck
or no phone. I showed that marked-down lushworker, I thrun his moldy
baloney on the floor. 'There's yer breakfast,' I told him straight."

Sparrow was too preoccupied with his own woes to listen to any cabbie's. "The captain's gonna see I get all the breaks I got comin'," he brooded now upon Bednar's words. "How the hell did he *mean* that?"

Yet knew in his heart just how Record Head had meant that.

"Tomorrow I'm gettin' out," the cabbie decided aloud, as he decided around this time every night, "first thing I'm goin' to the Rye-awlto. You guys remember Eddie Cicotte? I knew a guy once used to pinch-hit fer Rockferd in the T'ree-Eye League. My old man never hit a bar in his life but he kept a little bottle in the medicine cab'net, he said it was his healt' tonic. The old lady was hitched to him twenny-eight years before she found out it was Old McCall. You guys know some good pinched-hitters? She did say she'd noticed he'd act a little strange on Saturday nights. Swap me a couple cigarettes, soldier?"

All Sparrow could see of the cabbie was one tattooed forearm wrapped about the bars. "I ain't no soldier," he assured the cabbie, "I got rejected for moral warpitude." And a dull calamitous light like a madhouse light began filtering dimly down from somewhere far above, making an uphill queue of shadows aslant the whitewashed walls. Nudging each other upward inch by sullen inch, they gathered strength for some sudden and swift descent by midnight behind queues of shadowy escapees from a hundred other cells. Down to a shadowed street.

Between the bars and down the disinfected corridors, unseen by captain's men and soft-clothesmen, undetected by the confidence detail the sullen shadows sidled, by-passing the pawnshop patrol and the cartage squad while the auto-theft hawks were giving tomorrow's winners to two dog-tag detectives and a single plain-clothes bull. Past pressmen and citizen-dress men, evading fire dicks and gumboots, fingerprint experts and rookies in harness, the night's last bondmaker and the morning's earliest, most eager bailiff, down many a narrow long-worn wrought-iron way, to be delivered at last from the grand-jury squad and the Bail Bond Bureau into the dangers of the unfingered, unprinted, unbetrayed and unbefriended Chicago night.

"You should see my Gracie," the cabbie invited everybody, waking or asleep, "she's a hundred per cent 'n her petticoat hangs like crazy. But I got a good record too, I never hit a mailman in my life. Never hit a conductor. Who wants a couple lousy cigars for a couple tailor-made cigarettes?" He laughed derisively.

Then added as apologetically as though suddenly confronted by a teetotaling judge: "I been in five rackets, sir, but I supported my sister's kids two years, that's in my favor. Once I lost a hunderd-eighty in a fixed crap game, worked overtime t'ree mont's to make it back 'n then got rolled by my best friend for a hunderd-ten. Didn't even get downhearted, just started on that overtime slave deal again, pinchin' them little red pennies, gettin' back on my feet wit' the little woman helpin' all the way 'n never askin' nothin' except once a while a piece of my little pink body. Never heard her squawk once. 'My little red wagon is hitched to yours, DeWitt,' she tells me, 'I take the bad wit' the good, the bitter wit' the sweet.' So I knocked her off the back porch to learn her some sense.

"You know where a man goes wrong? It's on them dirty gas bills every time. I didn't owe a dime in the world yesterday afternoon—then she sent me out to square up wit' People Gas Light 'n Coke 'n I stopped off for a quick one 'n all I got to do now is restitute the *insurance* company for a four-hunderd-buck plate-glass window 'r do it on the knees. 'Let's settle this out of court,' I says. 'Wit' *what?*' they want to know—can you beat that? They'd been to see Gracie awready 'n found out I don't own a dime of my own 'n now Friendlier Loans knows where I'm at too. Them dirty gas bills is a man's downfall every time."

"Go back to the beginning," Sparrow requested politely, "I lost tract in the middle." But DeWitt was too busy hauling that little red wagon of piled-up woes to heed anyone.

"Can they get their money back if I do a stretch?" he asked himself with a sort of angry perplexity. "They won't get penny-one that way 'n that's where I got 'em by the old jalino. I'm goin' to work for them plate-glass people till the *insur-ance* people is all squared up—so now all I'll have to do is drop one of them windows now 'n then 'n I got me a steady slave deal the rest of my dirty life.

"All I hope is that bartender don't clunk the bucket, the cop said he got cut pretty bad when he went t'rough the glass. If he clunks it, then it's all over. Then it's on the knees the rest of the way 'n no Gracie, no gas bills, nothin'.

"Bills 'n humiliations, troubles 'n degradations," DeWitt told himself softly, "'n it's on the knees the rest of the way all the same."

"I'm a lost-dog finder myself," Sparrow informed the cabbie brightly. "You want to buy a Polish airedale?" but DeWitt remained too preoccupied. "I try to get the fool salty at me but the fool won't salt. Brings me cigarettes 'n says she's still wit' me. If she's still wit' me how come she fergets the matches? Are they *all* like that? Once I shoved her out of the cab 'n all she done was sniffle a little 'n come up lame. I should of shoved her harder. But one thing they can't pin on

me, I never hit a mailman in my life. Say, who wants to swap me a couple cigarettes for a couple lousy stogies—where'd I get these things in the first place?"

"The same thing happened to a fellow in Pittsburgh," Sparrow consoled
DeWitt.

"How many in there?" the lockup wanted to know.

"One," Sparrow told him and the lockup, peering closer, recognized the punk
in the dimness. "Oh, it's you—the captain says any time you want to get in touch
with a lawyer, just say the word." And moved on to ask DeWitt, sitting hoarse
and limp from his night-long efforts, "Are you the guy was hollerin' all night?"

"No, sir," the little cabbie lied meekly, "I just been settin' here waitin' for the
brother-law."

"Who's he?"

"He's a sergeant detective wit' the attorney's office."

"What attorney?"

"State's attorney."

"Don't give me that cheap romance. You're a loose bum with a streak of
pimp 'n if you got a brother-law he's pimpy too. Yer whole fam'ly's pimpy."

The outraged cabbie rose, tore the top button off his shirt to give his throat
room, squeezed his forehead forward between the bars till the temples were
pinched by the steel.

"You insultin' my *fam'ly?* Awright, let's have your number, fellow, you're
gonna be on the job as long as John was in the army 'n John wasn't in there
long. Don't try givin' *me* the business, when Big Eye Lipschultz gets here we're
puttin' in a little beef on you to the state's attorney 'n there goes your number.
No use tryin' to shove me around from one station to another neither—I'm
the guy got friends in *all* of 'em, Big Eye 'n me don't care *what* bond you set,
Big Eye's takin' over this case person'lly now. Ever hear of Defamation of
Character, sucker? That's what you just done. Ever been sued for false arrest?
Ever heard of the U.S.A. Constitution?"

"I didn't even know the fellow was sick," the turnkey advised DeWitt solic-
itously at last. "Could you let me know when he gets back to town?" He turned
softly away, thinking soft and killing thoughts. "I *tawt* that was the guy was hollerin'," he explained further up the tier, "I just wanted to make sure. For when
he starts askin' favors."

"I'll need favers from you like I need a chop in the head with a dull ax!" DeWitt
had found his voice again all right. "You lead wit' yer nose!" Then bent his troubled

forehead against his fist and his fist about the cold blue bars, brooding desperately upon the duplicity of policemen in general and Chicago cops in particular.

"You got to know a desk man or a bailiff if you want to get out before Monday," Sparrow consoled him, "but you're a man all the same, cabbie. You're a victim of circumstance but you're a man all the same." Sparrow laid it on heavy in the hope of getting DeWitt started on the turnkey again.

"I'm just a nobody," DeWitt decided gloomily, confessing himself aloud. "Just a down-'n-out, hard-luck, no-good, slow-dwindling drip." Adding wistfully, "But Gracie's a hunderd per cent."

"That lockup wouldn't of talked that way if there hadn't been bars between you, champ," Sparrow flattered the little man as if picturing him as some oversized strongarmer not likely to be subdued by less than four patrol-loads of the city's finest.

"I couldn't whip *nobody,* pal," the moody DeWitt resumed his self-denunciation like a man with a fixed idea. "I couldn't battle my way out of a wet paper bag. I'm just a know-it-all, know-nuttin' jerk. A drag-ass ignoramus. A stooge. A bottom-of-the-heaper. I guess I'm the biggest bust out of the museum. Small potatoes 'n few in the hill, that's me."

"Yeh," Sparrow agreed, "but he didn't have to call you no bum. You want to buy a dog?" Implying that a dog, any dog, was the one certain solution, in an uncertain world, to any cabbie's troubles.

"I couldn't buy the lice off a sick cat," the cabbie answered from the very depths of self-deprecation.

"I wouldn't sell you one with lices," Sparrow assured him lightly. "I take the lices off 'n sell *them* sep'rate."

"I wouldn't buy one wit' out no licenses." DeWitt's confusion grew.

Then down the dusty jailhouse hours Sparrow stood watching the long light rise and spread, shift slowly when the noon chow cart tinkled and ebb drowsily down, like feathered hours, upon the sleeping strays. All through that brief December day the castoffs and the outlaws slept, rebels and wrecks and heat-broken bummies, cell after cell and tier upon tier, wakened only by the weary chow cart's call or the sudden clanging of a cell door upon some forenoon coneroo, afternoon penny matcher or early evening lush arguing fiercely while being locked up for cooling off.

Watched and remembered Frankie Machine and the arm that always held up. Remembered in the evening light, when cards are boxed and cues are racked, straight up and down like the all-night hours with the hot rush hours past. Remembered that golden arm.

Till he saw how Bednar would beat it at last.

Pokey came past dragging a drunk by the scruff of the neck and the toes turned toward the ceiling: he bounced by wearing a smile of serenest peace, as if fancying he were riding in a cab while his heels scuffed stone and his arms dangled like a puppet's on broken strings. Pokey held him with one ham of a hand while opening the next cell with the other.

Sparrow heard the body land like a sack, Pokey's twin cats tiptoed up to see whether they'd surveyed this particular abomination before and nodded to each other judicially: "It's him again all right"—and tiptoed tastefully out of sight.

"Cats are all stooges anyhow," Sparrow felt an old preference, "a dog'll never squeal on a pal"—as his own predicament began breaking in on him at last.

Going. This time he was *really* going.

He heard a girl's voice crying out a single question, she was being brought in off the street a full floor above him; but in a voice so agonized it seemed she spoke directly to himself:

"Ain't anybody on *my* side?"

She was really asking him.

"Nobody, sister. Not a soul," Sparrow answered, she suited his own mood so well. "You're all on your own from here on out. Ain't nobody on anybody's side no more. You're the oney one on your side 'n I'm the oney one on mine."

But no one, on the long streets above, off which both had been taken, cared one way or another. For up there each was the only one on his own side. Under one moon or another, he knew not one man on the side of men.

"Hey! Pokey!" DeWitt had heard the girl's anguished cry too and was back at the bars ready to do fresh battle with the lockup. "Hey! Pokey! They just fished a Clark Street whore out of the river—run up 'n see if it's your wife!"

Really going. Going for good and it wasn't a gag and no vaudeville stuff about being ready to come down and do thirty days any time would get him out of an hour of the whole long dirty unlivable years. "I don't want to go," Sparrow whimpered in a terror that wrung his heart. For Bednar's own great hand had reached within and found that heart at last.

When Pokey came past, to see what the cabbie had to say for himself this time, Sparrow reached one thin arm through the bars and touched the pokey's shirt sleeve.

"I'll make that phone call now," Sparrow told Pokey.

This year there was no party. There was only a four-foot Christmas tree, bearing a single star from the five-and-dime, to stand beneath the luminous Christ against the hallway wall.

And like a child waking from a dream of a single star, Sophie spoke the words she had spoken all the Christmas seasons of her life: *Gwizadka tam na niebie*. A starlet there on the heavens. For one more year.

On New Year's Eve there came a brief challenge of cardboard horns from the bar below; and a single silvery siren called to them both from far away. Then all was still: the long, long year was gone and the new year had begun, borne in upon a revelry of cardboard trumpets blown by strangers. Blowing like their very own lives to somewhere far away.

Frankie had not gone to work. He went to sleep just after 2 A.M.

Slept. And had bad dreams.

Dreams of iron footsteps upon a spiraling stair with just time enough left to reach a pane blurred by either last year's rains or tomorrow's tears—only time enough left to get his hand on the latch and feel it grate with rust as old as the rains and all the strength went out of his fingers: through the streaked and spotted glass a monkey with a jaunty green fedora on his head returned his gaze. A small red feather in the fedora's band was wilting in the rain. Bent in a sort of crouching cunning there on the other side of the pane, it gave Frankie the look which womenish men employ in sharing an obscenity with their own kind.

Frankie felt himself struggling to waken, for the monkey was tucking the covers about his feet, still wearing that same lascivious yet somehow tender look. Felt the unclean touch of its paw and saw its lips shyly seeking his own with Sparrow's pointed face. To kiss and be kissed, and he wakened from the very pit of his stomach, with a bounding leap of his heart—the window was open, the dark shade was rustling, something was going wrong with him and someone was knocking softly and stealthily at his own hallway door.

The furtive knocking of one who wishes to waken but one sleeper in a room where a friend and a foe lie sleeping; and felt Sophie stir beside him.

He went to the door in his naked feet and asked, as softly as the hand that knocked, "Who's knockin' this time of the morning?"

Kvorka from Saloon Street, out of uniform, sweaty about the collar and whitish about the mouth, stood in the hall with the knuckles of his red-mittened right hand raised as if to conceal some evidence there of the new year's earliest felony. Frankie shut the door noiselessly behind him.

"The punk is cryin' off, Dealer," Cousin had come to say. "Bednar come out of the room half an hour ago with the paper in his hand. The wagon men got the warrant, they're havin' coffee at the Coney 'n then they're on their way." He started to give Frankie his hand, thought better of it and turned toward the stairs with his one last embarrassed plea: "Don't feel too hard on the punk, Dealer. He bucked the old man in five different stations thirty dirty days before he bust. He been cryin' downstairs there all night since he done it. Don't feel too hard."

"Thanks, Cousin." Listening to Cousin's hurried step down the leaning stairs, he called over the railing, "Look out for the loose board."

Cousin was already safely past the open tread and safely out on the open street. Frankie turned, numb from cold or fear, back to the room, feeling for the knob as though he were still dreaming. Then came to with a sharp command to his own numb toes: "Move fast, feet. Jump off." And the cold hall draft nudged him anxiously, like a nudge from an anxious stranger: the downstairs door had swung open of itself and would bang back and forth there till the Jailer sent Poor Peter down to fasten it securely.

He had his his left lace tied and his hands upon the bow of the right when the right hand started to tremble. It shook for a whole half minute while he watched it with a wan despair; then pressed his thumb down upon the knot and tied it with his left hand. When it was tied the trembling stopped as suddenly as it had begun; yet something continued to flutter there. Within his pulse's fluttering.

"Where the hell *you* casin' off to?"

"Just goin' down for rolls, Zosh."

"Was somebody here?"

"Just the paper kid."

"You got to wear a clean shirt to buy rolls these days?"

"It's Sunday, Zosh. What kind you want?"

"The custard kind."

"They don't have that kind on Sunday."

But she had fallen asleep again, into a dream of fresh custard rolls every day of the week and chocolate éclairs on Sunday. He slipped his GI shaving kit into his combat jacket, fingers fumbling on the buttons, saw a couple bandages on the shelf and took those too, he didn't know why. Then picked up an empty half gallon from under the sink, tapped his wallet to be sure there was still something in it and didn't even look toward the bed to see whether she slept or watched as he left.

Standing on the open street with the empty in his hand, he hesitated to go to the left or to the right for the refund. It wasn't that he needed the dime that badly—though he knew he was going to need every dime he could trap soon— but rather that it just didn't seem right to be hunted by the police with a half-gallon empty in his hand. He couldn't remember Burt Lancaster doing it that way at all. Burt never seemed to need a ten-cent refund.

For what Frankie sought, in that hesitating moment, was the place that would return him a refund on his very life, fleeing headlong, down back street and alley, so fast and so far he didn't know whether he'd ever recapture it again.

The nearest open bar was the Widow Wieczorek's and he moved into it with the hand that held the empty already bluish with cold. It wasn't any kind of a morning to be on the lam—how the hell was a lamster supposed to stay warm in January anyhow?

Right at the front of the bar Umbrella Man stood as if he'd been leaning against it all Saturday night, waiting for Sunday morning's earliest customer.

He certainly looked like he was battling the booze, Frankie saw. Umbrellas looked like he was dying for a beer. But he spoke no word as Frankie passed: only leaned forward and begged with his eyes, rolling them like a dying dog's toward Frankie. Frankie shook his head. No.

Umbrellas leaned back once more against the bar to wait for someone who would say yes.

In the rear of the bar the Widow Wieczorek was stoking up the stove and Frankie sat studying the usual legends till she came to serve him. Feeling Umbrellas' eyes upon him all the while.

Don't say 'charge it,' one legend urged, *this isn't a battery station.*

Don't stare at the bartender, another requested, *you may be goofy yourself someday.*

Frankie hunched forward over the rail, pretending he was back in the Kentucky Tavern in Brussels, where he'd spent a riotous three-day pass just before his last convoy. When he opened his eyes the Widow was looking down at him and asking, "How's by you?"

"Is by me okay," Frankie assured her and shoved the empty toward her; but she shook her head, no soap. It was a Fox 400 and she had switched to Canadian Ace.

"Take it anyhow," Frankie told her. "I just want to set a minute to get warm. You got a warm beer?"

The Widow brought him a warm beer and he let it stand while trying to guess which of his two pursuers he might dodge the longest. Bednar or McGantic. How long was he going to be able to stay out of sight when he started getting sick? He was good for forty-eight hours at the most—then he was going to have to score for M, and he'd have to do it in strange territory.

He knew, as every West Side junkie knows, of the one-arm restaurant at a Madison Street transfer point that carries junkie traffic all night long. There the sallow unkjays sit, over coffee growing cold, facing windows which allow them to spot anyone pushing the stuff in any of four directions.

A convenient arrangement for both sides in the ceaseless battle for possession of heroin, morphine and cocaine. Convenient to the junkies and convenient to the narcotic squad, which could pick up any particular junkie—the squad knew most of the old-timers—without pursuing him all over the city. After the squad had picked up the one they wanted, those left behind felt a sense of ease, knowing they would not be troubled again for a few hours and could go about their business in relative peace.

The junkies were Sergeant Dugan's business and Sergeant Dugan was theirs. There was an understanding between them which made it possible for him to pick them up like a father taking a wayward child home. They liked to be regarded as children, and it was as sick children that Dugan regarded them. They went with resignation. Occasionally one sought him out to give himself up, asking to be sent to Lexington for the cure, and Dugan would arrange the pauper's writ for such a surrenderer. If he felt such surrender sincere. He would wish the junkie luck in kicking the habit.

Six months later Dugan would be cruising about with one eye out for that same truce-bearer and a warrant in his pocket.

Dugan was an earthy man and wished other men to stay on the ground. When he saw one propelling himself through Cloudland simply by twitching his nose like a rabbit, Dugan felt obliged, by decency as well as by duty, to bring him back down. Though the junkie might howl his protest all night long.

The junkies had nicknamed the restaurant the Cloudland. For it was precisely at this transfer point that those for whom there was nothing to do and nowhere to go on the ground got their transfers to the stratosphere. "It's better up there than down here," they agreed, yawning a bit, having themselves a bit of a scratch together. But you had to know somebody who'd sell you a transfer before you could go visiting up there. The peddlers didn't chance it, selling to some panic man and then having him pull his badge and say, "That did it, Fixer, now come along nice or come along dead."

"I'll have to chance it there, it's the only place I know around Madison," Frankie knew with the first faint sinking touch of dread. That McGantic was working for Bednar now, blocking him off into just those very places where the captain would look for him first.

The man with the thirty-five-pound monkey on his back was running him down and between that one and Bednar he had most to fear from McGantic. That was the wiser pursuer. For he knew Frankie's next move before Frankie himself. Indeed, he told Frankie where to go and could wave to Bednar: "Here he comes." He would never shake off Bednar unless he shook off the sergeant first.

Yet for the moment Frankie felt that neither the captain nor the sergeant had really begun the hunt in earnest. Bednar would have to wait at least till Frankie's innards began to tighten with the need of a charge.

Out of the corner of his eye he saw Umbrella Man scoop a roach off the bar in a movement surprisingly swift for one so sluggish—and in the same movement jam it between his teeth. Frankie's hand stopped on the glass: here came Umbrella Man, the bug's blood streaking down teeth and chin and the bug itself crushed—feelers still waving between the teeth—"*Man! Wash! Gimme wash!*"—pleading between the clenched teeth and his smeared face right up to Frankie's.

Frankie turned his head away, shoved the beer toward Umbrellas and didn't turn his head back till he heard Umbrellas drain the glass to the last drop.

"He never done anythin' like that before," Frankie complained to the Widow Wieczorek. "What's gettin' into *him?*"

"He does it all the time now," Widow explained with a certain pride; as if she had taught him such a trick.

When Frankie left the empty behind him on the Widow's bar, and Umbrella Man leaning in the exact spot he'd leaned when Frankie had entered, Frankie felt as if he were leaving a burden of some kind behind. Though he saw no certain possibility of ultimate escape, yet a reasonless confidence had him feeling that somehow he could find a way. He had not felt so light and free since the day of his discharge; when everything was going to be as it had always been because he had a paper in his hand that guaranteed it to be so.

"They'll never catch up with the boy with the golden arm," he boasted to himself while warning his feet: "Feet, just be careful where you take me."

For he still felt he had one clandestine door in which to duck both Bednar and McGantic.

Molly Novotny's door. Wherever that might be this night.

What was the name of the place Meter Reader had said he'd seen her? The Kit-Kat Klub, something like that, one of the jungle clubs between Madison and Lake. "Wherever it is, it'll be safer than the Cloudland," he decided. He wouldn't try the Cloudland till he'd tried to find Molly first.

He went south down Paulina to Huron and the day was so overcast that, though it was still morning, Christmas-tree lights and red-bulbed holly burned, here and there, as if it were already evening. "They ought to throw those things away now," Frankie thought irritably, "Christmas is over."

He paused in a doorway, took a drugstore bandage out of one pocket and a five-dollar bill from his wallet. Folding the bill carefully, he plastered it onto the inside of his right arm right below the elbow. An old precaution. Strongarmers hesitated to pull a bandage off a man if he were wearing it near a vein. The police, however, with their greater courage, would yank a bandage off a man's jugular for the sake of a two-dollar bill.

When Frankie reached Ontario he cut over to Ashland and caught a trolley south. One block south of Lake he got off under a black-and-yellow sign: Maypole Street.

Maypole Street is a long, cold street, and it runs both ways to the end of the line. Frankie blew on his hands and fished, with numbed fingers, all his identification out of his wallet and tossed the papers—voter's registration card, photostated discharge and a season pass to the clubhouse at Sportsman's Park for 1947—into an alley bonfire. "My name is Private Nowhere now," he told himself with his wry half grin. "Private Nowhere from every place but home. And I won't be here long."

As he stood by the fire that burned out of an ashcan, warming his hands and liking the way the smoke curled so tenderly about the buttons of his jacket, a half-pint Negro girl came skipping down the alley hauling a quarter-pint one by the hand, the little one trying to skip just as high and fast as Half Pint. Both of them were wrapped tightly in some old red-sweatered rags and right in front of the fire Half Pint whirled Quarter Pint with one deft motion of her hand on the crown of the little one's pigtail, crying, "Now you're a human merry-go-round!" Then both whirled on without so much as having seen Mr. Nowhere from No Street at All.

Once he fancied he was being watched from somewhere above, but when he glanced up all he saw was an open window with a white curtain fluttering like a pennant there. Something about that fluttering made him feel homesick for someplace where he'd been nearly happy. The only place he'd ever had that had felt like his own. The one place to which he'd belonged at last. Had belonged so well he'd almost gotten straight in it.

A room with two lamps, one red and one blue. A heart-shaped face, so dear, so dear, that came to him out of the gloom. Near a candle red as wine.

He came to the open street and from somewhere near at hand, as if borne by the wires overhead, heard the familiar revelry of some old juke-box tune.

Directly across the street, above a tavern built below street level, an unlit neon legend announced:

PINK KITTEN KLUB
All cats welcome

That must be the joint, he hoped vaguely, and just as he went down the steps, as if they'd been waiting all morning only for his arrival, the neon legend lit up in green and red and the juke-box tune came clearer.

"I wonder who's boogin' my woogie now?"

Frankie touched the bandage below his elbow where his fix money was wadded; his drinking money was in the half-dozen halves and quarters in his pockets. He pushed at the big red door.

"Looks like some cats swing right here," Frankie observed, looking all about.

The captain felt impaled. It had been a bit too long since he had laughed. Felt joy or sorrow or simple wonder. When a light ripple, half protest and half mockery, moved down the other side of the wall he felt somehow appalled that caged men should laugh at anything. The ragged edge of that careless laughter hung like a ripped scarf upon an iron corner of his heart.

An iron heart, an iron life. Laughter and tears had corroded in his breast. In the whitish light of the query room a tic took a corner of his mouth and his lips worked trying to stop it, like a drunk trying to work off a fly.

For something had happened to the captain's lips as well as to his heart. All his honest policeman's life he had guarded both so well, knowing how little time there was, in the roistering world, for pity and loose talk and always too much traffic in the sort of thing anyhow. Too many women holding out pity like a day-old sweet roll out of a greasy bag—"We are all members of one another"—what had that half-crazed priest of the line-up meant by *that?*

Something that even the punk had seemed to know when he'd said, "Everybody's a habitual in his heart"? What did it mean that all the guilty felt so certain of their own innocence while he felt so uncertain of his own? It was patently wrong that men locked up by the law should laugh while the man who locked them there no longer felt able even to cry. As if those caged there had learned secretly that all men are innocent in a way no captain might ever understand.

"I know you," Bednar assured them quietly, "I know you all. You think you're all members of one another, somethin' like that."

They thought they were putting something over on him in there; while all the while it was himself who was putting it over on them.

Yet the glare in his eyes seemed to fill some small part of a need he had never felt before. And the unrecorded arrest slips littering his desk seemed written in a code devised by ancestral enemies.

"If you don't pull out of the blues you'll be writin' your own name on the sheet," Cousin Kvorka had joked with him that forenoon. Since that moment Bednar had been trying to rid himself of a compulsive yearning to write his name there where for so long he had written only the names of the guilty and the doomed.

The guilty and the doomed. He saw that steerer's small white face, exhausted like a child's from crying in his cell, and in one moment his own heart seemed a bloodstained charge sheet with space left upon it for but one more name.

In a suffocating need of absolution he took the pen and wrote, in a steady hand, corner to corner across the sheet, the meaningless indictment: *Guilty.*

Immediately he had done that through his mind there careened a carnival of rogues he had long forgotten. All those he'd disposed of, one way or another, from behind this same scarred desk. A shambling gallery of the utterly condemned. With that same exhausted small white face following everyone so anxiously, from so far behind. "I only done my honest copper's duty," the captain defended himself against the steerer and against them all, his fingers spreading involuntarily to conceal the word written across the sheet.

Yet somewhere along the line a light in his heart had gone out like an overcharged light bulb, leaving only some sort of brittle husk for a heart; a husk ready to crumble to a handful of dust. "My honest copper's duty," he repeated like a man trying to work a charm which had once worked for someone else: to cast out blue-moon moods, low-hanging memories and all bad dreams.

He said it twice and yet guilt like a dark bird perched forever near, so bald and wingless and cold and old, preening its dirty feathers with an obscene beak. "I'm one sick bull," Bednar decided, "it's time to go home." But it had been time to go home for hours and yet he sat on as though manacled to his unfiled arrest slips and that single word so firmly written beneath his hand.

He dried the sweat off his forehead with a blood-red bandanna, then tossed the rag aside as if he had touched his temples with the blood of others. "He wasn't nothin' to nobody, the punk," the captain recalled.

Then why did it feel like turning informer, why did he feel he had sold out a son, like being paid off in gold? For if everyone were members of one another—he put the notion down. That would mean those on the other side of the wall were his own kind.

It could not be. For if they were anything less than enemies he had betrayed himself a thousandfold. It would be too much to make a traitor out of a man for having done his simple duty. But what if he had done traitor's work all his life without realizing it? He tried to rise, for he had to find out, he had to find out what he had done to himself by doing his simple captain's duty.

"Cut out that racket in there," he warned the ceaseless murmur behind the wall: for a moment he had the delusion that they were examining his anguish through some peephole, nudging each other and winking, as convicts do, as they watched. "I never hated a man of you," he tried to appease them. And heard a knowing reply: "Nor loved any man at all."

Heard his own lips say that and felt himself growing angry. What ghostly kind of good would it have done a soul if he had? What except to delay justice awhile? For every man of them, he knew, had been guilty to the hilt, guilty of every sort of malice of which the human heart is capable. What they hadn't done to others had been only through indolence and lack of a proper chance.

For every man was secretly against the law in his heart, the captain knew; and it was the heart that mattered. There were no men innocent of intent to transgress. If they were human—look out. What was needed, he had learned long ago, was higher walls and stronger bars—there was no limit to what they were capable of.

Somewhere along the line he had learned, too, that not one was worth the saving. So he'd been right in saving none but himself. And if that had left them all to be members of one another, then it had left him to be a member of no one at all. Had, indeed, left him feeling tonight like the most fallen of anybody.

The captain realized vaguely that the thing he had held secretly in his heart for so long against them all was simply nothing more than a hostility toward men and women as men and women.

And now so lost to all men and women that the murmur beyond the walls troubled him like the voices of friends he had denied ever having known. "The bums 'r gettin' my goat, that's all," he decided, pulling himself together. They had begun by stealing his sleep. He listened in fevered hope of hearing them call out to all the world that he was no better than the very worst of them. That he knew as well as themselves who was guiltiest tonight.

Silence. They blamed no one. They had the brassbound nerve to take the rap and forgive him for everything. Everything.

So that suddenly the captain wished to do something so conspicuously noble, something at once so foolish and so kind, so full of a perfectly useless mercifulness toward the most undeserving of all, that prisoners and police alike would laugh openly at him. Would laugh without pity as at an old enemy gone balmy at last.

He wished them all to speak to him directly, without trace of respect, make some sort of obscene joke out of his uniform and his badge and his unassailable record—he wished suddenly to be insulted so grievously and accused so unjustly that there would be no use of defending himself: so hopelessly misunderstood by everyone that there would be nothing left to do but keep his silence while everything he had labored so long and so faithfully to build was torn down, overnight, right before his eyes.

His heart paced with the prospect of such a fall as if in anticipation of an orgy. Then slowed, stanching its own excitement. "It sounds like they're all on their knees prayin' for me in there," he fancied. And did not wish to be prayed for.

For it was time to be stoned. He had been so proud to be an enforcer of the laws men fell by, of being the kind of man who tempered Justice with Mercy. Now it was time to see himself whether there were any such things at all. If there were neither one nor the other for himself, he would do without. An iron life, an iron heart, he could wish for an iron death.

Alone below the glare lamp in the abandoned query room, stifled by a ravaging guilt, he knew now those whom he had denied, those beyond the wall,

had all along been members of himself. Theirs had been the common humanity, the common weakness and the common failure which was all that now
could offer fresh hope to his heart.

Yet he had betrayed them for so long he could not go to them for redemption. He was unworthy of the lowliest—and there was no court to try any captain for doing his simple duty. No place was provided, by church or state,
where such a captain might atone for everything he had committed in his heart.
No judge had been appointed to pass sentence upon such a captain. He had
been left to judge himself.

All debts had to be paid. Yet for his own there was no currency. All errors
must ultimately be punished. Yet for his own, that of saving himself at the cost
of others less cunning than himself, the punishment must be simply this: more
lost, more fallen and more alone than any man at all.

Thieves, embezzlers and coneroos, all might redeem themselves in time.
But himself, who had played the spiritual con game, there was no such redemption. There was no salvation for such self-saviors.

Only his own heart might redeem him: through tears or laughter. His heart
that felt stopped by dust.

It had been too long since the captain had laughed. Even longer since he had
wept.

Someone—could it still be that steerer?—cried out in sleep on the other
side of the wall—bringing him, out of the wisdom of some ancestral dream,
news of salvation to policemen and prisoners, dealers and steerers and captains, blind men and hustling girls, cripples and priestlike coneroos alike.

To the hunter as well as the hunted.

Record Head wept.

Crocodile tears: he belonged to no man at all.

Long after Bednar's men had come and gone and the whole great gray tenement had murmured once and grown still, Sophie sat on by the window and
saw the snow, in a slow, suspended motion, begin to measure her hours. Heard
the clock above the dresser begin keeping count with the snow; like a clock
with a broken heart.

Counting out the weather in all the streets of evening with no true hope for
the bright alarm of morning any more. Each tick suggested, to her stunned
and brooding mind, a slow dying down of wheels, till everything would be the

same as though she and Frankie Majcinek had never been born to listen to clocks. Nor see the slow snow trailing the evening trolleys.

Tavern and tenement, all was still, under the new year's first still snow. Bakery and brothel, carbarn and bar, all lay under the dreaming snow. The night's first drunks came padding through it: out of the Safari, out of the Widow Wieczorek's, out of the Tug & Maul. Sometimes one cried a name up to her with the glow of the neon like drifting fog on his face and passed on in a neon-colored mist. Once a whole group of them stopped to look up together, laughed a single knowing laugh right in her face and went off laughing together about what they had just done.

The smell of despair, the odor of whisky and the scent of the night's ten thousand dancers, the perfume and the powder sprinkled across the deep purple roar of barrelhouse laughter, the armpit sweat cutting the blue cigar smoke and the hoarse cries of those soon to grow hoarser with love, scents and sounds of all things soon to be spread up through a thousand rooms into her own room. Till the drinkers and the dancers, the gamblers and the hustlers and the yearning lovers came dancing and loving, came gambling and hustling in a wavering neon-colored cloud down her walls.

And died away forever in the room's coldest corner as the neon beer signs died one by one along the street below.

Leaving her nothing but the dull gray clamor of those same night-weary locals she had heard when she had first yearned toward Frankie, in this same room, between the night's last local and the morning's first express, out of the very pit of sleep.

Now, between the wavering warning flares, the all-night locals paused, as always, and passed across the thousand-girdered El down the tunnel of old El dreams and were gone.

All night she saw the January watchfires flicking the swirling snow. And could not sleep for saying his name to the swirling snow. The snow that changed to rain, from time to time, while the radiator's suggestive whisper was drowned, each time it changed, by the oncoming thunder of the cars: as their thunder receded the same secret gossiping would begin again.

Gossiping of whisperers who paused, fingers to lips, as the rattling clatter of the empties shook the old house and bent the vigil flares, like a single flare, all one way; and not another whisper then till the flares had come upright once more all down the line. To guard the constant boundaries of night.

Then heard them go right back at it again and it was lies, all lies. They told each other Frankie's name, and named things he'd been doing she knew he hadn't done at all no matter how tired he might have gotten. The nastiest sort of gossip and not a word of it true, they'd never get her to believe a single word. Then pretending they hadn't said any such a thing, she had just imagined someone had said it—it must have been somebody else they'd tell her. Who ever would *dream* of saying such a thing about Frankie?

And the whispering would die away like a whisper dying within a dream.

Till all her nights seemed suddenly to have passed like local stops seen hurriedly from some long Loopbound express through windows streaming with an unabating rain. A violet city, in an unabating rain. So swiftly they all had gone, and could not come again: the handsome blond boys with the laughing mouths dancing her around and around: that would not dance her again. The brief and magic nights in Frankie's arms, so sinewy, tight and warm: never ever so briefly to hold her so again.

Her fingers plucked phantom specks, like phantom memories, from the blanket across her knees. Old Pin Curls turned on the radio down the fourth-floor hall and its beat, without words or music or even a tone—only that muffled beat-beat-beat to which one's fingers must keep plucking time like threads forever—it stopped and she lay back as slowly as though the back of the chair was sinking beneath her weight and passed her hands once over her eyes.

Voices, deliberately muffled—right next door. Schwiefka was running his game in there, she heard Sparrow and Blind Pig and Meter Reader and once, just once, Nifty Louie's voice, all making one soundless laugh together at the way she had slept in this same chair while Frankie had slept with that piece of trade one flight down. All night. And how, when he'd come crawling back upstairs, everyone in the house but herself had known.

A lie. Just one more of Nifty Louie's lies. Making up things about Frankie like that because he wanted to get Frankie's job in the slot and then—because of a sudden they knew she was listening they all stopped their gossiping at once, gesturing to each other that she was there at the wall again listening for all she was worth: they winked quietly at each other then. She knew. For she heard the cards going around.

Heard cards slapping softly or sharply down and drew a circle about her temple to show them what she thought of them all and then as plain as day one said, "That one ain't worth a nickel," and the latch shook with the long El's passing.

Under its roar they all took their chance to laugh, so strange and noiselessly, till it had passed.

To pretend then no one had laughed at all.

When she looked up it was a night without a moon and the luminous crucifix on the wall had begun to glow dimly. She wheeled toward its small sorrowing face, wondering that it could seem so filled with some inner motion while the whole great house could seem so still. With no light down Division Street nor either way down the El.

It had seen all things that had passed in this room since she and Frankie had first slept in it together, she saw now. It had watched her every time she had taunted him, it alone had known that she had wished him to be as crippled as herself.

Mad, of course, quite mad. The Christ above her eyes, she saw, was no less mad for seeming so gentle: and knew she shared that madness. That she had become wiser and more gentle than anyone in the world for sharing it.

With no light in the long cold hall, nor down the steep and treacherous stair.

Only the flowering neon glare of streets where nothing grows save a far-off glimmer of track or girder, crosslight or carbarn or rail.

All the way down to the streets where the dark people live and Frankie Machine drank alone.

Two monkeys were caged above the bar, huddling and blinking together, with ancestral wisdom, down upon the barflies shrieking insults at them from below: "Bingo bongo bongo—how'd you like it in the Congo?"

Across the tables, above the piano and over the tiny stage there hung some sort of pungent pall, a bit like the autumnal odor of stale blood dried on a leaf-strewn walk the day after a sudden death between the curbing and the wall. A little, too, like the wet yellow smell of insanity when the white ward wakes in the midwinter Monday morning. A little something, too, of the flowered scent of a young girl's armpits in first love. Something of death in autumn, something of early summer love, and something as flowered as the last day of April—touched by something as cold as a surgeon's glove.

And something as bittersweet as the slow irresistible seep of marijuana in a darkened, curtained, locked and windowless room.

Out on the narrow Negro streets the wind blew the rain and the snow down from the Saloon Street Station, searching together in every alley and dim-lit rooming-house hall between Record Head Bednar's desk and the monkeys who yearned for the Congo.

Frankie Machine sat among the strange cats of the Kitten Klub, drinking the dark people's beer.

He'd been sitting here all afternoon and the five-spot that had been plastered to his arm was remembered there now only by a single end of a bandage still clinging to the skin.

The high-yellow M.C., whose sole wage was in the nickels and dimes tossed at his feet, was doing his first stint of the night, with a sort of merriment part strut and part convulsion.

"This show'll kill you, folks," he threatened everyone in the place, "them it don't kill it'll cripple."

Nobody laughed.

"It's the cocktail houah, cats," the high-yellow urged them all, "get drunk 'n *be* somebody."

"It's better to be yourself, friend," Frankie thought mechanically, he'd been through that particular hope before. A pair of deadpan amber strippers waiting for a live one at the table beside his own purred softly in agreement.

The M.C. began a mock strip himself, down to a pair of lacy orange silk shorts, till some paid-by-the-shot-glass shill shouted, "Take 'em off, Mr. Floor Show!" And Mr. Floor Show picked up the paid-in-full challenge by retorting, "Oh, I wouldn't *dare!*" And began an idiotic crooning with a wild backflinging of his head and a demented weaving of his arms. "Bless your little G strings," he called familiarly to the deadpan brass ankles waiting so quietly in the shadows, "you're *so* sweet! And now we'll have a little song entitled 'Honey, If This Isn't Love You'll Have to Wait Till I Get More Sleep'—that's right, we're giving you the best show in the country. I don't know about the city. And it's all for youah benefit—most of you look like you need a benefit." And laughed with the lightest, most silvery sort of laugh to veil the whole wide gray world's despair. "Get off youah hands! What youah want? *Blood?*"

Frankie got off his hands. "You tell 'em, Mr. Floor Show," he applauded weakly; and drank on in the hope of somehow postponing the sickness. "Can't afford to get sick now," he mourned the long-gone fiver.

"I knew there was *somebody* out there," Mr. Floor Show observed, squinting far over the little line of red-white-and-blue footlights, "I heard *breathing*"— and resumed his fluttering about in the orange shorts for want of anything better to do, like a crazed burlesque queen, pausing only to stamp his foot with a girlish petulance and assert, "I'll have you know I'm every inch a man!" Then, seeming suddenly to tire of everything, began torturing himself in a voice full of a hoarse glee at its own pain: "Boop-de-oop-doop 'n razz-muh-tazz, kizz muh feet 'n kizz muh azz—interdoosin' to you ouah supah-sulphous walkin'-talkin' see-*eep*ia doll, ouah tiny mite of dynamite—*Miss Dinah Mite!* Meet her 'n greet her! Come *out,* honey! Mello as a cello 'n merry as a berry—Boys! The strain from hernia!" The three-piece band began beating it out while Miss Mite took over.

"I wonder who's boogin' my woogie now."

Yet the strange brown cats of the Kitten Klub all sat wanly smiling, like copper cats that never bled, whose blood was formed of others' tears.

Copper cats out of some plastic jungle wherein only the neon kitten above the bar felt pain, only the Budweiser bottles sweated tears of joy, and only the monkeys overhead knew better.

FEED THE KITTY

the legend below the neon kitten commanded. Off and on, off and on, with a sort of metallic beggary unmatchable by any human panhandler.

GET UP A PARTY
FEED THE KITTY
GET UP A PARTY
FEED THE KITTY

An outsized octoroon venus began galloping about on spindle legs just to make her belly shake—it was distended as if with some malignant growth; her absurd finery flew behind her, she paused only to beg breathlessly:

"Daddy, I want a diamond ring
'N everything—"

Her G string was upheld by court plaster and a gilded cardboard crescent swung for some reason from her navel while she went into a convulsive series of bumps; like some dark Diamond Lil just fed on Spanish fly.

"You got to get the best for me—"

with the G string bounce-bounce-bouncing.

Frankie Machine squeezed his temples, to keep the panic down till it ebbed back down his nape. Leaving him a reasonless desire to go hurrying out through the snow to the nearest station, whatever the cost, in the hope of getting some sort of charge at County. "They *got* to give it to you when you're really sick," he assured himself, "they can tell when a guy *got* to have it, doctors can tell, they ain't like cops, they help a guy get to sleep."

—and the ram-bam of the drums going into "Song of the Islands."

Above the empty iron-banging din a waitress dropped a trayful of drinks. The shattering of the glass tinkled, in the sudden silence that followed, like an echo of soiled laughter along any soiled bar and Frankie applauded clumsily, numb with bar whisky and an utter weariness.

"Tough it out, kid, tough it out," he tried to urge himself, feeling the first line of sweat forming along his forehead. But the whole business of escape seemed so hard, so useless, so endless and so long, a voice like another's voice answered his anguished blood: "Tough it out for what? What for? What's it all for anyhow?"

A brownskin buck feigning drunkenness bumped the edge of his table, upsetting his beer, then pretended to apologize by wiping it all into Frankie's lap with a blue silk handkerchief. Frankie stood up weaving. "What you up to, cousin?"

"I wasn't lookin', man," the buck apologized, "I'm tryin' to get my bearin's, where the people are." He went off waving the silk handkerchief as if trying to dry it on the drifting smoke.

Then the noise came on again, the juke began, the singing seemed more shrill, the lights changed from a delicate nursery pink to a raw and bleeding scarlet so that the barflies' faces beamed, one moment, like so many tawny-pink cooks in a Cream of Wheat ad and in the next were flushed by an apoplectic light as though caught, in the very instant of the hemorrhage that bathes the brain without warning, into so many cream-colored plastic horrors.

> *"Bingo bango bongo*
> *I don't want to leave the Congo . . ."*

The monkeys above the clamor regarded each other in genuine fright, for the octoroon war horse was on the loose again, charging furiously about in a skirt of pale pink grass while Mr. Floor Show pursued her playfully, bounding like a man trying to goose a butterfly and finally leaning over the piano to deal the pianist a blow as weak as his humor. "I could just *smaaash* you!" In one corner somebody sniggered.

"I want the frim-fram sauce,"

the war horse went into some two-year-old novelty tune,

> *"With the aussenfay*
> *And cha-fa-fa on the side."*

"We go till gangrene sets in!" Mr. Floor Show threatened everyone with ferocious gaiety and under the curtain of perfume and smoke, under the pall of all their lives, poisoned by the shame they had somehow been taught to feel at not being white, their voices ceased altogether, the singing and the laughter ceased; and only the dead-flat whirring of the fans came on like a wind rising from the world they had left behind their tenement doors. In the sudden silence one of the brass ankles at the next table put her palm slantwise beneath her nose, sniffed once and said with prim pride: "This is *one* thing you don't see *me* do" and right outside the door someone smashed a bottle on the walk, the juke cried out, the music went on, the laughter picked up in the very teeth of that dead-flat warning wind.

While out of the years when the world had gone only half wrong the juke picked up a faded and raggedy tune.

> *"Red sails in the sunset,*
> *All day I've been blue."*

Till the strange cats looked all around.

It was time to be going home, if he could just find out where one was. It was time for bed, time for a drink, time for a charge and time to give himself up. There was nothing left for Frankie Machine, with his hands pressed so hard to his temples, but the bottles behind the bar, the age-old monkeys above the bottles, and the voice of the wind, bringing snow, rain and sleet, down all the streets where the squadrols sought him.

"Nobody can stand gettin' this sick," Frankie told himself. "Nobody can stand gettin' this sick 'n not havin' no place to go."

Afraid to stay and afraid to leave, afraid of those at the tables about him and wanting to fight them all, he sat on with his right hand trembling so that he had to use the left to bring a glass of beer to his lips; he tried to keep the tiny stage in focus as he drank on.

A white girl with a mouth like a baby carp's was trotting around up there as though being moved on strings, singing in a tinny little sing-song.

"When the lights go on again
All over the world . . ."

with three sets of lights and carrying the battery concealed in one hand. "Take
'em off, honey," someone called. "The war's over!"

But all she did was to prance like a little circus pony with the light on her
navel flickering weakly, like a symbol of all such purchased humanity: purchased, marked-down, remaindered and sold out.

In the uproar and the odor, in the heavy sweat and the crash of bottles, within
the smash of the drums and Mr. Floor Show's incessant shrieking, watching the
passion of the octoroon venus and studying Frankie Machine's dead-cold
despair, the two amber strippers sat wanly on and on.

Once one laughed restlessly while the other drank without pleasure. Idling
over the amber glasses, both were careful, Frankie saw, to put the glasses down
softly after drinking so as not to clink them vulgarly upon the table; both drank
and put them down together, in some sort of cunning pact, then raised their
brown eyes each to each.

And both sat wanly smiling.

"That's how I got sin-ukul,"

the baby carp bawled to the neon cat.

"Ya put me on a pin-ukul
'N then ya let me do-ow-own,"

and went up so high on "down" that the neon kitten closed his eyes, drew in his
ears and arched his back a bit to indicate his suffering. For only the neon cat felt
pain and only the bottles wept small tears. Only the monkeys yearned for home.

"Bingo bango bongo
I don't want to leave the Congo . . ."

While all sat wearily, wisely, wanly. All sat faintly smiling.

A brown and white chorus came out one by one, seemingly too indifferent
toward each other to come out together, till there were five. Though each wore
only slippers and a G string, all seemed overdressed, so studiously had their nakedness been donned. Each pore powdered, each taut pink nipple tinted with fingernail polish and dusted with some mauve talc, the armpits shaven and deodorized,

each navel dusted and the hair swept back behind each small catlike ear.

The last one came out shading her eyes with her hand while bumping list-lessly, as if half in shame. It was only the glare in her eyes and a general indif-ference to her public. When she'd bumped out of the glare she dropped her hands, wetted the fingertips with her tongue in a gesture Frankie knew so well that his hands came away from his temples—it took his heart in a single hot, tightening stitch and would not let the taut heart go and would not let him breathe. She daubed each naked nipple moistly, threw back her head and began stroking the hair coiled on her nape in a slow and sensual indolence. He brushed his shot glass off the table and stood up.

Molly could not see him weaving against the table out there in the dark while he was trying to understand to himself whether it was time for him to leave, before she saw him, or time to go to her before he lost her again.

He felt a sickening sort of shame, this was just the way he wished not to be in finding her again: broke, sick and hunted. What was it someone had said of her long ago? "She's the kind got the sort of heart you can walk in 'n out of with boots on."

Then the act was done and she was gone, they were all gone as if they hadn't been there at all. As though the whole act had been a kickback from an over-charge, something he'd formed in his brain out of beer fumes and smoke.

Yet went weaving heavily through smoke and fumes toward the tiny dress-ing room offstage.

Wearing army brogans on his feet.

All that day, aslant the window, a long-forgotten, tangled black aerial wire touched continually at the pane as if Poor Peter had at last found another game than that of planting paper daisies to pass his days. He was jerking it from the roof just to taunt her—who else would be up there in such weather, with the wind like a whip and the ice on the walks? She turned on the radio to muffle its constant tap-tap-tapping; but all she could get was some fire-eating preacher offering her a choice of salvation or brimstone and even that was better than the tapping. What troubled her most was that, even when the wind seemed still, yet the wire tapped on.

She pried the sash up an inch with a shoehorn. But it dangled on just out of her reach. So she shut the window, realizing it was just one more trick they were playing on her.

And that Vi was no better than the rest of them any more. For all her fine talk about poor man's pennies, the way she was carrying on with the Jailer, it seemed she thought more of landlord's nickels these days.

Vi and the Jailer and that Frankie, leaving without so much as a word of good-by, all he ever thought of was himself. The preacher, droning eternally on and on, began hinting certain things about certain people, he was worse than any of them and in sudden fitlike fury she pulled the radio off the dresser, wheeled into the hall and dropped it over the rail without so much as looking to see whether some-one might be coming up the stairs to catch damnation on the point of his skull.

She heard the crash below and the Jailer's startled voice: "Who t'rows t'ings?" The set had missed him by inches.

"It's that priest talkin' against me again," Sophie explained, knowing she'd done just right, and wheeled back into the room, locking the door behind her. Then called, to answer the Jailer's angry rapping, "You'll all get just what you got coming! I'm giving it to all of you now!"

There was no further knocking at her door all that endless afternoon. Only, toward evening, the rapping of Jailer's hammer where he was putting a couple final raps to the radio. "He's always better at knockin' somethin' apart than puttin' somethin' together anyhow," Sophie told herself with pleasure.

The evening of the night that no one came at all and she wanted the moon to move.

Only the moon to move, it seemed so little to ask, for it moved for every-one else.

All anyone ever did for her was to flush the toilet down the hall and when would he ever quit flushing that nasty thing anyhow?

Not one of them heard, hours later, the stranger's step in the hall below, lis-tening there to hear whether he were expected, then begin coming on heavily, like one almost too tired to mount one more flight. She peered out, the door an inch ajar, like an animal expecting pursuit and knew: "It's Frankie comin' home." To make it all up to her for leaving like that without even saying goodbye.

Without even telling her what it was for that the wagon men had wanted him. Without even telling her it was all a lie about him and that public hide on the first floor front. Without giving her so much as a word to fight with when the neighbors said things behind her back. It would serve him right if she told him now: "You've brought it all on yourself. It's every bit your fault." But by the way he came on, so heavily with every step, she could tell how sorry he really was. He was sorry at last, truly truly sorry, he'd come back to make it all up to her now.

To make it all up, and have something to eat, a place to sleep and a place to hide—what was the difference whether he'd slept with this one or that, whether he'd hit some other bum on the head sometime or other—the main thing was he was coming back, he was sorry, for he loved her after all. She bit her nails with excitement.

Heard the struggler below lean for breath hard against the rickety rail—she hoped he just wasn't drunk again. If he was she'd have to get him sober right away, she would have to work fast and be ever so still, he'd be so tired, so hungry and sick and broke and everyone against him—he would need her so badly and she whispered through the door all the way down the stairwell: "Hurry, honey," as loudly as she dared.

Then that same old fool down the hall, who by right should have been in bed for hours, began the same old record on the same dreary old all-night vic.

"It all seems wrong somehow . . ."

The struggler heard, she heard him turn, he thought there was a party going on and had best not take such a chance after all. The door closed though the record went on.

"That you're nobody's baby now."

When it stopped she realized he must be going around the block, he was going to use the fire escape and fool them all, she would have to have the fire-escape door open for him.

Then down the hall he would come so softly, no one would hear his step at all. No one would know where her Frankie was so safely hiding.

No one, not even that Vi would know, she would feed him and bathe him and make him sleep and take care that passers-by didn't waken him.

But the moon seemed too bright. Past all the blind doors to the rust-colored escape window that only long disuse had fastened: she got the shoehorn between the door and the sash and it came wide with a tiny flaking of rust onto the blanket across her knees. She had to stand up to let him know it was safe now to come up from the alley shadows.

Yet heard no steps on the iron stairs. No feet feeling for rusted rungs. No low whistle in the winter night to tell he was coming at last to her now.

Leaning upon the rust-colored wall, her feet felt blindly for the iron, her eyes blurred with winter moonlight; a tenement moon, a fire-escape moon, so bright, so steady, so unmoving—if it would move just ever so little, then he could come—he was afraid while it was shining so bright, and from behind her, from the room where the vic had played, a woman's head was thrust out of a bright-lit door to ask, "Who's prowlin' around here?"

Then saw the vacant wheelchair and Sophie leaning for support upon the rail. From the moonlit air above, the troubled air below and the unbalanced air all about Sophie heard their voices clamoring toward her.

She could walk by herself if they just didn't all hold her so tightly, she knew.

"Take it easy, sister. One footsy at a time. That's our girl."

She was going, much too fast, down the gutter-colored hall between two square-capped voices and the pin-curled neighbors in their doors watching all the way down to the very last door of all. Where that double-crossing Vi stood wringing her hands because everything in the world happened to her even when it happened to somebody else.

"All night she been wheelin', back 'n fort', back 'n fort'," someone complained, "I couldn't get a wink, but I know what troubles she's had so I let her be, I'm not the kind to make trouble for others, I've had too much myself."

Then Violet's compassionate voice, telling the neighbors just how everything had happened. "Them two, him 'n her, wantin' to love each other just ever so long. Wantin' so much 'n never knowin' how, neither one of 'em."

Sophie felt the Division Street wind slap her cheek and the winter air nip at her throat—it had been so long since she'd been in the open. Then the air came close and stuffy, houses and store fronts and people were passing in great dips exactly as though she were riding the roller coaster once more. And laughing softly to herself at such a pleasant surprise, felt herself coasting right down into some whitewashed hall toward a cornerless room.

In the city's cornerless heart.

Little dull red lights burning all in a row and the terrible odor of insanity, yellow and cloying, forever just one door down, almost underfoot and just overhead and following softly forever like a moving pall in the disinfected, bought-and-measured air. Seeping out from behind some whitewashed door where, so remote, so lost to all, some lost one sang in a young girl's voice, like a voice circling endlessly on a lopsided merry-go-round.

"I feel so gay
In a melancholy way
That it might as well be spring . . ."

While Somebody nearer at hand kept asking faraway questions of Someone who'd rather laugh than answer a sensible word.

Someone who kept turning her head so daintily instead of answering like she should. Till Somebody took her arm and everyone pretended to be a little sad, going down the hall all together without touching the floor at all till they came to a certain numbered door where nobody had a key.

"We're all locked out," Sophie told them solemnly, and they laughed, though why that was so funny nobody knew.

The room was bare from the ceiling to the cold stone floor except for a built-in cot covered by one clean and well-worn sheet and a familiar-looking khaki blanket across its foot.

She felt a sick dread of the walls, they were as white as the corridors, as white as the cot, as the sheet, as the ceiling and as the faces that urged her inside: she drew back, sensing she would not return from here, making a polite child's excuse. "Somebody lives here, I mustn't go inside—but I'll come back tomorrow and we'll all have a little talk."

They turned on the light to show her there was no one waiting for her here. Though she knew whoever lived in here was only hiding—he would come when they had gone and the light was out and the door locked behind her.

A room with neither window nor door, a room within many other rooms unlighted at evening by either neon or moonlight, where neither the city's sounds nor Frankie's cherished voice would sound for her again. But, feeling herself urged on either side, went forward with the crushed docility of the utterly doomed.

Heard the door click behind her for keeps and something locked in her heart with that same automatic key. When she looked around from where she lay on the clean and well-worn sheet, she saw no way to tell where the door had been at all: the walls merged into the door in a single whitewashed surface. Her slow eyes followed for some corner that would rest them, but wall merged into wall in a single curve and there was no place for the eye to rest. Around and around and around, on a whitewashed merry-go-round, ceiling to floor and back again. Till the heart grew sick and the sick brain wheeled, around and around and around.

Till the whiteness was a dull pain on the eyeballs, then a weight on the lids, and the merry-go-round slowed down, slowed down; till it moved on only to the timeless tunes of sleep.

She wakened in a low, sad light, with rumors of evening all down the hall and hearing, from the other side of the wall, a low animal moaning. It was that Drunkie John beating that poor hide of a Molly Novotny again, he was beating her harder than ever before, he was beating her with a certain contentment.

"If he loves her, what are a few blows?" Sophie thought with sudden clarity. "If a man tells you you're his—what are a few slaps to *that?*" Then, relapsing into an infantile smile as the nurse entered, asked, pretending to lisp a little, "Nursy, I want to brush my toothies, please."

And after her teeth had all been nicely brushed began telling the nurse, still with the same babyish lisp, all the names she knew.

"Sparrow. Vi. Stash. Rumdum. Zygmunt. Old Doc D. Piggy-O. Nifty Louie." Saying each one aloud lying on her stomach while the nurse sponged her back with something cool. Picturing their strange lost faces, faces never truly cherished at all and yet now seeming, suddenly, so dear, so dear.

Saying them like a child counting numbers. "Umbrella Man. Cousin Kvorka. Record Head. Schwiefka. Chester from Conveyor. Meter Reader from Endless Belt. Widow Wieczorek. Jailer Schwabatski and Poor Peter. Shudefski from Viaduct. Molly N. Drunkie John."

And not till after the nurse had left, only then and more tenderly than any, softer than all, somehow more terribly, she whispered at last the last sad name of all—

"Francis Majcinek. We got married in church."

The sorrowful name of Frankie Machine.

And now they had been hunting him three weeks already. And where, in all Chicago, a junkie stud-poker dealer might be hiding, this season of thunderous winds and bitter skies, Zygmunt the Prospector might inquire, Antek the Owner might surmise, a certain ward super had to know; and Record Head Bednar could only try to find out. The captain had not reckoned on a woman whose heart could be trod upon by army brogans.

For none but God and Molly Novotny knew for sure.

They had searched the back-room stud sessions and listened in the gin mills for mention of a name. Beneath the hollow merriment of the backstreet cabarets they had watched the midnight creepers and the last-jag weepers; they had questioned forty lushes and pinched one hyped-up Purple-Heart blond. They had let the 26-girls cheat them without a rumble: the music and the traffic passed, great freighters forced the river ice, the murmurous bridges strained slowly upward, paused and as slowly fell. The clocks in all the railroad depots were synchronized to a second's fraction; yet no one heard that name. The night's last drunk left with the wind at his heels and the snow turning into a smoke-colored rain.

They followed drunks in a driving sleet and finished following a changeable rain. A rain that wandered aimlessly, like any hatless drunk, down sidestreet and alley and boulevard looking for any open door at all. In a Lake Street alley they found a five-foot-seven Pole wrapped in an army overcoat, with the marks of the needle like two knotted nipples tattooed into the breasts of a nude on his arm. So they beat him in a different station at exactly the same hour every evening for five nights running. Then kicked him out right on the sixth night's hour.

Just as the smoke-colored rain began once more.

They picked up a six-foot-four North Clark Street drummer with a stick of marijuana in his wallet almost as long as himself and on South State they found an aging stripper who wept, "That's the same guy walked out on me wit' my watch after we run up a twenty-six-dollar tab at the Jungle Club—he said I could go to work doubling for Thelma Todd any time I wanted—Who the hell is Thelma Todd?"

They picked up weed hounds, shook down every peddler they spotted coming out of the Cloudland, badgered tavern hostesses and talked price with the hustling girls. And God help the weary hustler without a connection then.

Weed hounds, peddlers, hostesses and hustlers, all gave the law the names of half a hundred other hustlers and hostesses. Then names, alibis, threats, protests and counterthreats, all ran down and were drowned in the snow that, white as uncut morphine, melted in whitish surgical streams along the city's walks and drains.

They had searched the Polish taverns, they had stood listening in the washroom at Guyman's Paradise and had inspected the stag line at St. Wenceslaus Kostka. They had picked up four blond dealers, three with broken noses and one with no nose at all, and Bednar himself still conducted the showups at Central Police with the unwavering knowledge that, sooner or later, the West Madison Street dragnet would seine up his fair-haired smash-nosed boy.

But his fair-haired boy wasn't in the Polish bars and he wasn't on West Madison. He slept on an army cot in a two-room first-floor cold-water flat where no one knocked but a Negro housekeeper called Dovie and the only other white who entered was Molly-O herself.

"Everythin's blowed over," Frankie assured Molly-O, "there ain't been a line in the papers about it."

"If there ain't nothin' in the papers about it," Molly told him, "it just means they're keepin' it out so you'll get careless 'n walk into the chair for them."

Frankie sounded hurt. "There ain't no chair about it, Molly-O. It's manslaughter is all. Happens every day of the week."

"It must be nice not to have to worry about a little thing like doin' one to twenty then," she feigned admiration of anyone so lucky.

He grinned wryly. "Don't forget that good-conduct time. I may get out in sixteen."

"You couldn't behave yourself that long if they handcuffed you to the warden."

Of course Molly-O was right, she had that way of knowing what was wisest and best for Frankie; it was only for herself she couldn't tell what was wisest.

"One to twenty'd be worse than the chair for you," she told him. "The shape you're in you wouldn't live four." Then she was sorry for saying it like that and came to him, he looked so beat, where he sat at the bare little table where he always sat, dealing to men he'd never deal to again; and took the deck from his hand. "Nothin' blows over Record Head's head but smoke," she told him, and perched on his lap with her hands on his shoulders. "You never did tell me what happened that night." It was by now only her right to know.

He squinted out across the littered Negro yard next door, where February's first touch of thaw was glinting along the rubbled earth. A wheelless, one-fendered chassis of something that might once have been a Chalmers or an Overland stood there with little puddles along its single fender. How many wheelless, one-fendered years it had rusted there no neighbor could have told.

"I come in contack with that certain guy."

He'd lost so much weight off his shoulders, face and forearms since that night, albeit his bit of a beer paunch had clung nicely to him through it all, that she really couldn't imagine him knocking a full-grown man down unless he were armed with a couple house bricks.

"I slugged him." The toughness was still in the grin if not in the biceps, the arms making a loose, outswinging gesture which she took to mean he'd first tried shoving that certain guy off. "Then his neck made a sort of dead sound 'n I knew that was it."

"His mouth, you mean."

"No. His neck." Now the grin came one-sided, both tough and weak, like that of a fighter who knows he's beat trying to convince everyone he can take still more. He lifted the thin wrists toward her as naïvely as a child. "Wit' these." He locked the fingers till the knuckles cracked and the fingers reddened faintly at the tips. "It's all in the wrists," he told her thinly, "I used to have the touch."

She ran her hands over the locked fingers curiously, trying to feel what power had been in them that was there no more, then parting the fingers slowly; as though they had been manacled too long to open of themselves. They dropped onto his lap of their own weight and the very hopelessness of the way he'd let them fall reached at her heart. To put strength back into those fingers and the light back into those eyes was what Molly Novotny wanted and there was a gladness in her just at having such a chance.

"When you feel useless you don't think nothin' of throwin' yourself away," she'd once told him. "One way is as good as another." She didn't feel like throwing herself away any more, for she couldn't do that and still be of use to Frankie Machine. "I never did somethin' real good like this for anybody," she realized quietly, standing behind his chair with her hands on his shoulders, as he had too often stood behind Sophie. "Nobody give me the chance."

He shut his eyes and put his head back and she held his face cupped in her palms a long time. At night he ground his teeth and jumped wide awake, jerking with fear, if she touched him.

One night he'd shaken her roughly. "Where's the punk?" he'd demanded.

"In jail," she'd told him quickly.

"Poor punk," he'd told her and lay back with his lips still moving in sleep.

Had they let the punk out on bond or had they put the hammers to him? Sleeping or waking, he was troubled not to know. "How can I know where *I'm* at when I don't know where he's at?" he wanted to know of Molly-O.

"You'll never know where you're at till you kick that habit—Jack the Rabbit," she teased him: it was a kinder nickname than his own of "Frantic McGantic."

They could afford a thin little jest or two about the habit. It had been three full weeks since he'd been sick—she'd never want to see anyone that sick again all her life. She'd pulled him out of his last tailspin with nothing more than codeine.

He wouldn't let her think for a minute that he'd kicked a thing. "I kicked it once," he told her, "'n nobody kicks it twice. You get off that hook once you're the luckiest junkie in Junkietown—but nobody gets that lucky twice. You get hung up again you're on the hook to stay. Jesus Christ hisself couldn't come down off *that* cross."

"Why'd you get back on the stuff, Frankie?" He irritated her at the way he still drove the nails into his palms.

"The troubles started pilin' up on me the day I got back in that room with Zosh," he remembered. "I didn't know how to get out from under 'n the more they piled up the more it felt like it was all my fault, right from the beginning, when me 'n Zosh was little stubs together 'n I made her do the things she wouldn't of done with nobody else. Whatever happened to me, it seemed like, was just somethin' I had comin' for a long time, I don't know why. It's why I rolled up all the little troubles into one big trouble."

"If you kicked it once you can kick it again," Molly decided firmly; it was in her nature to hope for others against all reason and against all odds. "God has more than He has spent," she liked to quote an old proverb; out of a ragbag of many old proverbs.

So all she'd do for him, when the cold sweats came, was to get him the codeine that kept the sickness down for an hour or two. It eased him a bit toward sleep if she sat beside him and eased him too.

But codeine had no drive, no tingle. "The stuff don't *hit*," he complained like a child.

"It ain't supposed to, fool," she reminded him. "That's the point. We can't afford no more tingles 'n drives."

There were days when he needed and wanted to bathe, yet couldn't stand the idea of water touching his skin. It was one of those mysteries of the ever-changeful blood. He would sit saying wanly, "I'd like to take a bath, Molly-O— but I couldn't stand the touch." Then he would get up to straighten a skirt or a jacket hanging crookedly on the back of a chair: "I can't stand things to hang crooked." A drawer left open a minute troubled him till it was shut. A light bulb left swinging touched panic in him till it was stopped.

At night she walked him around the block as if she were walking a dog, staying close to him for fear he'd try to duck her and score somewhere for morphine. For she knew he wasn't telling her how really badly he was needing it; it troubled her that, after all this time, she had not yet gained his trust. She had to lock him in, when she left for the club, with his codeine, his deck and a couple dated copies of *Downbeat*.

She hadn't let him come near the club since that first night, for the police knew the place too well. The law was always seeking someone beneath the sign of the neon cat.

One night she brought him home a practice board she'd bought off one of the drummers, more battered even than his old one had been. The next morning he wakened her early, tapping lightly on it. All that day he kept hard at it with the radio murmuring the beat beside him; and no lush at all, not even a glass of beer. He didn't even go for the codeine.

When she returned that midnight he looked happier than she'd seen him since the long-ago time when he'd taken her to the dance at St. Wenceslaus. "You look like it's going good, Dealer."

"Call me 'Drummer,' " he asked her, "'cause I'll never deal another hand. I'm really gettin' the swing of these sticks now." He turned the radio on to a program of dance recordings and followed the record all the way without missing a beat. Just to show her.

Yet hadn't told her the best thing about it: that he had used both hands all day and the right had been as steady as the left. All day.

"Once you got the touch it never leaves you," he boasted to her like a boy.

He passed the first week of March between the practice board and the bed. He would simply go at the board till he was too tired to work longer and would fall into the sack and sleep, only to return to the board on waking. On the first sunny day of that month he made up his mind. "I got to get out 'n get a drummin' job," he declared, "this practicin' thing is goin' on long enough. If things ain't blowed over now they never will."

"There ain't a safe job for you in this town, Drummer."

"I'll drive a cab then. Hack all day 'n get a drum job nights."

"They'll print you the first day 'n fire you the second 'n here comes the man on the third." She crossed her wrists to indicate the man from the law.

"I'll hustle freight by Kinzie Street."

"They'll print you."

"I'll drive a truck. I'll go to work in a factory. I'll get a mill job in Gary."

"They'll print you."

"We'll case out of town then."

"We can't blow town on nothin', Frankie."

She never mentioned Drunkie John.

Yet, when she tried telling him she'd lost ten dollars of her pay playing twenty-six, he asked her simply: "You mean John is cuttin' in again?"

"He wants me to come back to him."

"Why lie?" Frankie wanted to know. "You know as well as I do John don't want you or any woman. You're payin' him 'cause he's found out I'm sleepin' here 'n he's promised to button up. Why not just say it straight, Molly-O?"

"I didn't see what good makin' things worse for you'd do," she confessed miserably. "Just when you're startin' to get back on your feet, lookin' like you used to look the night we went dancin'." Suddenly she dropped the past and all its broken promises. "I'm afraid *not* to give him the money, Frankie."

"What good is any lush's promise?" he asked her. He was lying stretched out on the army cot and she sat on its edge with her hand holding the hair back out of his eyes. "You can't keep payin' him off all your life, Molly-O."

"I got to cut your hair tonight," she told him, and put a finger to his lips. "I don't know what I'd do if you weren't waitin' for me when I come back at night."

"You'd be back on the lush yourself," he told her truthfully. And saw how the past months had tired her. She was twenty-four and looked thirty, with a sort of unsatisfied compassion in her eyes he had never seen before. It made him want to fathom the dark well of her love. "What makes you take care of a no-good guy like me, Molly-O?" was the only way he had of putting it.

She laughed a pleased little laugh, shrugged and told him, "I don't know, Frankie. Some cats just swing like that."

But her face looked careworn.

A short, cold spring. By morning a musk-colored murmuring drifted down from all the flats above and the amber afternoons passed with music-making: a snatch of rhythm by the door, shouts from porch to porch and laughter rocking down the stairs. Till all the weekday morning murmurs, all the back-porch calls and all the laughter on the stairs mounted to a single Saturday night shout, when the whole house shook with Negro roistering. To the din above his head Frankie would tap away on his practice board though hardly able to hear the radio's beat for the slap and slam, the shambling and the clattering of heavy feet, right overhead all night long.

He slept on the army cot and Molly on a couch which served, by day, as his orchestra pit. On nights when his single blanket wasn't enough to keep him warm she took him beside her on the couch and kept him warm till morning.

A listless sort of light seeped in, toward noon ice would be melting down the windows. He kept the little fuel-oil stove going most of the day but shut it off, for economy's sake, as soon as the nights began growing a bit less cold. At noon they used it for heating coffee or a can of soup or beans. The only sink was out in the hall, it was there she washed the plates and forks; she felt it unsafe for him to be seen in the hall. Sometimes one of the Negro women came out of her own private cavern with a couple cracked plates and a handful of tarnished silver to say "Good morning, ma'am," and share the sink. Molly kept such conversations down to the barest formalities.

As his restlessness grew he took to sneaking out for round-the-block walks while she slept. When she wakened she would see the mud on his shoes and would realize he couldn't be pent up much longer. Once, when he returned smelling like a brewery, she became the outraged mother, locked him in and wouldn't take him for their evening walk between shows by way of punishment. "Remember that the first time you're picked up for drunk 'n disorderly you're on your way to where you won't come back," she scolded him. "Why *do* you take such chances, hon?" His face lighted up with that half-malicious little grin. "Some cats just swing like that, Molly-O."

He knew. He knew, yet each day wandered nearer the haunts of home. He had to get to someone who knew the score on the punk before he could make another move. He had to get it off his mind and thought of walking straight up Schwabatski's steps and asking for Vi.

On the first warm day of March, while Molly was washing dishes in the common sink, he took off without a word, but she saw him leaving and called to him.

"I'm just gonna look around, the places where the people are," he reported over his shoulder.

"When you get enough of them on your tail run the other way," she offered her final warning.

On Damen and Division he spotted Meter Reader, empty-eyed and empty-handed, and ducked him; he didn't want to hear how proud Meter Reader was of his boys. Instead he slipped around to Antek the Owner's side door and waited just inside the door till Antek motioned him toward the back room and followed Frankie there. Antek's short-haired wife nodded to Frankie sullenly and went up to take care of the bar while Antek filled two shot glasses and drank off his own before looking straight at Frankie.

"You're hotter than ever, Dealer," Antek told him at last, "you won't cool off till after the elections. They got out another handbill about 'Alderman's Sluggers Go Free in Strongarm Murder,' somethin' like that. What I know is the super is gonna lose his job if Record Head don't clear the books on Louie.

They're pertendin' now that somebody got paid off to slug Louie 'n you're the guy Bednar needs to clear hisself."

"Skip the politics, Owner," Frankie cut him short. "What's the score on the punk?"

"It's the punk who's in the crack, Dealer. That's for sure. Bednar got him thinkin' he can beat the rap if he plays along. He's had two continuances 'n he's out stealin' everythin' in sight to pay off the lawyers. They don't want him in a jacket till after he's fingered you, so the aces got him out stealin' everythin' layin' loose, they know what's layin' loose 'n it's up to him to snatch it 'n turn it over. Every time he tries to holler about somethin' they got lined up for him, they got to go through it all over again for him, how one more conviction adds up to life 'n no parole—'n all the time they're gettin' so much on him he *can't* say no. They got enough on him now to hang him—but what's the punk gonna do? Either he goes along or he's gone for keeps."

"Don't he know he's gone for keeps anyhow?" Frankie felt a cold disgust with everyone. "Don't he know the day he crosses me in court like he's promisin' Bednar, Bednar's gonna cross him the day after?"

"The punk just can't figure it that far, Frankie," Antek tried to soften Frankie, "*nobody* can figure that far. A guy *got* to hope, it's all the punk got left now is hopin'. He thinks they'll cut down his time if he plays along 'n that's all he can think of. He can't back up now, he got to keep goin' no matter what's at the end for him 'r you 'r anybody. The day they fixed his bond he come in here 'n tells me, 'I won't do more'n a year 'n a day, Owner. I got the captain's word. Then I'll make the street like a little woolly lamb.' 'N he looked that sick when he said it I had to pour him two on the house. He looked that sick when he said it, you'll never know how sick. Trouble is he's spendin' more than they let him keep. He don't bother pourin' the stuff into shot glasses no more—he goes right for the bottle, like he thinks it's the last one he'll get his hands on all his life."

Antek paused to go for a small one from the bottle himself, then set the bottle down with a certain decision; the drink had convinced him it was time to wise the dealer up all the way.

"God knows it wasn't him rolled Louie, Frankie." For a moment Antek looked like a man caught rolling a corpse himself.

"I had a good hunch it wasn't all along," Frankie decided, things coming clearer at last. "I get it now. Pig *had* to frame the punk that night with the package to save his own hide. Bednar guessed that the punk was the one guy who could give him the straight story on Louie and he guessed right."

"It was a dirty one awright," Owner agreed, "puttin' Pig on the payroll to get the punk." Antek looked white about the mouth. "You can see the spot *I* was in, Frankie, just to keep *my* nose clean—but don't think we're blamin' *you*. You done what you had to do, it wasn't just *one* guy's fault. We all got caught in it one way or another."

Frankie got his shot down. "It's hard to tell whose fault a thing like that is," he told Antek. "There's so many things seem like they're *all* my dirty fault, I don't know just why. Even the punk got plenty to blame me for now, I wanted to jam him up—but I didn't want to jam him so's he couldn't get out, ever. Seems like everyone I get close to ends in the vise—what's the score on Zosh?"

If Antek had looked white before, he looked as red as the label on the bottle now; yet came up with the answer straight enough. Somebody had to say it. "Your Zosh is one sick chick, Frankie. She flipped her wig the Sunday you left, right up there in the hall. My Mrs. went to see her once when she was at County 'n Vi goes to see her too. Only she ain't at County no more. She's at the end of the Irving Park line 'n it ain't your fault there neither, like you're thinkin' it is awready."

As though he had known it secretly, without acknowledging it to himself, Frankie just stood looking down at the bottle. "How's Vi doin'?" he asked at last. Just to ask something and be on his way.

Antek's voice was relieved that Frankie had changed the subject. "You'd never recognize that woman, Frankie. All squared up. 'Lips that touch liquor will never touch mine' is her motto these days, 'n she's got the Jailer off the bottle too. It's just about half my rent gone to hell there, between the two of them. You know she's hooked up with the Jailer legal? 'N all they do is count their money? Schwabatski moved her into his own flat 'n his dimwit is goin' to a school fer tardy children, somethin' like that. Even that broken-wind hound is off the lush, Frankie." For a moment Antek looked torn between tears and laughter. "You should just see the four of 'em goin' down Division Saturday nights, the dummy with a big new picture book all about flowers under his arm, leadin' the hound with a new dog collar 'n all brushed 'n combed—you wouldn't even recognize the hound. He goes for milk 'n dog biscuit now 'n brings home the newspaper instead of a bottle in his teeth."

"Where they goin' down Division on Saturday nights if they don't go by whisky taverns?" Frankie asked suspiciously.

"Oh, they're handin' out literture on Milwaukee 'n Ashland, all about guardin' an old lighthouse, somethin' like that, they're in a tailspin on some religious kick. That loose board we used to razz the Jailer about ain't never gonna get fixed now, looks like, unless the dummy gets smart enough in that school to fix it hisself. Looks like the loose board is in the Jailer's head these days."

"He could do worse than Vi," Frankie felt, slapping his checkered cap on the back of his head.

Antek held him one moment.

"Stay out of sight till after elections, Frankie. They'll have to get the punk into a jacket by then, he can't keep on gettin' continuances 'n once he's on his way you'll be cooler. You won't have to be afraid of no one-to-twenty rap if you can stick it out till November. You'll beat the rap altogether if you can get a grand together. Zygmunt's beat tougher raps than yours for less. I'd pitch in a c-note myself 'n the other boys'd come along. Even Schwiefka'd have to pitch in the way we'd put it to him. We'll hold a raffle every night here to get the clout together for you. How much you need right now?"

"Slip me five to keep me alive," Frankie singsonged. And as he took it heard Antek add in an embarrassed undertone, "Lay off that happy gas, Frankie. If you can beat *that* we'll beat Bednar. Is it a deal?"

"It's a deal." Frankie gave him the grin and the grip. Such deals are so easily made.

With the fiver in his pocket he let Antek scout the street both ways for him before he took off. "If you can stick it till November—" Antek was beginning all over again.

At the corner a whole billboard, taken up by the features of the man behind Record Head Bednar, begged shamelessly in five-foot letters:

VOTE FOR UNCLE MIKE

"I'll vote for you, Uncle dear," Frankie assured him and reminded himself, of both the weather and the place: "The patch is pretty warm for March."

As he passed the iron-fenced yard of the McAndrew School he paused to watch a group of punks shooting craps in a shadowy corner: the identical corner in which he'd been caught shooting craps on his last day of school. He walked on with the children's cries rising above the traffic's clamor like voices heard undersea: then realized he wasn't hearing the children who shouted and cried out on this day at all, he was hearing cries that had followed him out of the schoolyard twenty years past and he shuffled on, the checkered cap shading his eyes and the threads, from where his overseas stripes had been torn off, hanging loose from the jacket's patched sleeve.

He turned down a familiar alley, crossed a familiar street, caught a familiar trolley and, where the Ashland Avenue car rolls down Paulina toward Madison, returned to the streets of his exile. Overhead ran the Lake Street El and underneath its checkered light the Negro missions crouched. Missions, taverns and bazaars in long unpainted rows. He cut down the home alley to Maypole Street.

As his hand touched the knob he sensed trouble. Molly sat on the couch, her back against the wall and her legs drawn up protectively under her. Drunkie John was leaning over her.

"Don't kick me," Frankie heard her begging. "Don't kick me." A plea as simple as that. Of a man with a face that belonged on the bottle on the table. John wore some sort of leather headgear, a boy's helmet with chin straps dangling; apparently his latest fancy was that he was some kind of aviator. The face it framed, as it turned toward Frankie, was seared to a purplish red on one side and sunken and pale on the other, giving it a paralytic look; a look borne out by his old trick of speaking, without any movement of the lips at all, from the unseared corner of the mouth. "All in a muddle, like a whore's handbag," he was saying, holding Molly's purse in his hand. "She thinks I drink too much," John told Frankie; but put the purse down. Frankie pushed him toward the door.

"All in a muddle," John laughed quietly even while he went stumbling and came up against the wall with a sly and sheepish little smile. "The joke's on you," he told Frankie, "I'm not as drunk as you think."

"You've done a damned good job of trying," Frankie told him.

"I ain't really drunk till I stagger around," John defended his condition with anxious pride. "One glass of beer all morning 'n I spit that one out, it tasted green."

"Some of it must of trickled down," Frankie suggested, and turned to Molly. "You all right, Molly-O?"

"Make him go, Frankie. Tell him we can't give him no more."

Frankie relayed the information. "We can't give you no more."

"She'll give it or get it," John answered, staying close to the open door.

"Don't hit him, Frankie," Molly cautioned, "don't make him mad."

It was true. Nobody could afford to make this amateur airline pilot angry. So Frankie just stood studying that debauched phiz with its out-thrust jaw and eyes as closely set as those of a baby alligator's. All he could see there, for the life of him, was a little knock-kneed gin-mill fink held together by a kind of poolroom poise. "He's good with a cue too," went through Frankie's mind. "Case out, lush," he told John without touching him at all. "I'm the big dog in this kennel now."

"You caught the right word for it at that, junkie," John told him, taking sudden courage. But was half through the door before he reproached Molly: "I took two jolts in the workie when you'n me was together 'n you never took one. Not one. But your turn is comin' up, sister. This McGantic man, he's gonna fall a long way 'n you're gonna fall right with him. I took two jolts 'n you didn't take one. Not one." They heard him leave.

Frankie closed the door softly, hoping the housekeeper hadn't heard the row. "*Now* what?" he asked Molly-O.

The door opened behind him and Drunkie John stuck his mug back in.

"The *bottle,* buddy—the *bottle.*"

Frankie took a long slug out of it, tossed it to John and heard him go at last.

"That one won't lose much time," Molly-O told him as if he didn't know.

"I'll make it myself now," he pretended, yet with real fear that she might let him try going it alone. When she came to him he felt her trembling. "Don't worry, he won't be comin' back, you can stop shakin'," he assured her.

"It ain't why I'm shakin'," she told him. "It's account of what you said, makin' it yourself now. How about *me?* What if *I* can't make it *my*self?"

"You'll fall if you stick to me now," Frankie warned her.

"I'd rather fall with you than make it without you, Frankie." He held her head on his shoulder and knew this was finally true too: it wasn't just himself needing her any longer, it wasn't just taking without any giving. It was nearer fifty-fifty now and that felt better than he'd ever known a thing like that could be. "I couldn't make it a week by myself," he confessed, "'n you know it. I'd be back sleigh-ridin' in two days without you, Molly-O. If I had to steal to get it."

"Then let's not lose each other again," she decided for keeps. "I'll get work in a South Side joint 'n we'll take care of each other. Just us two."

"Workin' in a South Side joint ain't playin' it safe at all, Molly," he had to remind her as she had so often reminded him. "They'll be lookin' for me through you. You can't stay in the strip racket or the man with the manacles'll come to take us both."

"Okay—so I'm a waitress—look!" She pranced about bearing an imaginary tray. He caught her and brought her back to the business at hand. "You'll be a waitress at Dwight if you don't start gettin' your things together. Let's case."

He stuffed his pockets with cigarettes, toothbrush, shaving cream, a razor and a couple blades. "Just like I'm takin' my rations down to the Rue Pigalle," he laughed reminiscently while she put on her very best shoes—the little silver-heeled open-toed jobs—and filled a small brown five-and-dime overnight bag with underclothing, nylons and her one best dress. He caught her looking lonesomely toward the closet where other dresses hung. "No help for it, Molly-O. We got to travel light."

"It ain't only that," she mourned. "I got six days' pay comin' from the club—how about *that?*"

"Forget it. I loaned a fiver off Antek this morning, it'll get us a room for a day or two. Out the back way, Molly-O. The patch is hot."

The patch was hot all right. The patch was burning. They were half-way down the narrow gangway to the alley when he heard the tires wheel into the alley. She'd played waitress ten seconds too long. "Back in the house," he told her.

But in a white fear she clung to him, her hand pressing him hard against the wall. He wheeled her about by her shoulders and shoved her hard. "Stall them."

The little silver heels went tap-tap-tapping like a silver hammer on stone down the concrete and up the little flight of stairs, like tapping up the little flight of stairs into her dressing room, and the door slammed behind her. Good girl. She'd do as he'd told her.

Just like he'd told her, plus a year and a day, and what tapping the little silver heels would do after that wouldn't amount to much. A bit on the backstreet pavements after dark perhaps and not much more. Then his own position broke upon him.

One squad in front and one in the back and the aces in the alley sitting there playing it safe.

"That John must have said I was packin' a rod to make hisself look good," Frankie guessed. Well, the boy with the golden arm had been lucky once, a long time ago, this must be the spot where the old luck started coming back—just when it couldn't get worse. He got back down the gangway and down the half flight to the basement. To listen one moment at the basement door for the housekeeper's heavy step, heard nothing but a rat's light scuttling and ducked into the gaseous darkness, bending under the low-hung piping to the single ground-level window.

Overhead he heard the military clumping, from small room to small room all down the hall, the banging at doors and the calling up the stairs, the shoes and shouts and threats of the Lake Street aces. He swung the window open from the inside, latched it carefully onto a little rusty hook in the basement ceiling and got out onto the stone walk between the walls.

He had gained the distance of the building's breadth, nothing more. He would be that much farther away from the aces when he hit the alley, their eyes would be just a second slower to spot him when he walked into view, if he hit the alley in the spot a next-door neighbor would hit it. He pulled his cap down low and shoved his hands in his pockets to give him that fraction of a second it would take for them to make certain he was their man.

"If she can hold them two more minutes," he prayed, feeling the brick against his back.

A lanky Negro in a baseball cap paused, on the walk that fronted the house, to rest a bat on the toe of his left shoe and study Frankie as gravely as a scout out looking for pitching talent. "They get out for spring practice early around here," Frankie thought hurriedly, crossing himself for the first time since he'd left County. He was going to need *somebody's* help, that was for sure. And came out into the alley standing up thirty feet behind the squadrol.

Shambling along like any early afternoon bottle boy, he counted four El girders before he heard the aces rumble. "Man out the basement!" someone called and ten yards ahead, with two girders still to pass, the iron steps of the El waited in the checkered sunlight.

"You down there!"

Now he was for it and yet shambled listlessly on—a deaf, dumb, half-blind drunk of almost any color at all going nowhere in no particular hurry—he'd be good for one warning shot and the ace gave it to him: it whined high overhead into the ties, the next shot would be for promotion and he went low, assault-course fashion, zigzagging with the girders sheltering his back, thinking, "I done this three times awready—it's all in the Service Record," and up the iron steps three at a time, the promotion shot whammed into the iron inches below and a brief, cold, painless flame, like the needle's familiar touch, brushed his heel. He went past the ticket taker head down, heard her call once and then yank the cord. *Bong!* "Mister!" and the *bong* was lost in the oncoming thunder of the Loopbound El pulling up, pausing and pulling away.

Leaning flat against the door, he caught one brief flash of the car in the alley below and then the alley was gone in a rush of city sunlight. "Bednar's gonna be awful mad at someone for this," he thought softly; and stopped hiding. He was on his way.

Sitting with one arm across the open window while the city rocked along below, he wiped sweat off his forehead with his cap and felt the sweat clear down to his socks. "I only hope they don't go too touch on Molly-O," and felt the old pang of conscience: something happened to everyone, it seemed, who came too close to the man with the golden arm. "I'll make it all up to her some day," he eased himself out of the vise.

But it was hard, with the breath hardly back in his lungs, to ease himself far. He counted three stations: they had just passed Franklin and Wells when the sweat in his socks began stinging and he looked down.

He was on his way all right. With a sockful of blood.

A sockful of blood and an hour and a half to the rush hour. Frankie coughed a bit into his hand, the little dry junkie's cough that starts coming on when trouble starts coming. He looked down the car: there were only a couple women sitting, with their backs toward him, down at the other end. And felt the first cold surge of the sickness. "I'll stop by the drugstore 'n get cough medicine," he decided, pinning all his hope now on codeine.

Knowing that, without Molly-O, neither codeine nor paregoric could do it. He undid the shoe's lace with fingers that weakened momentarily. When the conductor passed he crossed his ankles to conceal the bloody shoe and looked out the window all the way to State and Dearborn. The car began filling.

If he could score for just half a grain he'd be good for two days; and fingered the fiver in his pocket. "I'll double back on them." He walked, limping as lightly as he might, across the transfer bridge. "Old Doc D.'ll remember me, he'll patch the foot 'n Owner'll let me have the dough to hide out with till it blows over 'n Zygmunt can fix it. I'll make it up to everybody."

With each step downward to the northbound platform he let his hopes go up an inch. If he could just make it back to the Division Street Station ahead of the rush-hour crowd, before he got just too damned sick. The Logan Square El rumbled up with the spring's last snow rusted along its roof.

"They're runnin' right on time today," he congratulated the CTA, reminding himself with mock seriousness: "I still owe 'em fifteen cents."

The moment he felt the El picking up speed as it left the Loop he began fancying the aces waiting for him, harness bulls and soft-clothes dicks, on every West Side platform: twice he changed seats to get away from the station side. At every stop the car got more crowded; till there wasn't one seat a restless rider might change for his own.

When the conductor called "Madison!" he knew he wasn't going to make it to Division, he'd be flat on the floor of the car by then. The ice was under his heart and the bones were beginning to twist. He got off just in time to keep from being pinched by the El door.

The air, after that of the closed car, brought the sickness down and when he got to the bottom of the Madison Street El stairs at Damen he saw a bundle of tabloids, bound, for return, by newspaper twine and picked them up on a hunch as fast as he'd ever had on a pair of dice or a last closed card. "Makes me look like the corner paper hustler," he decided. "Innocent-like." He felt himself growing more sly by the moment, limping east, block after block, toward the Cloudland, down a pavement thronging with overalled winoes, past curbs littered with bottles and butts. Once having to step a bit to one side to allow a white-aproned bartender, busily backing out of a bar door with his hands wrapped about the ankles of a drunk so limp he would have seemed only a bundle of ragged clothes except for the gleam of the sun on the naked white ankles: when he had the wreck in the middle of the walk the bartender simply left him there and went back to work. Leaving the ruined sleeper lying flat on his back with his fly open to the blue and mocking sky.

Two doors down Frankie felt himself going and turned, holding the papers he had forgotten in a sudden sly flicker of pain in his groin, into a hallway bearing a simple invitation:

HOTEL
Men Only

And now it was time to ride the whitewashed merry-go-round once more with laughter all the way. So she closed her eyes and made the secret finger signs that started the music and the wheels, spreading her fingers over her lips to let the laughter through. She was going farther than ever this time. Yet—feeling the roughness of the flannel nightgown—no one could go calling like *this*. Where were her garters and stockings and skirt?

They had taken her garters, they had taken her purse, they had taken her hand mirror and locked her door. They had taken her dark, loose-fitting dress and her white, tight-fitting pride. "How do you expect a person to look neat without even a little mirror to peek into?" she asked the doctor. "How am I supposed to comb my hair?" Coming so close to him that he held her hands to her sides, not seeming to trust her at all, though she liked the touch of the hands. Then before he had time to say a word, got one finger loose, pointed it at his little mustache and laughed right in his face: "Look at the cooky duster, girls!"

She would fix them all. If they didn't let her have the things a decent person should have, she'd just let herself go, hair, face, figure and nails. Till they'd be so ashamed they'd come in with a little white dressing table and fingernail polish and she'd make herself proper again; for when proper people came to see her.

Sometimes at night she heard the proper people coming down the hall and not any of your West Division Street hides either. Real refined devils from Augusta Boulevard. But when they heard how badly she was dressed they kept right on going; to call on someone a bit more in the fashion.

So she'd have to go visiting just as she was and all in her own strange way. Rocking herself on the cot's iron edge with a pillow behind her back as though fancying herself still in the wheel chair, her knees came up slowly toward her chin, her head went ever so slowly and sleepily forward into her cupped and waiting hands. Rocking herself gently and steadily so, she felt herself going into the dark on the one-way merry-go-round, rocking along to somewhere ever so pleasant she had been sometime, somewhere, before. A rocketing, darkening, winding trip, all the way to Sometime Street where there was always dancing down the whitewashed, lopsided walks.

But mustn't speak to a single soul on the way or they'd come and take her back. She had to let everything go, keep both eyes closed and never peek, that was the whole trick of riding the whitewashed merry-go-round to the whitewashed lopsided streets. The merry-go-round that rolled in, rolled out, rolled right along through night and day, down the ceaseless carnival that kept all-day holiday now in her brain: nurses and card dealers, doctors and all, policemen and landlords and priests and blind peddlers—not a word to a single soul, she had to let everyone, all of them go and never look back at any.

For when they found out where she was trying to ride they would force her back on the iron cot. There was some sort of house rule that forbade her to leave by either the door to the room or on the merry-go-round: she would waken with her spine throbbing and her wrists still hurting from where they'd been twisted to force her back and she would know they had found her out again.

She mustn't do that, they told her, ever again. She mustn't go *there*, for some night she wouldn't get back at all. She would find it was darker and colder there than she'd ever thought; so dark and so cold and so far that no one could help her find the way back. They stood around looking down at the stray-haired woman with such peace and light in her eyes; and when they were quite through telling her what she must and must not do she looked at them all and, very slowly, told them everything *they* had to do.

For she was on to all their tricks and knew a thing or two she wasn't telling. She wasn't telling one of them of the magic skate she wore which got her back, all the way, every time, because of a certain skater who showed her the way, far up ahead with a sort of light about him no matter how dark and cold it was behind.

Small wonder they didn't want her to leave, they were getting paid well enough to keep her. What they were really afraid of was that she'd bring her business elsewhere.

That was why they wouldn't return her clothes, why they kept on taking her temperature to pretend they thought she was sick. That was why they took to surprising her. The door would open without warning in the middle of the night and the light would go on—they'd catch her at it then, her head in her hands and her knees drawn up. It got to be something of a game: when she lost she got the needle.

They never knew of the times they never caught her at all.

At first she had fought against them, spat their thermometers out on the floor, bitten a nurse's hand and refused their food, their voices, their hands and their terrible eyes.

Then, too abruptly, had turned strangely docile. "That's a *real* good girl," she heard the nurse tell the doctor. "She's just as *good* as she can be now, Doctor, we're *ever* so proud of her." Without looking at their eyes Sophie was pleased. She had caught the falseness of the nurse's tone and sensed her sudden docility had them more worried now than had her hostility. They didn't know how to bring her out of it. They knew that her docility was feigned; but couldn't reach her through it. For it wasn't docility. It was a wall.

Behind it she began evading them. So what they wanted of her now was exactly what they had first punished her for: to weep against them, to curse them, to beg them to let her go and to throw the food on the floor in a biting spite.

Now she ate only so long as they guided her hand to her mouth and not one spoonful more.

"Just try eating this yourself. You can eat and walk too. If you just wanted to." Underneath the warmth of the nurse's tone was a concealed rage at this one who wouldn't come out of the shell and was wiser in her spite, somehow, than any of them.

Right along with breakfast, the next morning, the nurse brought a deck of cards to test this one's wisdom, and Sophie understood right away. When she had all the cards in the world counted she could go home. That would show them she was as smart as could be, so they would have to let her go.

So it was that, knowing they watched her secretly, yet feeling wonderfully at peace with herself, she sorted the cards most carefully and counted them one at a time to be sure not to make a single mistake and spoil all her chances. She could tell by the way they stood, a bit to the side, so white and stiff and proper, the way good doctors and nurses must always stand until they are told to go away.

Sorted and counted so carefully, according to some strange, wanton pattern drifting like a rainbow-colored fog bank through her mind, counting by color and whim and a wayward cunning the way she'd counted falling snow from a window that faced the El.

And when they were all properly counted began throwing them one by one, selecting this one and rejecting that, because this one was a good little card and that one had been naughty—and always somehow picking the one they hadn't expected at all—the very one she knew they hadn't seen, since it had been hiding from everyone but herself. Tossing them according to the slow suspended motion of the snow that had fallen so slowly all night long and he hadn't come home at all.

Tossed them toward the cot's iron corners, making each one come down face up or face however she wished, just by telling each, in her mind, which way to land as it fell; so each did his trick just as he was told.

When it was all done at last and time to go home she looked up and told the doctor pleasantly, "Now you must tell the precinct captain to bring my new-look dress and the green babushka so I can go home looking nice," and added, just because it always pleased her to say it, "you with the cooky duster."

"I'll tell the precinct captain," Cooky Duster assured her, his grave gray eyes never leaving her face for a moment. "I'll tell him you're moving to another precinct."

She looked at them both then, with such seeming trust, that something of pity stirred beneath the white-starched hospital jackets. For they saw a child's face, puffed by some muted suffering she could never tell. The face she had rouged, from the nurse's compact, so it was that of a child painted to look like a clown's.

And the eyes so dark and buttoned so tightly. So pinched by that private, midnight-colored grief.

The doctor nodded to the nurse, saying something Sophie wasn't supposed to hear at all. So she spoke right up and told them to their faces, "You can just tell them the whole business is a dirty lie and everyone has to stop pretending it isn't right this minute." She saw their look of genuine amazement and paused in a quick fear that somehow she had given herself away and would not be going home after all. For both at once urged her to say more, say something more, anything more. She made a slow, weaving motion then with her hand and sang teasingly, just for Cooky Duster to hear: "Oh, *Doctor*—you do me *so* much good." Then hid herself behind her eyes and grew so rigid, under the nurse's stroking, that the doctor had to tell the woman to stop.

"There's *real* spite for you," Sophie heard the nurse decide.

That night, just to show what she thought of them both, Sophie went down the street lined with the picture-postcard trees, pushing herself on the single skate; trying to keep the skater ahead in view all the way to the porch with the leaves strewn along the arc lamp's broken light.

But there, for the first time, she was left all alone in the dark. It was later than ever before and he had not waited to show her the way back. So dark, so cold, so far to go with leaves rustling so darkly all around. Till the chimes of old St. Stephen's rang once and the wind began blowing the flies away. The lights went on and a voice said right in her ear: "What are you thinking of right now, Sophie?"

She drew her knees to her chin and showed the voice what it was like to be dead.

Whenever they peered into the whitewashed room after that they saw only a gently rocking shadow in a long gray nightgown on the built-in cot, her head in her hands and her knees to her chin with the playing cards scattered and forgotten. Like everything else she had scattered and forgotten, across the cold gray concrete at her feet.

When they gathered the cards off the floor at last and took them away in a neat little box she said in a whisper, for she knew then she had won: "The wind is blowing the flies away. God has forgotten us all."

Nor ever asked again for anything more but a sense of a white-washed still-ness about her rising each day higher and more white.

The everlasting walls of Nowhere Land, higher than any hospital wall.

From which is no returning.

The wind had blown the summer flies away. God had forgotten His own.

As soon as he got the shoe off he pried at the naked heel with a razor blade to get at the lead in the flesh. But the blood began again, the wrist went weak as water and he lay back with the blood-smeared paw across his forehead and the naked foot resting upon the crumpled tabloids with the pain beating straight through the morning line to the unclean cover on which he lay. He felt the blood drying on the dated headline under his ankle.

Once he got up, fetched a scrap of soap off the washstand and began rubbing it across the ankle to get the blood off. But the light was too strong and he fell back on the bed with his checkered cap doubled under his head for a pillow, still clutching the sliver of soap in his hand. He wished that somebody would make the light stop swinging or shade it.

A red paper poppy clung to the chicken wire directly overhead and he couldn't remember tying it there at all. "Must of been drunk again last night," he decided vaguely. Unless that Peter had tied it there. He must still be drunk, he needed a drink so bad, a drink of anything at all and all the way down. His throat felt like that left foot looked—smeared with something dark, stale and brown. Something that had to be washed off and not a blessed drop for throat, foot, or tongue. "Fightin' again," he decided about the blood. "Who was I bat-tlin' this time?"

He sat up suddenly. What was he doing here lying flat on his pratt when there was so much to be done? It was late, it was almost too late, there was just time left to pull back the last open chair and say, "Deal me in."

It was blackjack and the dealer's eyeshade was pulled down too far over the eyes just as he had always liked to wear the shade himself; while the sucker to whom he dealt wore his own checkered cap. He stood aside and watched them both. He was both sucker and dealer; yet felt he cared nothing for what hap-pened to either. Under the night light's feral glare a single soiled silver dollar lay stained with his own wet blood.

"If I win that buck they'll find out I killed some guy," the sucker realized as the dealer flipped him the ace of diamonds. The dealer was laughing behind the eyeshade and around the board many Bednars smiled behind their cards; each holding them before his mouth so that no sucker might guess they were on to the dealer's game: to stick the sucker with the bad-luck buck that meant one to twenty and maybe life.

"Don't take *everything* you can get," Molly-O told him ever so softly from just the other side of the wall and the girl knew what she was saying all right because the bad-luck buck lengthened under the light into a glistening new hypo with two full caps beside it. About the board, behind their cards, all those sly fat Bednars smiled: they hadn't come here to play blackjack at all.

They had come to watch Frankie Machine take the one big fix and someone began pumping his arm to get the slow blood moving. He wakened with the desk clerk tugging at his wrist. "What's wrong in here?" he wanted to know right away. "Where'd you get hurt?"

"I stepped on a nail is all." Frankie grinned weakly through the smear of blood across his cheek. "I'm not the kind makes trouble, Doc," he pleaded feebly. "Can I get a drink of water?"

But there was nobody there any more and he could not tell whether he had really seen or merely imagined the clerk. It made no difference, he had to get up and phone Antek to come and get him. Antek would get here in no time at all to help him downstairs into the car so there wasn't any use worrying, everything was as good as done, he'd just float on his back a minute to let all the little waves wash him clean. The sun hurt his eyes, he was getting too far out, he could hardly see the beach for the glare. He sat up shaking his head to clear it.

About the bulb a little rainbow-colored halo burned, the bulb swinging a bit in its colored shell as though someone had been in here and set it swinging again while he'd floated off. He mustn't float off again that way, he had to hold on. Hold on hard and figure out how much time he had. What was it the fellow had asked: "How did you get hurt?" He sat up with sweat ringing his throat, it slid like the beads of a rosary about his neck when he turned his head; and wished to Christ the bulb would stop its endless swinging. It hurt his eyes yet he had to follow its tiny arc. There was something about it he needed to understand and slowly he saw it: framed within that rainbow-colored halo Frantic McGantic looked down with gentle mockery in his eyes.

Sergeant McGantic had come to call and the sergeant brought his own small mercies. The sergeant wasn't one to let a good junkie down. Frankie's eyes went seeking about the room to see what the sergeant had brought him and found it at last. It didn't make any real difference now that there was no hypo to this fix at all.

It was enough that the sergeant had tossed, across the bedpost and in a reach of a good junkie's hand, one thin double strand of yellow newspaper twine.

Leaning upon one elbow, there on the bed soiled by sweat and blood, Frankie asked himself aloud, squinting at the brassy glint of the bedpost beneath that swinging bulb, "What am I waitin' for?" For the roll of the squadrol's tires? For the ice in the blood to reach the heart? Or for the tread of heavy boots following a flashlight up the stairs?

"I hope Molly-O stays clear of John after she does her time," he made a bit of a prayer for Molly—but there was even less time for praying than for hoping. He got off the bed, favoring the naked left foot, and supported himself against the brass of the bedpost: he felt the chill that years of flophouse nights had trapped in the metal like the chill trapped deep in his own bones. Who was it had told him, "That's the other side of the wall—it's worse there when it's still"?

One flight below a Madison Street trolley charged past in a stream-lined, cat-howling fury that left him strengthened by an odd excitement. Before the trolley's scream had died he had the double strand in his hands and his fingers working on it as surely and steadily as if making paper jazzbows for Solly Saltskin out of yesterday's *Form*.

"It's all in the wrist 'n I got the touch," he told himself in a surge of ice-cold confidence and far, so far it told him he was still seconds ahead of them all, the siren's first metallic cry fluttered the shade, whimpering faintly along the chicken wire and then a bit louder till it was a moaning telegraphic code shaking a wavering message across the waves of the brain—"Have a good dream you're dancin', Zosh"—and the words were whirled like leaves in a dead-cold wind blowing up from the other side of the wall. Into one brief strangled whimpering.

To rustle away down the last dark wall of all.

WITNESS SHEET

STATE OF ILLINOIS)
COUNTY OF COOK)
      BEFORE THE CORONER OF COOK COUNTY
INQUEST ON THE BODY   )
      OF   ) FIRST AND FINAL HEARING
FRANCIS MAJCINEK   )

Transcript of the testimony taken and the proceedings had at an inquest held upon the body of the above-named deceased, before WILLIAM HACKETT, a DEPUTY CORONER OF COOK COUNTY, ILLINOIS, and a jury, duly impaneled and sworn, at 199 N. Ashland Avenue, Chicago, Illinois, April 1, 1948. At the hour of 3 p.m.

LORRAINE REPORTING SERVICE
R. Jackson, stenographer.

The first witness, having been duly sworn, was then examined by Deputy Coroner Hackett and testified as follows:

Q. What is your name and occupation?

A. Anthony Witwicki. Tavernkeeper.

Q. What was the full name of the deceased?

A. Frankie—that is Francis, I think—Majcinek the *right* name—Frankie Machine, how people say.

Q. His address?

A. Same as mine only upstairs.

Q. His age?

A. Thirty, thirty-one, around there.

Q. Was he married or single?

A. He was married, his wife is invalid that happened one night he got drunk—

Q. Where was he born?

A. Why, right there on Division, he had a secondhand car that time, I forget the make—

Q. Where was his father born?

A. Poland same as mine. Both dead a long time now.

Q. And his mother?

A. That was a stepmother, he called it "foster mother"—they got along all right. She is married again, went away, I don't know where. He never spoke of this, that was forgotten.

Q. What kind of work did he do?

A. When he come to see me he had no work.

Q. Before that. Before he went and got into all this trouble with the police.

A. He was in jail a little now and then. Nothing serious.

Q. Before he was in jail, did he work for you?

A. No, no, he did one thing. Dealt cards. Made pretty good when he worked. Sometimes he couldn't work every night though, how those things are.

Q. What other work did you know him to do in the past?

A. When he was a boy one summer he was a caddy, every day, the whole summer. We went together, I think they called the course Indian Hill, something like that. Once when he owed me for drinks he fixed the furnace. He could work good but not every day, he got restless then and start to drink. When he don't work, then he don't drink so much.

Q. Did he always drink, before all this trouble?

A. Sometimes he was a heavy drinker, then for a while he don't drink at all, like he's thinkin' about somethin'. Then if he got drunk it would be awhile before he begin again. A week, maybe two weeks with hardly a drink. Just a beer or two.

Q. Does he owe you money now?

A. Nothing, nothing.

Q. When did you last see him?

A. Yesterday in the morning, I just opened up and there he was waiting, I didn't know who it was one minute, he didn't say. Just standing there saying nothing in the dark. I said, "Who's there?" and he says then, "You alone, Owner?" When I go up to him I see. He looks like chicken with the soup out. He looks like just out of hospital.

Q. You knew the police had been looking for him. You knew it was your duty to call the police right then.

A. Nothing I knew. All I know is sometimes he is in jail a little, what for isn't my business. I knew he was in some trouble but I don't ask about such things, I don't mix in politics. I just serve whisky and beer.

Q. Did he tell you he wished he were dead, that he wanted to die, that sort of thing?

A. No, no, no. That one never talked like that. *Never.* All he talked was he's going to work for Gene Krupa, play "hot drums" he calls it someplace downtown—then he laughs, he don't really think so, he just like to hear how it sounds when he talks big like that.

Q. Was he nervous during this last conversation?

A. Never nervous. Just don't feel good, too much domestic trouble, too many bills, too much beer, that's all.

Q. Did you know of him taking anything more stimulating than beer?

A. Whisky. That's all. Whisky.

DEPUTY: Line 16. That's right, the full name. Your address right below it. Thank you. Next witness.

The second witness, having been duly sworn, was then examined by Deputy Coroner Hackett and testified as follows:

DEPUTY: What is your name, Sergeant?

OFFICER: L. H. Fallon.

Q. Were you the officer who found the deceased?

A. That's right. Myself and Officer Otto Schaeffer. A bit after midnight it was.

Q. And that was at?

A. 1179 W. Madison Street, a small hotel there, we got the call on Sangamon and Adams—this is the gentleman here who called, he'd gone up to see what this fellow was hollering about.

CLERK: I went up there the first time and saw he'd been hurt some way, so I went back down to the phone and while I was phoning I heard something else and ran right back up. I couldn't get in the door, we don't have keys but he'd put something up against the knob. I jumped up and looked down through the top—we have that chicken-wire top like according to the Board of Health it's permitted and I seen him hanging but I couldn't cut him down, I couldn't get inside. I figure this ain't my job now it's up to the officers—I work in this place almost three months now and it's the first time anything like this happened except once, my first week. As soon as this man come in it seemed to me—

DEPUTY: Let the officer tell what he found.

OFFICER FALLON: When we broke in the door the deceased had fallen, the wire had given way—the wire he'd hooked the rope onto but the rope was still around his throat, it was soaped, there was still a bit of soap in his hand. He was up against the bed, huddled there like, he must have hit the bedpost with his forehead when the wire gave, it was bruised there where he hit it and tore the sleeve of his jacket. The knees were bent—like under him and the head hung on one side, toward the shoulder.

DEPUTY: Was he fully clothed?

OFFICER: Fully clothed, except for one shoe, he just had the right one on. The heel of the foot without a shoe had been torn by a .38-caliber shell. We removed him to the Polish-American Hospital where he was identified as the man who escaped them earlier in the day. There was a murder warrant out on him. He was pronounced dead by Dr. Blue and removed to the County Morgue.

Q. How was he dressed when you found him?

A. He was wearing army clothes, mostly. A combat jacket, suntans, army shirt dyed green, army brogans.

Q. Were there any valuables?

A. A few dimes in one pocket. No papers. A good-conduct medal in his wallet.

DEPUTY: Line 17, Sergeant. Thank you. Next witness.

The third witness, having been duly sworn, was then examined by Deputy Coroner Hackett and testified as follows:

Q. You're the young woman being held in connection with the death of Francis Majcinek?
A. That's right.
Q. When did you last see the deceased?
A. Around one, maybe two o'clock yesterday.
Q. Where was this at?
A. The house on Maypole Street where the police came.
Q. What is that? A hotel?
A. Rooming house.
Q. You lived there with the deceased?
A. Since winter.
Q. I see. Did you get along well together?
A. Very well. No trouble at all.
Q. What was the matter with him?
A. Just worried all the time, no work, sorry for things he'd done, blaming himself, all like that.
Q. What I mean is, weren't there other things—bad habits he'd picked up depressing him?
A. Drinking, that was his one bad habit.
Q. Did you ever hear him threaten to commit suicide?
A. Never. Not once. Oh well, he used to like to say things, but it didn't mean anything.
Q. Tell us what you mean.
A. Just swing talk like musicians use. He liked to say "Some cats swing like that." Then he'd laugh, just a saying he had, it didn't mean anything.
Q. Did you know he was wanted for murder?
A. He never told me that.
Q. But did you know it?
A. *Nobody* told me that.
Q. I see. And you just met him recently?
A. I know Frankie ten years. We went together before he got married.
Q. Do you understand the charge against you?
A. They haven't told me yet.

Q.   It's called "Accessory after the Fact," that's very serious, you will have to go
     to jail if you're found guilty.
A.   Are you trying me here, Coroner? If not I'd rather let the lawyers decide
     in court.

DEPUTY: Thank you. Line 18. Just write "no address." The statement of the
coroner's physician is as follows: "In my opinion death was due to asphyxiation
by strangulation." Is there any reason why this inquest shouldn't be closed?

     (No response.)

DEPUTY: Let the record show no response. The verdict of the coroner's jury
will read that the deceased came to his death from asphyxiation by strangulation, with a rope around his neck extended from a wire roofing put on with his
own hands with suicidal intent, at the above-mentioned location between midnight of March 31st, 1948, and 12:20 A.M. of April 1st while temporarily
insane. Close the case.

EPITAPH   The Man with the Golden Arm

It's all in the wrist, with a deck or a cue,
And Frankie Machine had the touch.
He had the touch, and a golden arm—
"Hold up, Arm," he would plead,
Kissing his rosary once for help
With the faders sweating it out and—
Zing!—there it was—Little Joe or Eighter from Decatur,
Double trey the hard way, dice be nice,
When you get a hunch bet a bunch,
It don't mean a thing if it don't cross that string,
Make me five to keep me alive,
Tell 'em where you got it 'n how easy it was—
We remember Frankie Machine
And the arm that always held up.

We remember in the morning light
When the cards are boxed and the long cues racked
Straight up and down like the all-night hours
With the hot rush hours past.

For it's all in the wrist with a deck or a cue
And if he crapped out when we thought he was due
It must have been that the dice were rolled,
For he had the touch, and his arm was gold:
Rack up his cue, leave the steerer his hat,
The arm that held up has failed at last.

Yet why does the light down the dealer's slot
Sift soft as light in a troubled dream?
(A dream, they say, of a golden arm
That belonged to the dealer we called Machine.)

REMEMBRANCES

LETTER TO JOE HAAS

Nelson Algren

Introduction

Bettina Drew

In 1952 a young man named Joseph Haas, who had earlier reviewed *The Man with the Golden Arm* and was then stationed with the U.S. Army during the Korean War, began a correspondence with Algren about literature. Feted, flush with money, and about to begin writing the long essay on literature and Cold War culture that would be published as *Nonconformity,* Algren was in an expansive mood. He responded to Haas's questions in the following letter, which remains the best description of Algren's experiences and feelings while writing the story of Frankie Machine. (Letter courtesy of Rare Books and Manuscripts, Ohio State University Libraries.)

Gary, Ind. March 1

Dear Joe,

I'd judge that I rewrote "Golden Arm" a dozen times in
some places, and more in most others. I suppose there were,
for some sections, forty rewritings that still aren't right.
If Mr Doubleday hadn't come and wrenched the thing away
from me by brute strength I'd still be up there on Wabansia
Avenue , rewriting away. Unless, by this time, they would
have come and wrenched me away, shrieking Don't Let Them
Take My ~~Babywayx~~ Baby's Daddy Away.

No, it didn't pour, It comes in lumps, and each lump
has to be smoothed and grained down and then, when it's
just so shining and smooth you read it over aloud to your
self and love the sound of every perfect word, you find
you can t use it, it doesn't tie in, it's fine in itself
but it diverts the whole story. So you gulp and put it
away assuring yourself you'll make a ~~xxxy~~ use of it another
day and sometimes you do, if you remember what drawer you
put it away in. Sometimes it's like a squirrel looking for
the acorns he hid the fall before last- he knows it's somewhere in the neighborhood, ~~but~~ and digs up the whole plot
and when he finds it, it's gone to seed in two years.

It's a hardy trade, Joe, with a boot as quick as a
fiver.

But there were never days when I felt I wouldn't complete it. I knew that, unless the army got me again or a
Buick bumped me, I'd get a story put together, because I
had the parts to put together. My ~~xxxxxxxx~~ self-doubts
weren't concerned with whether it would be completed, but
only whether it would ~~say~~ anything, and say it well, as
nobody else could have said it, when it was done. All
those things came true, to a limited degree, so I feel
it was a lucky book, and a lucky time now past, and I
was lucky to write it.

No, I wasn't wild with delight in the writing- but
certainly not unhappy. I had more kicks, aside from
~~writing~~ in that time, than ever before, and was moderately happy, and still am. I don't think you have to
suffer as savagely as you suspect. Jst so long as you
don t get complacent, and self-satisfied, you're alright

Actually, I don't think I gave any particular thought, at the
time, as to whether I was happy or not, and still don't. Don't
have the time to find out. Or, rather, not particularly interested, one way or another. So I guess if I had been, or
were now, I'd know it.   " words to
    I never recall having an anger that brought them to
flow like tears."First place, the words never flowed for me,
out of any emotion, and I never believe I ever got that mad.
In a sense, I suspect, I'm mad all the time. But it isn't up
where it interferes with my life. Nobody could get that mad
about anything so long as he has a remaant of a sense of humor. Because I understood, a long time ago, so long ago I can't remember where or how I first found it out, that it's all a crazy
sort of joke on us all; that there isn t any true meaning to
anything that wont be untrue in half an hour, and if you can
live through it you're doing fine. If you can live through it,
and have a few of the good things on the way- music, a girl.
a sense of work that you like, then you're as lucky as possible. I think that, once you get rid of the notion that the
world is going to hell unless you keep it from going there
personally, you're bettr off. It frees you to do and say what
you think, to talk back and not fall for the hundred myths
with which we're deluged with every day, and not to expect
too much. After all, it's only your life.
    Nathanael West was somebody who would have been one of
the greatest and the best if he'd just a few short years to
live. I have his "ACool Millions" so
    The dramatization, for which you generously gave thought
to backdrops, is off. We hadn't even reached the script stage
when you started buying props. My collaborator couldn t do it.
He's the third one who's had to give up. I'm going to try a
guy on the West Coast next.
    Don't trouble yourself about my using my valuable time
to answer your letters. If I feel like writing to somebody I
do, if I don't I throw the letter away. I do more tasteful
things with my priceless hours. Write when you like, xxx
                    there you go,   Algren

ARM

A MEMOIR

John Clellon Holmes

In 1959, when I first met Nelson Algren, he was fifty years old, and he was wearing the loud, checked jacket and wide, Day-Glo tie of a short-odds bettor at the two dollar window of a downstate Midwest racetrack. We were sitting at a table in the middle of the Oak Bar of the Plaza Hotel in New York, and our waiter was trying to disguise his bemusement at Algren's Runyonesque get-up. "I always stay here when I come to New York," Algren said in his deliberate Chicago drawl, "but I can never get a rise out of them."

When I last saw Algren, in the autumn of 1971, he had gate-crashed a party at the Playboy Mansion in Chicago, a party to which he had pointedly not been invited, by masquerading behind a large, well-kept moustache. "I'm thinking of moving to New Jersey," he said mysteriously—Algren who, for three decades, had been Chicago's premier literary personality.

In the twelve intervening years, I got to know Nelson about as well as anyone but his oldest cronies—that is, I ate Chinese with him on Mott Street after escaping from the literary cocktail parties we both hated; I passed him in the shadowy upstairs hall of my house in Connecticut where, insomniacs both, we separately prowled, preparing the next day's sentences; we wrote a hundred-odd sportive letters to one another across a couple of continents and several oceans; and once, in a musing mood, having the first drink of the evening, he said to me: "What we do, you know—

writing these books—the kind of books we write—It's not *wanted*, John Clellon."
He looked at me, his lean, sharp-nosed face bleak and hard in the fading light, his
eyes without the raillery that usually lay banked within them. "Don't kid yourself, kid.
It's a loser's game."

Actually, it was American literature that was the loser. This writer, whom
Hemingway had called one of the finest American writers after Faulkner, whose best
novel, *The Man with the Golden Arm*, was the first winner of the National Book
Award, and who had claimed a portion of contemporary American reality as his personal bailiwick, wrote nothing of lasting importance after *A Walk on the Wild Side* in
1956. He has been all but forgotten in the years since his death in 1981, his books
out of print, his hard eye and sucker's heart out of fashion, and his style—that unique
amalgam of Villonesque lyricism and Chekhovian compassion—exerting little or no
influence on our national letters. Pity.

For his vision was his own. On the literature of the Chicago Renaissance, he
wrote: "The search went down Main Street in Winesburg, Ohio, and down Main
Street to the edge of town, to where the towns's last gas-lamp makes fence and
wagon-road look haggard. And on either hand, in town or out, in the General Store
or on backland farms, faces of men and women living without alternatives were
revealed.... A search past 3 a.m. gas-stations and darkened farms under a moon
that said Repose, Repose. Past field and suburb, to where the arc-lamps of Chicago
begin; down streets Jennie Gerhardt knew. And everywhere, awake or sleeping,
revealing men and women trapped without repose."

In beer tavern and hired room, at racetrack and police lineup, Algren depicted the
reposeless with a deadwall humor and a moonlit poetry that embodied a moral
imperative as unique as his style: "I submit that literature is made upon any occasion
that a challenge is put to the legal apparatus by a conscience in touch with humanity.... The hard necessity of bringing the judge on the bench down into the dock has
been the peculiar responsibility of the writer in all ages of man."

This is not the vision, nor the credo, of a flash-in-the-pan scribbler. His style, its
long-line, street-smart vernacular (more blues than jazz) always verging on minor-
key lament, is the genuine article, a Midwest prose commensurate to mean streets
and hard times and starved hearts. And his contention that literature should be the
voice of the voiceless, the embodiment of Whitman's claim that "I belong to these
convicts and prostitutes myself," is a faith that cuts to the bone of the original
American social compact, and it's time we asked, and not without discomfort, whatever happened to Nelson Algren?

That first night, which began at the Plaza, was fairly typical of the public Algren
of those years. During the first hour, as he wide-eyed the bill and fumbled with his
money, he seemed to have a bad case of Second City paranoia, a sudden

onslaught of nervous Hickism, and I marveled again at New York's ability to intimi-date even the most illustrious out-of-towner. As the evening unwound, however, I saw that a lot of this was an elaborate put-on, the act of a man secretly bored, secretly aggravated by most things around him, and trying to amuse himself. He was sizing me up with his small, alert eyes as we headed west and south towards Times Square, saying: "I used to hang out around Stillman's Gym when I came to New York, you know, but now I'm getting into this theater crowd. You can't do *everything*.... How about Chinese?"

We went to what seemed to me a carefully chosen, second-rate Chinese restau-rant off Broadway in the forties. Over sweet-and-sour, he brought up a piece I had written on existentialism and the novel for the *Chicago Review*, in which I had stated that Algren was "the only American novelist, whose point of view matured during the Depression, that we can read today." It was this comment that had led him to write to me, suggesting that we meet.

"What about Nathanael West though?" he said carefully. "He was no second-rater. And *Native Son*'s the only sure-as-hell existentialist novel we ever wrote over here. Don't anyone read Dick Wright anymore?"

We ate a lot of the mediocre food (upon which I made no comment, good or bad, nonplussing him), and talked a lot, and I studied him. He was a shrewd customer, with a flimflammer's taste for subterfuge, something of an actor. Too young to have shared the social didacticism of the Steinbecks and Farrells, who typified the liter-ature of the thirties, his first novel, *Somebody in Boots* (1935), had been wrongly seen as belonging to their genre. Too old to be really at ease with the Mailers and Kerouacs of my generation, he was honestly bewildered by our feeling that *The Man with the Golden Arm* was the single novel of the forties that was prophetic of our group's emerging attitudes. Thus, he was an outsider, a loner, a man between two stools, and his way of dealing with this was to so exaggerate his personality in the direction of eccentricity that Mailer dubbed him the "Grand Odd-Ball" of our litera-ture. "I've got to see this woman over on the West Side after eleven," he said, choos-ing a red toothpick as we paid the bill. "How about catching some hot music first?"

We wandered under Times Square's canopy of soiled neon, among the hustlers and the whores, the gawkers and the geeks, and Algren's spirits rose. As I learned, he was always at home in the tenderloin of any city. He gravitated to its air of forth-right larceny, naked appetite, no-shit con. He was invigorated by the people who worked there, the "racket people" (as he called them), who service the outlaw instincts that lie below the false veneer most citizens show the world. And he was no Saturday night slummer. These were his chosen people. As man and as writer, he felt himself their partisan. Above everything else, he respected the tight-mouthed code, the bottom-line loyalty, the hard-bitten *ethics*, of those on the margins of life.

The essence of his work was to bring the day-to-day, deal-to-deal, fix-to-fix lives of these people out of the shadows, to reclaim their special perspective for our literature, a vision on-the-bias, on-a-slant, exposing by comparison the impoverishment of most middle class values.

As it happened, I'd always had a similar taste for gamy neighborhoods, for night-towns, for the smalltime Raskolnikovs and Nastasya Phillipovnas of the Underside, and though I felt at ease drinking at the Plaza Hotel, I never would have stayed there. The fact that he had chosen it as his New York residence only struck me as revealing of his current state of mind when I got to know him better, and we turned into the Metropole's battery of brassy noise, feeling distinctly comradely.

In those days, the Metropole was a long, dark Broadway bar, offering Dixieland musicians (lined up like life-size, paid-for bottles) along the backbar, a place as raucous and redolent as a wholesale meat market. Algren ordered schooners of beer and produced stogies, and nothing would do but that we have a souvenir photo taken by one of those hustling girl-photographers who work the tourist joints—another example of Algren's complicated put-on of—what? I decided it wasn't me, but rather some supposed image of himself, the Poet Laureate of Division Street, of which he wanted to disabuse me. I fell into the charade, and we laughed and laughed, talking about B-movie actors of the thirties. He could be infectiously funny if you got on his wavelength, his savvy eyes aglow, his drawling delivery a little theatrical, and I warmed to him. Beneath the surface, he seemed an intensely private man, who never showed his hand openly, who feinted and hinted, a man who carefully eschewed the vocabulary and attitudes of the intellectual but had an artist's hard-earned respect for language and a thoughtful man's awareness of the rings of implication radiating outward from events. He was a person whom the world seemed to have put at odds with himself.

He was meeting his date at Downey's, a show biz restaurant on the edge of the theater district, and we were early. "I ought to buy her some flowers, I guess," he deadpanned, "but they're a little dear around this neighborhood. Say, maybe you know her—"

I didn't.

She was Geraldine Page, and she was appearing up the street in Tennessee Williams' *Sweet Bird of Youth*. "I usually see her these days when I'm in town," he added, and I remembered that his long affair with Simone de Beauvoir, renewed each time she came to the States, had been so carefully compartmentalized from the rest of his life that no one knew about it until she wrote a barely fictionalized account in *The Mandarins*. "I'll just run over there and pick her up," he said, checking his watch. "Keep your eyes open for Sylvia Sidney."

In a few minutes, they were back. "Gerry" (as he insisted I call her), who had just spent three hours playing the disintegrating movie star Alexandra del Lago to Paul

Newman's Chance Wayne, was makeup-less, in a tweed skirt and cardigan, as fresh scrubbed and round faced as a farm wife, but distracted by her evening's work. "I'm real pleased to meet you," she said, as if I was the twentieth person she'd been introduced to in as many minutes.

"Tony Curtis!" Nelson said, sotto voce, behind his hand. "Yes, that's right. I just shook his hand backstage—"

The next hour was occupied with what he called "the theater crowd"—Actors Studio types in jeans, agent types with pompadours and that day's *Wall St. Journal*, wide-eyed starlet types with the careful unction of so many Eve Harringtons—even Shelley Winters, who craned over the back of our booth and asked when "one of you writer-types" was going to write a meaty role for her. I got the impression that Algren had met her before, perhaps during one of his stints in Hollywood, and knew she was on to him. But with everybody else, he was droll, faintly sardonic, like a big butter and egg man with a famous actress on his arm, enjoying the attentions that celebrity elicits from the cold noses pressed to the windows of the banquet hall.

It seemed to me as good an arrangement as any, and a moment later I succumbed to it myself when Newman and Joanne Woodward took the booth opposite ours. Frankly, they were the most stunning couple I had ever seen; there was a kind of golden glow to them that wasn't merely Bloomingdale's chic or cinema magic, but bespoke the natural accretive process by which character develops, a certain completeness of spirit, that made me gawk with the rest of the room at the sight of people who seemed so fortunate, so fair. They epitomized everything (money, fame, integrity, love) for which all the compacted hungers of that place longed. Nelson exchanged a few words with them, and then left them to their quiet supper amid the hubbub. After a while, I pleaded weariness (it was almost 1:30), and left with a suddenness that later Nelson told me had convinced him that I had remained unimpressed with everything.

That wasn't true. The theater crowd hadn't meant much to me, having known enough actors by then to enjoy them as you enjoy talented children without mistaking them for the roles they played, but Algren *had* impressed me. I was intrigued by his personality, which was like a series of Chinese boxes, each smaller than the one that preceded it. The last, the smallest of all, contained what I had encountered in so many American writers who were especially gifted and peculiarly prescient to the drift of things—a sort of quiet, objectless anger, an anger born of a special hurt.

Over the next decade, during which my friendship with Algren richened and deepened, I got to know something about its origins and effects. I saw Algren, a man I considered a major American writer just due to crest into his full creative force, lose his way, resort to repeating whole paragraphs book to book as if they were litanies that reassured him that he still had the music, and finally become a bizarre parody of his own finest self, as baroque and mandarin at heart as the late Hemingway.

Some of it was honest outrage. Chicago, the sandlot ballpark of his boyhood, the literary turf of his maturity, had rejected him. The Polish community had attempted to get the city to ban his second novel, *Never Come Morning* (1943), while he was a private in the army in Europe. His bitter valentine, *Chicago: City on the Make* (1951), certainly one of the most original and eloquent tributes to a city ever written, had evoked squalls of outrage and scorn in the very streets it immortalized. Algren, a perennial outsider who wanted *in* but wouldn't compromise, had learned the consequences of celebrating hard truths in square America, and despite his laconic exterior, I think he sulked with rejected love. Like all writers, he believed that truth would carry everything before it, and like all writers he was baffled to discover that nothing could be farther from the fact. He had honestly thought the burghers and aldermen would approve his seamy portrait of their town, and stood exposed in his *naiveté* when they didn't—just like all writers who care enough to go down into the dark where the real ore lies, and are offered ten cents on the dollar, and a ticket out of town, when they return.

It may have been, as well, that Algren was a victim of his own good reviews. It sometimes happens. After he was touted for the lyric compassion with which he dealt with Frankie Machine's heroin addiction in *The Man with the Golden Arm*, he began to talk about writing a long, detailed, no-nonsense novel that would deal frankly and exhaustively with all the boring, day-to-day minutiae of the dope racket, talk that went on for years, even after it became clear that the book would never be written, particularly after Burroughs's *Naked Lunch*. When critics failed to applaud the wacky strain of gallows humor in *A Walk on the Wild Side*, and concentrated instead on "its large cast of human derelicts," he went on to compose the bitterly sophomoric burlesques of the literary scene that at times made *Who Lost an American?* (1963) such an embarrassment. Increasingly, he seemed to be contending with an image of himself that originated in the typewriters of reviewers.

No truly original writer of my acquaintance can bear for long the Byzantine intrigues of the New York literary life, and Algren was no exception, yet he seemed drawn to them like a suicidal moth to a candle flame. When I asked him about a new novel in a letter in early 1960, he wrote back: "No, no novel. I'd as soon attempt that as I would open a pizza joint on Chicago's Westside without getting protection first. My only chance of getting out of hock is to quit writing.... Anyhow, who *for*? I used to think it was for some vague assemblage called 'readers.' I used to think it was for people named Cowley and Sartre and such, too. But all it turns out it is for is someone like Rapietta Greensponge, girl attorney of Predator, Cormorant, Lunge and Gore.... I'll be in NY around the 20th of Feb. Would shore admire to see you."

He was there as advertised, having decided (or planned for months—who could tell?) to go to Europe for the first time in years. Shirley and I went to a bon voyage party given for him by a mutual friend. The apartment was too long, too narrow, and too badly illuminated for the crowd that jammed it. Your nerves jangled instantly on entering. Nelson was off-balance, ricocheting like a pinball between knots of antagonistic people from different parts of his life. Norman and Adele Mailer, with their entourage, studiously ignored Jay and Fran Landesman, with theirs. Horse-players and prizefighters and poker-buddies milled with literary agents and magazine people and book reviewers. The bedroom was a snarl of overcoats, the kitchen was a seethe of hostilities. Nelson drew me aside into a closet, and said hurriedly: "Don't split. We'll cut out of this and have a quiet dinner.... The trip? Oh, yeah, de Beauvoir wants to tour the Middle East, and I'm tagging along—"

Later, he wrote me from the S.S. *United States:* "Sorry our evening was aborted. I used up all my brain power trying to figure how to get a party of 4 out of a party, but once we hit the street I became confused and that is how we wound up at La Pomme de Terre or wherever it was. Write me at 11 Rue Schoelcher, Paris, and let me know what I can do for you in the existentialist line. Socks? Underwear? Cezanne?"

His letters arrived almost weekly thereafter from London, Paris, Madrid, Barcelona, Mallorca, Istanbul, Athens, and Crete, most of them mysteriously signed "ARM," all of them written in his strangely elliptical, satiric style, beneath which I gathered that, among other things, he was hawking my work to European publishers. Eventually, he managed to get a German sale for my novel, *The Horn,* a fraternal gesture, writer to writer, that remains unique in my experience. Indeed, he was selling me everywhere: "I like your letters and try to get them over to Mme. de B., for the same reason that I try to explain the importance of baseball, certain cartoons in the *New Yorker,* or a good column by Art Buchwald. Being American, I don't like her to think, and never did, that it consists entirely of overweight organization men hollering around the Alhambra, 'You can't git ham un eggs in this country in less than an hour an' a half!'" In the end, Mme. de B. sent me an autographed copy of her monograph on Brigitte Bardot, a work of the same approximate weight as my mostly spoofing letters to Nelson.

When he got back from Europe in September, he escaped to Saybrook after a few hectic days in New York, for the first of many such visits. We gave him a big spare bedroom with a desk, he set up a portable electric typewriter, Shirley showed him the ropes in the kitchen, and we forgathered for drinks and dinner in the evenings. He was an unobtrusive, thoughtful, and convivial guest. He liked Shirley from the start, and flirted with her as if she were his hostess for Derby week, and she became his fierce partisan overnight. We swam for an hour every afternoon (always his exercise of choice), and finally talked for real, and I came to know something of the complex man behind the complex masks.

He was part Jewish and had changed his name. He had gone to the University of Illinois and had ridden the rails up and down the country during the Depression. He had a degree in journalism and had been an itinerant farm-worker in the Southwest. He had been jailed for stealing a typewriter in Texas, and was an editor of the Illinois Writers' Project of the WPA. He had married the same woman twice, and was very funny about the kind of "sap" who would do such a thing.

Also, he remained—right into the middle of the eruptive sixties—an old-fashioned radical of the Middle Border, who revered the likes of Big Bill Haywood, Eugene Debs, Clarence Darrow, and Theodore Dreiser—those stubborn idealists devoured by an era of dehumanizing ideologies, to whom egalitarianism was an article of simple decency, and the fraternity of working people only common sense. The motto over his writing desk might well have been Chekhov's statement: "It is not the business of writers to accuse or prosecute, but to take the part of guilty men once they have been condemned and are undergoing punishment." Algren's deepest and most natural instincts went out to those he called "The tricked, the maimed, the tortured and the sly, doers of small deeds from the nation of furnished rooms," and there seemed to be no place for him in a world of SDS, LSD, psychedelics, and electronic cacophony. He lunged about like a wounded lion in a shopping mall, growling at shadows.

Sometimes the growls were mean-spirited, as when I described, in a letter, the growing psychic confusion that was overtaking Jack Kerouac as a result of his sudden celebrity: "I can understand F. Scott Fitzgerald getting spiritually bankrupt," Algren answered, "and I believe what he wrote in *The Crackup* was all true—he *had* had it and he *had* spent it, and he was broke both ways. But I can't get up a thing for Kerouac (and others) because they went broke without spending a crying dime. Fitzgerald had a right to feel he'd been run over, but if Kerouac has been run over it was by a toy automobile."

Later, this same streak of mean-spiritedness came out concerning James T. Farrell, an indication that Algren's resentments certainly weren't generational. I had read a story in the *New York Post* that depicted a Farrell reduced to living in a furnished room, writing squibs for upstate newspapers for five dollars an item, his memory fading in and out of focus, broke and bewildered, too absentminded to even wipe the fingerprints off his eyeglasses. Perhaps it was this last detail that got to me, but I sent Farrell twenty-five dollars anonymously, thanking him for *Studs Lonigan* (a book which had meant a good deal to me the summer I was sixteen), and alerted everyone I knew to his predicament.

Nelson was conspicuously unmoved: "The stuff he's doing now is probably unreadable," he wrote back. "I never liked his books, even 'Studs' seemed belabored and slow, tho he was always right about who he was against, I wish he'd get a substantial package out of his movie [they were filming *Studs* at last], buy a modest joint in the Florida keys, get himself a Cuban girl-friend to cook, and spend the next twenty years fishing." There was no check enclosed. His literary opinion may have been close enough to the mark, but his pettiness appalled me.

To such lengths of ill-feeling does the competitive, dog-eat-dog, who's-in-who's-out nature of commercial publishing in America drive even our most generously endowed writers, and once again I pondered what kind of future there could possibly be for a culture in which writers felt compelled to direct their ire at each other, instead of at all the forces of mass trivialization that made for such poverty of spirit here.

Algren, like many American writers in middle age, was exhausted by his efforts to maintain with some degree of purity the vision of his youth, in the face of years of piddling advances, unfair contracts, botched movie deals, the self-advertising egos of book reviewers, and the weekly trauma of *The New York Times'* Bestseller List. Algren, like most of us, groused and grew bitchy, worried and wasted time, harassed agents and bad-mouthed peers, until gradually, secretly, with a cold thrill of fear, the suspicion that we had lost it, were written out, were out-of-date, were impotent, began to dawn on us one sodden dawn after a well-liquored night. And we made the first damaging adjustments.

"Completed a trip to the U. of Washington for $650.00 and sucked and smiled and wheedled and lapped and meached and dandled and fondled and whinnied and altogether played it *so* winning and coy that I may get invited back next year," Nelson wrote at one point. "A man who won't demean himself for a dollar is a phony to my way of thinking."

This was a few years after Hemingway shot himself, and Nelson abruptly booked himself on a freighter for the South Pacific to brood on time, literature, Papa, and style. His letters from such ports as Singapore, Manila, and Calcutta were not so sprightly as the ones from Europe and the Near East. In fact, they were downright ruminative for Nelson, and eventually resulted in his odd, and oddly moving, book, *Notes from a Sea Diary* (1965), part travel memoir, part essay on Hemingway.

A writer who becomes obsessed with style is often a man who is inexorably losing touch with the wellsprings of his talent (which always rise out of the rich bottom lands of content), and something like this may have been happening to Algren. In any case, he was thinking with dead seriousness and unusual precision about the relationship between a man's words and his special vision: "Style is that force by which a man becomes what he most needs to become. When this need is one common to multitudes and the man's force suffices, we call him an artist, because in saving himself he saves others."

Hemingway, above all other twentieth century writers, drives other writers to brood this way on the mysteries of style—on the sequence of information release, on a word's specific color and weight, on the subtle music, in the sentence itself—and his suicide out of the despair of personal and creative impotence silenced most of us for a while.

Nelson was the only writer I knew who had actually visited the *finca* in Cuba, spent time with Hemingway, been recognized by him, and I wondered what he would have to say. Hemingway has always been baited by lesser men. His posturings invited it, his self-mythification encouraged it, his petty hectorings of dead friends seemed to demand it, but whether Algren recognized some of these failings in himself is not germane. He went back to the clear, hypnotic, and masterfully poised prose that is Hemingway's triumph, dismissed the public man, and wrote his valedictory to the artist.

Except for a piece by fellow-novelist Wright Morris, I've read nothing on Hemingway to match a few sentences of Algren's: "He was the historian who noted how many letters littered the field where the Austrian dead lay face-down in the sun with their hip-pockets emptied: and he was the Austrian face down in the sun. He was the English girl dreaming herself dead in an Italian rain. He was the chronicler of mules with their forelegs broken drowning in the port of Smyrna.... His risks were of the kind that, failing, the taker fails alone; but succeeding, succeeds for everyone." These seem to be the words of a man who realizes, after an important death, that he is going to be lonelier from now on, and they are stark evidence of how fragile and personal American literature is to those who make it.

There were girls in these years. He brought some to Saybrook. We theatered and restauranted with others in New York. There was Judy who was studying in New Haven, and there was Madeliene from Montreal on her way to Paris. I remember sitting with her, again in the Oak Bar, as Nelson, still at war with the waiters there, pressed the rubber bulb on his novelty bow-tie, which promptly lit up, and elicited a widening of eyes from the normally imperturbable waiter, and a snort of victory from Algren.

He was attentive with women, particularly when wooing them, but clearly his was a man's world, and he liked "broads" who fitted into it, along the lines of Lauren Bacall. He bored easily, he was no good at adjusting to women's schedules, and there was a streak of the perverse in him which made him willfully change his mind just to establish his right to do it. But also he was wearying, I think. At one point, he became seriously infatuated with the screen image of the starlet Diane Varsi, who, after a brief and promising career, had quit Hollywood and retired to Vermont. He talked about her with barely disguised urgency. "I feel she's for me," he said, "I just feel it." A week later, he actually wrote her a letter, proposing God knows what. But nothing ever came of it. He seemed oddly hurt, as if redeemed in his suspicion that there was no one at the other end of the tenuous line of human communication that began in his typewriter.

"It's not *wanted*," he said again and again. "The only choice they give you is break your heart or break your balls. Who wants to spend two years, and then get dumped on by the likes of Norman Pederast or Dwight Mac-dum-dum? Ain't they in the same horse race? It's a sucker bet, I tell you." And his small eyes were as narrowed as those of a fox who's gone to earth.

During this period, I taught for two semesters at Paul Engle's Writers' Workshop at the University of Iowa. Like Nelson, I'd always managed to avoid the choice between teaching or starving that catches up with most American writers whose books have little Hollywood or Book Club appeal. I'd ghostwritten, I'd hustled for the trade magazines, I'd become fast and reliable at all kinds of articles. But in late 1962, a novel just completed and at least a year to go before I could expect to see any real money out of it, I caved in to the promise of a steady salary and went to Iowa City. Nelson was hilarious and a little snide about this move.

"Christ," he said, "better to get lucky at the track or at high stakes poker, or just put your woman on the street.... Don't play tight-ass with those guys! They'll ruin your style, man—"

My style survived the experience, and so did I. Then in 1965, Nelson suddenly announced that he was going to get married: would Shirley and I come in to New York to meet the bride? Because he needed to talk about something. We went in, and met Betty, a handsome, savvy woman, with a sharp eye out and a reserved mouth, and over dinner in an expensive midtown restaurant, Nelson said that he'd succumbed to "that campus gold," and they, too, were going to Iowa for a year.

"I want to get it off to a good start," he added, somehow suggesting that he meant the marriage rather than the job. "How little bullshit can I get away with?" I assured him that for anyone who liked to talk books and writing, teaching a workshop was a license to steal. A simplification I came to regret.

I heard almost nothing from Algren during the year he spent at the Writers' Workshop, but stories got back to me from colleagues and ex-students. For the obligatory literature course (instructor's choice of books), he taught only Truman Capote's *In Cold Blood*. He taught it slowly, exhaustively, appreciatively, and then he taught it again. And possibly again, depending on the degree of bafflement or outrage on the part of the teller of the tale. His conferences on the students' writing became an instant Workshop-legend. If he liked something, he would talk for hours, ranging far afield, suggesting markets, even soliciting editors. If he didn't like what he read, he sniffed: "This is crap. Forget it." And that was that. The Algren Forty-Five Second Conference, it was called.

Then there were the poker games. A student of mine, a young man so infatuated with Algren that he had become a dealer in Las Vegas after reading his books, went back to Iowa City when he heard that Nelson was going to be there, and I got the story from him. A high stakes game that went on every weekend. Nelson sitting under a green eyeshade. Everyone nervous to be playing with Frankie Machine, the man with the golden arm. Nelson betting high, Nelson over-betting, Nelson losing. Week after week after week. The marriage turning sour, then ugly, then—I never found out. But five months after leaving the Workshop, Nelson scrawled on the bottom of a Christmas card: "My sole accomplishment at Iowa was to push a Taiwanese lady into the *Atlantic*. And to lose the bankroll I went there for. Ever best, ARM."

After that, we drifted apart. There was never a breakup, there was never a disagreement. The occasional card was warm, but remote and uninformative. It was as if he had turned a corner and come into my life for reasons that I was too flattered by him to explore, and just as abruptly had turned another corner and gone out of it. It was as if there were many rooms in his days, each mutually separate from all the others, and when one of them had been furnished and lived-in and used up, he simply closed the door, and changed his address. For a time, I puzzled over it, wondering whether I had done or said something, or failed to say or do something else, but my conscience was clear. We'd been close, and then all at once we weren't close anymore.

Sometimes, remembering that Frankie Machine's arm was both his fortune and his curse, that he dealt cards with it as no one had ever dealt cards before, and that he shot heroin into it to numb a lifetime of secret hurts that haunt even the most favored men, I wondered if there wasn't some sort of clue in Frankie to Nelson's enigmatic signature. But I didn't know.

All I knew for sure was that Algren had written for an America that was vanishing before the onslaught of the bulldozers, the housing projects, and the color televisions that were wiping out neighborhoods and neighborhood loyalties; an America in which the dream of brotherhood, even among the lawless and the dispossessed, was a sucker's dream; an America that was no longer stirred by the great word-slingers who had made its literature part-epic, part-lyric, a wildly inflated boast of heroic dimensions, and a sadly depleted whimper of waste, neglect and bitterness. Algren had ended up like so many writers before him (some better than he was, some worse), writers who had outlived fame into obscurity, and a waning of powers.

In 1885, a British visitor to our shores had written of Herman Melville: "I sought everywhere for this Triton, who is still living somewhere in New York. No one seemed to know anything of the one great writer fit to stand shoulder to shoulder with Whitman on that continent." The same indifference greeted the later years of William Saroyan and James M. Cain, of Henry Roth and Edna St. Vincent Millay, of Kerouac and Farrell—

What can you say? Must we always end up protesting *after* the death of our writers, "My God, I didn't know he was still *alive*!"? Must we always be shamed too late by realizing how carelessly we wasted such human richness, how cruelly we forgot the achievements of the past, merely because of a change in cultural fashion?

Algren once complained: "What country is there for a white man that isn't white?" And I wonder why it is that the most native of our writers, who have always been either red or black under the skin, end up tamed or gelded or dead too young? Why can't we respect honorable work, even work that scares the horses, just for itself alone?

These thoughts were on my mind the last time I saw Algren. In October of 1971, *Playboy* magazine held a Convocation of Writers in Chicago—a week of panel discussions, readings, dinners, and deal-making, to which it invited a hundred or more writers and their mates, everything (including round trip air fare) on the magazine; a tax write-off of stupendous proportions.

One of the last events was a party at Hugh Hefner's mansion on the near Northside. I hadn't expected that Algren would be at any of the meetings, knowing he'd had some kind of *brouhaha* with the magazine a few years before, and Shirley and I milled around in the half-dark of the vaulted reception room, trying to get a drink from one of the two working bars. Finding room on a divan, I watched Max Lerner doing the Hully-Gully to a rock band, John Cheever with his dinner jacket and sad spaniel-eyes, Studs Terkel in a red-checked shirt, shaking his silver mane, and arguing good-naturedly with someone, and a man with a prominent moustache kissing my wife.

It was Nelson, and the three of us made our way downstairs to the Woo Grotto where it was quieter, to watch Alan Watts cavorting nude in the swimming pool with a couple of Bunnies. We talked for half an hour. Nelson seemed just like he'd always been, but graver, more caustic, less fun. I don't remember what we talked about, but when we parted a little later at the door of the mansion he said he thought he'd be moving to New Jersey eventually, that he was on to something. "A big one, I think. Something I can go all out on. It might take years." His smile was blurred by the smoke and the noise. And then he turned and went out the door and into the Chicago night.

He did move to New Jersey, and it was said that he got involved in the case of a prizefighter who had been jailed for murder. It was said he was writing a book about the case, along the lines of *In Cold Blood*. Then it was said that he had decided to turn it into an out-and-out novel. Then, some years later, I heard he had moved to Sag Harbor, a ritzy town far out on Long Island, across Great Peconic Bay from the place where I had spent all my summers as a boy. Then he was dead.

For me, still, it has that unfinished quality that is one of the toughest pills that growing older forces us to get down. I have no sense of an ending, and now it's too late. I think of him and smile, and I try not to wonder what he might have written had things been different. For he was the real McCoy, and I miss him.

"For keeps and a single day," as he often said.

ALGREN'S GOLDEN PEN

Mike Royko

I remember almost to the moment the first time I saw the name Nelson Algren.

It was in a tent in Korea about three decades ago. The guy in the next bunk flipped a paperback book at me and said: "Hey, here's a book about Chicago. You want it?"

I glanced over the blurbs on the cover to see what it was about. One blurb said something to the effect that this book was set in a "slum" In Chicago. And it described the slum as being the Division Street area.

Slum? I was offended. That was no slum. That was my neighborhood.

Curious, I went ahead and read the book, and I was stunned. It was the first time I had read a novel that was set in a place I knew. And Algren, with *The Man with the Golden Arm*, had captured it. He had the people, the sounds, the alleys, the streets, the feel of the place.

It's a strange sensation to read a novel about a place you know well. It had never occurred to me, growing up in that neighborhood, that it contained the stuff a great book can be made of. The great books, as they were force-fed to us in the schools, were about other countries, other cultures, other centuries. And the duller they were, the greater they were.

But here was somebody named Nelson Algren writing about Division Street and Milwaukee Avenue, and the dope heads and boozers and the card hustlers. The kind of broken people Algren liked to describe as responding to the city's brawny slogan of "I Will" with a painful: "But What If I Can't?"

I didn't know it then, but many Chicagoans weren't pleased by Algren's book, even though it won the first National Book Award for fiction, sort of an Oscar for writers.

Among those who were displeased were the so-called leaders of the city's Polish community—people who were big on joining the Polish National Alliance and other such organizations.

They believed that because many of his characters were Polish, Algren was presenting them in a poor light. I guess they would have preferred that he write a novel about a Polish dentist who changed his name and moved from the old neighborhood to a suburb as soon as he made enough money.

So for years they sniped at Algren, tried to keep him out of the libraries, and made themselves look foolish. As one of them—an insurance broker—once said to me: "I didn't know anybody like the characters in his books." Well, I did. And I saw some of them off when they went to prison or the morgue.

After reading my first Algren novel, I made a point of finding his other works. He had done other novels, and a wonderful prose poem about Chicago called *Chicago: City on the Make*.

But my favorite of all his writings was his collection of short stories called *The Neon Wilderness.* Bitter-sweet stories. Funny-sad stories. I think they're among the finest short stories written by an American.

I told him that the first time I met him, about seventeen years ago. He had invited me to a gathering in his walk-up flat overlooking Wicker Park, near Damen, North, and Milwaukee.

That's where he lived for most of his years in Chicago. It's a funny thing about the rewards of the writing trade in this country: You can pick up a *People* magazine and see this or that commercial, best-selling hack lounging by his pool in Beverly Hills, or swaggering about his estate on Martha's Vineyard. Or you can read about some wordsmith who stole the plot of *Moby Dick*, turned the whale into a white shark, and made a fast million or two.

Meanwhile, someone like Algren never got out of Wicker Park and couldn't always make the rent until a small check for a book review came in the mail.

But, he would have to admit, that's the kind of thing that always happened to the losers in his stories, so why not to the author of those stories?

Not that he ever beefed about life around Wicker Park. It had many advantages.

For one, there were the Luxor Baths on North Avenue, once considered the finest steam bath joint in town. When it opened in the 1920s, Mayor Big Bill Thompson himself showed up to honor it by accepting a squirt of steam on his big gut.

Although I always argued that the Russian Baths on Division Street had more class, Algren preferred the Luxor and would spend many hours soaking up steam and listening to the bookies, loan sharks, precinct captains, and his other favorite creatures discussing events of the day.

He could always find a poker game in the back of a barber shop or saloon, or an ex-prizefighter to describe how he almost became a contender.

And when there was nothing else going on, he could sit on his third-floor porch and watch the passing scene—which often included somebody with a brick chasing somebody with a wallet.

In many other countries, a writer of Algren's stature would have given a chair at a university, assured of a reasonable income, and asked only to write to his heart's content. They do that in this country, too, but usually for dull writers who know how to play university politics and act properly at the dean's wife's teas. Algren tried it briefly, but he talked too tough for them, and I think he pinched a few coeds, so they asked him to go away.

He moved from Chicago a few years ago, and had a great time announcing that he no longer liked this city, and that it had never appreciated him. Neither statement was true, and he knew it. But he liked saying such things to create a controversy. We had dinner the night before he left and the fact was, he was moving because he felt like moving.

He tried New Jersey for awhile, and finally wound up in a pretty, old whaling town on Long Island, New York. That's where he died a few days ago and was buried on Monday.

If the mayor and some of those stiffs in the city council can see their way clear, it would be a nice gesture for them to rename one of the little streets around Wicker Park after him. Algren Court, or Algren Place. Nothing big. He wouldn't expect it.

And if you get a chance, you might want to read some of his writings. Any good bookstore can probably order them for you.

You might even come across a 1967 printing of those short stories I mentioned, *The Neon Wilderness*.

If you do so, check the printed dedication. As I said earlier, the first time I met him, I told him I thought the short stories were the best things he ever wrote. I was afraid he might be offended, since he considered himself foremost a novelist. But he listened, nodded politely, and said: "That's interesting."

A few years later, a new, hardcover edition of the short stories came out. He had a little party to celebrate, and when we went home, he handed us each a book.

It wasn't until a few days later that I opened it and saw the printed dedication. It said: "For Mike Royko."

It's still one of the nicest things anyone ever did for me.

ALGREN AS I KNEW HIM

Kurt Vonnegut

According to the diary of my wife Jill Krementz, the photographer, the young British-Indian novelist Salman Rushdie came to our house in Sagaponack, Long Island, for lunch on May 9th, 1981. His excellent novel *Midnight's Children* had just been published in the United States, and he told us that the most intelligent review had been written by Nelson Algren, a man he would like to meet. I replied that we knew Algren some, since Jill had photographed him several times and he and I had been teachers at the Writers' Workshop of the University of Iowa back in 1965, when we were both dead broke and I was forty-three and he was fifty-six.

I said, too, that Algren was one of the few writers I knew who was really funny in conversation. I offered as a sample what Algren said at the Workshop after I introduced him to the Chilean novelist José Donoso: "I think it would be nice to come from a country that long and narrow."

Rushdie was really in luck, I went on, because Algren lived only a few miles to the north, in Sag Harbor, where John Steinbeck had spent the last of his days, and he was giving a cocktail party that very afternoon. I would call him and tell him we were bringing Rushdie along, and Jill would take pictures of the two of them together, both writers about people who were very poor. I suggested that the party might be the only one that Algren had given himself in his entire life, since, no matter how famous he became, he remained a poor man living among the poor, and usually alone. He was living alone in Sag Harbor. He had had a new wife in Iowa City, but that marriage lived about as long as a Junebug. His enthusiasm for writing, reading and gambling left little time for the duties of a married man.

I said that Algren was bitter about how little he had been paid over the years for such important work, and especially for the movie rights to what may be his masterpiece, *The Man with the Golden Arm*, which made huge amounts of money as a Frank Sinatra film. Not a scrap of the profits had come to him, and I heard him say one time, "I am the penny whistle of American literature."

When we got up from lunch, I went to the phone and dialed Nelson Algren's number. A man answered and said, "Sag Harbor Police Department."

"Sorry," I said. "Wrong number."

"Who were you calling?" he said.

"Nelson Algren," I said.

"This is his house," he said, "but Mr. Algren is dead." A heart attack that morning had killed Algren at the age of seventy-two.

He is buried in Sag Harbor—without a widow or descendants, hundreds and hundreds of miles from Chicago, Illinois, which had given him to the world and with whose underbelly he had been so long identified. Like James Joyce, he had become an exile from his homeland after writing that his neighbors were perhaps not as noble and intelligent and kindly as they liked to think they were.

Only a few weeks before his death, he had been elected by his supposed peers, myself among them, to membership in the American Academy of Arts and Letters— a certification of respectability withheld from many wonderful writers, incidentally, including James Jones and Irwin Shaw. This was surely not the first significant honor ever accorded him. When he was at the peak of his powers and fame in the middle of this century, he regularly won prizes for short stories and was the first recipient of a National Book Award for Fiction, and so on. And only a few years before his death the American Academy and Institute had given him its Medal for Literature, without, however, making him a member. Among the few persons to win this medal were the likes of William Faulkner and Ernest Hemingway.

His response to the medal had been impudent. He was still living in Chicago, and I myself talked to him on the telephone, begging him to come to New York City to get it at a big ceremony, with all expenses paid. His final statement on the subject to me was this: "I'm sorry, but I have to speak at a ladies' garden club that day."

At the cocktail party whose prospects may have killed him, I had hoped to ask him if membership in the American Academy and Institute had pleased him more than the medal. Other friends of his have since told me the membership had moved him tremendously, and had probably given him the nerve to throw a party. As to how the seeming insult of a medal without a membership had ever taken shape: this was nothing but a clumsy clerical accident caused by the awarders of prizes and memberships, writers as lazy and absentminded and idiosyncratic in such matters as Algren himself.

God knows *how* it happened. But all's well that ends well, as the poet said.

Another thing I heard from others, but never from Algren himself, was how much he hoped to be remembered after he was gone. It was always women who spoke so warmly of this. If it turned out that he had never mentioned the possibility of his own immortality to any man, that would seem in character. When *I* saw him with men, he behaved as though he wanted nothing more from life than a night at the fights, a day at the track, or a table-stakes poker game. This was a pose, of course, and perceived as such by one and all. It was also perceived back in Iowa City that he was a steady and heavy loser at gambling, and that his writing was not going well. He had already produced so *much*, most of it in the mood of the Great Depression, which had become ancient history. He appeared to want to modernize himself somehow. What was my evidence? There he was, a master storyteller, blasted beyond all reason with admiration for and envy of a moderately innovative crime story then appearing in serial form in the *New Yorker*, Truman Capote's *In Cold Blood*. For a while in Iowa, he could talk of little else.

While he was only thirteen years my senior, so close to my own age that we were enlisted men in Europe in the same World War, he was a pioneering ancestor of mine in the compressed history of American literature. He broke new ground by depicting persons said to be dehumanized by poverty and ignorance and injustice as being *genuinely* dehumanized, and dehumanized quite *permanently*. Contrast, if you will, the poor people in this book with those in the works of social reformers like Charles Dickens and George Bernard Shaw, and particularly with those in Shaw's *Pygmalion*, with their very promising wit and resourcefulness and courage. Reporting on what he saw of dehumanized Americans with his own eyes day after day, year after year, Algren said in effect, "Hey—an awful lot of these people your hearts are bleeding for are really mean and stupid. That's just a fact. Did you know that?"

And why didn't he soften his stories, as most writers would have, with characters with a little wisdom and power who did all they could to help the dehumanized? His penchant for truth again shoved him in the direction of unpopularity. Altruists in his experience were about as common as unicorns, and especially in Chicago, which he once described to me as "the only major city in the country where you can easily buy your way out of a murder rap."

So—was there anything he expected to accomplish with so much dismaying truthfulness? He gives the answer himself, I think, in his preface to another novel, *Never Come Morning*. As I understand him, he would be satisfied were we to agree with him that persons unlucky and poor and not very bright are to be respected for surviving, although they often have no choice but to do so in ways unattractive and blameworthy to those who are a lot better off.

It seems to me now that Algren's pessimism about so much of earthly life was Christian. Like Christ, as we know Him from the Bible, he was enchanted by the hopeless, could not take his eyes off them, and could see little good news for them in the future, given what they had become and what Caesar was like and so on, unless beyond death there awaited something more humane.

GLASSES

Studs Terkel

Glasses. Once upon a time, they were the mark of the vulnerable. At least to me. Not the pince-nez of Woodrow Wilson; his was the emblem of the Sunday school-master, the wrinkled prune, the bloodless. Nor the pince-nez of FDR, which, in its off-again, on-again behavior, became as insouciant a sign as his tilted cigarette holder. Nor the pince-nez of my mother, which, considering her tough credo, became as antic and outrageous a symbol as Bobby Clark's painted-on glasses. No.

When Lee Meadows appeared on the pitching mound for the Pittsburgh Pirates, it was, for me, a revolutionary moment. He was the first major leaguer to wear glasses. And then came Carmen Hill. And George Torporcer. And when a slugger, Chick Hafey, decided to wear them, I knew that a corner had been turned. And when, some time later, another bespectacled slugger, Bull Connor, turned the hose on people, I no longer had to worry about the daily fate of "four-eyes." Nor feel inordinately tender.

It was, apparently, not so for Billie Holiday. As recently as 1956, she was soft on those who wore specs. I had gone to see her at the Budland. It was a short-lived jazz club in a South Side Chicago cellar. I was in the process of working on a children's jazz book. "Sure, baby. Come on," she said at the other end of the phone. Nelson Algren accompanied me. He was, at the time, wearing glasses.

Billie's voice was shot, though the gardenia in her hair was as fresh as usual. Ben Webster, for so long big man on tenor, was backing her. He was having it rough, too. Yet they transcended. There were perhaps fifteen, twenty patrons in the house. At most. Awful sad. Still, when Lady sang "Fine and Mellow," you felt that way. And when she went into "Willow, Weep for Me," you wept. You looked about and saw that the few other customers were also crying in their beer and shot glasses. Nor were they that drunk. Something was still there, that something that distinguishes an artist from a performer: the revealing of self. Here I be. Not for long, but here I be. In sensing her mortality, we sensed our own.

After her performance, Algren and I shambled into her dressing room. Dressing room, did I say? It was a storeroom: whiskey cases stacked against the walls, cartons of paper napkins, piles of plastic utensils strewn about, this, that, and the other. It didn't matter. She was there, with the gardenia in her hair. Lady, in the gracious manner of a lady, bade us be seated. Algren slouched into a chair against the far wall, in the semidarkness. He appeared a character out of one of his works: Bruno or Frankie or Sparrow or Dove.

Patiently, she answered questions that I'm sure had been put to her too many times before. About the white stoops of Baltimore, of the others for whom she scrubbed, about Miss Bessie, about her grandmother, about club owners, the honest and the venal. When there was trouble remembering, her eyes half-shut as in a slow blues, her hands poised in midair. If, by chance, I hit upon the right name, her fingers snapped. That's it, baby. No words were needed; the gesture said it.

And when the conversation ended, as casually as it had begun, and the waiter had brought her a tumbler of gin—"Lemon peel, baby"—she indicated the man in the shadows, Nelson Algren. She had been aware of his presence from the beginning; there had been mumbled introductions. Now she murmured inquiringly, "Who's that man?" Algren explained that she and he had the same publisher. *The Man with the Golden Arm* and *Lady Sings the Blues* had both been put out by Doubleday.

"You're all right," she said to him.

"How do you know?" he asked.

"You're wearin' glasses."

He laughed softly. "I know some people with glasses who got dollar signs for eyes."

"You're kind."

"How can you tell?" he persisted. How could she tell? He was half-hidden in the shadows.

"Your glasses." She was persistent, too.

Nelson Algren no longer wears glasses, but he's still a funny man. He may be the funniest man around. Which is another way of saying he may be the most serious. At a time when pimpery, lick-spittlery, and picking the public's pocket are the order of the day—indeed, officially proclaimed as virtue—the poet must play the madcap to keep his balance. And ours.

Unlike Father William, Algren does not stand on his head. He just shuffles along. His appearance is that of a horse player, who, this moment, got the news: he had bet her across the board and she came in a strong fourth. Yet, strangely, his is not a mournful mien. He's chuckling to himself. You'd think he was the blue-eyed winner rather than the brown-eyed loser. That's what's so funny about him. He *has* won. A hunch: his writings may be read long after acclaimed works of Academe's darlings, yellowed on coffee tables, will be replaced by acclaimed works of other Academe's darlings. To call on a Lillian Hellman phrase, he is not "the kid of the moment." For in the spirit of a Zola or a Dreiser, he has captured a piece of that life behind the billboards. Some comic, that man.

At a time when our values are unprecedentedly upside-down—when Bob Hope, a humorless multimillionaire, is regarded as a funny man and a genuinely funny man (until his bad choice of lock-pickers) was regarded as our President—Algren is something of a Gavroche.

"The hard necessity of bringing the judge on the bench down into the dock has been the peculiar responsibility of the writer in all ages of man." It was something Algren wrote in 1961, as an added preface to his prose-poem, *Chicago: City on the Make*. The original work had been composed a decade earlier. It's a responsibility to which he has been obstinately faithful. He's openhearted to Molly-O and Steffi and Margo and Aunt Elly's "girl," who are forever up against it; who are forever in the pokey for turning a five-dollar trick with the wrong guy. (That fee is absurd today. You must remember his heroines subsisted long, long before inflation.) He's mail-fisted to their judges, the Respectables, who turn a trick for no less than a hundred G's. So, too, this piece of writing from the same essay:

> "We have to keep Chicago strong and America mighty," I heard his Honor proclaim before sentencing the girl with a record for addiction. "A year and a day! Take her away!"
>
> Blinking out of the window of an Ogden Avenue trolley at the sunlight she hadn't seen for almost a year, "I guess I was lucky I done that time," the girl philosophized. "Chicago still looks pretty strong and America looks mighty mighty."
>
> Still nobody seems to be laughing.

What Algren observed fifteen years ago applies today in trump. And in that prose-poem put down some twenty-odd years ago—and what odd years they've been—the ring of a city's awful truth is still heard. Only louder. As with all good poets, the guy is a prophet.

It was no accident that he wrote *The Man with the Golden Arm* so many centuries before posh suburban high schools fretted about junkies in their blue-eyed midst. The fate of Frankie Machine presaged adolescent hells to come.

In *Never Come Morning*, Algren gave us Bruno, the doomed young jack-roller. How different is he, the desperate city ethnic, from the young black mugger? Law and Order is the cry today, as Algren so eloquently italicized in the old poet's prophecy: "The slums will take their revenge." Call it ghetto, if you wish.

Yet, I'm thinking of Nelson Algren, the funny man. The antic sense is there, of course, in Dove Linkhorn, the innocent, of *A Walk on the Wild Side*. It's there in Frankie's colleague, Sparrow, the hapless shoplifter. It's there in Some Fellow Willie, who always looked suspicious because he always suspected himself of one thing or another. It's there in Lost Ball Stahouska of the Baldhead A.C.'s. He was something, that one. Remember when his conscience bothered him because he shoved an in-play baseball in his pocket, though he was unperturbed when cracking a safe with the help of three Chicago cops? As to the latter caper, Stahouska explained, "Oh, *everybody* does that."

Again, you have it. Turning a two-dollar trick is a sin and prickly to the conscience. Turning a hundred-thou trick, that's something else again. Lost Ball, were he around today, could well appreciate the workings of ITT, Lockheed, Penn Central, and the late Howard Hughes. Recurring in all of Algren's work—novel, short story, poem—is the theme of the rigged ball game. Offered in his unique lyric style, they are memorable.

In his poetic evocation of the Black Sox scandal of 1919, he asks the ever-impertinent question: How is it that front office men never conspire? However do senators get so close to God? Or winners never pitch in a bill toward the price of their victory?

Though today's literary mandarins treat the man with benign neglect—he has in the past twenty-five years become something of a non-person—he is highly regarded in unexpected quarters.

About two years ago, in the streets of London, I ran into a voluble Welshman. On learning I was an American—let alone a Chicagoan—he bought me a whiskey. I had no idea Americans were so popular with the people from Rhondda Valley. But it wasn't that at all. He could hardly wait to blurt out, "You're an American, you must know of Nelson Algren." He proceeded to rattle off, in mellifluous tongue, all the titles of Algren's novels and short stories. On discovering that I actually knew the man, he bought drink after drink after drink. And on miner's pay, at that. How I got back to the hotel shall forever remain a mystery to me.

In New York, an old freight elevator man, a small battered Irishman, whose one claim to immortality was an encounter with Fiorello LaGuardia, asked me, between floors, if I'd ever heard of a writer named Algren. He had read *The Neon Wilderness*. As far as I know, he owned no coffee table.

Recently, in a conversation with a woman on welfare, his name came up. It was she, not I, who introduced it. She had been reading one of his paperbacks and saw herself in it. She had also been having her troubles with the Welfare Department and neighborhood cops. As far as I know, she owned no coffee table.

Maybe Nelson Algren's horses usually run out of the money. Maybe his luck at the poker table is not that good. Maybe he'll never be endowed by a university; nor be earnestly regarded by literary makers and shakers. But he has good reason to just shuffle along like a laughing winner. And he may be the funniest man around.

NELSON ALGREN'S POLITICS

Stuart McCarrell

Like much of his life and work, Nelson Algren's politics were at once complex yet simple, tragic yet heroic.

Far from being a politically active radical with ties to the Communist Party (as the FBI pretended to think), Nelson was politically inactive for the last thirty years of his life. In the late 1940s and early 1950s Simone de Beauvoir faulted him for this political inactivity—faulted him as much as she dared, since she was deeply In love with him. In the years when I was quite close to him (the 1960s and early 1970s), he greatly approved of my activity as a radical journalist, often visited me in my office, and even let us use one of his poems on our journal's front page. But he would never take part in any of the meetings, rallies, or campaigns that we (or any other left groups) organized against racial oppression and the Vietnam War.

From some of our wonderful long post-midnight talks I got the feeling that Nelson had never read much of Marx or other Marxist theoretical writings. But he would never discuss such things directly. He always subtly, humorously, insistently switched the subject back to books, sports, plays, people. I believe that, like most Americans, Nelson shied away from "theory" because he regarded himself as a "practical" man. He rightly saw how for too many people theory becomes not a tool for seeing recurring patterns and thus making sense out of the confusing rush of reality but instead a way of oversimplifying both people and events. He knew that such a righteous and ungenerous attitude toward life and human beings was fatal to any attempt to create good art. He told me of some bitter experiences that he and Richard Wright had had with various doctrinaire Party officials in the 1930s and early 1940s, which had confirmed a natural inclination on his part against ambitious doctrines of any type.

But while Nelson after his early thirties was not committed to any party or movement, he was for all his long life a "gut radical" who never wavered in his insight into and testimony against the worst evils of the selfishness, smugness, and arrogance that have dominated post–World War II America. And he did not believe, as did Cold War "liberals," that "politics" could stop at the water's edge.

In H.E.F. Donohue's *Conversations with Nelson Algren*, Donohue tries to correct Nelson's thinking:

> Donohue: Then you must think that the United States is an imperialist country?
>
> Algren: She's an imperialist son-of-a-bitch. We still own Guatemala. When I say we own it, I mean we backed the fruit company that owns it, and when things go against us…we put our man in. The other guy becomes a Communist. He was no Communist. He was a man for land reform, which means taking land from the United Fruit Company. We back [the fruit company] by force. It's an imperialist country.

Needless to say, in the 1950s it was such talk and such writing that brought down on Nelson's head the wrath of the academic cold warriors like Leslie Fiedler and Norman Podhoretz. To them his basic commitment to "American values" was under suspicion. So was his writing ability. They accused him of being a shallow, sentimental writer who idealized the poor, prostitutes, and the underclass in general. If "sentimentality" means easy, faked pseudo-emotions, it will be obvious to anyone reading Algren that such charges are false. Of course, if it means a capacity for warmth, tenderness, empathy, and imagination, then Nelson must plead guilty. Probably it is these qualities, which Nelson shares with other great writers such as Dreiser, that such critics really resent.

There are two other vital qualities in which Nelson far exceeds Dreiser (and almost all other great American novelists): poetry and humor. Fiedler and Podhoretz are blind to these also; selfishness, smugness, and arrogance are their strong suits. No wonder they think of themselves as so "American," so well adjusted, so "with it."

In addition to the savage critical attacks discussed above—which eliminated Nelson's work from many libraries and from the serious literary agenda for over three decades, until Dan Simon and Seven Stories Press turned things around in the 1990s—there were two other areas in Nelson's life where he was also made to pay a high price for his "politics," as they were understood by the FBI and assorted cold warriors.

In 1950, when Nelson's *Man with the Golden Arm* was both a critical and a popular success, the brilliant photographer Art Shay prepared and had accepted by *Life* magazine a long photo essay on Nelson and his work. But suddenly the publication was delayed, and then rescheduled. On the newly scheduled date it mysteriously did not appear. Perhaps the editors suddenly realized that Nelson was not the type of artist to be honored in a Henry Luce publication—or perhaps they were reminded by a friendly government agency. In any case, the essay was soon officially canceled, without an explanation. So great was both the prestige and the circulation of *Life* at the time that many of us feel that if that article had run, Nelson's whole life might have been much easier. The Podhoretzes and Fiedlers of the world might not have been able to blight his career so effectively and for so long.

Algren suffered for his politics in his personal as well as his professional life. In the early years of Algren's love affair with Simone de Beauvoir they were both striving desperately to make it work. In the long run they did not succeed. In the first two or three years, when the pattern was not yet set, and when he wanted so much to be able to visit her in Paris, he could not: the State Department would not issue him a passport. When it finally did, in 1960, it was too late. By then the relationship had changed subtly but decisively. De Beauvoir was as intelligent and as dedicated as Algren, and deeply in love with him. Surely the great love of his life, she was his best hope for the long, important, loving relationship that he wanted so much, and never had.

In the last two years of his life, because of new friendships with Joe Pintauro, Kurt Vonnegut, and Joe Heller, Algren felt much less alone. But for thirty years he had endured neglect and misrepresentation stoically and without flinching or copping out. No matter what the political or literary pressures were, he never ceased to speak "for the least of these." He spoke against the power structure and against conventional wisdom for those who had no other spokesman. He was a radical both before and after it was fashionable to be radical.

Algren's heroes were four great "prairie radicals": Dreiser, Altgeld, Darrow, and Debs, the stubborn truth-saying prophets "who could be broken but who could not be bent." Surely now we can add a fifth name—Algren—to that honored list.

PHOTOGRAPHING NELSON ALGREN

Layle Silbert

As I look at contact sheets of pictures I took of Nelson Algren more than twenty years ago, I'm surprised, almost startled, at how sad his expression is in many of the frames. What were we talking about as I photographed? What was he thinking at those moments? Easy enough to speculate that he was engrossed in characters he'd written about; or was it the state of civilization in America as set forth in his *Noncomformity: Writing on Writing*? I remember nothing that serious in our conversation on those occasions. Even on frames where he smiled, his expression has traces of sadness.

Nelson had been photographed throughout his writing life; this made him an easy subject. And here I was on the heels of Arthur Shay, for one, whose photographs are on Nelson's recent books. Other photographers as well in Chicago had followed him around with their cameras. Each of us had seen him in his or her own way. As I was doing, they'd focused, concentrated, searching for that special aura, that almost unknowable quality or character, of the particular writer. As for me, I think of trying to get under the skin of the writer I see through the viewfinder.

Nelson and I had run into one another in front of the now defunct Eighth Street Bookstore, a reunion of two Chicagoans. Next I went to Greenwich House for a talk he was giving: that is when I first photographed him.

Not long after, on a fine summer day, I found myself in the bus terminal looking for a bus in accordance with Nelson's instructions. So thorough a New Yorker had I become that this was to be my first time in Paterson, New Jersey. Nelson met me at the bus and off we went to a pleasant bar with the setting sun shining through the window. As I finished off my ladylike gin and tonic, I turned down an offer of another. I was scornfully rebuked, but did not give in.

That evening we watched boxing matches in the open, which only began to interest me when a couple of lady boxers came on. Ah ha, I thought as I ran to be close enough to photograph them, women can do anything they want these days. I was adding a new dimension to my collection of photographs and to my experience in this life. For Nelson it was ordinary; boxing was what he went to for entertainment, for relaxation, where he took his guests, like me.

What did we talk about? Easier to say what we didn't talk about. Not about Simone de Beauvoir, even though I kept remembering his remark, "She doesn't baby her privacy, does she?" Nor about Vietnam, not much anyway, maybe a few sentences about his dislike of the Vietnamese when he was looking for a place to stay in Saigon, on assignment for *Esquire*. So he chose to stay in Cholon among Chinese. Since I'd lived among Chinese myself in Shanghai, I approved. However, I was able to read more about Nelson in Saigon in *The Last Carousel* much later. Nor did we talk about the movie made from *The Man With the Golden Arm* and the stupendous amount of money it was assumed he'd made. He hadn't.

Then in the fall, I went with Nelson to Aqueduct, another place I never thought I'd be, although I knew there was an Aqueduct somewhere around. On a subway line new to me, we came right to the place. From a box we watched real live horses running, a sight not to be compared to the same on TV or sports section photographs, no more than a live theater performance can be compared to a movie. Easy to learn to stand up at the right moment, even get excited. Whether Nelson made any bets or won some money I do not remember. More wary, I didn't consider betting.

This, I confess, was not my first time at the races. In Rangoon, where my husband was working on a UN mission, he and I went to the races in the same spirit we went to look at the Shwedagon temple. Racing, the institution and the structure itself, left behind by the British, was patronized by anglicized Burmans and a few British who'd stayed on. Its air of elegance reminded me of Jacques Lartigue's photographs in Paris. No such air hung over Aqueduct. Furthermore, as part of America, it was to be taken seriously. And that could be in part the reason Nelson went to the races, as he delved into other aspects of America many of us neglect, overlook, ignore, or know nothing about.

I found out why he was in New Jersey, not in Chicago, where I'd thought his heart lay. He'd given up his apartment, he said. But who gave up apartments even in those days? He was doing what he came to do, to write about Hurricane Carter, a prizefighter in jail nearby. He was never to go back except for a visit he told me about, when he'd gone downstate to see a friend in some low profession. I'm not sure of what it was anymore, but it was a profession that could have been followed by some character in his novels.

As other people in Chicago had wondered when I was still there, I also wondered why a nice young man from Wicker Park wrote about such unseemly characters, and with such respect. He'd broken caste. What made him write about Division Street? I knew Division Street too—not the block with saloons from end to end, but a nice vegetarian restaurant I used to go to for farmer's chop suey, made up of tomatoes, radishes, and iceberg lettuce under a heavy topping of sour cream.

Nelson gave me a hand to get over figurative fences into a part of the world which until then I knew mostly from books, including his of course. For this and much else, I thank him.

EARLY RECEPTION

NELSON ALGREN
THE IRON SANCTUARY

Maxwell David Geismar

When I first looked at Nelson Algren's *The Man with the Golden Arm*, after it had won the National Book Award in 1950, I regarded it as a piece of virtuoso prose writing. I was wrong. Having just read it again, along with the rest of his books, I realize now that, like most serious works of literature, it asks the reader to participate also. A writer can never be better than his audience; but you must pay the price of admission he has set. Such books as *Moby-Dick* or *The Financier*, as well as the classic modern example, *Ulysses*—all such novels have their special language, which you must translate, as it were, to learn the real intention of the artist.

Yet to live completely in Nelson Algren's world is a strange and somewhat exhausting experience. This is very different from the standard tours around the Lake Country of the English poets or that of Hardy's Wessex. This is a world of ruins—but living ones. And prison is the safest place for Nelson Algren's people to be. It is the "iron sanctuary" which puts at rest their fevered and distorted hopes. It is, as he says, "the play for which all had rehearsed many times," and whose chorus consists of snickerers:

> Already the snickerers were waiting restlessly, in darkened rows, to identify the man who'd slugged the night watchman and the one who'd snatched the purse through the window of the moving El; for he who'd chased somebody's virgin daughter down a blind alley or forged her daddy's signature; tapped a gas main

or pulled a firebox; slit the janitor's throat in the coalbin or performed a casual abortion on the landlord's wife in lieu of paying the rent. All the things that had to be done to help someone else out of a jam. The little things done in simple fun and the big things done for love.

These prison scenes are remarkable achievements in Algren's work; they are recurrent and almost nightmarish episodes in which the writer, like the police captain Bednar in *The Man with the Golden Arm*, is haunted by an eternal procession of "bucket workers and bail jumpers, till tappers and assistant pickpockets, square johns and copper johns; lamisters and hallroom boys, ancient pious perverts and old blown parolees, rapoes and record-men; the damned and the undaunted, the jaunty and condemned." They come on and on and on, and where they come from no captain knows.

I am being polite and omitting the more flagrant cases of crime and vice who record their twisted destinies on the prison walls toward which they have moved just as surely as the young executives of middle-class American life aspire to join the country club. As early as 1935, in *Somebody in Boots*, his first novel, Algren had confronted the standard interpretation of American life—prosperity and success—with his own chronicles of poverty and failure. His first hero, a "poor-white" Texas boy, growing up during the depression years, takes to the road and becomes a vagabond and petty criminal. The book is dedicated to "those innumerable thousands: the homeless boys of America." It may remind you of Jack London's earlier study of American tramps and vagabonds called *The Road*, or of certain parts of John Dos Passos' *The 42nd Parallel*. There is indeed a whole body of literature dealing with this area of the national scene, as far back as the 1890s, which is seldom referred to in the classroom.

The emphasis of Algren's first novel is on the scenes of brutality which mark the life of the "lumpen-proletariat," the social scum, the passively rotting mass of people who lie at the bottom of the social scale. A boy is beaten up and crippled by a drunken father, a little Mexican child is crushed by the wheels of a train, a Negro woman gives birth to a stillborn baby in a sealed boxcar, a cat's head is twisted off, and worse. Those in "boots" represent authority: the police, the owners of property, the system of capitalism itself. But the novel is also in the straight documentary style of the 1930s: a thesis novel of social protest in which the characters are social types—if they are lucky. The prose is "poetic" in the bad sense; the tone of the novel is sentimental and melodramatic. *Never Come Morning*, seven years later, in 1942, was a very different story.

What happened to Nelson Algren himself during these seven years, I have been unable to find out. We are told he was born in Detroit, has lived in Chicago for many years, is an ex-GI, and a graduate of the life he depicts. He has been called the "Poet of the Chicago Slums" by Malcolm Cowley; both Ernest Hemingway and Carl

Sandburg have praised his work highly. But for a writer who has no scruples of gentility or false refinement, who is tough and blunt and calls a spade a spade only when he is at a loss for a richer phrase, he is extraordinarily reticent, it seems, about his own life, which I happen to like. The hero of *Never Come Morning* is Bruno Lefty Bicek, a young Polish boxer—or rather a young Polish hoodlum who dreams about being a champion in the way it is done in the movies and the comic strips. The early sections of the novel describe the plight of the Polish immigrants and their children in the barbaric slums of the new world.

The Polacks are on the ropes, though "Iron Man Bicek" doesn't know it yet; the immigrants, Algren is saying, have been betrayed, too. The barber Bonifacy is no longer sure about anything. "They were always trying to cheat him in this country." What is this fight business, the Widow Rostenkowski asks Bruno. "Is *crooked* business?"

"Ever'thin's crooked, Widow," he says easily, and glibly, for he has just passed from boyhood to manhood, from vandalism to hoodlumhood. The old people are bitter and despairing; the young people—starved, warped, ignorant little egoisms— are still warmed by the celluloid light of fame and wealth the quick way. The new city light glares on the "old-world face" of Steffi Rostenkowski, when she is seduced by Bruno, and then abandoned by him, in fear and drunken frustration, to the wolf pack of tougher hoodlums whom he calls his friends.

There is only one thing that Bruno Lefty Bicek is wary about. "The slot machine syndicate was big business—and big business didn't fool." (And one remembers Jack London's prophecy of the great battle between the business community and organized crime.) But Bruno is haunted by Steffi's ruin; he has killed her in his heart. The actual murder of the Greek, which he has committed in a blind fury of rage and revenge for Steffi, seems to him the best thing he has ever done. "For once he had done something right in his life." His visit to prison is inevitable. "Knew I'd never get t' be twenty-one anyhow," he thinks—"And the bell."

"To the greater understanding of our times, *Never Come Morning* portrays what actually exists in the nerve, brain, and blood of our boys on the street, be they black, white, native, or foreign-born," Richard Wright said in his introduction to the novel. Perhaps the best comparisons are with the Chicago Irish of James T. Farrell's novels and the tormented black souls of Wright's own work; but you get in Algren's book even more clearly the sense of stunted (and potentially vicious) children. Bruno Lefty Bicek tears apart a doll he has won at the circus because he hates "stuffed things," while to the police captain Tenczara of the story he is just a "strange animal." The realism is cold and brutal. It is only indeed in the love affair of Steffi and Bruno—in the range of normal emotions—that the novel falters and becomes somewhat artificial or theatrical. But in this literary orbit of bitter, angry lusts, of stunted emotions and stuffed lives, it may be that love itself is a luxury—or another path to crime.

The stories in *The Neon Wilderness* (1948) are in a softer vein: provided that you have read the other Algren books. For the first time women appear here, not only as credible human beings, but as a source of comfort and aid, however briefly, in the fast run between the womb and the grave. There is the sketch, reminiscent of Sherwood Anderson's midwestern vein, of the workingman who gambles and drinks his week's pay away on Saturday night because his wife had not been home to meet him; but she comforts him with her flesh at the end. "So nothing important has been lost after all." There is the stupid miserable creature who calls herself "the girl that men forgot awright," but there is also Wilma who gave all her love to another of Algren's boxers, and kept him straight, until her past caught up with her. There is the gambler who believes in "lucky bucks, fast money, and good women"—this glittering vista of Algren's Chicago slum world at its highest peak. And there is the tale of Railroad Shorty—a "halfy" or legless man—who clubs a young bartender to death in a casual brawl.

Algren's powerful effects are usually in his big scenes rather than in the portrayal or development of character. He is almost at his best in this volume of short stories where he can suggest the whole contour of a human life in a few terse pages. There is more warmth and humor here, too, than in the earlier books. It is, all in all, an excellent collection of short stories, perhaps one of the best we had in the 1940s. And, opening the new decade of the 1950s, *The Man with the Golden Arm* brought together the various strains in Algren's work.

The hero is Frankie Machine, in the Americanized version of Francis Majcinek, whose golden arm has brought him local fame as "the Dealer" in a gambling club. His pal and protégé is the "Sparrow," unnoticed by God, as Algren implies, befriended by Frankie; and the doorman or "steerer" in the same club. One of the Sparrow's other rackets is dog-stealing; his close little room has never lost "the special smell of shanghaied dogflesh," where poodles would emerge looking like debauched terriers or "Cocky Spaniards." There is quite a brilliant satiric episode of the Sparrow's love affair with Violet, who, inflamed with passion, drives her "Old Husband" into the clothes closet and finally out of the window. Other characters include the Jailor, the landlord of the Division Arms Hotel; the bartender Antek, called Owner; the blind man Piggy-O; and Nifty Louie, the morphine peddler at the Safari Club.

It takes quite a while to discover all this; almost as long as in a Faulkner novel perhaps. The structure of the book is panoramic; there are a host of minor characters, and the language is rich, if not ornate with the idiom of punks, cranks, and petty gangsters. This is, as it were, a *Winesburg, Ohio* of the demented slum dwellers; and one remembers that Sherwood Anderson wrote his nostalgic country tales while living in one of these miserable Chicago buildings, at the ragged end of life, where the streets run on and on, "out of nowhere into nothing." For Frankie Machine had cracked up an automobile while he was drunk. His crippled wife uses the accident as her revenge upon him. He has become a "junkie"—has taken to dope—and not even his love for Molly Novotny can save him from the inevitable trip—the classic denouement of all Nelson Algren's novels—to see the police captain. Record Head Bednar is the recording angel, the weary voice of justice and destiny, in this subluminous world of frustration.

The point is that Algren's typical figures are failures even at vice. They are the underdogs of sin, the small souls of corruption, the fools of poverty, not of wealth and power. Even the murders they commit, out of blind rage or through sheer accident—or through another ironic twist of their impoverished destiny—are not important. It is a political feud in an election year which dooms Frankie Machine, not justice. The police are no more interested in him than are the social workers or penal psychologists whom Nelson Algren loves to take for a ride—or than the respectable citizens of the republic, including teachers and literary critics perhaps, who read and then forget these chronicles of violence; or who say, conveniently, that such a world doesn't really exist, or that nothing can be done about it anyhow. But in one sense, this is almost true. For when Algren's hero does finally reach the iron sanctuary which promises a relief from both his hopes and his vices, you almost get the impression, to paraphrase Freud's morose dictum, that his whole life has merely been the attempt to choose his own method of dying. His final act of human dignity is to hang himself through the cunning of the golden arm.

Thus Algren's work represents an extreme phase of the native American realism which opened, in the 1900s, with Stephen Crane's *Maggie*, Frank Norris' *McTeague*, and Dreiser's *Sister Carrie*. All these authors were concerned with the dispossessed, but still retained the notion of hope and chance in a blind and very often hostile but not absolutely fatal universe. And there are obvious limitations and aesthetic dangers in the social area and the kind of human material that Algren has made his own. The quality of Dreiser's art, for instance, was evident in the fact that he could move from the lowest to the highest reaches of American society—from Carrie and Jennie Gerhardt to Frank Algernon Cowperwood and then back again halfway to Clyde Griffiths. This writer saw human character both as a social and as a biological product; or, rather, he did not see character as a "product" at all, but as that "mystery of personality" which fascinated him continually. Yet Algren himself has moved steadily from the documentary novel of social misery, the typical art form of the 1930s, to the depiction of human beings who are caught in the trap of social circumstances, which is quite another thing.

The present period is one of literary reaction against the whole current of realism and naturalism in the United States. In my own view we have regarded perhaps too highly, and uncritically, such figures as Henry James, Franz Kafka, or T. S. Eliot. We have condemned without trial, and often without reading, such masters as Dreiser himself and his descendants. To a certain degree the tradition of social protest which Algren belongs to is unfashionable today (though half the world is in the throes of social revolution), and he must regard himself at times as an isolated figure.

But he also represents a solid and enduring part of the American heritage of dissent. He should take comfort from the past, even while he writes, as all artists do, for the future; and, in his own words, he is still in there, "toughing it out."

NELSON ALGREN

George Bluestone

*The only really ugly thing on earth is the death that comes before true
death arrives.*

—Nelson Algren

Nelson Algren is known as a Chicago novelist, but he is only secondarily an urban
writer. He has chosen, rather, to explore the theme of death and survival among our
Lumpenproletariat. Of his four novels, all of one and two-thirds of another are set
entirely outside Chicago. In *The Neon Wilderness*, his collection of stories, at least
one third take place outside the urban world. In brief, only slightly more than half his
published fiction is centrally concerned with Chicago. It is true, as Blanche Gelfant
has shown, that Algren is an ecological novelist, that *The Man with the Golden Arm*
is perhaps "the fullest treatment of the world of the socially dispossessed and the
inwardly dissociated." But even though Algren moves in the world of Dreiser, Farrell
and Richard Wright, his sensibility is his own. He is not a naturalist, and to read him
in the naturalist tradition is to misread him. It was, perhaps, Algren's curious
disjuncture between conventional setting and offbeat prose that moved Stanley
Edgar Hyman, at a symposium on the novel, to refer to *The Man with the Golden
Arm* as a "weird duck." But the disjuncture becomes less weird in the light of
Algren's whole development.

393

[...]

In *The Man with the Golden Arm*, all of Algren's exploratory motifs merge for the first time to form a satisfactory whole. The humor, the incantatory style, the graphic eye, the poetic imagery all elucidate a central pattern. The reasons for this success, however, are not easily fixed. True, the characters are more clearly etched than ever before. Frankie, Sparrow, Zosh, Molly-O, Vi, Stash, Schwiefka, Nifty Louie, Blind Pig, Bednar are composites of earlier women, gamblers, petty thieves, drunks, drug addicts, dope pushers, police. True, Algren combines the leisurely, episodic narrative of *Somebody in Boots* with the spare, more tightly unified structure of *Never Come Morning*, lending the novel new tension and density. It is also true, as Blanche Gelfant has pointed out, that at least one reason for the ruin of these characters is rendered more persuasively here than in Algren's earlier work. The characters are haunted by the guilt of dispossession, "the great, secret and special American guilt of owning nothing, nothing at all, in the one land where ownership and virtue are one." But it seems to me that none of these, singly or in combination, is responsible for the novel's special aura. It is not even the maturity of Algren's style, which magically fuses colloquial dialogue and heightened prose, nor the problem of dope addiction, which has given the book its popular notoriety. In a celebrated interview in *The Paris Review*, Algren points out that the problem of Frankie's addiction was added at the request of an agent after a draft of the book had been completed. Clearly, the problem of drug addiction is not Algren's main concern.

The real center, it seems to me, lies in an advancement of the love-death theme we have traced before. More specifically, it lies in the complex relationship between Frankie and Sophie on the one hand, and between Frankie and Molly on the other. From the beginning, Frankie is haunted by a sense of guilt at his role in the automobile accident which led to Zosh's crippling. Before the accident, we may assume, Frankie and Zosh enjoyed the kind of innocent pleasures which Cass and Nancy, Bruno and Steffi experience only briefly. Since the accident, Zosh has been continually faced with the possibility of losing Frankie. And because the loss of Frankie represents the loss of love, Sophie binds him to her with the only weapon at her disposal, Frankie's guilt. Her physical and psychological crippling are finally indistinguishable.

Molly Novotny, on the other hand, represents another possibility for a redemptive love, a way out of Frankie's daily round of drugs and gambling and Sophie's endless harping. Molly returns his love, but like Mary in "Design for Departure," she loses him to prison, and, like Mary, degenerates soon after. Like Cass McKay and Bruno Bicek, Frankie tries one more reconciliation only to discover that he is too late. Frankie's second major crime, the inadvertent killing of Nifty Louie, the dope-pusher, catches up with him at last. The police close in, aborting the symbolic act of Frankie's "cold turkey," his last ditch effort, with Molly's help, to throw the "thirty-pound monkey" off his back.

Haunted by his own destructive past, hunted by the police, Frankie is driven out into the deserted streets to loneliness and suicide. Frankie's destruction of Zosh has made Molly's love impossible. It is this double focus in Frankie's identity that gives the digressions, the mood pieces, and the reveries their structural significance.

A pervasive sense of disaster, following love's ruin, reverberates throughout the book. The fear of a loveless life gives Sophie her characteristic awareness of death and drives her, ultimately, to madness. Like Steffi, she is continually plagued with images of a deserted world, presaging some future evil: "… why did it feel as though the all-night movies had all been emptied, why did it feel they must be showing broken reels to empty rows and that the all-night bakery fires had gone out: that the loaves would grow cold and mold slowly to dust in ten thousand rusting stoves?" Such visions soon become habitual.

A passage depicting Frankie's reveries in prison makes the same point in another way:

> Along the tier a hundred thieves argued in sleep with unseen turnkeys: the unseen pokies of all thieves' dreams who stride, jangling the special keys to each thief's private nightmare, down all the lonely corridors of despair. There was no delivery from the dead end of lost chance. No escape from the blue steel bars of guilt.
> Somewhere far above a steel moon shone, with equal grandeur, upon boulevard, alley and park; flophouse and penthouse, apartment hotel and tenement. Shone with that sort of wintry light that makes every city chimney, standing out against it in the cold, seem a sort of altar against a driving sky.

The echoing power of the prose becomes quite comprehensible under even rudimentary explication. The passage abounds in verse techniques—repetition: "thieves," "unseen," "all," "no," "keys"; assonance: "thieves… unseen… keys," "dead end," "city chimney"; fragments of iambic lines: "Along the tier a hundred thieves…," "down all the lonely corridors of despair." It reveals characteristic tropes, the dead city, the dark light, the wind image implicit in "driving sky," the obliteration of distinctions between nature and industrial life ("steel" is attributed to "moon" as well as "bars"). In general, it evokes the image of a dark, metallic, deserted city, symbolic of the living death associated with love's failure.

Finally, I would like to explore the figure of the altar, for it represents a recurrent thread which Algren has suggested in his previous work but has never before so fully woven into his texture: an inverted use of Christian myth to comment ironically on the action. In Sophie's plaintive meditation on the disordered world around her, she decides at one point, "It's just the way things would be if that Nifty Louie was God 'n Blind Pig was Jesus Christ." It is significant that the first movement of the novel, "Rumors of Evening," is framed by Captain Bednar's guilt-ridden meditations on the derelicts who march endlessly before him; that his guilt becomes identified with the guilt of his victims; that his role as judge and sufferer is underlined in terms of crucifixion. Much of the repartee between the Captain and his captives, reminiscent of the patterned dialogue between Bruno and Tenczara, is lifted straight from Algren's story, "The Captain Has Bad Dreams." But where the Captain of the story merely has a troubled conscience, Captain Bednar is haunted by what a defrocked priest has told him: "We are all members of one another." Bednar is almost envious of the criminals who have sentences hanging over their heads "like the very promise of salvation." And when he fails to take the warning advice he gives himself, "Come down off that cross," Algren's image becomes explicit: "The Captain was impaled." This new level of inverted Christian imagery functions ironically because in Algren's world there is no hope of an afterlife. In themselves, the Christian terms would be no more significant than other recurrent images if they did not have a special meaning. This secular appropriation of religious ritual is pertinent to Algren's central theme. For in this novel, Algren's prose approaches a very individualized kind of incantation, like the chanting of ritual itself. The incantatory style continually makes implicit judgments on the action. If, as Algren makes abundantly clear, morality is not to be found in the law, the church, in criminal ethics, in social struggle, in any normative standards for success, then where is the moral authority? Only in love. But if love is doomed by the social milieu, or by some inexplicable destructive instinct, where does redemption lie? In the stubborn ingenuity that guarantees these characters' survival? Yes, to some extent, Algren seems to say. The details of this drama can be very funny, as Sparrow's antics prove, but surely mere survival is not enough. Then is redemption to be found nowhere at all? The peculiar intensity of Algren's prose seems to support the harsher judgment. If man is deprived of salvation in an afterworld, if he must make his way in this world or not at all, then life is truly harsh. Indeed, Algren's final image, despite the humor, despite the intensity, despite the struggle to survive, is one of hopelessness and desolation. In this world, death is inescapable.

What possible approaches are open to the narrator who wishes to communicate such a vision? He can laugh; or he can lament. Algren does both supremely well. But the laughter is edged with bitterness; before the reality of death, it sadly falls away. It reminds us of Steffi's curious vision: "When she saw people bending with laughter, she fancied, for a moment, that they were weeping at some final disaster."

The lament, on the other hand, becomes at once a threnody of pity and a defense against terror. It enables Algren to look at his Medusa without turning to stone, as if the act of writing itself had become an amulet for evil. For Algren, then, the incantatory style is a surrogate for prayer.

A final word about the structure of this novel, since much has been made of its weaknesses. Blanche Gelfant argues that the book is held together less by virtue of structural necessity to theme, plot and characterization than by relevance to setting, as though intensity of tone and atmosphere substitute for, and even obscure the absence of, sustained theme. If I am right about the central pattern of Algren's prose, one sees that not only is a very real theme sustained, but that the structure is the only one really suited to it. "Rumors of Evening" is an elaborate record of Frankie's unsuccessful attempt to rid himself of the drug habit, and thereby of his guilty tie to Zosh. "Act of Contrition" traces Frankie's failure to win, through Molly's love, another lease on life. If the novel gives the impression of separate pieces of cloth loosely stitched together, or, in Blanche Gelfant's phrase, of parts that fit together "like pieces of mosaic," it is simply because no other scheme will do. If Algren is concerned with the living death that follows love's destruction, then one can understand the succession of timeless moments, each indistinguishable from the rest, like a series of stills in which action is both palpable and frozen. Postures succeed each other without correlative shifts in consciousness. Only moments of love—or love's destruction—can create new states of being. What lies between these points is the echoing wind of death. Everyone meets death at the end; the loveless meet it sooner.

That is why Frankie's relationship to Zosh, then to Molly, is more terrible than the murder of Nifty Louie or Frankie's self-destruction. That is why events seem to zigzag so, why strange ellipses occur between successive scenes, why the passages that deal with prison, or with Sparrow's amorous adventures, or with Frankie's all-night dealing have a curious dreamlike effect, as if time has wholly stopped. The meaning of all the digressions is precisely in their pointlessness. A more conventional development, conforming to traditional standards of plot, crisis and resolution, would constitute a different kind of novel. To reject Algren's structure, then, is to reject his central vision. When his vision changes, then his structure, too, will change. He is too careful a writer to have it otherwise.

A VOYEUR'S VIEW OF THE WILD SIDE

NELSON ALGREN AND HIS REVIEWERS

Lawrence Lipton

"What final pleasure we find in his [Algren's] novels we find, alas, as voyeurs," concludes Leslie A. Fiedler in his review of Nelson Algren's *A Walk on the Wild Side*. "We" are, of course, the people who read magazines like *The Reporter*, where his review appeared, and, I suppose, the reviewers and readers of other magazines for nice middlebrow men and women of good will. People who are normal and conformist except for a slight leftist independence of thought in their politics, which in anyone over forty today means a tinge of nostalgia for his New Deal honeymoon days. They would stiffen with indignation if you called them self-righteous, yet they cannot read about characters like Algren's without feeling like slummers. Not snooty slummers but slummers who are a little sad at what they see and yet keep their distance, glad to get back to the right side of the tracks again. Social workers are not encouraged by their supervisors to live in the same neighborhood as their "clients," but few would anyway. Laboratory technicians who work with unpleasant and pathological "specimens" develop a similar professional detachment. Algren, however, does not think of himself as either a social worker or a laboratory technician. Like that now rare type of doctor, the general practitioner of the small town or the city slum, he brings to his work the human compassion without which there can be no true diagnosis and the tender loving care (TLC our family doctor calls it) without which there can be no true healing. People like Leslie Fiedler, confronted with the same human material, feel like *voyeurs*. Even the pleasure they find in Algren's books is, alas, a guilty pleasure, like a respectable citizen's at a peep show.

In Fiedler's case it is complicated by another sort of guilt, the guilt of former association. He loses no opportunity in print to confess the guilt of his "innocence" during the New Deal "united front" thirties, and the only way he can explain Algren's continued preoccupation with "The Noble Savages of Skid Row" (that is the title of his review) is that Algren "was made, unfortunately, once and for all in the early 1930s, in the literary cult of 'experience' of those times," and has "stood still" since that time "as our literature has moved on and left him almost a museum piece—the Last of the Proletarian Writers." The implication is that if Algren would confess to the political innocence of which Fiedler, too, confesses himself guilty he would cease to be "isolated from the real life of his time," that is, he would forget all this nonsense and sentimentality about bums, tramps, whores, and pimps, all this wild talk about the losers on the wild side of the street, the gamblers and the junkies and the lost people, and see the real life of his time as one of Permanent Prosperity, the New Capitalism, the Highest Standard of Living in the World, in short, the world of Cash McCall and the Man in the Grey Flannel Suit. I'm sure that Mr. Fiedler and his admirers would find fault with summation of his views, but *Life* and *Time* would find no fault with it; and it is not recorded that Mr. Fiedler has ever found fault with *Life* and *Time* in such matters. He calls Algren's world "this expurgated universe" and complains that there is no room in it for "workers or teachers or clerks." Admittedly whores are not workers in the respectable sense of the word, and pimps are not ordinary clerks, although both, as well as bookies, are expected to report their earnings and pay income taxes, and who should know better about such things than congressmen and tax collectors? (As for teachers, I do not press the point. Whatever it is that Algren's whores, junkies, pimps, and bums have to teach us, it is not in the standard curriculum and no oath is required to teach it.) But, if Algren's characters are not workers, how can it be said that he is "the Last of the Proletarian Writers"? Unless Fiedler would class them with the *Lumpenproletariat*, in which case he is, alas, once more guilty by association—word association, which is the worst kind—for the communists have always held the view that the *Lumpenproletariat* are not workers. Guilt by association, especially word and thought association, is a tricky thing. There may have to be a new round of subpoenas and television trials now that anti-Stalinism is official communist policy, with all the Friendly Witnesses trooping back to the witness stand again to clear themselves of a new heresy. The breast-beater's lot is not a happy one.

Clearly Algren is not among the confessed, the cleared, the brain-washed, or the saved. But how does it happen that the reviewers were so long finding it out? Fiedler offers the ingenious explanation that Algren didn't write his first book first. "Algren has finally got to his [first novel] six books deep in his career." My own guess is that the reviewers have discovered something about Algren six reviews late in *their* careers. They have discovered that Algren really *means* it.

Reviewing *A Walk on the Wild Side* in *The New Yorker*, Norman Podhoretz remarks that "this time Mr. Algren knows what he wants to say. What he wants to say is that we live in a society whose bums and tramps are better men than the preachers and the politicians and the otherwise respectable" (June 2, 1956). Of the same book, *Time* magazine's reviewer has this to say:

> One of the literary cliches that takes a long time dying is the notion that prostitutes have hearts of gold and that bums are somehow more steeped in humanity than people who work. No living U.S. writer has done more to keep the idea alive, and no one has done it with more literary authority than Chicago novelist Nelson Algren. (May 28, 1956)

The *Time* reviewer concludes that Algren's "old admirers have to reconsider their admiration. They may well wonder if his sympathy for the depraved and degraded has not carried him to the edge of nonsense," and sums up with the observation that "he means the book to be a caress for the most degraded members of society and a protest against social injustice… but in supposing that human virtue flourishes best among degenerates, Novelist Algren has dressed his sense of compassion in the rags of vulgarity." In basic agreement Norman Podhoretz concludes that "as a celebration of wine, women and song, the book is more in the spirit of the boozy sentimentality of the broken-down Shakespearean actor declaiming to the boys on the barroom floor than an expression of Rabelaisian exuberance."

If the whore and the pimp are degenerates, what does that make the good citizen from the other side of the tracks who patronizes them, or the conventioneer on the loose, or the police and judges and politicians who "protect" them? The victims always stand lower in the pecking order than their exploiters. They are fair game, and so is any writer who essays to speak for them, on the principle, no doubt, that first you "get" the accused, then you go after his defenders, a principle that has been followed in practice by all pseudo-juridical inquisitorial bodies. And here, as in all such proceedings, even the terms of the indictment are phony. The notion that prostitutes have hearts of gold is of course a literary cliché, and you will find it in much of the slumming fiction of the past; but nowhere in Algren's books is there any prostitute with a heart of gold. *Time*'s reviewer would find himself hard put to it to find a single line in *A Walk on the Wild Side*, or *Never Come Morning*, where prostitution is part of Algren's theme, that could be quoted or twisted to support the notion. Algren's prostitutes are people, good, bad, and indifferent, like any other women. If they perform a good deed or an unselfish act their motives are as mixed as those of any wife or sweetheart—or any businessman on the make for a buck. As for the bums, the charge of idleness is itself a cliché. It was always leveled against itinerant workers, "tramps," "hoboes," who followed the harvest or preferred pick-up jobs to punching a time-clock. For Dove Linkhorn in *Wild Side* it is work or starve from start to finish, and he is seldom idle. Far from being a bum in the *Time* reviewer's sense of the word (as distinguished from "people who work"), Dove is clearly intended to be a parody of the young man on the make for money and sucess, or, if you prefer, The Great American Goof who pursues the bitch goddess till he finds out she is making a fool of him. It is not surprising that the author who chooses such a theme should be slapped down by the reviewer of a magazine that makes America the Land of Opportunity an article of faith and a test of loyalty—while at the same time, unwittingly, documenting its falsity in the pages of *Time, Life*, and *Fortune* week after week and month after month. All it succeeds in proving is that America is the land of opportunity for those on the make, those who are willing and able to "play the game," and if the game is not an honest or a moral game you can prove that from their pages too. *A Walk on the Wild Side* is part of such a documentation.

This theme is not a new one for Algren. It was already fully developed in his first book, *Somebody in Boots.* How does it happen then that *The New Yorker*'s and *Time*'s reviewers have only now discovered it?

The case of *The New Yorker* is simple. *New Yorker* policy is liberal, eclectic, sophisticated, urbane. In its "Talk of the Town" pages a deadpan interview with an unwashed prophet of doom may be followed by equally deadpan cocktail talk with a perfumed princess. The dandy with the quill pen and the monocle is free to go anywhere and talk with anybody. *Noblesse oblige*, brought up to date with a touch of parlor pink. Right down to the Clifton Fadimentals of things, and with a bright, smart Bennett Cerface. The tip-off is the winking owl opposite the Knickerbocker dandy in the masthead which adorns the "Talk of the Town." That wink is telling Altman & Co., Black Starr and Gorham, and Chanel No. 5: Yoo-hoo, I didn't mean *you*. And to the sophisticated reader it is saying: Yoo-hoo, *you* know what I mean, even if I didn't say it in so many words. I have heard it called satire and irony, but the only things in the magazine that occasionally approach the ironic or the satirical are the captions under the cartoons. The Town Talk pieces, the profiles and the special articles stick pretty close to the It's a Mad World my Masters sort of attitude; at their most daring they approach H. L. Mencken's 1920s brand of smart set cynicism. Everyone in the country should by now be familiar with this type of *New Yorker* schizophrenia. It is the occupational disease of Madison Avenue and the Exurbanites. The analytical couches on Central Park South could document it by the bookful if they were wired for sound.

Up to the publication of *The Man with the Golden Arm* Algren rated little in *The New Yorker* besides a ribbing of the title of *Never Come Morning* by Stanley Edgar Hyman who was writing Perelmanesque humor in those days ("How Green Is My Truelove's

Title," June 13, 1942). My own title, *Brother, the Laugh Is Bitter*, also came in for a rib-bing. I remember it now only because Algren's title was originally the working title of my own book and I relinquished it to him at the suggestion of our mutual editor at Harper. Algren's own title was *I Should of Stood in Bed*. He should have stuck to it.

The Man with the Golden Arm rated something more than a brush-off and a bit of New Yorkerese ribbing. It had not only been praised by Ernest Hemingway (more about that later) but it gave Mr. Knickerbocker a chance to *noblesse oblige* himself to the point of virtual sainthood. Nothing gives the sophisticated intellectual *noblesse* such a lift as the opportunity to sit in literary judgment on an interesting case history straight out of the slum and give it the nod of approval that will raise it to the level of literature. The juvenile delinquents of *Never Come Morning*, and their basement gang-shags, might be called powerful, poignant, significant, and what not, and the *New Republic* might call the book's author a poet of the slums and Sandburg's suc-cessor: but this was not yet the stuff that calls for a nod from the man with the mon-ocle. Frankie Machine was more like it. A Golden Boy gone wrong, a champ who goes down under the seductions of the needle as other champs in the past went down with the bottle. True he failed the billboards all down the line, failed the Altman ads and Black Starr and Gorham, failed Tee and Green and Audax Minor and the On and Off the Avenue Christmas shopping guide; but he was there slugging all the time, he was trying to Rise, trying to Make Good. He—and his author—were worthy of a Helping Hand from the man with the monocle.

But the creator of Dove Linkhorn and *A Walk on the Wild Side* is another story, something that calls for an agonizing reappraisal. *The Man with the Golden Arm,* the *New Yorker* reviewer now tells us:

> was a book full of half-realized attitudes identifying themselves only in a distant whisper; it was a book that never quite discovered what it wanted to say, which accounts for the uneasiness one felt in reading it. A Walk on the Wild Side is a far more self-conscious, purposeful novel. There are no whispered intimations; the shouts are loud and clamorous enough for all to hear. This time Mr. Algren knows what he wants to say. What he wants to say is that we live in a society whose bums and tramps are better men than the preachers and the politicians and the other-wise respectable. This startling proposition he attempts to demonstrate through a complicated satire on America's claim that it is the land of opportunity.

Half-realized attitudes and whispered intimations were things the owl could wink at. The champ who swings wild and falls on his face trying to make good, that's one thing. But a hero who rejects the American dream, a Candide who gets wised up and in the end turns his back on the grey flannel suit, the men of distinction, and Countess Mara, who crosses over for good to the wild side of the street where there is no Brooks Brothers branch, no Commander Whitehead, no Schweppervescence, where Merrill

Lynch, who is willing to go almost anywhere, never goes at all, nor even Pierce, Fenner, or Beane—such a hero has forfeited all claim to slick paper recognition. Back with him to the newsprint liberal weeklies which specialize in lost causes and willful failures, where loud shouts, "clamorous enough for all to hear," are more welcome than whispered intimations. Perhaps they will not mind it so much if Algren, "to make double sure that Dove stays put on the loser's side of the street… contrives to have him blinded in a savage fight with an embittered cripple." The blinded on the loser's side of the street are not to be confused for one minute with a Baron Wrangell wearing an eye patch and a Hathaway shirt in a *New Yorker* color page. Dove Linkhorn, diseducated, re-educated and disaffiliated, will never again be a prospect for the $10,000 mink, the gift that says Merry Christmas all through the year, or even the little dream of a pince-nez, the lenses not much bigger than dragonfly wings, ground to prescription for only eighteen dollars, to give his girl friend. He will never get close enough to ask the man who owns one. In creating such a character, Algren has failed the slick paper critics all down the line. To *The New Yorker*'s Norman Podhoretz he is now "The Man with the Golden Beef"—a sly reference, of course, to the ingratitude of an author who has already seen sizeable royalty checks and important movie money. He has looked the Trojan gift horse in the mouth and reported predatory teeth and moral halitosis.

The case of *Time* magazine is a bit more complex. To the tone of *noblesse oblige*, *Time* likes to add the gesture of *largesse*. Once the directive goes into the inter-office memos and the teletypes that so-and-so rates boldface type in the People department, whether he be a tycoon or a crooner, a prize fighter, or a poet, he is henceforth "Timeworthy." Nothing is too good for the Timeworthy, but the honor, like being received at Sing-Sing or the Court of St. James, involves a certain etiquette. Once he has been named and rated he is expected to remain true to the character in the dossier. *Time* doesn't make mistakes. This is a Fact, and it is maintained with all the tenacity and force of a legal fiction.

Nelson Algren became Timeworthy upon publication of *The Man with the Golden Arm*, having been sponsored at Court by long-time Timeworthy Ernest Hemingway. What bare-knuckle-machine-gun-prose Hemingway saw in the rhapsodic prose poetry of Algren is little more than a puzzling "attraction of opposites" till you stop and take into account the highly subjective character of all of Hemingway's literary judgments. I suspect that what Hemingway saw in the Golden Boy was the hero who lives by the Hemingway Code. The hero who, as John W. Aldridge described him in *After the Lost Generation*, "is tough, numb, and simple-minded… a man 'things are done to,'" whose code is to suffer nobly and make a "good show" of himself. This was the formula that made Hemingway Timeworthy in the first place, and a living legend that *Time* had done so much to propagate and keep alive—a formula that somehow broke down in *To Have and Have Not*, much to *Time*'s dismay, and which was greeted with the full treatment in *Life* when Hemingway recaptured it in *The Old Man and the Sea*. That Spanish adventure of Hemingway's, with a hero who instead of becoming disillusioned becomes angry, who fights back, and in the process betrays his creator—and the Code (as Aldridge has pointed out)—nearly got him stricken from the Court Circular; men have been broken and demoted to light-face type for less in *Time*.

Frankie Machine was near enough to the formula to satisfy Hemingway, despite the difference in literary style. That there were other, deeper, differences—between Frankie Machine and the Frederick Henrys, the Nick Adamses and the Jake Barneses—seems to have been lost on Hemingway at the time, if indeed he has discovered them since. Algren's characters are, to be sure, consistently unsuccessful people, but the secret of their unsuccess is not to be found in Hemingway's formula or Hemingway's Code. They are Victims. They do not fight violence with violence, they fight it with cunning, the devious underground cunning of the hopelessly poor; shop-lifting, petty pilfering, purse-snatching, pimping, and prostitution. Petty crime is their only form of social protest. The only major crimes they commit are committed accidentally, in the act of attempting a minor crime and—characteristically—muffing it. I can see how all this endeared them to *Time*, but I can't for the life of me understand how it went down with Hemingway; unless, as I suspect, he had read nothing of Algren's before *The Man with the Golden Arm*, and had then given little thought to what makes Frankie Machine tick, either. A generous gesture for Papa to make, but a confused and perhaps impulsive one.

For *Time*, on the other hand, it was the correct one—at the time. For the Timeline was, had been for many years, the pious one that *The poor ye have always with you*. It was Scripture, it was History, it was a law of Human Nature. In *Time*'s socio-economic theology it was the dogma of Original Sin. Only in this mystical sense could the poor be blamed for their poverty, but, by the same dogma, neither could the rich be blamed for their wealth, a position that Mr. Luce's Bright Young Men managed to bolster up—by semantical tricks and malquotation—from the "moral man and immoral society" of Reinhold Niebuhr, the Court Theologian. But, just as there was Divine Grace in heaven, so there was Management and Technology on earth, and *Fortune* was its prophet. Pope Henry was in his tower, in Mr. Rockefeller's Cathedral of Commerce. Any further questions were certain to find infallible answers. In a pinch there were always the ten volumes of Toynbee, the Court Historian, unabridged and incontrovertible.

That was the Timeline in 1950 and the rumdum poor of Algren's books seemed to fit as snugly into it as the tough, numb, and simpleminded of Hemingway's. The *New Republic* had nominated Algren as poet of the Chicago slums ten years before, with *Never Come Morning*. Now *Time* made it official, and All American, with Poet of the Slums. For *Time*, Algren was a Bourke-White—with a soft-focus lens. He turned poverty into poetry.

But since then the Line has changed. With all the media of communication securely muzzled by firings, jailings, and blacklisting, Management and Technology have decided to take over heaven as well as earth. Now, instead of Grace, it is to be Salvation by Works: the steel works of Bethlehem, Pennsylvania, the automobile works of Detroit, the chemical works of Dupont. Now the Line is no longer *The poor ye have always with you*, but *The poor ye have no longer with you, at least, not for long*. The richest nation on earth is creating a society without poverty. Today the nation, tomorrow the world.

Like all absolute Truth, the new Line must be protected against Heresy. Already holding the portfolio of culture, *Life-Time-Fortune* also took over the portfolio of cultural brain-washing. It had held itself more or less aloof from the smearing, jailing, and blacklisting of the film, radio, and theater people. Perhaps it preferred to wait and have a go at the creative writer himself, and the literary cirtics who expound and support him. In 1951 *Life* was able to give a measure of support to John W. Aldridge's *After the Lost Generation*. In 1955 the manifesto of the New Line was published in *Life* (Sept. 12) and by 1956 Aldridge's *In Search of Heresy* was on the rack, as was also my own *Disaffiliation and the Art of Poverty* (*Chicago Review,* Spring 1956), for the crime of heretical dissent from the new line. And now Nelson Algren, the Poet of the Slums in 1950, is down-graded to "poet laureate of Skid Row," Skid Row being all that is left of the slum in the land of The New Capitalism, The New Conservatism, and Prosperity Unlimited. Salvation by works is simple. Sin against the *Time-Life-Fortune* line and they'll give you the works.

Gilbert K. Chesterton, who had his own brand of New Conservatism (he would have preferred to call it radicalism, or course), once took it upon himself to defend the slum novel and the slum novelist on the ground that "in religion and morals... the sins of the educated classes [are] as great as, or perhaps greater than, the sins of the poor and ignorant." (For Chesterton the rich were always the edcuated and the poor were the ignorant.) The medieval ethic, which he held up as a model for his time, made much of the sin of pride, "because it would be quite obvious that the rich have it more than the poor." "We are always ready," he went on to say, "to make a saint or prophet of the educated man who goes into cottages to give a little kindly advice to the uneducated. But the medieval idea of a saint or prophet was something quite different. The medieval saint or prophet was an uneducated man who walked into grand houses to give a little kindly advice to the educated. The old tyrants had enough insolence to despoil the poor, but they had not enough insolence to preach to them. It was the gentleman who oppressed the slums; but it was the slums that admonished the gentleman."

He was quite prepared to defend the slum novels of Arthur Morrison and Somerset Maugham (he was referring to Maugham's *Liza of Lambeth*) because they provided a much needed "shock to the imagination" of the educated upper classes, and he saw quite clearly that the slum novelist should live in the slum and share the life of the poor; but he insisted that the writer should emphasize the pleasures of poverty rather than its hardships and illnesses, as Maugham did in that first novel of his. For it was Chesterton's Christian Catholic conviction that the poor are the blessed and the rich are ever in peril of their souls' damnation. What he demanded of the slum novelist is that he should present the slum dweller not as a poor man but simply as a *man.*

> The nearest approach to it in our ordinary life would be the promptitude with which we should consider mere humanity in any circumstance of shock or death. We should say, after a somewhat disturbing discovery, "There is a dead man under the sofa." We should not be likely to say, "There is a dead man of considerable per- sonal refinement under the sofa." We should say, "A woman has fallen into the water." We should not say, "A highly educated woman has fallen into the water." Nobody would say, "There are the remains of a clear thinker in your back garden."[1]

This simple humanity, he says, "was native to St. Francis of Assisi. It was native to Walt Whitman." It also describes, I submit, the ethical approach of Nelson Algren to the poor of the slums. This is the chief quality that Fiedler, Podhoretz, and Gissen would have found, I think, in *A Walk on the Wild Side,* if they had been prepared to think of its characters as men and women, not as freaks put on show for the guilty pleasure of the *voyeur.*

There *is* a peep show in *A Walk on the Wild Side,* a *real* peep show in which Dove Linkhorn puts on a rape act in the whorehouse for paying customers at the peephole, and it is interesting to read what Algren himself has to say about these *voyeurs.*

> Each watcher was affected differently. One paled slowly as he looked and, after a minute, left for good thinking how sad such things were so. Another laughed smugly deep in his liver, to see proven at last what he had long suspected: a man was a two-legged animal and a woman a four-legged one, nothing more.... Yet a third looked thoughtful, as at a demonstration in carpet weaving: see, there was still money to be made in small enterprise. Another felt stale lusts grow swift and bit his lips for lack of cash: had he every dollar in town tonight, all would be spent by morning. But the great cripple neither laughed nor paled. Only the lines of his heavy head hardened and he swung his torso on its tiny wheels and wheeled off down the hall, making a rolling thunder to hide his indignation.

Each of these represents an attitude not only toward a peep show but toward the *whole* show, to the life of our time. Only the cripple turns away with indignation, the same cripple who in the end blinds Dove Linkhorn in a saloon brawl over a woman.

Only one reaction is lacking here, that of the novelist himself, and this is found every- where else in the book, from the first page to the last: compassion. A compassion that *Time*'s reviewer says is "dresed in the rags of vulgarity," that Podhoretz called "boozy

sentimentality," and that Fiedler calls his "pose ... tance ... platitudes and sentimentality." For them it is not true compassion because it is misplaced. His characters are
not worthy of compassion. They would not have him choose his worthy ones as a phil-
anthropist, or a social worker, perhaps, chooses the "worthy cases." Fiedler makes
much of the fact that Dove Linkhorn is on the make for money and success the same
as the banker or the big time operator, failing to see that what Algren is presenting here
is a parody of the Success Story. The banker and the big time operator have their
reward—and their court poets. Algren is the poet of the losers, the lost who believed,
believed all the promises, and were betrayed, betrayed from within and from without.
"The book," he tells us in the jacket copy, "asks why lost people sometimes develop
into greater human beings than those who have never been lost in their whole lives.
Why men who have suffered most at the hands of men are the natural believers in
humanity, while those whose part has been simply to acquire, to take all and give nothing, are the most contemptuous of mankind. Why the laughter of old survivors rings
more true than those whose laughs have to be bought."

"These are not, of course, ideas," Fiedler tells us, "but sentimental indulgences—
a refusal to see the very characters the authors imagines or remembers except
through a haze of forgiving tears." To evaluate dispassionately, to judge, to classify—
perhaps to arrest and punish?—is that more blessed than to forgive? And who is the
author, who is the critic, who are we to take it upon ourselves to forgive? Algren has
said it more than once: the writer's place today is with the accused, guilty or not
guilty, with the accused.

It has always puzzled the nice people why it is that writers and artists so often go
to the slums for their material, why they keep such bad company, with the unsuccessful, the losers on the wrong side of the tracks, on the wild side of the street. The
answers is at least two thousand years old, also in a parable:

> A certain man made a great supper; and he bade many: and he sent forth his servant
> at supper time to say to them that were bidden, Come; for all things are now ready.
> And they all with one consent began to make excuse. The first said unto him, I have
> bought a field, and I must needs go out and seed it; I pray thee have me excused.
> And another said, I have bought five yoke of oxen, and I go to prove them; I pray
> thee have me excused. And another said, I have married a wife, and therefore I can-
> not come. And the servant came, and told his lord these things. Then the master of
> the house being angry said to his servants, Go out quickly into the streets and lanes
> of the city, and bring in hither the poor and maimed and blind and lame....

Note

1. Gilbert K. Chesterton, *"Slum Novelists and the Slums,"* in Heretics *(London, New York: John Lane, 1906), 267 ff.*

NEW VIEWS

ALGREN'S QUESTION

Daniel Simon

He would hang his coat neatly over the back of his chair in the leaden station-house twilight, say he was beat from lack of sleep and lay his head across his arms upon the query-room desk.

—The Man with the Golden Arm

I am looking at a photograph of Nelson Algren on the evening he received the very first National Book Award. It adorns the most prominent wall in the Seven Stories Press offices where, were we another kind of business, we would have our diplomas, our first dollar bill, or our celebrity photo. Algren was the first author I published, beginning a year or two after he died, and the photo, a recent find in the archives of the National Book Foundation, shows me a happier vision of this person than the one I have grown accustomed to over the last fifteen years. Nelson stands beside Eleanor Roosevelt, who presented him with the award. It is March 1950. He is biting down on a cigar and grinning to himself like a hard-boiled Mona Lisa, unmistakably a man who has taken on the world and won, and even more surprisingly, a man who had expected to win all along.

Taking on the world, for Algren, meant changing it through the proper use of his literary voice. His heroes were the Russian writers he admired, who could take for granted what on American soil can seem like a grandiose notion: that literary and social aims fit together. Algren was, like Tolstoy and Dostoyevsky, a novelist with the heart of a radical reformer (just precisely the kind of writer HUAC deemed "un-American"), and like his contemporary, the playwright Arthur Miller, he is representative of what many still consider to be the best American literary tradition of the postwar period. When his goal of revolutionary change through literary means seemed impossible, his life depressed him, even made him suicidal on at least one occasion; when the goal seemed within reach, as on this cool night in March 1950, he became elated and all was right with him.

Since Algren fought losing battles on a regular basis, winning, for Algren, held a special glory. But no surprise. And since he had chosen to write about a world of extreme dysfunction and despair, his strategy for making it habitable and enjoyable for his readers had to be complex and even a bit far-fetched. In order to mine this world for gemstones of joy and hope, Algren had to be both in his particular historical moment and outside it, and given the sensitive and difficult subject matter he had chosen, he had to approach his readers gingerly, not pointing a finger but asking questions, hopefully questions that could be a bridge from his time into the future.

He had won the award for his astonishing novel *The Man with the Golden Arm*, completed and published in the prior year, 1949. And the mysterious moment captured in the photo is best understood in terms of this specific work. Not because it is his only monumental achievement. It isn't. The earlier novel *Never Come Morning* (which actually sold more copies), his gracious story collection *The Neon Wilderness* (still the favorite among his works of many fellow writers, as Mike Royko writes in these pages), the book-length prose poem *Chicago: City on the Make*—each of these is of comparable stature and strength. But it is his *Golden Arm*, nonetheless, that is his greatest triumph, his greatest victory, his winningest hand—because its language is so densely laid down and so lyrical, its momentum so sustained, because the familiar Algren characters here are possessed of so much insight. To say it the way I imagine Algren might have: because it is the book he put the most into. Or as Nelson actually described his feelings about the novel, in a letter written just after he completed it (included in this volume), "So I feel it was a lucky book, and a lucky time now past, and I was lucky to write it."

The story line of *The Man with the Golden Arm* is simple, but hidden. It is not the story of a man falling prey to drug addiction, since that happens offstage and prior to the novel's start. Nor is it an account of a marriage breaking up, since that also happens in the wings, before the novel's opening. Nor is it the account of a murder, unless in a most unusual sense, since the murder plays only a small part of the monumental drama that is played out in these pages. *The Man with the Golden Arm* is, plainly and simply, an account of a junkie trying to go straight, or, in more universal terms, a man pulling his life together—and failing miserably at it. Hooked on morphine at the end of the war, Frankie kills his dealer in a fit of pride and disgust. Saddled with a miserable marriage, he begins seeing a girl, an old acquaintance with a heart of gold, and can foresee a time when he has put his marital troubles behind him. Jailed on a minor theft, he hero-ically "buries his monkey," kicks his habit cold turkey, because jail is the one place he can get that job done. Frankie Majcinek is only trying to improve his life. But Algren's world is an essentially upside-down, tragic place. Good things happen too late to mat-ter, or not at all. In the end, it's all the same difference. After paying so steep a price to get clean, Frankie goes back on morphine anyway. So what keeps us, Algren's read-ers, trudging along with hope in our hearts?

Algren embraced contradictions: he wrote unromantically, yet sentimentally; he wrote hopefully about characters with no way out; he wrote about a drab and almost colorless world in a splendidly rich, densely poetic, and colorful prose style. He turned Aristotle on his head as well, writing about "low" comedic characters as if their stories were high tragedy—and to Algren they were, because what happened to them mattered so very much to him. That he came along when he did, at a time of suffocating conformity, only adds to the magic of what he accomplished. But where lies the pull of Algren's novels? And—a related question—could it be a mat-ter of importance both in his historical period and in ours?

The Man with the Golden Arm is a book about identity, not action. The engine that powers the narrative forward is not the impact of the doer but the drama of the witness—of Sparrow, who sees the murder and helps drag the body out of plain view to buy Frankie time; of the many other neighborhood denizens, who rightly assume they know who done it, and approve; of Record Head Bednar, who interrogates the endless parade of the accused and condemned, only to feel that he alone, he who has done nothing wrong, is the real guilty party. Action here always has a dreamlike, otherworldly quality. People's jobs—Steerer, Record Head, Fixer, Meter Reader—are usually running gags of irrelevance, and even Frankie's—Dealer—becomes one by the end. Algren's characters here watch themselves with the distance and objec-tivity of unpartisan witnesses. They reveal what they are made of not through their actions, but by how they bear witness.

The lead actor in another Algren drama, the novel *Never Come Morning*, says at one point, in response to a sure death sentence, "Knew I'd never get t'be twenty-one anyhow." And what takes our breath away is precisely the spectacle of someone observing his own demise, coolly and with a hearty and humorous appreciation of the irony his life embodies. And so, the pounding the reader hears in his ears throughout *The Man with the Golden Arm* is only partly the expiring, exhausted breathing of Frankie Machine, victim, and partly the pulsing of the attentive hearts of Sparrow, Record Head, Molly-O, Frankie himself, Algren himself, alert, listening, watching—witnesses.

Questions give rise to other questions. Whose identity is at stake here? (Sparrow's? Frankie's? Algren's? The reader's, as Bill Savage argues persuasively in these pages?) leads to, And how much responsibility rightfully belongs on the witness's shoulders, anyway? This more than any other may be Algren's question, the one he had to ask of himself, and of the rest of us. It would have concerned him, as a soldier who had only a few years earlier served in a world war that was already the second of this century. And, as it would other writers of conscience, it would come to haunt him, as a writer who only a few years hence would have his passport application denied and the publication of a book of his hurriedly refused by his publisher because of his political affiliations (he was honorary cochairman of the Chicago chapter of the Save Ethel and Julius Rosenberg Committee). He, and we, similarly, could speak of a century in which we have come to know so much and seem to be able to do comparatively little, a century in which genocide has been followed by the words "Never again," and then more genocide, and in which the fight against totalitarianism is routinely used to justify totalitarianism. And it is in this context that the question of the witness, Algren's question, keeps returning, demanding an answer. We all know we are bystanders of horror. Is there something about the nature of standing by and watching that Algren teaches? It is a question each reader of Algren will ask, and every reader will answer a little differently.

Since Algren's novel is a work of identity, not action, the reader experiences it on several planes, only one of which is narrative, and thus only one of which is hopeless. Whatever happens, there are residues of personality, of humor, of grace, that outlast and outshine the botched beginnings and miserable ends. It is almost as if Algren's novels were written in several literary genres simultaneously, as if at the end of *The Man with the Golden Arm*, the novel were superseded by a parallel work, a drama, and what resonates most strongly is an irreducible lyric quality, what Algren would have called poetry. And as if confirming this notion of multiple and parallel works within the novel, Algren in fact gives us three separate endings to the book, the first set in the hotel room where Frankie has holed up, fading in and out of consciousness and leaving the reader also without a sure grip on reality, followed by the police report, which is as it were absolutely narrative, followed by the poem with which Algren closes the book, *letting go* of the novelist persona, stripped naked. He calls the poem "Epitaph: The Man with the Golden Arm," and in its last stanza he poses this question: "Yet why does the light down the dealer's slot / Sift soft as light in a troubled dream?"

It was Algren's friend and agent Candida Donadio who first suggested to me that Algren was sentimental. I had to think about that. I'm still thinking about it. She was asking me to see sentimentality as a positive attribute, since Candida wasn't criticizing Algren when she said it—just describing him. We usually think of sentimentality as the distortion of a true emotion. It can also be a bridge there.

In the early 1960s, about twelve or thirteen years after he'd completed the writing of *The Man with the Golden Arm*, Nelson himself spoke on the subject to H.E.F. Donohue, for the book *Conversations with Nelson Algren:*

> [Sentimentality] is an indulgence in emotion. You want men and women to be good to each other and you're very stubborn in thinking that they want to be. Sentimentality is a kind of indulgence in this hope. I'm not against sentimentality. I think you need it. I mean, I don't think you get a true picture of people without it in writing.... It's a kind of poetry, it's an emotional poetry, and, to bring it back to the literary scene, I don't think anything is true that doesn't have it.

As the soul-grinding narrative of *The Man with the Golden Arm* is nearly completed toward the end of the novel, there is a scene in which Sparrow watches Frankie shoot up:

> "It kills me in the heart, how you are now," Sparrow couldn't keep from saying. "It just ain't like bein' Frankie no more."
> "That's the hardest thing of all for me to be, Solly," Frankie told him with a strange gentleness. "I'm gettin' farther away from myself all the time. It's why I have to have a charge so bad, so I can come back 'n be myself a little while again. But it's a longer way to go every time...."

As the scene continues, Frankie pelts Sparrow with questions: "You know who I am? You know who you are? You know who *anybody* is any more?" Sparrow says he doesn't know. And then, abruptly, Frankie asks: "Then tell me just this—why do some cats swing like this?" Sparrow doesn't know that either. But for a moment, as happens at key points throughout the book, the different planes of the novel speak in harmony. The scene is heavy with plot, propelled by Bednar setting Sparrow up to deliver Frankie his morphine, which allows Bednar to put the heat on Sparrow to rat on Frankie about Louie's murder. The dramatic plane is present in Frankie's own awareness of his dead-end position. And the poetic plane comes through in Frankie's words. Action expresses alienation from being; being itself marks a diminishing trail; and in the end it is in their self-awareness, self-deprecating, often funny, and bought at a steep price, that Algren's characters find their unearthly power.

THE QUALITY OF LAUGHTER
ALGREN'S CHALLENGE TO THE READER

William J. Savage Jr.

In the one passage of overt social critique in *The Man with the Golden Arm*, Nelson Algren's narrator describes the scene as Frankie Machine looks around at his fellow prisoners in the Saloon Street Station lockup one morning. Frankie sees men with "faces bloody as raw pork ground slowly in the great city's grinder," who all share "the great, secret and special American guilt of owning nothing, nothing at all, in the one land where ownership and virtue are one" (1990, 16–17). Society's rejects, they have watched "the truer Americans mount the broad stone stairways to success . . . without enough sense of honor to climb off a West Madison Street Keep-Our-City-Clean box" (17). For these men, "the city itself seemed some sort of open-roofed jail with walls for all men and laughter for very few" (17). Yet they are redeemed, decisively, by humor, by an ability to laugh: despite their alienation, "yet they spoke and yet they laughed; and even the most maimed wreck of them all held, like a pennant in that drifting light, some frayed remnant of laughter from unfrayed years" (17). As beaten down as these men are, they still can laugh, they still hold on to their human dignity.

Algren's emphasis here on the humanizing, redemptive power of laughter is a key to this novel. As the scholar June Howard (1985, x) has observed, most naturalist and realist novels that focus on the American ghetto feature either a character or a narrator who acts as a stand-in for the presumed middle-class reader, a tour guide who from a privileged position observes and analyzes the inhabitants of the exoticized urban jungle. While Algren can hardly be characterized as a run-of-the-mill naturalist (he has the modernist writer's concern for highly wrought prose, which most American naturalist writers have thought beside the point) his subject matter is very much in the mainstream of what James R. Giles has characterized as "late naturalism" (1989, 17). It might seem at first reading that Algren violates this naturalist convention, as the novel seems unremittingly focused on the *lumpenproletariat* of Damen and Division, inhabitants of the proverbial lower depths of Chicago's slums: it is as though middle-class Chicago does not exist.

But in one key passage, the lineup scene that ends the first section of the novel, Algren subtly introduces to the book anonymous, faceless characters representative of the middle-class audience. Giles has argued that this scene is key to the book in relation to the influence of existential philosophy on Algren, because in it the reader must confront his own relationship to the down-and-out characters of the novel and acknowledge a common humanity born out of suffering (1990, xi). But this scene, like the earlier passage in the lockup, also firmly connects Algren to American literary traditions based in vernacular humor, linking this text back to writers like Ambrose Bierce, Finley Peter Dunne, and Mark Twain, writers who satirically exploited the dark humor latent in the direst of situations. Whatever else might be going on in this scene, as Algren's friend Studs Terkel reminds us often, humor is the key to understanding *The Man with the Golden Arm* (and Algren's work in general) here because the scene pivots on a question of laughter. Or, to be more precise, the reader's laughter.

In this scene, Algren dramatizes the act of reading the novel. The lineup is characterized as a play: the accused, including Frankie, wait "offstage" (189) and feel "festive," "as if a play for which all had rehearsed many times was to have an audience on the other side of the footlights at last" (188). The "snickerers," the middle-class victims of and witnesses to crime who have come to identify the guilty, are repeatedly referred to as the "audience." Physically, the setting resembles a theater: the accusers enter from the "clean well-lighted street" (199) and sit in darkened rows watching the accused, who enter from "backstage" (190), speak into a microphone, and are blinded by the glare of the lights. Captain Bednar stands between them at a podium, with the charge sheets, where he acts like the director of a play, or the emcee of a vaudeville show, a comic routine.

The dramatic tension in this scene, as well as Algren's thematic concern with humor, is generated by the jokes Bednar makes in response to the lies told by the accused in response to the charges and the airing of their criminal pasts:

> "How'd you like it in the pen?" he asked in old routine.
> "I didn't."
> "Why not? Wouldn't the warden give you his job?" That was always the answer to that one. They always stepped into it in the same way. (191)

The captain has been through this drama so many times that he has his timing down pat and his jokes memorized; it's an old routine, and a successful one. As one of the accused puts it, "Very funny.… Captain, you're killing me" (195). Yet the metaphor of stepping into it, as a boxer might step into his opponent's punch, is telling: this exchange might resemble a comic routine, but it has an underlying and barely disguised violence, the perpetuation of a corrupt and ruthless system, a system that brutalizes those at its bottom while providing entertainment for those privileged enough to sit in the audience.

The stagy, dramatic setup dehumanizes the accused by exposing their every flaw and stressing the ideological structures within which the audience perceives them. While they stand visible and vulnerable before the objectifying gaze of the snickering audience, they themselves can see nothing:

> Frankie stood with a backstage view of the rows where, here and there among the listeners, a police badge glistened and all faces were dark and featureless.
>
> While upon the stage all faces were lined up under a glare that brought out every wrinkle, pimple, and scar. (190)

And what this staged situation reveals to the snickering audience is not even accurate. The glare of the lights

> made any man look like a plastic job with a prefabricated expression grafted on, according to some criminologist's graph or other, to fit the crime of which the captain's charge sheet had him accused: here was a pickpocket's deadpan mask and there a shoplifter's measured manner. Here the brutal lines of the paid-in-full premeditated murderer and there the coneroo's cynical leer.
>
> Yet the man behind the murderer's mask was under the lights for stealing a bushel of mustard greens and the coneroo's leer had been picked up for oversleeping in a Halsted Street hallway. (192)

As in melodrama, the expectations of the audience about the stock characters matter the most: the individual human reality of the person under the lights becomes submerged in preconceptions of how a criminal should look. Such ideas are the cultural remnants of nineteenth-century social Darwinist criminologists like Cesare Lombroso, who were obsessed with finding physical attributes marking people thought to be inherently inferior and predisposed to crime, and who distorted their data to produce graphs delineating the sort of looks associated with different criminal types (Gould 1981, 122–43). The men and women in the lineup are, in a vital sense, not real to the audience: they are the products of expectations about the criminal that the audience brings in with it from the clean, well-lighted street, expectations that inform how the audience responds to what it sees.

Nonetheless, heartfelt humor, real emotion, can still take place in the midst of this action. Frankie has been arrested after a shoplifting expedition with Sparrow had gone awry; the six electric "eye-rons" he was stealing ripped through the bottom of a paper shopping bag and bounced away down the escalator, attracting, as one might well imagine, the amused attention of the house detectives. When questioned about it by Bednar, "Frankie grinned. He could still see those damned irons bouncing" (195). The comical absurdity of the whole situation, being arrested for such a bonehead move in such ridiculous circumstances, is funny even to Frankie. Just as in the earlier scene in the lockup, genuine humor can still exist even in the midst of a dehumanizing situation.

Finally, though, the captain gets stumped, and the routine of the comedy is shown up for the empty exercise it has become. He asks one "gaunt wreck in a smudged clerical collar,"

> "Are you a preacher?" The captain sounded puzzled.
> "I've been defrocked."
> "You were still pretty good when it comes to cashing phony checks. What were you defrocked for?"
> "Because I believe we are all members of one another."
> That one stopped the captain cold. He studied the wreck as if suddenly so uncertain of himself that he was afraid to ask him what he had meant by that. "I don't get it," he acknowledged at last. (198)

Presented with a statement for which he has no ready-made response, no automatic retort, the captain doesn't get it, just as someone doesn't get a poorly told or unfunny joke. Giles characterizes this moment as the captain confronting his own humanity, a humanity he shares (like it or not) with the criminals before him. The confrontation can also be analyzed in terms of the dynamics of humor. The Chicago depicted in *The Man with the Golden Arm*, as in the rest of Algren's work, displays the relentlessly hierarchical nature of American culture, the dehumanization of those on the bottom and the alienation from themselves of those on the top. The captain simply cannot understand—or let himself understand—a claim that this hierarchy is unreal, that humanity is all of a piece, that we are all members of one another. He subconsciously recognizes the dilemma, but has no ready-made solution, no easy quip to get past the rough spot in the old routine.

Finally, for Bednar—and for Algren and his readers—the problem comes down to the quality of laughter, the way in which the middle-class audience, both within the line-up scene and of the novel, reacts to the human reality behind the easy banter of crime and punishment. How does the audience laugh? Bednar thinks that

> Worst of all were the witnesses who snickered after every questioning. If only, just once, one of them would laugh out from the heart.... What was it that the defrocked priest had said? "We are all members of one another." What had the

holy-sounding fraud meant by that? Why had several snickered then and not one
had laughed out from the heart? (197, 200 my ellipsis)

The difference between snickering and laughing out from the heart is the difference
between a callous objectification of another person as the mere butt of a joke and a
sympathetic identification with another human being as a human being (or, as Giles
analyzes it, Sartre's distinction between regard, the dismissal of another as an object,
and reciprocity, the recognition of another as an equal). The difference between snickering and laughing out from the heart is the difference between laughing at someone
and laughing with someone. This quality of laughter is what Algren wants us to focus
on and to consider as we confront the characters and the situations he depicts.

The varieties of humor he uses throughout the novel complicate this challenge.
We can laugh easily at the various malapropisms that perfectly capture the characters' personalities, as when Sparrow complains of being kept out of military service
for "moral warpitude" (12) or when Frankie tells Sophie she's had a "repercussion,"
like she's "been bounced on [her] head twice" (36). But we have to think more carefully about how we take The Great Sandwich Battle, the extended scene in which a
drunken Vi and Sparrow ridicule Old Husband, a part of the book that daringly mixes
violence and farce and ends with the old man being arrested because he doesn't
have any money to pay off the cop. And throughout the novel we meet grotesque
neighborhood characters like Blind Pig or Umbrellas, characters whose grotesque
nature has an antic comic edge. The humor grows organically out of the neighborhood situation and the characters' personalities, and there are many laughs in the
book: but with the lineup scene Algren warns us to consider how we laugh.

Here in "the one land where ownership and virtue are one," Algren's challenge to his
audience still stands. Giles points out that "Lineups… served Algren as metaphors for
respectable society's depersonalization of the criminal Other" (1989, 53), and this
depersonalization pivots on how we laugh. As readers, we are like the viewers of the
lineup; we sit, unseen, and pass judgment on the characters Algren presents. Do we
identify with the people he portrays, who once would have been called denizens of
the lower depths, who we now might describe as the marginalized economic and criminal Other? Do we see them as human beings, Americans like ourselves, or do we
objectify them? Algren characterizes this choice as one involving the quality of our
laughter: either we snicker at his guilty "innocents," or we laugh out from the heart with
them; either we distance ourselves from them or we identify with our shared humanity and see that "we are all members of one another." Bednar's realization of this
dilemma leaves him "impaled," unable either to laugh or to cry, as dehumanized by
the system he has upheld as those like Sparrow and Frankie, crushed beneath it. We
should, as readers a half-century after the publication of this novel, recall Algren's challenge and ask ourselves how we laugh.

Works Cited

Algren, Nelson. *The Man with the Golden Arm*. New York: Seven Stories Press, 1990.

Giles, James R. "The Harsh Compassion of Nelson Algren." Introduction to Algren, *The Man with the Golden Arm* (New York: Seven Stories Press, 1990), vii–xvii.

———. *Confronting the Horror: The Novels of Nelson Algren*. Kent, Ohio: Kent State University Press, 1989.

Gould, Stephen Jay. *The Mismeasure of Man*. New York: Norton, 1981.

Howard, June. *Form and History in American Literary Naturalism*. Chapel Hill: University of North Carolina Press, 1985.

THE STORY OF DECLINE
AND THE OCTOBER CITY

Carlo Rotella

When Nelson Algren got back to the Near Northwest Side of Chicago in 1945 after two years of military service, he got back to work. He was a writer, and his job as he understood it was to write about Chicago. If the city seemed to have changed in his absence—"The last of Chicago's gaslamps had gone out," and "Flourescent neon lit brands of beer never named before"[1]—he still could pick up where he had left off before the war. After making a name for himself with a first novel, *Somebody in Boots* (1935) and short stories in the 1930s, he had begun to win significant acclaim for his novel *Never Come Morning* (1942). In 1945 he was poised to make his mark on the literary world. Working from observation of postwar Chicago, his wartime experience, and a base of stories and poetry he had written in the 1930s and 1940s, Algren produced three Chicago books in relatively short order: a collection of short stories entitled *The Neon Wilderness* (1947) set the stage for two longer works, the novel *The Man with the Golden Arm* (1949) and the book-length prose poem *Chicago: City on the Make* (1951). *Golden Arm*, which was awarded the first National Book Award for fiction in 1950, was Algren's best and best-received work. It sold well, and influential writers and critics like Richard Wright, Ernest Hemingway, and Malcolm Cowley identified Algren as a major postwar novelist on the rise. They, and the publicists at Doubleday, whose ad copy for *Golden Arm* urged readers to "add the name NELSON ALGREN to the honor roll of Chicago authors... who have entertained you and inspired you with novels that have made American literary history," agreed that Algren was the next big Chicago writer: one in a line that extended back through Wright and James T. Farrell to Carl Sandburg, Theodore Dreiser, and other masters who had explored the literary implications of industrial urbanism as exemplified by Chicago.[2]

In retrospect, though, the fanfare accompanying Algren's arrival as a Chicago writer marks the the end of his most productive period, and he never wrote another sustained, original treatment of the city with which he was so closely identified. *Golden Arm* and *City on the Make* were his last Chicago books, and together they drew a portrait of midcentury Chicago as a city in steep decline—if not in ruins— about which Algren would not have much else to say. The two books are a literary epitaph for the city Algren knew and the city he wrote.

Algren was identified as a Chicago writer, but he had never been a civic booster. From the very beginning of his writing career, he marked out the sphere of the desperately dispossessed as his literary territory, and his body of work advanced a critique of the arrangements of power and meaning in the industrial city. The workers and drifters who populate his books always play hopeless hands against a house that stacks the political, economic, and cultural deck against them. Like the Chicago novels of Farrell and Wright, who shared with Algren the project of representing the industrial city's neighborhoods, Algren's Chicago novels and stories are overhung with a sense of the inevitable: people without access to wealth and power will be ground up by urban business as usual—the production and consumption of goods, services, and the status quo.

If Algren's postwar writing sustained the terms of critique he had developed before the war, it put them to a new purpose. *Golden Arm* and *City on the Make*, refitting the language and imagery of his earlier work and of the Chicago tradition in which he placed himself, move from the urgent contemporaneity of social critique toward the retrospective, elegiac mood of the decline narrative. Midcentury Chicago was in many ways a boomtown, beginning to flower into new, postindustrial shape under pressure from suburbanization on the periphery and redevelopment in the center, but for Algren it was an aging industrial city that was rapidly exhausting both its productive vigor and its cultural importance. At midcentury, Algren looked back upon high-industrial Chicago, which had been the subject of his starkest renderings of urban modernity, as the capital of a golden age populated by outsize heroic figures: not just the working men and women who made the industrial city in the late nineteenth and early twentieth centuries, but also great reformers like Jane Addams, literary icons like Carl Sandburg, larger-than-life victims like Shoeless Joe Jackson, and even the fantastically villainous industrialists, owners, and politicians who exploited and opposed them. *Golden Arm* and *City on the Make* narrate a decline from this golden age to a debased, reduced present. They do not so much advance a critique of industrial urbanism as imagine—and nostalgically mourn—its passing.

In *Golden Arm*, something has gone obscurely and finally wrong in midcentury Chicago. The novel's characters, operating within the tightly circumscribed limits of neighborhood life in the Polish urban village around Division Street and Milwaukee Avenue, can sense the local effects of massive change without being able to specify its dimensions or causes. The invalid Sophie Majcinek, sitting at her window in a wheelchair late at night, reads intimations of apocalypse in the crowded, low-rise landscape of walk-up apartment buildings, roominghouses, factories, churches, and elevated train tracks:

> Moonlight that had once revealed so many stars now showed her only how the city was bound, from southeast to the unknown west, steel upon steel upon steel; how all its rails held the city too tightly to the thousand-girdered El.
>
> Some nights she could barely breathe for seeing the flat and unerring line of cable and crosslight and lever, of signal tower and switch. For the endless humming of telephone wires murmuring insanely from street to street without ever really saying a single word above a whisper that a really sensible person might understand.
>
> For the city too was somehow crippled of late. The city too seemed a little insane. Crippled and caught and done for with everyone in it. No one else was really any better off than herself, she reflected with a child's satisfaction, they had all been twisted about whether they sat in a wheelchair or not...
>
> She grew tense to see how the nameless people were bound, as they went, to the streets as the streets seemed bound to the night and the night to the nameless day. And all the days to a nameless remorse.[3]

The news is bad, but incompletely articulated: the vista murmurs to Sophie of nameless remorse and an imminent but unspecified disaster. All she knows for certain is that things were better in the old days, when "some happier, some might-have-been, some used-to-be or never-was Sophie" lived in a world that had not yet "gone wrong, all wrong." If that receding golden age of the 1920s and 1930s was like spring, then at midcentury Chicago has reached October, when the year begins its steep decline into Chicago's famously brutal winter:

> Sultry September had come and gone and the wind was blowing the flies away.
> "God has forgotten us all," Sophie told herself quietly....
> The wind was blowing the flies away. God was forgetting His own. (99)

The year's decline and fall seems to resonate with a larger, parallel decline and fall of the world she knows.

The world she knows is the industrial city, and more precisely the industrial neighborhood order, that flourished between the Chicago fire of 1871 and World

War II. Chicago was the paradigmatic American city of that period, the model of industrial modernity and the kinds of urbanism associated with it. Migrations from Chicago's various hinterlands—not only the small-town and rural Midwest and South but also Germany and Ireland, Scandinavia, Eastern Europe, southern Europe, Mexico, the Philippines—brought people of modest means to Chicago to work in its factories and the service industries they engendered. For foreign immigrants, the urban villages that grew around factory workplaces, streetcar lines, and local institutions were staging grounds in which they came to terms with the transition between the Old Country and America. European immigrants and their descendants dominated the urban villages of industrial Chicago, which ringed the downtown core in a vast patchwork. The urban villages, and the ways of life they housed, were the heartland of the industrial city's social landscape, formed on an armature of rail lines, port facilities, factories, and other infrastructure dedicated to circulating raw materials, manufactured goods, and the people who processed and bought them. Sophie sees this world from her window—the old neighborhood bound to the rail lines, "steel upon steel upon steel"—and obscurely mourns its passing as she reviews her own hard luck and the intimations of personal disaster still to come.

Unlike *City on the Make*, which narrates the rise and fall of Chicago on the grand scale and surveys a panoramic landscape peopled with well-known historical figures, *Golden Arm* portrays the decline as a neighborhood tragedy so claustrophobically local in scope that the reasons for imminent catastrophe must remain mysterious and inchoate. The transformation of postwar Chicago becomes one of the novel's principal subtexts, a crisis gathering force beyond the close horizons of the old neighborhood. Sophie Majcinek, penned within that narrowing world, senses only the vague outlines of decline in the "rumors of evening" that filter down to her in murmurous, coded fragments. Nelson Algren, whose own windows looked out on a similar vista in the 1940s and early 1950s, could feel the change coming, too. He could not have known then that *Golden Arm* and *City on the Make* would be his last Chicago books, but one can feel his unease, like Sophie's, with the intimations of change he felt moving through the familiar landscape of the neighborhoods he lived in and wrote about. Algren's literary subject was industrial urbanism; his literary project was to represent the industrial city and infuse it with meanings, as had a number of celebrated Chicago writers before him. He understood the decline of industrial Chicago to mean the end not only of the neighborhood order he knew but also of the literary tradition in which he worked.

Any city at any time is going to hell in one sense or another. Narratives of decline seem to spring from the overlap of orders in time and space: the overlap of established residents and newcomers; of pieces of social landscape arranged to serve different sets of people and functions; of different institutional arrangements for making money, exercising power, making life meaningful, living poorly or well. However, specific arguments for decline have historical and generic provenance that can be traced to period and place, to particular structures of thought and traditions of representation. Nelson Algren's version of Chicago's decline was part of a larger literature of urban decline that thrived at midcentury, and has since become a staple of postwar urbanism. That literature embraces a variety of fictional and nonfictional accounts, written by a range of variously accredited and influential urban intellectuals, many of whom agreed on little else.

"In the years just after the Second World War," observes Robert Beauregard, "the trauma of the country's large central cities could hardly be avoided." That "trauma" was most evident in the great industrial cities of the Midwest and Northeast, and it was most immediately the result of "15 years of depression, war, and inflation"[4] in which specifically urban problems had been pushed to the back burner: factories, civic buildings, and especially overcrowded neighborhoods were physically deteriorating; cities' economies, especially factory production and downtown retailing, were showing signs of long-term erosion; pollution was increased and traffic congestion exacerbated by the proliferation of cars in streets originally designed for the horse and wagon; city governments were denounced as weak and corrupt, while federal government was potently committed to suburbanizing the nation; many cities' tax bases shrank as poor in-migrants, especially Southern blacks, settled in the inner city while middle-class whites and businesses dispersed into the suburbs. The trauma was also, however, part of a larger change in the form and function of cities. The industrial cities that had for generations been the leading models of American urbanism were undergoing a profound transformation. The gradual shift of primary economic function from manufacturing to services, the prodigious rise of the suburbs as places to live and work, the expansion of the black inner city and the erosion of the industrial village—these were the big groundswells, just beginning to shake the foundations of industrial urbanism, that would make urban history in the second half of the century. One can perceive their effects, as well, in the way urban intellectuals wrote and thought about cities. There had always been a vigorous literature of antiurbanism in American culture, and there was a long tradition of equating cities with specifically moral decline, but a particular genre of decline narrative— promulgated especially by people who loved cities—appeared after World War II and has descended to us as one of our fundamental ways to think about and represent inner cities. In many different versions, and pursuing an enormous range of particular subjects that range from traffic to class conflict, the postwar narrative of decline considers the causes, effects, and meaning of the endlessly complex set of changes that add up to postindustrial transformation.

Chicago, the paragon of industrial urbanism, provided an especially resonant setting for the postwar decline. "There is an opinion," observed the *New Yorker* essayist A. J. Liebling in 1952,

> advanced by some men who worked in Chicago transiently during the twenties, as well as by many native Chicagoans, that the city did approximate the great howling, hurrying, hog-butchering, hog-mannered challenger for the empire of the world specified in the legend, but that at some time around 1930 it stopped as suddenly as a front-running horse at the head of the stretch with a poor man's last two dollars on its nose. What stopped it is a mystery, like what happened to Angkor Vat.[5]

Jack Lait and Lee Mortimer, New York newspapermen who had worked more than transiently in Chicago before World War II, made a similar claim in their hard-boiled insider's guide, *Chicago Confidential* (1950): "In 1910 Chicago breezily and confidently expected to surpass New York by 1950; in 1950 it no longer talks of growing bigger than New York—it wonders when it will be smaller than Los Angeles."[6] Liebling, Lait, and Mortimer, reporters all, did not claim to have formulated the story of Chicago's decline; rather, they claimed to have collected it as it circulated ready to hand in the culture around them. Having gone to Chicago to do what amounted to follow-up pieces on the well-known story of its remarkable growth into a world city in the half-century before the Great Depression, they had returned with stories of decline.

The reporters' claims to having found the next chapter of the Chicago story in the narrative of decline found support from Carl Sandburg, whose literary persona continued to enjoy a close identification with the story of industrial Chicago in the ascendant, a story he had definitively told in the early twentieth century. Sandburg was not a "native Chicagoan," but he was poet laureate of Illinois and author of the city's semi-offi cial poem, "Chicago" (1914). That poem had been quoted and referred to so consistently (even by people who had not read it or any other poems) that over time what Liebling simply calls "the legend" of Chicago had become condensed into a few of its richly freighted phrases: "Hog Butcher," "Big Shoulders," and so forth. Sandburg wrote in *Holiday* magazine's special issue on Chicago in 1951, "There is a question that occurs: Is Chicago less vivid and strident than in former generations? That could be, might be, I'm not sure."[7] Like Liebling, Sandburg employed a passive construction—"There is an opinion…," "There is a question that occurs…"— that imputed to the decline the status of received wisdom. The hesitant tone of Sandburg's answer to the "question that occurs" at midcentury makes a striking contrast to the belligerently assertive language of his celebrated poem. In 1914, he had imagined industrial Chicago issuing a challenge:

> Come and show me another city with lifted head singing so
>   proud to be alive and coarse and strong and cunning

> Flinging magnetic curses amid the toil of piling job upon job,
> here is a tall bold slugger set vivid against the little soft
> cities.[8]

At midcentury, Sandburg's drastically changed tone seemed to concede the loss of the youthful vigor and prospects with which his earlier poetry had infused its portrait of the industrial city. The *Holiday* article repeats the poem's language, like the word "vivid" (which seems to be associated with productivity), but drains the words of their original stridency. Writing about midcentury Chicago, Sandburg seemed to be unsure of what to say about it.

If midcentury Chicago as a literary subject was still importantly defined by themes and language evolved in the late nineteenth and early twentieth centuries in response to the shocks of industrial modernity, then the passing of industrial urbanism suggested a decline and demanded a revision of the Chicago story. If Sandburg was not prepared to write it, others—like Liebling, Lait and Mortimer, and Nelson Algren—were. The story of decline, literary and journalistic, told of Chicago's passage from a bygone moment of limitless promise to a reduced and dispirited present day. Variants of the decline appearing in the late 1940s and 1950s told of Chicago's fall from aspiring world city to the humbler estate of one regional capital among many, from industrial dynamo to rusting postindustrial dinosaur (anticipating by decades the Rust Belt elegies that accompanied the city's great period of deindustrialization in the 1970s), from literary capital to cultural wasteland, from vigorous city of neighborhoods to blighted inner city eclipsed by prosperous suburbs, from a vital congeries of white-ethnic villages and Black Metropolis to an archipelago of white enclaves surrounded by pathologized black ghetto. The story of decline argued for the passing of a moment when Chicago had been the right place at the right time. It had once been the way station between metropolitan America and its resource-rich frontier, the destination of immigrant laborers drawn to the industrial city, the cultural capital of the Middle Border during the maturing of urban America and the revolt against Main Street. Now it was at best like everywhere else, and at worst a ruin.

Especially because the story of decline tends to treat the city like a single individual—who is getting old and fat, who once aspired to better things, and so on—it tends to reduce complexity to simplicity or mysticism. The imputation of general decline tends toward analytical vagueness, always begging the question, In what sense? Because a city, like a nation, is complex enough to be simultaneously rising and falling by any number of measures, the story of decline acquires coherence and authority by both specifying and mystifying its terms to evolve a kind of symbolic shorthand. On the one hand, the story tends to range in great leaps across the spectrum of historical information, unifying disparate but evocative details into a grand impressionistic whole. For instance, the failure of Chicago to become a center for the manufacture of automobiles, the departure of important literary figures in the 1920s, and the passing of its great criminal entrepreneurs hang together thematically in Liebling's account in ways that suggest an across-the-board failure of the city's creative energies. On the other hand, the decline tends to condense drastically in order to make sense, identifying a particular Chicago in time and space and making it stand for the whole. Thus, the decline formula can be adapted to recount the transformation or disappearance of many different or overlapping golden-age Chicagos: the Middle Border capital raised by hard work and entrepreneurial inspiration from the swamps and the ashes of the Great Fire; the city of European immigrants negotiating through hard work and solidarity the passage from horse-and-wagon days to American modernity; the midwestern literary capital that produced stark realists, prairie modernists, muckraking reporters, and dialect humorists and was in turn produced discursively by them.

Although they infused the formula with different sets of meanings, most of the versions of Chicago's decline agreed upon the general contours of the story. All assumed that the city had enjoyed a golden age of promise more than a generation before. Lait and Mortimer only specify that in 1910 the golden age had not yet elapsed. Liebling dates the city's moment of ascendance from around 1890, when the census employed by Frederick Jackson Turner to argue for the closing of the frontier also showed that Chicago had passed Philadelphia to become the nation's second city, to about 1930, when Chicago mysteriously collapsed in the stretch of its run at First City status. He notes that in the 1920s Colonel Robert McCormick's incorrigibly boosterish *Tribune* was still printing daily on its editorial page a "Program for Chicagoland" that featured as Article 1 an injunction to "Make Chicago the First City of the World." By midcentury, the *Tribune* had dropped this grandiose program, which Liebling takes as tacit acquiescence to the notion of decline. The novelist James T. Farrell, a leftist who otherwise had little in common with the famously right-wing and anti-union McCormick, provides a similar periodization of the golden age. He remembered that he "grew up inside of the city of Chicago, and after the city had passed its period of greatest hope," which he defined as a stretch from 1880 to 1910 in which Chicago's bankers and industrialists had created a world capital and its progressive liberals had given the city intellectual life and conscience.[9] Farrell saw the city as somehow broken by its failure to deliver on its golden-age promise of high productivity tempered by social justice.

Like Farrell, Nelson Algren understood himself to have been born during the city's age of promise (Farrell in 1904; Algren in 1909) and come to maturity as the city declined toward eventual ruin. In the autobiographical *City on the Make*, Algren presents the end of the golden age as coinciding with his first disillusionments: the Black Sox scandal of 1919 marks in retrospect the end of "the silver-colored yesterday" dominated by "giants." The humiliations endured in preadolescence by the poem's autobiographical narrator for believing in his baseball heroes feed into a city-wide sense of loss that has grown through midcentury. Algren's account of the fall or departure of giants—Shoeless Joe Jackson, Theodore Dreiser, Eugene Debs, Jane Addams, even self-serving "clowns" like the politician Big Bill Thompson and the traction magnate Samuel Insull—nicely illustrates Liebling's observation that, at mid-century, "Chicagoans are left in the plight of the Greeks at the beginning of history, when the gods commenced ceasing to manifest themselves."[10] The present, then, as imagined in both *City on the Make* and *Golden Arm*, constitutes a postheroic age extending from the 1920s to the distant but foreseeable end of history.[11]

Algren's postwar writing bears the marks of its historical moment: in its sense of liter-ary-historical desperation as well as its awareness—sometimes obscure or deflected, but always potent—of the flows of capital and population already transforming Chicago's social landscape. *Golden Arm*, the definitive story of decline in novel form, stands as a culminative masterpiece of the Chicago realist tradition that grew around the task of exploring the literary and social consequences of industrial urbanism. The novel's richly imagined October City affords us a way to consider a midcentury moment suspended between the industrial and postindustrial eras, between a prewar urban literature and formative genres that would rework and replace it. (At midcentury, Gwendolyn Brooks, Saul Bellow, and others were already taking Chicago literature out of its industrial era and into territory that Algren would often characterize as not his kind of Chicago writing.) The pervasiveness of the El in the October City's landscape—as mapped in both *Golden Arm* and *City on the Make*—invites us to consider the rela-tionship between Chicago and the city constructed by its literary tradition: both the material city and the imagined city grew around their railroads, which thereby acquired a powerful symbolic charge that survives well into the age of the expressway that began around midcentury. The El's great rusting trestles, many of prewar vintage, con-tinue to this day to serve as a resonant shorthand for Chicago: they still carry loads of meaning, just as they still bear trains filled with flesh-and-blood passengers. The El reminds us that with all the midcentury talk of decline, apocalypse, and the "disap-pearance" of Chicago, the prewar city did not fall overnight into ruin but instead became absorbed into a new landscape that was just beginning to emerge when Algren wrote *Golden Arm*.

Notes

1. Nelson Algren, *introduction to* The Neon Wilderness *(1947; reprint, Hill and Wang, 1960), cited in Bettina Drew,* Nelson Algren: A Life on the Wild Side *(Austin: University of Texas, 1989), 171.*

2. *The Doubleday advertisement appeared in* The New York Times Book Review, *2 October 1949, 11.*

3. *Nelson Algren,* The Man with the Golden Arm *(1949; New York: Seven Stories Press, 1990), 96. Further references in the text.*

4. *Robert Beauregard,* Voices of Decline: The Postwar Fate of U.S. Cities *(Cambridge: Blackwell, 1993), 3, 109. In* Voices, *Beauregard definitively collects and analyzes the journalistic and policy literature of decline.*

5. *A. J. Liebling,* Chicago: The Second City *(New York: Knopf, 1952), 12.*

6. *Jack Lait and Lee Mortimer,* Chicago Confidential *(New York: Crown, 1950), 9.*

7. *Carl Sandburg, "Introduction to Chicago,"* Holiday *(October 1951), 33. Holiday, a handsome large-format travel magazine, devoted most of its October 1951 issue to a series of articles that together made a portrait of Chicago at midcentury. Noted contributors to the issue included Gwendolyn Brooks, the neighborhood novelist Albert Halper, Colonel McCormick (publisher of the Tribune), gossip columnist Irv Kupcinet, Robert Hutchins (president of the University of Chicago), and Nelson Algren, whose prose poem "One Man's Chicago" (so retitled by Holiday's editors, apparently to make it clear that Algren's dark portrait was a dissenting view) was an early version of City on the Make. That Sandburg asked his "question that occurs" about the city's decline in his introduction to this issue made it clear that decline would be a principal theme, sometimes explicit and always implicit, of the articles that followed. The subtext of decline grated against a competing narrative of the city's continuing growth and physical vigor, embodied in the skyscraper skyline, that took form around the monumental development of the Loop and North Side. The troubled coexistence of these two narratives— one about the city of neighborhoods and the decrepitude of Sandburg's "tall bold slugger," one about the enduring vitality of the increasingly service-oriented urban core in a suburbanizing age—gave Holiday's portrait of Chicago an edgier inner life than is typical of travel magazine features. A train of regrets and grievances cut across the powerful generic tendency of the magazine toward a determinedly sunny tone and upward-curving narrative lines.*

8. *Carl Sandburg, "Chicago," in* Chicago Poems *(New York: Henry Holt, 1916), 3–4.*

9. *James T. Farrell, quoted in* Lewis Fried, Makers of the City *(Amherst: University of Massachusetts Press, 1990), 121.*

10. *Liebling,* Chicago, *143.*

11. *This periodization acquired a continuing life. A popular history of Chicago written in the 1970s, for instance, contains a chapter entitled "Golden Age" that deals in large part with "those twenty years following the fair" (1893–1913) that constituted "a golden age for the cultivated people of Chicago" in which great writers and other artists converged on the city in waves. The history,* Finis Farr's Chicago *(New Rochelle, N.Y.: Arlington House, 1973), closes with an Atlantean passage extending the logic of decline from the end of the golden age through the troubled present—all he could say for the city of 1968 was that "one hoped it might survive"—to the very end: "All we can now write with certainty is that Chicago was wonderful in its time, and its story will be often repeated, until Lake Chicago comes back to cover the ruins, and the land falls silent under the sky" (400–401). Farr's history, like* City on the Make, *moves from consideration of larger-than-life characters in the golden age to an image of depopulated ruin.*

THE HEART OF THE MATTER

Bettina Drew

Unlike many other writers, who wrote in a gritty minimalism influenced by Hemingway that has become a mainstay in American literature, Nelson Algren was a lyrical writer in the tradition of Melville, Faulkner, Poe, and Thomas Wolfe, a poet of the numberless rooms in fourth-rate hotels and the countless lonely shadows cast by the El. And in *The Man with the Golden Arm,* Algren's poetic rendering of the lives of lost people reached its zenith. Algren's emotionally and aesthetically rich descriptions lend his characters, in Carl Sandburg's words, "a strange midnight dignity"; they are not simply tragic but capable of joy and humor and happiness. And it's a measure of Algren's understanding that in trying to make us care about the addict, thief, and stripper, he used poetry, the most emotionally direct means available and the language that cuts through rationalization. Algren also saw his characters lyrically because he loved them, and the story of the life and death of Frankie Machine ends fittingly with a poem.

But Algren was more than word-drunk. He was driven by a social and moral vision of the fundamental unfairness of American society that he never abandoned, even when it became unpopular. He acquired it on the road during the Great Depression and later by living in Chicago's declining Polish neighborhoods; and he expressed it best through the techniques of literary naturalism. Unlike late-nineteenth-century realism, which despite its lifelike descriptions tended toward romantic, "storylike" endings, naturalism was politically charged. Naturalism saw the individual not simply as the product of his own will and personality but as subject to ungovernable forces including biology, economics, society, and even chance, and naturalistic novels were almost always works of social criticism. The best-known naturalistic writer, the French novelist Emile Zola, used it to create the devastating depiction of French coal miners in near-slavery in *Germinal*, and in the late nineteenth and early twentieth centuries it became the method of choice for writers around the world. In Russia, the early Maxim Gorky employed it in his play *The Lower Depths*, as did Alexander Kuprin in his novel set in a brothel, *Yama*, which so influenced Algren's earlier novel *Never Come Morning*. In America, naturalism found expression in Stephen Crane's *Maggie, Girl of the Streets*, in Frank Norris's depiction of the crushing power of the railroads and the wheat industry in *The Octopus* and *The Pit*, and most famously in the work of Theodore Dreiser, America's greatest naturalistic writer. But unlike Dreiser, with his decidedly unstylistic renderings, Algren was virtually the only writer to combine the techniques of naturalism with lyrical prose, and he added to this a strong element of unconscious psychological self-destruction. The wounds suffered in corrupt and hideously mechanistic Chicago, the heart of "the one land where ownership and virtue are one," have penetrated into his character' souls. And *The Man with the Golden Arm* was the last naturalistic novel of stature to reach a wide audience before the Cold War, with its stifling lid on social dissent, clamped down.

But *The Man with the Golden Arm* is more even than lyrical naturalism; it is a profoundly moral and philosophical work, tinged with elements of a nonreligious but nevertheless Christian socialism. "Okay, kid, you beat Dostoevsky," Hemingway told Algren, for the themes of crime, punishment, guilt, and expiation are central to *The Man with the Golden Arm*. Though his wife Sophie's troubles are psychologically motivated, Frankie's guilt lies in believing he crippled her in a car accident while driving drunk, and he expiates it by taking morphine. When after a brief dispute at the poker table he kills his pusher Louis Fomorowski—whose own crime is that he justifies all actions that make money—Frankie pays with his final "Act of Contrition." In Algren's world, guilt, while a terrible burden, is a sign of humanity. And it is in the police captain Bednar's recognition of his guilt that Algren's most profound moral message comes through.

Bednar, pursuer of the doomed Frankie Machine, has been sending people up for twenty years, believing he was doing his honest copper's duty. But one night in the lineup a human wreck in a clerical collar who's been passing phony checks tells him that "we are all members of one another." And Bednar, stopped cold, begins to have a crisis of faith. "What did it mean that all the guilty felt so certain of their innocence while he felt so uncertain his own?... As if all those caged had learned secretly that all men are innocent in a way no captain might ever understand" (295). Amid images of being nailed to a cross from which he is finally unable to come down,

Bednar senses his guilt at all those years passing judgment, and his spiritual death for failing to have loved humanity. He tries vainly to justify himself. But in jailing Frankie's sidekick Sparrow to make him finger Frankie for Louis's murder, he wonders, "Why did he feel he had sold out a son, like being paid off in gold? For if everyone were members of one another—he put the notion down. That would mean that those on the other side of the wall were of his own kind. . . . [And] if they were anything less than enemies he had betrayed himself a thousandfold" (298). He understands finally that they are indeed less than enemies, and that his punishment is to be "more lost, more fallen, and more alone than any man at all"(298).

Clearly, Algren believed that we are all members of one another, and that, in a world of survival and oppression, as the critic George Bluestone put it, "love is the only way human beings may meaningfully relate. Nothing else is finally reliable." The price of our failure to recognize that the Frankie Machines of this world are of our own kind and worthy of love is spiritual death. But we have a chance at redemption, for *The Man with the Golden Arm* moves us to make that recognition.

NELSON ALGREN
THE VALUE OF DISSENT

James R. Giles

In a capitalistic society that assigns value only to those things, and even to those people, that bring a high purchase price, Algren's outcasts can purchase nothing, not even the power to define themselves. Thus, they are unfaithful to American society because they fail to accumulate things and, in turn, become themselves not worth preserving. Record Head Bednar can appropriate and exhibit them for the passing amusement of the middle-class audience. Moreover, Record Head intuitively understands linguistic power; he is a master at appropriation through naming. By imposing labels on the principal actors in his theater, he takes away their genuine identities; for him, they become "habituals" rather than human beings. It is only when the "defrocked preacher" refuses to go along with the captain's exercise of hegemonic control that Bednar is "impaled." Capitalistic power over these powerless individuals continues even after their deaths, society coldly discarding most while choosing a few to cut open (in of course a "sanitary" manner). One of the most unforgivable offenses of the "habituals" is precisely their failure to be "sanitary," their potential for intruding upon the inhumanly clean and repressive morality of representatives of middle-class authority like Bednar.

One could hardly find a novelistic passage that better exemplifies Jeremy Bentham's concept of the Panopticon, famously extended by Foucault to include all of capitalistic society's controlling institutions, than the police line-up scene. Bednar puts the powerless outcasts who fall under his power on display while denying them the right to see their audience.

437

Throughout their lives they are under a constant societal surveillance that threatens to "discipline and punish" them while systematically denying their humanity.

Algren has been dismissed as an old-fashioned practitioner of social protest fiction, one who believed naively in the potential of literature to change society. Yet his entire aesthetic conveys a sophisticated, almost a postmodern, awareness of the limitation of social protest. To see this, it is only necessary to compare *The Man with the Golden Arm* to a text like John Steinbeck's *Grapes of Wrath*. There is no Ma Joad in Algren, no idealized voice of an oppressed, but innately noble, common man or woman. Such Algren "common men" as Blind Pig, Sparrow Saltskin, and even Frankie Machine are hardly noble. None of them could or would give a Tom Joad "I'll be there" speech. In contrast to Steinbeck, Algren stands back from the urban "wonders" who populate his fiction, often seeming even to mock and ridicule them. He thus takes a narrative stance outside and above his creations, a stance that would be comparable to Bednar's except that it is from the first impaled by the pain of the "habituals." He seems to have possessed a Foucaultian understanding of the irresistible power of modern capitalism, of its power to transform counter-hegemonic assertions of rebellion into linguistic modes of control.

To a degree, the continuing academic neglect of Algren is a result of the inherent difficulty in labeling him. Not a traditional social protest writer, he nevertheless focused upon urban outcasts. Intuitively grasping critical concepts of postmodern thought, he was not interested in theoretical approaches to human beings or in elaborate linguistic game-playing, insisting instead upon the most graphic forms of dramatization. He did not want to construct simulacra of urban anguish, but was committed to exploring the very real anguish of twentieth-century urban American lives. His sense of the absurd was comparable to Celine's; and like Celine he depicted the urban powerless engaged in ridiculous and even criminal activities, while affirming their humanity—a humanity not fundamentally different than that of the middle-class spectators safely hidden behind the mirror in Bednar's interrogation room.

Moreover, the causes of Algren's unfashionableness transcend academia. American society has increasingly evolved, just as he predicted in the 1950s, into a "third-person society." In the last analysis, Algren's aesthetic rests upon an affirmation of compassion, and compassion is not highly valued in contemporary America. One thinks of the current controversy in the Republican party over millionaire George W. Bush (possibly the ultimate "third-person" presidential candidate) and his doctrine of "compassionate conservatism." Algren would almost certainly have appreciated the visible distress experienced by Steve Forbes and other Republicans when forced to pronounce the "c" word and, perhaps most of all, the absurdity of their proclamations that neglect constitutes a higher form of compassion. Above all, Algren's aesthetic rests on the moral necessity of affirming the human presence of the powerless. Whether art or politics can ultimately help them, the urban outcasts, the "habituals," are still there.

GOLDEN ARM'S SONG OF SWEET SURRENDER

Lee Stringer

As I sit down to do this bit on *The Man with the Golden Arm*, three things spring to mind. The first is my recent first-time visit to Chicago, where I spent an afternoon haunting Nelson Algren's shadow, hosted by the affable Art Shay, Algren's once–trolling partner and photobiographer. We started in the shadow of a bridge—at the Busy Bee Bar & Grill, where Shay and Algren once put in serious elbow-bending time. As I trailed to a table at the elbow of the rectangular bar, my eyes were everywhere at once, anticipating that this might be the real-life incarnation of the infamous Tug & Maul, where Division Street down-and-outers in *The Man with the Golden Arm* convened in that desperate brand of low-roar carousel peculiar to folks who have gotten a good glimpse of the end of their own rope.

Shay took a few stabs at dredging up a bit of past color, between bites on a burger, but I was only half listening. My ears were cocked toward the center of the room, hoping to be privy to some latter-day Sparrow Saltskin unwinding yet another doomed, hapless scheme to his half-soused cronies. But the place was tame and sober as an Elks lodge on bingo night. The only hint that the Busy Bee may have once provided any grist for Algren's gritty mill was a dim photo of him—sporting a mischievous, crooked grin—amidst the other black-and-white portraiture adorning the even dimmer walls.

Next, we revved up Shay's groaning museum of a car and hit "Polish Town," the pulse of whose mean streets throbs throughout *The Man with the Golden Arm*. Shay playing the dutiful tour guide, dropping an anecdote here, a demographic aside there as we snaked along boulevards and twisted down side streets, I rubbernecked and ogled for signs of anything Algrenian—some mope wandering from the alleyway, dragging the sad sack of his ruined life behind; a distant cousin to Pig, perhaps, that grotesque, blind misanthrope of *The Man with the Golden Arm* with the raw, half-eaten nostrils, who prevails upon the generosity—or guilt (either one, for all the difference it makes)—of sighted people to fete him to a tidy shot or two at the Tug & Maul.

But only the standard-issue busyness of lives lived out of walk-ups a single day at a time was in good evidence—weary women at their shopping; leathered laborers crawling home from the early shift; withered old folk out for a few sweet lungs full of what remained of their lives—nothing so uncommon to whatever middle American city as to suggest that we were in Algren's Chicago.

Our mini-pilgrimage dead-ended at the foot of Algren's house—a walk-up affair that we treated as a shrine, taking time out for silence and photographs. A loose-leaf-sized plaque was posted by the door, quietly certifying that, yes, Nelson Algren once lived here. I closed my eyes, tried to imagine him, cloistered up there in the shank of a frigid Chicago night, sleeping an uneasy poet's sleep. But even my mind's eye refused to take it for anything more than it was: an old wood-frame house of no particular note—except for its rude, impromptu design—amidst row after row of old wood-frame houses.

I left Chicago feeling cheated—like a kid who'd gone to the circus and couldn't get in to see the freak show—realizing only much later that what I was looking for could not be had all in one place, all at one time, in real life, and that my search for Algren's Chicago was superfluous. For I had already seen the soul of that city more keenly and more intimately than otherwise possible, by the trick of a book called *The Man with the Golden Arm.*

The second thing that comes to mind is what a rare breed of writer Algren was and how misunderstood he is because of this. While it should never be the case that you have to understand an author to enjoy his work, with Algren—whose writing greatly turned on understanding himself—having a bead on where he is coming from flushes out the great graces that fill his books.

I have had three readings of this particular book, the first and last of which fell before and after my having the occasion to ply similar turf writing about my own protracted down-and-out residence on the streets of this city. And the thing about attempting to portray people who have become all but invisible to the rest of society is that they are not likely to sit for a formal interview, an approach that wouldn't be satisfying in any event, as far as I'm concerned. The challenge, therefore, is to extract from the evidence of the present—from who they are now, what they have become— the truth of each character's past.

In my case, I found myself peeling away assumption after assumption until it became clear to me that—no matter who the subject, hero or villain—it was neces- sary to find a part of that person in myself in order to do the job successfully, by which I mean compellingly. The remarkable thing about doing this—and its reward as well—is that it inevitably leads to compassion. So while one might imagine Algren possessed of an almost superhuman sense of compassion that he could bring to bear on his work at will, I would suggest that for him writing was less the wielding of his compassion than its genesis.

We more or less tend to presume about great authors that they proceed with superior clarity and deliberation of purpose and that this, when subjected to the dic- tates of craft, emerges as literature. Algren himself, however, bravely deflated such myth. Pressed in one interview to dissect his own work—a dangerous exercise for any- one valuing creative purity as much as he did—Algren declared, "The only good writ- ing is done by people who don't know what they are doing. They just go all out." Perhaps the grandest distinction of *The Man with the Golden Arm,* then, is that it is the work of a writer not so much intent on suprising us as willing to be surprised himself, a writer not merely cagey enough to master the writing process but with balls enough to surrender to it.

This brings me to the third thing, the book itself; how enduring it is, how relentlessly American it is, and how much the fate of its protagonist, Frankie Majcinek, turns on this question of wile versus surrender—or so it strikes me. There's an old seaman's prayer, since adopted by any number of religions and fellowships, that speaks to this in the following simple words:

> God grant me the serenity to accept the things that can't be changed, the courage to change the things that can, and the wisdom to know the difference .

Perhaps the most vivid aspect of Algren's characters—cops, politicians, hoods, bums, punks, and fat cats alike—is the sense they have each in their own way come to accept, however grudgingly, that—any attempts to co-join fate and ambition notwithstanding—they have not, so far as this life is concerned, been put in the driver's seat. And each bit of poise they manage to wring out of the rude bargain they have made with their fate stands as a miracle of the ever-resilient human spirit.

"I was a Lily of the valley in my time," a ruined flower of her day with whom a younger Frankie Machine once had a dalliance laments with crude, ragtag grace. "Now I'm just Lily of the Alley—say, didn't I turn out to be a beauty!"

Or take Sparrow Saltskin, a dognapper, peeping Tom, and occasional bar change pilferer who seems to have little quarrel with the fact that his chosen "professions" lead regularly to residence in a Saloon Street Station house cell.

"How many times I been pinched now?" he asks Record Head Bednar, the precinct captain for twenty years. "You keeping tract for me? When I hit a hunnert I'm gonna volunteer for Leavenswort."

As for the captain himself, he may hold the fate of petty punks like Sparrow in his hands, but even he is aware that he does his business merely as a dupe for those higher up the feeding chain—so much so that his only rational response to this is to entertain the notion of booking himself.

Sad as the predicament of all these characters might be, if you weep for any of them, you revel in them as well. There is a certain bittersweetness in their surrender.

But Frankie Majcinek, you will notice, seldom sheds his soldier's cloak. And the soldier's code is "no surrender." He is a card shark whose stock-in-trade is cheating a certain fate. He is also an American—for my money the quintessential post–World War II "can do" American, in that he banks on skill and cunning alone to get him through. Standing alone among his Division Street compatriots, fending off their sorry concerns with a passive, smirking humor, clinging to the myth of his golden arm despite that it ever fails to deliver him any gold, Frankie's ugly secret is his contempt for the pettiness of their lives, which has so objectified the pettiness of his own—leaving him without love as well as out of luck. In the end, all this earns him a footnote of sorts, a bleak epitaph on whatever blotter notes the lives of those who come to no good end. But it earns him nothing in life but a peculiarly American brand of angst—the fear and shame of having lived and died merely as a man.

Then there is Sophie, Frankie's wheelchair-bound wife. At a casual glance you would assume that she and Frankie are simply a mismatched couple. But upon closer inspection you can see that both of them are cut from the same cloth. That there is no love left between them—that both of them, in their stubbornness, are largely incapable of love—does not deter her from manipulating Frankie, as deftly as he manipulates a stack of fifty-two, into maintaining their failed union regardless. Not to give anything away, but as things develop hers may be the cruelest trick of all.

Such is the compassion with which Algren writes that it is quite plausible to see Frankie Machine as a hero being ground, inch by miserable inch, into the grave by a postwar America immersed in an orgy of conspicuous consumption. And from that perspective *The Man with the Golden Arm* serves up potent commentary not only on the emerging American Dream of the1940s and 1950s, but also on what has become the American Century.

If *Golden Arm* achieved nothing else, I might be exalting Algren here as a great journalist, a tag he was loath to have pinned on him. But I have yet to see to my satisfaction any book devoted merely to pursuing issues that has a fat chance of standing as literature over the long haul.

Algren does sketch out here, layer by layer, the multitiered class structure of our "classless" society. And there are indications that he set out to skewer what in the 1960s we would refer to as "the system." As a longtime habitué of Chicago's more desperate streets, he most certainly bore witness to enough social cruelties to make any man's blood boil. And he once went so far as to publicly let on that for him writing was an act of revenge. But if indeed Algren had been the type of writer who "knew what he was doing," muscling that original impulse onto the page, *The Man with the Golden Arm* might have been mere social commentary dressed up as a novel and much less of a book. Less sympathetic. Less humane. Certainly less enduring.

Fortunately something happened en route.

"I was going to write a war novel." Algren later revealed of his intentions for this book. "But it turned out to be this *Golden Arm* thing. I mean the war kind of slipped away, and those people with the hypos came along and that was that."

My guess is—getting back to the subject of surrender—that Algren ultimately surrendered his angry notions about getting even with society to his honesty as a writer, that as his war novel began to unwind he found he had something fundamentally bigger than the system in his sights, which was that, in fact, the most dynamic effects of war are on a nation's psyche.

We see some of this right from the start of the book. It's the different feel of things along Division Street that Frankie, fresh from war, readily notices and which Sparrow offhandedly explains away as "just a new way of walking." And later on, when Frankie Machine broods over the desolation of Skid Row, it is not the poverty itself that oppresses him but his guilt over it, the "great, secret and special American guilt of owning nothing, nothing at all, in the one land where virtue and ownership are one."

So it would seem that it is not cruel circumstance itself grinding Frankie Machine into the grave, but his stubborn, guilt-laden, and unaccepting response to it. And Frankie Machine may well be not the hero but the foil.

You tell me if this isn't a war book after all. Maybe not about the more obvious conflicts—those battles between nations that some of us are occasionally called upon to fight. But about the less obvious wars of the soul to which duty every beating heart is called.

The first roll of film I shot after giving up reporting on *Life* for photography in 1949 showed Nelson in this Division Street poker game being dealt to by "Doc," his probable model for Frankie Machine in *The Man with the Golden Arm*.

At Nelson's ten-buck-a-month pad on Wabansia Street, another friend demonstrated how a junkie shot up (inset). This was just for my camera. Nelson hated this deadly process and had seen it before.

(Far left) Algren always cased neighborhood bars before entering.

(Above) Cruising tough old Madison Street in my 1949 Pontiac, Nelson excitedly pointed out the poor "halfie" on his little cart. Shooting past Nelson's shoulder, I made "Sunday Morning on Madison Street."

(Left) Nelson with the tragic love of his life, Simone de Beauvoir, in front of his pad at 1523 Wabansia.

George Bluestone, literary scholar and film producer, was author of *Novels into Film* (1957).

Bettina Drew's biography, *Nelson Algren: A Life on the Wild Side*, was a finalist for the *Chicago Sun-Times* Book of the Year and received a Special Citation in the PEN Gerard Fund for Emerging Women Writers. Her essays have been cited in Best American Essays and nominated for Pushcart Prizes, and her collection *Crossing the Expendable Landscape* won a Special Citation in the PEN New England/L. L. Winship Award. The recipient of a fellowship in nonfiction literature from the New York Foundation for the Arts, she lives in New Haven.

Close friend of Nelson Algren, **Maxwell Geismar** was a prolific and influential literary critic, historian, and scholar. Among his many books are *American Moderns: From Rebellion to Conformity* (1958), *Rebels and Ancestors: The American Novel, 1890–1915* (1953), *The Last of the Provincials: The American Novel, 1915–1925* (1947), and *Writers in Crisis: The American Novel between Two Wars* (1942).

James R. Giles has been a member of the Department of English at Northern Illinois University since 1970. Giles is the author of *Confronting the Horror: The Novels of Nelson Algren* (1989), *The Naturalistic Inner-City Novel in America* (1995), *Understanding Hubert Selby, Jr.* (1998), *Irwin Shaw: A Study of the Short Fiction* (1992), and the Twayne U.S. Authors Series volumes on Claude McKay, James Jones,and Irwin Shaw. He is also the co-editor of *The James Jones Reader* (1991).

Poet, essayist, and novelist **John Clellon Holmes** is perhaps best known for his 1952 *New York Times* essay "This Is the Beat Generation," which introduced his friend Jack Kerouac's definition of the Beats to America. His novels *Go* (1952) and *The Horn* (1958) chronicle the intellectual counterculture of New York in the immediate postwar years.

Lawrence Lipton was a political activist, novelist, poet, teacher, and critic. His most widely read work, *The Holy Barbarians* (1959), was one of the first critical studies of the Beat Generation.

Stuart McCarrell is a Chicago playwright and poet. His play *Voices, Insistent Voices*—in which Nelson Algren was featured—had an extended run in New York in 1986. Xenia Press has five of his plays and three of his books of poetry in print. A close friend and protégé of Nelson Algren, he founded the Nelson Algren Committee in 1989.

Carlo Rotella is the author of *October Cities: The Redevelopment of Urban Literature* (University of California Press, 1998), from which this essay is excerpted, and teaches at the University of Massachusetts-Boston. He is currently writing a book about boxing, blues, gambling, and other forms of urban culture. A native of Chicago's South Side, he first read *Golden Arm* because Mike Royko kept recommending Algren in his newspaper column.

Mike Royko was Chicago's—and America's—preeminent urban newspaper columnist for nearly four decades, writing for the *Chicago Daily News*, the *Chicago Sun-Times,* and finally the *Chicago Tribune*. Daily from 1963 to 1997, readers relied upon his straightforward prose, political sense, incisive wit, generous spirit, and sense of humor to give them a picture of their city at its best and its worst. A posthumous collection of his columns, *One More Time: The Best of Mike Royko* (University of Chicago Press, 1999), has been a regional best-seller.

William J. Savage Jr. wrote his doctoral dissertation, *Starting Points: Canons, Genre, the Preinterpretive Field and the Literary Reputation of Nelson Algren*, at Northwestern University, where he is currently visiting assistant professor.

Celebrated photojournalist **Art Shay** is the author-photographer of seventy-nine books, including *Nelson Algren's Chicago* (University of Illinois Press, 1988), which was hailed by Chicago newspapers as "a masterpiece" and a "Chicago treasure, like its author." His play *Nelson, Simone, and Sartre* had its first stage reading in 1999.

Layle Silbert has made her career as a photographer, mostly of writers, and has had about thirty exhibits in the United States, Ecuador, and Mexico. She has published stories, poems, and a handful of personal essays, but thinks of herself chiefly as a writer of short stories, more than one hundred of which have appeared in literary magazines. She has published a book of poems and five short fiction collections. *The Freethinkers: Stories of the New World* (Seven Stories Press, 2000) is her first hardcover publication.

Seven Stories Press publisher **Daniel Simon** is coauthor, with Jack Hoffman, of *Run Run Run: The Lives of Abbie Hoffman* (Tarcher/Putnam, 1993), and translator of *Van Gogh: Self-Portraits* by Pascal Bonafoux (Wellfleet Press, 1989). Since 1985 he has overseen the rerelease of Nelson Algren's fiction, and in 1996 he edited, with C. S. O'Brien, Algren's *Nonconformity: Writing on Writing* (Seven Stories Press, 1996), for which Simon wrote the critical afterword.

Lee Stringer is the author of *Grand Central Winter: Stories from the Street* (Seven Stories Press, 1998). Formerly the editor of *Street News*, he has emerged as a unique literary voice to remind us that human states such as homelessness are not crimes. His *Grand Central Winter* has been translated into ten languages. Lee Stringer's newest book is a collaboration with Kurt Vonnegut, *Like Shaking Hands with God: A Conversation about Writing* (Seven Stories Press, 1999) He is currently at work on a second memoir.

For decades **Studs Terkel**'s nationally syndicated daily radio show on WFMT, Chicago, has broadcast the life stories of everyday people—from waitresses to statesmen, construction workers to actors, writers to police officers—to a vast listenership of everyday people. Winner of the Pulitzer Prize, Terkel has also received international acclaim for his best-selling books; he is not only our greatest listener but also one of our greatest writers. Among Terkel's books are his excellent autobiography *Talking to Myself: A Memoir of My Times* (1977), *Working: People Talk About What They Do All Day and How They Feel About What They Do* (1974), and *Race: How Blacks and Whites Think and Feel About the American Obsession* (1992).

Kurt Vonnegut is among the very few grandmasters of twentieth-century American letters, one without whom the very term "American literature" would mean much less than it does. His newest books are *Bagombo Snuff Box: Uncollected Short Fiction* (G. P. Putnam's Sons, 1999), a collection of his early stories; *Timequake: a novel* (G. P. Putnam's Sons, 1997), *Like Shaking Hands with God: A Conversation about Writing* (Seven Stories Press, 1999), with Lee Stringer; and *God Bless You, Dr. Kevorkian* (Seven Stories Press, 1999), imaginations of the afterlife. All of the nearly twenty book-length works of fiction by Kurt Vonnegut are always recommended reading.

ACKNOWLEDGMENTS AND CREDITS

"A Note on the Critical Edition of *The Man with the Golden Arm*" by William J. Savage Jr. and Daniel Simon. Original contribution. Copyright © 1999 by William J. Savage Jr. and Daniel Simon.

"Arm: A Memoir" by John Clellon Holmes. Originally published in *Representative Men: The Biographical Essays*, Selected Essays by John Clellon Holmes, volume 2 (Fayetteville: The University of Arkansas Press, 1988), pp. 243–62. Reprinted here by permission of the estate of John Clellon Holmes. Copyright © 1988 by the estate of John Clellon Holmes.

"Algren's Golden Pen" by Mike Royko. Originally published in the *Chicago Sun-Times/Daily News* on May 13, 1981, and collected in *One More Time: The Best of Mike Royko* (Chicago: The University of Chicago Press, 1999), pp. 147–50. Reprinted with special permission from the Chicago Sun-Times, Inc. and Judy Royko. Copyright © 1999 by the Chicago Sun-Times, Inc.

"Algren as I Knew Him" by Kurt Vonnegut Jr. Adapted from the introduction to Nelson Algren's *Never Come Morning* (Seven Stories Press, 1987). Copyright © 1986 by Kurt Vonnegut Jr.

"Glasses" by Studs Terkel. Adapted from *Talking to Myself: A Memoir of My Times* (The New Press, 1973), pp. 225–229. Reprinted here by permission of the author and The New Press. Copyright © 1973 by Studs Terkel.

"Nelson Algren's Politics" by Stuart McCarrell. Original contribution. Copyright © 1999 by Stuart McCarrell.

"Photographing Nelson Algren—and More" by Layle Silbert. Original contribution. Copyright © 1999 by Layle Silbert.

"Nelson Algren: The Iron Sanctuary" by Maxwell Geismar. Originally published in *College English* (March 1953), pp. 311–15. Copyright © 1953 by Maxwell Geismar.

"Nelson Algren" by George Bluestone. Adapted from "Nelson Algren," originally published in the *Western Review* (Vol. 22, Autumn 1957), pp. 35–44. Copyright © 1957 by George Bluestone.

One of the most neglected American writers and also one of the best loved, Nelson Algren wrote once that "literature is made upon any occasion that a challenge is put to the legal apparatus by conscience in touch with humanity." His writings always lived up to that definition. He was born March 28, 1909 in Detroit and lived mostly in Chicago. His first short fiction was published in *Story* magazine in 1933. In 1935 he published his first novel, *Somebody in Boots*. In early 1942, Algren put the finishing touches on a second novel and joined the war as an enlisted man. By 1945, he still had not made the grade of Private first class, but the novel *Never Come Morning* was widely praised and eventually sold over a million copies. Jean-Paul Sartre assisted in the translation of the French-language edition. In 1947 came *The Neon Wilderness*, his short story collection which would permanently establish his place in American letters. *The Man with the Golden Arm*, winner of the first National Book Award and generally considered his finest novel, appeared in 1949. Then came *Chicago: City on the Make* (1951), a prose poem, and the novel *A Walk on the Wild Side* (1956). Algren also published two travel books, *Who Lost an American?* (1963) and *Notes from a Sea Diary: Hemingway All the Way* (1965). *The Last Carousel*, a collection of short fiction and nonfiction, appeared in 1973. He died on May 9, 1981, within days of his appointment as a fellow of the American Academy and Institute of Arts and Letters. His last novel, *The Devil's Stocking*, based on the life of Hurricane Carter, was published posthumously in 1983. *The Texas Stories of Nelson Algren* appeared in 1995, and *Nonconformity: Writing on Writing*, a lost 1952 essay on the art of writing, in 1996.